MARG~~ARET O~~

(1828–1897) w~~as~~ ~~born in Edinbu~~rgh and
lived in Scotla~~nd until~~ ~~1834, when~~ her family
moved to Liver~~pool, and then Birk~~ead. Her mother
was an Oliphant b~~y birth, but littl~~e is known of her father,
Francis Wilson, ex~~cept that h~~e once "took affidavits" in a
Liverpool Customs House. She wrote her first novel at the
age of sixteen while nursing her mother through an illness,
but her first published work was *Passages in the Life of Mrs
Margaret Maitland* (1849), and in 1851 she was introduced
to the Scottish firm of Blackwoods, who were to be her
principal publishers, and to whose *Blackwoods Magazine*
she remained a regular contributor until her death.

In 1852 she married her cousin Francis Oliphant, an
architectural glass painter and associate of Pugin. The
greater part of the family income, however, came from her
journalism and Scottish regional novels such as *Katie
Stewart* and *The Quiet Heart* (1854). In 1859 she found
herself a widow with three small children and £1000 in
debt: from then on she was always under pressure to write
to educate her sons (her daughter died in 1864), and also to
support her brothers, nephew and nieces.

One of the greatest women of the Victorian Age, Mrs
Oliphant eventually published almost 100 novels, of which
the best known are the "Carlingford Chronicles": *Salem
Chapel* (1863), *Miss Marjoribanks* (1866), and *Phoebe
Junior* (1876). Other important works include *Harry
Joscelyn* (1881), *The Ladies Lindores* (1883), *A Country
Gentleman and His Family* (1886), *Lady Car* (1889), *Kirsteen*
(1890) and *Sir Robert's Fortune* (1895). She also wrote
supernatural tales, biographies, literary histories, trans-
lations and travel books. Her last years were overshadowed
by the deaths of her nephew Frank in 1879, and her sons
Cyril and "Cecco" in 1890 and 1895. Remembered by J.
M. Barrie as "of an intellect so alert that one wondered she
ever fell asleep", Mrs Oliphant died in Wimbledon at the
age of sixty-nine.

Aurella Wein
August 29, 1984
Oxford, England

HESTER

A STORY OF CONTEMPORARY LIFE

MRS OLIPHANT

With a New Introduction by
JENNIFER UGLOW

Virago

Published by VIRAGO PRESS Limited 1984
41 William IV Street, London WC2N 4DB

First published in Great Britain in 3 volumes by Macmillan and Co. 1883
First published in 1 volume by Macmillan and Co. 1884
Virago edition offset from Macmillan and Co. 1884 edition

British Library Cataloguing in Publication Data

Oliphant, Margaret
Hester.—(Virago modern classic)
I. Title
823'.8 [F] PR5113.H4

ISBN 0–86068–515–2

Printed in Finland by Werner Söderström Oy, a member of Finnprint

" A springy motion in her gait,
A rising step, did indicate
Of pride and joy no common rate
    That flush'd her spirit:
I know not by what name beside
I shall it call: if 'twas not pride,
It was a joy to that a'lied
    She did inherit.

*　　*　　*　　*　　*

She was trained in Nature's school,
    Nature had blest her.
A waking eye, a prying mind,
A heart that stirs, is hard to bind :
A hawk's keen sight ye cannot blind,
    Ye could not Hester."
                                CHARLES LAMB.

CONTENTS.

CONTENTS.

CONTENTS.

INTRODUCTION

HESTER is a witty, ironic, forceful tale of women who run their lives either by choice or by necessity without the support of men—fatherless girls, old maids, widows, domineering sisters. But being alone, as its author knew, is not the same as being independent, and all the women in the book are presented in different ways as being entangled in complicated nets which hamper their freedom of action; almost invisible chains woven of family duty, financial need and the unspoken codes which governed "correct behaviour" for their sex and class. The main narrative traces the struggles of Hester Vernon between the ages of fourteen and twenty-three. She cannot expect a "good marriage" and her temperament, in any case, drives her to want an independent career, but at every attempt to create her own destiny she encounters the strength of these hidden bonds. Despite the title the novel has two heroines, Hester and her elderly second cousin Catherine, who seems at first to be the spider sitting in the centre of the web in which the girl is caught. The book's real romance, although Hester has a succession of suitors, is between these two women, a version of *Pride and Prejudice* in which misunderstanding, resentment and jealous independence mask similarity and attraction; "I think you and I have hated each other because we were meant to love each other, child."

They are opposed in age and youth, wealth and poverty,

cynicism and idealism, but are united in their pride, their abundant energy, their emotional fervour and their desire to work, to be of use in the world. In the end, despite appearances, both are equally constrained. Catherine is head of the Vernon family, running the family bank for thirty years after saving it from near ruin precipitated by mismanagement on the part of Hester's father John. She fills a local house with her pensioners including the widowed "Mrs John" and daughter; she settles her nephews in the bank to ensure the future of the dynasty; she dominates local society. She seems free and rational but she too is presented as vulnerable, enmeshed and blinded by her emotions, her loneliness and craving for love.

The main elements in this powerful story—loneliness, family ties, money, work, strong women dictating to weak men—were all constant themes of Mrs Oliphant's novels and of her own life. As a child, she felt that the "dim figure" of her father was completely overshadowed by her mother Margaret, sharp-tongued, energetic, overseer of the family finances and a natural story teller who filled her with a romantic idea of her own side of the family, the Oliphants, "an old, chivalrous, impoverished race". She herself clung to this heritage, as Catherine does to the Vernon name, signing her name with a flourish after she married her cousin Francis as Margaret Oliphant W. Oliphant. She also always retained her tart Scottish accent, cherishing her outsider's claim to a clearer view of English manners.

As a young wife in the 1850s she was clearly disappointed by the lack of success of her unbusinesslike husband, whose craft of glass painting was rendered unfashionable by the decline of Gothic Revival architecture. Like many other professional women writers whose family depended largely on their earnings (the widowed Mary Shelley, Mrs Beeton, Mary Braddon), she worked incessantly, pausing only briefly for births or for bereavements (her mother and

two of her babies), an existence vividly conjured up by
Frank's note to Blackwoods in February 1855, "Our poor
little darling left us as we feared, about half past three
yesterday afternoon. Mrs Oliphant would beg as a favour
that her article on Charles Dickens which was to have
appeared in the Magazine for March, might now be arranged for April."

Frank's own health failed in 1858 and after suffering
through a dank Florentine winter with their two small
children, and a summer in Rome, he died in November
1859. He never told his wife that even before their disastrous Italian trip he knew his illness was terminal, a
"cruel deception" she never entirely forgave. Her son
Cecco (Francis) was born in December and she returned to
England the following February. "When I thus began the
world anew," she wrote, "I had for all my fortune about
£1000 of debt, a small insurance of, I think, £200 on
Frank's life, our furniture laid up in a warehouse, and my
own faculties, such as they were, to make our living and
pay off all our burdens by." Her loneliness was intensified
by the sudden death of ten-year-old Maggie, also in
Rome, in 1864. "Here is an end of all. 1 am alone, I am a
woman. I have nobody to stand between me and the
roughest edge of grief." And her burdens were increased
by her brother Willie, an alcoholic, who after an initial
attempt to become a Presbyterian minister, drifted into an
indigent life at home and then in Italy. Ten years later she
also undertook to support her widowed brother Frank, a
failed businessman, and his four children.

Her novels, not surprisingly, are full of strong efficient
women, who carry the loads placed on them by ineffectual
men, many of whom "go to the bad" and in *Hester* she links
the plight of her fictional heroines with memories "deep
down in the recollection of many a woman of whom the
world knows no history". Her autobiography is a short,
heartrending document, but one of her most extraordinary
features was her resilient spirit, "almost criminally elastic"

as she herself said, a quality defined in *Hester* as "that heroism of necessity which is more effective than mere will". In the 1860s, the first decade of her widowhood, she established her reputation with the "Carlingford Chronicles" and immediately after Maggie's death wrote *Miss Marjoribanks*, one of the funniest novels of the day. Contemporaries and juniors, like J. M. Barrie, remembered her not as a tight-lipped martyr but as an opinionated, entertaining woman, "In talk she was tremendously witty without trying to be so . . . and she was of an intellect so alert that one wondered she ever fell asleep."

Surveying her enormous output we too may wonder if she ever had time to sleep, for in addition to her novels, biographies, travel books and critical works she maintained "a lightly flowing stream of magazine articles, and refused no work that was offered to me". A great deal of her criticism and fiction endures remarkably well, but her best works have been forgotten along with those which she admitted were written for the "boiling of the family pot". In the mid 1870s, determined to live in style and to send her boys to Eton and Oxford, she frankly decided "with a metaphorical toss of my head", to put aside dreams of producing a masterpiece and "to set myself steadily to make as much money as I could . . . it had to be done, and that was enough".

Although her books sold well and her name was widely respected, she was not a consistently best-selling writer except for a brief period in the 1860s. Indeed professional jealousy as well as concern for "respectability" in literature may explain the vehemence of her attack in *Blackwoods* in 1867 on "sensuality" in the works of women writers such as the romantic Rhoda Broughton and the outstandingly successful sensation novelist Mary Braddon. For despite her "toss of the head", she was very sensitive about her popularity and literary reputation, and at the end of her life suffered from the feeling that her talents had been largely wasted; "No one even will mention me in

the same breath as George Eliot. And that is just." In fact
she under-estimated herself; at her death Henry James in
his *London Notes*, evoked her inimitable quality, "She was
really a great improvisatrice, a night working spinner of
long, loose, vivid yarns, numberless, pauseless, admirable
repeatedly, for their full, pleasant, reckless rustle over
depths and difficulties." Several later critics have compared her analysis of provincial life with that of Eliot and
Trollope.

The tension behind the preoccupation with work in
Hester may come from the way her own writing was never
considered "real work" in the same way that a man's
occupation or profession would be, no matter how solid her
reputation, or how many people depended on her earnings. Instead a fiction remained that her writing was an
amateur activity, done in her "spare time". She wrote her
early novels while her mother did needlework at the
family table, and she maintained the habit in later life,
always making herself available during the day for her
family and friends, working in "the little second drawing
room where all the (feminine) life of the house goes on;
and I don't think I have ever had two hours uninterrupted
(except at night, with everybody in bed) during the whole
of my literary life".

By the 1880s however, the pretence had begun to pall.
She thought up schemes for journals she could edit,
appealed to her editor George Craik at Macmillan to look
out for something of "a permanent character, which would
relieve me a little from the necessity of perpetual writing"
and lamented the advantage which most literary men had
of a regular salary in addition to their freelance earnings. I
think it was her experience of never being taken seriously
as a professional writer which swayed her feelings more
and more in support of the feminist cause. In her *Blackwoods* articles of the 1850s and 60s, although she showed
sympathy for the *actual* oppression of women and acknowledged the logic of demanding the vote for women house-

holders, she defended the notion of separate spheres with
defiant pride: "we are women, not lesser men. We are
content with the place in the world's economy which God
has given us."

But while the explicit arguments of her articles upheld
the status quo, the implicit arguments of her novels were
beginning to challenge it. In 1865 *Miss Marjoribanks*
provided a graphic and very funny illustration of the waste
which resulted from confining a woman of immense capabilities to using her talents solely in the domestic and
social spheres, and in 1866 *Agnes* offered a tragic (auto-
biographical) vision of a disillusioned wife. These themes
are repeated again and again and gradually the hidden
anger found its way into her articles. At the end of a wide-
ranging piece in *Fraser's Magazine* in 1880 she cried out
openly against the "ungenerous" attitude of men towards
women; "whatever women do, in the general, is undervalued by men in the general, because . . . it is done by
women", and she declared that legal disabilities are "mere
evidences of a sentiment which is more inexplicable than
any other by which the human race has been actuated, a
sentiment against which the most of us, at one period or
another of our lives, have to struggle blindly, not knowing
whence it originates, or how it is to be overcome."

Hester, written in 1883, may surprise readers today by its
overtly feminist tone, since if they have any preconceived
image of its author, it is likely to be the anti-feminist of the
1850s or the upholder of moral purity revealed in the
attack on *Tess of the D'Urberville's* in the 1890s. But while
Mrs Oliphant always retained conservative views on
female sexuality she became increasingly radical in her
perception of the widespread and disabling sexism rooted
in the consciousness of both men and women. It is this
prejudice, rather than legal or social institutions, which
she attacks in *Hester*. If we read the novel as a polemic,
then the crucial passage must surely be that where Hester

presses Edward, her declared lover, to explain his business transactions to her, begging,

> "But tell me, only tell me a little more."
> He shook his head, "Hester, he said, "that is not what a man
> wants in a woman; not to go and explain it all to her with pen
> and ink, and tables and figures, to make her understand as he
> would have to do with a man. What he wants, dear, is very
> different—just to lean upon you—to know that you sympath-
> ise, and think of me, and feel for me, and believe in me, and
> that you will share whatever comes".
> Hester said nothing, but her countenance grew very
> grave.

She is shaken still further by her own mother's agreement
that for a man to discuss business with a woman shows a
lack of respect.

> There was indeed a sort of awe in the girl's perception of her
> mother's perfectly innocent, perfectly assured theory of what
> was right in women. What wonder that a man should think so,
> when women themselves thought so?

By 1883 not only had Mrs Oliphant changed her personal views about the rightness of the dictum "men must
work, women must weep", but concrete gains had been
won which, superficially, indicated an improvement in the
status of women; access to higher education, the Married
Women's Property acts, the extension of the municipal
franchise and involvement of women in local government.
But the ridicule which every campaign aroused made her
painfully aware of the deep-seated resistance to change
and of the underlying belief in the weakness and inferiority of the female sex. *Hester* has an ironic subtitle "A Story
of Contemporary Life", for the main action is not contemporary, but begins at the end of the 1860s when the
first shock of widespread assaults on traditional attitudes
were still reverberating through the country. The impli-
cation is that little had really changed in the fundamental
attitudes of men to women in the intervening decade.

As an indictment of social attitudes *Hester* is all the more effective because it makes no mention of violent public debates. Everything is on a small scale; the scene is not London, but Redborough, and the emotional and moral boundaries of the heroine's world are equally limited, by family ties and monetary obligations, while her possibilities of action are firmly controlled by Catherine, head of the family and of the bank. (In this version one cannot talk glibly about patriarchal institutions). The way Catherine exerts her authority constantly, cynically and in the only way open to her, through "womanly charity" is a telling comment on the delicate subject of Victorian philanthropy as an expression of power. In the town she becomes a kind of provincial Angela Burdett-Coutts, a local saint, but in the family she is seen as a none-too-benevolent despot; "she is more than the Queen; the house belongs to her, and the furniture, and everything". There is a constant conflict between dependence and dignity, gratitude and rebellion. Her personal tragedy is that, despite her keen intelligence, she is blind to the existence of this conflict in her adored protégé Edward, which drives him to hypocrisy, furtiveness and rejection. At the time of writing Mrs Oliphant was experiencing a growing estrangement from her eldest son and in the relationship of aunt and nephew she provides a bitter, ironic picture of a passion and betrayal which can be just as much part of parental and filial as of romantic love.

Catherine's public prestige and control, which endow her with an illusion of invulnerability, derive from her tight hold on the purse strings. Almost everyone in *Hester* is obsessed by money, with the exception of the Morgans, Catherine's maternal relations, who provide a counter image to her paternal family, the Vernons. In Redborough a social hierarchy based on land and birth is gradually being superseded by one dictated by wealth. The old order is overtly respected, for example in the seating arrangements at a grand Christmas party, but it is quite clear that even genteel poverty now equals powerlessness. Edward is therefore right in a sense when he forces Hester to ask "Does it all come down to money?" But Mrs Oliphant's analysis goes further. What really counts in the eyes of society is the appearance of wealth or rather the sheer *belief* in the existence of wealth, just as it is the appearance of unity which is important for a family, and the public observation of the rules of correct behaviour which define "a lady". The two central institutions of Victorian society—capitalism and the family—(how brilliant to make Vernon's a family bank) are shown to be fictions supported by faith. Vernons seems "solid as the Bank of England", yet within pages mere rumours and doubts threaten a run on the bank which would leave a whole neighbourhood ruined. The disaster is stemmed not by hard evidence of cash in the vaults but by the appearance of a Vernon (Catherine) smiling in the doorway. Private bankers depended entirely on reputation and Catherine, incidentally, provides a perfect model of the behaviour recommended in such a crisis by George Rae in his classic *The Country Banker* (1885). It is credibility, not money, which must be restored.

Yet the vision of *Hester* is not simply an easy exposé of the hollowness and hypocrisy of Victorian life. Rather it is a recognition that all relationships are analogous with financial ones, systems of debt and obligation. And that social institutions, commercial or domestic, do have value if governed by disinterested, trusting, watchful people. The delicate systems of agreement and accepted custom are in fact necessary to hold these institutions together when they are threatened, and extreme individualism, whether it takes the form of "male" capitalism (Edward's speculation) or "female" romance (Hester's longing to elope) can destroy society. Both characters envisage freedom in the same terms, as a fierce wind, exhilarating and terrifying, "the strong gale of revolution". One of the things which makes this novel exciting and uncomfortable is the tension the reader experiences between the sad loss of hopes of personal freedom and the recognition of the importance of maintaining the fabric of social life. Edward measures his "slavery" by cups of tea and Hester is held back from flight by the most slender of barriers, her mother's pleasure that they will be able to make strawberry jam in a fortnight.

It is entirely appropriate that such a momentous decision should hang on such a trivial remark. For Mrs Oliphant suggests that for most people, especially women, time is measured chiefly in terms of personal experience and daily life. The novel contains no dates; Captain Morgan, who is over eighty, remembers the Battle of Trafalgar, but Mrs John dates her youth by the songs of Mrs Haynes Bayley and the fashion for ringlets and spotted muslin. The mood of the late 1860s and early 1870s is evoked, not by mention of appropriate public events such as the 1866 collapse of Overend and Gurney which ruined thousands of small investors, but by the decline in fashion of large crinolines, by the craze for *Thé Dansants*. The point is not the "realism" of her details, but their value, as expressions of the possibilities of women's lives; Mrs John's repeated references back to "when I was young" within the novel, and the way in which the younger generation laugh at the fashions and furniture of their elders are echoed by the narrator's voice referring back from the 1880s to attitudes "in those days", reminding us constantly that all social norms are products of particular historical conditions.

It is on this level that the social comedy is most effective. Several women characters, like Hester's mother, function both as quite complex individual portraits and as types of womanhood of the period. Ellen Vernon is a fairly mild provincial copy of the fast young woman caricatured in late 60s journals as having "an inordinate love of gaiety, a bold determined manner, a total absence of respect towards her parents . . . Her conversation is full of

slang—so repulsive in a feminine mouth", while Emma
Ashton, the Morgan's granddaughter with her total lack of
imagination and self-consciousness and constant reference
to "my chance" is a ludicrous illustration of the mercenary
attitude to marriage. The men too are recognisable comic
types: Vernon Ridgeway, the fussy, bitchy bachelor
worried about his heating bills; Roland Ashton, the romantic outsider with melting eyes; and Harry Vernon, the
upright, manly, honest Dobbin figure who seems to offer
Hester the promise of a married life spent in endlessly
scoring at village cricket matches.

Another of the reasons why *Hester* is disconcerting to
readers familiar with the self-consistent worlds of most
Victorian novels, is that Hester and Catherine seem so out
of place in this nicely realised semi-comic realm. They fit
no stereotypes, a fact which is made clear on Hester's first
introduction, "she was not what people call unselfish—the
one quality which is supposed to be appropriate to feminine natures. She was kind and warm-hearted and affectionate, but she was not without thought of herself." It is
also a fact which grates on other characters in the book,
"Ladies in this country have nothing to do with business—
by the way, I am forgetting Aunt Catherine."

Catherine should be "a type" because she is an "old
maid", as Hester's father had joked that she would be,
with "one of those laughs with which a coarse-minded man
waves the banner of his sex over an unmarried woman".
But she is credited with neither the embittered frustration
nor the sentimental gentleness associated with the opposing clichés of spinsterhood. Because she has wealth and
opportunity, Mrs Oliphant is able to present her independence as a boon rather than an impediment. The situation
of the growing numbers of single women was a much
discussed issue in the nineteenth century, and this portrait
illustrates two interesting aspects of the discussion. The
first was the insistence that it was not just material depend-
ency but internalisation of the ideal of marriage which

made spinsterhood a "problem", as Josephine Butler had maintained, "There is abundance of work to be done which needs men and women detached from domestic ties; our unmarried women will be the greatest blessing to the community when they cease to be soured by disappointment or driven by destitution to despair." Again it is a problem of consciousness, or "sentiment". The second is that by the 1880s spinsterhood was beginning to be seen as a positive condition, allowing freedom of action often denied to married women, a point noted in an article on "The Future of Single Women" in the *Westminster Review* in 1884 which declared "The unmarried woman of today is a new, sturdy and vigorous type . . . The world is before her in a freer, truer and better sense than it is before any individual, male or female."

There is a sense of excitement about the presentation of Hester and Catherine, which we remember almost more than the pessimism of their story. They are large, hungry, healthy, restless, associated with words like "triumph", "energy", "pride" and they seem always to be bursting out of the domestic interiors which confine them. Catherine paces up and down, sweeping majestically from room to room, and in all formal scenes, whether frozen in humiliation at Catherine's evening parties or waltzing feverishly at Ellen's balls, Hester is uncomfortable and constrained. The central image is of her walking, alone, as in Lamb's poem, with "springy gait", or escaping to walk on the common with the old Captain, whose memories offered her access to a larger world where "there were great storms and fights, there were dangers and struggles and death lurking round every corner . . . Why was not Hester born in that day! Why was she not a man!" Neither woman can be contained in the inner world appropriate to their sex. All the emotional crises take place outside, on the porch, at the gate, beneath the trees, and above all on the road which links their two houses and which gives a kind of symbolic axis to the novel. And these scenes of excitement or decision also invariably take place at night as if Hester's intensity does not belong to the mundane behaviour of everyday life.

Towards the end of the book, the plot is forced to a denouement by conventions of betrayal and revelation which belong more to sensation novels than to ironic comedies. The action is halted at crucial moments, reminding one of tableaux from melodramas or the dramatic composition of popular paintings and increasingly the characters themselves are made to sense their own symbolic power, as when Hester, full of premonitions, finds herself remembering the snaky locks and petrifying glance of Medusa. Almost every description attains the quality of metaphor, referring not only to Hester's situation but to that of so many passionate, intelligent women whose dreams of change seemed doomed to disillusionment:

> "I think—I had better go home—to my mother" the girl said, looking along the road with a dreamy terror. She was afraid of the dark, the solitude, the distance—and yet what was there left for her but to go home, which she seemed to have quitted, to have fled from, with the idea of never returning, years ago. Catherine put out her hand and grasped her. She was by far the most vigorous of the two.

It is Catherine, the old maid, who is the embodiment of strength for the future and who points the way forward, not only for Hester, but for the new breed of "odd women", the solitary heroines of the 1890s.

Jennifer Uglow
Canterbury, 1983

HESTER.

CHAPTER I.

VERNON'S.

THE Banking House of the Vernons was known through all the Home Counties as only second to the Bank of England in stability and strength. That is to say the people who knew about such matters, the business people, the professional classes, and those who considered themselves to be acquainted with the world, allowed that it ought to be considered second: but this opinion was not shared by the greater proportion of its clients, the shopkeepers in Redborough and the adjacent towns, the farmers of a wide district, and all the smaller people whose many united littles make up so much wealth. To them Vernon's bank was the emblem of stability, the impersonation of solid and substantial wealth. It had risen to its height of fame under John Vernon, the grandfather of the present head of the firm, though it had existed for two or three generations before him. But John Vernon was one of those men in whose hands everything turns to gold. What the special gift is which determines this it is difficult to tell, but there can be little doubt that it is a special gift, just as it is a particular genius which produces a fine picture or a fine poem. There were wiser men than he, and there were men as steady to their work and as constantly in their place, ready for all the claims of business, but not one other in whose hands everything prospered in the same superlative

way. His investments always answered, his ships always
came home, and under his influence the very cellars of the
banking-house, according to the popular imagination, filled
with gold. At one period of his career a panic seized the
entire district, and there was a run upon the bank, by which
it was evident anybody else must, nay, ought, to have been
ruined ; but John Vernon was not ruined. It was understood
afterwards that he himself allowed that he did not understand
how he had escaped, and nobody else could understand it : but
he did escape, and as a natural consequence became stronger
and richer, and more universally credited than ever. His son
after him had not the same genius for money, but at least he
had the genius for keeping what he had got, which is next best.

Edward Vernon, however, was not so fortunate in his
family as in his affairs. He had two sons, one of whom died
young, leaving a little daughter to be brought up by her
grandfather; the other " went wrong." Oh, never-ending
family tragedy, never ending, still beginning, the darkest
anguish that exists in the world ! The younger son went
wrong, and died also in his father's lifetime, leaving a
helpless little family of children, and a poor wife stupefied
with trouble. She did her best, poor soul, to bring up her boy to
ways the very opposite of those in which his father had stumbled and fallen, and it was supposed that he would marry his
cousin Catherine Vernon, and thus unite once more all the
money and prestige of the house. He too was John Vernon,
and resembled the golden great-grandfather, and great things
were hoped of him. He entered the bank in old Mr. Vernon's
time, and gave every promise of being a worthy successor as
long as the senior partner, the head of the house, lived. But
when the old gentleman died and John Vernon became in his
turn the head of the house, there very soon appeared signs of
change. In the first place the marriage with his cousin never
came to pass ; things had seemed to promise fairly so long as
the grandfather with whom she lived was alive. But after,
there was an immediate cooling of sentiment. Whose fault
this was nobody knew. She said nothing on the subject even
to her dearest friends; nor did he say anything; but he
laughed and waved aside all questions as a man who " could
an if he would "—— His mother, for her part, said a great
deal. She ran between them like an excited hen, shaking her
tail feathers and cackling violently. What did they mean by
it ? What was it for ? She asked her son how he could

forget that if Catherine's money went out of the business it
would make the most extraordinary difference? and she bade
Catherine remember that it would be almost dishonest to
enrich another family with money which the Vernons had
toiled for. Catherine, who was not by any means an ordinary
girl, smiled upon her, perhaps a little sadly, and entered into
no explanations. But her son, as was natural, scoffed at his
mother. "What should you know about the business?" he
said. Poor Mrs. Vernon thought she had heard enough of it to
understand it, or at least to understand the intentions of those
who understood it. But what is the use of a mother's remonstrances? The new generation will please itself and take
its way. She scolded and wept for years after, poor soul, in
vain, and yet could never learn that it was in vain, but began
anew day after day weeping, entreating, remonstrating, falling
into nervous crises of passion a hundred and a hundred times
over. How much better for her to have held her tongue! but how
could she help it? She was not of that placid and patient nature
which can be wise. And gradually things began to go badly
with John. He married a young lady belonging to a county
family, but with no money to keep up her pretensions.
He had his stables full of horses and his house full of company. "What is it all to come to?" cried his poor, anxious,
angry, disappointed, despairing mother, seeking opportunities to have a few words with him, to speak to him
seriously, to remind him of his duty. To be sure she did a
great deal more harm than good. She drew many a blow
upon herself which she might have escaped had she been content to allow that his life had passed far beyond her guidance;
but the poor lady would not be taught. And it was quite
true what John Vernon said. It would take a long time, he
told her, before a few horses and pleasant company would
affect Vernon's bank. As the head of that establishment he
was expected to be hospitable, and keep almost open house;
the country which trusted in him knew he could afford
it. The Redborough people went further, and liked to see the
confidence with which he spent his money. What could that
do to Vernon's? He had never lived up to his income yet, he
believed. So he told his mother, who was never satisfied, and
went on till the day of her death always seeking a few words
with him—an opportunity of speaking seriously to her son.
Poor mother! nothing went very well with her; perhaps she was
not clever either at managing her children or her money. The

partisans of the Vernons said so at least ; they said so of all the
wives that were not Vernons, but interlopers, always working
harm. They said so also of Mrs. John, and there his mother
thought they were not far wrong. But none of her children
turned out very satisfactorily; the girls married badly ;
Edward, her younger son went into the Church and never
was more than a vicar, and their money matters would not
go right. Certainly she was not a fortunate woman. But she
died, happily for her, before anything material happened to
realise her alarms in respect to John.

It is astonishing how money grows when it is in the way of
growing—when it has got the genuine impulse and rolls every
kindred atom near it, according to some occult law of attraction, into itself. But just as wonderfully as money grows
does it melt away when the other—the contrary process—has
begun. John Vernon was quite right in saying that the bank
justified, nay, almost demanded, a certain amount of expendi-
ture from its chief partner. And he was more, much more,
than its chief partner. Catherine, though she was as deeply
interested in it as himself, took no responsibility whatever—
how should she, a girl who knew as much about money as
her pony did ? She took less interest, indeed, than in ordinary
circumstances she would have done, for there was certainly
something, whatever it might be, which had interrupted the
natural intercourse between the two cousins. They were not
at ease with each other like brother and sister, as everything
suggested they ought to have been—not sufficiently at ease to
consider their mutual interests together, as partners ought to
have done. This, one of them at least thought, would have
been ridiculous in any case. When his lawyers asked what
Catherine thought on this or that subject, he laughed in
their faces.

"What should she think? What should she know? Of
course she leaves all that to me," he said. "How can a girl
understand banking business?"

But this did not satisfy the respectable firm of solicitors
who advised the banker.

"Miss Vernon is not a girl any longer," said Mr. Pounce,
who was its head ; upon which John Vernon laughed, one of
those offensive laughs with which a coarse-minded man waves
the banner of his sex over an unmarried woman.

"No," he said, "Catherine's growing an old maid. She
must look alive if she means to get a husband."

Mr. Pounce was not a sentimentalist, and no doubt laughed sometimes too at the unfortunate women who had thus failed in the object of their life; but he respected Miss Vernon, and he was very doubtful of her cousin.

"Husband or no husband, I think she ought to be consulted," he said.

"Oh, I will take Catherine in my own hands," was the cousin's reply.

And thus life went on, very gay, fast, amusing, and expensive on one side; very quiet and uneventful on the other. John Vernon built himself a grand new house, in which there were all the latest improvements and scientific luxuries, which the most expensive upholsterers filled with the most costly furniture, and for which the skilfullest gardeners all but created ready-made trees and shrubberies. He filled it with fine company—names which the clerks at the bank felt were a credit to the establishment, and which the townsfolk looked upon with admiring awe; and there was nothing in the county to equal Mrs. John Vernon's dresses and diamonds. What is all that to a great bank, gathering money every hour?—nothing! Even Mr. Pounce acknowledged this. Personal extravagance, as long as it is merely hospitality and show, must go a very long way indeed before it touches the great revenue of such a business. It was not the diamonds nor the feasts that they were afraid of. But to be lavish with money is a dangerous fault with a man who is a business man. It is a very common sin, but there is nothing more perilous. In Manchester or Liverpool, where they turn over a fortune every day, perhaps this large habit of sowing money about does not matter. People there are accustomed to going up and down. Bankruptcy, even, does not mean the end of the world in these regions. But a banker in a country town, who has all the money of a district in his hands, should not get into this reckless way. His clients are pleased—up to a certain limit. But when once the first whisper of suspicion has been roused it flies fast, and the panic with which rural depositors rush upon a bank which has awakened the ghost of an apprehension, is even more cruel and unreflecting than other panics. It went on a long time, and where it was that the first suggestion came from, nobody ever knew. Probably it did not come from any one—it was in the air, it struck two people, all at once, talking to each other, and the electricity of the contact found a single syllable of utterance.

When that was done, all was done. Everybody had been waiting for this involuntary signal ; and when it came, it flew like
lightning through all Redborough, and out into the roads and
lanes—to distant farmhouses, into the rectories and vicarages,
even to the labourer's cottage. "It's said as Vernon's bank's
a-going to break," the ploughmen in the fields said to each
other. It did not matter much to them ; and perhaps they
were not sorry that the farmer, who grew fat (they thought)
on their toil, should feel that he was also human. The farmers
had something of the same feeling in respect to their land-
lords, but could not indulge it for the furious terror that took
possession of themselves. Vernon's bank! Safer than the
Bank of England, was what they had all said exultingly.
Very few of them had sufficient command of themselves to
wait now and inquire into it and see how far the panic was
well founded. To wait would have been to leave the chance
of salvation to other men.

Mrs. John Vernon was considered very refined and elegant
according to the language of the day, a young lady with
many accomplishments. But it was the fashion of the time
to be unpractical just as it is the fashion of our time that
women should understand business and be ready for any
emergency. To wear your hair in a high loose knot on
the top of your head, with ringlets straying down your
cheek, and across the always uncovered whiteness of your
shoulders, and to sing the songs of Mr. Haynes Bayley,
"Oh no, we never mention her," or "The Soldier's Tear"—
could anything be more entirely inconsistent with business
habits? Mrs. John would have considered it a slight to the
delicacy of her mind to have been supposed to know anything
about the bank ; and when the head clerk demanded an
audience at an unseasonable hour one summer ·evening she
was entirely taken aback.

"Me! do you mean that it is me Mr. Rule wants to see?"
she asked of the servant in consternation.

"He did ask for master, ma'am," said the man, "but
as master's from home he said he must see my lady. He
looks very flustered. I'll say that for him," he added.

To be sure William had heard the whisper in the air, and was
more or less gratified that Mr. Rule should be flustered ;
but as for his lady, she saw no connection whatever between
Mr. Rule's excitement and herself.

"I do not see what good I can do him, William ; and it's

not an hour at which I ever receive people. I am sure I don't know what he can want with me."

"It's business, I think, ma'am," said the servant, with a little eagerness. He wanted immensely himself to know what it was, and it did not occur to him as possible that his mistress, so much more interested than he, should be without anxiety or concern.

"Business!" said Mrs. John, "what do I know about business? However," she added, "if he is so desirous, perhaps you had better show him up. Your master is always pleased when I pay a little attention to the clerks. He says it does good."

"Yes, ma'am," said William.

Being a reasonable human creature he was touched in spite of himself by the extraordinary sight of this poor, fine lady, sitting in her short sleeves on the edge of the volcano, and knowing nothing about it. It was too bad of master, William thought, if so be—— To leave the poor lady entirely in the dark so that she did not know no more than a baby what the clerk could want with her. William speculated, too, on his own circumstances as he went down stairs. If so be—— It was a good place, and he would be sorry to lose it. But he remembered that somebody had said the Sandersons were looking out for a butler.

"Mrs. Vernon will see you, sir," he said in the midst of these thoughts; and Mr. Rule followed him eagerly up stairs.

But what could Mrs. John do? Her dress was spotted muslin, as most dresses were in those days; it was cut rather low on the shoulders, though she was not dressed for company. She had pretty little ringlets falling upon her cheeks, and short sleeves, and a band round her waist with a shining clasp. She was considered brilliant in conversation, and sang, "We met, 'twas in a crowd," and the songs previously mentioned, with so much feeling that people had been known to weep as they listened. The clerk had heard of all these accomplishments, and as he hurried in, his eye was caught by the harp in its corner, which was also one of the fashions of the time. He could not help being a little overawed by it, notwithstanding his dreadful anxiety. Poor lady! the thought passed through his mind as similar thoughts had passed through William's—would all this be sold away from her? White muslin dresses with low necks have the advantage that

they quite seem to separate their wearers from everyday life.
We have no doubt that the dying-out of chivalry, and the
way in which women nowadays insist on doing their own
business, and most likely other people's too, is in great part
to be put down to high dresses and long sleeves. In these
habiliments a lady looks not so very much different from other
people. She feels herself free to go into common life. But
Mrs. John sat there helpless, ignorant, quite composed and
easy in her mind, with pretty feet in sandalled slippers
peeping from under her dress. Mr. Rule had time for all
this distressed, regretful sympathy before he could stammer
out in a hurry his anxious question—or rather his hope—that
Mr. Vernon would be home to-morrow—early?

"I am sure I don't know," said Mrs. John. " It would be
scarcely worth his while to go away if he was to be back so
soon. He said perhaps to-morrow, but more likely next
week."

"Next week!" cried Mr. Rule; "then he may just as well
stay away altogether ; it will then be too late."

"Dear me!" said Mrs. John, politely, willing to show an
interest ; but she did not know what more to say.

"Perhaps you know where he is, ma'am," said the anxious
clerk : for this was the time when people said ma'am. "We
might send an express after him. If he were here, things
might still be tided over. Excuse me, Mrs. Vernon, but if
you can give me any information——"

"Dear me," said Mrs. John, "my husband was going to
London, I think. Is it about business, or anything I may
know?"

"All the world will know to morrow," cried the agitated
clerk, "unless you can give me some assistance. I don't like
to trouble a lady, but what can I do? Mrs. Vernon, to-
morrow is market day, and as sure as that day comes if he
is not here to make some provision for it, we shall have a
run on the bank."

"A run on the bank!" said Mrs. John, dismayed. "What
does that mean?"

"It means that we shall have to pay every note that is presented us in gold : and that everybody will rush upon us
with our notes in their hands : and all the people who have
deposit accounts will withdraw their money. It means Ruin,"
said Mr. Rule, very much flustered indeed, wiping the per-
spiration from his brow. He had an account himself, and a

considerable sum to his credit. Oh, the fool he had been to let it lie there instead of investing it! but then he had been waiting for a good investment, and in the meantime, Vernon's was as safe, safer than the Bank of England. He had believed that till to-day.

Mrs. John sat looking at him with bewildered eyes. "I don't understand," she said. "The bank of course is for that, isn't it? I never understand how you do it," she added, with a little of the sprightliness for which she was distinguished. "It has always been a mystery to me what good it can do you to take all the trouble of paying people's bills for them, and locking up their money, and having all that responsibility; but I cannot deny that it seems to answer," she concluded with a little simper.

The harassed clerk looked at her with a pity that was almost tragic. If she had not been so handsome and so fine, and surrounded with all these luxuries, it is very likely he would have been impatient, and considered her a fool.

He replied gently—

"I dare say, ma'am, it is difficult for you to form an idea of business; but I am almost forgetting, sitting talking to you, how dreadfully serious it is. If I knew where Mr. Vernon was, I would send a post-chaise directly. We are lost if he is not here. They will say—God knows what they may not say. For God's sake, ma'am, tell me how I am to find him?"

"Indeed, Mr. Rule, I am very, very sorry. If I had known! but I rather encouraged him to go. He was looking so poorly. He was going to town, I am sure—first: and then perhaps to Bath: or he might go across to France. He has been talking of that. France—yes, I suggested it. He has never been on the Continent. But now I think of it, I don't think he will go there, for he said he might be home to-morrow—though more likely next week."

"It seems very vague," said Mr. Rule, looking at her with a steady look that began to show a gleam of suspicion; but this was entirely out of place. Mrs. John answered lightly without any perception even of what he could mean.

"Oh yes, it was vague! it is so much better not to be tied down. I told him he ought to take me; but it was settled in a hurry, he was feeling so poorly."

"Then he has forsaken us!" cried the clerk in a terrible voice, which shook even her obtuse perceptions. She gazed at him with a little glow of anger.

"Forsaken you! Dear me, surely a little holiday never can matter. Why, the servants could go on without me for a time. It would never come into Mr. Vernon's head that you could not manage by yourselves even for a single day."

The clerk did not answer; it was all such a terrible muddle of ignorance and innocence, and perhaps of deep and deliberate guilt. But anyhow, there was the result beyond all uncertainty. The bank must come down. Vernon's, which it had taken the work of generations to build up; Vernon's, which was safer than the Bank of England. Mr. Rule had been a clerk there, man and boy, for about twenty years. He had been one of old Mr. Vernon's staff. He had a pride in the bank as if it had been his own. To give up Vernon's to destruction seemed more than giving himself up. But what could the clerks do without the principal? A lieutenant may fight his ship if the captain fails, or a subaltern replace his leader, but what can the clerks do without the head of the establishment? And he had no authority to act even if he had known how to act; and every two or three minutes there would come across him a poignant recollection of his own deposit. Oh, the Alnaschar hopes he had built upon that little fortune, the ways in which it was to serve him! He tried honestly, however, to put it away from his mind.

"We could have done well enough on an ordinary occasion," he said, "and Mr. Vernon generally settles everything before he goes; but I thought he was only absent for the day. Mrs. Vernon," he cried, suddenly, "can't you help us? can't you help us? It will be ruin for you too."

She stared at him for a moment without speaking, and then—

"You make me quite wretched. I don't understand. I have only a little money in the house. Would that do any good?" she said.

"How much have you?" said the clerk in his trouble.

She ran to a pretty ornamental desk and opened it nervously.

"I dare say there may be about twenty pounds," she said.

He laughed loudly, harshly, a laugh that seemed to echo through the large, unoccupied room.

"If it were twenty thousand it might do something," he said.

"Sir!" said Mrs. John Vernon, standing in a fine attitude of displeasure by her desk, holding it open with one hand.

She looked like a picture by Sir Thomas Lawrence, her scarf, for she wore a scarf, hanging half off her pretty white shoulders, caught upon one equally white arm, her ringlets waving on her cheek. His laugh was rude, and then he was only a clerk. She was all angry scorn from the high knot of brown hair on the top of her head to the point of her sandalled shoe.

Poor Mr. Rule was as penitent as man could be. He was shocked beyond measure by his own brutality. He had forgotten himself—and before a lady! He made the most abject apologies.

"But my interest in the bank will, I hope, be some excuse. I feel half distracted," he said; and he added, as he backed out at the door with painful bows, "perhaps, ma'am, if you can think of any means of communicating with Mr. Vernon, you would let me know; or I will call later, if we could send an express; nothing is too much for the chance of having him back to-morrow."

"Well," said the lady, "you are strange managers, I must say, that cannot get on without my husband one day."

"It is not that, ma'am; it is not that."

"I don't know what it is. I begin to think it is only making a fuss," Mrs. John said.

CHAPTER II.

Poor Mr. Rule rushed out into the night in a state of despair. It was a summer night, and the streets of Redborough were still full of the murmur of life and movement. He came down from the slope on which Mr. John Vernon's grand new house was situated, into the town, turning over every thing that it was possible to do. Should he go to the Old Bank, the life-long rival of Vernon's, and ask their help to pull through? Even such a humiliation he would have endured had there been any chance of success. Should he go to the agent of the Bank of England? He could not but feel that it was quite doubtful whether between them they could make up enough to meet the rush he expected; and were they likely to do it? Would not the first question be, Where is Mr. Vernon? And where was Mr. Vernon? Perhaps gone to Bath; perhaps to France, his wife said. Why should he go to France without letting any one at the bank know, saying he was only to be absent for a day? There was no telegraph in those days, and if he confided Mr. Vernon's story to the other banks, what would they think of him? They would say that Vernon was mad, or that he had—gone away. There could be no doubt of what they would say. Rule was faithful to his old service, and to the honour of the house which had trained him. He would say nothing about France or Bath. He would allow it to be understood that Mr. Vernon had gone to London to get the assistance necessary, and would come back in a post-chaise before the offices were open in the morning. And perhaps, he said to himself, perhaps it was so. God grant it might be so! Very likely he

had not thought it necessary to enter into the matter to a
lady. Poor thing, with her twenty pounds! that showed how
much she knew of business; but it was very high-minded and
innocent of her to offer all she had. It showed there was
at least no harm in her thoughts. It gave a momentary ease
to the clerk's mind to think that perhaps this was what Mr.
Vernon must mean. He must have known for some time how
badly things were going, and who could tell that the sudden
expedition of which he had made so little, only saying when
he left the bank the day before "I shall not be here
to-morrow," who could tell that it was not to get help to
surmount the crisis, that he had gone away? Rule turned
towards his own house under the solace of this thought,
feeling that anyhow it was better to get a night's rest, and
be strong for whatever was to happen to-morrow. It would
be a miserable to-morrow if Mr. Vernon did not bring help.
Not only the bank that would go, but so many men with
families that would be thrown upon the world. God help
them! and that money which stood to his own credit, that
balance of which two or three days before he had been so
proud, to see it standing in his name on those well-kept
beautiful books! All this hanging upon the chance that Mr.
Vernon might have gone to town to get money! No, he could
not go in, and sit down at the peaceful table where Mrs.
Rule perhaps would be hemming a cambric ruffle for his shirt,
or plaiting it delicately with her own fingers, a thing no
laundress could do to please her—and the children learning
their lessons. He felt sure that he could not rest; he would
only make her anxious, and why should she be made anxious as
long as he could keep it from her. It is difficult to say how
it was that the first suggestion of a new possibility took hold
of Mr. Rule's mind. He turned away when he was within a
stone's throw of his own house, saying to himself that he
could not go in, that it was impossible, and walked in the
opposite direction, where he had not gone far until he came
in sight of the bank, that centre of so many years hard work,
that pride of Redborough, and of everybody connected with
it. Vernon's! To think that Ruin should be possible, that so
dark a shadow could hover over that sacred place. What
would old Mr. Vernon have said, he who received it from
his father and handed it down always flourishing, always
prosperous to—not to his son. If his son had lived, the
eldest one, not he who had gone wrong, but the eldest,

who was John too, called after his grandfather, he who was the
father of— It was at this point that Mr. Rule came to a dead
stop, and then after a pause wheeled right round, and without
saying another word to himself walked straight up Wilton
Street, which as everybody knows was quite out of his way.

The father of —— Yes, indeed, indeed, and that was true !
The recollection which called forth this fervour of affirma-
tion was a pleasant one.　All the youth of Redborough at one
time had been in love with Catherine Vernon.　The bank
clerks to a man adored her.　When she used to come and go
with her grandfather—and she did so constantly, bringing him
down in the morning in her pony carriage, calling for him in
the afternoon, running in in the middle of the day to see
that the old gentleman had taken his biscuits and his wine—
she walked over their hearts as she crossed the outer office,
but so lightly, so smoothly, that the hearts were only thrilled,
not crushed by her footfall, so firm and swift, but so airy as it
was.　She knew them all in the office, and would give her
hand to the head clerk, and send a friendly glance all round,
unaware of the harm she was doing to the hapless young men.
But after all it was not harm.　It was a generous love they
felt for her, like the love of chivalry for a lady unapproach-
able.　That young princess was not for them.　None of
them grew mad with foolish hopes, but they thought of her
as they never thought of any one else.　Mr. Rule was at the
end of Wilton Street, just where it meanders out towards the
edge of the common, before he took breath, and began to ask
himself what Miss Vernon could do for him.　Was not one
lady enough to appeal to ?　She whom he had already seen
had nothing for him—no help, no advice, not a suggestion
even.　And yet she was more closely connected with the
bank than Catherine Vernon, who had disappeared from
all visible connection with it at her grandfather's death, notwithstanding that a great deal of her money was in it, and
that she had in fact a right to be consulted as a partner.　So
it had been settled, it was said, by the old man in his will.
But she had never, so far as anybody knew, taken up this
privilege.　She had never come to the bank, never given a
sign of having any active interest in it.　What then could
she be expected to do ?　What could she do even if she wished
to help them ?　Mr. Rule was aware that there was no very
cordial feeling between her cousin's house and hers.　They
were friends, perfectly good friends, but they were not cordial.

While he turned over these thoughts in his mind, however, he walked on steadily and quickly without the least hesitation in his step. There was even a sort of exhilarated excitement in him, a sentiment quite different from that with which he had been disconsolately straying about, and painfully turning over possibilities, or rather impossibilities. Perhaps it was a half romantic pleasure in the idea of speaking to Miss Vernon again, but really there was something besides that, a sense of satisfaction in finding a new and capable mind to consult with at least, if no more.

Miss Vernon lived in the house which her grandfather had lived in and his father before him. To reach it you had to make your way through the delta of little streets into which Wilton Street ran, and across a corner of the common. The Grange was an old house with dark red gables appearing out of the midst of a clump of trees. In winter you saw the whole mass of it, chiefly old bricks, though these were thrown up and made picturesque by the fact that the oldest part was in grey stone. Broad large Elizabethan windows glimmered, lighted up, through the thick foliage this evening; for by this time the summer night was beginning to get dark, and a good deal too late for a visit. Mr. Rule thought as he knocked at the door that it was very likely she would not see him. But this was not the case. When he sent in his name as the head clerk at the bank he was received immediately, and shown into the room with the Elizabethan windows where she was sitting. By this time she was of mature years, and naturally much changed from the young girl he had known. He had been one of the young clerks in the outer office, whom she would recognise with a friendly smiling look, and a nod of her head all round. Now, however, Miss Vernon came up to him, and held out her hand to Mr. Rule. "You need not have sent me word who you were," she said with a smile. "I knew quite well who you were. I never forget faces nor names. You have not come to me at this time of night on a mere visit of civility. Don't be afraid to tell me at once whatever there may be to say."

"From the way you speak, ma'am," said Mr. Rule, "I conclude that you have heard some of the wicked reports that are flying about?"

"That is exactly what I want to know," she said, with all her old vivacity. "Are they wicked reports?"

"A report is always wicked," said Mr. Rule sententiously, "which is likely to bring about the evil it imagines."

"Ah!" she cried. "Then it is no further gone than that; and yet it is as far gone as that?" she added, looking anxiously in his face.

"Miss Vernon," said Rule solemnly, "I expect a run upon the bank to-morrow."

"Good God!" she said, clasping her hands; which was not a profane exclamation, but the kind of half-conscious appeal which nature makes instinctively. "But you have made all preparations? Surely you can meet that."

He shook his head solemnly. The credit of the bank was so much to him that when thus face to face with the event he dreaded, poor Rule could not articulate anything, and the water stood in his eyes.

"Good God!" she said again: but her face was not awe-stricken; it was that of a soldier springing instantly to the alert, rallying all his resources at the first word of danger; "but you don't mean to say that my cousin—does not John know this? They say everybody knows these things before the person concerned. Why, why did you not warn him, Mr. Rule?"

Rule shook his head.

"It isn't possible that he could have been ignorant. How could he be ignorant, ma'am? God knows I have not a word to say against Mr. Vernon—but to think he should forsake us in our moment of trial!"

"Forsake you!" A sudden flush flew over Miss Vernon's face—a spark shot out of her eyes. Indignation and yet doubt was in her face. "That is not possible," she cried, holding her head high; and then she said anxiously, "Mr. Rule, tell me what you mean?"

"I dare say it is the falsity of appearances," said poor Rule. "I am sure I hope so. I hope Mr. Vernon has gone away to get help, personally: you can do that so much better than writing; and that he may be back in time to-morrow."

"Has he gone away?" she said in a low tone.

"Unfortunately, Miss Vernon—I can't help saying unfortunately, for it paralyses everybody else. We can do nothing at the bank. But I cling to the hope that he will be back before the bank is opened. Oh, yes, I cling to the hope. Without that——"

"Everything will be lost?"

"Everything!" cried he, who was so proud of being the head clerk at Vernon's, with tears in his eyes.

And then there was a pause. For a minute or two not a word was said. The daughter of the house was as much overcome by the thought as was its faithful servant. At last she said faintly, but firmly—

"Mr. Rule, I cannot believe but that you will see John to-morrow when the bank is opened, with means to meet every demand."

"Yes, Miss Vernon, that is my conviction too."

But in what a faltering voice was this conviction stated! The room was not very light, and they did not distinguish very clearly each other's faces.

"But in case of any failure—" she said, "for of course one never can tell, the most tiresome nothings may detain you just when speed is most important; or he might not have succeeded as he hoped. In case of any—delay—I shall be there, Mr. Rule; you may calculate upon me, with every penny I can muster——"

"You, Miss Vernon!" the clerk said, with a cry of relief and joy.

"Certainly; who else, when the credit of the bank is at stake? I have been living very quietly, you know. I spend next to nothing; my mother's money has accumulated till it is quite a little fortune, I believe. What had I best do? send to Mr. Sellon and ask him to help us on that security? I don't think he will refuse."

"If you do that we are saved," said Rule, half crying. "That is the thing to do. What a head for business you have!"

She smiled, and gave him a little nod, like one of those happy nods she used to give to the young clerks in her fine youthful days, in which there was a kind acknowledgment of their admiration, a friendly good fellowship with themselves.

"I hope I am not old Edward Vernon's granddaughter for nothing," she said, beginning to walk up and down the room with a buoyant impatience, as though longing for the moment of exertion to come. "I had better write to Mr. Sellon at once; there is no time to lose."

"And if you will let me I will take the note directly, and bring you an answer."

"Bravo! that is promptitude," cried Miss Vernon; and she went up to him and held out her hand. "Between us we will keep the old place going," she said, "whoever may give in."

If Mr. Rule had not been the steady, bashful Englishman he was, he would have kissed that hand. He felt that there was in it enough to save everything—the bank first, and then his own little bit of money, and his situation, and his children's bread. He had not allowed himself to think of these things in the greatness of his anxiety in respect to Vernon's; but he did think of them now, and was ready to cry in the relief of his soul.

Never was an evening more full of occupation. Mr. Sellon, who was the agent of the Bank of England in Redborough, was fortunately at home, and responded at once to Miss Vernon's appeal. Mr. Rule had the gratification of walking back with him to the Grange, whither he hastened to reply in person, and of assisting at the interview afterwards with a sense of pride and personal advancement which heightened the satisfaction of his soul. Miss Vernon insisted strongly on the point that all these preparations were by way of precaution merely.

" My cousin will no doubt be back in time, fully provided ; but of course you never can be perfectly certain. Horses may break down, shafts be broken ; the least little accident may spoil everything. Of course John put off such a step till the last moment, and thought it better to keep it entirely to himself."

" Of course," cried Rule, speaking out of his corner ; and " Of course," but much more faintly, Mr. Sellon said.

"That is so evident that it requires no repetition : but just as naturally Mr. Rule was alarmed, and had the good sense to come to me."

All this was by way of convincing Mr. Sellon that the whole matter was perfectly simple, and that probably his resources would not be called upon at all. To be sure, as in every case of a similar kind, Miss Vernon might have saved herself the trouble, the circumstances being far more clearly known to Mr. Sellon than to herself. He was very sure that John Vernon would not return, and that his intention was to get himself out of it. Everybody had known it was coming. It was just as well to humour a lady, and accept her version as the right one ; but he was not for a moment deceived.

" Of course the bank," he said, " will make it up to you afterwards."

" Of course," she said ; "and if not, I don't know who is to stop me from doing what I like with my own."

He asked a few questions further, in which there was a good deal of significance, as for instance something about Mrs. John Vernon's marriage settlements, which neither of the others for the moment understood. Rule saw Mr. Sellon to the door, by Miss Vernon's request, with great pride, and went back to her afterwards, "as if he were one of the family," he described to his wife afterwards.

"Well," she said, "are you satisfied?"

"Oh, more than satisfied, happier than I can tell you," cried the clerk. "The bank is saved!"

And then she, so triumphant, buoyant, inspired as she was, sank down upon a chair, and put her head in her hands, and he thought cried; but Rule was not a man to spy upon a lady in the revulsion of her feelings. When she looked up again she said to him quickly—

"In any case, Mr. Rule, we are both sure that my cousin is doing all he can for the bank; if he succeeds or not is in other hands."

"Oh yes, Miss Vernon, quite sure," Rule replied promptly. He understood that she meant it to be understood so, and determined within himself that he was ready to go to the stake for the new dogma. And then he related to her his interview with Mrs. John, and her willingness to give him up her twenty pounds to save the bank.

Miss Vernon's first flush of indignation soon yielded to amusement and sympathy. She laughed and she cried.

"That shall always be remembered to her credit," she said. "I did not think she had any feeling for the bank. Let us always remember it to her credit. She was ready to give all she had, and who can do any more?"

Mr. Rule was somewhat intoxicated with all these confidences, and with the way in which Miss Vernon said "we" —his head was a little turned by it. She was a woman who understood what it was to have a faithful servant. No doubt, after the sacrifice she was making, she would, in future, have more to do with the business, and Rule could scarcely keep his imagination from straying into a consideration of changes that might be. Instead of merely being head clerk, it was quite possible that a manager might be required; but he pulled himself up, and would not allow his thoughts to carry him so far.

Next day everything happened as had been foreseen. There was a run on the bank, and a moment of great excitement;

but when Miss Vernon was seen at the door of the inner
office smiling, with her smile of triumphant energy and
capability, upon the crowd, and when the Bank of England
porters appeared bringing in those heavy boxes, the run and all
the excitement subsided as by magic.   The bank was saved ;
but not by John Vernon. The outside world never was aware
how the matter was settled.   But John did not come back.
He would have met nothing but averted looks and biting
words, for there could be no doubt that he had abandoned his
post, and left Vernon's to its fate.   Messrs. Pounce and
Seeling had a good deal to do about the matter, and new
deeds were drawn, and old deeds cancelled to a serious extent ;
but the bank ever after remained in the hands of Miss
Vernon, who, it turned out, had more than her grandfather's
steady power of holding on, and was, indeed, the heir of her
great-grandfather's genius for business.   The bank throve in
her hands as it had done in his days, and everything it
touched prospered. She deserved it, to be sure, but everybody
who deserves does not get this fine reward. There is something
beyond, which we call good luck or good fortune, or the favour
of Heaven ; but as Heaven does not favour all, or even most,
of the best people in this way, we have to fall back upon a
less pious phraseology.   Is it, perhaps, genius for business, as
distinct as genius in poetry, which makes everything succeed ?
But this is more than any man can be expected to understand.
Rule attained all the heights of those hopes which had vaguely
dawned on him out of the mist on that July evening when his
good angel suggested to him Catherine Vernon's name.   He
was raised to the dignity of manager as he had foreseen.   His
salary was doubled, his sons were provided for, and he grew
old in such comfort and general esteem as he had never
dreamed of.   " This is the man that saved the bank," Miss
Vernon would say.   And though, of course, he deprecated
such high praise, and declared that he was nothing but the
humblest instrument, yet there can be no doubt that he
came to believe it in the end, as his wife and all his children
did from the beginning.

Miss Vernon's was a reign of great benevolence, of great
liberality, but of great firmness too.   As she got older she
became almost the most important person in Redborough.   The
people spoke of her, as they sometimes do of a very popular
man, by her Christian name.   Catherine Vernon did this and
that, they said. Catherine Vernon was the first thought when

anything was wanted either by the poor who needed help, or
the philanthropist who wanted to give it.   The Vernon Almshouses, which had been established a hundred years before,
but had fallen into great decay till she took them in hand,
were always known as Catherine Vernon's Almshouses.   Her
name was put to everything.   Catherine Street, Catherine
Square, Catherine places without number.   The people who
built little houses on the outskirts exhausted their invention
in varying the uses of it.   Catherine Villas, Catherine
Cottage, Catherine Mansion, were on all sides ; and when it
occurred to the High Church rector to dedicate the new
church to St. Catherine of Alexandria, the common people,
with one accord, transferred the invocation to their living
patroness.   She was, at least, a saint more easily within
reach, and more certain to lend a favourable ear.

CHAPTER III.

THE VERNONRY.

THESE things all happened a great number of years before the beginning of this history. Catherine Vernon had become an old woman—at least she was sixty-five; you can call that an old woman if you please. Sometimes it may mean the extreme of age, decrepitude and exhaustion : but sometimes also it means a softer and more composed middle age—a lovely autumnal season in which all the faculties retain their force without any of their harshness, and toleration and Christian charity replace all sharpness of criticism or sternness of opinion. Sometimes this beautiful age will fall to the lot of those who have experienced a large share of the miseries of life and learnt its bitterest lessons, but often—and this seems most natural—it is the peaceful souls who have suffered little to whom this crown of continuance is given. Catherine Vernon belonged to the last class. If her youth had not been altogether happy, there had been fewer sorrows and still fewer struggles in her life. She had gone along peacefully, her own mistress, nobody making her afraid, no one to be anxious about, no one dear enough to rend her heart. Most people who have gone through the natural experiences of life are of opinion with the Laureate, that it is

" Better to have loved and lost
Than never to have loved at all."

But then we do not allow the other people to speak who know the other side of the question. If love brings great happiness it brings many woes. Catherine Vernon was like Queen Elizabeth, a dry tree—while other women had sons and daughters. But when the hearts of the mothers were torn with anxiety, she went free. She had the good of other people's children in a wonderful degree, but it was impossible she could have the harm of them—for those whom she took to were the good children, as was natural, the elect of this world. Her life had been full of exertion and occupation since that night when Rule called upon her at the Grange and set all the world of her being in movement. What flagging and loneliness might have been hers—what weariness and longing had ended at that time. Since then how much she had found to do! The work of a successful man of business increased, yet softened by all the countless nothings that make business for a woman, had filled her days. She was an old maid, to be sure, but an old maid who never was alone. Her house had been gay with young friends and tender friendship. She had been the first love of more girls than she could count. By the time she was sixty-five she was a sort of amateur grandmother in numbers of young households. A woman with plenty of money, with a handsome, cheerful house, and a happy disposition, she had—at least since her youth was over—never had occasion to remember the want of those absorbing affections which bind a married woman within her own circle. The children of the barren in her case were more than those of any wife. If ever in her heart she said to herself, like Matthew in the poem—

> "Many love me, yet by none
> Am I enough beloved,"

the sentiment never showed, and must have occurred only as Matthew's did, in moods as evanescent as the clouds. Her face was not without lines, for that would be to say that it was without expression; nor did she look too young for her age: but her eye was not dim, nor her natural force abated. She had a finer colour than in her girlhood, though the red was not so smooth, but a little broken in her soft cheek. Her hair was white and beautiful, her figure ample, but graceful still. At sixty she had given up work, entering upon, she said, the Sabbatical period of her life. For the rest of her days she meant to keep Sunday, resting from her labours —and indeed, with perhaps too close a following of the divine example for any human creature to venture upon, finding them very good.

It follows as a matter of course that she had found somebody to replace her in the bank. There were so many Vernons,

that this was not very difficult to do.   At least it was not
difficult to find candidates for so important a post.   Descend-
ants of the brothers and sisters of the great John Vernon,
who had first made the bank what it was, were plentiful, and
from among them Catherine Vernon selected two hopeful
young men to carry on her work.   One of them, Harry
Vernon, was descended from the daughter of the great John,
who had married a relation and continued to bear the family
name.   The other went further back and traced his descent
from a brother of that great John.   The parents of these
fortunate young men acquiesced with delight in the proposals
she made to them.   It was a certain fortune—an established
living at once—far better than the chances of the Bar, or the
Indian Civil Examinations, or Colorado, which had begun to be
the alternative for young men.   Indeed it was only Edward
Vernon who had parents to be consulted.   Harry had but a
sister, who had come to live with him in the fine house
which the last John, the one who had put the bank in such
deadly peril, had built.   Edward lived with Miss Vernon
herself.   Five years had passed since their inauguration as
partners and managers, with very little change in their feelings towards the old cousin, who had done so much for them,
and whom they called Aunt Catherine.   She was Aunt
Catherine to a great many people, but these three, who were
the nearest to her in blood, were disposed to give themselves
airs, and to punish intruders who presumed upon a fictitious
relationship.   They were to all appearance quite satisfactory
young people, if perhaps not brilliant ; and pious persons
said that Miss Vernon had got her reward for her kindness to the poor, and her more than kindness to her poor
relations.   She was surrounded by those who were to her
like children of her own.   No mother could have had sons
more respectful and devoted.   Good and virtuous and kind
children—what could a woman have more ?

Perhaps this was rather a flattering and ideal statement of
the case ; but at all events one of the young men satisfied all
Miss Vernon's requirements, and they were both steady-
going, fine young fellows, paying every attention to business, keeping everything going.   Ellen perhaps was not
quite so satisfactory.   She was young and headstrong, and
not sure that Catherine Vernon was all that people made
her out to be.   There was nothing wonderful in this.   To
hear one person for ever applauded is more likely than

anything else to set an impatient mind against that person
—and Ellen kept her old cousin at arm's length, and showed
her little affection. Nobody could doubt that this must have
vexed Miss Vernon, but she took it with wonderful calm.

" Your sister does not like me," she said to Harry ; " never
mind, she is young, and she will know better one day."

" You must not think so," Harry said. " Ellen is foolish
and headstrong, but she has a very good heart."

Catherine Vernon nodded a little and shook her head.

" It is not a heart," she said, " that is disposed towards
me. But never mind ; she will think better of it one day."

Thus you will see that Miss Vernon escaped from the worst,
and had the best, of motherhood. What a bitterness to her
heart would this alienation have been, had Ellen been her child !
but as the troublesome girl was not her child in reality, the
unkindness vexed her in a very much less degree. She was able
to think of the boys, who were so good, without being disturbed by the image of the girl, who was not so good. And
so all things went on serenely, and the years went by, gentle,
unremarkable, tranquil years.

Several years before this, before indeed the young people
had entered into her life, the old house, called the Heronry,
came into Miss Vernon's hands. It was at some distance on
the same side of the common, but a little further out towards
the country than the Grange—a large old red brick house, in
the midst of a thin but lofty group of trees. Though it was
so near the town, there was something forlorn in it, standing
out against the west, the tall trees dark against the light, the
irregular outline of the old house flush against the sky, for it
was a flat country, no hills or undulations, but everything that
was tall enough showing direct against the horizon in a way
that was sometimes very impressive. This great old house
Miss Vernon made a curious use of. It contained a multitude
of rooms, not any very large except that which occupied the
centre of the area, a sort of hall, with a great staircase going
out of it. From the moment it came into her hands, she
made, everybody thought, a toy of the Heronry. She divided
it into about half a dozen compartments, each with a separate
entrance. It was very cleverly done, so as not to interfere in
any way with the appearance of the place. The doors were
not new and unsightly, but adapted with great care, some of
them being windows a little enlarged. What was it for ? All
kinds of rumours ran about the town. It was some sort of

a convent which she was going to institute, a community of
an apostolical kind, a sisterhood, a hospital, a set of almshouses. Some went so far as to call it Catherine Vernon's
Folly. She spent a great deal of money upon it, elaborating
her whim, whatever it might be. It was fitted up with
apparatus for warming, which would make the dwellers in it
independent of fires, people said, and this looked like a
hospital everybody allowed. There was no end to the conveniences, the comforts of the place. The old-fashioned
gardens were put in order, and the greatest trouble taken to
make the old pool—which had got the place its name, and
where it was said that herons had actually been seen in the lifetime of some old inhabitants—wholesome and without prejudice
to the health of the house. The pool itself was very weird
and strange to be so near the dwelling of ordinary life. It
lay in the centre of the clump of trees which had once been a
wood, and which round it had grown tall and bare, with
clumps of foliage on the top, and straight, long stems mount-
ing to the sky, and shining in long lines of reflection in the
still, dark water. Several gaunt and ghostly old firs were
among them, which in the sunset were full of colour, but in
twilight stood up black and wild against the clear, pale sky.
This pool was about as far from the Grange as Miss Vernon
could walk with comfort, and it was a walk she was very fond
of taking on summer nights. The common lay between the
house and the town ; beyond it spread the long levels of the
flat country. In the summer all was golden about, with gorse
and patches of purple heather, and the abundant growth of
wild, uncultivated nature. What did Catherine Vernon mean
to do with this house ? That was what all Redborough wanted
to know.

By the time at which this story properly begins, Redborough
had been acquainted for years with Miss Vernon's intentions ;
they were indeed no longer intentions, but had been carried
out. The Heronry had changed its name, if not formally, yet
in familiar parlance, throughout all the neighbourhood, and
was called the Vernonry even by people who did not know
why. The six dwellings which had been contrived so cleverly
were all occupied by relations and dependents of the family,
members of the house of Vernon, or connections of the same.
They made a little community among themselves, but not the
community of a sisterhood or a hospital. It was said that
they had their little internal feuds and squabbles, as people

living so close together are always supposed to have, but
they were sufficiently well bred, or sufficiently in awe of their
cousin and patroness, to keep these quarrels decorously to
themselves. How far they were indebted to her for their
living, as well as their lodging, nobody knew, which was not
for want of many a strenuous investigation on the part of
the neighbourhood ; but the inmates of the Vernonry were
clever enough to keep their own counsel on a matter which
involved their own consequence and credit. Disagreeable
things were indeed said about " genteel almshouses," and
" poor relations," when it first became a question in Redborough about calling on the new residents. But as it turned
out, they were all persons of pretensions expecting to be called
upon by the county, and contemptuous of the townspeople.
Five of the six apartments into which the old house had been
divided were occupied, when Redborough was startled by the
extraordinary intelligence that the last and best had been
reserved for no less interesting an inmate than Mrs. John
Vernon, she who had left the town in circumstances so painful.
John Vernon, the unfortunate or the culpable, who had all but
ruined the bank, and left it to its ruin, had died abroad.
His wife's marriage settlement had secured their income, but
he had spent as much as it was possible to spend of that,
and forestalled every penny that he could manage to forestall.
His debts were such that his widow's income was sadly
crippled by the necessity of paying them, which it was said
she would not herself have seen so clearly but for the determined way in which it was taken up by her child, a very
young girl, born long after the catastrophe, but one who was
apparently of the old stock, with a head for business, and a
decision of character quite unusual in a child. Mrs. John's
return caused a great sensation in Redborough. She was very
well connected, and there could be no question on anybody's
mind as to the propriety of calling on a woman who was aunt
to Sir John Southwood, and first cousin to Lady Hartingale.
How she could like to come back there, to live within sight
of her own beautiful house, and to be indebted for shelter to
Catherine Vernon, was a much more difficult matter to understand. But as everybody said, that of course was Mrs. John's
own concern. If she could make up her mind to it, certainly
nobody else had any call to interfere.

But what a change it was from the fatal day when poor
Mr. Rule, all anxious and miserable, was shown in by the
curious servant to the costly drawing-room in which John

Vernon's wife, in her spotted muslin, sat ignorant of business, but confident and satisfied in her good fortune, and in the certainty that all would go well with her! Poor lady! she had learned some few things since that day, but never had grasped the mystery of her downfall, nor known how it was that everything had collapsed in a moment, tumbling down like a house of cards. She had not, indeed, tried to understand at that terrible time when it all burst upon her—when the fact that she had to leave her house, and that her furniture was going to be sold in spite of all her indignant protestations, compelled her understanding, such as it was, into the knowledge that her husband was ruined. She had too much to do then, in crying, in packing, in appealing to heaven and earth to know what she had done to be so cruelly used, and in trying to make out how she was to travel, to be able to face the problem how it had all come about. And after she went away the strangeness and novelty of everything swept thought out of her mind, if, indeed, it ever entered there at all. Perhaps it was only after that life was over, and when widowed and growing old she came back to the strange little house which Catherine Vernon had written to offer her, that she remembered once more to ask herself the question. Or, perhaps, even then it was not she who asked it, but Hester, who, greatly excited, with eyes large with curiosity and interest, clinging to her mother's arm in a way she had, which looked like dependence, and was control, went all over the new-old place with her, drinking in information. Hester led her mother wherever she pleased, holding her arm embraced in her own two clasped hands. It was her way of holding the helm. She was a tall girl of fourteen when she came to the Heronry, out-growing all her frocks, and all her previous knowledge, and thirsting to understand everything. She had never been in England before, though she prided herself on being an English girl. She knew scarcely anything about her family, why it was they lived abroad, what was their history, or by what means they were so severed from all relationships and friendships. The letter of Catherine Vernon offering them a house to live in had roused her, with all the double charm of novelty and mysterious, unknown relationship. " Who is she? Cousin Catherine? Papa's cousin! Why is she so kind? Oh yes, of course she must be kind—very kind, or she would not offer us a house. And that is where you used to live? Redborough. I should think in a week—say a week

—we might be ready to go." It was thus that she carried her
mother along, who at the first did not at all intend to go.
Hester arrived at the curious old house, which was unlike
anything she had ever seen before, with eyes like two notes of
interrogation, brilliant, flaming, inquiring into everything;
and as soon as her mother had rested, and had taken that
cup of tea which is an Englishwoman's comfort, the girl had
her out to see what was to be seen, and led her about, turning
the helm now one way, now another. The Grange was visible
as soon as they got beyond their gate, and on the other
side of the red roofs of Wilton Street, standing on the only
height that exists in the neighbourhood, there was the white
and splendid "elevation" of the White House, still splendid,
though a little the worse for wear. Mrs. John stood still,
resisting the action of the helm unconsciously, and all at once
began to cry. "That is where we used to live," she said,
with little sobs breaking in, "that—that is where we lived
when we married. It was built for me ; and now to think I
have nothing to do with it—nothing ! "

It was then that the question arose, large, embracing
the entire past, and so many things that were beyond the
mother's knowledge—" Why did papa go away ? " Mrs. John
cried, she could not help it, feeling in a moment all the
difference, the wonderful change, the downfall and reversal
of everything that in those days she had expected and hoped.
She dried her eyes half a dozen times, and then burst out
again. "Oh, what have I done that so much should happen
to me! and Catherine Vernon always the same," she said.
After a while Hester ceased to ask any questions, ceased to
impel her mother this way or that by her arm, but led her
home quietly to the strange house, with its dark wainscot,
which was so unfamiliar, and made her lie down upon the sofa.
Mrs. John was not a person of original impulses. What she
did to-day she had done a great many times before. Her
daughter knew all her little ways by heart. She knew about
how long she would cry, and when she would cheer up again ;
and in the meantime she did her best to put two and two
together and make out for herself the outline of the history.
Of course she was all wrong. She had heard that her father
was the victim of a conspiracy, and she had never seen him
on any but his best side. Her idea was he had been wronged ;
perhaps he was too clever, perhaps too good, for the designing
people round him, and they had laid their heads together and
procured his ruin. The only thing that puzzled Hester was

the share that the unknown Cousin Catherine had in it. Had
she been against him too ? But, if so, why was she kind to
his wife and child ? Perhaps out of remorse and compunction ?
Perhaps because she was an old woman, and wanted to make
up a little for what she had done ? But this was all vague,
and Hester was prudent enough not to make up her mind
about it until further inquiries. She put her mother to bed
in the meantime, and did all the little things for her which
were part of Mrs. John's system. She brushed her hair, still
so pretty ; she tied nicely, as if it were an article of full dress,
the strings of her nightcap ; she put all her little things by
her on the table by her bedside—her Bible and prayer-book,
the novel she had been reading on the journey, a biscuit in
case she should wake up feeling faint in the night. There was
quite an array of small matters. And then Hester kissed her
mother and bid her go to sleep. " You will not be long of
coming to bed, dear ?" Mrs. John said ; and the girl promised. But she went away, carrying her candle into one
wainscoted room after another, asking herself if she liked
them. She had been used to big white rooms in France. She
saw gleams of her own face, and reflections of her light in the
deep brown of these walls with a pleasant little thrill of alarm.
It was all very strange, she had never seen anything like it
before ; but what was the reason why papa left ? What had
he done ? What had been done to him ? One of the down-stairs
rooms opened upon a pretty verandah, into which she was
just about stepping, notwithstanding her dread that the wind
would blow her candle out, when suddenly she was met by a
large and stately figure which made the heart jump in Hester's
breast. Miss Catherine had come out, as she did so often at
night, with a white shawl thrown over her cap. The road
was so quiet—and if it had been ever so noisy Catherine
Vernon could surely dress as she pleased, and go as she
pleased, from one place to another in Redborough and its
neighbourhood. She saw coming out upon her in the light of
a candle a pair of brown eyes, large and wide open, full of
eager curiosity, with a tall girl behind them, somewhat high-
shouldered, with clustering curly short hair. Catherine
Vernon was not without prejudices, and she did not like
Mrs. John, nor did she expect (or perhaps intend) to like her
daughter. There was something in the girl's face which
disarmed her suspicion ; but she was not a person to give in,
and give up her foregone conclusion on any such trifling
occasion as that.

CHAPTER IV.

A FIRST MEETING.

CATHERINE VERNON had come to see with her own eyes that her guests or tenants had arrived, and that they were comfortable. They were relations, which justified the want of ceremony; but, perhaps, if they had not been poor, and she had not been their benefactor, she would scarcely, in so very easy a way, with a shawl over her cap, and at an hour not adapted for visits, have made the first call upon them. She would have been more indignant than any one at such a suggestion; but human motives are very subtle, and, no doubt, though she was not in the least aware of it, this was true. To be sure, there were circumstances in which such a visit would have seemed, of all things, the most kind, but not, perhaps, with persons so little in sympathy as Catherine Vernon and Mrs. John. She knew she had been substantially kind. It is so much easier to be substantially kind than to show that tender regard for other people's feelings which is the only thing which ever calls forth true gratitude; and perhaps Catherine had not altogether escaped the deteriorating influences of too much prosperity. In her solitude she had become a great observer of men—and women: and was disposed to find much amusement in this observation. Miss Vernon was half aware that other motives than those of pure benevolence affected her mind as she went that evening to the Vernonry. Curiosity was in it. She could not but wonder how Mrs. John was feeling, what she thought of all these changes. She was glad that her cousin's widow had come home where she could be looked after, and where it would be seen that nothing happened to her; but she had wondered

above measure when her offer of shelter and a home had been
accepted, not knowing, of course, anything about that very
active factor in Mrs. John's affairs, who was known to the
people in Redborough only as "the little girl." Catherine
Vernon thought that she herself, in Mrs. John's position, would
have starved or worked her fingers to the bone rather than
have come back in such a humiliated condition to the neighbourhood where she had held so different a place. She was rather
glad to feel herself justified in her contempt of her cousin's
wife by this failure in her of all "proper pride"; and she
allowed curiosity and a sense of superiority and her low
estimate of Mrs. John's capacity of feeling, to carry the day
over her natural sense of courtesy. What so natural, she
said to herself, as that she should run out and see whether
they had arrived, and if they were comfortable, and establish
friendly, easy relations at once, without waiting for formalities ?
Qui s'excuse s'accuse. Miss Vernon certainly knew, at the
bottom of her heart, that sorrow and downfall merited a more
respectful accost ; but then Mrs. John had none of those
delicacies of feeling, or it was not in nature that she would
have come at all. And nothing could be more substantially
kind than Catherine knew she had been. She had engaged an
excellent servant for them—a woman who had been in her
own house, and who was a capital cook, and capable of taking
a kind of charge as housekeeper if Mrs. John still remained
incapable as of old ; and, no doubt, Miss Vernon thought,
there would be a foreign *bonne* of some sort or other to take
care of "the little girl." Her own maid accompanied her to
the gate, then went round to the humbler entrance while Miss
Vernon walked through the garden to the pretty verandah
newly put up (but in excellent taste and keeping, everybody
said), which was intended to form a sort of conservatory in a
sunny corner, and give the inhabitants a little more elegance
and modern prettiness than the other houses afforded. She
had done this on purpose for Mrs. John, who had got used, no
doubt, to foreign ways, sitting out of doors, and indulgences
of that kind. Could anything have been more kind ? And
yet, at the bottom of her heart, Miss Vernon was aware that
if she had resisted her impulse to come and spy upon the poor
traveller this first night, and investigate her feelings, and how
she was supporting the change, and all the recollections to be
called forth by her return, she would have been far more really
kind. She felt this, yet she came. What is there in the

human bosom more strong than the desire to see how the gladiators die? Poor Mrs. John was no gladiator, but she was upon the point of that sword of suffering which some writhe and struggle upon, and some allow themselves to be wounded by, in silence. Miss Vernon was very anxious to know how she was bearing it. The daylight, which had come to an end altogether in the dark wainscoted rooms inside, was still lingering without. Behind the trees there was a golden clearness upon the horizon, against which every branch stood out. The stars were only half visible in the faint blue. The walk had been delightful. It was the time she preferred to be abroad, her mind undisturbed by those cares which pursue less peaceful people, yielding itself up entirely to the spell of universal tranquillity and repose.

But when Miss Vernon, opening the glass door of the verandah, suddenly came in sight of a figure which was quite unexpected, which she could not identify or recognise, she was, for the moment, too much startled to speak. A tall girl of fourteen, in that large development which so many girls attain at that early age, to be "fined down" into slim grace and delicacy afterwards—with rather high shoulders, increased by the simple form of her dress; hair of a chestnut colour, cut short, and clustering in natural rings and twists—not curled in the ordinary sense of the word; a complexion in which white predominated, the creamy whiteness of a sanguine temperament, with but little of the rose; and two large, eager brown eyes, full of curiosity, full of life, evidently interrogating everything, coming out, even upon the twilight and the tears of departing day, with her lighted candle and all-questioning eyes. There was so much warmth of life and movement about Hester, that it was difficult not to feel a certain interest in her; and there was something wonderfully characteristic in her attitude, arrested, as she stepped out, like an explorer, with her candle in her hand.

"I don't know you," said Catherine Vernon, who, from her general popularity and the worship administered to her all round, had, perhaps without knowing it, acquired the familiar ease of expression which belongs to kind and well-intentioned despots. The tone of her voice, Hester thought, who was accustomed to that distinction, was as if she said "*tu.*" And it depends a great deal upon circumstances whether it is affection or insult to *tutoyer* a stranger. "I don't know you," she said, coming in without any invitation, and closing the glass door

behind her. "I suppose you must have come with Mrs. John
Vernon. It is not possible," she cried a moment after, "that
you are the little girl?"

"I am all the girl there is. I am Hester; but I don't
know you either," the girl said, determined not to show any
poltroonery or to veil her pretensions for any one. "Are you
Cousin Catherine?" she added after a moment, with a quick
drawn breath.

"Yes, I am Cousin Catherine. I came to see how you have
got through your journey, and how your mother is. I suppose
she is your mother? It is quite astonishing to me to see you
look almost like a grown up young woman, you whom I have
always thought of as the little girl."

"I am fourteen," said Hester. "I never was very little
since I can remember;" and then they stood and looked at
each other under the glass roof, which still let in some light
among the flowers, their two faces lit up by the flame of the
candle. Hester stood in front of the door which led into the
house, and, indeed, had something the aspect of a guardian of
the house preventing the visitor from going in. There was a
sort of resemblance to each other in their faces and somewhat
largely developed figures; but this, which ought to have been a
soothing and comfortable thought, did not occur to either.
And it cannot be denied that the first encounter was hostile
on both sides.

"I should like to see your mother : to—welcome her—home."

"She has gone to bed. She was—tired," Hester said ; and
then, with an effort—"I do not suppose it is quite happy for
her, just the first night, coming back to the place she used to
live in. I made her go to bed."

"You take good care of her," said Miss Vernon; "that is
right. She always wanted taking care of." Then, with a
smile, she added, "Am I not to go in? I came to see if you
were comfortable and had everything you want."

"Mother will be much obliged," said Hester, stiffly. She
did not know any better. She was not accustomed to visitors,
and was altogether at a loss what to do—not to speak of the
instinct of opposition which sprang up in her mind to this
first new actor in the new life which lay vaguely existing
and unknown before her feet. It seemed to her, she could
scarcely tell how, that here was an enemy, some one to be
held at arm's length. As for Catherine Vernon, she was
more completely taken aback by this encounter than by any-

thing which had happened for years. Few people opposed
her or met her with suspicion, much less hostility ; and the
aspect of this girl standing in the doorway, defending it, as
it were, preventing her from entering, was half comic, half
exasperating. Keeping her out of her own house! It was
one of the drawbacks of her easy beneficence, the *defauts de
ses qualités*, that she felt a little too distinctly that it was
her own house, which, seeing she had given it to Mrs. John,
was an ungenerosity in the midst of her generosity. But
she was human, like the rest of us. She began to laugh,
bewildered, half angry, yet highly tickled with the position,
while Hester stood in front of her, regarding her curiously
with those big eyes. "I must rest here, if I am not to go
in," she said. "I hope you don't object to that ; for it is as
much as I can do to walk from the Grange here."

Hester felt as if her lips were sealed. She could not say
anything ; indeed she did not know what she ought to say.
A vague sense that she was behaving badly made her uncomfortable ; but she was not going to submit, to yield to
the first comer, to let anybody enter who chose. Was she
not the guardian of her mother, and of her quiet and repose?
She shifted her position a little as Miss Vernon sat down on
one of the creaking basket chairs, but did not even put her
candle out of her hand, or relax in her defensive attitude.
When her visitor laughed again, Hester felt a flush of hot
anger, like a flame, going over her. To be ludicrous is the
last thing a girl can bear : but even for that she would not
give in.

"You are a capital guardian," Catherine said, "but I
assure you I am not an enemy. I shall have to call my
maid Jennings, who has gone to the kitchen to see Betsey,
before I go home, for I am not fond of walking alone. You
must try and learn that we are all friends here. I suppose
your mother has told you a great deal about the Vernons—
and me?"

"I don't know about any Vernons—except ourselves,"
Hester said.

"My dear," said Miss Vernon, hastily, "you must not get
it into your little head that you are by any means at the head
of the house, or near it. Your grandfather was only the
second son, and you are only a girl—if you had been a boy
it might have been different ; and even my great-grandfather,
John Vernon, who is the head of our branch, was nothing

more than a cadet of the principal family. So don't give
yourself any airs on that score. All your neighbours here
are better Vernons than you——"

"I never give myself any airs—I don't know what you
mean," said Hester, feeling a wish to cry, but mastering
herself with all the strength of passion.

"Don't you, my poor child? I think you do. You are
behaving in a silly way, you know, meeting me like this.
Your mother should have taught you better manners. I
have no desire but to be kind to you. But never mind, I
will not say anything about it, for I dare say you are all put
the wrong way with fatigue and excitement; otherwise I
should think you were excessively uncivil, do you know,"
Miss Vernon said.

And Hester stood, fiery-red, and listened. If she had
spoken she must have cried—there was no alternative. The
candle flickered between the two antagonists. They were
antagonists already, as much as if they had been on terms
of equality. When Miss Vernon had rested as long as she
thought necessary, she got up and bade her young enemy
good night. "Tell your mother that I have done my duty
in the way of calling, and that it is she now who must come
to me," she said.

Hester stood at the door of the verandah, with her candle
flaring into the night, while Catherine went round to the other
door to call Jennings, her maid, and then watched the two
walking away together with a mixture of confused feeling
which filled her childish soul to overflowing. She wanted to
cry, to stamp with her feet, and clench her fists, and grind
her teeth. She was like a child in the unreasoning force of
her passion, which was bitter shame as well. She had
behaved like a savage, like a fool, she knew, like a little
silly, ill-tempered child. She ought to be whipped for her
rudeness, and—oh, far worse!—she would be laughed at.
Does not every one remember the overwhelming, intolerable shame and mortification which envelope a young creature like a sudden flame when she perceives that her
conduct has been ludicrous as well as wrong, and that
she has laid herself open to derision and laughter? Oh, if
she could but wipe that hour out of her life! But Hester
felt that never, never could it be wiped out of her life. She
would remember it if she lived to be a hundred, and Miss
Vernon would remember it, and tell everybody what a sense-

less, rude, ignorant being she was. Oh, if the earth would
open and swallow her up! She did not wish to live any
longer with the consciousness of this mistake. The first
time, the first time she had been tried—and she had made
herself ridiculous! The tears came pouring from her eyes
like hail-drops, hot and stinging. Oh, how she stamped upon
the floor! Never more could she hold up her head in this
new place. She had covered herself with shame the very
first hour. All the self-restraint she could exercise was to
keep herself from flying up stairs and waking her mother in
order to tell her all that had happened. She was not what
people call unselfish—the one quality which is supposed to
be appropriate to feminine natures. She was kind and warm-
hearted and affectionate, but she was not without thought
of herself. Her own little affairs naturally bulked more
largely to her than everything else in the world. She could
scarcely endure to keep all this to herself till to-morrow.
She had indeed flown up stairs with a cry of "Mother,
mother!" open-mouthed : and then it had occurred to her that
to wake her mother would be cruel. She was very tired,
and she had been more "upset" than Hester had ever seen
her. Probably she would be still upset in the morning if
she were disturbed now in her slumber. Hester's fortitude
was not sufficient to make her go to bed quietly. She was
almost noisy in her undressing, letting her hair-brush fall,
and pushing the furniture about, hoping every moment that
her mother would wake. But Mrs. John was very tired, and
she was a good sleeper. She lay perfectly still notwithstanding this commotion ; and Hester, with her heart swelling, had to put herself to bed at last, where she soon fell
asleep too, worn out with passion and pain—things which
weary the spirit more than even a day on the railway or
crossing the Channel when there are storms at sea.

Miss Vernon went home half amused, but more than half
angry. Edward Vernon had not very long before taken up
his abode at the Grange, and he was very attentive to Aunt
Catherine, as many of the family called her. He came out
to meet her when she appeared, and blamed her tenderly for
not calling him when she went out.

"I do not think you would have been the worse for my
arm," he said. He was a slim young man with a black
beard, though he was still quite young, and a gentle expression in his eyes. He was one of those of whom it is

said that he never gave his parents an anxious hour; but
there was something in his face which made one wonder
whether this was from genuine goodness, or because he had
never yet come under temptation. This doubt had passed
through Catherine Vernon's mind when she heard all that his
enthusiastic family had to say of him; but it had worn
away in beholding the sweetness of his disposition, and his
gentle, regular life. To see him so dutiful and gentle was
a relief and comfort to her after the encounter she had just
had.

"It would have given you a sensation," she said, "I
promise you, if you had come with me, Edward. I have
just had a meeting with a little spitfire, a little tiger-cat."

"Who is that, Aunt Catherine?"

Miss Vernon threw her shawl off her cap, and sat down on
the sofa to take breath. She had walked home faster than
usual in the excitement of the moment.

"If you will believe me," she said, "I don't even know
her name—except of course that it is Vernon, John Vernon's
daughter. I suppose she must have been warned against me,
and instructed to keep me at arm's length."

"To keep *you* at arm's length? That is not possible."

"Well, it does not look likely, does it?" she said, somewhat mollified. "People are not generally afraid of Catherine
Vernon: but it is singular sometimes how you will find your
own family steeled against you, when everybody else likes
you well enough. They see you too near at hand, where there
is no illusion possible, I suppose; but that could not be the
case with this little thing, who never set eyes on me before.
She let me know that her mother was not to be disturbed,
and even refused me admission—what do you think?—to
my own house."

"Are you quite sure there is no mistake?" said Edward;
"it seems incomprehensible to me."

"Oh, I do not find it incomprehensible. She is Mrs. John's
daughter, and there never was any love lost between us. I
always felt her to be a vacant, foolish creature; and no one can
tell what a venturesome, ridiculous hoyden she thought me."

Here Catherine Vernon felt herself grow hot all over, as
Hester had done, bethinking herself of an encounter not
altogether unlike the present, in which she had enacted
Hester's part, and exposed herself to the ridicule of Mrs.
John. Though this was nearly half a century ago, it had

still power to move her with that overwhelming sense of
mortification. There are things which no one ever forgets.

"When I heard of that woman coming home, I knew
mischief would come of it," Miss Vernon said.

"But forgive me, Aunt Catherine, was it not you that
asked her to come?"

Catherine Vernon laughed.

"You have me there," she said. "I see you are quick, and
I see you are honest, Edward. Most people hearing me say
that would have been bewildered, and thought it not possible.
No, I did not bring her. I only said to her, if you are
coming, there is a house here which you are welcome to if you
please. What else could I do?"

"She is not penniless, I suppose. You might have let her
settle where she pleased."

"She is not penniless, but she is heedless, and heartless,"
said Miss Vernon, with a sigh; "and as for settling where
she pleased, of course anyhow she would have come here. And
then I never expected she would take it."

"You thought she would come here, and yet you never expected she would take it; and you knew she would make
mischief, yet you invited her to come. That is a jumble. I
don't make head or tail of it."

"Nor I," cried Miss Vernon, with another laugh. "You
shall carry the problem a little further, if you please. I
feared that her coming would disturb us all, and yet I am
half pleased in my heart, being such a bad woman, that she is
going to make a disturbance to prove me right. You see I
don't spare myself."

"It amuses you to make out your own motives as well
as other people's: and to show how they contradict each
other," Edward said, shaking his head.

This little bit of metaphysics refreshed Miss Vernon. She
became quite herself again, as she told him her story.

"The little firebrand!" she said, "the little spitfire! facing
me on my own ground, defying me, Catherine Vernon, in the
very Vernonry, my own creation!"

"I wonder what the child could mean by it; it must have
been ignorance."

"Very likely it was ignorance: but it was more; it was
opposition, firm, healthy, instinctive opposition, without any
cause for it; that is a sort of thing which it refreshes one to
see. It must have been born in her, don't you see? for she

didn't know me, never set eyes on me. The little wild cat!
She felt in every nerve of her that we were in opposition, she
and I."

"Don't you think you give too much importance to the
nonsense of a girl? I know," said Edward, with a very
serious nod of his head, "what girls are. I have six sisters.
They are strange beings. They will go all off at a tangent in
a moment. Pull a wrong string, touch a wrong stop, and they
are all off—in a moment."

"You forget that I was once a girl myself."

"It is a long time ago, Aunt Catherine," said the ruthless
young man. "I dare say you have forgotten: whereas I, you
know, have studied the subject up to its very last development."

Miss Vernon shook her head at him with a playful menace,
and then the tea was brought in, and lights. As he went on
talking, she could not refrain from a little self-congratulation.
What a wise choice she had made! many young men hurried
out in the evenings, made acquaintances that were not desirable, involved themselves in indifferent society. Edward seemed
to wish for nothing better than this soft home atmosphere,
her own company, his books and occupations. What a lucky
choice! and at the same time a choice that reflected much
credit on herself. She might just as well have chosen his
brother, who was not so irreproachable. As she sat on the
sofa and took her tea, her eyes sought the figure of the young
man, pacing quietly up and down in the dim space, filling the
house and the room and her mind with a sensation of family
completeness. She was better off with Edward than many a
mother with her son. It was scarcely possible for Miss
Vernon to divest herself of a certain feeling of complacency.
Even the little adventure with the stranger at the Heronry
enhanced this. Mrs. John, to whom she had been so magnanimous, to whom she had offered shelter, had always been
against her; she had foreseen it, and if not content with this
incident, was so with herself.

CHAPTER V.

NEXT MORNING.

WHEN Mrs. John awoke, confused, and not knowing where she was, very early on the next morning, she was dismayed by the story which was instantly poured into her half-awakened ears. Hester, it is to be feared, had not shown that respect for her mother's slumbers which she had enforced upon Miss Vernon. The girl was too impatient, too eager to tell all that had happened. "Of course I was not going to let her come in and disturb you," she cried. "Is that how people behave in England? She had not even a bonnet on. No. I did not ask her to come in. It was so late : and besides, I never heard of people making calls at night; people you don't know.

"Oh, my dear!" said Mrs. John, in dismay. "Oh, Hester! what have you done? Catherine Vernon turned away from the door! She will never forgive you, never, as long as she lives."

"I don't care," said Hester, almost sullenly. "How was I to know? Even if I had been quite sure it was Cousin Catherine, I should not have let the Queen come in, to disturb you."

"The Queen of course would never want to come," said Mrs. John, who was very literal, "but Catherine Vernon! she is more than the Queen; the house belongs to her, and the furniture, and everything. It is all warmed with hot water pipes, and servants kept, and every comfort. I shouldn't wonder if she turned us out after what you have done."

"If she does, mother, I will be your servant. I will keep good fires and keep you warm, never fear," cried Hester, paling and reddening in panic, yet courage.

"Good fires!" said Mrs. John; "do you think fires can be got for nothing? and we have so little money." She looked very pale and worn, supported among her pillows in the early morning light so penetrating and so clear; and at this she began to cry. "Oh, why was I so foolish as to leave you to mismanage everything? I might have known! Whatever Catherine Vernon wanted, you ought to have let her have it. She can turn us out in a moment if she pleases, and she will never forgive you, never. And just when we were going to be so comfortable!" the poor woman cried.

"Don't cry, don't cry, mamma. You know I always said I should give lessons. We will get two nice little rooms somewhere, much nicer than these. If she is such a hard woman, I don't want to be obliged to her. Oh, mother, mother, don't cry! *I* can take care of you."

"Oh, hold your tongue, hold your tongue, child! what do you know about it? Let me get up. I must go to her at once and tell her you are only a child, and constantly doing silly things."

This to Hester, who was so conscious of being not only her mother's prop and support, but her real guide in life. She was so utterly aghast, that she did not know how to reply.

"Put me out my best crape," said her mother. "Catherine will like to see that even in a foreign place where it is so difficult to get things as one ought, proper respect was paid. Everybody said that she meant to marry your poor papa when she was young; but he saw me—Oh, dear, dear, when I think of all that has happened since then—and she never has liked me. I think that was quite natural: and now that you have gone and made everything worse—Put me out my best dress with the crape."

"It is only five o'clock," said Hester, half penitent half irritated, "there is nobody up. The people in England must be very lazy in the morning. Does no one go to early mass?"

"Five o'clock!" said Mrs. John, fretfully. "I think you must be going out of your senses, Hester. Is that an hour to wake me, when I have not had my first sleep out? draw down the blinds and close the shutters, and let me get a proper rest. And for goodness' sake," she cried, raising her head before she settled down comfortably among the pillows, "for goodness' sake! don't go about talking of early mass here."

Hester did as her mother ordered, but with an impatient heart. It was bitter to have thus put into the hands of the poor

lady who was her kingdom, and for whom she had legislated
for years, the means of shaking off her sway—a sway which
Hester was firmly persuaded was for her good. John Vernon
had not been much of a guide for either mother or child. He
had not cared very much about them. His wife's monotonous
feebleness which might have been well enough in the tranquillity of the luxurious sheltered life at home to which she
was born, was nothing but tiresome in circumstances where
an energetic woman might have been of some use; and his
daughter was a creature he did not understand—a child, a chit,
who ventured to look disapproval at him, to his indignation
and wonder. What you are used to from your birth does not
affect you much, and Hester had not suffered any heartache
from her father's neglect. She accepted it as the order of
nature, but the result had been that from her earliest consciousness almost, she had taken upon herself the charge of
her mother; and to be thus threatened with deposition, and
criticised by her helpless subject, appalled her. So active
and young as she was, and full of superfluous strength, it was
impossible for her to return to her pillow as her mother had
done. When she had closed the shutters and drawn the
curtains, she stole softly out on tiptoe down the old oak staircase which creaked at every footfall. In the glory of the
early morning the house was not dark. In rooms which the
sun had reached, the black old wainscot was glimmering full of
reflections, and all the world out of doors lay resplendent in
that early gladness. Hester had heard all her life from many
a discontented mouth, of the gloomy skies and dark days of
England, of a climate always obscured with fog, and a sky
where there was no blue. Accordingly it was with a kind of
indignant ecstasy that she stepped out into the intense delicious
radiance, so soft and fresh, yet so all-powerful. The birds had
got their early twitterings over, and were in full outburst of
song. The flowers were all in intensest dewy bloom, and
everything taking the good of that sweet prime of the morning
in which they bloomed and sang for themselves, and not
officially, on behalf of the world. The girl forgot her vexation
as she came out to the incense-breathing garden, to the trees
no longer standing out black upon the sunset, but in all their
sweet natural variations of colour, basking in the morning
light. The pond even, that had looked so black, was like a
basin of pure gold, rimmed with rich browns and greens. She
opened the gate and looked out upon the road which was all

silent, not a shadow upon it, swept by the broad early blaze of
the morning sun.   Not a sound except the chorus of the birds,
the crackle of the furze bushes in the stillness, the hum of
insects.   She had all the world to herself, as the poet had on
that immortal morning when the houses of quiet London all
lay asleep, and Thames flowed onward at his own sweet will.
Standing apart from the road, among its shrubberies, was the
Grange with its red gables and its eyelids closed—farther
off the light rebounded softly from the roofs of the town, and
behind the town, revealed in partial shadow, rose the white
distant front of the house in which her mother had told
Hester her early married life had been passed.   She had it
all to herself, nobody to disturb or interrupt.   And what
in human form could have given a more complete impersonation of the morning than this girl, fresh, fair, and strong,
with such a world of latent possibilities in her?   The cloud
of last night's perversity blew away.   She met the eye of
the day with a gaze as open and as confident. Neither Nature
nor Hester had any fear.   She was like her namesake in the
poem, whom the "gentlehearted Charles" beloved of all men,
could not, though she was dead, give up the expectation of
meeting as heretofore, "some summer morning."

> " When from thy cheerful eyes a ray
> Had struck a bliss upon the day,
> A bliss that would not go away,
> A sweet forewarning."

And this glorified world, this land of light and dews, this
quiet sweetness and silence and ecstatic life, was the dull
England of which all the shabby exiles spoke with scorn !
Hester felt a delightful indignation flood her soul.   She went
out all by herself with a little awe, and walked round the
common which was all agleam with blobs of moisture shining
like diamonds in the sun :—

> " A springy motion in her gait
> A rising step did indicate,
> Of pride and joy no common rate
> That flushed her spirit.

> " I know not by what name beside
> I shall it call : if 'twas not pride
> It was a joy to that allied
> She did inherit."

Hester was a great deal too young for a heroine, but as it

chances there could not be a better portrait of her than that
of Lamb's "sprightly neighbour." She went out with that
springing motion, stepping on air, with the pride of life and
youth and conscious energy in every vein. A certain youthful
contempt for the inferior beings who lay stupid behind those
closed shutters, losing all this bloom and glory, was in her
heart. She was very black in the midst of the bright landscape in her mourning frock, with a white kerchief tied round
her throat like a French girl, but her curly locks shining like
everything else in the sun. She did not mind the sun. She
had not yet learned that she had a complexion to care for ;
besides, the sun could do nothing to the creamy-white of her
tint. Perhaps she was not very sensitive, not thin-skinned
at all, either in body or soul.

Now it happened, curiously enough, that as Hester passed
the gate of the Grange, at which she gazed very anxiously
with a half-formed intention of making her way in, in face of
every obstacle, and making her peace with Cousin Catherine,
—a project which only the early hour prevented her from
carrying out—the said gate opened softly and a man appeared. Hester was more startled than she could explain to
herself. Why should she be startled? It was not so early
now—six o'clock or later. He was a young man of middle
height, with a very dark beard and bright eyes. Hester felt
that he was somewhat unsuitable to the scene, not English in
her opinion—Englishmen had fair hair, rosy complexions,
blue eyes—they were all *blonds* : now this man looked like
those to whom she was accustomed. Was he, she wondered,
going to early mass? He had a portfolio in his hand, a small
box strapped to his shoulders. The first Englishman she had
seen ; what was he going to do? What he did first was to
look at her with considerable curiosity. She had hastily put
on her hat on seeing him, that there might be no impropriety
in her appearance, an action which put out, so to speak, one
of the lights in the landscape, for her hair was shining almost
as brightly as the blobs of dew. He crossed the road to the
common, and then he paused a moment on the edge of it and
looked at her again.

"I wonder if you are my little cousin," he said.

It was on Hester's lips to protest that she was not little at
all, but quite as tall as he was, but she waived this point on
second thoughts.

"Are you a Vernon—*too ?*" she said.

"Yes, I am a Vernon—too. Edward, at your service. I am glad to see you keep such early hours."

"Why?" she asked, but did not wait for any reply. "What are you going to do?"

"I am going," he said, "out upon the common to look for a rare flower that grows here, only I have never been able to find it. Will you come and help me?"

"A flower!" said Hester, confounded. "Do Englishmen look for flowers?"

"Englishmen as well as others—when they happen to be botanists. Does that surprise you? I am obliged to get up early, for I have no time in the day."

"What do you do in the day?" the girl asked.

"I am at the bank. Have you never heard of Vernon's Bank? the business from which we all take our importance here. The Vernons are great or they are small, don't you know? according to their connection with the bank."

"Then you are one of the great ones," said Hester with decision. "Do any of the Vernons live in that great white house—that one, do you see?—on the other side of the red roofs?"

"The White House? Oh yes, Harry lives there, another cousin, and his sister."

"Are they in the bank too?"

"Harry is; he and I do the work between us. Ladies in this country have nothing to do with business——by the way, I am forgetting Aunt Catherine."

"That is a pity," said Hester, not noticing his exclamation. "Then I suppose my father must have had something to do with it, for do you know, though we are poor now, he once lived there?"

"Yes, I know."

"Then why did he go away?" said Hester musingly; "that is what I should like to find out. Do you know Cousin Catherine? you must, if you live in her house."

"I call her Aunt Catherine," said the young man.

"Why? Is she your aunt? And I call her cousin; but she cannot be my cousin. She is so much older. Was she angry —do you know—last night? I did not know who she was— and I was—rude."

He laughed, and she, after a doubtful glance, laughed too.

"Oh yes, I am afraid I did know who she was—that she

was Cousin Catherine; but then, who is Cousin Catherine? I had never seen her before. Mother thinks she will be very angry. Could I let her come in and disturb my mother after she was in bed? Mother thinks she will not let us stay."

"Should you be sorry to go?"

Hester cast a long look all round from east to west, taking in the breadth of the common glistening in the morning dew, the dark roofs of the Heronry against the trees, the glittering vanes and windows of the town on the other side.

"It is very pretty," she said with a little sigh. "And to think what they say of England! They say it is always fog, and the sun never shines. How can people tell such lies? We should not go, we should take some small rooms in the town, and I would teach."

"What could you teach?"

Hester looked at him with half resentment.

"Do you know many languages?" she said.

"Many languages? no!—a smattering of Greek and Latin."

"I don't call them languages. I mean French and Italian and German: for I know them all. I know them as well as English. I haven't a bit of the accent Britannique: Madame Alphonse said so, and I hope she is a good authority. I will give *cours*, as many as they please: French one day and the others the next. Not only should I be able to help mother, but I should make a fortune, they all said. Three *cours* always going: I should make a great deal of money, and then in ten years or so I could retire, you know. In ten years I should only be"—here she paused in the fervour of conversation and eyed him a little with doubt in her face. Then she said quite calmly, "I forget the rest."

Edward Vernon listened with great edification; he forgot the flower which he was going to search for.

"I am very sorry to discourage you in your plans: but I don't think Aunt Catherine will turn you out."

"Don't you think so?"

Hester, after her brag, which was perfectly sincere, and of which she believed every word, felt a little disappointed to be thus brought down again.

"No, I don't think so. She told me that you were rude, but she was not angry; she only laughed."

At this Hester grew wildly red, and stamped her foot. "She shall not—she shall not—nobody shall laugh at me," she cried. "I will tell mother we must go away."

"Don't go away. You must consider that your mother
will be a great deal more comfortable here than in lodgings in
town. And you know you are very young. You had better
be a little older before you begin to give *cours*. Don't be
angry: but if you were to mount up to the desk with your
short frock" (here Hester looked down at her feet, and in
a sudden agony perceived the difference between her broad,
old-fashioned shoes, and the pointed toes of her companion)
"and short hair ——" But this was more than she could
bear.

"You are laughing at me! You too!" she said, with a
poignant tone of mortification.

"No, my little cousin, I will not laugh; but you must let
me be your friend, and show you what is best; for you *are*
very young, you know. One can't know everything at——"

"Fourteen," said Hester. "Fourteen is not so very young;
and girls are older than boys. Perhaps you are thinking
that a boy of fourteen is not much? That is very true; but
it is different with me. Mother is not strong. I have to do
most of the settling, not to tire her. What I think is always
what will be the best——"

"For her? To be sure," said Edward; "so you must make
up your mind to be civil to everybody, and not to quarrel."

"Quarrel! I never quarrel. I would not for anything in
the world; it is so childish."

"I don't think I shall find my flower this morning," he
said. "I will walk home with you if you will let me, and we
can talk about everything. Have you seen the other people
who live in the Heronry? Some of them will amuse you.
There are two old ladies—Vernons, like the rest of us."

"Is it Cousin Catherine that has brought us all here?"

"All of us. She is not a person to be made light of,
you see."

"And why did she bring *you?* Were you poor? Had you
no father like me? Is she fond of you that she has you to
live in her house? Do you love her?" said Hester, fixing her
large curious eyes on the young man's face.

He laughed. "Where am I to begin?" he said. "I have
a father and mother, little cousin. They are not poor precisely, but neither are they rich. I can't tell you whether
Aunt Catherine is fond of me. She brought me here to work
in the bank; the bank is everybody's first thought; that
must be kept up whatever fails; and she was so good as to

think I would do. It was a great advancement for me. If I had stayed at home I should have had to struggle for something to do along with all the other young men. And there are a great many young men in the world, and not so much for them to do as could be wished. Have I satisfied you now?"

"There is one question you have not answered," said Hester. "Do you love her?—that is the chief thing I want to know."

"Love her? Come, you must not go into metaphysics. I like her very much. Aunts are excellent things. I have a great respect for her. Won't that do?"

"I looked at her last night," said Hester. "I got her by heart. I shall either love her or hate her. I have not made up my mind which."

"There is something between these violent sentiments," said Edward; "at least I hope so. You must not hate me."

"Oh, you!" said Hester, with friendly contempt, "that is a different thing altogether. You are not of any consequence. I think I like you, but you may be sure I shall never hate you; why should I? You can't do anything to me. But when there is one that is—that is—well, almost like God, you know—" said the girl, dropping her voice reverentially. "It is astonishing, is it not, that one should be so much more powerful than others. They say in France that men are all equal; but how can that be when Cousin Catherine—What gives her so much power?"

"That is all a fallacy about men being equal. You will see through it when you get older," said Edward, with gentle superiority. He had laughed at her cavalier mention of himself, but he was very willing to instruct this self-opinioned young person. "You are mixing up circumstances and principles," he added. "It is circumstances which make Aunt Catherine powerful; chiefly because she is rich—rich and kind; very kind in her way; always ready to do a charitable action."

The colour wavered in Hester's cheek. "We don't want charity," she said; and after this walked on very stately, holding her head high. The Vernonry towards which they were going had begun to wake up. Smoke was rising up into the clear air from one or two of the chimneys; a few blinds

had been drawn up; a gardener, with his wheelbarrow and
his scythe stood in the gate, throwing his shadow across the
garden. Edward Vernon thought there was in the air a
vague perfume from the cups of tea that were being carried
about in all directions to the bedsides of the inhabitants.
The people in the Vernonry were all elderly; they were all
fond of their little comforts. They liked to open their eyes
upon the world through the refreshing vapour of those early
cups. All elderly—all except this impersonation of freshness
and youth. What was she to do in such a place, amid the
retired and declining, with energy enough for every active
employment, and a restless, high, youthful spirit? Poor girl!
she would have some bitter lessons to learn. Edward,
though he had won the heart of his powerful relation by his
domestic character and evident preference for her society, had
not been able to divest himself of a certain grudge against the
author of his good fortune. The feeling which Hester expressed so innocently was in his mind in a more serious
form.

When they reached the gate, Hester stopped short.

" You must not come in now," she said in her peremptory
tones, "for mother is not up yet. I must go and make her
coffee before she gets up. I will make you some, after dinner
if you like. You cannot make coffee in England, can you ? "

" No more than we can make the sun shine," said Edward
with a smile. " I shall certainly come for my coffee in the
evening. I may be of some use to you as your difficulties
increase ; but I should like to know your name, and what
I am to call you ? "

" Are you sure that our difficulties will increase ? " said
Hester, aghast, opening her mouth as well as her large eyes.

" Unless you know how to deal with them. I shall set up
a series of lectures on fine manners and deportment."

Hester's countenance flamed upon him with mingled resentment and shame.

" Do you think me a savage ? " she said. " I—do you know
I have been brought up in France ? It is in England that
there are no manners, no politeness."

" And no sunshine," said Edward with a laugh. Thus
saying he took off his hat with a little exaggeration of respect,
and waving his hand to her, turned away. If Hester had
been older, she would have known that to stand and look

after him was not according to any code. But at fourteen the
soul is bold and scorns conventional rule. She stood,
shading her eyes with her hand, watching him as he walked
along; still the only figure that broke the blaze and the
silence of the morning. It was true, as she had said, that
he was not of any consequence. Perhaps that was why she
felt quite at her ease in respect to him, and on the whole
approved of him as a pleasant feature in the new life.

CHAPTER VI.

IN the morning, the inhabitants of the Vernonry were to be seen a little before or after noon, according to the season, appearing and disappearing in the immediate neighbourhood of their house. It was a little community perfectly at leisure, called out by no work in the morning, returning with no more punctuality than pleased them. As a matter of fact they were exceedingly punctual, coming and going as by clockwork, supporting their otherwise limp existence by a severe mechanism of rule. Those who have least to do, are often most rigorous in thus measuring themselves out; it gives a certain sense of something real in their lives. It was a little after eleven when Mr. Mildmay Vernon appeared. His residence was in the west wing, nearest to the pool and the trees, and he thought it was probably owing to the proximity of the water that his rheumatism troubled him so much in winter. It did not trouble him at this fine season, but he had the habit of leaning on his stick and talking in a querulous voice. He came out with his newspaper to a little summer-house where the heat was tempered by the foliage of a great lime. He had very good taste; he liked the flicker of the sunshine which came through those green-silken leaves, and the shelter was very grateful when the sun was hot. The worst of it was that the summer-house was not in his portion of the common grounds, and the ladies, to whom it ought to have belonged, and to whom it was so convenient to do their work in, resented his constant presence. In winter, he seated himself always on a sunny bench which was in front of the windows now belonging to Mrs. John, but she was not as yet aware of this peculiarity. The Miss Vernon-Ridgways occupied the space between Mr. Mildmay's house and Mrs. John's. They were not in the direct line, and they felt that they were treated accordingly, the best of everything being appropriated to those whom Catherine Vernon, who was so proud of her name, considered nearest to the family stock. These ladies were convinced that the blood of the Ridgways had much enriched the liquid that meandered through the veins of the Vernons; but in Catherine Vernon's presence they kept silence as to this belief. The rooms in the wings were much the best, they thought, and they had even proposed an exchange to Mr. Mildmay when he complained of being so close to the pool. But he had only grinned and had not accepted; he knew better. Of course he would have grumbled if he had been lodged in Windsor Castle, the ladies said; but he knew very well in his heart that he had been preferred to the best place. On the other side of the house, towards the road, lived Mrs. Reginald Vernon, the young widow of an officer, with her four children, of whom everybody complained, and an old couple, in reality not Vernons at all, but relations of Catherine's mother, who were looked down upon by the entire community, and had clearly no business in the Vernonry. The old gentleman, Captain Morgan, had been in the navy, and therefore ought to have been the equal of any one. But the people on the road-side kept themselves very much to themselves; the aristocracy lived on the garden front. When Mrs. John Vernon made her appearance in her deep mourning, there was a great deal of excitement about the place. Mr. Mildmay put down his paper and came out, bowing, to the door of the summer-house.

"Between relations I do not know if any ceremony of introduction is necessary," he said. "It gives me great pleasure to welcome you back to England. Poor John and I were once great friends. I hope you will allow me to consider myself at once an old acquaintance."

"Oh, how thankful I shall be for some one to speak to!" cried Mrs. John. "Though my family were of this county, I seem to have lost sight of every one that used to know me. A great many changes happen when one has been thirty years away."

"Poor John! I suppose he never came back to this country again?" Mr. Mildmay said, with sympathetic curiosity, and that air of knowing all about it which is some-

times so offensive ; but Mrs. John was simple-minded. She
was not even displeased by the undertone of confidential
understanding.

"Never! it would have broken his heart; what was left
to him to come for? He always said that when ladies
meddle with business everything goes wrong. But, dear
me, I oughtn't to say so here," Mrs. John added, with a
little panic, looking round.

"Why?—you need not be afraid of expressing your sentiments, my dear lady, before me. I have the greatest respect
for the ladies—where would we be without them? 'Oh,
woman, in our hours of ease,' &c.—you know. But I think
that mixed up with business they are entirely out of their
place. It changes the natural relations—it creates a false
position——"

"John always thought so. But then I was so silly—so
dreadfully silly—about business ; and he thought that women
should all be like me."

"That is certainly the kind of woman that is most attractive to men," said Mr. Mildmay, with a gallant bow; "and
in my time ladies thought much of that. I hope, however,
that you will like this retirement, and be happy here. It is
very retired, you see—nothing to disturb us——"

"Oh, Mr. Mildmay, I dare say I shall do very well," said
Mrs. John, putting her handkerchief to her eyes; "but
seeing *that* " (she waved her hand towards the front of the
White House in the distance) "from the window, and knowing
every day how things are going on at the bank, and all the
old associations, I cannot be expected to be very happy. That
was not thought of when I came here."

"My dear lady!" Mr. Mildmay said, soothingly; and
then he saw his way to inflicting another pin-prick upon
this bleeding heart so easily laid open to him. "I suppose
you know that Catherine has put her nephew ˙Harry and his
sister—he is no more her nephew than I am—one of Gilbert
Vernon's boys : but she took a fancy to him—in the White
House? It belongs to her now, like everything else in the
neighbourhood. Almost the whole of Redborough is in her
hands."

"Her nephew?" said Mrs. John, faintly, "but she has no
nephew—she was an only child. My Hester is nearer to her
than any one else." Then she paused, and added with conscious
magnanimity, "Since I cannot have it, it doesn't matter to

me who has got it.   We must make ourselves as contented as
we can—Hester and I."

It was at this moment that the two ladies appeared who
considered the summer-house their special property. They were
tall women with pronounced features and a continual smile—
in dresses which had a way of looking scanty, and were
exactly the same.   Their necks were long and their noses
large, both which characteristics they held to be evidences of
family and condition.   They followed each other, one always
a step in advance of the other, with a certain pose of their
long necks and turn of their shoulders which made some
people think of the flight of two long-necked birds.   Mr.
Mildmay Vernon, who pretended to some scholarship, called
them the Cranes of Ibycus.   They arrived thus at the
peaceful spot all chequered with morning light and shade, as
with a swoop of wings.

" Dear lady ! " said Miss Matilda, "we should have waited
till we could make a formal call and requested the pleasure of
your acquaintance as we ought; but when we saw you in
our summer-house, we felt sure that you did not understand
the distribution of the place, and we hurried out to say that
we are delighted to see you in it, and *quite* glad that you
should use it as much as ever you please."

" Oh ! " cried Mrs. John, much disturbed, " I am so sorry
if I have intruded.   I had not the least idea——"

" *That* we were sure you had not—for everybody knows
that Mrs. John Vernon is a lady," said the other.   " It is
awkward to have no one to introduce us, but we must just
introduce each other.   Miss Martha Vernon-Ridgway, Mrs.
Vernon ; and I am Matilda," said the spokeswoman, with a
curtsey.   " We are very glad to see you here."

At this Mrs. John made her curtsey too, but being unready,
found nothing to say : for she could not be supposed to be glad
to see them, as everybody knew the sad circumstances in
which she had returned to her former home : and she seated
herself again after her curtsey, wishing much that Hester was
with her.   Hester had a happy knack of either knowing or
suggesting something to say.

" We hope you will find yourself comfortable," said the
two ladies, who by dint of always beginning to speak together
had the air of making their remarks in common ; but Miss
Matilda had better wind and a firmer disposition than her
sister, and always carried the day.   " You are lucky in having

the end house, which has all the fresh air. I am sure we do
not grudge you anything, but it always makes us feel how we
are boxed up; that is our house between the wings. It is
monotonous to see nothing but the garden—but we don't
complain."

"I am sure I am very sorry," Mrs. John began to say.

"Your favourable opinion of the end houses is very complimentary," said Mr. Mildmay. "I wish it were founded on fact.
My windows look into the pool and draw all the miasma out of
it. When I have a fire I feel it come in. But I say nothing.
What would be the good of it? We are not here only to
please ourselves. Beggars should not be choosers."

"I hope, Mr. Mildmay Vernon, that you will speak for
yourself," said the sisters. "We do not consider that such an
appellation applies to us. We are not obliged, I beg to say,"
Miss Matilda added, "to live anywhere that does not suit
us. If we come here as a favour to Catherine Vernon, who
makes such a point of having all her relations about her, it
is not that we are beggars, or anything of the sort."

"Dear, dear me!" said Mrs. John, clasping her hands, "I
hope nobody thinks that is the case. For my poor dear
husband's sake, and for Hester's sake, I could never submit—;
Catherine offered the house out of kindness—nothing but
that."

"Oh, nothing but that," said Mr. Mildmay Vernon, with a
sneer.

"Nothing at all but that," said the Miss Vernon-Ridgways. "She said to us, I am sure, that it would be a favour
to herself—a personal favour. Don't you remember, Martha?
Nothing else would induce us, as you may suppose, Mrs.
John—my sister and me, who have many friends and resources
—to put up with a little poky place—the worst, quite the
worst, here. But dear Catherine is very lonely. She is not
a person, you know, that can do with everybody. You must
understand her before you can get on with her. Shouldn't
you say so? And she is perhaps, you know, a little too fond
of her own way. People who can't make allowances as
relatives do, are apt not to—like her, in short. And it
is such a great stand-by for her—such a comfort, to have
us here."

"I should have thought she was very—independent," said
Mrs. John, faltering a little. She did not even venture to risk
an opinion; but something she was obliged to say. "But I can

scarcely say I know her," she added, anxiously, "for it is
thirty years since I was at Redborough, and people change
so much. She was young then."

"Young! she must have been nearly forty. Her character must have been what one may call formed by that time,"
said Mr. Mildmay; "but I know what you mean. Our
dear Catherine whom we are all so fond of——"

"You are quite right," said Miss Matilda, emphatically,
"*quite* right, though perhaps you mean something different,
for gentlemen are always so strange. We *are* very fond of
dear Catherine. All the more that so many people misunderstand her, and take wrong ideas. I think indeed that you
require to be a relation, to enter into the peculiarities of the
case, and take everything into consideration, before you can do
dear Catherine justice. She is so good, but under such a
brusque exterior. Though she never *means* to hurt any one's
feelings—that I am certain of."

"Oh *never!*" cried Mr. Mildmay, with mock enthusiasm,
lifting up his hands and eyes.

Mrs. John looked, as each spoke, from one to the other with
a great deal of perplexity. It had seemed to her simple mind
at first that it was with a real enthusiasm that their general
benefactress was being discussed; but by this time she had
begun to feel the influence of the undertone. She was
foolish, but there was no rancour in her mind. So gentle a
little shaft as that which she had herself shot, in vindication,
as she thought of her husband, rather than as assailing his
successor, she might be capable of; but systematic disparage-
ment puzzled the poor lady. She looked first at the Miss
Vernon-Ridgways, and then at Mr. Mildmay Vernon, with
a bewildered look, trying to make out what they meant.
And then she was moved to make to the conversation a
contribution of her own—

"I am afraid my little girl made a sad mistake last night,"
she said. "Catherine was so kind as to come to see me—
without ceremony—and I had gone to bed."

"That was so like Catherine!" the Miss Vernon-Ridgways
cried. "Now anybody else would have come next day at
soonest to let you have time to rest and get over your journey.
But that is just what she would be sure to do. Impatience
is a great defect in her character, it must be allowed. She
wanted you to be delighted, and to tell her how beautiful
everything was. It must be confessed it is a little tiresome.

You must praise everything, and tell her you are *so* comfortable. One wouldn't like it in anybody else."

"But what I regret so much," continued poor Mrs. John, "is that Hester, my little girl, who had never heard of Catherine—she is tall, but she is only fourteen, and such a child! Don't you know she would not let her in? I am afraid she was quite rude to her."

Here Mrs. John's artless story was interrupted by a series of little cheers from Mr. Mildmay, and titters from the two sisters.

" Brava!" he said. "Well done!" taking away Mrs. John's breath ; while the two ladies uttered little laughs and titterings, and exchanged glances of pleasure.

"Oh, how very funny!" they cried. "Oh, what an amusing thing to happen! Dear Catherine, what a snub for her! How I wish we had been there to see."

" I should like to make acquaintance with your little Hester, my dear lady," said Mr. Mildmay. "She must have a fine spirit. Our respected Cousin Catherine is only human, and we all feel that to be opposed now and then would be for her moral advantage. We flatter her ourselves, being grown-up persons : but we like to know that she encounters something now and then that will be for her good."

"I must again ask you to speak for yourself, Mr. Mildmay," said the sisters; "flattery is not an art I am acquainted with. Dear, dear, what a sad thing for a beginning. How nervous it must have made you ! and knowing that dear Catherine, though she is so generous, *cannot* forgive a jest. She has no sense of humour; it is a great pity. She will not, I fear, see the fun of it as we do."

"Do you think," said Mrs. John, with a little tremor, "that she will be dreadfully angry? Hester is such a child —and then she didn't know."

The sisters both shook their heads upon their long necks. They wished no particular harm to Mrs. John; but they would not have been sorry so to frighten her, as that she should go away as she came. And they sincerely believed Catherine to be as they represented her. Few people are capable of misrepresenting goodness in the barefaced way of saying one thing while they believe another. Most commonly they have made out of shreds and patches of observation and dislike, a fictitious figure meriting all their anger and contempt, to which they attach the unloved name. Catherine

Vernon, according to their picture of her, was a woman who, being richer than they, helped them all with an ostentatious benevolence, which was her justification for humiliating them whenever she had a chance, and treating them at all times as her inferiors and pensioners. Perhaps they would themselves have done so in Catherine Vernon's place. This at all events was the way in which they had painted her to themselves. They had grown to believe that she was all this, and to expect her to act in accordance with the character they had given her. When the sun shone into the summer-house, and routed the little company, which happened just about the time when the meal which they called luncheon, but which to most of them was dinner, was ready, Mrs. John carried back with her to her new home a tremulous conviction that any sort of vengeance was possible. She might be turned out of this shelter, or she might be made to feel that her life was a burden. And yet when she got back to the low cool room in which Hester, doubtful of Betsey's powers, was superintending the laying out of the table, it seemed to her, in the prospect of losing it, more desirable than it had been before. There were three windows in deep recesses, one of them with a cheerful outlook along the road that skirted the common, in which was placed a soft, luxurious chair, which was exactly what Mrs. John liked. Nothing could have been more grateful, coming out of the sunshine, than the coolness of this brown room, with all the little glimmers of light in the polished wainscot, and the pretty old-fashioned furniture. Mrs. John sighed as she placed herself in the chair at the window. And the smell of the dish which Betsey soon after put upon the table was very appetising. It turned out to be nicely cooked, and the table was laid with fine linen and pretty crystal and old-fashioned silver—everything complete. The poor lady in her wandering and unsettled life had lost almost all this needful garniture which makes life so much more seemly and smooth. She had been used to lodging houses, to *pensions*, greasy and public, to the vulgarity of inns; and all this daintiness and freshness charmed her with a sense of repose and personal property. She could have cried to think that it might be put in jeopardy by Hester's childish petulance.

"Oh, why did I let you persuade me to go to bed? Why didn't I stay up—I could have done it quite well—and see Catherine Vernon? Why are you so self-willed, child? I

think I could be happy here, at least as happy as I can ever
be now; and what if I must give it all up again for you?"

"Mother, if we have to give it up, we will do better,"
said Hester, a little pale; "we shall get pretty lodgings like
Ruth Pinch, and I will give lessons; and it will not matter
about Cousin Catherine."

"Oh child, child, what do you know about it!" Mrs. John
said.

CHAPTER VII.

SETTLING DOWN.

THESE alarms, however, did not come to anything, and as the days passed on Mrs. John accustomed herself to her new position and settled down to it quietly. She got used to the little meetings in the summer-house or on the bench in front of her own windows, and soon learned to remark with the others upon the freedom with which Mr. Mildmay Vernon took the best place, not taking any trouble to remark to whom it really belonged. He was a great advantage to the ladies of the Vernonry in giving them a subject upon which they could always be eloquent. Even when they could not talk of it openly, they would give each other little looks aside, with many nods of the head and an occasional biting inuendo; and this amused the ladies wonderfully, and kept them perhaps now and then from criticising each other, as such close neighbours could scarcely fail to do. But even more interesting than Mr. Mildmay Vernon and his mannish selfishness was Catherine, the universal subject on which they could fraternise even with Mildmay Vernon himself. He was caustic, and attacked her keenly; but the sisters never failed to profess a great affection for their cousin, declaring that from Catherine one accepted anything, since one felt that it was only her *gauche* way of doing things, or the fault of her education, but that she always meant well. Dear Catherine! it was such a pity, they said. Mrs. John never quite adopted either style of remark, but the subject was endless, and always afforded something to say; and there was a little pleasure in hearing Catherine set down from her superior place, even though a gentler disposition and simpler mind

prevented Mrs. John herself from adding to the felicities of
the discussion. Catherine had taken no notice of the unlucky
beginning which had given so much alarm to Mrs. John, and
so much amusement to the other members of the establishment. When she came in state to call on the mourner,
which she did a few days after, with that amused toleration
of the little weaknesses of her dependents which was as
natural in Catherine's position as the eager and somewhat
spiteful discussion of her was in theirs, Miss Vernon had
tapped Hester on the cheek, and said, "This is the good
child who would not let me disturb her mother." But when
Mrs. John began to apologise and explain, Catherine had
stopped her, saying, "She was quite right," with a decisive
brevity, and turning to another subject. The magnanimity
of this would have touched Hester's heart, but for the half-
mocking smile and air of amusement with which it was said,
and which made the girl much angrier than before. It
cannot be denied that this was to some extent the tone unconsciously adopted by Catherine in her dealings with the
poor relations who were so largely indebted to her bounty.
There was a great deal that was ridiculous in their little
affectations and discontents, and the half-resentment, half-
exaction with which they received her benefits. These might
have made her close her heart against them, and turned her
into a misanthrope; but though the effect produced was
different from this, it was not perhaps more desirable. Catherine, though she did not become misanthropical, became
cynical, in spite of herself. She tolerated everything, and
smiled at it; she became indulgent and contemptuous. What
did it matter what they said or felt? If they learned to
consider her gifts as their right, if they comforted themselves
in the humiliation of receiving by mocking at the giver, poor
things, that was their misfortune—it did not harm her upon
her serene heights. She laughed at Hester, tapping her
cheek. Had she been perhaps less tolerant, less easy to
satisfy, she would not have excited that burning sense of
shame and resentment in the girl's heart.

But Catherine was very kind. She came in the afternoon
in the carriage and took them out with her for a drive, to the
admiration of all beholders. The Miss Vernon-Ridgways inspected this from behind their curtains, and calculated how
long it was since Catherine had shown such a civility to
themselves, and how soon Mrs. John would find out the brief

character of these attentions. And the drive was perhaps
not quite so successful as might have been expected. Mrs. John
indeed gave her relative all the entertainment she could have
desired. She became tearful, and fell away altogether into her
pocket-handkerchief at almost every turn of the road, saying,
" Ah, how well I remember ! " then emerged from the cambric
cloud, and cheered up again till the next turn came, in a
way which would have afforded Catherine great amusement
but for the two blazing, indignant, angry eyes of Hester
fixed from the opposite side upon her mother's foolish little
pantomime and her patroness's genial satisfaction, with equal
fury, pain, and penetration. Hester could not endure the
constant repetition of that outburst of pathos, the smiles that
would follow, the sudden relapse as her mother was recalled
by a new recollection to a sense of what was necessary in her
touching position ; but still less could she bear the lurking
smile in Catherine Vernon's eyes, and her inclination to draw
the poor lady out, sometimes even by a touch of what Hester
felt to be mock-sympathy. The girl could scarcely contain
herself as she drove along facing these two ladies, seeing, even
against her will, a great deal which perhaps they themselves
were only half-conscious of. Oh, why would mother be so
silly ! and Cousin Catherine, this rich woman who had them
all in her power, why had not she more respect for weakness ?
Hester turned with an angry longing to her idea of putting
her own small young figure between her mother and all those
spurns and scoffs, of carrying her away, and working for
her, and owing nothing to anybody.

When they stopped at the door of Kaley's, the great shop of
Redborough, and half-a-dozen obsequious attendants started
out to devote themselves to the lightest suggestion of the great
Miss Vernon, Mrs. John cleared up, and enjoyed the reflected
distinction to the bottom of her heart ; but Hester, pale and
furious, compelled to sit there as part of the pageant, could
scarcely keep still, and was within an ace of jumping out of
the carriage and dragging her mother after her, so indignant
was she, so humiliated. Cousin Catherine threw a little *fichu*
of black lace into the girl's lap, with a careless, liberal, " You
want something for your neck, Hester," which the girl would
have thrown at her had she dared ; and it would not have
taken much to wind her up to that point of daring : but
Mrs. John went home quite pleased with her outing. " It
was a melancholy pleasure, to be sure," she said. " All those

places I used to know so well before you were born, Hester—
and Kaley's, where I used to spend so much money. But,
after all, it is a pleasure to come back among the people that
know you. Mr. Kaley was so very civil, did you notice? I
think he paid more attention to me even than to Catherine ;
of course he remembered that as long as I was well off I
always used to go there for everything. It was very sad, but
I am glad to have done it. And then Catherine was so kind.
Let me see that pretty lace thing she gave you? It is exactly
what you wanted. You must be sure to put it on when we
go there to-morrow to luncheon." Hester would have liked
to tear it in pieces and throw it in Miss Vernon's face ; but
her mother regarded everything from a very different point
of view.

Catherine Vernon, on her side, talked a great deal to
Edward that evening of the comical scene, and how she could
not get the advantage of poor Mrs. John's little *minauderies*
because of that child with her two big eyes. " I was afraid
to stir for her. I scarcely dared to say a word. I expected
every moment to be called to give an account of myself,"
she said. It added very much to her enjoyment of all the
humours of her life that she had this companion to tell them
to. He was her confidant, and heard everything with the
tenderest interest and a great many amusing comments of his
own. Certainly in this one particular at least her desire to
be of use to her relations had met with a rich reward. No
son was ever more attentive to his mother ; and all his habits
were so *nice* and good. A young man who gets up to botanise
in the morning, who will sit at home at night, who has no
evil inclinations—how delightful he is to the female members
of his family, and with what applause and gratitude they
repay him for his goodness ! And Miss Vernon felt the force
of that additional family bond which arises from the fact that
all the interests of the household, different as their age and
pursuits may be, are the same. Nothing that concerned the
one but must have an interest for the other. Perhaps Edward
did not speak so much about himself, or even about the business, which was naturally of the first interest to her, as he
might have done, but she had scarcely as yet found this out :
and certainly he entered into all she told him on her side
with the most confidential fulness. "The Vernonry has
always been as good as a comedy," she said. " I have to be
so cautious not to offend them. And I must be on my ps and

qs with this little girl. There is a great deal of fun to be got out of her; but we must keep it strictly to ourselves."

"Oh, strictly!" said Edward, with a curious little twist about the corners of his mouth. He had not told the story of his own encounter with the new subject of amusement, which was strange; but he was a young man who kept his own counsel, having his own fortune to make, as had been impressed upon him from his birth.

There were only two other members of the Vernon community with whom the strangers had not yet made acquaintance (for as has been already said Mrs. Reginald Vernon, the young widow who was altogether wrapped up in her four children, and old Captain and Mrs. Morgan on the west side of the Vernonry scarcely counted at all), and these were its gayest and most brilliant members, the present dwellers in the White House, Harry and Ellen Vernon, the most independent of all the little community. Stories were current in it that Harry in business matters had begun to set himself in something like opposition to Catherine Vernon not long after she had given up the conduct of the bank into his hands: while Ellen detached herself openly from her Aunt Catherine's court, and had set up a sort of Princess of Wales's drawing-room of her own. It was some time before they appeared at the Vernonry, Harry driving his sister in a phaeton with a pair of high-stepping horses which seemed scarcely to touch the ground. The whole population of the place was stirred by the appearance of this brilliant equipage. Mrs. Reginald Vernon's little boy, though bound under solemn penalties never to enter the gardens, came round and hung upon the gate to gaze. Even old Captain Morgan rose from his window to take another look. Mr. Mildmay Vernon came out with his newspaper in his hand, and if the sisters did not appear, it was not from want of curiosity but because Ellen Vernon had not received their civilities when she came to Redborough with the cordiality they had a right to expect. Catherine Vernon's fine sleek horses made no such impression as did this dashing pair. And the pair who descended from the phaeton were as dashing as their steeds. Ellen was very fair, with hair half flaxen half golden, in light little curls like a baby's upon her forehead, which was not the fashion in those days and therefore much more effective. She was dressed in a rich red-purple gown, charitably supposed to be "second mourning" by the addition

of a little lace and a black ribbon, with yards of silken train
sweeping after her, and sweeping up too all the mats at
the doors as she went in.   Harry was in the lightest of
light clothes, but he had a tiny hat-band supposed to answer
all necessities in the way of "respect" to John Vernon
deceased, or to John's widow living.   Hester standing shyly
by, thought this new cousin Ellen the most beautiful creature
she had ever seen; her daintiness and her fineness, her airy
fairness of face, set off by the rich colour of her dress, was
dazzling as she came into the brown room, with its two inhabitants in mourning, and the tall, light-coloured young man
after her.   Mrs. John made them her little curtsy, shook hands
with them, gave her greeting and a smile or two, and then had
recourse to her handkerchief.

"Oh, yes, thanks," she said, "I have quite settled down.
I am very comfortable, but everything is so changed.   To
go away from the White House where I had everything I
wished for, and then to come back—here; it is a great
difference."

"Oh, but this is so much nicer than the White House,"
cried Ellen; "this is so delightfully old fashioned!   I would
give the world to have the Vernonry.   If Aunt Catherine had
only given it to us when we came here and taken the White
House for the ——" pensioners she was about to say, but
paused in time, "other relations!   I should have liked it so
much better, and probably so would you."

Mrs. John shook her head.

"I never could have gone back to it in the same circumstances," she said, "and therefore I would prefer not to go to
it at all."

"But oh, you must come and see me!" said Ellen; "and
you too," turning to Hester.   "I am so fond of getting among
little girls and feeling myself quite young again.   Come and
spend a long day with me, won't you?   I will show you all my
things, and Harry shall drive us out, if you like driving.   May
she come?   We have always something going on.   Aunt
Catherine's is the old set, and ours is the young set," she said
with a laugh.   She spoke with a little accompaniment of chains
and bracelets, a soft jingle as of harness, about her, being very
lively and full of little gestures—pretty bridlings of her head
and movements of her hands.

Harry behind backed her up, as seemed to be his duty.

"She is dreadfully wild," he said; "she would like to be always on the go."

"Oh, Harry, nothing of the sort; but if we don't enjoy ourselves when we are young when are we to do it? And then I say it is good policy, don't you think so, Mrs. Vernon? You see we are just like shopkeepers, all the people hereabouts are our customers. Aunt Catherine gives big dinners for the old fogeys, but we do just as much good, keeping the young ones jolly; and we keep ourselves jolly too."

"Indeed, Miss Ellen," said Mrs. John, with some dignity, "I never heard such an idea that bankers were like shopkeepers. Catherine must have made great changes indeed if it is like that. It never was so in my time."

"Oh," said Ellen, "you were too grand to allow it, that is all, but it is the fashion now to speak plain." And she laughed, and Harry laughed as if it had been the best joke in the world. "But we mustn't say so before Aunt Catherine," cried the gay young woman. "She disapproves of us both as it is. Perhaps not so much of Harry, for she likes the boys best, you know; but oh, dreadfully of me! If you want to keep in favour with Aunt Catherine—isn't your name Hester?"

"I don't," said Hester abruptly, without further question.

"Oh, Harry, look here, here's another rebel! isn't it fun? I thought you were nice from the very first look of you," and here Ellen rose with a still greater jingle of all her trappings and touched with her own delicate fair cheek the darker oval of Hester's, which coloured high with shyness and pleasure. "I'll tell you what I'll do, I'll come for you one of these days. Are you doing lessons now? What are you learning? Oh, she may have a holiday for one day?"

"That is just what I ought to be inquiring about," said Mrs. John. "A governess—I am afraid I am not able to carry her on myself. I have taught her," the poor lady said with pride, "all she knows."

Hester listened with a gasp of astonishment. What Mrs. John meant was all she knew herself, which was not much. And how about her teaching and her independence and the *cours* she felt herself ready to open? She was obliged to overcome her shyness and explain herself.

"I don't want to learn," she said, "I want to teach. I can speak French, and Italian, and German. I want to open a *cours*; don't you think I might open a *cours*? I know that

I could teach, for I am so fond of it, and I want something
to do." Having got all this out like a sudden shot from a
gun Hester stopped short, got behind her mother, and was
heard no more.

"Oh!" cried Ellen, "teach! that little thing!" and then
she turned to her brother, "Isn't it fine?" she said, "it
would be a shame to stop her when she wishes it. French
and Italian and German, only fancy. I don't know what a
cours is, but whatever it is you shall have it, dear. I promise
you. Certainly you shall have it. I will not have you kept
back for the want of that."

Hester was a great deal too much excited to laugh, and
here Mrs. John interfered. "You must excuse me," she said
nervously. "Do not think I don't feel the kindness. Oh,
you must excuse me! I could not let her teach. My poor
husband would never have suffered it for a moment. And
what would Catherine say?—a Vernon! Oh, no, no! it is
impossible; there is nothing I would not rather do. She has
spoken of it before: but I thought it only childish nonsense.
Oh, no, no! thank Heaven, though we are poor," cried the
poor lady, "and fallen from what we were—we are not
fallen so far as that."

"Oh, but it isn't falling at all," said Ellen, "you see you
are old-fashioned. Don't be angry. I don't mean any harm.
But don't you know it is the fashion now for girls to do
something? Oh, but it is though! the best girls do it;
they paint, and they do needlework, and they sing, and they
write little books, and everybody is proud to be able to
earn money. It is only when they are clever that they can
teach; and then they are so proud! Oh, I assure you, Mrs.
Vernon! I would not say so if it were not quite the right thing.
You know, Harry, people do it in town constantly. Lady
Mannion's daughter mends old lace, and Mrs. Markham paints
things for the shops. It is the fashion: the very best families
do it. It will be quite aristocratic to have a Vernon teaching.
I shall take lessons myself."

"That's the thing," said the good-natured Harry. "Nell,
that's the best thing. She shall teach you and me."

"Oh, he wants to make a hole and corner thing of it," said
Ellen, "to hide it up! How silly boys are; when it is the
very height of the fashion and will bring us into notice
directly! There is old Lady Freeling will take her up at once:

and the Duchess. You may do whatever you please, but I will stand by her. You may count upon me, Hester, I will stand by you through thick and thin. You will be quite a heroine : everybody will take you up."

Mrs. John looked from one to the other aghast. " Oh, no, no, pardon me; but Hester—I cannot sanction it, I cannot sanction it; your poor papa—" faltered Mrs. John.

It was characteristic that in the very midst of this discussion Ellen Vernon got up with all the ringing of her caparison, and took her leave, declaring that she had forgotten that she had to go somewhere at four o'clock, "and you know the horses will not stand, Harry," she said, " but whenever we are happy anywhere, we forget all our engagements—we are two such sillies, Harry and I." She put her arm round Hester's waist as they went through the passage, and kissed her again at the door. " Mind, you are to come and spend a long long day with me," she said. Mrs. John interrupted in the midst of her remonstrances, and not sure that this dazzling creature would not drive off straight somewhere or other to establish Hester in her *cours*, followed after them trying to put in another word. But Ellen had been placed in her seat, and her dust-cloak arranged round her, before the poor lady could say anything. And she too stood spellbound like all the rest, to see the beautiful young couple in their grandeur, so fair, so handsome, so perfectly got up. The only fault that their severest critic could find with them was that they were too fair; their very eyelashes were flaxen, there were no contrasts in their smooth fair faces; but this in conjunction with so much youth and daintiness had a charm of its own. Mr. Mildmay Vernon had been watching for them at the window, losing all the good of his book, which was from the circulating library and cost twopence a night; consequently he threw away at least the half of a farthing waiting for the young people to come out. When they appeared again he went to his door, taking off the soft old felt hat which he wore habitually out of doors and in, and kissing his hand—not it is to be feared very much to his advantage, for these two fine young folks paid little attention to their poor relations. The Miss Vernon Ridgways looked out behind their curtains watching closely. How fine it is to be young and rich and beautiful and on the top of the wave ! With what admiration all your dependents look upon you. Every one in the Vernonry was breathless with excitement when Harry took the reins and the groom left the horses' heads, and the phaeton wheeled round. The little boys at the gate scattered as it wheeled out, the small Vernons vindicating their gentility and relationship by standing straight in the way of the horses. And with what a whirl and dash they turned round the sweep of the road, and disappeared from the longing view! Mildmay Vernon who had taken such trouble to get a glance from them crossed over to the door of the verandah where Mrs. John, with the streamers of her cap blowing about her, and her mind as much disturbed as her capstrings, stood still breathless watching the departure. "Well," he said, "so you've had the Prince and Princess in all their grandeur." Mrs. John had to take a moment to collect herself before she could even make out what he had said. As for Hester, she was so dazzled by this visit, her head and her heart so beating and throbbing, that she was incapable of putting up with the conversation which always made her wicked. She ran away, leaving her mother at the door, and flew to her own room to recollect all that had passed, and to go over it again and again as lovers do. She put her hands over her eyes and lived over again that moment, and every detail of Cousin Ellen's appearance and every word she had said. The jingle of her chains and trinkets seemed to Hester like silver bells, a pretty individualism and sign of her presence. If she went into a dark room or if you were blind, Hester thought, you would know by that that it was she. And the regal colour of her dress, and the black lace of her bonnet all puffed about those wonderful light locks, and her dainty shoes and her delicate gloves, and everything about her! "A long, long day," and "You may count upon me, Hester." Was it possible that a creature so dazzling, so triumphant had spoken such words to her? Her heart was more elated than it had ever been before in her life. And as for the work which she had made up her mind to do, for the first time it seemed possible and feasible. Cousin Ellen would arrange it for her. She was far too much excited and awed to be able to laugh at the mistake Cousin Ellen had made in her haste about buying a *cours* for Hester, not knowing in the least what it meant. In this way with all sincerity the dazzled worshippers of greatness lose their perception of the ridiculous in the persons of those who have seized upon their imagina-

tions. Hester would have been revolted and angered had
any one noted this ludicrous particular in the conversation.
Through the open window the girl heard the voices of her
mother and the neighbours, now including the sharp voice of
Miss Vernon Ridgway, and the sound made her heart rise
with a kind of indignant fury. They would discuss her as if
they had any understanding of such a creature, as if they
knew what they were speaking about! they, old, poor, spiteful
as they were, and she so beautiful, so young, so splendid, and
so kind. "The kindness was the chief thing," Hester said to
herself, putting her fingers in her ears not to hear the ill
nature down stairs. Oh, of course, they would be taking
her to pieces, pouring their gall upon her! Hester felt that
youth and happiness were on her own side as against the
envious and old and poor.

For days after she looked in vain for the re-appearance of
that heavenly vision, every morning getting up with the conviction that by noon at least it would appear, every afternoon making up her mind that the dulness of the lingering
hours would be brightened by the sound, the flash, the wind
of rapid movement, the same delightful voice, the perfumed
fair cheek, the jingle of the golden caparisons. Every day
Mrs. John said, first cheerfully, then querulously, "I wonder
if they will come for you to-day." When it began to dawn
upon Hester at last that they were not coming, the sense of
deception which came over her was, in some sort, like the
pangs of death. She stood still, in her very being astounded,
unable to understand what had happened. They *were not
coming again*. Her very heart stood still, and all the wheels
of her existence in a blank pause like death. When
they began to move again reluctantly, hoarsely, Hester felt
too sick and faint for any conscious comment upon what
had happened. She could not bear the commentary which
she was almost forced to hear, and which she thought would
kill her—the "Poor child! so you've been expecting Ellen
Vernon?" which Miss Matilda next door said to her with
an insulting laugh, almost drove her frantic. And not
much less aggravating to the sensitive girl were her mother's
frequent wonderings what could have become of them, whether
Ellen could be ill, what had happened. "They said they
would come and fetch you to spend a day with them, didn't
they? Then why don't they come, Hester?—why don't they

come ? " the poor lady said.   Hester's anger and wretchedness
and nervous irritation were such that she could almost have
struck her mother.   Was it right, in addition to her own disappointment, that she should have this question thrust upon
her, and that all the pangs of her first disenchantment should
be discussed by contemptuous spectators ?   This terrible
experience, which seemed to Hester to be branded upon her
as by red-hot irons, made a woman of her all at once.   To
her own consciousness, at least, she was a child no more.

CHAPTER VIII.

NINETEEN.

SUCH were the scenes and the people among whom Hester
Vernon grew up. Her first *désillusionment* in respect to
Cousin Ellen, who for one bright and brief moment seemed
about to bring glory to her young existence, was very poignant
and bitter: but by the time Hester was nineteen she had
ceased to remember that there had been so sharp a sting in
it, and no longer felt it possible that Ellen, with all her
finery, could at any moment have affected her with any particular sentiment. These years made a great deal of difference
in Hester. She was at the same time younger and older at
nineteen than at fourteen. She was less self-confident, less
sure of her own powers to conduct everything, from her
mother—the most easily guided of all subject intelligences in
the old days—upwards to all human circumstances, and even
to life itself, which it had seemed perfectly simple to the girl
that she should shape at her own pleasure. By degrees, as
she grew older, she found the futility of all these certain-
ties. Her mother, who was so easily guided, slid back again
just as easily out of the groove into which her child had, as
she thought, fixed her, and circumstances defied her altogether taking their own way, altogether uninfluenced by her
wishes. Mrs. John Vernon was like the "knotless thread"
of the Scotch proverb. Nothing could be more easy than to
convince her, to impress her ductile mind with the sense of
this or that duty; but, on the other hand, nothing could be
more easy than to undo next moment all that had been done,
and turn the facile will in a new direction. Between this soft

and yielding foundation of her life upon which she could find
no firm footing, and the rock of Catherine Vernon who
remained quite immovable and uninfluenced by her, coming no
nearer as the years went on, yet hemming in her steps and
lessening her freedom, the conditions of existence seemed all
against the high-spirited, ambitious, active-minded and
impatient girl, with her warm affections, and quick intelligence, and hasty disposition. The people immediately about
were calculated to make her despise her fellow-creatures
altogether : the discontented dependents who received everything without a touch of human feeling, without gratitude
or kindness, and the always half-contemptuous patroness
who gave with not much more virtue, with a disdain-
ful magnanimity, asking nothing from her pensioners but
that they would amuse her with their follies—made up a
circle such as might have crushed the goodness out of any
young mind. Even had she herself begun with any enthusiasm for Catherine, the situation would have been less
terrible; but as this, unfortunately, had not been the case,
the poor girl was delivered over to the contemplation of one
of the worst problems in human nature without shield or safeguard, or any refuge to creep into. Fortunately her youth,
and the familiarity which deadens all impression, kept her, as
it keeps men in general, from a conscious and naked encounter
with those facts which are fatal to all higher views or natural
charities. She had in her, however, by nature only too strong
a tendency to despise her neighbours, and the Miss Vernon
Ridgways and Mr. Mildmay Vernon were exactly of the order
of beings which a young adventurer upon life naturally treats
with disdain.

But Hester had something worse in her life than even
this feeling of contempt for the people about her, bad as
that is. She had the additional pang of knowing that habit
and temper often made her a partaker of the odious sentiments which she loathed. Sometimes she would be drawn
into the talk of the women who misrepresented their dear
Catherine all day long, and sneered bitterly at the very bounty
that supplied their wants. Sometimes she would join involuntarily in the worse malignity of the man to whom Catherine Vernon gave everything that was good in his life, and who
attributed every bad motive to her. And as if that was not
enough, Hester sinned with Catherine too, and saw the
ridicule and the meanness of these miserable pensioners with

a touch of the same cynicism which was the elder woman's great defect, but was unpardonable in the younger, to whom there should as yet have been no loss of the ideal. The rage with which she would contemplate herself when she yielded to the first temptation and launched at Cousin Catherine in a moment of passion one of those arrows which were manufactured in the Vernonry, the deep disgust which would fill her when she felt herself, like Catherine, contemplating the world from a pinnacle of irony, chill but smiling, swept her young spirit like tempests. To grow at all in the midst of such gales and whirlwinds was something. It was not to be expected that she could grow otherwise than contorted with the blasts. She came to the flower and bloom of existence with a heart made to believe and trust, yet warped to almost all around, and finding no spot of honest standing-ground on which to trust herself. Sometimes the young creature would raise her head dismayed from one of the books in which life is so different from what she found it, and ask herself whether books were all lies, or whether there was not to be found somewhere an existence which was true? Sometimes she would stop short in the midst of the Church services, or when she said her prayers, to demand whether it was all false, and these things invented only to make life bearable? Was it worth living? she would ask sometimes, with more reason than the essayists. She could do nothing she wanted in it. Her *cours* had all melted into thin air; if it had been possible to get the consent of her authorities to the work she had once felt herself so capable of, she was now capable of it no longer. Her mother, obstinate in nothing else, had been obstinate in this, that her poor husband's daughter should not dishonour his name (alack the day!) by becoming a teacher—a teacher! like the poor governesses for whom he had felt so much contempt; and Catherine Vernon, the last auxiliary whom Mrs. John expected, had supported her with a decision which put all struggles out of the question. Catherine indeed had explained herself on the occasion with a force which had almost brought her within the range of Hester's sympathies, notwithstanding that the decision was against herself. " I am here," Miss Vernon had said, " to take care of our family. The bank, and the money it brings in, are not for me alone. I am ready to supply all that is wanted, as reason directs, and I cannot give my sanction to any members of the family descending out of the position in

which, by the hard work of our forefathers, they were born.
Women have never worked for their living in our family, and,
so far as I can help it, they never shall."

"You did yourself, cousin Catherine," said Hester, who
stood forth to learn her fate, looking up with those large eyes,
eager and penetrating, of which Miss Vernon still stood in a
certain awe.

"That was different. I did not stoop down to paltry work.
I took the place which—others had abandoned. I was wanted
to save the family, and thank Heaven I could do it. For that,
if you were up to it, and occasion required, you should have
my permission to do anything. Keep the books, or sweep the
floors, what would it matter?"

"It would matter nothing to me," cried Hester, clasping
her nervous hands together ; and then it was that for a
moment these two, the old woman and the young woman,
made of the same metal, with the same defects and virtues,
looked each other in the eyes, and almost understood each
other.

Almost, but, alas! not quite : Catherine's prejudices against
Mrs. John's daughter, and her adverse experiences of mankind
and womankind, especially among the Vernons, intervened,
and brought her down suddenly from that high and serious
ground upon which Hester had been capable of understanding
her. She turned away with one of those laughs, which still
brought over the girl, in her sensitive youthfulness, a blush
which was like a blaze of angry shame.

"No chance, I hope, of needing that a second time : nor of
turning for succour to you, my poor girl."

It was not unkindly said, especially the latter part of the
sentence, though it ended in another laugh. But Hester, who
did not know the circumstances, was quite unaware what that
laugh meant. She did not know that it was not only Catherine Vernon's personal force and genius, but Catherine
Vernon's money, which had saved the bank. In the latter
point of view, of course, no succour could have been had from
Hester ; and it was the impossibility of this which made Miss
Vernon laugh. But Hester thought it was her readiness, her
devotion, her power of doing everything that mortal woman
had ever done before her, which was doubted, and the sense that
she was neither believed in nor understood swept in a wave
of bitterness through her heart. She was taken for a mere
schoolgirl, well-meaning perhaps—perhaps not even that : in-

capable—she who felt herself running over with capacity and strength, running to waste. But she said nothing more. She retired, carried further away from Catherine in the recoil, from the manner of the approach to comprehending her which she felt she had made. And after that arrest of all her plans, Hester had ceased to struggle. In a little while she was no longer capable of the *cours* to which she had looked so eagerly. She did not know anything else that she could do. She was obliged to eat the bread of dependence, feeling herself like all the rest, to the very heart ungrateful, turning against the hand that bestowed it. There was a little of Mrs. John's income left, enough, Hester thought, to live upon in another place, where she might have been free to eke out this little. But at nineteen she was wiser than at fourteen, and knew that to risk her mother's comfort, or to throw the element of uncertainty again into her life, would be at once unpardonable and impossible. She had to yield, as most women have to do. She had to consent to be bound by other people's rules, and to put her hand to nothing that was unbecoming a Vernon, a member of the reigning family. Small earnings by means of sketches, or china painting, would have been as obnoxious to Catherine Vernon's rule as the *cours :* and of what use would they have been? It was not a little money that Hester wanted, but work of which something good might come. She yielded altogether, proudly, without another word. The arrangement of the little household, the needlework, and the housekeeping, were nothing to her young capabilities ; but she desisted from the attempt to make something better of herself, with an indignant yet sorrowful pride. Sometime Catherine might find out what it was she had rejected. This was the forlorn and bitter hope in her heart.

The only element of comfort which Hester found at this dark period of her life was in the other side of the Heronry in the two despised households, which the Miss Vernon Ridgways and Mr. Mildmay Vernon declared to be "not of our class." Mr. Reginald Vernon's boys were always in mischief ; and Hester, who had something of the boy in her, took to them with genuine fellow-feeling, and after a while began to help them in their lessons (though she knew nothing herself) with great effect. She knew nothing herself ; but a clear head, even without much information, will easily make a path through tho middle of a schoolboy's lessons, which, notwithstanding

his Latin, he could not have found out for himself. And
Hester was "a dab at figures," the boys said, and found out
their sums in a way which was little short of miraculous.
And there was a little sister who called forth all the tender
parts of Hester's nature, who had been a baby on her first
appearance at the Vernonry, and to whom the girl would
gladly have made herself nurse and governess, and everything that girl could be. Little Katie was as fond of Hester
as of her mother, and this was a wonderful solace to the heart
of the girl, who was a woman every inch of her, though she was
so much of a boy. Altogether the atmosphere was better on
that side of the establishment, the windows looked on the common, and the air was fresh and large. And Mrs. Reginald,
if she would have cared for it, which was doubtful, had no
time for gossip. She did not pretend to be fond of Catherine,
but she was respectful and grateful, a new feeling altogether to Hester. She was busy all day long, always doing
something, making clothes, mending stockings, responding to
all the thousand appeals of a set of healthy, noisy children.
The house was not so orderly as it might be, and its aspect
very different from that of the refined gentility on the other
side ; but the atmosphere was better, though sometimes
there was a flavour of boots in it, and in the afternoon of
tea. It was considered "just like the girl," that she should
thus take to Mrs. Reginald, who had been a poor clergyman's
daughter, and was a Vernon only by marriage. It showed
what kind of stuff she was made of.

"You should not let her spend her time there—a mere
nursery-maid of a woman. To think that your daughter
should have such tastes! But you should not let her, dear
Mrs. John," the sisters said.

"*I* let her!" cried Mrs. John, throwing up her hands; "I
would not for the world say a word against my own child,
but Hester is more than I can pretend to manage. She always
was more than I could manage. Her poor papa was the only
one that could do anything with her."

It was hard upon the girl when her own mother gave her
up; but this too was in Hester's day's work ; and she learned
to smile at it, a little disdainfully, as Catherine Vernon did;
though she was so little hardened in this way that her lips
would quiver in the middle of her smile.

The chief resource which Hester found on the other side of
the Vernonry was, however, still more objectionable to the

feelings of the genteel portion of the little community, since it was in the other little house that she found it, in the society of the old people who were not Vernons at all, but who quite unjustifiably as they all felt, being only her mother's relations, were kept there by Catherine Vernon, on the money of the family, the money which was hers only in trust for the benefit of her relations. They grudged Captain Morgan his home, they grudged him his peaceful looks, they grudged him the visits which Catherine was supposed to pay oftener to him than to any one else in the Vernonry.   It is true that the Miss Vernon Ridgways professed to find Catherine's visits anything but desirable.

"Dear Catherine!" they said, "what a pity she has so little manner! When she is absent one can recollect all her good qualities, how kind she really is, you know, at bottom, and what a thing it is for her to have us here, and how lonely she would be, with her ways, if she had not us to fall back upon. But when she is present, really you know it is a struggle! Her manner is so against the poor, dear! One is glad to see her go, to think, *that* is over; it will be some time before she can come again ; for she really is much better, *far* better, than she appears, poor dear Catherine !"

This was how they spoke of her: while Mr. Mildmay shrugged his thin old shoulders. "Catherine, poor thing, has too much the air of coming to see if our houses are clean and our dinners simple enough," he said.

Even Mrs. John chimed in to the general chorus, though in her heart she was glad to see Catherine, or any one. But they were all annoyed that she should go so often to those old Morgans. They kept an account of her calls, though they made believe to dislike them, and when the carriage was heard on the road (they could all distinguish the sound it made from that of any other carriage), they all calculated eagerly at what house she was due next. And when, instead of coming in at the open gate, which the old gardener made haste to open for her, as if he had known her secrets, and was aware of her coming, she stayed outside, and drew up at the Morgans, nobody could imagine what a commotion there was. The sisters rushed in at once to Mrs. John, who had a window round the corner, and watched to see if it was really true, and how long Catherine stayed. They made remarks on the little old gentleman, with his white head, when he came out to put her into the carriage.

"What hypocrites some people are," they cried. "We are always as civil as ever we can be, and I hope dear Catherine, poor thing, *always* feels that she is welcome. But to make believe that we have enjoyed it is more than Martha or I am equal to." They watched until the fat horses had turned round, and Catherine's bonnet was no longer distinguishable. "That is the third time in a month, to my certain knowledge," Miss Matilda would say.

"Be thankful, my dear ladies, that it is on old Morgan, not on you, that she bestows her favours," Mr. Mildmay would remark.

Mrs. John was not always sure that she liked this irruption into her house. But she too watched with a little pique, and said that Catherine had a strange taste.

"Oh, taste dear Catherine; she has no *taste!* Her worst enemy never accused of her *that,*" the other ladies cried.

And when it was known that these old Morgans, the Captain and his wife whom Catherine Vernon distinguished in this way, had gained the heart of Hester, the excitement in the Vernonry was tremendous. Mr. Mildmay Vernon, though he was generally very polite to her, turned upon his heel, when the fact was made known to him, with angry contempt.

"I draw the line at the Morgans," he said. Much might be forgiven to the young girl, the only youthful creature (except Mrs. Reginald's boys, whom he detested) among them, but not this.

The sisters did not, alas, pass it over so briefly. They themselves had never taken any notice of the old couple. The utmost they had done had been to give the old captain a nod, as they did to the tradesmen, when he took off his hat to them. Mrs. Morgan, who never went out, did not come in their way, fortunately for her. So strange was this departure on Hester's part from all the traditions of the place that, to do them justice, they would not believe in her iniquity until the fullest proof had been secured. But after she had been seen about half a dozen times, at least, seated in the round window which commanded the road, and was the old gentleman's delight, and even, strange girl, without any sense of shame, had made herself visible to everybody walking with him on the edge of the common, and standing talking to him at his door, there was no further possibility of doubt on the subject. The only thing that could be thought was to cut Hester, which was done accordingly by all the garden front, even her own mother being wound up by much exhortation, as for the advantage of her daughter's soul, to maintain a studied silence to the culprit by way of bringing her to her senses. But it may be supposed that Mrs. John did not hold out long. A more effectual means of punishment than this was invented by Mr. Mildmay Vernon, who declared that it was a very clever way of currying favour with Catherine, and that he only wondered it had never been adopted before. This, indeed, touched Hester to the quick : but it did not detach her from her friends. The objects of all this enmity were two very simple old people without any pretension at all, who were very willing to live peaceably with all men. Captain Morgan was an old sea-captain, with all the simplicity of homely wisdom, which so often characterises his class ; and his wife a gentle old woman, entirely devoted to him, and, by this time, not capable of much more than to keep the record of all his distinctions and to assert his goodness. It was he who helped her down stairs every day to the chimney corner in winter, and in summer to the large chair in the window, from which she could see everything that went on in the road, all the people that passed, and the few events that happened. A conviction that little Ted, Mrs. Reginald's third boy, would be run over, and an alarmed watch for that incident, were the only things that disturbed her placid existence : and that she could not accompany him on his walks was her only regret.

"He dearly loves somebody to walk with," she said : "except when he was at sea, my dear, I've gone everywhere with him : and he misses me sadly. Take a little turn with the captain, my dear."

And when Hester did that which so horrified the other neighbours, old Mrs. Morgan looked out after them from the window and saw the tall slim girl walking by the side of the stooping old man, with a pure delight that brought the tears to her eyes. When you are over eighty it does not take much to make you cry. Hester, who was the subject of continual assault in every other place, was adored and applauded in this little parlour, where they thought her more beautiful, and good, and clever, than ever girl had been

before. The old captain, who was screwed and twisted
with rheumatism, and stooped with age, held himself almost
straight when his young companion started with him upon
his daily walk.

"When a young lady goes with me," he said, "I must
remember my manners. An old fellow gets careless when
he's left to himself."

And he told Hester stories of all the many-chaptered past,
of the long historic distances, which he could remember
like yesterday, and which seemed endless, like an eternity, to
her wondering eyes. He had been in some of the old sea-
fights of the heroic days—at Trafalgar, though not in Nelson's
ship; and he liked nothing better than to fight his battles
over again. But it was not these warlike recollections so
much as the scraps of his more peaceful experience which
entranced the young listener. She liked to hear him tell how
he had "got hold" of a foolish young middy or an able
seaman who was "going to the bad," or how he had subdued
a threatening mutiny, and calmed an excitement; and of
the many, many who had fallen around him, while he kept on—
fallen in death sometimes, fallen more sadly in other ways.
A whole old world seemed to open round Hester as he talked
—a world more serious, more large, than this, in which
there were only the paltry events of the day and her foolish
little troubles. In Captain Morgan's world there were
great storms and fights; there were dangers and struggles,
and death lurking round every corner. She used to listen
breathless, wondering at the difference—for what danger was
there, what chance of mortal peril or temptation, here? In that
other universe the lives of hundreds of people would sometimes
hang upon the decision and promptitude, the cool head
and ready resource of one. Why was not Hester born in that
day? Why was not she a man? But she did not sufficiently realise that when the men were going through these
perils, the mothers and sisters were trembling at home, able
to do no more than she could. After these walks and talks,
she would go in with the captain to pour out his tea,
while Mrs. Morgan, in her big chair, restrained herself and
would not cry for pleasure as she was so fain to do.

"Oh, my dear, it was a good wind that blew you here, the
old lady said. "The trouble it has been to me not to be
able to go about with him! Indoors we are the best companions still; but he always liked his walk, and it is

dreadful not to be able to go out with him.   But he is happy
when he has a young companion like you."

Thus they made a princess of Hester, and attributed to
her every beautiful quality under the sun.   When a girl is
not used to enthusiasm at home, it does her good to have
somebody believe in her, and admire all she is doing.   And
this was what made her strong to bear all the jibes of the
fine people, and even that detestable suggestion that she
meant to curry favour with Catherine.   Even the sting of
this did not move her to give up her old captain and her
humbler friends.

CHAPTER IX.

"IF you will not think me an old croaker, ma'am, I would say that you retired from work too soon. That was always my opinion. I said it at the time, and I say it again. To give up before your time is flying in the face of Providence."

"I know you are fond of a fine preacher, Mr. Rule," said Catherine Vernon; "don't you remember what the Scotch Chalmers said, that our lives were like the work of creation, and that the last ten years was the Sabbath—for rest?"

"We are not under the Jewish dispensation," said the old clerk, as if that settled the question.

Catherine laughed. She was seated near old Mrs. Morgan in the round window, her carriage waiting outside. Mr. Rule, who was a neighbour, having retired upon a handsome pension and occupying a handsome house, had come in to call upon the old couple, and these two, so long associated in labour and anxiety, had begun, as was natural, to talk on a subject which the others with difficulty followed—the bank. Mrs. Morgan never did anything save sit contentedly in her chair with her hands clasped, but the captain sat by the table working away at one of his models of ships. He was very fond of making these small craft, which were admirably rigged and built like miniature men-of-war. This one was for Alick Vernon, the middle boy of Mrs. Reginald's three. In the background, half hidden by the curtains and by the captain's seat, Hester had taken refuge in a deep elbow-chair, and was reading. She did not want to hide herself, but she had no desire to be seen, and kept in the background, of her own will. Catherine Vernon never took any special notice of her, and Hester was too proud either to show that she felt this, or to make any attempt to mend matters. She had risen up on her cousin's entrance, and touched her hand coldly, then sank back into her former place, and whether any one remembered that she was there at all she did not know.

"If one works till sixty, one does very well," Miss Vernon said.

"You did not think that applicable to me, ma'am," said the clerk. "You would not let me give up till I was near seventy."

"For the sake of the bank—for the sake of the young men. Where would they have been without a guide?"

"Ah!" said old Rule, shaking his head, "there is no guide like the chief. They might turn upon me, and laugh in my face, and tell me 1 am old-fashioned; but they could not say that to you."

"Well, well! the young men fortunately have gone on very well, and have shown no need of a guide."

To this there was no reply, but a little pause pregnant of meaning. The thrill of the significance in it roused Hester altogether from her book : she had not been reading much to begin with, and now all her faculties were awakened. She understood no reason for it, but she understood *it*. Not so Catherine, however, who took no notice, as so often happens to the person chiefly concerned.

"Thirty years is a long spell," she said. "I was at it late and early, and did not do so badly, though I am only a woman."

"Women—when they do take to business—are sometimes better than men," said the clerk, with an accent almost of awe.

"That is natural," said old Captain Morgan over his boat, without raising his head. "For why?—it is not the common women, but those of the noble kind that ever think of trying : so of course they go further and do better than the common men."

"I don't think that is a compliment," said Catherine, "though it sounds a little like one. You have a turn for those sort of sayings, Uncle Morgan, which seem very sweet, but have a bitter wrapped up in them."

"Nay, he never was bitter, Catherine," said the old lady. "He knows what he is talking of. He means no harm to the common women—for his wife is one of them."

"We will not inquire too closely what he means," said Catherine Vernon with a smile. "Anyhow it is very sweet to be able to retire while one has still command of all one's faculties, and see the young ones come in. Of course one does not expect to live for ever. We are all in the Sunday period of our lives, all of us here."

"Not I," said the old clerk, "with respect be it spoken : I have had my Sunday and I am ready to begin again, if there should be any need of me."

"Which there is not, thank God," she said heartily. And again there ensued that little pause. Was it possible she did not observe it? No one echoed the sentiment, no one even murmured the little nothings with which a stillness, which has a meaning, is generally filled up by some benevolent bystander. What did it mean? Hester asked herself. But Catherine took no notice. All had gone so well with her. She was not afraid of evil tidings. Her affection for the young men, her relations and successors, was calm enough to secure her from the anxious prescience of love. She took her life and all that was connected with her, with that serene and boundless faith which is the privilege of the untried soul. Catherine would have resented beyond everything else the imputation that her life was without experience. She had gone through a great deal, she thought. The evening long ago, when she had been told that the credit of the Vernons was at stake, and had roused herself to redeem it, had been the highest crisis and turning-point of existence to her. What had happened since had been little in comparison. She had not known what anxiety meant in the deepest sense of the word, and what had happened before was so long over, that, though she recollected every incident of that early time, it was apart from all her after-life, and never influenced her practical thoughts. She did not pay any attention to that pause which might have awakened her suspicions. There was no foundation in her for suspicion to build upon. She was so sure of all connected with her, and of herself, the first necessity of all.

"I will never forget," said old Mr. Rule, after a pause, "that night, when I had to go and warn you that all was lost unless you would help. What a night it was! I recollect now the light on Wilton Street; the sunset shining in the Grange windows as I rushed through the shrubbery. You were a young lady then, Miss Vernon, and I could not tell

whether you would do it or not. Mrs. John, poor thing, that
I went to first, was never very wise——"

Here a sudden fit of coughing on the part of the captain,
and a stirring of Hester in the background, showed the old
clerk his mistake.

"I beg your pardon, Miss Hester," he cried, "I was just
going to tell something of your mother that would please you.
When I told her we wanted money, she ran to her desk and
got out all she had. It was twenty pounds," said the old
clerk, with a little laugh; "twenty pounds, when we wanted
twice as many thousands! But what did that matter? Some
people have laughed when I have told that story, and some
have been nearer crying."

He was an old man, and tears and laughter get mixed up
at that age; he was nearly crying himself at the end.

Hester's heart gave a bound of mingled pleasure and pain.
Perhaps even she had never done justice to her simple-hearted
mother. She sat bolt upright in her chair, listening with all
her might. Catherine Vernon seemed to retire from the
principal place she had hitherto held in the conversation, and
Hester came forward in her stead. She looked at the old
clerk steadily.

"You speak," she said, "of ladies only. Where was my
father?" holding Rule with her eye, so that he could not
escape.

"Your father!" he faltered, his very lips quivering with
surprise and consternation.

"I don't know why we should bring up all these old stories
to-night," said Catherine, suddenly, "nor what led us to introduce the subject. Let bygones be bygones, Mr. Rule.
We old fogeys have our little talks together, and tell over
our old adventures to amuse ourselves for want of something
better; but that is what the young ones never understand."

"Do you wish me to go away, Cousin Catherine?" said
Hester with her usual pale defiance, rising up with the book
in her arms.

"Oh no, not I. It does not matter in the least whether
you stay or go. I can remember, Uncle Morgan, when the
same sort of thing I am now saying to Hester you used to say
to me : and it does not seem so very long ago either. Now we are
all old together, and not much difference between us," she said
with a little laugh. It still gave her a certain amusement
to think that she was old like these old people, and yet it was

true; for though sixty-five and eighty-five are very different, nobody can doubt that sixty-five is old. It was still strange, almost ludicrous, to Catherine, that it should be so.

"I am of all ages," said the old captain, "for I can remember all. I'll sail my boat with Alick to-morrow, and enjoy it like a small boy (it's a capital little boat, and will sail, I can tell you, Catherine, if you took any interest in it), and then I shall walk on the common with a young lady, and talk of poetry and love."

"Fie, captain!" said his old wife; "but he does not mean all that nonsense, Hester."

"If love is nonsense, and poetry, she and I will go to the stake for them," said the captain. "We'll take a longer walk to-night, my dear, to prove to that old woman how wrong she is."

"I can't wish you a pleasanter thing, captain—and now I must be going," said old Rule, inconsequently.

Catherine, who had been sitting thoughtful since the moment when she interfered, all unthanked and misunderstood to save Hester, rose when the old clerk did, and went out before him, with her rich black silk gown sweeping and rustling. The presence of the elder people made her look blooming, and capable, and young. The old couple watched her from their window, as Rule, gratified and beaming, put her into the carriage.

"She looks young enough to do as much again," said Captain Morgan, standing in the window with his gum-bottle in his hands, with which he was working.

"Oh, captain!" said his wife, "but where's the money?" shaking her old head.

Hester behind peered out between these two aged heads, pale with interest, and antagonism, and attraction. She could never think of any one else when Catherine was near, though all her instincts were in arms against her. The words that passed between the old people were as a foreign tongue to her. She had not the slightest perception what they meant.

Meantime Catherine spoke a warning word to her former prime minister, who had abdicated later than herself.

"You were very near giving that child a heartache," she said. "Take care not to say anything before her. She need never know that her father deserted his post. The creature has a quick sense of honour, and it might wound her."

"She is not like his daughter," said the clerk, "nor that

poor lady's either. She is one of the pure old Vernon stock."

"Do you think so?" said Catherine, indifferently. "I rather dislike her than otherwise; but I would not do the child any harm." And then the fat horses put themselves in motion, and she gave a smile and a bow to all her retainers and worshippers—and the Miss Vernon-Ridgways drew away from Mrs. John's window, where as usual they had been watching Catherine, as she, amid all these visible signs of her wealth and sovereignty, disappeared from their eyes.

"I suppose, Captain Morgan," said Hester that evening, when she walked out with him as usual, "that Cousin Catherine was young once?"

It seemed an absurd question, but it was put with the utmost gravity; and Hester knew what she meant, as perhaps the reader will too.

"About your age, my dear," the captain said, promptly "and not at all unlike you."

"Like me!"

"You think you are very different now, but there is not much more difference than that of years. She was the same kind of girl as you are—masterful—very sure that her own way was the right one—obstinate as a mule in her mind, but not so difficult to move by the heart."

"Am I all that?" said Hester, wondering; "not in some things, for I am never sure that I am right—or any one else— except you, perhaps. No, it is the other way, quite the other way! I am very sure that I am wrong, and every one else— except you."

"A large rule and a small exception," said the old man; "but it is the same thing. Catherine was rich and had everything her own way. You are—in the midst of a poor community where we can have nothing our own way. And at your age you can't discriminate any more than she could at hers."

"Then does it come to this, that money is everything?" asked the disciple with some bitterness, but without, as may be supposed, the slightest intention of accepting the master's teaching on this point.

Captain Morgan made no reply. What he said was—

"I should like to interest you in Catherine, my dear; all that happened, you know, before we came here, while we were busy with our own life, my wife and I; but I have put this

and that together since. Catherine was, as people say, crossed
in love, notwithstanding her wealth and all her qualities. So
far as I can make out, the man preferred a woman that could
not hold the candle to her; not so pretty, not so clever, altogether inferior. That must be rather a blow to a woman!"

"A blow! What sort of a woman would she be that
cared for a man who did not care for her?"

This somewhat inarticulate sentiment Hester delivered with
an indignant blush and flashing eyes.

"That is all very fine, my dear; but you are too clear-
headed to be taken in by it," said the captain. "A woman
might not show it, perhaps. I have no reason to suppose that
Catherine showed it. But you must remember that a woman
is not a woman in the abstract, but Catherine or Hester as the
case may be, and liable to everything that humanity is liable
to; and she would be a poor creature indeed if she were
incapable of falling in love generously, as a man is supposed
to do."

"I don't know what you mean by generously!"

"Ah, but you do—none better. Something however
occurred after, much worse than his preference of another
woman. The man turned out to be an unworthy man."

Hester had been following every word with breathless
interest. She grew quite pale, her lips dropped apart, her
eyes blazed out of the whiteness of her face upon her old
instructor. He went on without taking note of this change,

"I should think for my part that there cannot be any such
blow as that. Don't you remember we agreed it was the
secret of all Hamlet's tragedy? It is the tragedy of the
world, my dear. I told the old woman we were going to
talk of love and poetry. You see I was right."

"But—Catherine?"

Hester was, as became a girl, far too much interested in the
individual case to be able to stray to the abstract, and in fact
she had only assented to her mentor's theory in respect to
Hamlet, not having begun such investigations for herself.

"Ay, Catherine. Well, that is just what happened to her,
my dear. The man first showed that he had no appreciation
of herself, which we will allow must have wounded her; and
then after, when that was all over, proved himself unworthy,
dishonourable—in short, what the young men call a cad."

"Who was he?" asked Hester, in a low and awe-stricken
tone.

Then Captain Morgan turned to look at her, apparently with some alarm ; but his fears were quieted by her face. She had evidently no clue to who it was.

"I never knew the man," he said quickly. "One has no wish to know anything about him. The interesting person is the woman in such a case. Here, Hester, you must be the teacher. Tell me, what would that discovery do to a girl, a daring, masterful spirit like you ?"

"Oh, captain, I am not daring or masterful," cried the girl clasping her hands ; "don't you know it is cruel to call me so —I that can do nothing, that am only like a straw tossing on the water, carried the way I would not. If I were masterful, I would go away from here. I would do something for myself."

"All that is no answer to my question," the old captain said.

Hester was used to follow his leading at a touch. There was a kind of mesmerism in the effect he had upon her.

"I cannot tell," she said in a low and hurried voice. "I don't see: it would turn all the world wrong. It would—— But," she added, collecting herself, "she would throw him away from her like a dead thing. He would be dead. She would think of him no more. Unworthy ! One shakes one's self free—one is done with that ! "

"Look again," said the old man, with a half smile, shaking his head.

"I don't wish to look again. Is not that enough ? I suppose it would make her very unhappy. She would struggle, she would try to find excuses. Oh, Captain Morgan, don't press me so ! I suppose everything would turn round and round. There would seem nothing to stand on, nothing to look up to, the skies would all whirl and the solid ground. It makes my head swim to think of it," the girl cried, covering her eyes with her hands.

"That was how it was with Catherine, so far as I know. She had to exert herself to save the bank, and that saved her."

"Had he anything to do with the bank ?" she asked quickly.

"My dear, I tell you I was not here at the time," said the wary old man. "I had no knowledge of the circumstances. I never wish to know who he was, lest perhaps I should fail in charity towards him. It is Catherine I want you to

think of. The bank troubles came afterwards, and she had
to get up and put her shoulder to the wheel, which saved
her. But do you think the world ever looked the same after?
Hamlet would never have discovered what traitors those young
courtiers were, if his mother had not turned out a fraud, and
his love a delusion—at least that is my opinion. The wonder
is, he did not misdoubt Horatio too. That is what I should have
done if it had been me. But there is the good of genius,
Hester; the Master who knew everything knew better.
Catherine had a sort of honest Horatio in old Rule, and she
had that work to do, which was the best thing for her. But
you may be sure the world was all dissolving views, and
nothing solid in it for years to come."

Hester, after the shock of the realisation which had been
forced upon her, as to what the result of such a calamity
would be, felt exhausted and sick at heart, as if all her strength
had been worn out.

"Why did you want me to know this?" she said at last.
"I see no signs of it in her. She looks so triumphant, as if
nothing had ever happened or could happen. She sees through
everybody and laughs at them, as if all their lies could never
touch her. Oh she sees very well how they lie, but is never
angry, only laughs; is that the way to make one love her?
And she does not know the false from the true," the girl cried
with an access of indignation. "She considers us all the
same."

"No—no—no—no," said the old man, patting her arm,
but he did not press her any further. He had said as much
as he wanted to say. They went further than usual over the
common as he had threatened to his wife, and as they returned
the old captain owned himself fatigued and took Hester's arm.
"You must be my great-grandchild in the spirit," he said.
"We had a little girl once, my wife and I. I have often
fancied her grown up and married and having children in her
turn. Oh, I am a great dreamer and an old fool. You remember Elia's dream children, and then Tennyson, though he
was not old enough to know anything about it, making the
unborn faces shine beside the never-lighted fire. These poets
make fools of us all, Hester. They know everything without
any way to know it. I fancy you are one of little Mary's
grandchildren. She must be as old as Catherine Vernon,
though age, we may suppose, doesn't count where she is."

"You never told me about *her*."

"There was nothing to tell," he said cheerfully. "Her mother cries still if you speak of little Mary, but not I. It would have been a great thing for us if we could have kept her, but she would have married I suppose, and her husband might not have pleased me. I have thought of that. She would have been taken in probably, and brought us some man I could not put up with, though the children might have been an addition. I dare say she would have turned out a soft, innocent creature, taken in all round, something like your mother, Hester. You are tempted to despise that, you clever ones, but it is a great mistake."

"Oh, Captain Morgan, mother is taken in, as you say, because she thinks everybody true—but she is true always."

"*Always!*" said the old man with fervour, "and far happier because she does not find it out. My wife is the same. It is such souls as these that keep the world steady. We should all tumble to pieces if the race was made up of people like Catherine Vernon and you."

"I wish you would not say Catherine Vernon and me!" said Hester passionately; "there is no likeness, none at all—none at all!"

But the old captain only laughed, and turned her attention to the sunset, which was lighting up all the western sky. The pines stood up against it like rigid black shadows, cut out against the golden light which was belted with flaming lines of crimson. Overhead the sky ascended in varying tints of daffodil and faint ethereal greenness up to the deep yet bright summer blue. The last gleams caught the yellow gorse upon the common and turned every blossom into gold, and all the peaks of the Vernonry rose black against the radiance of the west.

"I wonder if the people *up there* have any hand in it?" said the old man. "I should like to think so. The old landscape painters, perhaps, that never had such colours to work with before. But in that case there would be nothing for me to do," he added with a laugh, "unless it was some small post about the gunneries. I was always fond of my guns."

To Hester this light suggestion, and the laugh with which it was accompanied, sounded profane. She shrank from anything which could take away the awe and mystery from death, just as the old man, who was so near the threshold, liked to familiarise himself with the thought of going over it, and still finding himself a recognisable creature there.

CHAPTER X.

A LOVER.

IT was about this time that Hester became aware of a circumstance the most important that could possibly happen in a young woman's life. There had been no opportunity for her to become acquainted with the emulations and rivalship of other girls. Girls there were none about the Vernonry, nor did they abound in the neighbourhood, in the class from which alone her mother's visitors were chosen. Mrs. John, it has been said, belonged to a county family, a fact of which she was as proud as it is natural and becoming a woman should be. She did not altogether frown upon the few callers from the town who thought it only their duty to Miss Vernon, the most hospitable entertainer in the neighbourhood, to take a little notice of the pensioners, as the poor ladies at the Vernonry were called; but she did not encourage these benevolent visitors. "They are all ladies, and as good as any of us," Mrs. Redfern had been heard to say, who was the mayor's lady, and considered herself a leader of society; and it was a beautiful sight to see Mrs. John, in her old-fashioned dark room and simplest black gown, receiving with kind condescension, and endeavouring to set at her ease, this very fine lady, who considered herself to be paying the poor widow a quite undeserved honour. Mrs. John returned cards only in acknowledgment of Mrs. Redfern's visit, and there the acquaintance ended. So that Hester lost altogether the opportunity of knowing how ordinary girls looked and talked, and what was the object of their ambition. She had not even, which may surprise some people, come to any conclusion

whatever in respect to her own personal appearance. Sometimes indeed, it cannot be denied, she had looked up in the
midst of a novel, where all the young persons in whom the
reader was supposed to take any interest were beautiful,
and asked herself vaguely, with a blush, feeling ashamed of
the question, whether she was pretty. But partly she was
ashamed to give the time necessary to the solution of the
problem, and partly she had not the data upon which to form
her conclusions. There was a beautiful girl in Redborough in
a humble position, upon whose claims everybody was agreed,
but she was a queenly creature, with dark hair and blue eyes,
and features of the most exquisite regularity, to whom Hester
could not flatter herself that she bore the slightest resemblance. Nor was she like Ellen Vernon, with her lovely
fairness, her look of wax and confectionery. Hester was not
ethereal at all. There was no smallness about her, though
she was slim as became her age. "The springy motion in her
gait," the swift, light step which never tired, were beautiful
in their way, and so was the eager outlook in her eyes, which
seemed to contract and expand according to the degree of
interest with which outside subjects moved them; but all
this rather as exponents of the mind within than as merely
physical features. Her hair had never grown long, not much
longer indeed than was just necessary to twist into the knot
behind which proved her to be grown up, and it remained full
of curl and ready to break the smoothness of outline then
thought necessary, on the smallest provocation. Her complexion was very variable, sometimes radiant with flutters of
sudden colour, sometimes relapsing into a rose-tinted whiteness, more white than pale. Her features were not much to
brag of; it was the play of prompt feeling in her face, the
interest, the indignation, the pity, the perpetual change and
vicissitude, that made it attractive, and on this point of
course Hester could not judge. Seeing that her mouth was
too large, and her nose too short, and her eyebrows too
marked, she concluded that she was not pretty, and regretted
it, though in her circumstances it mattered very little; her
friends liked her just as well, whether or not; and she was
never likely to produce the effect which the heroines in novels
—even though comparatively plain—did produce. So she
decided, with a little shame to think that she could have
been disturbed about the matter, that it was not worth going
into it further. All the same it is a pity, for the sake of

young readers, that all the girls in novels, with so very
rare exceptions—and Jane Eyre, if not pretty, probably was
less plain than she thought, and certainly was *agaçante*, which
is much more effective—should be beautiful and should have
so much admiration and conquest. The girls who read are apt
to wonder how it is that they have not the same fortune.
Hester, for her part, had a fine scorn of feminine victories in
this sort; they had never come within the possibilities of her
lot. She never went to balls, nor met in society gangs of
suitors contending for her smile; she did not believe in such
things, and she thought she despised them.

It was in the very midst of this scepticism that she suddenly became aware of certain facts which, as we have said,
were of the kind generally supposed to be most important in a
young woman's life. Harry Vernon had been for some time
alone in the splendour of the White House ; Ellen, who had
inflicted so deep a wound upon Hester's inexperienced girlhood, had married the previous summer, and in the lack of
young ladies worthy to swell her train on that occasion, had
selected Hester as one of her bridesmaids. Hester had never
forgiven her frivolous kinswoman for that first disenchantment of her youth, but her mother, upon whom her exclusion
from society and from all opportunities of distinguishing herself there weighed heavily, had insisted on the acceptance of
the invitation, and Hester had figured accordingly in a white
muslin frock, much too simple to match the toilette of the
other bridesmaids in the pageant, greatly to her own disquiet.
She was the only Vernon in it, and thus had been specially
put forward, and Ellen, altogether unconscious of previous
offence, had exhausted herself in demonstrations of affection
to her young relative. It was she whom Harry led out in
the morning's procession, and he had, in the intervals of his
duty to his guests, come back again and again to her side.
Hester, all inexperienced and unknowing, had paid little
attention to these early indications. She did not identify
him with his sister's guilt towards her. He was a weak,
good-natured, genial fellow, and no more. If Harry did
anything wrong, no doubt it was because of being led astray.
In himself he wished nothing but good to any one. He was
not clever, he was steady and stolid, and went through both
work and pleasure without much discrimination as to which
was which, carrying on both in the same way. When he
began to come to the Vernonry evening after evening, Hester

paid little attention to him. She would go out to walk with
old Captain Morgan in the very face of the young visitor
whose "intentions" all the community considered to be of
such importance. Hester never thought of his "intentions."
She had none herself in which he was anyhow involved.
She was perfectly friendly when they met, but she did not
care whether they ever met or not, and repulsed him as much
as steady indifference can repulse an obstinate and not very
clear-sighted young man. But this was not saying much.
Harry knew as well as any one that his suit was a wonderful
chance for his distant cousin; that Hester had no right to
look for such good fortune as that of being the object of his
affections. He knew that he was bringing in his hand everything a girl need wish for. And so far as Hester's course of
action was concerned, though he was much irritated by it
sometimes, he still felt that it was what she had a right to
employ in the circumstances. It "drew a fellow on;" she
was right to do what she could to obtain this so desirable con-
summation. He could not find fault with her even when he
was angry. Had she been too ready to meet him, he felt that
he would himself have despised what was so easily won. But
her coyness, her apparent indifference, her walking out to the
old captain from her lover, all helped to rivet his chains. It
was excellent policy, and he took it as such; it drew a fellow on.

And it would be impossible to describe the interest of the
Vernonry in this new development. Harry made his appearance first when they were all outside enjoying the beauty of
the summer evening, Mr. Mildmay Vernon occupying that
bench in front of the verandah, which was the most desirable
place in the evening, being just clear of the low sunbeams
which came into your eyes through the trunks of the pines,
penetrating like golden arrows. Mrs. John herself was
watering the plants in the verandah, which were a little
exhausted by the long, scorching day, and wanted refreshment. The Miss Vernon-Ridgways were walking about with
their long sashes extended and their large sleeves flying, the
one eagerly talking from a few paces behind her, to the other.
Their conversation was on the well-worn subject of "some
people who never knew their own place," and was aimed at
the tranquil gentleman on the bench, who when he had
secured his own comfort, which was the first thing to be
thought of, rather prided himself upon never interfering with
his neighbours. When Harry Vernon appeared, there was a

universal stir. The sisters made a little flight round him,
gazing at him. "I do believe it is Harry. Is it Harry?"
they said. Mr. Mildmay Vernon put down his paper in the
midst of a paragraph, and came forward with his most genial
air. "I hope this is a visit only. I hope there is nothing
wrong," he said.

"Wrong! what should be wrong?" said Harry, turning
his fair countenance wonderingly upon the group. "It's a
lovely evening, and I wanted a walk," he added, with a little
reddening of that too-fair face; "and besides, I've got a
message from Ellen to Mrs. John——"

"Dear Ellen! How is Ellen? When is she coming home?"
cried Miss Matilda. "When you write to her, give her our
love. But I suppose she is too happy to care about anybody's
love save one person's. Marriage will improve Ellen—
marriage will steady her. She used to be a little forgetful,
perhaps. Ah! marriage will do her a great deal of good.
She had everything too much her own way."

"But she is missed. It would be pretty to see her again—
forgetting," said Mr. Mildmay, "that she had ever set eyes
on you before."

"Ah, dear Ellen! We should not have known her without
her little ways!"

Now Harry was fond of his sister.

"I'll thank you to leave Ellen alone," he said, brusquely.
"I dare say we've all got our little ways. I had something
to say to Mrs. John if you'll let me pass, please."

"Politeness is characteristic of our family," said Miss
Matilda, drawing her skirts closely round her, and standing
ostentatiously, though she was not very near him, out of
his way.

Mrs. John stood looking on in the verandah with the
watering-can in her hand, not hearing much of what they
said, but feeling that it was uncivil, and putting on a little
deprecating, anxious smile—

"Come in," she said, "come in. The parlour, I think, is
almost cooler than the garden after this hot day. Shall I
make you a cup of tea?"

"These pensioners of Aunt Catherine's are odious people,"
said Harry. "It was you and Hester I came to see."

"You must not speak of them so—they would not like it,"
said Mrs. John, not thinking that she herself might be
spoken of in the same way, though rather pleased at the

bottom of her heart that Harry should make a distinction
between them. He threw himself down in a chair, which
creaked under his weight, and looked very large and mannish
in the little feminine room—rather, indeed, it must be allowed,
out of place there.

"I wonder how you can get on in such a poky little place,"
he said. "I should like to see you in handsome big rooms;
it would seem much more natural."

Mrs. John smiled again, a deprecating, half-apologetic
smile.

"Oh, I am very glad to be here. I did not expect ever
to have to live in such a poor place when I married, it is
true; but people's minds change with their circumstances. I
am glad to have it——"

"You oughtn't to—you should have been provided for in a
different way. Ah, Hester! I am so glad to see you," Harry
said, rising with some commotion to his feet. He took
Hester's hand and held it for a moment. "I thought I'd
come and tell you about Ellen," he said, with a blush.

"Hester," said her mother, giving her a little meaning
look, of which she did not understand the signification, "you
must give Mr. Harry a cup of tea."

And there he sat, to her great oppression, for an hour at
least. He did not even tell them about Ellen. He said
nothing in particular—nothing which it was necessary to
say. Hester, who had intended to go out with her old
captain, felt herself bound by politeness and her mother's
warning looks. She did not know what these looks meant,
but they held her fast. There was not very much conversation. He said a few things over and over, which made it
difficult to change the subject; and it was mostly Mrs. John
who replied, and who rather liked, also, to repeat the same
sentiment. Hester poured out the tea, and when the moment
came for that, lighted the candles, and sat down in the
background and took her work. She was not very fond of
work, but it was better than doing nothing at all. When
she took that seat which was beyond his point of vision,
Harry turned his chair round so as to face her, and took
up one of the candles and arranged it for her, that she
might see to work. "You should have a lamp," he said.
"I have a nice little lamp at home just the thing for you;
you must let me send it." What a long time he sat, and how
anxious he was to make himself agreeable! After that he

came three or four times in succession. Mrs. John began to
look for him, brightening up as the hour of his visit approached :
and the neighbours kept up a watch which it was impossible
to mistake. "If he comes to-night again I shall know what
to think," Miss Matilda said. But when he came that night
he met Hester at the gate in her out-door apparel. Harry's
countenance fell.

"Oh, you are surely not going out," he said, "not just
when I come? You couldn't be so unkind."

"I have been unkind to Captain Morgan very often," said
Hester. "I must not neglect him to-night," and she passed
him quickly with a little bow and smile. It made Harry
very angry, but still he felt that it drew a fellow on.

On one of these occasions, when Hester eluded him in this
way, Harry spoke his mind to Mrs. John.

"I'm very lonely up there by myself," he said, "and I
have nobody to please but myself. Ellen used to interfere
and keep me in order, as she said ; but now she's got somebody
else to look after. I've thought a great deal of Hester for
years back. That time when we came to see you first, you
know, when Ellen made so many advances and forgot all
about them—that was her way. She's not a bad sort when
you get safe hold of her—but it's her way. Well, from
that time I've thought of Hester, though I never liked to
say a word as long as Ellen was there."

"Oh, Mr. Harry," said Mrs. John, who was fluttered and
flattered as if a proposal were being made to herself. "She
was only a child in those days."

"I know ; but she isn't a child now. If she'll have me—
and I can't see why she shouldn't have me—we might all
make each other very comfortable. I'm not frightened of a
mother-in-law as so many fellows are. I believe that's all
bosh. I shouldn't wish to part you more than for the honeymoon, you know. There is plenty of room for you in the
White House, and it would be always nice for her to have you
there, when I happened to be engaged. I think we should hit
it off very well together. And as for money—I know she
has no money—I should never think twice about that. Of
course it would be to my own advantage to make as good
settlements as possible, which is always a good thing in
business when one never knows what may happen. We
might have to consult Aunt Catherine just at first, for she
always keeps a hold on the funds——"

"And there's Hester to consult—that is the most important," said Mrs. John.

"To be sure, that's the most important; but I can't see why she should object," said Harry. "Why, she has never seen any one, has she? I am the only man that has paid any attention to her. At Ellen's wedding there were one or two, but that was only once in a way. I don't say she likes me, but she can't like any one else, can she? for she has never seen anybody."

"Not that I know of," said Mrs. John; "but, Mr. Harry, girls are so fanciful. You cannot be sure of them in that way. They may have some ideal in their heads, though they have never met any one——"

"Eh?" said Harry, making a large mouthful of the word, and opening wide those blue eyes of his with the light lashes. And, indeed, he did not know much about that sort of thing. He returned to the question without paying any attention to this strange piece of nonsense. "There's nobody about but the old gentlemen, and Ned at Aunt Catherine's. Sometimes I've felt a little suspicious of Ned. Does he come and see you often? He is a great fellow for books and that sort of thing."

"Mr. Edward Vernon," said Mrs. John, a little stiffly, "*never* comes here. Hester, I believe, has met him at the Grange or elsewhere; but he never comes here. I scarcely know him, neither of course does she."

"Then," said Harry, taking no notice of the offence in her tone, but bringing down his hand vehemently upon his knee, "if it isn't Ned, there is no one she can have seen, and the field is all clear for me."

"That is very true," said Hester's mother, but her tone was doubtful. "At the same time," she continued, "perhaps it would be well to let me talk to her a little first, Mr. Harry, just to see, before you said anything."

"If she doesn't want to have me, I don't wish to force her to have me," said Harry, his pride taking alarm.

"Force—oh, Mr. Harry, do you think I would force my child? And indeed I couldn't;" cried Mrs. John, shaking her head. "She is far, far, stronger than I."

"She would be the cleverest of us all," said Harry, admiringly. "I believe she is as clever as Aunt Catherine. I dare say she might even find out dodges in the bank, like Aunt Catherine did. Perhaps on the whole it might be better if

you would sound her a bit, eh? and find out what she is up to.
What she thinks of me, for instance," said Harry, nodding
half with modesty, half with vanity. " Yes, I should like
that. I should like to be pretty sure before I committed
myself. A man doesn't like to make a fool of himself for
nothing," the young man said.

Mrs. John thought this was quite natural. And indeed all
her feelings were enlisted on Harry's side, who expressed
himself so beautifully. What better could happen to
Hester than to be thus uplifted to the heights of luxury
and wealth, the White House, and everything else that heart
could desire, with a nice husband, so good-looking, so tall, so
fair, and so anxious to be kind to her mother? Her imagination, not her strong point on ordinary occasions, was strong
enough on this, to jump at all the advantages of the match
with a rapidity which would not have disgraced Hester herself. To see her child the mistress of the White House was
the very height of Mrs. John's ambition. She did not feel
that the world held anything more desirable. Her mind made
a hurried rush through the rooms, all so familiar to her, and
which Harry, no doubt, would re-model in preparation for his
bride. With what pride and happiness would she see her child at
the head of the table, where she herself had once sat! It would
be a return more triumphant than any return in her own person.
And yet she would be there too, the happy spectator, the
witness of it all. She saw in her mind's eye, the wedding, the
beautiful clothes, the phaeton, and the high-stepping horses,
and perhaps a pony carriage which Hester herself would drive.
All this in a moment, while Harry was telling her that he
would like to be pretty sure before he committed himself.
Perhaps it was not a lofty sentiment, but she felt it to be
quite natural. A man with so much to bestow had a right to
see his way before him, and then for Hester's own sake it
was far better that she should not be taken by surprise.
She was a perverse girl, and if the young man walked straight
up to her without warning, and asked her to marry him, the
chances were that she would refuse. That was not a risk to
be run when so much was at stake.

"If you will leave it in my hands, I think you will have no
cause to regret it," she said, nodding her head at him with the
softest maternal smile. " You may be sure you will have my
good wishes."

They were both quite affected when he took his leave.

"I feel sure we should hit it off together," Harry said,
warmly grasping her hand ; and the water stood in her eyes.
She could almost have given him a kiss as he stood before her,
a little flushed and agitated with his self-revelation. Indeed,
she would have done so but for that doubt about Hester.
What would Hester say ? That was the one point upon which
doubt existed, and unfortunately it was the most important of
all.   There could not be the least uncertainty as to the many
advantages of the match; money, comfort, good position,
good connection, everything that can be wished· for in
marriage, and with no personal defects to be glossed over by
these advantages, but a fine young man, a husband any girl
might be proud of.   Elation and gladness filled Mrs. John's
heart, when she contemplated that side of the question ; but
when she turned to the other a chill came over her, a cloud
that swallowed up the sunshine.   What would Hester say ?
Oh the perverseness of girls that never know what is good
for them ! if it had been somebody quite ineligible, somebody
without a penny, the chances were that Hester would have
had no doubt on the subject.   Mrs. John could not remain
still after this momentous conversation.   She went from one
window to another, looking out, watching for her daughter's
return.   She had been vexed that Hester should have been
so uncivil as to go away for no better reason than to walk
with old Captain Morgan when Harry was coming.   But she
felt now that this contradictoriness on the girl's part had been
providential.   How full her head was with thoughts and plans
how to speak, and what to say, with artful approaches to the
subject, and innocent wiles by which to divert all suspicion,
and lead Hester unawares towards that goal !   She trotted up
stairs and down, from one window to another, framing dialogue
after dialogue in her mind.   She was astonished by her own
powers as she did so.   If she ever had been so clever in
reality as she was in this sudden crisis of imagination, she
felt that it might have made a difference in her whole life.
And one thing Mrs. John had the wisdom and goodness to do
in the midst of her excitement, she kept within her own house,
and did not so much as venture down to the verandah, where
she might have been seen from outside, and pounced upon by
the eager watchers, brimful of curiosity, who wanted to know
what it all meant.   Miss Matilda Vernon-Ridgway, as has
been intimated, had been conscious of an internal admonition that something critical, something decisive, something

throwing a distinct light upon the "intentions" of young Harry
would happen this night.   And Mrs. John knew herself, and
was aware that she never would be able to stand against the
questionings of these curious spectators. Her only safety was
in keeping out of their way.   Thus not only her imagination,
but her moral faculties, her power of self-control and self-
denial, were strengthened by the occurrences of this momentous evening.   She had not felt so important before since
Hester was born.

CHAPTER XI.

MOTHER AND DAUGHTER.

MRS. JOHN had a long time to wait. The old captain prolonged his walk as he was too apt to do beyond his strength,
and came home very slowly, leaning on Hester's arm ; and then
as every hindrance, when people are anxious, has a way of
doubling itself, Mrs. Morgan sent a polite message to say
that she hoped Mrs. John Vernon would not object if she
kept Hester to supper. Mrs. John objected greatly, but she
was weak, and had never set up her own will in the face of
any one else who made a stand for theirs. She said "Oh yes,
with pleasure," with a pitiful little smile to Mrs. Morgan's
maid. To deny Hester anything (except the power of making
a governess of herself and losing caste) was what she had
never done in her life. It always gave her a little pang
when her child left her to eat her solitary meal in the dark
little parlour which nothing would light up, but she had
trained herself to feel that this was very wrong, and that
young people need change. Hester was entirely unacquainted
with the series of little sacrifices which her mother thus made
for her. If she thought of them at all, she thought that the
poor lady "did not mind." Her old friends next door were
not gay, but they talked as Mrs. John was quite incapable of
talking, and lived, though they saw nobody, in a wider atmosphere, a bigger world than any of the others. The old captain's
stories, the people he had seen, the experiences both these
old people had gone through, were like another world to Hester.
Her mother was small and straitened, had seen without seeing,
and lived without living. In the days when Hester had

guided her about by the arm, taking her whither she pleased, making new eyes for her in the vividness of her own, it was enough for the girl to have that echo of all her sentiments, that little objection generally ending with agreement, that broken little stream of faint recollections which her mother would give forth. But Hester had long ceased to form part of that sort of dual being which is so often made by a mother and her only daughter. To feel your parent smaller and sillier than yourself is sad. A great many young people do it without any adequate reason, strong in their sense of being the reigning monarchs of the present, while their progenitors belong to the past. Perhaps indeed it is the nature of youth to take a pleasure in such superiority. But that is very different from the fact of actual incapacity on the mother's part to follow her child's thoughts or even to know what she meant. Mrs. John was very well aware of it herself, and declared with a smiling countenance that young people liked change, and that she was never so happy as when her child was enjoying herself. And Hester, though she was so much more clever, accepted all this, and believed and thought her mother was quite contented with the evening paper, or a book from the circulating library, and never missed her when she was away. She misunderstood her silly mother, far more than that silly mother did her. The lesser comprehended the bigger, not the bigger the lesser, as in the ordinary course of affairs. Mrs. John had a great many sacrifices to make, of which her daughter was quite unconscious. And to-night the poor lady felt it, as with her mind so full she sat down at her little solitary table, which she had made pretty for Hester. There was nothing on it more' luxurious than cold meat and salad, but the crisp greenness of the leaves, the little round loaf, the pat of butter in a small silver dish which was one of her relics, the creaming glass of milk, all set out upon a white cloth and lighted up by the two candles, would, she had flattered herself, call out an admiring exclamation when the girl came in out of the dark, a little dazzled for the first moment by the light. After she had said "Oh, yes, with pleasure," Mrs. John came in and sat down and cried. Such a pretty table laid out, and oh, for once, so much to say! her mind so overflowing, her news so all-important! There could not be anything so exciting to talk about, that was certain, on the other side of the partition, and this provoked and tantalised sense of having herself far better entertainment for Hester than she could be

having, gave an insufferableness to the position. At one moment
Mrs. John thought she must send for the girl, that she could not
put up with the disappointment, but she was much more used
to putting up with things, than to asserting herself. She sat
down very cheerlessly and ate a mouthful of bread and salad.
To eat alone is always miserable. Hester was making the table,
where the old Morgans sat, very lively and cheerful, talking
as she never talked with her mother. They sat and talked
quite late into the night. What with the captain's stories,
and Mrs. Morgan's elucidations and Hester's questionings, the
evening was full of interest. It flew away so quickly that
when the clock struck eleven the girl sprang up with a great
sense of guilt. " Eleven o'clock ! what will mother say ? I
have never been so late before," she cried. They were all
half proud of it, of having been so mutually entertaining.
"The poor little mother must have felt lonely," Mrs Morgan
said, with a passing compunction when Hester flew round the
corner, watched from the door to see that all was safe by
the maid ; but the captain took no notice. " It is delightful
to see how that child enjoys herself," he said, flattered in
spite of himself, "though it's no very intoxicating amusement
we furnish her." Captain Morgan was very soft-hearted,
and understood by his affections as well as with his understanding, but in this case something beguiled him, perhaps
a little complacency, perhaps want of thought.

When Hester ran in, in the dark, locking the door of the
verandah behind her, Mrs. John had gone up stairs and was
going to bed. She was chilly and "cross" her daughter
thought, who ran quickly up to her full of apologies. "We
got talking," she said, "you must forgive me, mother. The
captain's stories run on so, one into another—one forgets how
the time runs on too."

" I wish," said Mrs. John, with the tears very near the
surface, " that your mother was sometimes as amusing as the
captain." It was the greatest reproach she had addressed
to her daughter for years.

" Oh, mother ! If I had thought you minded," cried Hester
with wondering eyes.

Mrs. John was penitent at once, and did her best to make
things up. " I ought not to speak," she said, " after all—for
I was not so very lonely. Harry stayed a long time and kept
me company. It is only when you have him to yourself that
you see how nice he is."

"Is he so nice?" said Hester indifferently. "How lucky for him to find you alone," she added with a little laugh.

"Oh, Hester, how can you say so. As if it was me he came for! Whatever you may try to make yourself believe you can't think that."

Hester made no reply. She slept in a small room within her mother's, the door of which always stood open. She had taken off her out-door things and let down her hair to brush it. It hung about her in a cloud, running up into curls as soon as she let it free. Mrs. John seated in the easiest chair, sat contemplating this operation with a mixture of pleasure and pain. The mass of curls was pretty, but it was not the fashion. It was quite unlike the smooth brown glossy locks that had adorned her own head when she was young. But she said to herself that it suited Hester, and gazed at her child admiringly, yet anxiously, conscious of many things in which she might be improved: her hair for one thing: and her waist, which was not so small as Mrs. John's had been in her youth : and her nose, which was a little too short. And yet with all these defects she was pretty. When she was Harry's wife everybody would admire her. Perhaps it was only because she was not sufficiently seen that she had no more admirers now.

"I had a great deal to say to you, dear," she said. "I don't grudge you being away when you are enjoying yourself, but I had many things to say. It is not likely that Harry Vernon would sit with me for hours for nothing."

"I suppose," said Hester, from the midst of her curls, "that he finds it dull now without Ellen at the White House?"

"I could tell you a great deal about that," said her mother quickly, eager to seize an opening. But Hester yawned with discouraging demonstrations of fatigue.

"Don't you think it will keep till to-morrow, mother? We had a long walk, and I am sleepy. I think Harry can't be very urgent. To-morrow will be time enough."

"Oh, Hester, how strange you are," cried Mrs. John, "so pleased with those old people, ready to listen to all their old stories ; but when I begin to talk to you of a thing that is of the greatest importance——"

"Nothing concerning Harry Vernon can be of great importance to me," cried the perverse girl; and then she tried to turn off her wilfulness with a laugh. "The beauty of the

captain's stories is that they are of no importance, mother.
You can have them when you please. It is like going to a
theatre, or reading a book."

"I am not so clever as the captain to interest you," Mrs.
John said.

There was a plaintive tone in her voice with which Hester
was very well acquainted, and which betokened an inclination
to tears. She came and kissed her mother, and gave her a
few of those half-impatient caresses which generally soothed
the poor lady. The girl did not in the least know that any
consciousness was in Mrs. John's mind of the superficial character of those kindnesses. She was not without love for the
tender domestic creature who had been hers to use at her
pleasure since ever she could recollect, but she bestowed these
kisses upon her, as she would have given sweetmeats to a child.

"Go to bed, mother. Don't mind me. I will shut the
door; you shall not have the light in your eyes to keep you
from sleeping. Go to bed, mammy darling."

Mrs. John had liked this caressing talk when Hester was a
child. She was soothed by it still, though a faint sense that
there was something like contempt in it had got into her
mind : and she could not struggle against a will which was
so much stronger than her own. But she could not sleep,
though she allowed herself to be put to bed. She could not
help crying in the night, and wondering what she could do to
be more respected, to be more important to her child; and
then she prayed that she might be able to put Harry before
her in the best light, and stopped and wondered whether it
were right to pray about a young man. Altogether Mrs.
John had not a tranquil night.

But next morning she made a great effort to dismiss her
anxiety, to present herself at breakfast with a cheerful aspect,
and to get rid of that plaintive tone which she was herself
aware of, which she had so often tried to remedy. Instead of
it she tried a little jauntiness and gaiety, for extremes are
always easy. It is the *juste-milieu* which it is so difficult to
attain.

"I am afraid I scolded you last night, Hester. I was cross
when you came back. One can't help being cross when one
has a great many things to say and no audience," she said
with a laugh.

"I am very sorry, mamma. I did not mean to stay so
late."

"Oh, it was nothing, my dear. I had Harry. He sat with me a long time. He is—really—very—entertaining when you have him to yourself."

"Is he?" said Hester demurely. "I should not have expected that: but I am very glad, mother, for your sake."

"Because I am likely to see a great deal of him in the future? Oh yes, my dear. I hope so, at least. He is very kind to me. Nobody has spoken so nicely of me for many a year."

"I like him for that," said Hester honestly, yet with a blush of self-consciousness; for perhaps though she liked him for it, it did not improve her opinion of Harry's intellect, that he should find her mother's company so congenial.

"Oh, you would if you knew him better, Hester. He feels for me in my changed circumstances. You don't know how different things used to be, what a great deal people used to think of me when I was young. I don't complain, for perhaps it was silly of them; but it is a great change. But living where he does in my house, you know, Harry feels that: he says it is there I ought to be—in the White House. Even though nothing should ever come of it, it is nice that somebody should think so."

"Unfortunately nothing can ever come of it," said Hester. "However nice people may be they do not give up their house to you, or their living; for you would need his money as well, to be able to live in the White House."

"You say unfortunately, dear," said her mother, with eagerness. Mrs. John blushed like a girl as she began her attempt to hint out Harry's love-tale to her daughter. She was innocent and modest, though she was silly. No talk about lovers, no "petty maxims" about marriage had ever offended Hester's ears. Her mother blushed and trembled when she felt herself broaching the subject to her child. "Oh, Hester, it would be easy, very easy, to cease to be unfortunate—if you choose, dear. All that part of our life might fly away like a cloud—if you choose. We might be done with poverty and dependence and thinking of what Catherine will say and what people will think. The White House—might be yours if you liked, everything might be yours. You would only have to say the word."

Mrs. John's eyes filled with tears. She could not get to the end of a long speech like this without crying: and she was so anxious, that they found their way also into her voice.

"Mother !" cried Hester, opening wide her eyes. They were very bright and clear, and when they opened widely looked almost unnatural in their size. She was all the more startled that she had never been subject to any such representation before. "I don't know what you mean," she said. "What should we do with the White House? I think it is a vulgar, staring place, and far too big."

"Don't speak so, Hester. I can't bear it. My own married home that your poor papa took me to!"

"I beg your pardon, mother. I had forgotten that. Of course taste was different in those days."

"Oh, taste! Your poor papa had beautiful taste. There are some things there that just break my heart—the ormolu set that everybody admired so, and the picture of me over the mantel-piece in the little parlour. It used to be in the drawing-room, but you can't wonder at them changing it. The hair was worn high then, on the top of your head, and short sleeves. It was very becoming to me. And to hear you call it vulgar and staring——"

"It was a mistake, mamma. I did not think what I was saying. Forgive me, mother dear!"

"You know I would forgive you anything," cried Mrs. John, now fairly launched, and forgetting all prudential restraints. "But oh, Hester, my darling, when he speaks to you don't be hasty; think of all that is involved. I am not going to tell you what he wants to say—oh no, he would never forgive me. It is he himself that must tell you that. But Hester, oh, don't speak hastily; don't answer all in a moment, without thinking. Often, often a girl says what she is sorry for, not being prepared. Think, my darling, what it would be—not only to be rich, but to be independent—to have your own house, all your own, and no charity—to have as much money as you want, to be able to help the poor, and do everything you wish, and to make me happy, so happy, to the end of my days!"

It was thus that Mrs. John treated Harry's secret. She forgot all her precautions and her conviction that from himself only the proposal ought to come. The dialogues she had invented, the long conversations with Hester which she had held in imagination, delicately, diplomatically leading up to the main possibility, had all disappeared when the moment came. When she began to speak she had forgotten them altogether, and gone off impromptu without recollecting a syllable of all that had been so painfully prepared : and her own eloquence, if it did not affect her daughter, affected herself beyond description : her mouth quivered, the tears flowed out of her eyes. Hester, who could no more bear to see her mother cry (though she had seen that sight often enough) than to see the tears of a child, rose from her seat, and coming round hurriedly behind Mrs. John's chair put her arms caressingly round her, and laid her cheek to that wet one. She was not so entirely unprepared but that she understood well enough what this emotion meant, but she tried to look as if it had a different meaning altogether. She drew her mother's head to her breast and kissed her.

"Dear mother ! Is it really so bitter to you to be dependent ? and you never let me know that you felt it."

"What would have been the good," said the poor lady, "when we could do nothing? The thing was to put the best face upon it. But now when it is all in your power—"

"It was always in my power," said Hester, with a mixture of real earnestness and a desire to persuade her mother that she put a different meaning upon all that had been said ; "if you had not stopped me, mother ; but I have not lost my accent, and if you will only give your consent now—I am older, and people will trust me with their children."

"Oh, Hester, do not vex me so," cried Mrs. John. "Do you think that is what I mean? And besides, if I were to give you leave to-morrow, Catherine, you know, would never consent."

"If you will trust to me," said Hester, colouring high, "what Catherine pleases shall not be the last word."

Mrs. John wrung her hands, drawing herself out of Hester's arms, to gaze into her face.

"Oh, why will you make such a mistake? It is not *that*. I am not strong to stand out against you, Hester, but for your own sake. And Catherine would never let you do it. Oh, this is quite a different thing, my dear love ! Not to work like any poor girl, but to be far above that, to have everything that heart could desire. And all so right and so nice, and so suitable, Hester. If your dear papa had lived and all had gone well I could not have wished for a better match."

"Match ! " said the girl, colouring violently.

She had indeed understood well enough that Harry was behind all her mother's anxious insinuations, her promises and entreaties, but she had been confident in her power to defeat

Mrs. John by aid of her own confused statements always capable of bearing two meanings. This word match, however, was one upon which there could be no confusion, and she was immediately driven to bay. She drew herself away from the tender attitude in which she had been standing.

" I never thought," she said, " that this was a thing that could be discussed between us," with all the unreasonable indignation of a high-handed girl, determined to crush all attempts to influence her on the spot.

But Mrs. John, though she was conscious she could not stand against Hester, was too sure that she was right, and too deeply convinced of the importance of this great question to give in, as she usually did.

" Oh why should it not be discussed between us ? " she said. " Is there any one so much interested as I am ? I have heard people say it was a mother's duty. And Hester, abroad where we used to live, I should have settled it altogether—you would never have been consulted. I am sure I don't know that it is not the best way."

" It is a way—that could never have been taken with me," Hester said. She walked round to her own side of the table with a very stately aspect and sat down, and made a pretence of resuming her breakfast, but her hand trembled with excitement as she took up her cup. " It may be quite true what you say, that you are interested, mother. I suppose so. People consider a girl a piece of goods to be sold and disposed of."

" Oh, Hester, have I ever thought so ? I have been wanting in my duty," cried Mrs. John. " I have never tried to put you forward, to get you invitations, to have you seen and admired as other people do. You are so proud and so fanciful that I have never dared to do it. And when there comes one, without ever being invited, or thought of, or supposed possible——"

It seemed to Hester that the burning blush which she felt go all over her was capable of bursting into flame. It was not the shy shamefacedness with which every girl contemplates this subject on its first introduction, but bitter and scorching shame.

" Invited—thought of ; mother ! " she cried in a voice of girlish thunder, " is it possible that you could ever think of scheming—match-making—for ME ? "

No capitals could represent the fervour of her indignation.

She was entirely unconscious of the arrogance of self-opinion
that was in all she said. For ME. That a man should be
invited into her presence with that thought, that she should be
put forward, taken into society in order to be seen with that
view. Heaven and Earth! was it possible that a woman
should avow such possibilities and yet live?

"When I tell you that I never did it, Hester! though I
know it was my duty," Mrs. John cried with tears. Never
was woman punished more unjustly. She turned like the
proverbial worm at the supreme inappropriateness of this
judgment against her, and a sudden impulse of anger
sustained the gentle little woman. "I know it was my duty,"
she cried; "for who is to care for you, to see that you are
settled in life, but me? But I was afraid to do it. I was
obliged to leave it—to Providence. I just said to myself, it
is no use. Hester would never be guided by me. I must
leave it—to Providence."

It did not appear that Mrs. John had much opinion of
Providence in such matters, for she announced this with a
voice of despair. Then taking courage a little, she said with
insinuating gentleness—

"I was just the same when I was a girl. I could not
endure to hear about settlements and things. It was all love
I thought of—my darling. I was like you—all love."

"Oh, mother!" cried Hester, jumping to her feet. This
was more intolerable than the other. Her face flamed anew
with the suggestion that it was "all love." "For Heaven's
sake don't say any more about it, unless you want to drive
me out of my senses," she said.

Mrs. John stopped crying, she was so astonished, and gazed
with open mouth and eyes. She had thought this last tender
touch would be irresistible, that the child would fall into her
arms, and perhaps breathe forth the sweetest secret aspiration
of her heart—perhaps own to her that dark eyes and a
moustache had been her dream instead of Harry's fairness; or
that a melting voice or a genius for poetry were absolute
requirements of her hero. With all these fancies she would
have so tenderly sympathised. She would have liked to
discuss everything, to point out that after all a fair complexion was very nice, and a genius for poetry not profitable.
She remembered what occupation and delight these same
subjects had afforded herself in the interval before John Vernon
had proposed to her. She herself had dreamed of a trouba-

dour, a lonely being with a guitar, with long hair and misfortunes ; and John Vernon had none of these attractions.
She was talked over by her mother and sister and made to
see that the Bank and the White House were far better.
Hester, perhaps, would have been more difficult, but yet she
had felt that, confidence once established, the sweetness of
these discussions would have been unspeakable. When she
had got over her astonishment, she sank back in a despair
which was not unmingled with resentment. Had it come to
that, that nothing a mother could say would please a child
nowadays—neither the attractions of a great match nor the
tenderness of love.

This was how the great question of a young woman's life
was first revealed to Hester. It was not, to be sure, the last
word. That would come when she was placed face to face
with the aspirant for her favour and have to decide, so to
speak, upon the future of two lives. But to say " no " to Harry
would not have excited and confused her being, like this
previous encounter with all the other powers and influences
which were concerned—or which were considered to be
concerned, in her fate.

CHAPTER XII.

AN INDIGNANT SPECTATOR.

HESTER VERNON had been, during the most important years of her existence, a sort of outlaw from life. She had been unacquainted altogether with its course and natural order, out of all its usual habits, separated from every social way of thinking or discipline of mind. She belonged to a little community which thought a great deal of itself, yet had no foundation for so doing ; but, strangely enough, though she saw through the fallacy of its general pretensions, she yet kept its tradition in her own person and held her head above the ordinary world in unconscious imitation of the neighbours whom she knew to have no right to do so. She kept the spirit of the Vernons, though she scorned them, and thought them a miserable collection of ungrateful dependents and genteel beggars, less honourable than the real beggars, who said "thank you," at least. And she had no way of correcting the unfortunate estimate of the world she had formed from this group, except through the means of Catherine Vernon, and the society in her house, of which, at long intervals, and on a doubtful footing which set all her pride in arms and brought out every resentful faculty, she and her mother formed a part. If the Vernon-Ridgways and Mr. Mildmay Vernon were bitterly critical of Catherine, missing no opportunity to snarl at the hand that fed them, Catherine, on her part, was so entirely undeceived in respect to them, and treated them with such a cynical indulgence and smiling contempt, as if nothing save ingratitude and malice were to be expected from humanity, that Hester had found no relief on that side from her painful thoughts. She was so conscious in her own person of meanings more high, and impulses more noble, that the scorn with which she contemplated the people about her was almost inevitable. And when, deeply against her will, and always with an uneasy consciousness that her mother's pleasure in the invitations, and excitement about going, was childish and undignified, Hester found herself in a corner of the Grange drawing-room, her pride, her scornful indignation and high contempt of society grew and increased. Her poor little mother standing patiently smiling at all who would smile at her, pleased with the little recognition given her as "one of the poor ladies at the Vernonry," and quite content to remain there for hours for the sake of two minutes' *banal* conversation now and then, to be overlooked at supper, and taken compassion upon by a disengaged curate, or picked up by some man who had already brought back a more important guest, made Hester furious and miserable by her complacency. Hester herself was one of some half dozen girls in white muslin, who kept a wistful eye upon the curate in the hope of being taken down to the supper room down stairs, from which such a sound of talk and laughter came up to the forlorn ones left above. But no curate, however urgent, ever persuaded Hester to go down, to stand at the tail of the company and consume the good things on Catherine's table. She saw it all from that point of view which takes the glitter off the brightest surface. Why did those poor girls in white muslin, not being compelled, like Hester, continue to go ? There were two sisters, who would chatter together, pretending to be very merry, and point out to each other the pictures, or some new piece of furniture, and say that Miss Vernon had such taste. They were always of the number of those who were forgotten at supper, who were sent down after the others came up stairs with careless little apologies. Why did they come ? But Hester was not of a temper to chatter or to look at the pictures, or to make the best of the occasion. She stood in the corner behind her mother, and made it quite clear that she was not " enjoying herself." She took no interest in the pieces that were performed on the piano, or the songs that were sung, and even rejected the overtures of her companions in misfortune to point out to her the " very interesting photographs " which covered one table. Some of the elder ladies who talked to her mother made matters worse by compassionately remarking that " the poor girl " was evidently

"terribly shy." But, otherwise, nobody took any notice of
Hester; the other people met each other at other houses, had
some part in the other amusements which were going on,
and knew what to say to each other. But Hester did not
know what to say. Edward Vernon, her early acquaintance,
whom she would still often meet in the morning, and between
whom and Hester there existed a sort of half-and-half
alliance unlike her relations with any one else, took no open
notice of her; but would sometimes cast a glance at her as he
passed, confidential and secret. "How are you getting on?" he
would say; and when Hester answered "Not at all," would
shrug his shoulders and elevate his eyebrows and say "Nor
I" under his breath. But if he did not "get on," his manner
of non-enjoyment was, at least, very different from Hester's.
He was, as it were, Catherine Vernon's son and representative.
He was the temporary master of the house. Everybody smiled
upon him, deferred to him, consulted his wishes. Thus, even
Edward, though she regarded him with different eyes from
the others, helped to give a greater certainty to Hester's
opinion on the subject of Society. Even he was false here
—pretending to dislike what he had no reason to dislike, and,
what was perhaps worse, leaving her to stand there neglected, whom he was willing enough to talk with when he
found her alone.

Hester felt—with her head raised, her nostrils expanded,
a quiver of high indignation in her lip—that she herself
would never suffer any one to stand thus neglected in any
room of hers. Those women in their diamonds, who swept
down stairs while her mother stood and looked on wistfully,
should not be the first in her house. She would not laugh
and say "One of the Vernonry," as Catherine permitted
herself to do. It seemed to Hester that the poor and the
small would be the first whom she would think of, and
amuse and make happy. They should have the best of
everything, they who had not the best of anything in life.
Society (she thought, always in that corner, where there was
full time to make theories, and the keen prick of present
humiliation to give animation to them) should be a fine compensation to those who were not so happy as the others. A true
hostess should lay herself out to make up to them, for that one
genial moment, for the absence of beauty and brightness in
their lives. It should be all for them—the music, and the wit,
and the happy discourse. Those who lived in fine houses, who

had everything that wealth could give, should stand aside and give place to the less happy. There should be no one neglected. The girl whom no one noticed stood apart and invented her high magnanimous court, where there should be no respect of persons. But it was not wonderful if in this real one she felt herself standing upon a pedestal, and looked out with scorn upon the people who were "enjoying themselves," and with a sense of bitter mortification watched her poor little mother curtseying and smiling, pleased to go down to supper after the fine people were satisfied, on somebody's benevolent arm who was doing duty for the second time. "No, I thank you," Hester said to the curate, who stood offering his arm, tossing her head like a young princess. "I never go to supper." She was not without a consciousness either, that Catherine, hearing this, had been mightily amused by her airs and her indignation, and next time looked out for them as one of the humours of the night.

Thus it will be seen that all Hester's small experience of society taught her to despise it. She was outside of the life of families, and knew little or nothing of the ordinary relations of parents and children, and of that self-sustaining life where there are no painful bonds of obligation, no dependence, no forced submission of one set of people to another. She thought the mass was all the same, with such exceptions as old Captain Morgan and his wife, rarely appearing, and here and there a visionary, indignant soul such as herself, free as yet from all bonds, looking on with a proud consciousness that were but the power in her hands it should not be so. The great question of love had scarcely flitted at all across her firmament. She had indeed a trembling sense of possibility such as youth itself could not be youth if it were destitute of, a feeling that some time suddenly there might come down upon her path out of the skies, or appear out of the distance, some one—in whom all the excellences of earth should be realised; but this, it need not be said, was as entirely unlike an ideal preference for dark eyes and moustaches, as it was unlike the orthodox satisfaction in a good match which her mother had so abruptly revealed. It was like the dawn upon the horizon where as yet there is no sun and no colour, a visionary, tremulous premonition of the possible day. A girl who has this feeling in her heart is not only horrified but angry, when the fact comes down upon her in the shape of a dull man's proposal or a parent's recommendation. It is a wrong to herself and to him, and to the new earth and the new heaven which might be coming. Hester left her mother on that memorable morning with the glow of a fiery resentment in her heart. Everything seemed to grow vulgar under that touch, even things which were heavenly. Not a magnanimous hero, but Harry—not a revelation out of heaven, out of the unknown, but a calculation of his good qualities and the comforts he could bestow. All this no doubt was very highflown and absurd, but the girl knew no better. She felt it an insult to her, that her mother should have set such a bargain before her—and oh, worse than an insult, intolerable! when poor Mrs. John, in her ignorance, invited the confidence of this high visionary maiden on the subject of love. This drove the girl away, incapable of supporting such profanation and blasphemy. She went out upon the Common, where she could be quite alone, and spent an hour or two by herself beyond reach of anybody, trying to shake off the impression. She had nothing to do to occupy her mind, to force out of it an unpleasant subject. She could only rush out and secure for herself solitude at least, that she might master it and get it under her feet.

But sometimes to appoint a meeting with yourself to discuss such a question, ends in another way from that which has been foreseen. Sitting alone under a bush of whins, some chance touch of fancy made Hester think of her mother's aspirations towards the White House, the ormolu set, and the portrait in short sleeves. Thoughts arise sometimes in a curious dramatic order, to all appearance independent of the mind of the thinker, as if certain pictures were presented to it by some independent agency outside. In this way there gleamed across the mind of Hester a sudden presentation of her mother in those same short sleeves, her pretty dark hair in two large bows on the top of her head, her feet in white satin shoes with sandals, like an artless beauty out of the *Keepsake* or the *Forget-me-not*. The imagination was so sudden that in the midst of thoughts so different it tempted the girl to a smile. Poor mother, so young and pretty—and silly, perhaps! And then Hester recollected old Mr. Rule's story, how she had rushed to her desk and produced twenty pounds to save the bank from bankruptcy. The girl recollected, with an indignant pang of compassion, that Catherine had produced thousands of pounds, and *had* saved the bank. What virtue was that in her? She had the money whilst the other had not, and Mrs. John's helpless generosity was just as great. Poor little mother! and the house she was so proud of, her "married home," her ideal of everything that was fine and handsome. Hester's imagination after this made a jump, and beheld her mother in the widow's dress of black which she never left off, standing, glad of any crumbs of notice which might fall to her in the corner of the drawing-room where Catherine the successful reigned supreme. It angered the girl that her mother should be so humble-minded—but yet it was quite characteristic of her. And what a contrast was in those two scenes! Who made her think of this at the very moment when, rushing out to escape from her mother, she had felt the gulf of incomprehension between them more bitterly than ever before? It could not be anything but a kind influence that did it, a good fairy, or even perhaps a friendly angel, grieved at the emancipation of this child from the tenderest bonds of nature. Anyhow Hester thought, with a sudden moistening of her eyelids, of the pretty creature in the picture and the widow in the black gown at the same moment. From white satin to crape, from twenty to fifty— ah, and more than these, from the thoughtless prosperity of a creature who had never known anything different, to the humiliation borne so sweetly of the too-submissive artless soul. Her eyelids moistened, and the sun caught them, and amused himself making tiny rainbows in the long lashes. Hester's heart too was caught and touched. Poor *petite mère!* how much, as she would have said herself, she had "gone through!"

And then something occurred to Hester which made her set her white teeth and clench her hands. If she pleased she could set that right again which was so wrong. She could put back her mother in the White House she loved, take down the innocent portrait in white satin, and hang it in the place of honour once more; throw open finer rooms than Catherine's for the reception of, oh! so different a company—society in which no one should be overlooked, and in which Catherine's gentle rival should be supreme. She could do all this if she chose. The thought suddenly bursting upon her made her head go round. She could put her mother in the place from which it seemed (wrongly, but yet that was so natural an impression) Catherine had driven her, turn the tables altogether upon Catherine, and make a new centre, a new head, everything new. The girl raised her head with a little shake

and toss like a high-bred horse, as this strange and sudden
suggestion came into her mind like an arrow. She could do
it all. The suggestion that she could do it when it came
from her mother had been an insult and wrong; but when
it came as it did now, though there was horror in it, there
was also temptation, the sharp sting of an impulse. What
was the dreadful drawback? Nothing but Harry: no monster,
nothing terrible, a good fellow, a docile mind—one who had
never been unkind. Hester had judged him with his sister
for a long time, but of late days she had learned to separate
Harry from Ellen. He had always been *nice*, as Mrs. John
said—not great indeed or noble, but honest and kind in his
simple way. Once at least (Hester remembered) he had—
what was nothing less than heroic in the circumstances—
stepped forward, broken all the Redborough laws of prece-
dence, and "taken down" her mother at one of the Grange
parties, in entire indifference to the fact that ladies more
great were waiting for his arm. This recollection jumped
suddenly into her mind as she sat in the solitude thinking
it all over. He had always done his best, coming to her,
standing by her side, with not much to say indeed, but with a
sort of silent championship which Hester had laughed at, but
which she remembered now. He was not very often present
at the Grange parties; but when he was there, this was what
he had done. It was no great matter, but in the excited state
of her mind it told upon her. Edward came only by moments
when the company was otherwise engaged, and then spoke to
her rather by signs, by that shrug of the shoulders and elevation of the eyebrows, than in words. But Harry had penetrated to her corner and stood by her, making himself rather
larger than usual that everybody might see him. The ungrateful girl had laughed, and had not been proud of her
large-limbed champion; but when she thought of it now her
heart melted to him. *He* had not been afraid of what people
would say. And after all, to be able to set everything right, to
restore her mother's comfort and exaltation, to be free and
rich, with no greater drawback than Harry, would that be so
difficult to bear? She shivered at the thought; but yet, that
she did so much as ask herself this question showed how far
already her thoughts had gone.

After the untoward conversation of this morning, Mrs. John
took great pains to keep Harry back. She ventured even to
write a note to him, composed in great anxiety, very much

underlined and emphatic. "I have sounded her, and find her mind *a complete blank* on that subject. She has never thought about it, and *she has seen no one*, as you remarked. If you will but put off a little, I feel sure it will be followed by THE HAPPIEST RESULTS." Circumstances, as it happened, served Mrs. John's purpose, and made it indispensable to put off a little any formal advances. For Harry had to leave Redborough on business for a week or two. His consequent absence from the Vernonry was seen with great satisfaction by the neighbours, who knew no reason for that absence.

"He has seen his mistake in time," the Miss Vernon-Ridgways said, congratulating each other, as if the destruction of poor Hester's supposed hopes and projects was some gain to them; and Mr. Mildmay Vernon nodded his head over his newspaper, and chuckled and announced that Harry was no fool They all remarked with much particularity to Mrs. John that her visitor had not long continued his assiduities.

"But we can't expect you know that a young man should always be coming out here," said Miss Matilda. "What was there to gain by it? and that is the rule nowadays. Besides, dear Catherine does not like these nephews of hers, as she calls them—no more nephews than I am!—to see too much of *us*. They might hear things which she wouldn't wish them to hear."

Mr. Mildmay's remark was jaunty like himself. "So Harry has given you up! Young dog, it's what they all do, you know. He loves and he rides away. I was no better myself I suppose."

Mrs. John could have cried with humiliation and pain. She explained that Mr. Harry was absent; that he had told her he was going away; but these kind people laughed in her face. Perhaps this too had a certain effect upon Hester's mind. She heard the laugh, though her mother did all she could to keep her from hearing; and an impulse to show them her power—to prove once for all that she could have everything they prized, the money, and the finery, and the "position," which they all envied and sneered at, when she pleased—an impulse less noble, but also keener than the previous one, came suddenly into her mind. When Harry came back, however, Hester quailed at the thought of the possibility which she had not rejected. She saw him coming, and stole out the other way, round the pond and under the pine-trees, so as to be able to reach the house of the Morgans without

being seen. And when Harry appeared he had to run the
gauntlet of the three bitter spectators, the chorus of the
little drama, without seeing its heroine.

"Dear Harry, back again!" the Miss Vernon-Ridgways
cried; "how nice of you to come again. We made up our
minds you had given us up. It was so natural that you
should tire of us, a set of shabby people. And dear Catherine
is so fond of you; she likes to keep you to herself."

"I don't know that she's so fond of me. I've been in
town on business," Harry said, eager to escape from them.

Mr. Mildmay patted him on the shoulder with his newspaper. "Keep your free will, my boy," he said; "don't give
in to habits. Come when you please, and go when you please
—that's a man's rule."

Harry looked at this feeble Mephistopheles as if he would
have liked to kick him, but of course he did not; because he
was feeble and old, and "a cad," as the young man said
in his heart; and so went in by the verandah door to see
Hester, and found her not, which was hard after what he had
gone through. Mrs. John pinned him down for a talk, which
she was nervously anxious for, and which he, after the first
moment, liked well enough too; and perhaps it was as well,
he consented to think, that he should see how the land lay.

Meanwhile, Hester very cautiously had crept into the house
of the old people next door. The two houses were divided
only by a partition, yet how different the atmosphere was!
The keen inquisitions of the Vernonry, its hungry impatience
to know and see everything, its satirical comments, its inven-
tions of evil motives, were all unknown here. And even
her mother's anxieties for her own advancement put a weary
element into life, which in the peaceful parlour of the old
captain and his wife existed no more than any other agitation. The old lady seated in the window, putting down her
book well pleased when the visitor came in, was an embodiment of tranquillity. She had lived no easy life; she had
known many troubles and sorrows, laboured hard and suffered
much; but all that was over. Her busy hands were still, her
heart at rest. Hester did not know sometimes what this
great tranquillity meant, whether it was the mere quiet of
age, almost mechanical, a blank of feeling, or if it was the
calm after great storms, the power of religious consolation
and faith. It filled her sometimes with a little awe—sometimes with a sort of horror. To think that she, with all the

blood dancing in her veins, should ever come to be like that !
And yet even in her small round she had seen enough to
be sure that these old people had a kind of happiness in
their quiet which few knew. Mrs. Morgan took off her
spectacles, and closed them within the book she had been
reading, well pleased when Hester appeared. The captain
had gone out, she was alone; and perhaps she did not care
very much for her book. At all events, Hester was her
favourite, and the sight of the girl's bright looks and her
youth, her big eyes always full of wonder, her hair that
would scarcely keep straight, the " something springy in her
gait," pleased the old lady and did her good.

" May I stay and talk to you ? " Hester said.

" You shall stay, dear, certainly, if you think it right; but
I see everything from my window, and Harry Vernon has
just gone in to see your mother. Do you know ? "

" I saw him coming," Hester said, with a cloud upon her
face, which looked like displeasure, but was indeed the trouble
of her self-discussion and doubt as to what she should do.

" Something is wrong," said the old lady, " and you have
come to tell me. Are you going to marry Harry Vernon,
Hester ? "

" Would that be something wrong ? " cried the girl, looking
up quickly, with a certain irritation. She did not mean to
have so important a question fore-judged in this easy way.

" That is according as you feel, my dear ; but I fear he is
not good enough for you. Catherine says——"

Now the Morgans were altogether of Catherine's faction,
being her relations, and not—as the other members of the
community remembered with much resentment—Vernons at
all. It was a sinful use of the family property as concentrated
in Catherine's hand, to support these old people who had no
right to it. More or less this was the sentiment of the community generally, even, it is to be feared, of Mrs. John herself ;
and consequently, as an almost infallible result, they were on
Catherine's side, and took her opinions. Hester stopped the
mouth of the old lady, so to speak, hastily holding up her hand.

" That is a mistake," she cried ; " Catherine is quite
wrong ! She does not like him ; but he is honest as the
skies—he is good. You must not think badly of him because
Catherine has a prejudice against him."

" That is a rash thing for you to say. Catherine is a great
deal older, and a great deal wiser than you."

"She may be older, and she may be wiser; but she does not know everything," said Hester. "There is one prejudice of hers you don't share—she thinks the same of me."

This staggered the old lady.

"It is true—she does not understand you somehow; things seem to go the wrong way between times."

"Am I difficult to understand?" cried Hester. "I am only nineteen, and Catherine is sixty——"

"You are not quite so easy as A B C," said Mrs. Morgan, with a smile; "still I acknowledge that is one thing against her judgment. But you do not answer my question. Are you going to marry Harry Vernon?"

Hester, seated in the shelter of the curtain, invisible from outside, hardly visible within, looked out across the Common to the place where she had sat and pondered, and breathed a half-articulate "No."

"Then, Hester, you should tell him so," said the old lady. "You should not keep him hanging on. Show a little respect, my dear, to the man who has shown so much respect to you."

"Do you call that respect?" said Hester, and then she added, lowering her voice, "My mother wishes it. She thinks it would make her quite happy. She says that she would want nothing more."

"Ah!" said the old lady, "that means——" It is to be feared that she was going to say something not very respectful to Hester's mother, about whom, also, Catherine's prejudice told: but she checked herself in time. "That gives it another aspect," she said.

"Do you think it would be right to marry a man, only because your mother wished it?" asked Hester, fixing her eyes on Mrs. Morgan's face.

"Sometimes," said the old lady, with a smile.

"Sometimes! I thought you were like the captain, and believed in love."

"Sometimes," she said again. "It does not do in every case: that is what I object to the captain and you for. You are always so absolute. Love rejects suitableness; and if Catherine is not quite wrong——"

"She is quite wrong!" cried Hester again, vehemently. "She does not know Harry any more than she knows me. He is not clever, but he is true."

"Then marry him, my dear."

"Why should I marry him?—one does not marry every one whom Catherine misjudges—oh, there would be too many! —nor even to please mother."

"I am perhaps as poor a judge as Catherine, Hester."

"Now you are unjust—now you are unkind!" cried the girl, with anger in her eyes.

"Come," said Mrs. Morgan, "you must not assault me. You are so young and so fierce : and my old man is not here to take my part."

"I cannot ask him because he is a man." said Hester; "but I know what he would say. He would not say 'Sometimes' like you; he would say 'Never!' And that is what I think too."

"Because you are so young, my dear; and my old man, bless him, he is very young. But this world is a very strange place. Right and wrong, are like black and white; they are distinct and easy. The things that baffle us are those that perhaps are not quite right, but certainly are not wrong."

"Do you call it not wrong—to do what your heart revolts at to please your mother?"

"I call that right in one sense; but I would not use such strong language, Hester," the old lady said.

"This must be metaphysics," said the girl. "Sophistry, isn't it? casuistry, I don't know what to call it; but I see through you. It would be right to do a great many things to please her, to make my dress her way instead of mine, to stop at home when she wanted me though I should like to go out; but not—surely not, Mrs. Morgan——"

"To marry the man of her choice, though he is not your own?"

Hester nodded her head, her face glowing with the sudden blush that went and came in a moment. She was agitated though she did not wish to show it. The impulse to do it became suffocating, the shiver of repugnance stronger as she felt that the danger was coming near.

"I am not so sure," said the old lady in her passionless calm. "Sometimes such a venture turns out very well; to please your mother is a very good thing in itself, and if you are right about his character, and care for no one else, and can do it—for after all that is the great thing, my dear—*if you can do it*—it might turn out very well, better than if you took your own way."

"Is that all that is to be thought of, whether it will turn out well?" cried Hester, indignantly. "You mean if it is successful; but the best way is not always successful."

"Success in marriage means almost everything," the old lady said.

Then there was a pause. Separated only by the partition, Harry Vernon was discoursing with Mrs. John on the same subject. He was telling her all he would do for his wife when he got her. The White House should be refurnished; but if she pleased the best of the old things, "the ormolu and all that rubbish," Harry said, which gave the poor lady a wound in spite of her great and happy emotion, should be put into the rooms which were to be her rooms for life; but for Hester he would have everything new. And he thought he saw his way to a carriage: for the phaeton, though Ellen was fond of it, was not quite the thing, he allowed, for a lady. He had got just about that length, and was going on, a little excited by his own anticipations, and filling his future mother-in-law with delight and happiness, when Hester, on the other side of the wall, suddenly sprang up and cried, throwing up her hands—

"But I cannot do it!" in tones so painful and so clear that it was a wonder they did not penetrate the wainscotting.

Mrs. Morgan, who had been waiting for a reply, folded her old fingers—worn with the hard usage of life, but now so quiet—into each other, and said, softly—

"That was what I thought."

CHAPTER XIII.

CATHERINE'S OPINION.

IT is not to be supposed that Harry's visits, which made
so much commotion at the Vernonry, could have entirely
escaped the keen observation of the Grange. Catherine
Vernon shared, with most sovereigns and the ruling class in
general, the peculiarity, not indeed a very unusual one, of
liking to know everything that went on within her sphere.
It was not as gossip, nor, she would have said with some
reason, from curiosity alone. She had for so long been all-
powerful, and sure that the means were in her hand to help
those that wanted help, and to regulate affairs in general for
the benefit of the world, that it had become a necessity, almost
a duty on her part, to keep herself informed of everything that
went on. When an individual feels capable of performing
the part of a visible Providence, it becomes incumbent upon
that person, so far as possible, to know everything, to shut
his eyes to no detail, to note every little incident, and to
encourage not only the confidences of his possible clients
and *protégés*, but the observations of all surrounding them,
and every hint as to their motives, their intentions and purposes, that can be got at. The outside crowd, knowing
nothing of the meaning of these investigations, is apt to
mistake them altogether; but Catherine did not care much
about the outside world. It was her wish that everything
should be told to her, and she was perhaps too apt to think
that those who were not willing or able to open their hearts,
were people who had secrets in their life, and probably a good
deal that would not bear the light. She liked her friends to
bring her news, and never thought anything too trivial to

be added to the mass of information which was in her
hands. She knew the habits of her neighbours, and the
good and evil fortune that befell them, better sometimes than
they did themselves. Parents, who were doubtful about the
proceedings of their sons, had they asked Catherine, would
have known all about them. So the prince, in a little State,
may often interest himself graciously about the affairs of his
subjects, and monarchs are the best of genealogists, knowing
who married who all the world over, even outside of the
Almanach de Gotha. It is not a taste which can be indulged
without falling into an occasional appearance of pettiness; but
yet there is a great deal to be said for this degree of interest
in our fellow creatures, and there is no way in which it can
be kept up so well as in a country town, where everybody knows everybody else. This is perhaps rather an elabor-
ate preface to introduce the simple fact that Catherine Vernon
from the very beginning had known of Harry's visit to the
Vernonry. Her own woman, Meredith by name, shared her
mistress's task, without Catherine's fine reason for it, and
carried it deeper than Catherine, not refusing any garbage
of the lanes to satisfy her appetite. And she was a woman
who saw everything and knew everybody. It was no more
than Harry's second or third visit when she pointed him out
to her mistress, walking past in his summer morning suit,
which the long evenings permitted a young man to retain
while daylight lasted and he could be about. Harry was very
carefully got up; he wore light clothes, and ties of the most
interesting description. He had always the stick which was
in fashion, the hat of the moment; and a very pleasant sight
he was striding along in the summer evening, going where
love carried him, with honest intentions, and a simple heart.
He was not perhaps capable of a very refined or poetical
sentiment. He had at that time no doubt whatever that
Hester would accept him gratefully, not so much for himself (in which point he had an instinctive humility), but for
the good things he could give her. The glamour and the
thousand little enchantments of love were not in him, but he
was honest and true as Hester had said. He meant this poor
girl, whom most people, in Catherine's drawing-room and elsewhere, passed by without notice, though some thought her
pretty—he meant her as his wife to be a happy and much-
honoured woman. And what was more, he meant to be good
to his mother-in-law. He might have been a romantic

paladin, or a man of genius, and not have been so excellent, so worthy of all admiration as that. It never occurred to Harry to go another way, to conceal what he was about from prying eyes. He was not ashamed of what he was about. All the world might watch his steps so far as he cared, and it must have required a distinct effort on the part of any honest heart not to like the sight of him as he went a-wooing, and wish him a happy ending. Perhaps it would be too much to say that Catherine made that effort; but she was not favourable to Harry as to his cousin who was under her own roof.

It is scarcely possible for any eyes but those of a parent (and even the eyes of a parent are not always impartial) to look upon two young candidates for favour with exactly the same sentiments. If it is too much to say that one will be loved and the other hated, at least the balance will be un-equal. Edward had found means from the beginning to please his patroness and relative. He had been—is not this the grand reason ?—so good : he had been ready at her service when she wanted him, he had stayed at home, he had been son and daughter to the lonely woman. All that she knew of him was excellent, and she had no reason to imagine there was anything to know which was not equally good.

Catherine was one of the people who say that they do not look for gratitude. If Edward had not appreciated the kindness which picked him up as it were from the roadside, she would but have laughed ; she would not have shown either surprise or pain ; but the fact that he did feel her kindness, and devote himself to her, touched her deeply. She was as well off as if he had been her son, far better off than many mothers with sons. But Harry was very different. For a long time she had made up her mind that Harry was her great failure. He and his sister had never attempted to attach themselves to Catherine. They had considered their elevation to the White House, and the honours of the bank, as owing to their own merits, and had set up a sort of heir-apparent establishment always in opposition. With the natu-ral instinct of a woman, she had concluded it all to be Ellen's fault ; but Harry had not the good sense to separate him-self from his sister, or even to imply that he did not support her in her proceedings : far from that, he stood by her with the utmost loyalty. Though he never was anything but deferential and respectful in his dull way to his benefactress, he never would allow it to be supposed that he did not approve of his sister and back her up. If Catherine saw the merit of this faithfulness, it was in a grudging way ; and, as a matter of fact she did not like Harry. There was nothing in reality to find fault with in him. He was very steady at his business, notwithstanding the rival claims of cricket in summer and football in winter. And when he was asked to dinner at the Grange, he was as punctual as clockwork, with an expanse of shirt front that would have been a credit to any man. But he did not please Catherine. He had given her a reproof which stung, on that occasion when he "took down" Mrs. John, without waiting to know what person of importance should have gone before. Nothing that could have been said would have stung Catherine so much as that good-natured act, and it was all the more hard upon her that in her heart (always a good and generous one) she approved Harry. It was a reproach to her, and still more, it was a reproach to Edward, who had never taken the slightest notice of Mrs. John's presence, but left her among the neglected ones. Catherine had been doubly angry with Harry ever since that evening. She would not allow even that he was a handsome fellow.

"He is big enough," she would say, resenting the fact that he was a head taller than Edward, and twice as strong. "He is a fine animal, if you like : but I don't see how a man with white eyelashes can be considered handsome."

Edward did not oppose his aunt in this any more than in other things. "I allow," he would say, "that he is not clever." But he shook his head, as one who would deprecate a too true accusation when Miss Vernon held Harry up to ridicule. "No, he is not clever ; he will never set the Thames on fire," Edward said.

Miss Vernon saw Harry pass the third time he went to the Vernonry, and afterwards she looked for him regularly. "Who was it for ?" she asked, with an ardent feminine appreciation of the only motive which could induce a man to hurry over his dinner and get to the Vernonry in time for the humble community's tea. This was a question not very hard to answer, seeing that the next moment she added to herself, "Who else could it be ?" It could not be Matilda, or Martha, who were neither young nor fair. It was very unlikely to be Mrs. Reginald, though she was young enough, and not without beauty. "But Harry is not the man to

burden himself with a lot of children," said Catherine, with an
unnecessary scoff at the poor fellow who was not her
favourite. Thus there was only one person whom it could
be. It gave her a sort of pang of amusement when she
concluded upon this—Hester! that proud, troublesome creature—she who would never give in, who put on the airs of
a princess in the Grange drawing-room, and declined to go to
supper—she with the spirit of a revolutionary, and the
temper of a—demon—(no, no, this was perhaps too bad—
the temper of a—Vernon, Catherine said to herself with a
laugh)—she to fall to the lot of Harry! This was so
strangely funny, so paradoxical, so out of character, that it
amused Catherine altogether beyond description, yet gave her
a strange blow. What a ridiculous combination! If the
world had been ransacked for two who ought not to come together, these two would be that pair. What would they do
with each other? how could they ever pull together—the
one all eagerness and vigour, the other stolid and heavy?
Catherine was almost tempted to be sorry for the girl, but
the next moment she laughed again. Oh, it was easy to
understand! Mrs. John must have managed it all. She
would see in it a way of recovering all her lost glories, of
getting back her footing in that ridiculous White House,
which had been adapted to her silly taste from the beginning. Oh, no doubt it was her doing! She would talk the
girl over; she would persuade her into it, "with a host of
petty maxims preaching down a daughter's heart." And it
was with a gleam of vindictive amusement that Catherine
assured herself that Mrs. John would find herself mistaken.
After she had made the marriage she would be left in the
lurch. Harry was not a man to put up with a mother-in-
law. Thus Catherine Vernon, though she was a clever
woman, misconceived and misunderstood them all.

But yet it did give her a natural pang. That girl, who
compelled her attention somehow, though she had no favour
for her—who inspired her with a certain respect, notwithstanding the consistent opposition to herself which Hester
had always shown—to think of that ambitious creature, all
fire and life, being quenched in the dulness of Harry, put
out in the heavy tranquillity of his athletic existence—to
score at cricket matches, and spend long wearisome days
out in the sun, watching for the runs he got! But then
she would be well off, would have the White House and

all sorts of good things.   Oh, no occasion to be sorry for
her. She would get her compensation.   And then Catherine
thought, with a jealous displeasure which she felt angry
with herself for entertaining, of the arrangements which
Harry's marriage would make necessary.   Up to this time he
had more or less held his position at her pleasure, but she
had no reason, she was aware, to refuse to satisfy all her
engagements, and make him actually independent, as he had
been virtually for a long time back.   She would not have the
slightest excuse for doing it.   Everything had gone on perfectly well.   There were no complaints of him at the bank.
The business flourished and made progress.   But the thought
that Hester would be thus immediately placed on a sort of
equality with herself, and Mrs. John reinstated, vexed her.
It was a mean sentiment, but she could not help it.   It vexed
her in spite of herself.

The news had been, it is scarcely necessary to say, communicated to Edward at a very early stage.   Miss Vernon
had called him to her, after dinner, as soon as he came up
stairs to the drawing-room, to the window from which the
road was visible winding along the side of the common to
the Vernonry.

"Do you see that?" she said, pointing his cousin out.

What? He saw the Common lying in all its sweetness, its
roughness and undulations standing out in the level sunset
rays, every bush casting a shadow.   He was young, and he
had at least a scientific love of nature, and longed to be out
poking into those beds of herbage, feeling the fresh air on his
face; and it was with a secret grudge in his heart that he
realised the difference between the light, strong figure moving
along buoyant with life and liberty, and he himself in his
evening clothes in his aunt's drawing-room, seeing it all from
within four walls.

"What?" he said, thinking that he would rather not see
the fair outdoor evening world since he could have no share
in it.   "Why—is it Harry?" and then he felt that he hated
the fellow, who was his own master.

"He is going a-wooing," Miss Vernon said.

She was sitting in her favourite place which commanded
this prospect, the Common, the Vernonry, the tall pines, and
the red bars of the sunset behind.   The sunset was her
favourite entertainment, and in summer she always sat here.
Edward stood behind, looking out over her head.   She did not

see the grimace with which he heard these words. And he did not reply for some time. It gave him a shock more sharp even than that with which Catherine herself had heard it first, though to be sure there was no reason why.

"Ah!" he said indifferently, "who can he find to woo about here?" But he knew very well in his heart what the answer would be.

"Only one person, so far as I can make out. It must be that girl of Mrs. John's. I suppose she is what you call pretty, though she has never been a favourite of mine."

"But you can't confine prettiness to your favourites, Aunt Catherine," said Edward, with a sharp smile which he had sometimes.

"No, that's true. I deserved that you should hit that blot. She is pretty I know. Poor Harry, he will have his hands full, what with the mild mother and the wild daughter. I wonder at the girl though. She is an ambitious, energetic thing, and poor dear Harry will never set the Thames on fire as you say."

"Did I say it? No, I don't think he will; but he has solid qualities."

"Very solid—the White House and his share in the bank. Oh, there will be an equivalent! And to think that little schemer, that soft little woman that looks as if she could not harm a fly, should have managed to secure herself in this cunning way and get her daughter back to the point she started from! Who would have thought it? There is nothing so astute as simplicity."

Edward made no reply, and this was a thing Miss Vernon did not like. She required a response. Silence felt like disapproval, and as there was a strong silent protest in her heart against everything that was mean or petty in what she said, she was apt to resent this want of acquiescence all the more. She looked back at him when he did not expect it, and was startled to see a look she had never seen before, a look that astonished her, on his face. It was something like a snarl of contempt and despite, but it disappeared in a moment and she could not believe her eyes.

"Are you so sure that Hester will marry him?" was all that Edward said.

"Marry him! Why how could he have so much as looked that way without encouragement? To be sure she will marry him. Where could she find any one else who had so much to

offer? the girl is not a fool. Besides, her mother would
not let her if she wished it; and of course she would not wish
it, an ambitious girl to whom her present position is intolerable. Don't you remember her look on the Thursdays, which
we both remarked?"

Edward had remarked it, not exactly in the same way as
Catherine had done. Hester's look had made him ashamed of
himself, but he had not had the strength to go and display
himself by her side as Harry had done. It made him furious
to think of Harry standing there by her in the corner, not
caring what their patroness might think. It was a courage
of which he was not capable.

"Don't you think," he said softly, "that we are going too
fast, Aunt Catherine, in every way? Harry's visit may be a
chance one. There may be no purpose at all in it, or it may
have some other purpose."

"He was there last night and on last Saturday and Wednes-
day, and I don't know how many evenings besides. Oh no,
there can be no doubt on the subject. It will be a great
amusement for the Vernonry; the dear old ladies want something to amuse them."

This was said of the Ridgways and Mr. Mildmay, who
were all younger than Catherine, and one of them a man. But
that fact increased the pleasantry all the more.

The curious thing was that through all this Catherine was
aware that what she was saying was unworthy of her, and in
reality was disgusted with herself, and kept a mental reckoning of all the meannesses of which she had been guilty. There
were first her remarks upon Mrs. John, which indeed might be
true enough, but which she ought not to have made; and her
certainty that scheming and "encouragement" must have
been used to entrap Harry, and that Hester would marry him
for an equivalent. No moralist would have noted these faults
more clearly than she did herself, yet somehow she went on with
them all the same. But it vexed and annoyed her to find
Edward so constrained. He said, "Will you come and have
a turn in the garden?" but not in his usual tone. That turn
in the garden had been doubly pleasant to her, because he
had made it appear that it was pleasant to him too.

"I think not to-night," she said.

"There is a new moon. It is a lovely evening," said he.
"I think you ought to go. The sunset on one side, and that
clear, pale shining in the east on the other, make such a

beautiful contrast. Come, Aunt Catherine, it will do you good."

" You think it will blow the ill-natured thoughts out of my head," she said with a laugh.

" Have you ill-natured thoughts ? I was not aware of it," said Edward ; and then as she did not move he added—" If you will not come I think I must go and give a little attention to some papers I brought home with me. I had not time to look at them during the day."

" What papers ? " she said quickly.

" Oh, only some prospectuses and details about investments," he said with a careless air, and left her : to her great surprise.

He had been in the habit of telling her of any work he had, all about it, and of sitting with her for an hour or two at least. Catherine was surprised, but as is natural in a first shock of this kind, having got over the momentary prick of it, assured herself that it was accidental and meant nothing : yet was a little more vexed with *that* girl and with Harry, because in some way their concerns had brought about this little, little break, this momentary lapse in the continuance. She could not any longer amuse herself with the prospect of the Vernonry, and the little excitement of this dawning story. There were a great many pricks about the story altogether, sentiments and sensations of which, when left alone and without the support of any moral backer up, of Meredith's stimulating disclosures or Edward's assent, she felt ashamed. It was wrong to speak as she had done about the astuteness of Mrs. John's simplicity. Why should not the mother wish to place her child in the position which she, after all by no fault of her own, poor creature! had lost? Catherine escaped from the tingling of shame at her own pettiness which had gone through her, by considering the final arrangements which she would have to make in view of Harry's marriage. Practically she was always magnanimous ; she would have scorned a petty cutting off, a restraint of liberality, a condition to her gifts. Her givings were always large, and if her mind was warped by the sense of benefactions unappreciated, or kindness unprized, of reaping envy and resentment where she should have got gratitude and love, was it not the fault of her pensioners more than her own, the fault of human nature, which she had been forced to believe she saw through, and which—in order not to break her heart over it—she was obliged to laugh at and despise ?

It would have given Catherine Vernon a sharper shock still if she had seen into Edward's mind as he went away from her, bitterly feeling that while other men could taste the sweetness of freedom and of love, he was attached to an old woman's apron-strings, and had to keep her company and do her pleasure, instead of taking the good of his youth like the rest. It was a sudden crisis of this bitterness which had made it impossible for him to bear the yoke which he usually carried so patiently, and which she, deceived in this instance, believed to be pleasant to him, the natural impulse of a tranquil and home-loving disposition. Had she known how he regarded it, how violently he suppressed and subdued himself, the shock would have been a terrible one; for she was slow to put faith in those around her, and she clung to the one who had been able to impress her with a sense of trustworthiness, with a double tenacity. Edward breathed more freely when he got out of that drawing-room where he always seemed so entirely at home. The library in which he sat when he was alone was a little less oppressive in so far that he was alone in it, but the recollection of Harry going lightly along in his freedom, going a-wooing, had raised a ferment in the breast of the other which it was very difficult to quiet down. Since the morning when he made her acquaintance first, Hester had been an interest to the self-sufficing young man. Perhaps it was only a little warmer than the interest he felt in his botany, in a new specimen, but it had continued through all those years. When he spoke that little aside to her at the party, with his eyebrows and shoulders in a suppressed and confidential attitude which placed himself and her in the same category of compelled assistants at a lugubrious merrymaking where neither of them "got on"—he felt her in her poor little muslin frock and her high indignation to be far the most interesting person in the room, and he resented the necessity which made it impossible to him as the official host to separate himself from the more important people, and show the opinion he had of her. Here again the disabilities of his good fortune weighed upon Edward. He was the host; he was the first person there next to Catherine, her representative, the master of all her wealth. Harry was not of any authority in the house; so he could do as he pleased, and earn the gratitude of Hester; but Edward could neither go to her side in her corner, nor set out of a lovely evening in his pleasantest clothes to woo her, as a free man might. He was not sure

that he wanted to woo her, any more than as a fine specimen :
but he could not bear the impudence of the other fellow who
thought himself good enough to go after her, and whom
Catherine thought so sure to win. Edward could not contemplate with any self-possession the idea that Harry might
win. It made him angry, it made him furious ; it made him
for the moment too much a natural man, too sincere and real
to be capable of his usual self-suppression. Harry would
have an equal share with himself of the bank; they were
equal there in power and authority, and in the profits they
drew. Why then was it that Harry should be his own
master and Edward the slave of an old woman ! This was
the utterance of his passion, of the sincerity which was forced
upon him by the enticements of the summer night, the freedom
in the air, and the sight of all the privileges which Harry
exercised so easily without knowing they were privileges at
all. No doubt the fellow thought himself good enough for
Hester, perhaps believed that she would jump at him, and was
encouraging him, and ready to accept his proffered hand as
soon as ever he should hold it out. This thought made
Edward's blood boil, and the confinement of the Grange became
so oppressive to him that he did not know how to bear it. He
indemnified himself by plunging into the midst of the bundle
of papers which he had not chosen to describe to Catherine.
In these papers lay far more excitment than all Harry's privileges had yet supplied. A battery of artillery planted in
front of this peaceful Grange with all its matches alight
would scarcely have been more full of danger. There was
enough in the packet to tear the house up by its roots, and
send its walls flying in a whilwind of ashes and ruin. Edward
sat down to examine it as another man might have flown to
brandy or laudanum. Dreams were in it of sudden successes,
of fortunes achieved in a moment. Castles in the air more
dazzling than ever rose in a fairy tale. He revenged himself
on his bonds, on the superior happiness of his rival, on
Catherine above all, the unconscious cause of his imprison-
ment, by this.—Here was enough, all ready and in his hands,
to ruin them all.

CHAPTER XIV.

OF all the people who discussed his affairs and were interested in his prosperity, Harry Vernon himself would have
agreed most entirely with Catherine. He had no very elevated
ideal either of life in general or even of love, though that
influenced him at the present moment very powerfully. He
had got to be " very fond," as he would himself have described
it, of Hester. He thought her very pretty to begin with,
very delightful, attractive, and amusing—the sort of girl
with whom life never would be dull. He thought her clever,
one who would be able to manage his now somewhat too large
and unwieldy house and take the trouble off his hands ; he
thought that handsomely dressed, as of course she would be,
she would look very nice at the head of his table and make it
popular—better even than Ellen had done : for in Ellen's
time it had been somewhat fast and noisy, more than Harry,
with the instincts of a respectable citizen and man of business,
felt to be advantageous, though he had enjoyed it well enough.
In all these particulars he felt that his affections were leading
him wisely, and that not merely love—always avowedly more
or less folly—but discrimination and sense were in his choice.
But he would have thought Catherine perfectly right about
the advantages on Hester's side, and he would not have been
disgusted or offended by the suggestion that Mrs. John had
schemed to place her daughter in the White House, and done
her best not to let such an eligible suitor slip through her
hands. And quite right too, he would have said ! He knew
that he would be " a catch " for Hester, and that as she was
no fool, it was inconceivable that she should not jump at

him. This idea did not offend him at all; that she should
marry him because he could give her rank which otherwise
she would not have, was a natural, sensible, perfectly legitimate reason to Harry. Had there been a rival in the field
with greater things to offer, he would have felt that he had
a right to pause, to think what was most to her advantage.
But as there was nobody, he thought probably that Hester
would be a great fool if she made any difficulty. Catherine
had offended herself and offended Edward by her suggestion,
but she would not have offended Harry. "That is about it—
that is the true state of the case," he would have said. And
it is possible that he might have represented that notwithstanding the fact that she had no money, Hester would not be
an altogether bad investment; for she had connections. Mrs.
John might be a silly little woman, but she was Sir John
Westwood's cousin, and a little more backing up from the
county people would do the Vernons no harm. Thus he took
a very commonsense view of the whole concern, thinking it
perfectly reasonable that Mrs. John should scheme, and that
Hester should consider the advantages. He thought even
that she had probably calculated the uses of holding back,
and that her expeditions with the old captain, her disappear-
ances at the time of his own visits, were done with a distinct
intention of drawing a fellow on. It made him very angry,
especially as matters came to a crisis, to find her absent, and
only Mrs. John, very nervous and apologetic, waiting for him
when he went in: but after the first bitterness of the disappointment, he was ready to allow that it was good policy,
and that he was all the more anxious in the pursuit because
she thus played with him and kept him in uncertainty. If
Hester had but known that she was supposed to be "drawing
him on" by her absences! but fortunately she did not know.
And nothing could have made them understand each other on
that point. They belonged to two different species, and talked
different languages. But the superficial explanation which
Catherine was ashamed of herself for giving, and which
Edward despised, would have seemed quite natural to Harry,
though in many ways he was better than they were, and far
more true to his own system of morality. He neither hid nor
deceived, he did not cheat himself nor any one else; and truth
is so precious that even a low, matter-of-fact truth is better
than half a falsehood, however delicately and cleverly carried
out. Harry was all genuine throughout, not elevated in

kind, but never pretending to be what he was not. He liked to think that he had a great many advantages to bestow, and that the lady of his hopes had too much good sense not to take these advantages into consideration. This was different from wild impulse and passion, which some people think finer things. But Harry did not think so; he knew nothing indeed about them. He considered that a man (and on the other side perhaps an heiress) might "please his fancy," in the first place, about his wife, before thinking of other matters ; but that the girl should weigh the advantages, and strain a point to accept a good offer, was as clear to him as daylight. It would not in the smallest degree have vexed him to know that his own claims were thus reasonably weighed. He had the proud satisfaction of thinking that Hester was not very likely to get such another offer ; and he felt sufficient confidence in her good sense to be sure that this must have its just influence upon her. Why should not it weigh with her ? She was "no fool." She could not but see on which side the advantage lay.

The only thing was that he got tired of waiting for the decision. He thought it unreasonable that having so honourably and unequivocally displayed his intentions, he should not be allowed to carry them out. Summer began to wane and autumn to come on, and yet he had never been able to speak to the object of his affections. At last his patience failed him altogether. He announced his mind to Mrs. John almost with solemnity. "I can't go on much longer," he said; "the servants worry me to death. Ellen always took that sort of thing off my hands. But I don't want Ellen to get in her nose again and spoil my wife's chances when she does come. The truth is, I should like to get married before Christmas, if I am to be married at all. Why should Hester hold me off and on ? If she won't have me, let her say so, and I can look elsewhere. I don't think I should have much difficulty in finding—" he concluded, his annoyance going off in a half-smile of vanity as he caressed his light moustache.

A shiver ran through Mrs. John. Before Christmas ! Even if Hester would consent at all, was it possible that her reluctance could be overpowered so soon, or that she should be made to acquiesce in Harry's quite practical and matter-of-fact view. "No doubt you want a lady in the house," she said, sympathetically. "I am sure if I could be of any use——"

"Oh yes, of course you could be of use," said the straight-

forward lover, "after we are married; but it would be making
a laughing-stock of ourselves if I were to have. you before.
If there was any reason for putting off I might wait, but I
don't see any reason. Once it's settled, we could make our
arrangements comfortably. It is being hung up like this
from week to week which is such a nuisance to me."

He went away that evening almost angry. What was to
be done? Mrs. John's natural instinct was to "talk to"
Hester; but she had learned by experience that "talking to"
is not a very effectual instrument. All that she had been
able to say had been said, but without much apparent effect.
She had pointed out all the advantages. She had shown,
with tears in her eyes, what a change it would be—what an
unspeakable, delightful difference. Insensibly to herself, Mrs.
John had become eloquent upon the charms, if not of Harry,
at least of the White House. But this had suddenly been
brought home to her by her remorseless child, who said calmly,
"Mother, if I could marry the house, and let you have it, I
would do so in a moment," which stopped Mrs. John's mouth.

"Marry the—house!" she said, with a surprised cry.

"It is of the house you are talking. I know it is nice—or
at least I know you like it. I do not care for it myself."

"Oh, Hester, my first married home!"

"Yes, mother, I know. I wish I could get it for you—on
easier terms," the girl said, with a sigh. And this was about
all that ever came of talking to her. She was very obstinate :
and such a strange girl.

But sometimes Providence, so much appealed to—whom we
upbraid for not furthering us and backing up our plans—
suddenly did interfere. It was entirely by chance, as people
say. Mrs. John had gone out of the room not two minutes
before, and Hester, who had been walking and had just come
in, stood before the old-fashioned dark mirror, which occupied
the space between the windows, arranging her hair, which
had been blown about by the wind. It was, as has been
said, troublesome hair—so full of curls that the moment it
had a chance it ran out of the level and orderly into rings
and twists, which were quite unfashionable in those days. It
had been loosened out by the wind, and she was trying to coax
it back into its legitimate bondage, with her arms raised to
her head, and her back turned to the door. Harry came in
without knocking, and the first intimation Hester had that
the long-avoided moment had come, and that there was no

escape for her, was when she saw his large form in the glass, close to her, looming over her, his fair head above hers, looking down with admiration and tenderness upon her image. She turned round hastily, with a cry of astonishment, her rebellious locks escaping from her hands.

"Why shouldn't you let it stay so? It is very pretty so," Harry said, looking at the curly mass with a smile, as if he had a great mind to take a lock of it in his fingers.

Hester sprang away from him, and twisted it up, she did not know how.

"It is so untidy—there is so much wind." She was angry with herself for apologising. It was he who ought to have apologised. She pushed the hair away behind her ears, and got it fastened somehow. "I did not hear you knock," she said.

"I fear I didn't knock. The verandah door was open. I saw nobody about. I did not know whether I should find any one. You are so often out now."

"Yes, I walk with old Captain Morgan about this time. In the morning I am always at home."

"If I had known that I should have come in the morning," he said, "not regularly because of the bank, but I should have come once to see you. However, this is far better. I am so glad to find you. I have wished for this for months past. Has it never occurred to you that I was anxious to see you, Hester? You looked to me as if you were keeping away."

"Why should I keep away? I do always the same thing at the same hour. Captain Morgan is old—he requires to have somebody with him."

"And I—I am young, and I want somebody with me."

"Oh, it does not matter about young people," Hester said.

"I think it matters most of all, because they have their life before them; and, don't you know, the choice of a companion tells for so much——"

"A companion!—oh, that is quite a different question," said Hester. "It is teaching I have always wanted, never a companion's place."

"I have heard of that," said Harry. "When you were quite a little thing you wanted to teach, and Aunt Catherine would not let you. You—teaching! It would have been quite out of the question. Won't you sit down? Do come for once, now that I have found you, and sit down here?"

It was the little old-fashioned settee that was indicated, where there was just room for two.

"Oh! I have got things to do," cried Hester, in alarm. "My mother will be here immediately, but I—have got something up stairs——"

"Always when I come," he said. "Just once, because I am here, listen to me, Hester. It won't take very long. I think you use me very ill. You know I come here for you, and you will never let me see you. And now when I find you by chance, you insist that you have something to do. Leave it till to-morrow. Perhaps after to-morrow," said Harry, in a lugubrious voice, "I may not be coming any more."

"Is anything to happen to-morrow?" said Hester, betrayed by his seeming gravity.

Then Harry cheered up again, and became more at his ease.

"Not," he said, "if something should happen to-night. That's what I wish—that something should happen now. Sit down, please, and listen. Don't you know, Hester—they say women always know—that I've been in love with you ever so long?"

"No, I don't know anything about it," said Hester, though a sudden flush came over her face.

She had seated herself on the sofa in a kind of desperation, fearing that he meant to place himself beside her. And such had been Harry's intention; but some dim sense of fitness moved him to depart from this portion of his programme. He stood before her instead, looking down upon her, feeling now that he had it all in his own hands.

"It is true, though. What do you suppose I have been coming here for every night? I *think* I've been in love with you ever since I first saw you—when you were only a child. Now I'm alone since my sister is married, and quite free to choose where I like." He made a pause, but Hester did not say anything. She sat drawing patterns upon the carpet with her foot, listening—because she could not help it. She who was so full of eagerness and life, it seemed to Harry as if every line of her figure expressed the listlessness of a subject that wearied her. Now this was more than a fellow could stand, although even now he felt that it drew him on.

"By Jove!" he cried, "one would think you were getting offers every day of your life."

She looked up at him with a brightening countenance.

"No," she said. "If this is an offer, Cousin Harry, it is the first I have ever had."

"And you think no more of it than that!" he cried, with most natural feeling, flinging himself down in a low wicker-work chair at her feet, so that he made it shake and tremble. This restored Hester once more to herself. She began to be amused, which, in the dull life she was leading, told for so much.

"How should I take it? I don't know, indeed, for I never was in the circumstances before. It is true I have read about it in books," said Hester, considering. "A girl in a novel would say that it was a great honour you had done her, Cousin Harry," for he showed signs of natural impatience, jumping up and pacing noisily about the room. "Don't you see it is very difficult. You make a statement to me about your own state of mind, and then you look as if you expected something from me; but what am I to say? I am not in love with you—or anybody," Hester added quietly, as if by an after-thought.

He was coming towards her, with his lips apart ready to speak; but this quiet little additional word seemed to stop in a moment what he was going to say. He did not quite know how, nor did she know, whether she meant anything by it; but it had an immediate effect. He gave a gasp as if those arrested words almost choked him, then said "Nor any-body?" suddenly. It had seemed certain to him before that: she never could have seen any one, and she had informed him that this was her first "offer"; nevertheless he took these words—having them thrown at him, as it were, in a surprise—as a great concession. He drew a long breath, and said—

"Then, Hester, there is the more chance for me."

Thus in a moment their relative positions were changed. Harry had begun by feeling that he had a great deal to bestow—many things which no girl in her senses could neglect or reject. But in a moment he had been reduced to what in chivalry should be a lover's only standing-ground, the right of telling his love with or without response, waiting absolutely upon his lady's pleasure. hoping for her bounty—no more. He was so carried away by this new impulse that he did not understand himself, or the change worked in him; but with a gasp as for breath, turned from the nineteenth-century version of love-making to the primitive one, not knowing what he did.

"I don't know," said Hester. "Perhaps; I cannot tell. I don't know anything about it; and, if I must tell you the truth, Cousin Harry, I don't wish to know. It seems to me that all that is silly between you and me. You can come here as often as you like : my mother is always glad to see you. We are all very good friends. What advantage do you think there would be in turning everything upside down—in making a great fuss and disturbance and changing all our relations? I cannot see what object there is in it. I think we are much better to stay as we are."

"But I don't think so," said Harry stoutly. "If you're going to argue about it, I never was good at that sort of thing, and you might easily beat me. But *I* don't think so. I don't care about being good friends. I want you to belong to me, to live with me, you and your mother too. Why! we might go on as we are doing for a hundred years, and we never could be of any use to each other——"

Here Hester stopped him with raised hand and gesture. "Oh, yes, a great deal of use. To be friends is about the best thing in the world——"

"Not half so good," cried Harry, "as being man and wife! My house might all be at sixes and sevens, and you could not help me to manage it; living here, and you would never let me be of any use to you. Don't you see? if we were married I could give you everything you wanted, it would be natural. We should get on together, I know. I should never grudge you anything, and your mother could come back to her old home, and I should see to her comfort too. Whereas here, living as we are, what can I do?—or you for me?" said Harry. "Ah! that's all nonsense about being friends. It isn't your friend I want to be."

"What you say is very curious to me," said Hester. "There is a great deal that is very fine in it, Cousin Harry. To offer to give me all that is very nice of you, and I should like to help you to manage your house. I have often thought I should like to try—very likely I should not succeed, but I should like to try."

"It is the easiest thing in the world," he said with a smile that was tender, and touched Hester's heart. "As soon as ever you marry me——"

"But the preliminary is just what I don't like," said Hester. "I would rather not marry—any one. I don't see the need for it. We are very well as we are, but we don't know what a new state of things might do for us."

"I know," said Harry, "what it would do for me. It would

make me very happy and comfortable at home, which I am
not now. It would settle us both in life. A young fellow is
thought nothing of till he is married. He may go off to the
bad at any time, he may take a wrong turn ; and in business
he is never relied upon in the same way. When he has a wife
he has given hostages to society, they say—that is what it
would do for me. Except being richer and better off, and able
to make your mother comfortable, and so forth, I can't say, of
course, what it would do for you."

"Nor I either," she said gravely. "All these things would
be very good: but it might make me into something I shouldn't
like. I feel afraid of it. I have no inclination to it, but all
the other way."

"By Jove !" said Harry, which was an exclamation he
never used save when very hard bested, "that is not very
complimentary to me."

"Did you wish me to pay you compliments? No ; we are
arguing out the general question," said Hester, with her
serious face.

Harry was at his wits' end with impatience and provoked-
ness, if we may use such a word. He could have seized her
with his hands and shaken her, and yet, all the time, he was
still conscious that this strange treatment drew a fellow on.

"I suppose all this means that you won't have me?" he
said, after a pause.

"I think so, Cousin Harry. I am not satisfied that it
would do us any good ; but don't rush away in a temper," she
said, laying her hand lightly on his arm. "Don't be vexed ;
why should you? I don't mean to vex you. If I don't see a
thing in the same light as you do, that is no reason why you
should be angry."

"By Jove !" said Harry again, "if a man is not to be
vexed when he's refused, I wonder what you think he's made
of?—not flesh and blood."

"Sense," said Hester, "and kindness. These are things
you are made of, whether you are angry or not."

She had risen up, and stood looking at him, as he turned
round hastily and made for the door; but this flattery (if it
was flattery) stopped him. He turned round again and stood
looking at her, tantalised, provoked, soothed, not knowing
what to say.

"If you think all that of me, why won't you have me?" he
said, stretching out wistful hands towards her.

Hester shook her head.

"I don't want to have—any one," she said.

Mrs. John had been listening on the stairs. Not listening —she was too far off to hear a word—but waiting for the indications which a step, a sound of movement, the opening of a door, might give. The stair was an old oaken one at the end of the passage, hidden in the evening dimness ; dark at any time even in the day. When the door did open at last, though it did so with a little jar as from an agitated hand, yet two voices came out, and the sound of their conversation was not angry, nor like that of people who had quarrelled. But, on the other hand, it was not low like the talk of lovers ; and Mrs. John could not conceive it possible that if he had been accepted Harry would have left the house without seeing her. That was impossible. Either nothing had been said on the subject, or else— But what else ? She was con-founded, and could not tell what to think. Hester went out with him to the verandah door. It was she who did most of the talking. She called out to him something that sounded like "Don't be long of coming back," as he went out. Mrs. John by this time had hurried out of the staircase, and rushed to a window whence she could see him departing. He turned round and waved his hand, but he also shook his head with a look more completely lover-like than Mrs. John had yet seen him cast at her child. It was full of tender reproach, yet pleasure, disappointment, but also something that was far from despair. "It is all very well for you to say so," he said. What did it mean ? Mrs. John hurried down when he had disappeared, tingling with curiosity and anxiety. She found Hester sitting in the twilight quite unoccupied, her hands in her lap, her eyes gazing straight before her. Nothing could be more unlike her usual dislike to idleness. She was lying back on the settee, thinking, not even asking for lights. Mrs. John stole to her in the gathering darkness and gave her a sudden kiss. The mother was tremulous and shaken, the daughter very calm.

"Oh, Hester ! what has happened ? Have you accepted him ? " said Mrs. John : " have you refused him ? What has been going on ? Now it is over, you might let me know."

"I am just trying to think, mother," Hester said.

CHAPTER XV.

WHAT EDWARD THOUGHT.

THE day after this interview, which had excited everybody, and which, not only Mrs. John, but the chorus of attentive neighbours had felt in their hearts to be of the most critical importance, Hester had, as happened sometimes, a commission from her mother—or rather as she was the active house-keeper and agent in all their business, a necessity of her own, which took her into Redborough. Mrs. John had been brought up in the age when girls were supposed to be charming and delightful in proportion as they were helpless, and her residence abroad had confirmed her in the idea that it was not becoming, or indeed possible, to permit a young woman "of our class" to go anywhere alone. But what was it possible for the poor lady to do? She could not herself walk into Redborough, a distance which was nothing in the estimation of the young and energetic. All that Mrs. John was capable of, was to bemoan herself, to wring her hands, and complain how dreadfully things were changed, how incapable she herself would have been of going anywhere unaccompanied—all which galled, almost beyond endurance, the high spirit of Hester, whose proud consciousness of perfect capacity to guard herself wherever she chose to go, was yet so much embittered by the tradition of her mother's prejudice, that her expeditions, harmless as they were, always appeared to her as a sort of confession of lowliness and poverty, and defiance of the world's opinion. Thus she moved swift and proud about the streets, looking neither to the right hand nor the left, with a half-shame, half-scorn of her unprotectedness, which mingled oddly with her indignant contempt of the idea of wanting

protection at all.   No messenger ever went so quickly, or
returned so soon as Hester, under this double inspiration.
She skimmed along with "that springy motion in her gait,"
as straight and as light as an arrow ; and before the chorus of
the Vernonry had finished communicating to each other, the
exciting fact that Mrs. John had once more permitted *that*
girl to go into town by herself, and asking each other what
she could expect was to come of such proceedings—Hester
would walk back into the midst of their conclave with
such a consciousness of all their whisperings in the large eyes
with which she contemplated them as she passed to her
mother's door, as suddenly hushed and almost abashed the
eager gossips.

"She can't have been in Redborough," Miss Matilda would
say breathless when the girl disappeared.   "Nobody could go
so quickly as that. She has never been there at all. Dear Mrs.
John, how she is taken in !   She must have had some appointment, some rendezvous, there can't be any doubt of it."

"You know best, ladies, how such things are managed,"
Mr. Mildmay Vernon would say with his acid smile, which
was like a double-edged weapon, and cut every way.

This was the usual course of affairs. But on this particular
day she did not surprise them in their animadversions by
her rapid return. She was as long as any ordinary mortal. It
was already afternoon when she set out, and the early autumn
twilight had almost begun when she returned home. The
weather was no longer warm enough to permit of those hostile
meetings in the summer-house where the Vernonry disputed
and fraternised. They were all indoors, looking out—Miss
Matilda seated in her window, with her work-table displayed,
Mr. Mildmay making himself uncomfortable at the only
angle of his which commanded the gate, to watch for the girl's
return. If Harry accompanied her back the community felt
that this would be certain evidence as to what had happened ;
but they were still full of hope that Harry had not been such
a fool. It strung up their nerves to the highest pitch of
suspense to have to wait so long, especially as it was evident
that Mrs. John too was exceedingly nervous about her
daughter's delay. She was seen to go out, at least twice,
with a shawl over her cap, to look out along the road, and
twice to return disappointed. What was she anxious about ?
Very good cause she had to be anxious with a girl like *that*,
wandering no one could tell where about the streets !   And

where could she be? and whom could she be with? Of course
things could not go on like this; it must come to light sooner
or later; for the credit of the family it ought not to be allowed
to go on.   This was what the chorus said.

In the meantime Hester had done her business as quickly
as usual, but on her return she had found herself waylaid.
Edward, with whom her intercourse had been so broken, who
had established himself on the footing of a confidential friend
on the first day of her arrival, and at intervals when they
had met by chance since then, had spoken and looked as if
this *entente cordiale* had never been disturbed — Edward
was lingering upon the edge of the Common on this particular afternoon on his way home apparently, though it
was early.   It would be difficult to explain Hester's feelings
towards him.   He piqued her curiosity and her interest beyond any one of the limited circle with which the girl had
to do.   There were times when her indignation at the contrast between his fraternal and almost tender accost on their
accidental meetings, and the way in which he held himself
aloof on more public occasions, was uncontrollable; but yet
there rarely occurred any of these public occasions without a
meaning look, a word said in an undertone which conveyed to
Hester a curious sense of secret intimacy, of having more to
do with Edward's life than any of the fine people among
whom he was so much more visibly familiar.   She was young
enough to have her imagination excited, and kept in a state
of tantalised interest by these tactics, and also to be indignant
by any suggestion that this mode of treatment was not honourable on his part.   Not honourable!   The idea would have
roused Hester into proud indignation.   What was he to her
that it should matter how he behaved?   His blowing hot
and cold, his holding off and on, which a moralist would
have condemned summarily, which the gossips would have
delighted in commenting upon, what was it to her?   But it
amused her in the meantime with a constant curiosity and
frequent pique, exercising over her imagination something of
the same effect which her own waywardness had upon Harry,
when he declared that it drew a fellow on.   When she got
out of the streets, and saw before her walking slowly, as if
waiting for some one, the figure of this tantalising and uncertain personage, there was a slight quickening of Hester's
pulses and flutter at her heart.   He had never done anything
of this kind before, and she had a feeling that he had not

waited for her for nothing, but that some further revelation
must be at hand.

"I saw you from my office-window," he said. "I never
saw any one walk like you. I know you at once at any
distance, even in a crowd. Do you dislike so much walking
alone?"

"Why should I?" she asked quickly. "I always walk
alone."

"That is no answer. One may hate many things one has
to do habitually. Your walk says that you dislike it. It
says, Here am I, who ought to be guarded like a princess;
but I am poor, I have no escort of honour; yet here I walk, a
whole retinue, a body-guard to myself."

Hester's colour changed from pale to red, and from red to
pale, with mingled indignation and pleasure. It occurred to
her, against her will, that Harry might have seen her pass for
years without learning anything from her gait.

"I have to be my own body-guard, it is true," she said;
"but why should I want one at all? It is folly to suppose a
girl requires protection wherever she goes. Protection! who
would harm me?" she cried, lighting up with an almost
angry glow.

"I for one should not like to try," said Edward, looking at
her, with a look which was habitual to him when they were
alone. What did it mean? A sort of contemplative regretful admiration as of a man who would like to say a great deal
more than he dared say—a sort of, "if I might," "if I could,"
with an element of impatience and almost anger in the regret.
There was a pause, and then he resumed suddenly, and without
any preface, "So it is Harry—who is to be the man?"

"Harry!" Hester gasped, suddenly stopping short, as she
had a way of doing when anything vexed or disturbed her.
The rapidity of the attack took away her breath. Then she
added, as most people, and certainly every girl naturally would
add, "I don't know what you mean."

"Who else?" said Edward, calmly. "He has his freedom,
and he knows how to use it. And I approve him, for my
part. I am of the same opinion. It should be I, if I were
he."

It seemed to Hester that all the blood in her rushed to her
throbbing cheeks and aching forehead. She stamped her foot
on the ground.

"Is it of me you dare to speak so?" she cried. "Oh, I

understand you! When one has been brought up among
the Vernons, one knows what things mean. You venture to
tell me that Harry is the man :—who else ?—but that you
would have been so had you been free—the man," cried the
girl, with blazing eyes, that smote him with lightnings not of
a harmless kind, "to pick up out of the dust—me !—like
something on the roadside."

"You are very eloquent, my little cousin," said Edward,
"not that there is very much in what you say ; but your
looks and gesture are as fine as ever I saw. After all though,
is it called for? When I say that Harry is the man, I do
not suppose either that he is worthy of you, or that you think
so ; but you are a girl, what can you do? They would not
let you work, and if you could work nothing but daily bread
would come of it. And, my dear Hester, you want a great
deal more than daily bread. You want triumph, power ; you
want to be as you are by nature, somebody. Oh, yes," he
said, going on quietly, waving his hand to avert the angry
interruption which was on her lips ; "believe me it is so, even
if you don't know it. And how can you do this, save by
marrying? It does not make anything worse to recognise its
real character. You must do this by marrying. Harry is
the first man who offers. If you were to wait a little longer
you might do better ; but you do not feel that you can wait.
I do not blame you. I should do the same were I you."

All this was said very quietly, the speaker going on by
her side with his eyes turned to the ground, swinging his stick
in a meditative way. The soft measure of his voice, with
little pauses as if to mark the cadence, exercised a sort of
spell upon the girl, who with passion in all her veins, and a
suffocating sense of growing rage, which made her almost
powerless, and took away words in the very heat of her
need for them—moved on too against her will, feeling that
she could express herself only by tones of fury if she
attempted to express herself at all.

"Money does it all," said Edward, in the same meditative
way. "I am supposed to have as much as he has, but I am
tied to an old woman's apron, and would lose everything were
I to venture like he. Why should he be free and I a slave?
I know no reason. Caprice—chance made it so. He might
have been taken in at the Grange, and I at the White House.
Then I should have been the man, and he been nowhere. It is just so in life. Nothing but money can set

it right. Money does. You can believe in Providence when
you have money. I shall get it some day; but so far as
this goes, I shall be too late. For you, there are compensa-
tions," he said, giving a little glance at her. "You will
find him very manageable—more manageable than many
who would have suited you better—than myself for instance.
I should not have been docile at all—even to you—but he
will be. You can do what you please with him; there is
compensation in all——"

"Cousin Edward," said Hester, suddenly finding her voice,
"you told me just now that I disliked to walk alone, that I
was poor and had no body-guard. I said, who would harm me?
but you have proved that it was true, and I a fool. I did
want a body-guard, some one to see that I was not insulted,
to protect me, on a quiet country road, from—from—"

"Yes? from—whom? an unsuccessful suitor: a man that
always has a right to be insulting," cried Edward with a sort
of laugh, "to relieve his mind. True! to be sure all these
things are true. It is quite right that a girl needs protection. Men are stronger than she is, and they will insult her
if it is in their power, if not in one way then in another.
The weak will always go to the wall. If there is nobody to
take care of you, and nobody to punish me for it, of course I
shall treat you badly. If I am not any worse than my
neighbours I don't pretend to be any better. Do you think
I should have waited for you to-night if I had not wanted
to insult you? because you were alone and unprotected and
unfriended," he said, with a sort of snarl at her, turning
upon her with a fierce sneer on his face.

Hester was struck with a horror which stopped her indignation in full career. "Oh," she cried, "how can you make
yourself out to be so ignoble, so ungenerous! even when you say
it I cannot believe it; to insult me cannot be what you mean."

"Why not?" he said, looking at her, "you can't do anything to me. For your own sake you will tell nobody that
Edward Vernon met you and—said anything that he ought
not to have said. Besides, if you wished to ruin me with *her*,"
he waved his hand towards the Grange as he spoke, "in the
first place she would not believe you, in the second place if it
came to that I should not much mind. It would be emancipation anyhow, I should be no longer a slave bound to
follow a woman, in chains. If I lost in one way, I should gain
in another. But I am safe with you," he said with another

laugh, "I am free to irritate you, to outrage you as much as
I please, you will not complain : and in that case why should
not I take it out of you?" he cried, turning fiercely upon her.

Hester was too much startled to retain the violent indignation and offence of her first impulse. She was overwhelmed
with pity and horror.

"Cousin Edward," she said, "you do not mean all that. You
did not come here to insult me. You must have had some
other thought. You must be very unhappy somehow, and
troubled, and distressed to speak as you are doing now. It
comes out of yourself, it is not anything about me."

"Oh, yes, it is something about you," he said with a laugh.
Then after a pause, "but you have some insight all the same.
No. I'll tell you what it is; it is money, money, Hester,
that is what we all want. If you had it you would no more
marry Harry than old Rule; if I had it—And the thing clear
is that I must have it," said Edward, breaking off abruptly.
"I can't wait."

Hester went home very much bewildered, outraged by all
he said, yet more sorry than angry. He had not made any
reply to her appeal for his confidence, yet she knew that
she was right—that it was out of a troubled and miserable heart that he had spoken, not merely out of wounded
feeling on the subject of herself. She did not know whether
he understood what she said to him on the subject of Harry,
or if that penetrated his mind at all; but she went home at
once more miserable and more interested than she thought she
had ever been in her life. Had not she too drawn some conclusion of the same kind from her own experiences, from the
atmosphere of the Vernonry so full of ingratitude, unkindness,
and all uncharitableness? She came very slowly home, and
took no notice of the way in which Mildmay Vernon squinted
at her from his corner, and the Miss Ridgways waved their
hands from the window. Harry then had not come home
with her. "I knew he was not such a fool," the male observer
said to himself, and the sisters laughed and talked in quite an
outburst of gaiety for some time after. "Harry Vernon
think of *that* girl! of course he did not. Who would? so ill
brought up, with such manners, and hair that is nearly red,"
they said.

CHAPTER XVI.

WALKS AND TALKS.

"THEY tell me you are to be congratulated, Hester," said old Captain Morgan.

She had met him taking his evening walk, and in that and in his aspect altogether there was something altogether despondent—a depression and air of weakness which was not common with the old man. She had not gone with him for some days, and perhaps he had felt the desertion. The first thing Hester did was to draw his hand within her arm.

"You are tired," she said.

"Not very. I am a silly old fellow and always go too far. I have been thinking of you, my dear; and if you are to be congratulated——"

"No; I don't think so, Captain Morgan. What about?"

"About—— If anything so important had happened you would have come and told me, Hester."

"I am glad you see that at last. But yes, there is something to congratulate me upon. Nothing did happen. Is not that a great deal to say? For I was tempted, sadly tempted."

"My dear, I don't understand that."

Hester laughed.

"You see, Captain Morgan, you are wise and know a great deal; but you were never a girl—and a poor girl. It would have been so delightful to put my mother back in her nice house, and show Catherine——" Here she paused somewhat embarrassed.

"What of Catherine?" he said.

"Oh, not much—they were, perhaps, when they were young —on different sides. My mother has come down, and Cousin

Catherine has gone up. I should like to have put the balance straight."

"To bring Catherine down, and put your mother——"

"No, Captain Morgan. Catherine is always good when she is with you. I think I almost like her *then*. I would not harm her," said Hester, holding up her head, "if I had the power to do it. But she scorns every one of us; perhaps because we all consent to eat her bread. I would not, you know, if I could help it."

"I know you are ungenerous, Hester, in that respect."

"Ungenerous! Well, never mind, there are more kinds of ungenerosity than one. I am going in with you to tell Mrs. Morgan."

"I am not sure," said the old captain, "though it is a wretched piece of self-denial, that I want you to come with me to-night."

Hester opened her great eyes wide.

"Why!" she said. It was the one house in the world to which she felt she had a right.

"That is nonsense, however," said the old man; "for of course you must meet. We have got our grandson, Hester."

"I heard somebody had come, but I thought it was a gentleman. I did not know you had any—children—except little Mary."

"We have none—in this world; but do you think my wife would have been what she is with never a child? We all have our disabilities, my love. I have never been a young girl, and you have never been an old—pair."

They both laughed. Hester with the easily-recovered cheerfulness of youth, he in tremulous tones, which had as much pathos as mirth in them.

"This is the son of my daughter," he said. "She has been long dead, poor girl—happily for her. Unless when there is some business connected with them to be settled we don't talk much of them. My wife and I long ago went back to the honeymoon stage. We have had to live for each other: and very glad to have each other to live for. Children are very strange, my dear."

"Are they?" said Hester, with an awe which she could scarcely understand.

"Very strange. So dependent upon you for long, so independent after; so unlike you, that you cannot understand what you have to do with them. Perhaps it is a penalty of

living so long as we have done. I have a theory," said the
old captain, cheering up, "that after seventy, when you have
lived out your life, you begin another. And it is quite different. It is a pity we can't renew the old bodies—eyes and
ears and legs and all the rest of it. It would be a very interesting experiment."

"Like the people who found the elixir of life? or the
Wandering Jew?"

The girl spoke to humour him, herself wondering over every
word with that curiosity, mingled with pity and tenderness
and half disapproval, with which youth listens to the vagaries
of age.

"Not at all like the Wandering Jew; his life was continuous and one-ideaed," said Captain Morgan, delighted to
get upon his hobby. "And I miss a great deal in the stories
of those who get the elixir. They may renew their lives but
not themselves. There is one I recollect at this moment. St.
Leon. Of course you have never read St. Leon. He becomes
a beautiful young man, and the rival of his son, who, of
course, does not know him. But the old fellow knows *him*.
He is an old fellow notwithstanding his elixir: the soul of
him is just the same. That is not my point of view."

The old man had become quite erect and walked smartly,
animated by his fancy, leading Hester with him rather than
leaning on her.

"No," he repeated, "that is not at all my point of view.
The bodies keep old, the minds get—different. I have shaken
off my old burdens. I don't take any more responsibility
for those who—used to belong to me. They don't belong to
me any longer. They are labouring along in the former life.
I have started in the new."

"But Mrs. Morgan?" said Hester, with a quaver in her
voice.

"Ah! there's the blot," said the old man. "Of course,
she and I belong to each other for ever and ever. Oh, I don't
want to begin again without my old wife ; and she won't
give up the children, though they are children no longer.
Once a mother, always a mother, Hester. You women are
sadly fettered—you can't shake it off."

"Nor you either, Captain Morgan!" cried Hester, indignant. She could not bear that he should so wrong
himself.

"My dear, I could do it—without difficulty. Is it just, do

you think, that one human creature should be made the victim
of another, simply because he has been instrumental in bringing that other into the world? Supposing that they have
drained all that was best in me out of me for years? Supposing that they have made my life hard and bitter to me?
Supposing that they have grown alien to me in every respect—
thinking other thoughts, walking in other ways? And that
they are as old and more worldly than I am—older, less open
to any influences of nature—am I to go treating these old
rigid commonplace people as if they were my children still,
and breaking my heart about them? No; no."

This seemed a terrible speech to Hester. She kept patting
his arm softly with her hand, and saying, "Oh, Captain
Morgan! You do not mean that!" again and again. It was
dreadful that he should say this. A father to give up his
children! It hurt Hester to think such an idea could find
entrance into any mind.

"And as for the grandchildren, that is out of the question
altogether," Captain Morgan said; "I am not going to begin
a new life of trouble through them."

"I thought," said Hester, "that fathers and mothers never
could forget their children—it is in the Bible."

"'Can a woman forget?' It is a woman, my dear. There
is nothing about a man. My wife is horrified at what I say,
as much as you are. But for all that there is justice in everything, and one soul should not be sacrificed for another. Well,
will you come in? I do not forbid you; but don't take
much notice, I warn you, Hester, of the person you are going
to meet."

The person she was going to meet! This was enough to
make her curious, if not to prepossess her in favour of the
unknown, who, however, she expected to be introduced to her
in the shape of a schoolboy—perhaps a heavy schoolboy—a
sort of being for whom the girl had an instinctive dislike.
She followed the old captain into the house almost mechanically. Mrs. Morgan's chair, now that it began to be chilly in
the evenings, was placed so as to approach the fire, which in
the evening was now always lighted, and sent out a cheerful
glow. It was more cheerful than usual to-night, coming in
from the grey of the waning light outside. There was no
lamp, but only the leaping flame of the fire. The sound of
cheerful voices in conversation, even of laughter, was audible
as the door was opened. The quiet in which the old lady

generally sat waiting for her husband's return—a tranquillity
which was peace itself, yet a silent peacefulness—had always
seemed very sweet to Hester.   That soft stillness of waiting
had seemed to her the very atmosphere of love ; but now at
the door, even before she entered, she was conscious of a
difference.   Life had entered in.   The voices were not forced
or measured, but chiming with each other in the free interchange of familiar affection : the old lady's soft little laugh en-
ticing a louder laughter ; her voice alternating with the deeper
tones.   There was no pause in this lively conversation ; but
some one rose up against the firelight—a tall, straight figure,
no schoolboy, as was evident at the first glance—when they
went in.   But, indeed, the first glance was not supported by
any further revelation, for after the little commotion occasioned by their entrance, the stranger subsided into his chair
again, and remained to Hester, till her departure, a shadow
only, with a singularly soft and harmonious voice.   It got up
again to bow to her.   And it went on talking, out of the gloom,
as she, sitting in the full glare of the light, kept shyly by
Mrs. Morgan's side.   Why was she shy ?   It was not her disposition to be shy.   This evening a gentle embarrassment was
upon her.   She had a pleasure in sitting there by the old
lady's side, defended by the darkness from all necessity of
saying anything, sharing, she could scarcely tell why, the
content which trembled in every tone of her old friend's
voice.   The captain did not take any share in this talk.   He
sat down behind backs, saying that the fire was too much
for him, with a long-drawn breath that sounded like a sigh.
Once or twice he was appealed to by name, and made a brief
response ; but he took no part in the conversation.   On
ordinary occasions it was he who talked, Mrs. Morgan, in
her great chair, remaining quietly quiescent, now and then
making a remark.   It was very strange to see the captain
thrown thus into the background ; but, curiously enough,
Hester did not remark it, so much was she occupied with
the novelty of the conversation.   When the door opened she
was alarmed lest it should be the lights that were coming, so
much more satisfactory was it to let things remain as they
were.   The unseen speaker talked about a great many things
altogether unknown to Hester—his brothers and sisters, his
cousins, a throng of unknown Christian names, every one of
which it was evident had characteristics of its own with which
both the speakers were acquainted.   The listener felt as if a

throng of new acquaintances crowded softly in, filling the dim place with not unfriendly faces.

"And what is Elinor doing?" Mrs. Morgan said.

"It is easy to answer that question, grandmother. She is spoiling her children. And we all know so much better, we who have none."

"Yes, yes; that is always the way," said the old lady. "But, Roland, you must tell her from me that it is very foolish. She will not think it is ignorance on my part. Her mother, poor dear, was just the same," and here the old lady shook her head softly, with a glitter in her eyes, as if a tear was not far off; but if so, there was sweetness in the tear. She turned, after a time, to Hester, who sat by, with a strange sort of pleasure to which she was unaccustomed, listening, in surprised interest, without wishing to take any part.

"You are surprised to hear me so talkative, Hester? But it is not often I have a grandson to wake me up. You did not know I had one, perhaps? Ah! I have been hearing of so many people that I don't often hear of. That does an old body good."

"I like it too," said Hester, the firelight adding colour and animation to her face. "I did not know there were so many people in the world."

"That's very pretty of you to say, my dear," said the old lady. "I was afraid you would think it all gossip; but they are people who belong to me, the most of them. And letters don't tell you like the voice. You must run away when you are tired, for I think I shall go on asking questions till midnight. This young lady—this dear girl—Roland, is the comfort of our lives."

"I thought no less," said the voice out of the shadow, with a softness which went to Hester's heart, sending a little thrill of pleasure through her. She had not even seen his face—but she could not be unaware that he was looking at hers, from the protecting darkness on the other side of the fire. This curious pleasurable encounter, as through a veil, of two fresh souls, hitherto unknown to each other—a moment as full of enchantment as can be in this world—was suddenly broken in upon by the old captain, who jumped up, notwithstanding his rheumatism, as quickly as a boy, and, coming between, stood up with his back to the fire, interrupting the light.

"My old woman," he said, "your Elinors and your Emilys

are like a book to her.   It is like reading a chapter at hazard
out of a novel; but there is no end to the story and no
beginning, and she is at this moment deep in her own—approaching the end of the third volume."

"I should have said, to see Miss Vernon," said the stranger,
who was more a voice than ever, now that the old man interrupted what little light there was, "that she was at the
beginning of the first."

Was it the beginning of the first?   Hester felt a wave of
colour fly over her face, and thought in her heart that the
new-comer was right.   The initial chapter—surely this was
true; not even a beginning, but something that went before
any beginning.

"It never answers," said Captain Morgan, "to give an
opinion without knowledge of the facts.   You are a clever
fellow, Roland, but not so clever as that comes to.   You will
find, Hester, that round every human creature you come across
there is some kind of a world hanging 'bound with gold
chains about the feet of——'   That is the most uncomfortable
metaphor I know.   I wonder what Mr. Tennyson could have
been thinking of?   Did he think that this round world was
hanging on like a big ball, hampering the going of God, do
you suppose?   But there is something of that kind, true
enough, with men."

"If you mean that for me," said the old lady, smiling,
"you are wrong, Rowley.   God knows my heart yearns after
them all, great and small, and it is the greatest refreshment
and no hampering, to hear about them all—their pleasures and
their troubles.   What hurts me is to keep it all in and ask
no questions, as so often I have to do."

The old captain shook his head.   He kept on shaking it
gently.

"We have argued that question a great many times," he
said, "but I am not convinced."

What was evident was, that he intended this conversation
which had been so animated and pleasant to come to an end.
He could not surely be unkind?   But he placed himself, as it
were, in the midst of the current, and stopped its flowing.
A sensation of vexed displeasure and disappointment with
her old friend whom she loved rose in Hester's mind.   Was
it like him to reject the kindness of kin, to limit his wife in
her affections, to turn a cold shoulder on his grandson?   And
yet all these things he seemed to do.   "Roland" on the

other side (she knew no other name for him), had been
silenced. He had scarcely attempted to speak since the old
man took that place in front of the fire, from which his
shadow fell like a dark pillar across the room, dividing the
side on which Mrs. Morgan sat with Hester beside her, from
the other on which was the new being with whom Hester had
already formed almost an intimate acquaintance she felt,
though she did not know his name and had not seen his face.
This very uncertainty pleased her imagination, and inclined
her to the new-comer. But it was embarrassing to find herself in the midst of a scene, where so many confusing, uncomprehended elements were at work, and where something
which was not family harmony and peace lay evidently under
the surface. When she rose up to go away, the unknown
rose too ; but the captain was on the alert.

"You can now go back to your gossip," he said, "my dear :
for I mean to see Hester round the corner."

"No, Captain Morgan. It is very damp, and your rheumatism——"

"Bah! my rheumatism. There are worse things than my
rheumatism," he said, bustling to get his coat.

"Might I not replace you, grandfather? It would be a
pleasure, and I have no rheumatism."

This idea pleased Hester. It would be only for a moment ;
but he was something new. She was so sadly familiar with
every person and thing about that any novelty was delightful
to her. But the captain was not to be shaken off. He
pushed Roland back into his seat. "There are worse things
than rheumatism," he said. And he scrambled into his coat
and took Hester under his arm with unwonted formality.
She felt annoyed and angry beyond description, vexed with
her old friend. Why should he interrupt the innocent talk?
Why interfere so pointedly to prevent the simplest communication between her and the stranger? A mere politeness,
where could have been the harm of that? And then it was
quite unnecessary that anybody should see her home. That
the old man should risk an illness to do this, when she had
so often run unattended from one door to the other, was more
irritating than words could say. And, what was worst of all,
it made the captain less perfect in her opinion—the captain
of whom she had felt that, all the rest of the world failing
her, here was still an excellence upon which she could fall
back.

Since they had come in, though the interval was short, the autumn evening had closed in completely. It was very damp and cold. The Common lay in a white mist; the sky hazy, with a few faint stars looking down through veils of vapour; the atmosphere heavy.

"Why should you come out to catch cold?" Hester said. "I want no one. I am quite able to take care of myself."

"And I want no one, my dear, except myself, to have anything to do with you," said the old man. "I am not afraid to tell you my meaning, without disguise."

"Then stand at the door while I run home," she pleaded; but he would not spare her a step of the way. He hobbled along to the verandah, with his comforter twisted about his throat and mouth, speaking out of the folds of it with a muffled voice.

"If it was any girl but you I should be afraid to say it, lest the mere contradiction might be enough for them; but with you I am not afraid," he said.

Was his confidence justified? Was Hester too wise to be moved by that hint of opposition, that sense that a thing which is forbidden must be pleasant? It is dangerous to predict of any one that this will be the case; and, perhaps, the captain did his best to falsify his own hope. He took her to the very door and saw her admitted, as if there might be a chance up to the last moment of the alarming grandson still producing himself to work her harm. And then he hobbled back in the gathering mists. He even stood lingering at his own door before he went in to the fireside and the cheerful light.

"Neither Catherine nor Hester, neither the young nor the old," he said to himself. In his earnestness he repeated the words half aloud, "Neither Catherine nor Hester, neither money nor love." And then there came something of scorn into the old man's voice. "If his father's son is capable of love," he said.

CHAPTER XVII.

" I LIKE your Roland," said Miss Vernon. She had come to pay one of her usual visits to her old relations. The grandson whom Hester had made acquaintance with without seeing his face had now been nearly a week at the Vernonry, and was known to everybody about. The Captain's precautions had, of course, come to nothing. He had gone, as in duty bound, to pay his respects to the great lady who was his relation too, though in a far-off degree, and he had pleased her. Catherine thought of nothing less than of giving a great pleasure to her old friends by her praise. "He is full of news and information, which is a godsend to us country folks, and he is very good-looking, *qui ne gâte rien.*"

Mrs. Morgan looked up from her place by the fireside with a smile of pleasure. She sat folding her peaceful old hands with an air of beatitude, which, notwithstanding her content, had not been upon her countenance before the young man's arrival.

"That is a great pleasure to me, Catherine—to know that you like him," said the old lady. "He seems to me all that, and kind besides."

"What I should have expected your grandson to be," said Catherine. "I want him to see the people here, and make a few acquaintances. I don't suppose that our little people at Redborough can be of much importance to a young man in town; still it is a pity to neglect an opportunity. He is coming to dine with me to-morrow—as I suppose he told you?"

The old lady nodded her head several times with the same soft smile of happiness.

"You are always good," she said; "and you have done everything, Catherine, for me and my old man. But if you

want to go straight to my heart you know the way lies
through the children—my poor Katie's boys."

"I am glad that the direct route is so easy," Miss Vernon
said in her fine, large, beneficent way; "at least in this case.
The others I don't know."

Captain Morgan came and stood between his wife and the
visitor. To be sure it was to the fire he went, by which he
posted himself with his back to it, as is the right of every
Englishman. His countenance wore a troubled look, very
different from the happiness of his wife's. He stood like
a barrier between them, a non-conductor intercepting the
passage of genial sentiment.

"My dear Catherine," he said, with a little formality, "I
don't wish to be unkind, nor to check your kindness; but you
must recollect that though he is poor Katie's boy, she, poor
soul, had nothing to do with the up-bringing of him, and
that, in short, we know nothing about him. It has been my
principle, as you know, of late years, to insist upon living my
own life."

"All that, my kind old uncle, is understood," said Catherine.
"There are a great many people, I believe, who are better
than their principles, and you are one of them—that is all.
I understand that you know nothing about him. You are
only a man, which is a great drawback, but it is not to be
helped: we know, though we have seen no more of him than
you have. Isn't it so?"

She leaned forward a little, and looked across at the old
lady, who smiled and nodded in return. Old Mrs. Morgan
was not disturbed by her husband's disagreement. It did not
even make her angry. She took it with perfect composure,
beaming over her own discovery of her grandson, and the
additional happiness it had brought.

"My old man," she said, "Catherine, has his own ways of
thinking, we all know that; and sometimes he will act upon
them, but most commonly not. One thing I know, he will
never shut his doors on his own flesh and blood, nor deny his
old wife what is her greatest pleasure—the thing that has
been wanting to me all the time—all the time! I scarcely
knew what it was. And if the boy had been distant or
strange, or showed that he knew nothing about us,
still I should have been content. I would have said, 'Let
him go; you were right Rowley, and not I.' But it is not
so," the old lady went on after a pause, "there's love in

him. I remember when the girls were married there was something I always seemed to want. I found out what it was when the first grandchild was born. It was to feel a baby in my arms again—that was what I wanted. I don't know, Catherine," she added with humility, "if you will think that foolish?"

"If I will understand—that is what you are doubtful of—for I am an old maid, and never had, so to speak, a baby in my arms; but I do understand," said Catherine, with a little moisture in her eyes. "Well, and this great handsome fellow, a man of the world, is he your baby that you wanted so much?"

"Pooh!" said the old captain. "The great advantage of being an old maid, as you say, is that you are above the prejudices of parentage. It is possible to get you to hear reason. Why should my life be overshadowed permanently by the action of another? That is what I ask. Why should I be responsible for one who is not me, nor of my mind?"

"Listen to him! You would think that was all he knows," said Mrs. Morgan; "there is no fathoming that old man, my dear."

"What I have to say is, that we know nothing of this young man," said the captain, shaking his shaggy head as if to shake off his wife's comments. "You will exercise your own judgment—but don't take him on mine, for I don't know him. He is well enough to look at; he has plenty to say for himself; I dare say he is clever enough. Form your own judgment and act upon that, but don't come and say it's our fault if he disappoints you—that is all I have to say. Excuse me, Catherine, if I take a walk even while you are here, for this puts me out—I allow it puts me out," Captain Morgan said.

"What has made him take this idea?" said Miss Vernon when Captain Morgan had hobbled out.

"Oh, my dear, he has his fancies like another. We have had many things to put up with, and he thinks when it comes to the second generation—he thinks we have a right to peace and quiet in our old age."

"And so you have," said Catherine gravely, "so you have." She did not ask any questions. Neither she nor any one knew what it was with which, in the other part of their lives, these old people had been compelled to "put up." Nor did the old lady say. She answered softly, "Yes, I think so too. Peace is sweet, but it is not life."

"Some people would say it was better."

"They never knew, those people, what life was. I like to see the children come and go—one here, one there. One in need of your sympathy, another of your help, another, oh Catherine, even that—of your pardon, my dear!" This made her pause, and brought, what was so unusual, a little glistening moisture to the old lady's eyes. She was silent for a moment, and smiled, perhaps to efface the impression she had made. "If you can do nothing else for them you can always do that," she said.

Catherine Vernon, who was sixty-five, and knew herself to be an old woman, looked at the other, who was over eighty, as a girl looks at her mother—wondering at her strange experiences, feeling herself a child in presence of a knowledge which is not hers. She had not experience enough to understand this philosophy. She looked for a little at her companion, wondering, and then she said, soothingly—

"We must not dwell upon painful subjects. This young fellow will not appeal to you so. What I like in him is his independence. He has his own opinion, and he expresses it freely. His society will be very good for my nephew Edward. If he has a fault—and, indeed, I don't think that boy has many—it is that he is diffident about his own opinion. Roland, if he stays long enough, will help to cure him of that. And how does the other affair go on?" she added, with a perceptible pause, and in a voice which was a little constrained. "No doubt there is great triumph next door."

Old Mrs. Morgan shook her head.

"It is curious what mistakes we all make," she said.

"Mistakes? Do you mean that I am mistaken about the triumph? Well, they have very good reason. I should triumph too, if having been turned out of a great house, like Mrs. John, I managed to get back again, and recover all that I had lost by means of a thing so entirely my own creation as a daughter. Even a son would have been different—I suppose. You know I am not a judge on that point," Catherine said with a laugh.

The old lady continued to shake her head slowly.

"The only one that has not made a mistake is Harry. If he could have got what he wanted, it would have been the best thing that could have happened. There is no complication about that. For him it would have been the best."

"Do you mean to say," said Catherine, her eyes lighting up

with that fire of curiosity and interest which overcomes even
the languor of age. "Do you mean to say that—he is not to
get what he wishes? Oh, this is too much! That girl is
eaten up with pride. What is she saving herself for, I wonder?
What can she expect?"

Again old Mrs. Morgan shook her head, smiling softly as
at blunders upon which she could not be too severe.

"I have said already what mistakes we make, Catherine!
often in our own career, always about other people, my dear."

Upon this Catherine laughed, not having, though she
esteemed her old relation greatly, as much respect for her judgment as probably it deserved. Miss Vernon was too sensible
a woman either to feel or express any contempt for her own
sex, as clever women who were not sensible used to do in those
days; but there was an undertone in her mind of indifference, to say the least, of another woman's opinion. She had
a feeling that it could not be any better, and most likely was
not so good, as her own, for she had held a position not usual
among women, and knew that not many would have proved
equal to the emergency as she did. What the old captain said
would have impressed her more than what his wife said, and
this although she was perfectly aware that the old lady in
many cases was considered the most judicious of the two.

"I know you are both fanatics for Hester," she said, "who
is not my favourite as she is yours. You must take care that
Roland does not fall a victim to her. There are few girls
about, and in that case, when young men have a mind to make
fools of themselves, there is no choice. Do not shake your
kind head off; you know this is a thing in which we have
agreed we shall never think alike."

"Never is a long day," said the old lady, tranquilly. She
was well used to waiting. In her experience, so many things
had come to pass which no one expected. Even now, she said
to herself, if any one had told her that Roland Ashton would
one day be under her roof— She added quietly, "You are too
much alike to do each other justice."

At this Catherine grew red. It had been intimated to her
before, and she had scarcely been able to support the imputation. But she mastered herself with an effort. Nowhere
perhaps but in this house would she have done so; but these
old people had an ascendency over her which she could not
explain.

"We will say nothing on that point," she said, quickly.

" Your news has taken me so completely by surprise. Are
you sure of it ? Why should Mrs. John's daughter have
rejected so excellent a settlement ? She is looking for something better, I suppose ? "

" I think that was a mistake too," said the old lady. " She
says herself that Harry, though he is not clever, is good and
true. Ah ! it is you who shake your head now. In some
things even our Catherine fails ; he is not the equal of Hester ;
but it is not my opinion that a man need be always superior
to his wife. Where there is love, it does not matter. I
should have been pleased to see it ; but she is young ; she
thinks differently. She is looking for nothing consciously ;
but in her heart for love, which is the visitor one is always
looking for when one is young."

" Pshaw ! " said Catherine ; " it is the old people that are
romantic, not the young. It is the settlements that are the
things to be considered ; or perhaps she is thinking of a title ?
Her mother is capable of any nonsense," she said with a
scornful laugh.

Mrs. Morgan made no reply. Her peaceful aspect with her
folded hands, the soft little smile on her old mouth, the slight
shake of the head, was perhaps a trial of patience for the
other, who felt herself thrown back into the category of the
young and superficial by this calm expectation and quietness.
Catherine Vernon was still in the region of prejudice and
dislike. She had not lived into that superior sphere of toleration and calm. Impatience filled her veins. But she mastered
herself, the atmosphere subduing her. And Captain Morgan
came hobbling back, having calmed himself down too.

" Ellen has come back," said Miss Vernon, to change the
subject, " from Paris, with clothes enough for all the neighbourhood. It amuses me to think of her among the bonnet-
shops. What true enjoyment ! and scarcely less now to show
them to all her friends. Now there is a pleasure you cannot
enjoy, uncle. A man could not call his friends together to
look at his new hats."

" There is no telling what a young man can do in the way
of folly till he is put to it," said the captain. " I am loth to
recognise any inferiority. What do you think about all these
failures, Catherine ? or rather, if you have withdrawn from
it, what do the boys think ? "

" I hope I am still capable of giving an opinion," said Miss
Vernon. " None of them touch us, which is the chief thing.

For my part, speculation in this wild way is my horror. If
you could see the proposals that used to be put before me!
Not an undertaking that was not the safest and the surest
in the world! The boys are well indoctrinated in my opinions
on that subject. They know better, I hope, than to snatch at
a high percentage; and love the substance, the good honest
capital, which I love. I think," she continued, "there is a
little of a miser in me or perhaps you will say in all women.
I love to see my money—to count it over like the—— By the
way, it was the king that did that while the queen was eating
her bread and honey. That goes against my theory."

"A good many things go against your theory. They say
that there are no such wild speculators as women. It seems
easy to them that a sort of miracle should happen; that something should come out of nothing."

"They have not had my experience," said Catherine. "But
Edward and Harry are as steady as two churches; that is,"
she added with a complacency which they all recollected afterwards, "Edward is the head; the other fortunately has the
good sense not to attempt to think for himself."

"Hester would have done that for him," said Mrs. Morgan,
in an undertone; but Catherine caught it and went on with
heightened colour, for the idea that Hester—*that* girl!—might
have had something to say in the government of the bank,
struck her as if some one had given her a blow.

"Edward is the heart and soul of everything," she said.
"How fortunate it was for me that my choice fell upon that
boy. I should say he had an old head on young shoulders,
but that I don't like the conjunction. He is young enough.
He has always been accustomed to family life, and loves his
home."

"It is, no doubt," said Captain Morgan, kindly, "that he
has had the advantage of your own experience and teaching
more than the other, Catherine."

"That would be a delightful thought for me," Miss Vernon
said, with a suffusion of pleasure in her eyes. "Perhaps there
is some truth in it. I have done my best to share my lights,
such as they are, with him; but he goes beyond me. And to
think that I hesitated between Edward and Harry! I hope
I am grateful to Providence that turned me to the best.
The other family are following out their lot quite character-
istically. Ellen's husband has a good deal of worldly sense,
which is wanting to that bit of a butterfly. He is trying

hard to get her to make up to me. She has come to see me twice, full of pretty speeches about Algey's great respect for me. Human nature," said Catherine, with a laugh, "is as good, nay, far better, than a play. How cunning it thinks it is, but in reality how very easy to see through."

Here old Mrs. Morgan began to shake her head again, smiling always, but with an indulgent, gentle contradictori-ness which was more near making Miss Vernon angry than anything she had encountered in this house before.

"What does she sit there for, like a Chinese idol?" said the captain. "She has a wonderful opinion of herself, that old woman. Human nature may be easy to see through, but it is very hard to understand, Catherine. What is that the Bible says about 'deceitful above all things'? When you try to get hold of yourself, did you ever find a more slippery customer? There's a kind of amusement in it, when you are up to all your own dodges."

"Rowley, my dear!" said the old lady, surprised.

"It is true I am too old for slang : but one picks it up, and sometimes it is happy enough. I say when you are up to your own dodges ; but that is difficult, and takes a great deal of time. To find yourself trotting forth the same old pretences that you did at twenty, attempting to throw the same sort of dust in your own eyes, is wonderful. There is a sort of art-lessness in the artifice that is amusing, as you say ; but it is only amusing when you are strong enough to get the upper hand."

"When which of you gets the upper hand? for there seem to be two of you," said Catherine, not so much amused in her own person as she made a pretence of being—for this was certainly not her view.

"To be sure," said the old captain, "there are two of you, we all know that ; and in most cases one of you a very silly fellow, taken in on every hand, while the other man sniggers in his sleeve. Of course I am speaking from my own side—ladies may be different for anything I know. But after all," he went on, "I don't think so ; for I've been a woman myself, so to speak, through *her*, for sixty years—that is a long spell. I don't see much difference, though in some things she has got to the last word sooner than I."

"I think we mean different things," said Catherine, rising; "that was not the view I was taking. Yours is better in the moral aspect, for I suppose it is more profitable to judge ourselves than others; but one cannot always be studying one's self."

There was a half-apology in her tone, and at the same time a half-impatience. She did not desire to be turned from the comedy which she had in her way enjoyed for years, seeing through, as she said, all the little world of dependents that hung about her, drawing out their weaknesses, perceiving the bitter grudge that lay under their exterior of smiles, and the thousand ways in which they made up to themselves for the humiliation of being in her debt—in order to turn to what might prove the less amusing contemplation of her own weaknesses, or recognise the element of evil in that which was certainly not amusing. Her carriage was standing at the gate which admitted to the garden front of the Vernonry, and it was with a sense of comfort that she got rid of the old captain at his door, and threw a keen, half-laughing glance at the windows on the other side. Mr. Mildmay Vernon was making himself very uncomfortable at the only angle of his room which permitted him to see the gate, watching for her exit. He kissed his hand to her as she paused and looked round before getting into the carriage, and Catherine realised as if she had seen it, the snarl of mockery with which this salutation was accompanied. In the intervening space were the two sisters keeping the most vigilant watch for her re-appearance, counting the minutes which she spent on the other side of the house, and saying ill-natured things to each other as they nodded and waved their hands. She was aware of the very tone in which these speeches would be made, as well as if she had heard them, and it gave her a great sense of enjoyment to reflect that they were all sitting in rooms well warmed and carefully kept, and full of benevolent prevision of all their wants, while they thus permitted themselves to sneer and snarl at the bestower. Just as she drove away, Hester by chance opened the verandah door, and came out to gather some of the leaves of the Virginia creeper which were dropping with every blast. Hester's serious eyes met hers with scarcely any greeting at all on either side. Catherine did not know very well how it was that this girl came into the comedy. Had she been Harry's betrothed, Miss Vernon could have understood it, and though she could not but have felt the triumph of her old rival, yet it would have added delightfully to the commonplace drama in which everybody pursued their own mean ends under high-sounding pretences. She would have

been able to smile at the commonplace young fellow taken in
by the delusion that he was loved for himself, and laugh in the
conviction that Harry's was no deep affection to be wounded,
but that he could quite well take care of himself, and that
between these two it would be diamond cutting diamond.
But the present state of affairs she did not understand. All
that was amusing in it was the doubtless unbounded disappointment of the scheming little mother, who thus must
find all her fine schemes collapsing in her hands. She could
not refrain from mentioning the matter at dinner that evening, though Edward had a little failed on the former occasion,
in that backing up of all her opinions and feelings which she
had been accustomed to expect from him.

"I find there is to be no match such as that we were
speaking of," she said. "Harry has either drawn back or
he is refused. Perhaps it may be that he has thought better
of it," she added suddenly, without premeditation, grudging,
as perhaps was natural, to let her young antagonist carry off
the honours of the day.

"I thought it was not quite so certain as people seemed
to believe."

"Do you mean that Harry would persevere?"

"I mean that she would accept him, Aunt Catherine. She
is not a girl, so far as I can judge, of whom one could ever
be so sure."

"In the name of wonder," cried out Miss Vernon, "what
does she expect? Good heavens! where is she to get another
such chance again? To refuse Harry, for a girl in her position, is madness. Where does she think she will get another
such offer? Upon my word," said Catherine, with a little
laugh, "I can scarcely help being sorry for her poor little
mother. Such a disappointment for Mrs. John—her White
House and her recovered 'position,' that she loves so dearly,
and all her comforts—I could find it in my heart to be very
sorry for her," she said, with another little laugh.

Edward gave a glance up at her from his plate, on which
he had the air of being intent. The young man thought he
saw through Catherine, as she thought she saw through all
the other inmates of her little world. What he did see
through was the superficial badness which her position had
made, but he had not so much as a glimmering of the other
Catherine, the nobler creature who stood behind; and though
he smiled and assented, a sensation of disgust came into his

heart. He, too, had his comedy of human nature, which
secretly, under cover of his complacency and agreement with
Catherine's opinion, he regarded with the bitterest and angriest
scorn. What an extraordinary shock would it have been for
his companion, who felt herself to sit in the place of the
audience, seeing the puppets play their pranks upon the stage
and exhibit all their fooleries, to know that she herself was
the actor, turned outside in and seen through in all her
devices, to this boy whom she loved!

CHAPTER XVIII.

A FAMILY PARTY.

"A GRANDSON of Captain Morgan! Well, that is not much to meet us at our wedding dinner—at least, if it is not our wedding dinner— Oh, I know there was our state one, and we met all the old fogeys whom I detest!" cried Mrs. Algernon Merridew, born Ellen Vernon; "but this is only the second, and the second is quite as important as the first. She should have asked the county first, to introduce us properly — and then the town; but Aunt Catherine is one of the people who never do what's expected of them. Besides, I don't want to meet her relations on the other side. They're nobodies. She spends quantities of money upon them which she has no business to do, seeing it's the Vernons' money and not hers at all, if you come to that."

"Come, Nell," said her husband with a laugh. He was a dark young man, as was to be expected—seeing that she was so fair a young woman—good-looking, with whiskers, which were the fashion in those days, of a bushy blackness, and hair which suggested pomade. "Come, Nell," he said, "strike fair. Catherine Vernon does a great deal of good with her money, and doesn't spare upon the Vernons—all the town knows that."

"Oh no, she doesn't spare upon the Vernons—all those useless old creatures that she has up there in that horrid old-fashioned house! I think if she did a little more for real relations, and left those old fogeys alone, it would be more like—— Expecting one to call upon them, and take all sorts of trouble! And look at poor old Harry kept with his nose at his desk for ever."

"Poor old Harry is very lucky, I think. Fair play is a jewel. If she doesn't do all you want, who do you expect would ? "

"You, of course ! " cried Ellen, as was natural : and they were so newly married that he thought it very pretty ; "that is the good of you ; and if you go in for Aunt Catherine too, when you know I can't endure her——"

"Of course the good of me is to do whatever you want," he said, with various honeymoon demonstrations ; " but as for going in for Aunt Catherine—you must know this, Nelly, that I'm very proud of being connected with Catherine Vernon. I have heard of her all my life as a sort of goddess, you know. You must not put me off it all at once—I couldn't be put off it. There now, there's nothing to look sulky about."

"You are such an old Redborough person," Ellen said, with a little pout : which was very true. He was not, indeed, at all a good match for a Vernon ; but his whiskers—things much admired in those days—and her self-will had worsted all opposition. He was no more than the son of the perfectly respectable and very well-to-do solicitor, who was universally respected in Redborough, and though Algernon had been in town and sown his wild oats, he had never entirely got out of his mind the instinctive conviction that Redborough was the centre of the world ; and to feel himself within the charmed circle in which Catherine Vernon moved was a promotion which was intoxicating to the young man. Not even his devotion to his pretty wife, which was great, could bring him to disown that allegiance to Catherine Vernon which every Redborough man was born with. It was a sort of still more intoxicating proof of the dignity he had come to, that the pretty wife herself turned up her little nose at Catherine. That Mrs. Algernon should be so familiar with the highest excellence known to them, as to venture to do this, was to the whole family of the Merridews an admiration —just as a family entirely loyal might be flattered by having a princess among them who should permit herself to laugh at the majesty of the king ; but this did not shake their own fidelity. And Algernon, though he ventured with bated breath to say "Aunt Catherine" when he spoke of her in his own family, had not got over his veneration for Miss Vernon. He had taken her in to dinner on the occasion of the great banquet, which Ellen described so lightly, with a sensation

bordering upon the hysterical. Rapture, and pride, and panic
were in it. He did not know, according to the vulgar
description, whether he were on his head or his heels, and his
voice made a buzzing in his own ears as he talked. The
second time was to be in the intimacy of the domestic circle—
if it had been to meet a crossing-sweeper it would still have
been a bewildering gratification ; but all the more, his wife's
criticism and her indifference, and even discontent with the
notice which to him seemed so overpowering an honour,
pleased the young man. She felt herself every bit as good as
Catherine, and yet she was his—Mrs. Algernon Merridew !
The thought was one adapted to make his head swim with
pride and delight.

It was entirely a family party, as Catherine had said, and
a very small one. The Miss Vernon-Ridgways had been
invited, to make the number even, and their preparations for
the unusual honour had taken up four days at least. When
they sailed into the drawing-room at the Grange, having
spent ten minutes in shaking out the flounces and arranging
the flowers and ribbons with which they were ornamented, it
would be impossible to attempt to describe the disgust of the
bride. She turned her eyes upon her husband, who for his
part was in a state of beatitude not to be disturbed by
trifles, with a look of indignant rage which he did not understand. "To think she should ask those old things to meet
us ! I declare I have a great mind to go right away," she
whispered to Harry, who was more sympathetic. Harry
allowed that it was almost beyond bearing. "But I wouldn't
make a quarrel if I were you," he said. In the meantime
the sisters went up beaming to their dear Catherine, whom
they kissed with devotion. How well she was looking ! how
becoming her dress was ! but that lovely lace would be
becoming to any one ! they cried. Catherine received all
these compliments with a smile, and she took great pleasure
in Ellen's disgust, and the way in which she turned her ear
instead of her cheek to the salutations of the cousins, who
were rapturous in their admiration of her in all her bridal
finery. The entry of the stranger, who was unknown to any
of them, made a diversion. Roland Ashton, when he was
visible in the full light of Miss Vernon's drawing-room,
turned out, in appearance at least, a very valuable addition to
the society. Ellen, who was critical, and inclined by nature
to a poor opinion of old Captain Morgan's grandson, looked at

him with astonished, and indeed reluctant, approval. His whiskers were not so thick or so black as Algernon's ; but he had a fine mass of dark hair, wavy, and rather longer than is now permitted by fashion, fine features and dark eyes, with a paleness which was considered very interesting in those days. He was much taller and of more imposing aspect than Edward, whose stature was not great ; he was far more intellectual than Harry ; altogether of the four young men present, his was no doubt the most noticeable figure. They all appraised him mentally as he came in—Catherine first of all, with a sensation of pride that the one individual who was her relation, without being the relation of her family, was a creditable novelty to introduce among them ; the others, with various degrees of quickened curiosity and grudging. The grudge was intensified in the persons of the sisters, who could not endure this interloper. They had felt it their duty to draw the line at the Morgans long ago, and it was all they could do to behave with propriety at Catherine's table when they were seated beside the descendant of the old people on whom Catherine spent her money in what they felt to be an entirely unjustifiable way. They were the only persons present who kept up their grudge to the end. In Ellen's case it disappeared with the clear perception of his good looks. But when Mr. Ashton offered his arm to Miss Matilda Vernon-Ridgway, the look with which she received the offered courtesy was enough to freeze any adventurous young man into stone. It did not, however. It made him all but laugh as he glanced at Catherine, who for her part contemplated her cousins with much gratification. Miss Matilda placed the end of her finger upon the young man's arm. She kept at as great a distance as possible as she crossed the hall by his side. To the little speech about the weather, which he thought it his duty to make her, she returned a sort of inarticulate reply—a monosyllable, but conveying no meaning. When she was seated at table she flung herself, so to speak, upon her neighbour at the other side, who, as it happened, was Harry Vernon, and who was not prepared for the honour. All this was to Catherine as good as a play.

"What a climate, and what a poky old place this Redborough is," said Ellen, preparing to lead the conversation, as she finished her soup. She spoke apparently to Edward, but in reality to the company, which was not too large for general conversation. "It is dreadful to come back here in the beginning of winter from Abroad. I declare I quite envy you, you people who have never been Abroad ; you don't know the difference. Bright sunshine all day long, and bands playing, and the best of music, and all your friends to talk to, sitting out under the trees. Compare that with Redborough, where, beyond a few tiresome little dinner parties, and perhaps three dances at Christmas——"

"The White House used to be a great addition to the cheerfulness of the place," said Edward. "Harry will have no heart to keep it up by himself now you have left him."

"Oh, Harry shall marry," said Ellen. "I have made up my mind to that ; and as soon as we have got quite settled, I mean to set things agoing. I mean to have a Thursday, Aunt Catherine. We shall be glad if you'll come. It is to be a *Thé Dansante*, which is quite a novelty here. You learn so much better about all these things Abroad."

"Where is Abroad?" said Roland, in an undertone which was so confidential and intimate, that had he been anybody else, Miss Matilda must have yielded to its seduction. As it was she only gave him a look of surprise at his ignorance, and cleared her throat and shook her bracelets in order to be able to strike in.

"A *Thé Dansante* is exactly the kind of entertainment that suits me," Catherine said.

"Yes, won't it be nice?" said Ellen unconscious. "I learnt all the figures of the *cotillion*, which is the most amusing thing to end up with, and I made Algy learn it. As soon as ever our house is ready we shall start. It will be a new feature in society. As for Harry, till he's married he'll have to be content with bachelor's dinners, for I can't always be leaving Algy to look after him."

Here Harry murmured something, stammering, and with a a blush, to the intent that the bachelor's dinners would last a long time.

"We don't see you so often at our place as we used to do, Mr. Harry," said Miss Matilda, sweetly. "It used to be quite a pleasure to watch for you ; and the summer evenings were so tempting, weren't they? Oh, fie! it is very naughty to love and to ride away. We always said that was what was likely to happen, didn't we?" she said to her sister, on the other side of the table.

Miss Martha nodded and smiled in return, and cried—

"Oh, always," in a shriller tone.

"What's that you thought likely to happen? Then it didn't happen if it was Harry," cried Ellen, instinctively, ranging herself on her brother's side.

"But about this *cotillion?*" said Edward. "What is it? I thought it had something to say to a lady's dress. I am sure it had in the eighteenth century. We shall have to go to school to learn what your novelty means."

"She put me to school, I can tell you," cried Algernon, from the other end of the table. "I had to work! She is the most dreadful little tyrant, though she looks so soft."

"Dancing is neglected shamefully, nowadays," said Miss Matilda; "shamefully! We were taught very differently. Don't you remember, dear, Mousheer D'Egmont and his little violin, Martha? we were taught the minuet first on account of our curtseys—"

"Oh, the funny, old-fashioned thing! You *never* curtsey nowadays; even in the Lancers it is only a bob," said Ellen, "or a bend mostly with your head. You never see such a thing nowadays."

"My dear! In the presence of your sovereign," said Miss Matilda, with dignity, "it *always* continues necessary. There is no change in that respect so far as I am aware, Martha, is there? You were in the habit of attending Drawing-rooms longer than I."

"Oh, never any change in that!" cried Miss Martha, rising upon herself, so to speak, and erecting her head as she looked from one end of the table to another. It was not often that they had such a triumph. They had been Presented. They had made their curtseys to their Sovereign, as Miss Matilda said.

Silence fell upon the table, only broken by the jingle of Ellen's bracelets, which she pushed up her arm in her mortification; and there were so many of them that they made a considerable noise. Even she was cowed for the moment; and what was worse was, that her husband being simple-minded, and getting a little familiar with Catherine, now turned his looks of awe and veneration upon the Miss Vernon-Ridgways who were so well acquainted with the court and its ways.

And Catherine laughed.

"We are all behind in that respect," she said. "I am fond of pomp and ceremonial for my part. It is a pretty thing, but I like it best at a distance. It is my fault, I have no doubt, that your wife is ignorant of Drawing-rooms, Mr. Merridew."

"I always said so, Aunt Catherine," cried Ellen, who was ready to cry, in the midst of her triumph. "It is horrid for girls to have relations with those out-of-the-way notions."

Catherine only laughed; it was her habitual comment. She turned smiling to young Ashton by her side.

"You ought not to dislike state," he said, in an undertone; "you who are a kind of queen yourself—or, shall I say, grand duchess—in your own town?"

"A queen without any subjects," said Catherine, shaking her head. This time she did not laugh, and there was even a little glimmer of sadness in her eyes.

"Not so. I am a stranger, you know. When I go about the town, I hear of nothing but Catherine Vernon. They call you so, do you know—*tout court*, without miss or madam—that has a great effect upon one's imagination."

Young Merridew had thrust forward his head, and was listening, which perhaps was not very good manners.

"It is quite true," he said eagerly, "Ellen says I am a very Redborough person. I have been born and bred here. I can't remember the time when I didn't look up to—her, as if she was something above the human——"

"And yet you have married a Vernon!" said Catherine; but she was pleased. "It is not an uncommon thing in this world," she said. "People at a distance think more kindly of one than those who are near; but this is not talk for a dinner table. Not to interfere with Ellen's *cotillion*," she said, in a louder tone, "I am thinking of a party for Christmas, young people. As it is for you, you must lay your heads together and decide what it is to be."

Then there arose a flutter of talk, chiefly maintained by the ladies, but in which young Merridew was appealed to by his wife; and Harry, stimulated by the same hand, and Edward, mindful of his duties, took part.

Catherine and her young relative were left, as it were, alone, amid the babble of tongues.

"I cannot allow myself to look at it gravely," she said. "I laugh; it is the best way. They all take what they can get, but their opinions, if they were individually weighed, of Catherine Vernon, would surprise you. They don't think much of me. I dare say I quite deserve it," she said, after a pause, with another laugh. "Don't you think that in most cases enthusiasm is confined to those people who personally

know the least of the object of it? That's an awkward
sentence, but never mind."

"Isn't it the same thing as to say that a great man is never
a hero to his valet, or that a prophet has no honour in his
own country?"

"Not the last, at least," said Catherine; "for being no
prophet, you yourself say I have got some honour in my
country. As for the valet I don't know," she continued,
"but a maid, though she appraises you at your true value,
and is convinced you are a fool in many things, still is
not without a prejudice in your favour. She would like,
though she maintains her erect position, to see the rest of the
world bow down before you. That is amusing too."

"You are a philosopher," said the stranger, looking at her
with a tender regard in his eyes, which made a great impression generally upon younger women, and moved even Catherine
as with a sense of kindness—of kindness disproportioned to
their actual knowledge of each other, which is a thing which
conciliates everybody, looking as if it implied a particular
attraction.

"Your grandfather thinks me a cynic," she said. She
liked these few words of quiet talk in the midst of the mingled
voices of the others, and was grateful to the young man who
looked so sympathetic. "I don't know that I am a cynic, but
rather than cry, I prefer to laugh. Is that cynicism?" He
gave her a look which would have no doubt had a great effect
upon the heart of a younger woman, and which pleased
Catherine, old as she was.

"I think it is true philosophy; but some of us have feelings
that will not be laughed at," said Roland. He was accustomed to make great use of his fine eyes, and on this occasion
he did so with the greatest effect. There could not have been
more tender sympathy than was in them. Could he be really
so much impressed by her character and position, and the
failure of true gratitude and kindness? Catherine Vernon
would probably have laughed at any one else of her own age
who had been so easily persuaded; but it is always so much
more easy to believe in the sincerity of affection which is
called forth by one's self! Her eyes softened as she looked at
him.

"I think you and I, Roland, are going to be great friends,"
she said, and then turned with a slight little sigh, so small as
to be almost imperceptible, to the louder voices appealing to

her. "You must settle it among you," she said. "I give
Edward *carte blanche*. The only thing is that it must take
in everybody, all the Vernonry and our neighbours as well—a
real Christmas party."

"Oh, don't you think, Aunt Catherine, Christmas is such a
bore!" said Ellen, "and family parties! Let us have
strangers. Let us have people we never set eyes on before.
Christmas is so vulgar! Look at all the newspapers with their
little stories; the snow on the ground and the wanderer
coming home, and so forth. I am so glad we haven't got a
wanderer to come home."

"Christmas brings a great many duties I am sure," said Miss
Matilda. "Have you seen the charity flannel at Roby's,
Catherine? It is so good, almost good enough to wear one's
self; and the blankets really look like blankets, not horse-
cloths. Do you think that is good or bad? What you give
in charity ought to be different, don't you think? not to let
them suppose they have a right—"

"You forget," said her sister, eager to get in a word, "that
dear Catherine always gives the best."

"Ah! it is well to be Catherine," said Miss Matilda, "but
many people think there should be a difference. What do you
think, Mr. Harry? Catherine may consider poor people's
feelings; but there are some who think it is wrong to do so—
for who is like Catherine? She is always giving. She is
always so considerate. Whatever she does is sure to be the
best way."

"I am certain," said Algernon Merridew beaming with honest
loyalty from where he sat by Miss Vernon's side, "that all Redborough is of that opinion; and Redborough ought to know."

"You mean all but the people to whom I give," said Catherine, "there are not so many of them: but they are the best
judges of all, and I don't think they approve."

"There's nobody so unreasonable as the poor," said Ellen,
"they are never satisfied. You should just see them turning
over the pieces from my kitchen. Of course all the pieces
are quite nice; everything is, I hope, where I am housekeeper.
Oh, I know I am extravagant, I like the best of everything;
but nothing satisfies the poor. Cold potatoes now with mayonnaise sauce are what I adore, but *they* throw them away."

"Perhaps they don't have the mayonnaise sauce?" suggested
Edward.

"Oh, goodness! I hope not; that would be simply immoral,"

cried Miss Matilda. "But, Mr. Harry, you don't give your opinion, none of the gentlemen give their opinion. Perhaps that is because money is what they give, and one shilling is just like another. You can't have charity shillings. Oh, but I approve of charity flannel; and some people always like to make a difference in what they give to the poor. Poor ladies and gentlemen soon find that out, I assure you. People give you useful presents. If they want to invite you, they invite you when there's nobody there. They think a family dinner or high tea quite treat enough for you. And quite right, don't you think, when one is in the position of a dependent? It keeps people in their proper places. Dear Catherine buys the best flannel, better than I can afford, for her Christmas gifts. She is never like other people, always more liberal; but I should buy the whitey-brown, that is if I could afford any at all, you know."

"Don't attack me, Matilda," said Catherine, with a laugh, "all along the line."

"Oh, attack! *you* dear Catherine? not for the world. We all know what a friend you are. What should we do without you? Whether we are in Paris fashions or our old silks, don't we owe it all to you?"

There was a little pause round the table which was somewhat awkward; for what could anybody say? The clever ones were all non-plussed, but Harry who was the stolid one, suddenly became audible with his round rolling bass voice. "Whoever says that, and whether it was well meant or not, I say the same. It's all quite true. We owe everything to Aunt Catherine. I am always ready to say so, wherever I go."

"Have we come to Christmas toasts already?" said Edward intervening. "We had better not start that sort of thing before the time. We all know what we owe to Aunt Catherine."

"Hush, hush," she cried, waving her hand to him as she rose. "Now we shall release your noble intellects from the necessity of coming down to our level," Catherine said as she followed carefully Miss Matilda's long train. It was very long, though it was rather flimsy, and the progress of the ladies was impeded by it. Ellen swept out lightly in advance with a perfect command of hers. It was the first time she had preceded the old cousins in her dignity as a married woman, and the ring of her bracelets sounded like a little trumpet-

note. As she followed them out Catherine Vernon returned
to her habitual mood of amused indulgence. She had been
almost sentimental for a moment, she said to herself, beguiled
by that boy's sympathetic eyes, which no doubt he must make
great use of among the young ones. She laughed at herself
not unpleasantly, to think of the confidences she had almost
been beguiled into. But it pleased her to think that it was
her mother's blood which had exercised this influence upon
her. After all, it might be the Vernons only who were sordid
and ungrateful. The old captain and his wife had always
been exceptions to her sweeping judgment of human nature.
And now it was their descendant who had touched her heart.
Perhaps it was only the Vernonry after all. But she was
fully restored to her usual kind of amusement as she watched
the progress of her three companions into a temporary but
eager intimacy on the score of Ellen's Paris fashions which
they were eager to examine. The bride was as eager to exhibit
as they were to see, and was so well pleased with herself as to
be impervious to the little covert blows which Miss Matilda
gave under the shield of her flatteries. Catherine Vernon
established herself in her own chair, and gathered her costly
silken skirts about her, and took up the newspaper, which
people in the country have to read in the evening instead of
the morning ; but she did not read much. She was diverted
by the talk. " Crinoline is certainly going out," said Ellen.
"I heard it from the very best shops. Look at mine, it is
quite small, hardly to be called crinoline at all. This is the
very newest, from the Grangd Magaseens du Louvre. You
see yours are twice as big," Ellen added, making a little
pirouette to exhibit the diminished proportions of her hoops.
The Miss Vernon-Ridgways looked down upon their own
skirts with unquiet eyes.

" The French are always so exaggerated," said Miss
Matilda. " Ignorant persons have such strange ideas. They
think really nice people in England take their fashions
straight out of Paris, but that is quite a mistake. It has
always to be modified by English good taste——"

Ellen interrupted with a little shriek. " Oh, good taste !
You should just hear how they speak of that Abroad. Sometimes I could have cried. They say no woman knows how to
dress herself in England. And when I come back and really
see the dreadful things that are worn here—— This is
pretty," Ellen continued, drawing attention to a portion of

her dress. "The Empress wore one just the same at a ball."

"Dear Ellen," said Miss Matilda, "and you wear it at a little family party ! that shows the difference. I am sure it was done just to please us, to let us see what the new fashions are, in your unselfish way, dear !"

And Catherine laughed behind the newspaper. The honours of the occasion were to the old sisters after all.

In the meantime conversation of much more serious import, though scarcely more elevated, was going on round the table in the dining-room, where young Ashton had got the lead, though none of the others looked upon him with over-favourable eyes. There was no doubt that he was a very handsome fellow, and both Harry and Edward had that instinctive sense that he was a competitor likely to put them on their mettle, which is supposed to influence the bosoms of women alone. They thought (instinctively, and each in their different ways,) that he must be a coxcomb. They divined that he was the sort of fellow whom women admired, and scorned him for it—as women perhaps now and then indulge in a little sneer at a gentleman's beauty. But by and by he touched a chord which vibrated more or less in all their bosoms. He began to talk of the city, for which country men of business have a natural reverence. He revealed to them that he himself was on the Stock Exchange, and incidentally let fall an anecdote here and there, of the marvellous incidents, the fairy tales of commerce, that were taking place in those magic regions every day : of men who woke in the morning with the most moderate means at their command, and before night were millionaires. They gathered close about him as he added anecdote to anecdote. Edward Vernon was like tinder, prepared for the fire ; for all his thoughts for some time past had been directed in that way. And young Merridew was launching forth upon life, rather more lavishly than was consistent with his income and prospects. Harry was the least interested of the three, but even to him the idea of making a fortune in a few hours and being able to retire to the country to give himself up to dogs and horses, instead of going down to the bank every morning, was a beatific suggestion. The present writer does not pretend to be able to inform the reader exactly how it was, or in favour of which schemes, that the poet of the Stock Exchange managed to influence these rustic imaginations, but he did so. He filled their

minds with an impatience of their own slow business and its
mild percentages, even when he seemed to praise it.

"Perhaps it does feel slow work; I can't say. I think it
is a vast deal more wholesome. It is very hard to keep your
head steady, you know, when you feel that the chances of an
hour or two may make you the richest man in England."

"Or the poorest perhaps?" said Edward, more with the idea
of subduing himself than checking this flow of instruction.

"Ye-es," said Ashton, indifferently, "no doubt that's on
the cards : but it ought not to be if your broker has a head on
his shoulders. About the worst that can happen, if you take
proper precautions, is that you're no worse than you were to
start with, and better luck next time. I don't approve the
'gain or lose it all' system. But what will Miss Vernon say
if we stay here talking shop all the evening?" he added.

There was never a more clever conclusion ; it was like the
exciting close of an act in the theatre, for he could not be
persuaded to begin again. When they went reluctantly into
the drawing-room, Ellen thought her Algernon had taken too
much wine ; and even Edward, who never offended the proprieties in any way, had a curious light in his eyes, and did
not hear when he was spoken to. But Catherine Vernon,
for her part, did not notice anything except the filial kindness
of young Roland, and the sympathy and understanding which
shone in his eyes.

CHAPTER XIX.

CONFIDENCES.

"I WOULD not speculate if I were you," said Ashton. "What would be the good? You are very well off as you are. You are making your fortune steadily, far better than if you did it by a successful *coup*. Yes, yes, I can understand that a man should desire a little more excitement, and rebel against the monotony of a quiet life, but not you, Vernon, if you'll excuse my saying so. You don't go in for any sort of illegitimate pursuit. You don't play or bet; you have no claim upon you that you want extraordinary means of supplying—"

"How can you tell all that?" said Edward Vernon. "Do you think life's so easy a business that you can read it off from the surface, and make sure that everything is as it seems?"

"I don't say that. Of course, I go upon appearances. I can understand that perhaps you are tired of it——"

"Tired of it!" He twirled his stick violently in his hand, hitting at the rusty bramble branches and gorse bushes that bordered the Common as if they were his enemies. "I suppose one is apt to tire of anything that lasts and never varies," he cried with a forced laugh. "Yes, I am tired of it. Quiet life and safe business, and the hope of making a fortune, as you call it, steadily, in twenty or thirty years——Good life! Twenty or thirty years! Only think of the number of days in that, one after the other, one exactly like the other. I begin to feel as if I should welcome anything to break the monotony —crime itself."

"That means, old fellow," said Ashton soothingly, "nerves, and nothing more."

Edward laughed out, a laugh which was not harmonious

with the soft dulness of the autumnal atmosphere. "I have no nerves, nor tastes nor inclinations, nor any mind of my own," he said. "I do what it is the right thing to do. Though I am sick of it, I never show that. Nobody here has the slightest idea that I was ever impatient or irritable or weary in my life."

Ashton looked at him with some curiosity, but took no further notice. "Does Miss Vernon," he said, "take any share in the business of the bank—I mean, in the work, in the regulations?"

"Miss Vernon," said Edward, "takes a share in everything that is going on around her, it does not matter what. She has been so long used to be at the head of everything, that she thinks it her natural place ; and, as she is old and a woman, it stands to reason——"

"But she is a very intelligent woman ; and she must have a great deal of experience."

"The experience of a little country town, and of steady business, as you call it—oh, she has all that. But put your own views before her, or suggest even the advantages of the circulation of money, quick turning over, and balance of losses and gains——"

"I can understand that," said Ashton. "You don't appreciate the benefits of the Conservative element, Vernon. But for you and your steady-going banks, how could we operate at all? The money must be somewhere. We can't play with counters only in this game."

"There was no question of counters," said Edward ; "we have the money in our hands. It seems to me that you and I should change places : you to do the steady business here, and please Aunt Catherine—who has taken a great fancy to you, you must know—I, to watch the tide, how it comes and how it goes."

"There might be worse arrangements," Ashton said with a laugh : but he added quickly, meeting a keen, sudden glance from Edward, "if you could transfer to me your training, and I mine to you. I am counted rather bold sometimes, you must know," he added, after a moment, returning that look. They talked with great apparent readiness and openness, but with a curious dread of mutual observation going on under the current of their talk all the time.

"So much the better," said Edward, "so long as you know when to hold in."

They were going along the side of the Common between the
Grange and the Vernonry. It was Sunday afternoon—a dull
day, the sky hanging low, the green parts of the Common very
green, glistening with wetness, the gorse and brushwood very
brown and faded. Nobody was about on this day of leisure.
Even the slow country cart, the farmer's shandry, the occasional
roll of a carriage, was absent from the silent road. There were
no nursemaids and children from Redborough picking their way
along the side path. Captain Morgan, feeling his rheumatism,
had retired to his chimney corner; the young men had it all
to themselves. Ashton had been lunching at the Grange. He
was on the eve of going back to town to business from which
he declared he had been absent far too long. The object of his
visit was not very clear to any one : he had left his grandparents for years without showing so much interest in them.
But, whatever his motive had been, his expedition had not
been without fruit. He had discovered a new and wealthy
vein well worth working, and lit a fire which, no doubt,
would light up still further illuminations, in some inflam-
mable spirits. No one had received him more warmly than
Edward Vernon, but he was less easy to make out than the
others. He was less simple ; his life did not correspond with
the betrayals of his conversation, whereas neither Harry Vernon nor his brother-in-law had anything to betray. What was
evident, at least, was that Catherine Vernon smiled upon the
acquaintance which had been formed so rapidly between her
nephew and the stranger. She called Edward " your cousin " to
Ashton, then laughed and apologised, explaining that where
there were so many cousins it was difficult to remember that
her relation was not Edward's too. When Ashton replied,
" There is connection enough to justify the name, if it is
agreeable to Vernon," there could be no doubt that it was, at
least, agreeable to her. She smiled upon them from her window
as they went out together, waving her hand. And no foolish
mother could have been more unaware than Catherine, that
the knowledge that she was there, watching with tender looks
of affection the two figures as they went along, was to Edward
irksome beyond expression. He felt no charm of love in the
look, but substituted suspicion for tenderness, and believed
that she was watching them, keeping them in sight as far as
her eyes could carry, to spy out all they did, and make for
herself an explanation of every gesture. He would not even
have twirled his stick and cut down the brambles but in a

momentary fit of forgetfulness. When they got beyond her
range, he breathed more freely, but, even then, was not without a recollection that she had her opera glasses at hand, and
might, through them, be watching his demeanour still.

"Let us go this way," he said, turning into the road, which
slanted away on the nearer side of the Vernonry leading out
into the open country and brown fields.

Ashton hesitated a moment. "I am not sure that I am
not expected at home. It is my last day," he said.

"Home is a kind of irons," said Edward, "handcuffs, ankle-
chains. One is always like an unhappy cockatoo on a perch.
Any little attempt at flight is always pulled back."

"I don't think that is my experience. My old people are
very indulgent; but then, I am a mere visitor. Home does
not mean much to me," said Ashton. If he had been in the
presence of any lady he would have sighed as he said this—
being in absolute freedom with one of his own kind he smiled,
and it was Edward who sighed.

"There is such a thing as having too much of it," he said.
"What I suffer from is want of air. Don't you perceive it?
There is no atmosphere; every breath has been breathed over
and over again. We want ventilation. We welcome every
horror with delight in consequence—a murder—or even a big
bankruptcy. I suppose that is why bankruptcies are so
common," he added, as if struck with the idea. "A man
requires a great deal of original impulse before he will go the
length of murder. The other has a milder but similar attraction; you ruin other people, which shakes them up, and gives
a change of air."

"Ill-omened words," said Ashton, laughing and throwing
out the fore-finger and little finger of his right hand with a
play at superstition. "Ugly at all times, but especially when
we are talking of business and the Stock Exchange."

"Are you aware," said Edward, sinking his voice, "that
our predecessor, before Aunt Catherine, did something of the
kind?"

"Who was he?"

"A certain John Vernon. His wife lives yonder, with the
rest of Aunt Catherine's dependents in that red house. He
found it too much for him; but it was a poor sort of a flash in
the pan, and hurt nobody but himself."

"You would like to do more than that," said Ashton, still
with a laugh.

But in Edward's face there was no jest.

"I should like," he said, "if I broke down, to carry the whole concern along with me. I should like to pull it down about their ears as Samson pulled the temple, you know, upon his persecutors."

"Vernon," said Roland, "do you know that you are very rash, opening out like this to me? Don't you see it is quite possible I might betray you? I have no right to preach, but surely you can't have any reason to be so bitter. You seem tremendously well off, I can tell you, to a friendless fellow like me."

"I am very well off," said Edward, with a smile; "no man was ever better. I came out of a struggling family where I was to have gone to the colonies or something. My next brother got that chance, and here I am. John Vernon, so far as I can hear, was an extravagant fool. I have not the least sympathy with that. Money's a great power, but as for fine houses, or fine furniture, or show or dash as they call it—"

"I told you," said Ashton, "you have no vices."

Edward gave him a dark, suspicious look.

"I have even a contempt for it," he said.

"There are plenty of men who have that—a horror even; and yet can't do without the excitement."

"I prefer your sort of excitement. John Vernon, as I say, was a fool. He ran away, poor wretch, and Catherine stepped in, and re-made everything, and covered him with contempt."

"He is the father (is he dead?) of the—young lady—who is such a favourite with my grandfather?"

"Hester? Oh, you know her, do you? One of Aunt Catherine's pensioners in the Vernonry, as she calls it."

"It is a little hard upon them to be called dependents; my old people live there. They have their own little income to live upon. Miss Vernon gives them their house, I believe, which is very kind, but not enough to justify the name of pensioners."

"That is our way here," said Edward, laughing. "We are very ready to give, but we like to take the good of it. It is not respectful to call the place the Vernonry, but we do it. We are delighted to be kind; the more you will take from us, the better we will like you. We even—rather like you to be ungrateful. It satisfies our theory."

"Vernon, all that seems to me to be diabolical, you know,

I wish you wouldn't. Miss Hester is a little of your way of thinking, I fear. She makes it amusing though. There are parties, it appears, where she stands all night in a corner, or looks at photographs."

"She says that, does she?" said Edward. His smile had not been a pleasant one, but now it disappeared from his face. "And I suppose she tells you that I never go near her? I have to look after the old ladies and take them to supper. I have the honour of standing in the position of master of the house."

"I don't know that she blames any one," said Ashton indifferently. "It is more fun than anger. Talk of want of air, Vernon, that poor child wants air if you please. She is as full of spirit and life as any one I ever saw. She would like to do something."

"Something! What kind of something? Go on the stage —or what?"

"I have never heard of the stage or any thing of the kind. She wants work."

"Excitement!" Edward said, with an impatient gleam in his eyes.

"She is like you then," said Ashton, trying to laugh, but not with much cordiality, for he felt himself growing angry in spite of himself.

There was excitement enough now in Edward Vernon's face. It grew dark with passion and intolerance.

"A woman is altogether different," he said; then subduing himself with a change in his voice from rage to scorn. "She will soon have it in her power to change all that. Don't you know she is going to marry Harry Vernon, an excellent match for her—money and little brains—whereas she has much brains and little money, the very thing in marriage," he concluded, with a harsh laugh.

"Is that so?" said Ashton.

He had been listening quite at his ease, turning his face towards his companion, and it was a satisfaction to Edward to see that the stranger's countenance clouded over. He was astonished, and Edward could not help hoping more than astonished—for being sore and bitter himself he liked to see another feel the sting.

"That's well," Roland said after a moment, "if she likes it. I should not have thought—but a week's acquaintance does not show you much of a character. I am glad to hear it," he

said, after a pause, "if she likes it," which was but a dubious
sort of satisfaction after all.

Edward looked at him again with an expression of gratified
feeling. • He was glad to have given his new friend a little
friendly stab. It pleased him to see Roland wince. When
one is very uneasy one's self, that is always a little consolation.
He looked at him and enjoyed it, then turned away from the
subject which had given him this momentary pleasure.

"Let us return to our muttons," he said. "Tell me what
you think of these papers? I put them into my pocket to
show you. Now that we are fairly out of sight"—then he
turned back to glance along the still damp road, upon which
there was not a single shadow but their own—"and nobody
can spy upon us—for I distrust windows—we may think of
business a little," the young man said.

Ashton looked at him as he took the papers with a glance
as suspicious as his own. They had grown into a sort of
sudden intimacy in a single night. Edward had been exactly
in the state of mind to which Roland's revelation of chances
and possibilities was as flame to tinder. To have his impatient desires and longings made practical was everything to
him, and the prudence and business instinct left in him which
made him hesitate to make the plunge by himself without
skilled guidance, endowed the new-comer with an importance
which nothing else could have given him. He was at home in
those regions which were so entrancing and exciting, yet
strange to Edward. These communications had brought them
to something like confidential friendship, and yet they did not
know each other, and in many things were mutually anti-
pathetic, repelling, rather than attracting each other. This
interview, though it was to seal the connection between them,
made their mutual want of sympathy more apparent. Edward
had showed the worst side of himself, and knew it. He felt
even that his self-betrayal had been so great as to put him
almost in his companion's power, while at the same time
Ashton had impertinently interposed in the family affairs (a
point upon which Edward was as susceptible as any one) by
what he had permitted himself to say about Hester. Ashton,
on the other hand, whose temper in a way was generous and
easy, regarded the fortunate but ungrateful possessor of Catherine Vernon's sympathies with an indignant astonishment. To
have been so taken up by such a woman, to have her affection,
her confidence, her unbounded approbation and trust, and to

repay her so! It was incredible, and the fellow was ——.
Should he fling up all his pretence at sympathy with this cub,
and go off at once, rather abandoning the possible advantage,
than consenting to ally himself with such a being? This
was the point at which they stood for a moment; but beside
the pull of mutual interest how were they ever to explain the
sudden breach, should they follow their mutual inclinations
and make one? It would be necessary to say something, and
what could be said? and then there lay before Edward a world
of fabulous gain, of sudden wealth, of a hundred excitements
to which Roland seemed to hold the key; and before Roland
the consciousness that not only the advantage of having
Edward, but a whole population of eager country people
ready to put their money into his hands, and give him such
power of immediate action as he had scarcely dreamt of, depended upon his self-restraint. Accordingly the sole evidence
of their absolute distrust and dislike of each other, was this
mutual look, exchanged just before they entered upon the
closest relations of mutual aid.

It was a curious scene for such a beginning. The solitude
of the country road was complete; there was no one to interrupt them. Although they were in the freedom of the open
air, and subject to be overtaken by any passer-by, yet the
Sunday stillness was so intense that they might have been in
the most secret retirement on earth. Had they been seated
together in Edward's room at home, a hundred disturbances
were possible. Servants can never be shut out; if it is only
to mend the fire they will appear in the middle of the most
private conference. And Catherine herself, all unconscious
that her presence was disagreeable, might have come to the
door to summon them, or perhaps even to bring them, with
her own kind hands, the cups of tea which in his heart Edward
loathed as one of the signs of his slavery. They were the
drink of bondage—those poor cups that never inebriate. He
hated even the fragrance of them—the little steams ascending.
Thank Heaven no one could bring him tea out upon the high
road! The chill outer air, the faint scent of mossy damp
and decay, the dim atmosphere without a sparkle in it, the
absolute quiet, would have better suited confidences of a different
description. But if business is not sentimental it is at least
so urgent and engrossing, that it becomes indifferent to circumstances. The do-nothing calm of the Sunday closed curiously
around the group; their rustling papers and eager countenances

brought the strangest interruption of restless life into the almost
dead and blank quiet. The season, the weather, the hour, the
brown quiescent fields in which for the only moment of the
year no mystery of growth was going on, but only a silent
waiting for the seeds and the spring; this day of leisure when
everything was at rest, all the surrounding circumstances
united to throw into full relief the strange centre to the landscape—the two figures which brought a sharp interest of life
into this still-breathing atmosphere, and waiting stagnation,
and Sunday calm.

CHAPTER XX.

ROLAND.

ROLAND ASHTON had been in little doubt as to his own motives when he came after so many years' indifference to "look up" his old grandparents, and take up late, yet not too late, the traditions of filial duty. These traditions, indeed, had no existence for this young man. His mother, the victim of a dissipated and hopeless spendthrift, had died when her children were young, and her father and mother had stood aloof from all but the earliest years of the handful of boys and girls she left behind. The children scrambled up somehow, and, as is not unusual among children, whom the squalor of a parent's vice has disgusted from their earliest consciousness, succeeded in doing well; the girls making much better marriages than could have been hoped for; the boys, flung into the world on their own account at a very early age, finding the means of maintaining themselves, and even pushing forward to a position as good as that which their father had lost. That father had happily died and gone out of all power to injure them, a number of years before, and it was only on a rare visit to the elder sister, who alone knew much about the family connections, that Roland had learned something of the state of affairs at Redborough. Elinor was old enough to remember the time when the grandfather and grandmother had taken charge of the little weeping band of babies in their far-off helpless days, and she had kept up a certain correspondence with them, when, half ruined by that effort, they were saved by Catherine Vernon, the mysterious, wealthy cousin, of whose name everybody in

the family had heard. Elinor remembered so many details
when her memory was jogged, that it occurred to Roland that
it would be a very good thing to go down to Redborough and
pay his grandfather a visit. Catherine Vernon might turn
out to be worth cultivating. She had stepped in to save old
Captain Morgan and his wife from the consequences of their
own liberality to their daughter's children. She had a little
colony of pensioners about her, Elinor was informed. She
was very rich, so rich that she did not know what to do with
her money. There was a swarm of Vernons round her, eating
her up.

"We are her nearest relations on her mother's side,"
Elinor had said. "I do not see why we should not have
our chance too. Don't forget us, Roland, if you make any
way; and you ought to do something; for you have the right
way with women," his sister said, with some admiration and
a little doubt. Her faith was that he was sure to succeed,
her doubt whether his success would be of use to anybody but
himself; but, however it might turn out, it was always better
that one of the Ashtons should benefit by Catherine Vernon's
colossal fortune, than that it should all go into the hands of
the other people.

Roland himself was well aware that he had the right way
with women. This was not the result of art and calculation, but
was pure nature. The young man was bent upon his own ends,
without much consideration, in great matters, of other people.
But in small matters he was very considerate, and had a delightful
way of deferring to the comfort of those about him. And he had
the power of looking interested, and even of feeling interested
in everybody he addressed. And he had fine eyes! What more is
needed to enable a young man to make his way with women?
He was very popular; he might have married well had he
chosen to take that step; indeed, the chief thing against him
was, that he had wavered too long more than once, before he
could make up his mind to hurt the feelings of a sensitive girl
by not asking her to marry him. It was not, to be sure, his
fault, if they thought that was his meaning. A prudent girl
will never allow herself to think so until she is asked point-
blank; and when you came to investigate each case, there
really was nothing against Roland. He had made himself
agreeable, but then, that was his way. He could not help
making himself agreeable. The very tone of his voice changed
when he spoke to any woman who pleased him, and he was

very catholic in his tastes. Most women pleased him if they
had good looks, or even the remains of good looks ; or if they
were clever ; or even if they were *nice ;* and he was pleasant
to all, old and young. The quality was not without its
dangers ; but it had great advantages. He came to Redborough fully determined to make the conquest of Catherine
Vernon, whom, save that she was rich and benevolent, he
knew very little about. Very rich (according to Elinor),
rather foolishly benevolent, old—a young man who has the
right way with women could scarcely be indifferent to such a
description. He determined to find an opportunity in the
dull time of the year, when business was not too exacting, to
pay some of the long over-due respect and gratitude which he
owed to his grandfather. Captain Morgan professed to have
cut himself clear of all his relationships, but it was true that
twenty years before, he had spent everything he had, and
deprived himself of every comfort, he and his wife, for the
maintenance of his daughter's children. He had never got
any return for this from the children, who knew very little
about him. And it was full time that Roland should come
with his power of making himself agreeable to pay the family
debt—no harm if he did something for the family fortunes by
the way.

  And it has been seen that the young man fully proved, and
at once, the justice of his sister's description of him. His
grandmother, to be sure, was vanquished by his very name, by
a resemblance which she found out in his mouth and eyelids
to his mother, and by the old love which had never been extinguished, and could not be extinguished, in her motherly old
bosom. But Hester, by a mere chance encounter in the fire
light, without even seeing him, without knowing his name,
had been moved to a degree of interest such as she was not
conscious of having ever felt before. And Catherine Vernon
had yielded at once, and without a struggle, to his influence.
This was delightful enough ; but after all it did not come to
very much, for Roland found himself plunged into the midst
of a society upon which he had not at all reckoned. The
community at the Vernonry was simple ; he was prepared
for that, and understood it. But when he went to the Grange
and made acquaintance with the closer circle there, the young
men to whom Catherine had made over the bank and all its
interests, and especially Edward, who was established as if he
had been her son, in her house, a change came over Roland's

plans and anticipations. He had a strong desire for his own advantage and inclination to follow that wherever it might lead him ; but he was not malignant in his selfishness. He had no wish to interfere, unless it proved to be absolutely necessary, with another man's career, or to injure his fellow-creatures in promoting his own interest. And it cannot be denied that he felt a shock of disappointment which, as he found when he reasoned with himself on the subject, was somewhat unreasonable. How could he expect the field to be clear for him, and the rich, childless woman of fortune left at his mercy ? As if there were not crowds of other people in the world who had a quick eye for their own advantage, and clear sight to see who was likely to serve it ! But these discoveries put him out. They made his mission purposeless. They reduced it to the mere visit to his grandfather, which he had called it, but which he by no means intended it solely to be.

After this first shock of disappointment, however, Roland began to find himself at once amused and interested by the new community, into the midst of which he had dropped. The inmates of the Vernonry were all simple enough. To be very poor and obliged to accept favours from a rich relative, yet never to be able to escape the sense of humiliation, and a grudge against those who are better off—that is indeed too general : and it is even a conventional necessity of the imagination, that there should be bickerings and private little spites among neighbours so closely thrown together. Ashton did not see much of the Miss Vernon-Ridgways, who had refused to know him at Catherine's house, nor of their kindred spirit Mr. Mildmay Vernon; but he could imagine them, and did so easily. Nor was the gentle little widow, who was now on one side now on the other, according as the last speaker moved her, or the young heroine her daughter, difficult to realise. But Catherine, and the closer group of her relations, puzzled him more. That she should gauge them all so exactly, yet go on with them, pouring kindnesses upon their ungrateful heads with a sort of amusement at their ingratitude, almost a malicious pleasure in it, surprised him less than that among all who surrounded her there was no one who gave to her a real and faithful devotion. And her faith in Edward, whose impatience of her bonds was the greatest of all, seemed to Roland in his spectatorship so pitiful, that he could scarcely help crying out against it to earth and heaven. He was sorry for her all the more that she was so little sorry for herself, and it seemed to him that of all her surroundings he was the only one who was sorry for Catherine. Even his old people as he called them, did not fathom that curse of her loneliness. They thought with everybody else that Edward was a true son to her, studying her wishes, and thinking of nothing so much as how to please her. It appalled him when he thought of the snarl on Edward's lips, the profound discontent in his soul. It would be cruel above all things to warn her—she who felt herself so clear-sighted—of the deception she was the victim of ; and yet what could it come to but unhappiness ? Roland felt himself overpowered and almost overawed by this combination. Nobody but he, it seemed, had divined it. He had walked back with Edward to the Grange after their long talk and consultation, and had taken off his hat with a smile of kindness to the indistinct figure still seated in the window, which Edward recognised with a secret grimace. To see her seated there looking out for their return, was a pleasure to the more genial spirit. It would have pleased him to feel that there was some one who would look out for his coming, who would watch him like this, with tenderness as he went away. But then he had no experience of the kind in his own person, and Edward perhaps had too much of it. While the one went indoors with a bitter sense that he could go nowhere without being watched, the other turned away with a pleasant look back, waving his hand to Catherine Vernon in the window. She was not likely to adopt him, but she was kind to him, a pleasant, handsome old woman, and a most creditable relative. He was glad he had come if it were for that and no more. There were other reasons too why Roland should be glad he had come. He had found a new client, nay, a group of new clients, by whose means he could extend his business and his prospects—solid people with real money to risk, not men of straw. Though he was full of aspirations they were all of a practical kind. He meant to make his fortune ; he meant to do the very best for his customers who trusted him, as well as for himself, and his spirits rose when he thought what a power of extensive and successful operation would be given him by the money of all these new people who were so eager to face the risks of speculation. They should not suffer by it ; their confidence in him should be repaid, and not only his, but their fortunes would be made. The certainty of this went to his head a

little, like wine. It had been well for him to come. It had
been the most important step he had ever taken in his life.
It was not what he had hoped for, and yet it was the thing
above all others that he wanted, a new start for him in the
world, and probably the turning point of his life. Other
matters were small in comparison with this, and approbation or disappointment has little to do with a new customer in
any branch of business. As for other interests he might have
taken up on the way, the importance of them was nothing.
Hester was a pretty girl, and it was natural to him to have
an occupation of that sort in hand; but to suppose that he
was sufficiently interested to allow any thought of her to
beguile him from matters so much more serious, would have
been vain indeed. He felt just such a momentary touch of
pique in hearing that she was going to be married, as a
woman-beauty does when she hears of any conquests but her
own. If she had seen him (Roland) first, she would not have
been, he felt, so easily won; but he laughed at himself for
the thought, as perhaps the woman-beauty would scarcely have
been moved to do.

CHAPTER XXI.

WARNING.

"I THINK, if you will let me, I will send down Emma for a little fresh air and to make your acquaintance, grandmother. She is rather of the butterfly order of girls, but there is no harm in her. And as it is likely that I shall have a good deal to do with the Vernons——"

"What do you want with the Vernons? Why should you have a good deal to do with them?" asked Captain Morgan, hastily, and it must be added rather testily, for the old man's usually placid humour had been disturbed of late.

"In the most legitimate way," said Ashton. "You can't wish me, now that I am just launched in business, to shut my eyes to my own advantage. It will be for their advantage too. They are going to be customers of mine. When you have a man's money to invest you have a good deal to do with him. I shall have to come and go in all likelihood often."

"Your customers—and their money to invest—what do you mean by that? I hope you haven't taken advantage of my relationship with Catherine Vernon to draw in those boys of hers——"

"Grandfather," said Roland, with an *air digne* which it was impossible not to respect, "if you think a little you will see how injurious your words are. I cannot for a moment suppose you mean them. Catherine Vernon's boys, as you call them, are nearly as old, and I suppose as capable of judging what is for their advantage, as I am. If they choose to entrust me with their business, is there any reason why I should refuse it? I am glad to get everything I can."

"Yes, sir, there is a reason," said Captain Morgan. "I

know what speculation is. I know what happens when a hot-headed young fellow gets a little bit of success, and the gambling fever gets into his veins. Edward Vernon is just the sort of fellow to fall a victim. He is a morose, ill-tempered, bilious being——"

"Stop," said Roland; "have a little consideration, sir. There is no question of any victim."

"You are just a monomaniac, Rowley, my old man," said Mrs. Morgan.

"I know everything you can say," said the old captain. "All that jargon about watching the market, and keeping a cool head, and running no unnecessary risks—I know it all. You think you can turn over your money, as you call it, always to your advantage, and keep risk at arm's length."

"I do not say so much as that; but risk may be reduced to a minimum, and profit be the rule, when one gives one's mind to it—which it is my business to do."

"Oh, I know everything you can say," said the old man. "Give your mind to it! Give your mind to an honest trade, that's my advice to you. What is it at the best but making money out of the follies of your fellow-creatures? They take a panic and you buy from them, to their certain loss, and then they take a freak of enthusiasm and you sell to them, to their certain loss. Somebody must always lose in order that you should gain. It is a devilish trade—I said so when I heard you had gone into it; but for God's sake, Roland Ashton, keep that for the outside world, and don't bring ruin and misery here."

"What can I say?" said the young man. He rose up from the table where he had been taking his last meal with the old people. He kept his temper beautifully, Mrs. Morgan thought, with great pride in him. He grew pale and a little excited, as was natural, but never forgot his respect for his grandfather, who besides that venerable relationship, was an old man. "What can I say? To tell you that I consider my profession an honourable one would be superfluous, for you can't imagine I should have taken it up had I thought otherwise."

"Rowley, my old man," said Mrs. Morgan, "you are just as hot-headed as when you were a boy. But, Roland, you must remember that we have suffered from it; and everybody says when you begin to gamble in business, it is worse than any other kind of gambling."

"When you begin; but there is no need ever to begin, that I can see."

"And then, my dear—I am not taking up your grandfather's view, but just telling you what he means—then, my dear, Catherine Vernon has been very kind to him and me. She is fond of us, I really believe. She trusts us, which to her great hurt, poor thing, she does to few——"

"Catherine Vernon is a noble character. She has a fine nature. She has a scorn of meanness and everything that is little—"

The old lady shook her head. "That is true," she said; "but it is her misfortune, poor thing, that she gets her amusement out of all that, and she believes in few. You must not, Roland," she said, laying her hand upon his arm, "you must not, my dear lad— Oh, listen to what my old man says! You must not be the means of leading into imprudence or danger any one she is fond of—she that has been so kind to him and to me!"

The old hand was heavy on his arm, bending him down towards her with an imperative clasp, and this sudden appeal was so unexpected from the placid old woman, who seemed to have outgrown all impassioned feeling and lived only to soothe and reconcile opposing influences, that both the young man and the old were impressed by it. Roland Ashton stooped, and kissed his grandmother's forehead. He had a great power in him of response to every call of emotion.

"Dear old mother," he said, "if I were a villain and meant harm, I don't see how I could carry on with it after that. But I want you to believe that I am not a villain," he said, with a half-laugh of feeling.

Old Captain Morgan was so touched by the scene that in the weakness of old age and the unexpectedness of this interposition the tears stood in his eyes.

"When you do put your shoulder to the wheel, Mary," he said, with a half-laugh too, and holding out a hand to Roland, with whom for the first time he found himself in perfect sympathy, "you do it like a hero. I'll add nothing to what she has said, my boy. Even at the risk of losing a profit, or failing in a stroke of business, respect the house that has sheltered your family. That's what we both say."

"And I have answered, sir," said Roland, "that even if I were bent on mischief I could not persist after such an appeal —and I am not bent on mischief," he added, this time with

a smile; and so fell into easy conversation about his sister,
and the good it would do her to pay the old people a visit.
" I am out all day, and she is left to herself. It is dull for
her in a little house at Kilburn, all alone—though she
says she likes it," he went on, glad, as indeed they all were,
to get down to a milder level of conversation.

The old captain had not taken kindly to the idea of having
Emma; but after the moment of sympathetic emotion which they
had all passed through, there was no rejecting so very reasonable a petition. And on the whole, looking back upon it, now
that the young man's portmanteau stood packed in the hall,
and he himself was on the eve of departure, even the captain
could not deny that there had been on the whole more pleasure
in Roland's visit than he had at all expected. However he
might modify the account of his own sensations, it had certainly been agreeable to meet a young fellow of his own blood,
his descendant, a man among the many women with whom he
was surrounded, and one who, even when they disagreed,
could support his opinions, and was at least intelligent, whatever else. He had received him with unfeigned reluctance,
almost forgetting who his mother was in bitter and strong
realisation that he was his father's son and bore his father's
name. But personal encounter had so softened everything,
that though Roland actually resembled his objectionable father,
the captain parted from him with regret. And, after all, why
should not Emma come? She was a girl, which in itself
softened everything (notwithstanding that the captain had
recognised as a distinct element in Roland's favour that he
was a man, and so a most desirable interruption to the flood of
womankind—but nobody is bound to be consistent in these
matters). It was good of her brother, as soon as he was afloat
in the world, to take upon himself the responsibility of providing for Emma, and on the whole the captain, always ready
to be kind, saw no reason for refusing to be kind to this lonely
girl because she was of his own flesh and blood. He drew
much closer to his grandson during these last few hours than
he had done yet. He went out with him to make his adieux
to Mrs. John and her daughter. And Hester came forward to
give them her hand with that little enlargement about the eyes,
which was a sure sign of some emotion in her mind. She had
seen a great deal of Roland, and his going away gave her a
pang which she scarcely explained to herself. It was so much
life subtracted from the scanty circle. She too, like Edward,

felt that she wanted air, and the departure of one who had
brought so much that was new into her restricted existence
was a loss—that was all. She had assured herself so half-a-
dozen times this morning—therefore no doubt it was true.
As for Roland, it was not in him to part from such a girl
without an attempt at least to intensify this effect. He drew
her towards the window, apart from the others, to watch, as
he said, for the coming of the slow old fly from Redborough
which was to convey him away.

"My sister is coming," he said, "and I hope you will be
friends. I will instruct her to bring in my name on every
possible occasion, that you may not altogether forget me."

There is no likelihood that we shall forget you ; we see so
few people here."

"And you call that a consolatory reason ! I shall see
thousands of people, but I shall not forget *you*." It was
Roland's way to use no name. He said *you* as if there was
nobody but yourself who owned that pronoun, with an
inference that in thinking of the woman before him, whoever
she might be, he, in his heart, identified her from all women.

Hester was embarrassed by his eyes and his tone, but not
displeased. He had pleased her from the first. There is a
soft and genial interest excited in the breasts of women by such
a man, at which everybody smiles and which few acknowledge,
yet which is not the less dangerous for that. It rouses a prepossession in his favour, whatever may come of it afterwards ;
and he had done his best to fill up all his spare moments, when
he was not doing something else, in Hester's company. It
would be vain to say that this homage had not been sweet,
and it had been entertaining, which is so great a matter. It
had opened out a new world to her, and expanded all her
horizon. With his going all these new outlets into life would
be closed again. She felt a certain terror of the place without
Roland. He had imported into the air an excitement, an
expectation. The prospect of seeing him was a prospect full
of novelty and interest, and even when he did not come, there
had always been that expectation to brighten the dimness.
Now there could be no expectation, not even a disappointment ; and Hester's eyes were large, and had a clearness of
emotion in them. She might have cried—indeed, it seemed
very likely that she had cried at the thought of his going
away, and would cry again.

"Though I don't know," he added, leaning against the

recess of the window, and so shutting her in where she stood looking out, "why I should leave so many thoughts here, for I don't suppose they will do me any good. They tell me that your mind will be too fully, and, alas, too pleasantly occupied. Yes, I say alas! and alas again! I am not glad you will be so pleasantly occupied. I had rather you were dull a little, that you might have time now and then to remember me."

"You are talking a great deal of nonsense, Mr. Ashton— but that is your way. And how am I to be so pleasantly occupied? I am glad to hear it, but I certainly did not know. What is going to happen?"

"Is this hypocrisy, or is it kindness to spare me? Or is it——? They tell me that I ought to—congratulate you," said Roland with a sigh.

"Congratulate me? On what? I suppose," said Hester, growing red, "there is only one thing upon which girls are congratulated: and that does not exist in my case."

"May I believe you?" he said, putting his hands together with a supplicating gesture, "may I put faith in you? But it seemed on such good authority. Your cousin Edward——"

"Did Edward tell you so?" Hester grew so red that the flush scorched her. She was angry and mortified and excited. Her interest changed, in a moment, from the faint interest which she had felt in the handsome young deceiver before her, to a feeling more strong and deeply rooted, half made out of repulsion, half bitter, half injured, yet more powerful in attraction than any other sentiment of her mind. Roland was ill-pleased that he was superseded by this other feeling. It was a sensation quite unusual to him, and he did not like it. "He had no right to say so," said Hester; "he knew it was not true."

"All is fair in love and war," said Roland; "perhaps he wished it to be—not true."

"I do not know what he wishes, and I do not care!" Hester cried, after a pause, with a passion which did not carry out her words. "He has never been a friend to me," she said hastily. "He might have helped me, he might have been kind—not that I want his help or any one's," cried the girl, her passion growing as she went on. Then she came to a dead stop, and gave Roland a rapid look, to see how much he had divined of her real feelings. "But he need not have said what was not true," she added in a subdued tone.

" I forgive him," said Roland, " because it is not true. If it had been true it would not have been so easy to forgive. I am coming back again, and I should have seen you—changed. It was too much. Now I can look forward with unmingled pleasure. It is one's first duty, don't you think, to minister to the pleasure of one's grandparents? they are old ; one ought to come often, as often as duty will permit."

Hester looked up to him with a little surprise, the transition was so sudden ; and, to tell the truth, the tumult in her own mind was not so entirely subdued that she could bestow her full attention upon Roland's *double entendre*.

He laughed. " One would think, by your look, that you did not share my fine sense of duty," he said ; " but you must not frown upon it. I am coming soon, very soon, again. A fortnight ago the place was only a name to me ; but now it is a name that I shall remember for ever," he added with fervour.

Hester looked at him this time with a smile upon her mouth. She had recovered herself and come back to the diversion of his presence, the amusement and novelty he had brought. A half sense of the exaggeration and sentimental nonsense of his speech was in her smile ; and he was more or less conscious of it too. When their eyes met they both laughed ; and yet she was not displeased, nor he untouched by some reality of feeling. The exaggeration was humorous, and the sentiment not altogether untrue.

" Do you say that always when you leave a place ?" Hester said.

" Very often," he acknowledged ; and they both laughed again, which, to her at least, was very welcome, as she had been doubly on the verge of tears—for anger and for regret. " But seldom as I do now," he added, " you may believe me. The old people are better and kinder than I had dreamt of ; it does one good to be near them ; and then I have helped myself on in the world by this visit, but that you will not care for. And then——"

Here Roland broke off abruptly, and gazed, as his fashion was, as feeling the impotence of words to convey all that the heart would say.

It was very shortly after this that the white horse which drew the old fly from Redborough—the horse which was supposed to have been chosen for this quality, that it could be seen a long way off to console the souls of those who felt it could never arrive in time—was seen upon the road, and the last moment had visibly come. Not the less for the commotion and tumult of other feelings through which her heart had gone, did Hester acknowledge the emotions which belonged to this leave-taking. The depth and sadness of Roland's eyes—those expressive eyes which said so many things, the pathos of his mouth, the lingering clasp in which he held her hand, all affected her. There was a magic about him which the girl did not resist, though she was conscious of the other side of it, the faint mixture of the fictitious which did not impair its charm. She stood and watched him from the low window of the parlour which looked that way, while the fly was being laden, with a blank countenance. She felt the corners of her mouth droop, her eyes widen, her face grow longer. It was as if all the novelty, the variety, the pleasure of life were going away. It was a dull afternoon which was at once congenial as suiting the circumstances, and oppressive as enhancing the gloom. She watched the portmanteau put in as if she had been watching a funeral. When Roland stepped in after his grandfather, who in the softness of the moment had offered, to the great surprise of everybody, to accompany him to the station, Hester still looked on with melancholy gravity. She was almost on a level with them where she stood looking out ; her mother all smiles, kissing her hand beside her. " I wish you would show a little interest, Hester," Mrs. John said. " You might at least wave your hand. If it were only for the old captain's sake whom you always profess to be so fond of." Roland at this moment leant out of the window of the fly and took off his hat to her for the last time. Mrs. John thought it was barbarous to take no notice. She redoubled her own friendly salutations ; but Hester stood like a statue, forcing a faint ghost of a smile, but not moving a finger. She stood thus watching them long after they had driven away, till they had almost disappeared in the smoke of Redborough. She saw the fly stop at the Grange and Miss Catherine come out to the door to take leave of him : and then the slow vehicle disappeared altogether. The sky seemed to lean down almost touching the ground ; the stagnant afternoon air had not a breath to move it. Hester said to herself that nothing more would happen now. She knew the afternoon atmosphere, the approach of tea, the scent of it in the air, the less ethereal bread-and-butter, and then the dull long evening. It seemed endless to look forward, as if it never would be night. And Mrs. John, as soon as the fly was out of sight, had drawn her chair towards the fire and begun to talk. "I am sure I am very sorry he has gone," Mrs. John said. "I did not think I should have liked him at first, but I declare I like him very much now. How long is it since he came, Hester? Only a fortnight! I should have said three weeks at least. I think it was quite unnatural of the captain to talk of him as he did, for I'm sure he is a very nice young man. Where are you going? not I hope for one of your long walks: for the night closes in very early now, and it will soon be time for tea."

"Don't you think, mamma," said Hester, somewhat hypocritically, "that it would be kind to go in and keep Mrs. Morgan company a little, as she will be quite alone?"

"That is always your way as soon as I show any inclination for a little talk," said her mother provoked, not without reason. Then she softened, being at heart the most good-natured of women. "Perhaps you are right," she said, "the old lady will be lonely. Give her my love, and say I should have come to see her myself, but that—" Mrs. John paused for a reason, "but that I am afraid for my neuralgia," she added triumphantly. "You know how bad it was the other day."

Thus sanctioned Hester threw her grey "cloud" round her, and ran round to console Mrs. Morgan, while her mother arranged herself comfortably with a footstool, a book upon the table beside her, and her knitting, but with a furtive inclination towards an afternoon nap, which the greyness of the day, the early failing light in the dark wainscoted parlour, and the absence of all movement about her, naturally inclined her to. Mrs. John was at the age when we are very much ashamed of the afternoon nap, and she was well provided with semblances of occupation in case any one should come. But Mrs. Morgan was far beyond any such simple deceit. Eighty has vast advantages in this way. When she felt disposed to doze a little she was quite pleased, almost proud of the achievement. She had indeed a book on the table with her spectacles carefully folded into it, but she did not require any occupation.

"I had a kind of feeling that you would come, my pet," she said as Hester appeared. "When I want you very much I think some kind little angel must go and tap you on the shoulder, for you always come."

"The captain would say it is a brain-wave," said Hester.

"The captain says a great deal of nonsense, my dear," said the old lady with a smile, "but think of him going with Roland to the station! He has been vanquished, quite vanquished—which is a great pleasure to me. And Emma is coming. I hope she will not wear out the good impression—"

"Is she not so—nice?" Hester asked.

The old lady looked her favourite intently in the face. She saw the too great clearness of Hester's eyes, and that her mouth was not smiling, but drawn downward; and a vague dread filled her mind. She was full of love and charity, but she was full of insight too; and though she loved Roland, she did not think it would be to the advantage of Hester to love him.

"Roland is very nice," she said. "Poor boy, perhaps that is his temptation. It is his nature to please whomsoever he comes across. It is a beautiful kind of nature; but I am not sure that it is not very dangerous both for himself—and others."

It was fortunate that Hester did not divine what her friend meant.

"Dangerous—to please?" she said, with a little curiosity. She liked Roland so much, that even from the lips of those who had more right to him than she had, she did not like to hear blame.

"To wish to please—everybody," said the old lady. "My poor lad! that is his temptation. Your grandfather, if he were here—my dear, I beg your pardon. I have got into the way of saying it: as if my old man was your grandfather too."

"I like it," Hester said, with the only gleam of her usual frank and radiant smile which Mrs. Morgan had yet seen. But this made the old lady only more afraid.

"There is nobody he could be more fatherly to," she said. "What I meant was that if he were here, he would have something ready out of a book, as you and he are always going on with your poetries; but I never was a poetry woman, as you know. Life is all my learning. And I have seen people that have had plenty of heart, Hester, if they had given it fair play—but frittered it away on one and another, trying to give a piece to each, making each believe that she (for it is mostly upon women that the spell works) was the one above all others. But you are so young, my darling; you will not know what I mean."

A faint, uneasy colour, came on Hester's face.

"I think I know what you mean," she said. "I understand how you should think so of Mr. Ashton. You don't see so well as you did, dear Mrs. Morgan, when you have not got your spectacles on. If you did, you would see that when he talks like *that*, he is ready to laugh all the time."

"Is that so, my love? Then I am very glad to hear you say so," cried the old lady. But she knew very well that her supposed want of sight was a delusion, and that Hester knew it was only for reading that she ever used her spectacles. She felt, however, all the more that her warning had been taken, and that it was unnecessary to proceed further. "You are young and sweet," she said, "my dear: but the best thing still is that you have sense. Oh, what it is to have sense! it is the best blessing in life."

Hester made no reply to this praise. Her heart was beating more quickly than usual. What she had said was quite true: but all the time, though he had been ready to laugh, and though she had been ready to laugh, she was aware that there was something more. The tone of banter had not been all. The sense of something humorous, under those high-flown phrases, had not exhausted them. She was intended to laugh, indeed, if they did not secure another sentiment; but the first aim, and perhaps the last aim, of the insidious Roland, had been to secure this other sentiment. Hester did not enter into these distinctions, but she felt them; and when she thus put forward Mrs. Morgan's failing sight, it was with a natural casuistry which she knew would be partially seen through, and yet would have its effect. This made her feel that there was no reply to be made to the praise of her "sense," which the old lady had given. Was it her cunning that the old lady meant to praise? There was a little silence, and the subject of Roland was put aside, not perhaps quite to the satisfaction of either; but there was nothing more that could be said.

And presently the old captain came back, groaning a little over his long walk.

"Why do you never remind me," he said, "what an old fool I am. To drive in that jingling affair, and to walk back—two miles if it is a yard—well, then, a mile and a half. My dear, what was half a mile when you and I were young is two miles now, and not an inch less; but I have seen him off the premises. And now, Hester, we shall have our talks again, and our walks again, without any interruption——"

"Do not speak too fast, Rowley. There is Emma coming; and Hester will like a girl to talk with, and to walk with, better than an old fellow like you."

"That old woman insults me," said the captain. "She thinks I am as old as she is—but Hester, you and I know better. You are looking anxious, my child. Do you think we are a frivolous old pair talking as we ought not—two old fools upon the brink of the grave?"

"Captain Morgan! I, to have such a thought! And what should I do without you?" cried Hester, in quick alarm. This brought the big tears to her eyes, and perhaps she was glad, for various causes, to have a perfectly honest and comprehensible cause, in the midst of her agitation, for those tears.

"This was brought to my mind very clearly to-day," said the old captain. "When I saw that young fellow go off, a man in full career of his life, and thought of his parents swept away, the mother whom you know I loved, Mary, as dearly as a man ever loves his child, and the father whom I hated, both so much younger than we are, and both gone for years; and here are we still living, as if we had been forgotten somehow. We just go on in our usual, from day to day, and it seems quite natural; but when you think of all of them—gone—and we two still here——"

"We are not forgotten," said the old lady, in her easy chair, smiling upon him, folding those old hands which were now laid up from labour, hands that had worked hard in their day. "We have some purpose to serve yet, or we would not be here."

"I suppose so—I suppose so," said the old man, with a sigh; and then he struck his stick upon the floor, and cried out, "but not, God forbid it, as the instruments of evil to the house that has sheltered us, Mary! My heart misgives me. I would like at least, before anything comes of it, that we should be out of the way, you and I."

"You were always a man of little faith," his wife said. "Why should you go out of your way to meet the evil, that by God's good grace will never come? It will never come; we have not been preserved for that. You would as soon teach me Job's lesson as to believe that, my old man."

"What was Job's lesson? It was, 'Though He slay me, yet will I trust in him,'" Captain Morgan said.

"Oh, my Rowley!" cried the old lady, "I was wrong to say you were of little faith! It is you that are the faithful one, and not me. I am just nothing beside you, as I have always been."

The old captain took his wife's old hands in his, and gave her a kiss upon her faded cheek, and they smiled upon each other, the two who had been one for nearly sixty years. Meanwhile, Hester sitting by, looked on with large eyes of wonder and almost affright. She did not know what it meant. She could not divine what it could be that made them differ, yet made them agree. What harm could they do to the house that sheltered them, two old, good, peaceful people, who were kind to everybody? She gazed at them with her wondering young eyes, and did what she could to fathom the mystery: then retired from it, thinking it perhaps some little fad of the old people, which she had no knowledge of, nor means of understanding. The best people, Hester thought, when they grew old take strange notions into their heads, and trouble themselves about nothing; and of course they missed Roland. She broke in upon them in that moment of feeling, as soon as she dared speak for wonder, making an effort to amuse them, and bring them back to their usual ways; and that effort was not in vain

CHAPTER XXII.

DANCING TEAS.

IT was shortly after the departure of Roland that a new era dawned for Hester in social life. Mrs. Algernon Merridew had felt from the moment of her return from Abroad that there was a work for her to do in Redborough. It was not the same as in her maiden days, when she had been at the head of Harry's household, wonderfully enfranchised indeed, but still somewhat under the awe of Aunt Catherine. But now she was altogether independent, and nobody had any right to make suggestions, as to who she should invite or how she should entertain, to a married lady with an admiring husband, not to speak of brother—and sisters in-law, eagerly anticipating social elevation by her means, at her back. Ellen was not ill-natured. She was very willing to promote the happiness and prosperity of others, so long as she could do so without any diminution of her own—a negative goodness which the world at large is very well pleased to acknowledge as satisfactory. And it is not at all probable that the representations of Harry, or the good-humoured suggestions of Algernon inspired by Harry, to the effect that it would be sublimely good of her to take up and brighten the life of Hester, would have come to very much, had it not at the same time occurred to Ellen that Hester was the best assistant she could have on her own side of the house, in the indispensable work of making her Thursdays "go." Rather than that they should not "go," she would have embraced her worst enemy, had she possessed one; and she did not care to rely upon the Merridew girls, feeling as she did that she had condescended in entering their family, and that they must never

be allowed to forget that they owed everything to her, and
she nothing to them. But at the same time she required a
feminine auxiliary, a somebody to be her right hand, and
help to make everything " go." The result of her cogitations
on this subject was that she set out for the Vernonry one
afternoon in the little victoria, which Algernon, rather
tremulous about the cost, had set up for her, and which, with
the smart coachman who for the moment condescended to be
gardener too, and the boy on the box who was of quite a
fashionable size, looked a very imposing little equipage.
Ellen lay back in her little carriage enveloped in her new
sealskin, with a little hat of the same upon her head, and a
muff also of the same, and her light hair looking all the
brighter against that dark background, with bracelets enough
to make a jingle wherever she went, and which she had to
push up upon her arm from time to time, and a violet scent
about herself and all her garments, at least the scent which
is called violet at Piesse and Lubin's, which served her purpose. When she drove up in this state, it may be supposed
what a flutter she made in the afternoon atmosphere. The
inmates of the Vernonry rushed to their windows.

" It is that little doll Ellen, come to show off more of
her finery," said one sister.

" I wonder why she comes here, when you set her down
so, Matilda," said the other.

They kept behind the curtains, one over the other's
shoulder, that she might not see how curious they were.
But when Ellen floated in at the verandah door, and was
evidently gone to see Mrs. John, their astonishment was
boundless. They shrugged their shoulders and interchanged
glances with Mr. Mildmay Vernon, who, with his newspaper in his hand, had appeared at his window.

" Did he think she was going to see *him* ? " Miss Matilda
said even while addressing these satires in pantomime to
him. "What interest can he take in Ellen ? It is just
prying and curiosity, and nothing more."

The gentleman's comments were not more friendly. He
chuckled as he saw where Ellen was going.

" The old cats will think it a visit to them, and they
will be disappointed," he said to himself, all the same shrug-
ging his shoulders back again to Miss Matilda. They kept
on the watch all the time the visit lasted, and it was a
long one. The sisters discussed the victoria, the horse, the

little footman, the great fur rug which Ellen threw off as she
jumped lightly out of the carriage. It was somewhat hard
indeed that a little minx like Ellen should have all these
things, and her seniors, her betters, who would have enjoyed
them so much, none of them. But so it always is in this
unjust world.

On the other side of the partition from where the sisters
were sitting, Ellen's appearance had caused an almost equal
sensation. She was not looked for, and the proposal she made
was a very startling one.

"I am going to begin my *Thés Dansantes*, and I want you
to help me," she said abruptly. "I want you to be my right
hand ; just like my sister. You know I can't do everything
myself. Mrs. John, you shall come too, I never intended to
leave you out ; but I want Hester to help me, for she is the
only one that can help me. She is really my cousin. Clara
and Connie are only my sisters-in-law, and I don't care to
have them about me in that position. It would be nice for
me, and it would be giving Hester the best of chances. Now,
Mrs. John, I am sure you will see it in that light. What
could be better for a girl? All that she will meet will be
the best sort of people : and she would have her chance."

"I don't know what you mean by having my chance—and
I don't want any chance," said Hester, in a flush of shame and
indignation ; but Ellen put her down with a wave of her
gloved hand and arm, all tinkling with bangles.

"Of course you don't know anything about it," she said,
"an unmarried girl ! We don't want you to know. Your
mother and I will talk about that ; but you can understand
that a nice dance in a nice house like ours, will be something
pleasant. And you would be there not just like a visitor, but
like one of the family, and get a good deal of attention, and
as many partners as ever you liked."

"Of course, Ellen, of course," cried Mrs. John. "I am
sure *I* understand you. It would be very nice for Hester.
At her age every girl likes a little gaiety, and in my position
I have never been able to give it to her. It was very different
when my husband was alive, when we were in the White
House. I am sure I have never grudged it to you, but it made
a great difference. I was not brought up to this sort of
thing. I had my balls, and my parties, as many as could be
wished, when I was Hester's age. If her poor papa had lived,
and we had stayed in the White House, she would have held

a very different position.   It gives me a little prick, you will
understand, to think of Hester wanting anybody to be kind
to her ; but still, as it is so, and as you are her relation, I
never could object.   You will find no objection from me."

"No, I should think not," cried Ellen, throwing back her
warm coat.   It was at the time when sealskins were rare,
when they were just "coming in," and Mrs. John looked at it
with admiration.   She did not ask, as the Miss Vernon-
Ridgways did, why this little minx should have everything ;
but she remembered with a little regret the days when she
too had everything that a young woman could desire, and
wondered, with a little flutter at her heart, whether when
Hester married she would have a sealskin and a victoria, and
all the other crowns of happiness.   She looked with something of a pathetic look at her daughter.   Ah, if she could
but see Hester as Ellen was !

Meanwhile Hester was elevating her young head as was
natural, in special scorn of the "chance" which her cousin
meant to secure for her, and in defiance altogether of the
scheme, which nevertheless (for she was but human and
nineteen, and the prospect of a dance every week took
away her breath) moved her in spite of herself.

"When I was a child," Hester said, "when you first came
to see us, Cousin Ellen, you said you must see a great deal
of me, that I must go to your house, that you and Harry would
take me out, that I should have a share in your pleasures.
Perhaps my mother and you don't remember—but I do
How I used to look out for you every morning ; how I used
to watch at the window, thinking they will surely come or
send, or take some notice to-day.   I was very young, you
know, and believed everything, and wished so much to drive
about and to go to parties.   But you never came."

"To think she should remember all that ! " cried Ellen, a
little abashed.   "Of course I didn't.   Why, you were only
a child.   One said so to please you ; but how can you suppose
one meant anything ?   What could I have done with you
then—a little thing among lots of people ?   Why, you wouldn't
have been allowed to come !   It would have been bad for
you.   You would have heard things you oughtn't to hear.
You wouldn't have let her come, would you, Mrs. John ? "

"Certainly not, my dear," said Mrs. John, promptly.   To
tell the truth, it was she who had complained the most
though it was Hester who had been most indignant.   She

forgot this, however, in the new interest of the moment. "It would never have done," she said, with all sincerity. "Your cousin, of course, only spoke to please you, Hester. I never could have permitted you, a little thing at your lessons, to plunge into pleasure at that age."

"Then why—" cried Hester, open-mouthed; but when she had got so far she paused. What was the use of saying any more? She looked at them both with her large brown eyes, full of light and wonder, and a little indignation and a little scorn, then stopped and laughed, and changed the subject. "When I go to Cousin Catherine's," she said, "which I never do when I can help it, we stand in a corner all the evening, my mother and I. We are thankful when any one speaks to us—the curate's daughters and the Miss Reynoldses and we—— There is never anybody to take us in to supper. All the Redborough people sweep past while mamma stands waiting; and then perhaps some gentleman who has been down once before takes pity, and says, 'Haven't you been down to supper, Mrs. Vernon? Dear me! then let me take you.' You will please to remember that my mother is Mrs. Vernon, Ellen, and not Mrs. John."

"I only say it for—short," said Ellen, apologetically; "and how can I help what happens at Aunt Catherine's? I don't go in for her ways. I don't mean to do as she does. Why do you talk of Aunt Catherine to me?"

"It is only to let you see that I will not be treated so," the girl said with indignation. "If you think I will go to your house like that, just because you are a relation, I won't, Ellen; and you had better understand this before we begin."

"What a spitfire it is!" said Ellen, raising her hand with a toss of all her bracelets to brush Hester's downy cheek with a playful touch. "To think she should put all these things down in her book against us! I should never remember if it were me. I should be furious for the moment, and then I should forget all about it. Now, Hester, you look here. I am not asking you for your own pleasure, you silly; I am asking you to help me. Don't you see that makes all the difference? You are no good to Aunt Catherine. She doesn't need you. She asks you only for civility. But it stands to reason, you know, that I can't look after all the people myself if I am to have any of the fun. I must have some one to help me. Of course you will have every attention

paid you; for, don't you see, you are wanted. I can't get on
without you. Oh, *of course*, that makes all the difference!
I am sure your mamma understands very well, even if you
are too young and too silly to understand."

"Yes, Hester, your cousin is quite right," said Mrs. John,
eagerly. The poor lady was so anxious to secure her child's
assent to what she felt would be so manifestly for her advantage that she was ready to back up everything that Ellen
said. A spark of animation and new life had lighted up in
Mrs. John's eyes. It was not a very elevated kind of hope
perhaps, yet no hope that is centred in the successes of another is altogether ignoble. She wanted to see her child
happy; she wanted Hester to have her chance, as Ellen said.
That she should be seen and admired and made much of, was,
Mrs. John felt, the first object in her life. It would not be
without some cost to herself, but she did not shrink from the
idea of the lonely evenings she would have to spend, or the
separation that might ensue. Her mind, which was not a
great mind, jumped forward into an instant calculation of
how the evening dresses could be got—at what sacrifice of
ease or comfort. She did not shrink from this, whatever it
might be. Neither did she let any visionary pride stand in
her way as Hester did. She was ready to forgive, to forget,
to condone all offences—and in the long discussion and
argument that followed, Mrs. John was almost more eloquent
than Ellen on the mutual advantages of the contract. She
saw them all the instant they were set before her. She was
quite tremulous with interest, and expectation. She ran over
with approval and beaming admiration as Ellen unfolded her
plans. "Oh, yes, I can quite understand; you want to strike
out something original," cried Mrs. John. "You must not
think I agree with Hester about Catherine's parties. I think
Catherine's parties are very nice; and relations, you know,
must expect to give way to strangers, especially when there
are not enough of gentlemen; but it will be much pleasanter
for you to strike out something original. I should have liked
it when I was in your circumstances, but I don't think I had
the energy. And I am sure, if Hester can be of any use——
Oh, my darling! of course you will like it very much. You
always are ready to help, and you have plenty of energy—
far more than I ever had—and so fond of dancing too; and
there are so few dances in Redborough. Oh, yes, I think it
is a capital plan, Ellen! and Hester will be delighted to help

you. It will be such an opening for her," Mrs. John said,
with tears of pleasure in her eyes.

Hester did not say much while the talk ran on. She
was understood to fall into the scheme, and that was all
that was necessary. But when Ellen, after a prolonged visit
and a detailed explanation to Mrs. John, which she received
with the greatest excitement and interest, of all her arrangements as to the music, the suppers, and every other particular they could think of between them, rose to take
her leave, she put her hand within Hester's arm, and drew
her aside for a few confidential words.

"Don't think of coming to the door," she said to Mrs. John;
"it is so cold you must not stir. Hester will see me out.
There is one thing I must say to you, dear," she added, raising
herself to Hester's ear when they were out of the mother's
hearing, "and you are not to take it amiss. It must be a
condition beforehand—now please, Hester, mind, and don't be
offended. You must promise me that you will have nothing
to say to either of the boys."

The quick flush of offence sprang to Hester's face.

"I don't know what you mean. You mean something you
have no right to say, Ellen!"

"I have a very good right to say it—for I'm a married
lady, and you are only a girl, and of course I must know best.
You are not to have anything to say to the boys. Any one
else you like. I am sure I don't mind, but will do anything I
can to help—but not the boys. Oh, I know something about
Harry. I know you have had the sense to—— Well, I
don't understand how far it went, but I suppose it must have
gone as far as it could go, for he's not clever enough to be put
off with anything less than a real No. But you may have
changed your mind, or a hundred things might happen. And
then there's Edward; Aunt Catherine would be wild if anything got up between you and Edward. Oh, I think it's
always best to speak plain, and then one has nothing to
reproach one's self with after. She would just be *wild*, you
know. She thinks there is nobody good enough for him; and
you and she have never got on. Oh, I don't suppose there's
anything between you and Edward. I never said so; the
only thing is you must promise me to have nothing to say to
them. There are plenty of others—much better matches, and
more eligible: and it's always a pity to have anything to say
to a cousin in that way. You're sure to set the family by

the ears ; and then it narrows the connection, and you keep
always the same name; and there are ever so many drawbacks.
So just you promise me, Hester, there's a dear—never," said
Ellen, seizing her with both hands, and giving her a sudden
perfumy kiss, "never!" and the salute was repeated on the
other cheek, "to have *anything* to say to the boys——"

"The boys! if you think I care anything for the boys!
I shall have nothing to say to anybody," cried Hester, with
indignation, drawing herself out of this too urgent embrace.
Ellen tossed back all her bracelets, and shook her golden
locks and her sealskin hat, and made an agitation in the air
of scent and sound and movement.

"Oh, that's being a great deal too good," she cried.

Hester stood at the door, and looked on while Mrs. Algernon
got into her victoria and drew the fur rug over her, and was
driven away, waving the hand and the bracelets in a parting
jingle.   The girl was not envious, but half-contemptuous,
feeling herself in her poverty as much superior to this butterfly in furs and feathers, as pride could desire. Hester did little
credit to the social gifts, or the popularity or reputed clever-
ness in her own way, of her gay cousin who had been the
inspiration of Harry, and now was the guide of Algernon
Merridew. She said to herself with the downrightness of youth,
that Ellen was a little fool. But her own cheeks were blazing
with this parting dart which had been thrown at her. The
boys! She had a softened feeling of amity towards Harry,
who had done all a stupid young man could do to overcome
the sentence of disapproval under which Hester was aware she
lay. It had been embarrassing and uncomfortable, and had
made her anything but grateful at the moment ; but now she
began to feel that Harry had indeed behaved like a man, and
done all that a man could to remedy her false position, and
give her a substantial foundation for the native indomitable
pride which none of them could crush, though they did their
best. No ; she would have nothing to say to Harry. She
shook her head to herself, and laughed at the thought, all in
the silence of the verandah, where she stood hazily gazing
out through the dim greenish glass at Ellen, long after Ellen
had disappeared. But Edward! that was a different matter
altogether. She would give no word so far as he was concerned. Edward was altogether different from Harry. He
piqued and excited her curiosity ; he kept her mind in a
tremor of interest. She could not cease thinking of him,

when she was in his neighbourhood, wondering what he would
do, what he would say. And if it did make Catherine *wild*,
as Ellen said, that was but an inducement the more in Hester's
indignant soul. She had no wish to please Catherine Vernon.
There had not been any love lost between them from the first,
and Hester was glad to think she was not one of those who
had in any way pretended to her kinswoman's favour. She
had never sought Catherine, never bowed the knee before her.
When she went to the Grange it had been against her will, as
a matter of obedience to her mother, not to Catherine. If it
made Catherine wild to think that there was a friendship, or
any other sentiment between Edward and the girl whom she
had so slighted, then let Catherine be wild. That was no
motive to restrain Hester's freedom of action. All this
passed through her mind as she stood in the verandah in
the cold, gazing after Ellen, long after Ellen was out of sight.
There were many things which gave her a sort of attraction
of repulsion to Edward. He had tried to deceive Roland
Ashton about her, telling him she was about to marry Harry,
when he knew very well she had refused to marry Harry.
Why had he done it ? And in his manner to herself Edward
was two men. When they were alone he was more than
friendly ; he was tender, insinuating, anxious for her approval,
eager to unfold himself to her. But when he saw her in the
Grange drawing-room he never went near her. In early times
she had asked why, and he had answered with deceiving
words, asking how she thought he could bear to approach her
with commonplace civilities when she was the only creature
in the place for whom he cared at all, a speech which had
pleased Hester at first as something high-flown and splendid,
but which had not preserved its effect as time went on : for
she could not see why he should not be civil, and show some
regard for her presence, even if he could not devote himself
to her. And why could he not devote himself to her ?
Because it would displease Catherine. When Catherine was
not present, there was nobody for him but Hester. When
Catherine was there, he was unconscious of her existence.
This, of course, should have shown clearly to Hester that he
was not worthy of her regard, and to some degree did so.
But the conviction was mingled with so lively a curiosity in
respect to him, so strong an opposition as regarded her, that
Hester's moral judgment was confused altogether. She was
anxious, eager to overcome her adversary, excited to know

what Edward's meaning was. He would not stand up for her like a true friend, but at the same time he would never let her alone, he would still let her see that she was in his mind. She disliked him, yet—— She almost loved him, but still—— Nothing could be more tantalising, more entirely unlike indifference. To think of meeting Edward in society, yet not under Catherine's eye, made her heart beat loudly. She had never done this hitherto. She had met him by chance on the Common or in the country roads about, and his voice had been almost that of a lover. She had met him before the world, and he had scarcely seemed to know her. But how could these meetings test what he meant ? This it was that made Ellen's proposal exciting, even while she herself half scorned it.   Harry ? no !   Poor Harry ! she would not disturb his peace, nor say a word, nor even look a look which should put him in jeopardy. But Edward ? -ah ! that was a different matter. It was with all the vehemence of a quarrel that she snatched at the chance put into her hands, even when she had seemed to scorn it. To know what he meant—to know what was his real state of mind. If he would be afraid of what the world would say, as well as of what Catherine would say. In that case there was no scorn which Hester did not feel herself capable of pouring out upon her unworthy admirer ; but if things proved different ? Ah ! then she did not know what softening, what yielding, she might not be capable of. The very thought melted her heart.

And yet she had thought herself more " interested " (this was what she called it) in Roland Ashton than in any man whom she had ever heard of before. The world had seemed all blank to her when he went away. His step at the door had made her heart thrill : the commonplace day had brightened up into something smiling and sweet when he came in. But then she had not been fighting a duel with him half her life as she had been doing with Edward. She was not curious, *intriguée*, to know what Roland meant. She thought (with a blush) that she did know—more or less—what he meant. But Edward was a sort of sphinx ; he was an enemy to be beaten, a riddle to be read. She said to herself, what would please her best, would be to force him into self-abandonment, to carry him so out of himself that he should give up all pretences and own himself at her disposal, and then to turn her back upon him and scorn him. Would she have done so ? she thought she would, and that in this lay the secret of her interest in Edward and his crooked ways. And now, here was the trial approaching. She would see what was his true mettle, she would be able indeed to judge of him now.

"Hester," said Mrs. John appearing at the open door, "what do you mean by lingering in the cold, to get your death? You will be chilled to your very bones. You have not even a shawl on, and in this cold place. What are you doing? I have called you three times, and you never paid any attention. Even to stand here for five minutes freezes me."

"Then don't stand here, mamma," said Hester, taking hold of her mother's arm and thus leading her back in the old way. They did not walk about very much together now. Hester preferred her own thoughts to her mother's society, and Mrs. John was not sorry to be left quietly by herself at the fireside. How long it seemed since the time when she held her mother's arm clasped in hers whenever she moved, and used it as a helm to guide that timid and trustful woman wherever she would! A little compunction came over her as she made use of that well-known expedient again, and steered her mother (all the more gently for that thought) back to her own chair.

"Yes, yes, dear, this is very comfortable," said Mrs. John, "but I wish you had come at once, when I called you, for we must not lose any time in thinking about your dresses. You must do Ellen credit, that is one thing clear. I can't have you dowdy, Hester. The Merridew girls shall not have a word to say about the Vernons on your account. Oh, I know they will if they can; they will whisper and say how proud we all are, and give ourselves airs, and just look at Hester in a washed muslin! I would rather go without my dinner," said Mrs. John with vehemence, "for a whole year."

"But I shall not let you do that, mamma."

"Oh, Hester, just hold your tongue. What do you know about it? I would rather sell my Indian shawl, or my pearls—Dear me, what a good thing I did not part with my pearls! that is something nobody can turn up their noses at. And you can say you got them from your mother, and your grandmother before her—which is more than they ever had. But there are the dresses to be thought of," said the tender mother, looking in Hester's face, half awed, half appealing: for even in the pride of descent she was forced to remember that you cannot send your child to a *Thé Dansante* with nothing but a string

of pearls round her neck, however fine, and however long in
the family it may have been.

"Dresses! one will do," said Hester, with a little flush of
pleasure, yet determination to repress her mother's unnecessary
liberality. "You forget what you are talking of, mother dear.
One dress is as much as——"

"And to whom do you suppose you are speaking," said
Mrs. John with dignity; "there are a great many things which
you think you know better than I. Perhaps you are wrong there
too; but I am not going to bandy words with you. One thing
I must say, that when we talk of ball-dresses I know a great
deal better than you. Oh, but I do—I had to get everything
for myself in old days. Your father delighted in seeing me
fine, but he never pretended to have any taste. All the responsibility was on me. Considering that we are poor, and
that you are so young, I should think tulle would do: or even
tarlatan. Hester, I should like you to have silk slips, that
gives a character to a thing at once. A white one, a pink
one, and a blue one——"

"Dear mamma, a white frock, that is all I want. I am
sure that is all I want; we can't afford any more. And as
for silk slips——"

"Oh, hold your tongue, Hester, what do you know about
it?" cried Mrs. John, exasperated. "You have never been at
a ball in your life. You can't know what's wanted, like me.
There are quantities of other things besides. Shoes—you
must have satin shoes and silk stockings, and gloves, and something to wear in your hair. I don't even know what's worn
now. We used to have wreaths in my day, but perhaps that's
not the fashion at present. When I had not a maid—and of
course, poor child, you have no maid—I used to have a hair-
dresser to do my hair when I was going out. We wore it
quite high on the top of our heads, and now you wear it down
in the nape of your neck. What a thing fashion is! We
had gigot sleeves all puffed out with feather cushions,
and I used to wear a lace scarf which was very becoming.
We had muslins in my time, nice clear book-muslins, and
when you had worn it two or three times for balls you just
wore it out in the evenings at home. Tarlatan is not half
so profitable," said Mrs. John, with a very serious face, "but
you must have it, I suppose, all the same."

"Mother," said Hester, when her mother paused for breath,
"I feel quite horrified at all this. Why should I dress up so

fine for Ellen's parties? I shall only be a sort of poor
relation. My washed muslin will do very well. Nobody will
expect anything better from me."

"Then that is just why you shall have something better,"
said the poor lady, her pale countenance brightening with a
pretty pink flush. "You shan't go at all if you can't go as
my daughter should. You shall have a white first, and then
a—no, not a pink; pink used to be my colour, for you know
I was pale, and my hair was plain brown, not like yours.
Yours is a little too—auburn—for pink. You must have a
blue for your second, with silk slips made very simply, and
tarlatan over that. White shoes, and white gloves, and my
pearls. Oh, how glad I am I kept my pearls! It will be
such a pleasure, dear, to see you dressed, it will be like old
times again. And you must ask Ellen what to wear in your
hair, a wreath, or just one flower at the side, with a spray
hanging down over your neck. Mr. Ashton, I am sure, would
get it for me in town. For flowers and those sort of things
one should always send to London. And you must have a
fan. I wonder if my ivory fan would be old-fashioned? I
must ask Ellen. And, dear child, don't stand there doing
nothing when there is not a moment to lose, but ring for the
tea. We must have tea first. I always feel better after, and
then we must put everything down upon paper, and calculate
what it will cost, and how we are to do."

"I don't want all that," said Hester again : but the sound
of it flattered her youthful ears; for she was only a girl, when
all was said.

"Don't talk any nonsense, child, but ring for the tea," said
Mrs. John, feeling herself for once mistress of the occasion.
"But Hester," she added in so solemn a tone that Hester
came back half frightened to hear what it was, "if you ever
have children, as I hope you will, be sure you have one of your
girls taught how to cut out, and to look after the dressmaking.
If we only could have them made at home, what a saving it
would be!"

CHAPTER XXIII.

THE FIRST OF THEM.

YOUNG Mrs. Merridew's *Thés Dansantes* made a great commotion in Redborough. Dancing teas—what did it mean? It meant some nonsense or other. You might be sure it meant nonsense of some kind, as it was Ellen Vernon that was at the bottom of it, the elder people said; but the younger ones were of a different opinion. It did not matter to them so much that Ellen Vernon was silly; indeed the greater part of them were so dazzled by the furs and the bracelets and the victoria, if not by the brilliant fairness and beaming smiles and prettiness of the bride, that they did not remember Ellen Vernon had been silly, and thought Mrs. Algernon Merridew not only the leader of fashion, but the most amiable and good-natured of all queens of society, the most "easy to get on with" and most full of "go." Nothing like her and her dresses, and her house, and her company had ever been seen in the quiet, steady-going country town. She made it known graciously, that she was always at home at lunch, and there was scarcely a day that a merry party did not assemble at her house, filling the newly-furnished pretty room with chatter and laughter, and all the distracting devices of careless youth to get rid of a few of its golden hours. And already there had been half a dozen dinners, far too soon and quite unnecessary, as all the elders said. She ought to have waited until everybody had given her and her husband a dinner before she began to return their hospitalities. But Ellen had no idea either of waiting or returning the heavy dinners to which she, as a daughter of one of the reigning houses of the town, and her husband as belonging, if not to that rank, at least to the foremost respectability, were invited by all the principal people. The entertainments she gave were

reckless young dinners, where there was no solemnity at all,
and perhaps not much wit, but where laughter abounded and
all sorts of wild schemes of pleasure were invented. And just
as the solid people who had made a point of having a dinner
for the Algernon Merridews began to feel a little offended
at the goings-on of the young household which paid no attention to ordinary rules of civility, the younger portion of the
population was thrown into the wildest excitement by the
announcement of the *Thés Dansantes,* and frowning mothers
were courted to smiles again, by the anticipated pleasure of
their children. The old Merridews, the father and mother,
looked on with pride but misgiving, the brothers and sisters
with pride and delight, as they felt themselves already rising
high upon the topmost wave of society by means of their
brilliant sister-in-law.

"Only mind what you are about and keep hold on the
reins, my boy," old Merridew said to his son, which Algernon
promised with a laughing "Trust me for that."

"Trust Algey, indeed!" his mother said, shaking her head.
"I would not trust him a step further that I saw him
with that crazy little thing by the side of him; all my
hope is that being a Vernon her people will step in." They
were all sure that no great harm could happen to a Vernon
in Redborough. Harry, her brother, was always at her side, as
faithful as her husband, backing her up. And Catherine
herself could not disapprove, for she went to the house now
and then, and laughed when she was spoken to on the subject.
"Ellen was always like that," she said, "wild for pleasure
and amusement. She has asked me to her dancing teas,
as an entertainment quite suited to my years and habits." All
which things reassured the Merridews and the other anxious
persons about.

"And you are going to this dancing tea?" Catherine
Vernon said.

"I suppose so," said Edward, indifferently. "They would
think it strange if I did not go. And they expect you—
Merridew told me so. He said it would add such dignity to
their little party!"

There was something in the tone with which Edward said
this which Catherine did not like. It was true that she herself had always represented the invitation as ludicrous, yet it
was quite true that her presence would have added dignity to
the party, and there was nothing ridiculous in the idea that

Algernon Merridew thought so. This annoyed her a little,
but it was the annoyance of a moment. She said, "I
hope you will enjoy yourself," with a laugh, which Edward
on his side found as offensive: but he did not betray
this, and smiled in reply, as he knew she meant him to smile,
with a sort of apologetic indulgent air.

"I shall do the best I can," he said, and they both laughed.
She tenderly, thinking how good he was to take this trouble
in order to gratify the frivolous young pair and keep up the
Vernon traditions; he with a fierce question to herself, why
shouldn't he enjoy it? at least it would be an evening to himself, with nobody to keep watch over him and make a note of
every girl he danced with. Alas for Catherine! if she noticed
the girls he danced with it was in order to invite them afterwards (if she approved of them), for she had no jealous desire
to keep him to herself, but wanted him to marry. But then
there was one at least whom she could never have tolerated.
And the chief point in Edward's anticipations, as in Hester's,
was the freedom of intercourse permitted under Ellen's easy
young wing, and the opportunity he would have of seeing how
the eager, large-eyed girl would look among other girls, when
he could approach her freely. This gave him something of
the same sense of curiosity which was so warm in Hester's
mind. How would she look among other girls—how would
she receive him? It did not occur to him as probable that she
would resent that avoidance of her when under Catherine's
eye, which he had so often assured her made him wretched.
He felt that the little secret between them, the stolen glance
he would give her at the Grange parties, the little shrug with
which he pointed her attention to his bondage, would have an
attraction even greater than had he been always at her side;
and in some sense this was true. But he did not think of
Hester's judgment and of the natural indignation of her high
spirit; neither did he think of the comparison she made
between him and Harry, who had never hesitated to show his
devotion. To compare himself and Harry, seemed to Edward
impossible. A big idiot—a nonentity. She had more sense
than that.

Never was there such a spectacle seen in Redborough as the
first of the *Thés Dansantes*. The Merridews' house was near
the White House, and consequently on a little eminence, which
answered all the purposes of a great eminence in that flat
country. It stood in the midst of a little shrubbery above

which it rose on white steps, to make the position still more commanding. There was a long domed conservatory at one side, the windows were all plate glass, and when you consider that within and without the place was lighted up—like the Crystal Palace, people said—you may imagine something of the imposing effect. The conservatory was all hung with Chinese lanterns, and was fairy land to the young guests inexperienced in such glorious effects; the two drawing-rooms were both thrown open for dancing. There were very few chaperons; only here and there a middle-aged mother, too devoted to her charge, yawned behind her fan with nobody to speak to, not a lady of her own age to exchange experiences with, no elderly gallant to get her a cup of tea. All was youth, rampant, insolent, careless—feeling that the world was made for it, and rejoicing to shake itself free of every trammel. Mrs. Ellen set them the example in the most daring way.

"What do we want with the old things here?" she said; "they would much rather be in bed, and the best place for them. I don't suppose you mean to do anything wrong, any of you girls, and if you did they wouldn't stop you. If you can't take care of yourselves, if you want a chaperon, there's me. And there's Fanny Willoughby, and Lilian Melville, and Maud Seton; they've all been married as long as I have. Where could you find steadier married women? and ain't we enough to chaperon a couple of dozen of girls? I never pretend to ask old people, unless it was just to let them see how everything looks, poor old things, once in a way."

This being the creed of the mistress of the feast, it is not to be supposed that her disciples were more catholic. And there was no limit to the fun which the young people promised themselves. To do them justice, it was very innocent fun. The greatest sin on the conscience of the wildest romp in the place was that of having danced ten times with a favourite partner, besides sitting out all the square dances (of which there were only two) in his company. Algernon himself had insisted upon two. He said it was respectable: and he danced both with the least popular of the young ladies, that they might not feel themselves slighted, for he was a very good fellow.

"Did you ever see such a muff?" his wife said, who never condescended to the Lancers. "I do believe he likes to hop about with the ugliest thing he can pick up. I thought I had kept out all the ugly girls, but I haven't succeeded. If there is one, Algey is sure to find her out."

"To show you that you have no need to be jealous," some one said.

"Oh, *jealous!*" cried Ellen, with supreme disdain.

The young Merridews, brothers and sisters, thought her the most wonderful creature that had ever been born. Her light hair was in curls and frizzes (newly come in and extremely captivating) all over her head. Her dress was a sort of purple, a colour nobody but herself ventured to wear, but which threw up her fairness with the most brilliant effect. She had all her jewellery on, from the diamonds Harry had spent all his available money (under her own directions) in buying for her, to the little bracelet contributed by the clerks at the bank. Her arm was covered nearly up to the elbow, and the sound she made when they fell over her hands and she had to push them back again was wonderful. It was like a whole concert of fairy music, the bangles representing the higher notes, the big golden manacles furnishing a bass. She liked to hold up her hands and shake them back with a pretty little cry of "Tiresome! Why is one forced to wear all this upon one?" Ellen said.

And Mrs. John had accomplished her wish. She had got, if not three, at least two new dresses for Hester, one upon her shoulders at this moment, the other, the blue one, laid up all ready in the box. White of course was the first. It had the silk slip upon which Mrs. John had set her heart, which was so much more thrifty than anything else, which could be covered over and over again, as she pointed out to her daughter, and which at the present moment was veiled in floods and billows of tarlatan. Tarlatan was the fashion of those days: anything that was limp, that took—as people now love to say, "nice folds," being considered utterly dowdy. And when Hester appeared in those crisp puffings, with her pearls round her throat, and white flowers in the hair which her mother called auburn, even young Mrs. Merridew herself held her breath. She turned her cousin round and round to examine her.

"Well, I call that a *beautiful* dress," she said. "Who put it into your head to get a dress like that? Why, it is the height of the fashion! Those *bouillonées* are just the right thing to wear. And do you mean to say these are real pearls? Oh, go away, or I shall kill you! Why have not I pearls? They are far more *distingués*—oh, far more!—than my paltry bits of diamonds. Oh, take her away, or I shall

not be able to keep my hands off her. And such flowers!
they must have come from Forster's. I am certain they came
from Forster's. Mine are French, but they are not so pretty,"
Ellen said.

Hester stood and smiled while these comments were made,
though with a half sense of shame. She thought it annoyed
her very much to be subjected to such a survey, and so no
doubt it would have done had not the result been so satisfactory; but it is hard to be really displeased by approbation.

As for Ellen, she whispered behind her hand to Harry,
"The old lady must have a great deal more than we think for.
She must have been saving up. You don't get a dress like
that for nothing."

"It's not the dress—she always looks nice, whatever she
puts on," said faithful Harry.

His sister contemplated him with eyes full of contempt.
"What is the use of talking to such a silly?" she said.
"Not the dress! She never looked one ten-thousandth part
so well all her life, and that you know just as well as me."

No, she had never looked so well all her nineteen years.
Her dress was simple indeed, but it was perfect in all its
details, for Mrs. John had remembered everything. The
flowers were artificial, which also was the fashion then, but
they were from Forster's, procured by Roland Ashton and
brought down by his sister Emma, who had arrived that
same afternoon. The pearls were beautiful, more beautiful
than any other ornament in the room. Hester stood beside
her cousin to receive the guests with a sense that there were
no imperfections about her. In the days of the washed
muslin there was always a fear that the flounces were not
quite even, the bows not quite firmly sewed on, or something
else which at any moment might come to pieces and betray
the home-madeness of the garment. But she stood up in her
virgin robes with a sense of delightful security—a knowledge
that all was complete, which was exhilarating to her spirits.
She was not the one white swan in this little provincial
party: there were faces quite as lovely as Hester's, which,
as a matter of fact, was not so perfect as her dress; but there
was no one to whom the anticipated pleasure was so entirely
ideal. Her mind did not come down to practical delights at
all. She was going to be happy—was she going to be happy?
How does it feel to be happy? These were the questions in
her mind. She had been so, she was aware, as children are,

without knowing it; but this would be conscious, whatever it was.

The dancing began. It was a very pretty scene, and Hester, not in herself perhaps so overwhelmingly gay as the others about her, was caught upon that stream of careless youth and carried with it in spite of herself. An atmosphere of pleasure was about her; eyes looked upon her admiring, almost caressing, every glance was pleasant; the rougher part of the world had disappeared altogether. It was as if there was nothing but merry dancers, laughing engagements, an interchange of enjoyment, all about. Happy! Well, she could not say that this was not happiness. It might be so, for anything she could tell. There was not much that was ideal about it, but yet——. Just as she was thinking this, she felt in a moment of repose her hand suddenly taken, drawn into some one else's hand : and, looking round suddenly, saw Edward close to her, looking at her with a subdued glow in his eyes, a look of admiration and wonder. It was quite a steady, straightforward gaze—not furtive, not flying. She started at the touch and look, and attempted to draw away her hand, but it was held fast. But he had not lifted her hand, he had taken it where it hung half-veiled by her furbelows, and he had turned his back towards the company isolating her in a corner, while he inspected her. He drew a long breath apparently of satisfaction and pleasure.

"I am late," he said, "but this was worth waiting for. Cinderella, where have you left your pumpkin coach ?"

Hester's brow grew dark, her heart seemed to swoon away in her bosom altogether, then came to itself again with a rush of heat and indignation. She wrenched her hand out of that hold, a flood of colour came to her cheeks.

"I suppose you mean to insult me," she said ; "but this is not a place to insult me—I am among friends here."

"Why do you say so, Hester ? Insult you ? What an ungenerous thing to say ! as if I was in the habit of doing so, and must not here because you have friends. What a cruel thing to say !"

"Would you rather have it in your power to insult me always ? " said Hester. Her lip began to quiver a little. What an odious thing it is to be a woman, to be always ready when you would rather not, when you want to show yourself most strong and angry, to cry ! She clenched her hands tightly to keep herself down. "I am no cinderwench, Mr. Edward Vernon," she said. "I have given you no reason to call me so. It is a pitiful thing for a man to notice a girl's dress. If I am dressed poorly, I am not ashamed of it. It is not a sin to be poor."

"Hester! a girl of your sense to be so foolish! How could I mean that? What I meant was, that you have come out glorious, like the moon from the clouds. Nothing could be sweeter than that little house-frock you used to wear out on the Common. I liked it better than all the finery. But to-night you·are like a young princess. Why did I say Cinderella? Heaven knows; just because I was dazzled and bewildered, and because you are a princess; and the pleasure of seeing you made my head go round. Have I made my peace? Well, then, there's a darling, turn round and let me see you, that I may see all the finery, and everything that makes you so lovely, in detail."

"You may have made it a little better," said Hester; "but why do you go on talking like that? I am neither lovely nor a darling; and you shall not say so—you! that would not see me if this, instead of being Ellen's house, were the Grange."

"You have me at your mercy there," said Edward. "I confess you have me at your mercy, there."

Upon which Hester melted a little, and, perceiving the abashed look which he had put on, began to falter, and presently found herself guilty of the commonplace expedient of asking if he did not think it a pretty scene.

"Oh, very pretty," said Edward; "that is to say, I don't know anything about it. I looked for one individual when I came in, and as—as soon as I found her, she began to bully me violently, I feel a little muddled, and don't know what to think. Give me a little time."

By this time, as was natural, Hester began to think herself a monster of folly and unkindness, and to feel that she was ready to sink through the floor with shame.

"I did not mean to be cross," she said. "I thought—that is, I had been looking—that is——"

Here she stopped, feeling herself get deeper and deeper into difficulty. Her countenance changed from the girlish freshness of complexion, which everybody admired, into a burning red; her eyelids unable to keep up, her heart beating as if it would burst through silk slip, and tarlatan *bouillonée*, and all——

"Come, let us have this dance. I like the music," said Edward, drawing her hand suddenly through his arm.

"But I am engaged."

"Oh, never mind, if you are engaged. You were engaged to me before ever you came," he said, lightly, and drew her into the whirl. Hester was at the age (in society) when, to throw over a partner, looks like the guiltiest treachery. She could not take any pleasure in the dance, for thought of it.

"I must go and ask his pardon. I am sure I am very sorry. I did not intend to be so false; and there he is, poor man, not dancing."

These words Hester said breathless over the shoulder of the enterprising intruder, who had carried her off under the victim's eyes.

"Poor man!" Edward echoed, with a laugh. "I am glad he has nobody to dance with. What right had he to engage you? and you regret him; and you don't want me."

Here Hester rebuked her cousin.

"You have no right to say so. I might want—I mean I might like very well to dance with you when you condescended to ask me; but not to be run away with, without a word, and made to do a false thing. False things are what I hate."

"You say that with such meaning. You must be thinking of more than a dance. Am I one of the false things you hate?"

"I do not hate you," said Hester, as they came to a pause, looking doubtfully into his face; "but I do not think you are very true."

"You mean I don't blurt out everything I mean, and am capable now and then of keeping something to myself. I can keep my own counsel—not like that fellow there," Edward permitted himself to say: which was a mistake; for Hester looked up and saw the gaze of honest Harry dwelling upon her with some regret, and much tenderness, and was touched at once with sympathy and indignation.

"If you mean Harry, no one could ever doubt *him*," said Hester, in the warmth of her compunction. "If he is your friend, he is always your friend. He is not afraid of what any one says."

"Ah, Hester, you are always harping on that string," said Edward. "I know what you mean; but can't you understand the position I am in, and understand *me*? Don't you know I am in bondage. I cannot say my soul is my own. I dare not think nor feel but as I am told. If I were to follow my own heart without disguise, I think it would be my ruin. We will

not name any names, but you know. And I know what you
think about that big stupid there, but you are mistaken. It
is not that his heart is more true. It is that he has not
brains enough to see what is liked and what is not liked. He
is not even sympathetic enough. He does what he likes, and
never considers if it is good for him or not."

"Sympathetic !" cried Hester. "He is sympathetic with
me. When he sees me lonely and neglected he comes and
stands beside me. If he cannot do more, he does do that. I
don't pretend to say that he is very amusing," she continued,
with a laugh, "but he does what he can. He stands by me.
Oh! failing other things that are better, I like that. Rather
than being sympathetic with Catherine, I like him to sympathise
with me."

"There is no question of names," said Edward. "We must
not get personal. But I am glad you find Harry amusing. I
never heard that he was so before. He is standing by Ellen
now ; that's what he's here for. They will come to grief, these
young people. They are beginning a great deal too fast.
You know young Merridew, or old Merridew either, can never
keep up this. Ellen ought to know better. But Harry will
have scope for this great accomplishment that you appreciate
so highly. He will have to stand by his sister."

" And he will," Hester said.

She scarcely thought of the dancing, so much did this conversation—so unlike a conversation to be carried on in the
whirl of a waltz—occupy her. It occurred to her now, as
breath failed her, to remember how in all the accounts of a
first ball she had ever read, the heroine had felt all other
sentiments melt away in the rapturous pleasure of dancing
with the man of her heart. Novels were all Hester's experience. She remembered this, and it gave her a half comic,
half miserable sensation to realise that she was not thinking
about the dancing at all. She was carrying on her duel with
Edward. There was always a warm sense of gratification in
that—a stirring up of all her faculties. She liked to go on
carrying it a step further, defying and puzzling him, and
wondering on his side how much he meant, how much that he
left to be inferred, was true. The heroine in a novel is generally the point of everybody's admiration in the ball-room,
and to look at the perfection of the waltz which she and her
lover enjoy so deeply, the whole assemblage stands still. But
nothing of this kind occurred in Hester's case. As she had

so little experience, the chances are that she was by no means
the best dancer in the room, and certainly Edward was not
the other best.   Their waltz was the means of carrying on
the discussion which to both was the most attractive possibility.   When she realised this, Hester was a little amused,
but likewise a good deal disappointed. She felt a disagreeable
limit thus placed to her power to enjoy.

"Come into the conservatory," Edward said. "Don't you
think you have had enough? Oh, it is your first ball. I
suppose you like it ; but I am beginning to lose my relish
for those sort of affairs."

"You are not so old that you should give up dancing,
Cousin Edward."

"Old! No, I hope I am not old yet, and I don't intend to give
up dancing ; but I like to walk here better—with you. I like
to talk better—with you. I like to see your face, Hester, and
see how it changes from kindness to wrath, from friendship to
indignation, from a patient sense that I am endurable, to a
violent consciousness——Come and sit here."

"You seem to think I never do anything but think of you :
and that is the greatest mistake," Hester said.

Upon which he laughed.   The place he had led her to was
only partially lighted.   There were many other groups
scattered about among the plants and stands of flowers.
Flirtation was openly recognised in this youthful house as one
of the portions of the evening's entertainment, and large
provision made for it. There was nobody to notice with whom
it was that Edward was amusing himself, and he felt fully
disposed to take advantage of his opportunities. He laughed at
Hester's indignant disclosures. "If you did not think a little
about me, dear, you would not notice so distinctly my course
of conduct in other places, you could not be sure that it was
much more agreeable to me, instead of standing by your
side and trying to be as amusing as Harry, to lead down Mrs.
Houseman and old Lady Kearney to supper or to tea."

"My mother should go out of the room before either of
them," cried Hester.   "Do you know who she is? Sir John
Westwood is her cousin : a duke's daughter once married into
her family——"

"I quite understand you and agree with you, Hester. It is
nothing that she is a perfect little gentlewoman, and has far
better manners than any of us ; but because she is cousin to a
heavy baronet, who is not good enough to tie her shoe——"

"Edward!" The girl was so startled she could not believe her ears.

"Oh, I know very well what I am saying. You don't know me, that is all. You think I am a natural snob, when I am only a snob by circumstances. You yourself, Hester, do you really think your mother should stand upon her cousin and upon Lady Ethelinda (or whatever was her name), her great-grandmother, and not upon herself far better than either? I can't imagine you think that."

Hester was surprised and silenced for the moment. She had been so often reminded of the noble grandmother and the baronet cousin, and so hard put to it to find a ground of superiority on which her pride could take refuge, that this sudden appeal to her better judgment bewildered her. She was startled to find those advantages which were indisputable, and to which everybody deferred in theory, so boldly undervalued; but yet the manner of doing it made her heart beat with pleasure. Yes; people thought her dear little mother silly, and Hester was aware that she was not clever. Sometimes, in the depths of her own soul, she had chafed, as children will, at the poor lady's dulness and slowness of comprehension; but she *was* a perfect little gentlewoman. And he saw it! He felt in his heart that she was above them all—not because of Lady Ethelinda (she was Lady Sarah in reality) and Sir John, but herself.

"I did not know you were a Radical," she said. She knew nothing about Radicals, though instinctively in her heart she agreed with them. "I thought you cared for family and that sort of thing."

"Do you?"

Hester paused. She flung higher her young head, which was proud with life and a sense of power unknown. "I should like to be a king's daughter," she said, "or a great soldier's or a statesman's. I should like my name to mean something. I should like people to say, when they hear it, that is——"

"But you don't care much about Sir John?—that is what I thought. I am no Radical; I am all for decorum and established order and church and state. How could you doubt that? But, by the way, there is a person whom neither of us like, who certainly has the kind of rank you prize. Don't you know who I mean, Hester? When a stranger comes to Redborough, there is one name he is sure to hear. If she were a duchess she could not be better known. To be her relation carries a certain weight. We were always a leading family in the place, I suppose. But why are we, for instance, so much better than the Merridews and all the rest of the respectable people? She has something to do with it, I can't deny, though I don't like her any more than you."

"Edward," cried Hester breathlessly, "about that we ought to understand each other. I have no reason to like Catherine. Yes, I will say her name; why shouldn't I? She has not liked me. I was only a child, and if I was saucy she might have forgiven me, all these years. But she has taken the trouble on the contrary to humiliate me, to make me feel that I am nobody, which was unworthy. But you: she has been kind to you. She has been more than kind—she has loved you. I have seen it in her eyes. She thinks that nobody is worth thinking of in comparison with you. If—if—who shall I say?—if Sir Walter Scott came here, or Mr. Tennyson, she would rather have you. And yet, you that ought to be so grateful, that ought to love her back, that ought to be proud—oh, I should if I were you. If she were fond of me I should be proud. I hate all those wretched people who take from her hand, and then sneer and snarl at her, like dogs—no, not like dogs : dogs are far nobler—like cats ; that is better."

Hester's eyes were shining with eloquence and ardour ; the little movement of her head so proud, so animated, so full of visionary passion, threw back and gave a certain freedom to the hair which her mother called auburn. Her whole figure was full of that force and meaning which is above beauty. Edward looked at her with smiling admiration. If his conscience was touched, or his temper at least, he did not show it.

"Do you call me a cat?" he said.

"Oh, I am not in fun. I am as earnest as ever I can be. It is wicked, it is miserable, and I cannot understand you. All the others are as nothing in comparison with you."

He grew a little pale under this accusation ; he would not meet it directly. "But you know," he said, "why she hates you. It is for your mother's sake."

"My mother!" cried Hester astonished. "But no one could hate my mother." The suggestion took away her breath.

"It is true, all the same. I thought you did not know. She was to have married John Vernon, your father, and he preferred——that is the whole account of it ; then he got into trouble, and she had her revenge."

"Did she ruin-my father?" said Hester in a low whisper of horror.

"I—don't know if it went so far as that," Edward said.

A hesitation was in his speech. It was scarcely compunction, but doubt, lest a statement of this kind, so easily to be contradicted, might be injudicious on his part—but then, who would speak to Hester on such a subject? And her mother was a little fool, and, most likely, did not know, or would be sure to mistake, the circumstances.

"Don't let us talk of that: it is so long past," he said; "and here is a wretch, a scoundrel, coming up with his eye fixed upon you as if he was a partner. How I loath all your partners, Hester! Mind, the rest of the dances are for me. I shall watch for you as soon as you have shaken that fellow off."

But Hester did not care for the dances that followed. She went through them indifferently, faithful to the partners who had presented themselves before he came on the scene; and, indeed, the conversation in the conservatory had not drawn her nearer to Edward. It had given her a great deal to think of. She had not time in the whirl and fluster of this gaiety to think it all out.

CHAPTER XXIV.

A NEW COMPETITOR.

EMMA ASHTON had brought Hester's flowers, and though she was tired with her journey, had taken a great deal of interest in Hester's dress. When she came in to show herself to the old people in her white robes before her ball, the stranger had surveyed her with much attention. She had kissed her slowly and deliberately when introduced to her.

"Roland told me a great deal about you," she said. "I suppose we are cousins too. You look very nice. I hope you will enjoy yourself." She was a very deliberate, measured talker, doing everything steadily. When Hester was gone, she resumed her seat beside her grandmother.

"Roland admires her very much. She is pretty, but I should think she had a great deal of temper," Emma said.

"Temper is scarcely the word. She is a great favourite with your grandfather—and with me too—with me too."

"Roland told me," said Emma. "When I say temper I don't mean any harm. She would do much better for Roland if she had a good deal of temper. That is what he wants to keep him straight; for a man ought not to flirt after he is married, and he will, unless she keeps him in order."

"Married! but is he likely to marry? I did not hear anything of it."

"When a man can keep a sister he can keep a wife," said Emma, announcing this fact as if it were an oracle. "He has a house, and everything that is necessary. And of course I shall not stand in his way. I can go back to Elinor, where I am a sort of head nurse, and cheap enough at the

money ; or I can be a governess. That touches his pride—he
does not like that."

Here the old captain came back, who had been putting his
favourite carefully into the fly.

" Why has she not her mother with her ? " he said. " I like
a girl to have her mother with her. It is pretty, it is natural.
I do not like those new-fashioned, independent ways."

" But they are much more convenient, grandpapa," said
Emma. " Think how I should have been situated had a girl
always wanted her mother with her. Elinor, with her family,
cannot always be going out ; and when she goes she likes to
amuse herself, she does not go for me. A girl going out with
her mother means a devoted sort of old lady like the mothers
in books. Such nonsense, you know—for a girl's mother, when
she is eighteen or so, is rarely more than forty, and people
of forty like amusement just as much as we do. It is better,
on the whole, I think, when every one is for herself."

" Well, that is not my opinion," said the old captain,
shortly.

He was accustomed to do most of the talking himself, and
it startled him to have it thus taken out of his hand.

" I suppose an invitation will come for me," said Emma
calmly, " as soon as they know I am here ; and then Hester
and I can go together. Roland said there was no dancing,
but I think it always safest to bring a ball-dress. It is not
heavy, though it takes up a good deal of room ; but then you
can always take one box into the carriage, and the railway
only charges by weight."

" Roland is very busy, I suppose, my dear. You only see
him in the evening ? "

" I don't always see him in the evening. He has his own
friends, and I am getting a few acquaintances too. If he
gives me my living and very little to do I ought to be grateful
to him, but I would not let him give up his own amusements
for me. That wouldn't be fair. Oh yes, he is very busy.
He has found so many new people to do business for down
here."

" I hope to goodness he wont speculate with their money
and ruin them," Captain Morgan said.

" Ruin ! oh, I hope not. But Roland says there is nothing
so exciting as to be on the verge of ruin. He says it is better
than a play : for instead of looking on at the acting, the acting
is going on inside of you. But it is his trade to speculate,

isn't it, grandpapa? That is what he is there for, and he is
very good at it they say. I suppose this girl has not any
money? When they are pretty and nice they seldom have."

"What girl?" said Captain Morgan, almost haughtily
—as haughtily and harshly as the old gentleman could
persuade himself to speak.

"Doesn't he know, grandmamma?" said Emma, "the girl
Roland admired so much: and she would just do for him, if
she had some money: but so nice looking as he is, and so well
established in business, I don't think, unless there is money,
he should throw himself away."

"Is it Hester Vernon that you mean?" asked the captain
in an angry voice.

"She does not mean any harm, Rowley. Don't you see
Hester is just to her an abstract person, not the dear girl she
is to you and me. And Emma," said the old lady almost
with timidity, "I fear your ball dress will not be of much use.
Mrs- Merridew will not think of inviting you—she will not
perhaps know you are here."

"Roland met her, grandmamma," said Emma calmly. "He
told me; we are all cousins, I believe. She will be sure to
invite me, or if not, you will be able to get me an invitation.
People always exert themselves to get invitations for girls.
It is like helping young men on in business. We cannot go
and make acquaintances for ourselves as young men go and
set up offices, but we must have our chance, you know, as well.
Of course," said Emma in her deliberate way, "it is for
everybody's advantage that we should have our chance as
well as the men."

" And what do you call your chance?" said Captain Morgan.
He planted himself in the front of the fireplace with his legs
very wide apart, which, as his wife well understood, meant war.

" My old man," she said, " what do you know about the
talk of girls? They have one way of thinking, and we have
another. They are young and we are old."

"Hester is younger than she is," said the captain, "let
her alone. She is as ready to talk as there is any need
to . be."

"My chance, grandpapa?" said Emma with a slow little
laugh. " It is not necessary, is it, to explain? a girl's chance
is in making—friends. If one goes for a governess one's family
does not like it. They would rather you were your sister's
head nurse with all the trouble, and without any pay. Roland

has taken me now— and I do not require to work for my living; but it is not so very cheerful with Roland that I should not wish—if I could—to make a change. We must all think of ourselves you know."

"My dear," said the old lady in her soft voice, "in one way that is very true."

"It is very true, I think, in every way. It might be cheerful for me if Roland were to spend his evenings at home as Tom Pinch in Dickens did with his sister. But then Roland is not a bit like Tom Pinch, and I said to him when I came, 'You are not to change your life for me.' So that sometimes, you know, I am in the house all alone all day, and then if he is out to dinner, or if he has any evening engagement, I am alone all the night. And if he were to marry, why there would be an end of me altogether. So you see, grandmamma, wherever I am, it is very natural that I should wish to have my chance."

"How old are you?" said the captain abruptly.

"I shall be twenty-three at Christmas," said Emma, raising her eyes to his face. She was curious to know why he asked —whether he thought her older, or younger than her age, whether he thought it was strange she should still be un-married. "I was kept very much out of sight when I was with Elinor," she said half apologetically. She had not had her "chance" as she had always wished to have. She had not been very well treated she felt in this life, the youngest of seven. She had been passed on from one to another of her married sisters to make herself useful. All of them had said that Emma must "come out," but no one had taken any trouble about it. She had to scramble for a dress, a very cheap one, and to coax Elinor into taking her to some little local merrymaking, and so opening, as it were, the gates of society. As soon as she could say that she was "out" Emma had kept the idea of having "her chance" of making friends and getting invitations always before her. But her oppor-tunities had not been great, and Elinor had not devoted herself to her younger sister. She was still young enough to amuse herself, and it had not occurred to her to put so unimportant a person as Emma in the foreground. So that she had never been allowed to have much of a "chance." Emma had not much experience of the world. Of the many novels she had read, and which were her guides to life, a great many devoted themselves to the history and description of

young ladies at whose entrance into a ball-room every man
present fell metaphorically on his knees. She was acquainted
with many evening parties in fiction at which the fate of
countless young men and women was decided. The smallest
dance would be represented there as bringing people together
who were never more to be sundered. Emma herself had
not produced any such sensation at the small parties she had
hitherto gone to, but she felt that this glory must be awaiting
her, and especially that in a new place like this Redborough,
in some waltz or other, among some unknown assembly she
should meet her fate.

This being the case, it is not to be wondered at that she
should lose no time in announcing her certainty of an invitation to anything so likely to conduce to such an object as Ellen
Merridew's dancing teas. She had come down to Redborough
prepared to be cousin to all the world. Roland, indeed, had
taken pains to explain that Catherine Vernon's cousins were
not actually *her* cousins, but she had thought it better in
many ways to ignore this, and to descend upon the new scene
with the most amiable disposition to embrace as a near
relative every Vernon presented to her. Among them all,
what could be more likely than that her fate should be found?
She meant no harm to anybody. It would be doing no harm,
certainly, if any young man fell in love with her, to make him
happy by marrying him. She felt most strongly the supreme
necessity of marrying for her own part. She had no disguise
with herself on this subject, and with her grandparents she
did not think it necessary to have any disguise. Everything
was involved in it. Roland had taken the responsibility of
her upon himself and given her a home, with very little to
do, and enough to make her sufficiently comfortable. Emma
had always been brought up to consider everything from a
strictly practical point of view. She had been taught to
believe that she had no right to anything, that it was out of
their bounty and charity that her brothers and sisters, now
one, now another, afforded her a temporary home. And she
was very comfortable with Roland—but if he were to marry,
what then? The comfort of having a home of her own, a
husband of her own with a settled income, was to Emma in
prospect the crown of all good things. She would not have
been ashamed to say so if necessary; and it was in balls and
parties and picnics and social meetings generally, that a young
woman had her chance of suddenly obtaining, by looking

pretty, by making herself agreeable, all these good things at
a stroke. She made up her mind at once that heaven and
earth must be moved to get her an invitation to Mrs.
Algernon Merridew's *Thés dansantes.* She would not take, she
said to herself, any denial. She would see all the Redborough
people there, among whom there must certainly be some in-
dividuals of the class upon which depended Emma's fate. As
she sat unfolding so much of this as was needful with a calm
confidence in being understood, her grandparents, with a sort
of stupefaction, listened and looked on. Emma was knitting
all the time in the German way, with a very slight swift movement of her fingers and without looking at her work. She
spoke slowly, with an air of such undoubted fact and practical
commonplace about her, that those two old people, who each
in their several ways indulged in fancy and sentiment, were
daunted and silenced. Emma spoke in a sort of saintly
simplicity, as not knowing that anything beyond those solid
primitive foundations, anything like sentiment or fancy, was
in the world.

She was not handsome like her brother, and yet there
was something remarkable about her appearance which
some people admired. Her hair was dark, her features
sufficiently good. The strange thing in her was her eyes,
which were very light in colour—so light, that sometimes
there seemed no colour at all in them. This was not beautiful,
but it was *bizarre* and unusual, and as such Emma had her
admirers. But it was only in this particular, not in mind
or thoughts, that there was anything in her out of the
way.

"Well ?" said the old captain to his wife, when, after
having yawned softly over her work as a signal and preparation for bed-going, Emma rose with a smile at half-past
ten, and kissed them both, and asked if she might have
her candle. "I must not keep you out of bed," she said,
with that look of complacent consideration which, notwithstanding, was quite innocent and referred to her own
circumscribed horizon, in which everything connected
with herself was well in the foreground. Mrs. Morgan
did not meet her husband's eye as she had met it when
Roland was the visitor.

"She has not been well brought up, poor thing !" the old
lady said. "She has had no one to care for her—and,
Rowley, she is our own flesh and blood."

"That's the wonderful thing," the captain said, "Katie's child! My dear, I give it up; there seems no reason and no sense in it. I cannot think what the Lord can mean."

"Oh, hush, Rowley—nothing, nothing that is not good."

"One would say—that there must be just a crowd of souls ready to put into the new little bodies, and that one must slip down before the other that ought to come;—like that vile cad, you know, that slipped into the pool of Siloam before the poor fellow that had no servant could shuffle down."

"And that was all the better for your poor fellow as it turned out, Rowley, for he got his healing more sweetly out of the very hand—— And, poor little spirit, if it was not intended for this body, I can't think it has got very much by its deceit," Mrs. Morgan said, with a little laugh.

But the captain did not laugh. There was consternation in his soul.

"A girl," he said, "with her eyes open to all chances, looking out for a husband, and seriously thinking that is the right thing to do—to come from you and me, Mary—to come from you and me!"

The old lady gave him her hands that he might help her out of her chair, and when she stood upright, tottering a little—for she was not strong upon her legs—she gave him a little playful tap with her finger upon his old cheek.

"You are just a high-flown old sentimentalist," she said. "There is no harm in her. She is only prose to your poetry—which I've always been all our lives, and you've said so many a day."

"Don't blaspheme, old woman, don't blaspheme," the captain said.

But next day, when Hester came in to give them the account—which she knew the old people would expect—of all that had happened, Emma lost no time in making her desires known.

"It must have been a very pretty party," she said; "a conservatory lighted like that is always so nice. It is cool to sit in after you have got heated with dancing. I wish I could have seen you all enjoying yourselves. I am so fond of dancing, and I don't get much; for Roland does not care for dancing parties, and at Waltham Elinor never had time. I suppose you had an invitation, grandmamma, though you are too old to go?"

Here Hester explained, wondering, that there were very few chaperons, and nobody asked but people who were known to dance.

"Ellen says it only tires the others, and what is the use?" Hester said.

"That is very true; she must be judicious—she must have right notions. When do you think my invitation will come, grandmamma? I suppose people will call when they know I am here?"

Here there was a little pause, for even Mrs. Morgan was taken aback by this question, and did not know what to say.

"I am sure," said Hester blushing, after a minute's silence, "that if Miss Ashton would—like it so very much——"

"Oh, I should, of course, *very* much. I want to know the Redborough people. I like to know the people wherever I go. It is so dull knowing no one," Emma said. "And then it would be so convenient, you know, for I could go with you——"

To this Hester did not know what to reply; but it was well in one way that the new comer took it all for granted and gave no trouble. Emma made no account of embarrassed looks and hesitating replies. She did not even notice them, but pursued her own way deliberately, impervious to any discouragement, which was more equivocal than a flat "No." She had been used to "noes" very flat and uncompromising, and everything less seemed to her to mean assent. When she had disposed, as she thought, of this question, she went on to another which was of still greater importance.

"But I cannot expect cousin Catherine to call upon me," she said composedly. "She is too old, and she is always treated as a kind of princess, Roland says. And you are too old to take me, grandmamma. Perhaps I could go with Hester. Would that be the right thing? For they all say I must not neglect cousin Catherine."

Hester looked aghast upon the young woman, who contemplated them so calmly over her knitting, and talked of neglecting Catherine, and being called upon by the sovereign of society, who left even the Redborough magnates out, and called only upon those who pleased her. Emma went on quite placidly, knitting with the ends of her fingers in that phlegmatic German way, which is an offence to English knitters. The stocking went on dropping in longer and

longer lengths from her hands, as if twirling upon a leisurely
wheel.   She had explained that they were knickerbocker
stockings, for Elinor's boys, which she was always busy
with.

"She gives me so much for them, for every dozen pairs—and
the wool ; I make a little by it, and it is much cheaper for her
than the shops."

"Your grandfather will take you—some day," said Mrs.
Morgan hastily.

"Oh, that will do very well, but it ought to be soon,"
Emma said.   She returned to the subject after Hester had
given a further account of the merrymaking of the previous
night.

"Are you all great friends ?" said Emma, "or are there
little factions as there generally are in families ?   Elinor and
William's wife used always to be having tiffs, and then the
rest of us had to take sides.   I never would.   I thought it
was wisest not.   I was nobody, you know, only the youngest.
And when one has to stay a few months here and a few
months there, without any home of one's own, it is best to
keep out of all these quarrels, don't you think, grandmamma ?
Roland said there were some old things living here, some old
maids that were spiteful."

Now it is curious enough that though the Miss Vernon-
Ridgways were not at all approved by their neighbours, it
gave these ladies a shock to hear an outsider describe them
thus.

"Never mind that," said Mrs. Morgan, almost impatiently.
"Are you going further, Hester ?   If you want my old man,
tell him not to stay out too long, for the wind is cold
to-day."

"I am going to Redborough," Hester said.   "I have some
things to do for mamma."

"Oh, you must take me with you," said Emma—"just one
moment till I have turned this heel.   I never like to leave a
heel midway.   I want to see Redborough of all things.
Grandmamma, you will not mind me leaving you—I want
to see all I can, as I don't know how long I may stay."

"Do you mind, Hester ?" the old lady said in a little
alarm, as having finished the heel, and put her knitting carefully away in a long basket made to hold the length of her
needles, Emma went up stairs to get her hat.   Hester laughed
a little and hesitated, for though she was not moved to

enthusiasm by Emma, she was young enough to like the novelty of a new companion, whoever that might be.

"I hope she will not make me take her to see Catherine. Catherine would not be very gracious to any one whom I brought her. Dear Mrs. Morgan, I wanted to ask you—Was Catherine——Did Catherine——"

" What, my dear ? "

" Nothing—I can't tell you before any one. It was something I heard from——last night. Yes, I am quite ready, Miss Ashton," Hester said.

" It is grand to be called Miss Ashton, but I wish you would say Emma. It makes me feel as if I were some one's governess when you say Miss Ashton. I nearly was," said Emma. " You know we are a large family, eight of us, and we had no money. I am sure I can't tell how we managed to grow up. It was thanks to Elinor I believe ; she was the only one who could manage papa. And now they are all provided for, but only me. Elinor and Bee made very good marriages, and Kate didn't do so badly either, but she's gone to India. The others were to help me between them, but that is not very nice. They are always scheming to have as little of you as they can, and to make the others have too much. I never would give in to that. I always kept to my day. I used to say ' No, Bee, my time is up. I don't mind where you put me (for I never made any fuss in that sort of way, it turns the servants against you), I can sleep anywhere, but you must keep your turn. Elinor shan't be put upon if I can help it,' and the short and the long of it was that I had as nearly as possible taken a governess's place."

" That would have been better surely—to be independent," Hester said.

" In some ways. To have a paid salary would be very nice —but it hurts a girl's chance. Oh, yes, it does," said Emma, " there is no doubt of it : people say not when they want to coax you into it, but it does—and as all the others have married so well, of course I was very unwilling to do anything to damage my chance."

"What was your chance ? " said Hester with a set countenance : partly she did not know, and partly from the context she divined, and meant to crush her companion with lofty indignation : but Emma was not quick enough to perceive the moral disapproval. She was not even conscious that it was possible to disapprove of such an elemental necessity.

"Oh, you know very well," she said with a little laugh. "I have never been a flirt. I haven't got any inclination that way. Of course in my position I would think it my duty to consider any offer. But I was very nearly driven to the governessing," she continued calmly. "Elinor had visitors coming, and Bee was so ill-natured as to start painting and papering just as I was due there. Can you imagine anything more nasty? just to be able to say she could not take me in! I just said I must take a situation, and they were in a way. But I do really believe I should have done it had it not been for Roland. He said it would suit him very well to have me. He had just got a house of his own, you know, and I could be of use to him. So he took me, which was very kind. It is a little dull after being used to children, but I have scarcely anything to do, and he gives me a little allowance for my clothes. Don't you think it is very kind?"

"I would much rather be a governess," Hester said with a glow of indignant pride. This matter-of-fact description of the state of dependence, which was made without any sense of injury at all, with the composure of an individual fully capable of holding her own and looking for nothing else, had an effect upon her sensitive mind which it is impossible to describe. She shrank from the revelation as if it had been something terrible ; and yet it was not terrible at all, but the most calm historic account of a state of affairs which seemed perfectly natural to every one concerned. Emma knew that she would herself have employed any possible expedient to get rid of an unnecessary member of her household, especially such a detrimental as "the youngest"—and she was not angry with Bee.

"Ah, you don't know children," said Emma serenely. "I have been used to them all my life, and I know what demons they are ; and then it does so spoil your chances in life. Being with Roland is very nice you know, he never orders me about, and he gives me an allowance for my clothes, as I told you. But it is much duller. At Elinor's and Bee's, and even at William's, there's a little life going on. Now and then you can't help seeing people. Even when your sisters don't wish it, people will ask you out when they know you're there. And I must say that for Elinor, that when she's not worried she does take a little trouble about you, and always likes to see you look nice. To be sure with five boys and a husband in business, she is worried." Emma added with impartiality, "most of the time. What is that big house, that red one, so near the road? Nice people ought to live there."

"That is the Grange," said Hester, with a sudden flush, "that is Catherine Vernon's house."

"Oh—h! But then why should I lose any time? It would look better that I should go at once, the very first day. I suppose you run in whenever you please."

Hester's countenance flamed more than ever. "I never go —except when I go with my mother. Catherine would not care to see you with me. She is very fond of your grandfather and grandmother—but not so fond of us. And she is quite right, we don't deserve it so much," Hester said, flinging back her young head with that movement of natural pride which belonged to her. Just then, to make the situation more complicated, Edward came out from the gate, and seeing the two figures on the road, hesitated for a moment, conscious of Catherine's eye behind him, and Hester's keen consciousness before.

"Oh," said Emma again, "then there *are* factions? I am sure I am very glad grandpapa is on Catherine's side; for Elinor said, and then Roland told me——Who is that? Oh, then, there are *men* there? I thought she lived alone. He looks rather nice, though I like men to be taller than that. Mind you introduce me, and walk a little faster please, before he gets away."

Hester's response to this was naturally the indignant one of walking more slowly, so as to give the hesitating figure at the gate full time to get away. But Edward had thought better of it. On the whole, he found it more undesirable to encounter Hester's disdain than anything Catherine would be likely to say. And just at that hour after luncheon Catherine generally abandoned her seat in the window. It was true that he very seldom came back to lunch. He advanced accordingly a few steps from the door, and held out his hand. "I am glad to see you are none the worse of our dissipations last night," he said.

"Introduce me," said Emma, keeping her place close to Hester's side, "we are all cousins together, though we don't know each other. I wanted to go in at once to see Cousin Catherine, whom I have heard of all my life; but she will not let me. Perhaps you will mention it to Cousin Catherine. I will come as soon as I can get grandpapa to bring me. It is so much more formal than I thought. Among relations

generally one runs out and in, and never thinks twice, but
that does not seem to be your way here."

"No, it is not our way here.   We hold each other at arm's
length.   We are not even civil if we can help it," said
Edward, with a laugh and a glance at Hester, who stood,
the impersonation of unwilling politeness, holding herself
back, in an attitude which said as plainly as words, that
though their way was the same she did not choose to be
accompanied, by him, along even that common way.

"I see," said Emma.   "I am sure I am very sorry I made
you stand and talk, Hester, when you dislike it so much.   Of
course, among relations one understands all that.   Do you
live here?   I remember now Roland told me there were some
gentlemen-cousins, but I am quite a stranger, and I don't
know anything.   Hester is going to take me to see the little
town."

"You must not say 'little town' to any of the Redborough
people, Miss Ashton."

"Oh, mustn't I?   At Waltham nobody minds.   I should
like to see the Bank where all the Vernon money comes from.
The Vernon money has never done us any good I believe, but
still when one is connected with money one likes to see all
about it at least.   Do you think, Hester, this gentleman would
be so good as to see about my invitation?   I don't know if
Mrs. ——, I forget her name, who gives the dances—is your
sister, Mr. Vernon."

"Mrs. Merridew is my cousin," said Edward.

"Oh, cousin, is it?   I suppose we are all cousins.   Naturally
I should like an invitation: but I suppose it is because of the
splits in the family, grandmamma doesn't seem to wish to do
anything about it, and Hester hesitated, you know, just as
you hesitated, Mr. Vernon, before you came to speak to us.
What a pity that there should be such to-does: but where
there are a large number of people in a family, of course it
can't always be helped.   I have always found gentlemen were
more good-natured than ladies about getting one invitations.
If you were to tell Mrs. Merridew I am here, even if she
didn't think it right to call as most people would, at least she
might send me a ticket.   I can't have anything to do with
either side, seeing I only arrived yesterday, and don't know a
word about it: but I do like to make acquaintance with a place
wherever I go."

" I will see that my cousin sends you an invitation, Miss Ashton, at least if she will do what I ask her. I have got my work waiting me. Pardon me if I go on."

" Oh, we are going the same way. I suppose we are going the same way ? " said Emma, looking at her companion.

" You walk quicker than we do, and I daresay you are in a hurry," said Hester ungraciously. She did not respond to the look of mingled reproach and relief which he gave her. The very vicinity of Catherine Vernon's house stiffened Hester into marble, and Edward was very anxious to go on. He stood still for one moment with his hat in his hand, then hastened on, at a rate very little like his usual mode of progression. Hester on her part followed with studious lingering, pausing to point out to her companion the view over the Common, the roofs of the Redborough houses, the White House on the opposite slope. Emma naturally conceived her own suspicions from this curious piece of pantomime. They had been walking smartly before, they walked slowly now—and hers was what she thought a romantic imagination. She felt confident that these two were true lovers separated by some family squabble, and that they did not venture to be seen walking together. " I know we were going the same way," she said, " because there are not two ways, and you can see the town before you. I can't see why we might not have walked together. It is sinful to carry family tiffs so far," Emma said.

CHAPTER XXV.

A DOUBLE MIND.

EDWARD had drawn his bow at a venture when he made that statement about Catherine to Hester, and he was full of doubt as to how it would influence her. This was the first time almost that he had disregarded opinion and withdrawn the bolts and bars and let himself go. There was something in the atmosphere of the young house, all breathing of life and freedom, and daring disregard of all trammels, which got into his head in spite of himself. He had abandoned altogether the decorous habits of his life, the necessity which bound him as surely in a dance as at his office. On ordinary occasions, wherever a ball occurred in Redborough, Edward was aware beforehand which young ladies he would have to dance with, and knew that he must apportion his attentions rightly, and neglect nobody whose father or mother had been civil to him. He knew that he must not dance too often with one, nor sit out in corners, nor do anything unbecoming a young man upon whom the eyes of many were fixed. But the very air in the house of the Merridews was different from that of other places. There was a licence in it which existed nowhere else. He, the staid and grave, carried off Hester from her partners, appropriated her for a good part of the evening, sat with her hidden away among the ferns in the conservatory, and only resigned her when he was compelled to do so. Even then, by way of emphasising his choice of Hester, he scarcely danced at all after, but stood among the other disengaged men in the doorways, watching her and seizing every opportunity to gain her attention. He was startled at himself when he thought of it. He walked home in the middle of the night,

in the faint wintry moonlight, following the old fly he
heard lumbering off in the distance carrying her home, his
mind filled with a curious excitement and sense of self-abandonment. He had always admired her—her independence,
her courage, her eager intelligence, had furnished him since
she was a child with a sort of ideal. He had kept wondering
what kind of woman she would grow up; and lo! here she
was, a woman grown, drawing other eyes than his, the object
of admiring glances and complimentary remarks. When he
had seen her in her washed muslin at Catherine Vernon's
parties, she had still appeared to him a child, or little more
than a child. He had still felt the superiority of his own
position, and that the passing glance and shrug of familiar
confidential half-apology would probably please her more than
the ordinary attentions which he had to show among so many.
But Hester, by Ellen Merridew's side, a taller and grander
woman, well-dressed, with her mother's pearls about her white
throat, which was as white as they, was a different creature
altogether. To risk everything for a mere schoolgirl was one
thing, but a stately young creature like this, at whom everybody looked, of whom everybody said, " *That* Hester Vernon?
Dear me, I never thought she had grown up like that!" was
a different matter. The sight of her had intoxicated Edward.
Perhaps poor Mrs. John's pearls and the careful perfection of
her dress had something to do with it. And the place intoxicated him, There every one was doing what seemed good in
his own sight. There were few or none of those stern re-
minders which he had read elsewhere in the eyes of parents
whose daughters were waiting to be danced with, the "Was-
it-for-this-I-asked-you-to-dinner?" look, to which he had so
often succumbed. For once he had lost his head; he was even
vaguely conscious that he had come there with a sort of intention of losing his head, and for once thinking of his own
pleasure, and nothing more. No doubt this had been in his
mind: and the sudden sight of that white figure, all graceful
and stately, and of Mrs. John's pearls, had done the rest. But
he was a little nervous next morning as he thought over what
he had been doing; he did not bear Catherine's questioning
well at breakfast. When she asked him whom he had danced
with, he made answer that he had danced very little. But yet
he had enjoyed himself, oh yes. It had been so pretty a party
that it had been pleasure enough to look on. He described
the conservatory and its Chinese lanterns with enthusiasm.

" It must, indeed, have been like fairyland—or the fireworks
at the Crystal Palace," Catherine had said.   And he had felt
a bitter pang of offence, as she laughed.   He did not feel,
indeed, that he could bear any remarks of the kind, or depreciation of Ellen, for whom he felt a special kindness just now.
When Catherine said, " But all this must have come to a great
deal of money : Algernon Merridew has only a share in his
father's business, he has no private money, has he ?—but, of
course, I know he has no private means : and Ellen's little
money will soon go at that rate."

" I don't suppose Chinese lanterns cost very much," said
Edward.

" Your temper is doubtful this morning," said Catherine,
with a smile.   " It is ' on the go,' which is usual enough after
late hours and the excitement of a dance ; but I don't think
you are often so much excited by a dance.   Did you see some
one whom you admired, Edward ?   I am sure, if she is a nice
girl, I shall be very glad."

" Perhaps it would be as well not to try, Aunt Catherine ;
we might not agree about what a nice girl is."

" No ? " said Catherine rather wistfully.

She looked into his doubtful eyes across the breakfast table,
and, perhaps for the first time, began to feel that she was not
so very certain as she had once been as to what her boy
meant.   Was it possible, after all, that perhaps the words
upon which they agreed had different meanings to each ?   But
this was only a passing cloud.

" Who was the belle ? " she said smiling ; " you can tell me
that, at least, if you can't tell who you admired most."

Edward paused ; and then an impulse of audacity seized
him.

" I don't know if you will like it," he said, " but if I must
tell the truth, I think that girl at the Vernonry—Hester, you
know—who is grown up, it appears, and *out*—"

Catherine bore the little shock with great self-possession,
but she felt it.

" Hester.   Why should you suppose I would not like it ?
She must be nineteen, and, of course, she is *out*.   And what
of her ? " Catherine said with a grave smile.

She was vexed that Edward should be the one to tell her of
the girl's success, and she was vexed, too, that he should
think it would displease her.   Why should it displease her ?
He ought to have kept silence on the subject, and he ought

not to have seemed to know that she had any feeling upon it :
the suggestion hurt her pride.

"Ellen seems to have taken her up. She has grown up
much handsomer than I should have expected, and she was
very well dressed, with beautiful pearls——"

"Ah!" said Catherine, with a long breath; "then her
mother kept her pearls!" She laughed a moment after, and
added, "Of course, she would; what could I have expected?
She kept her settlement. Poor little thing! I suppose she
did not understand what it meant, and that she was cheating
her husband's creditors."

"I never quite understood," said Edward, "why you should
have brought her here, and given her a house, when she is
still in possession of that income."

"She has only a scrap of it. Poor little thing! She neither
knew it was wrong to take it, nor that if she did keep it, it
ought not to have been allowed to go for his after debts. She
got muddled altogether among them. The greater part of it
she mortgaged for him, so that there was only a pittance left.
Whatever you may think, you young men, it is a drawback
for a man when he marries a fool. And so she kept her
pearls!" Catherine added, with a laugh of contempt.

"Marrying a fool, however, must have its advantages,"
said Edward, "since a woman with brains would probably
have given up the settlement altogether."

"Advantages—if you think them advantages!" Catherine
said, with a flash of her eyes such as Edward had seldom
seen. "And certainly would not have kept the pearls—
which are worth a good deal of money," she added, however,
with her habitual laugh. "I think they must have dazzled
you, my boy, these pearls."

"I am sure they did," said Edward composedly; "they
took away my breath. I have seen her here often, a dowdy
little girl" (he scorned himself for saying these words, yet he
said them, though even his cheek reddened with the sense of
self-contempt) "with no ornaments at all."

"No," said Catherine; "to do Mrs. John justice, she had
as much sense as that. She would not have put those pearls
on a girl's neck, unless she was dressed conformably. Oh, she
has sense enough for that. I suppose she had a pretty dress
—white? But of course it would be white, at the first ball—
and looked well, you say?"

"Very handsome," said Edward, gravely. He did not look

up to meet the look of awakened alarm, wonder, doubt, and rousing up of her faculties to meet a new danger which was in Catherine's eyes. He kept his on his plate and ate his breakfast with great apparent calm, though he knew very well, and had pleasure in thinking, that he had planted an arrow in her. "By the way," he said, after an interval, "where did John Vernon pick his wife up? I hear she is of good family —and was it her extravagance that brought about his ruin? These are details I have never heard."

"It is not necessary to enter into such old stories," said Catherine, somewhat stiffly. "He met her, I suppose, as young men meet unsuitable people everywhere; but we must do justice. I don't think she had any share in the ruin, any more at least than a woman's legitimate share," she added, with a laugh that was somewhat grim. "He was fond of every kind of indulgence, and then speculated to mend matters. Beware of speculation, Edward. Extravagance is bad, but speculation is ruin. In the one case you may have to buy your pleasures very dear, but in the other there is no pleasure, nothing but destruction and misery."

"Is not that a little hard, Aunt Catherine? there is another side to it. Sometimes a colossal fortune instead of destruction, as you say; and in the meantime a great deal of excitement and interest, which are pleasures in their way."

"The pleasure of balancing on the point of a needle, over the bottomless pit," she said. "If I were not very sure that you have too much sense to be drawn into anything of the kind, I should take fright, to hear you say even as much as that. The very name of speculation is a horror to me."

"Yet there must always be a little of it in business," he said, with a smile creeping about the corners of his mouth.

"You think me old-fashioned in my notions, and with a woman's incapacity to understand business; but in my day we managed to do very well without it," Catherine said.

"To think of a woman's incapacity for business in your presence would be silly indeed. I hope I am not such an ass as that," said Edward, looking up at her with a smile. And she thought his look so kind and true, so full of affectionate filial admiration and trust, that Catherine's keen perceptions were of no more use to her than the foolishness of any mother.

He returned to luncheon that day as if for the purpose of obliterating all disagreeable impressions, and it was on leaving the Grange to return to the bank that he met Hester and

Emma. This confused and annoyed him for the moment. It was not so that he would have liked to meet the heroine of last night ; and her unknown companion, and the highly inappropriate place of meeting, made the encounter still less to his taste. But when he had hurried on in advance he began to ask himself what was the meaning of Hester's reluctance to walk with him, or even to speak to him, her attitude—drawing back even from his greeting, and the clouded look in her eyes. It was natural that he should not wish to speak to her at the door of the Grange, but why she should wish to avoid him he could not tell. It would have been a triumph over Catherine to have thus demonstrated her acquaintance with him at Catherine's very door. So Edward thought, having only the vulgar conception of feminine enmity. On the whole, seeing that he had sowed the seeds of suspicion in Catherine's bosom, it was better that Hester should hold him at arm's length. Yet he was piqued by it. When he reached the bank, however, news awaited him, which turned his thoughts in a different channel. He found Harry Vernon and Algernon Merridew in great excitement in the room which was sacred to the former. Ashton had made the first *coup* on their behalf. He had bought in for them, at a fabulously low price, certain stock by which in a few weeks he was confident they might almost double their ventures. To furnish the details of this operation is beyond the writer's power, but the three young men understood it, or thought they understood it. Of course a skilful buyer prowling about a crowded market with real money in his pocket, knowing what he wants, and what is profitable, will be likely to get his money's worth, whether he is buying potatoes or stock.

"I saw it was very low," said Merridew, "and wondered at the time if Ashton would be down upon it. I thought of writing to him, but on the whole I suppose it's best not to cramp them in their operations. They ought to know their own business best."

"They shell it out when there's a good thing going, these fellows do," said Harry, out of his moustache.

"And nobody has any money apparently," Algernon said, with a laugh of pleasure, meaning to imply *save you and me.* "When money's tight, that is the time to place a little with advantage," he said with a profound air. "I think you should go in for it on a larger scale, you two fellows that have the command of the bank."

" I wouldn't risk too much at once," Harry said.

Edward listened to their prattle with a contempt which almost reached the length of passion. To hear them talk as if they understood, or as if it mattered what they thought! His own brains were swelling with excitement. He knew that he could go a great deal further if he pleased, and that Harry's share in the decision would be small. Dancing on the point of a needle over the bottomless pit! It was like an old woman's insane objection to anything daring—anything out of the common way. Ashton's letter to him was far longer and more detailed than his communications with the others. He said plainly that here was an opportunity for an operation really upon a grand scale, and that there could be no doubt of a dazzling success. "You will communicate just as much or as little of this as you think proper to the others," Roland wrote, and it was all that Edward could do to keep up an appearance of replying to them, of joining in their gratification as he pondered this much more important proposal. "It is not once in a dozen years that such a chance arises," Roland said.

Now Edward had nothing of his own to speak of, far less than the others, who each had a trifle of independent fortune. All that he could risk was the money of the bank. The profit, if profit there was, would be to the bank, and even that large increase of profit would have its drawbacks, for Catherine, who liked to know everything, would inquire into it, and in her opinion, success would be scarcely less dangerous than failure. He could not stop in the drab-coloured calm of the office where these two young idiots were congratulating each other, and trying to talk as if they knew all about it. His scorn of them was unspeakable. If they gained a hundred pounds their elation would be boundless. They were like boys sending out a little toy frigate and enchanted when it reached in safety the opposite side of the puddle. But Ashton meant business. It was not for this sort of trifling work that he had set himself to watch those fluctuations, which are more delicate than anything in nature they could be compared to. The blowing of the winds and their changes were prose compared to the headlong poetry of the money-market. Edward felt so many new pulses waking in him, such a hurrying fever in his veins, that he could not control himself.

"You'll be here, I suppose, Harry, till closing time? I'm going out," he said.

"You going out—you that never have anything to do out of doors! I had to umpire in a match on the other side of the Common," said Harry, "but if you'll just tell Cordwainer as you pass to get some one else in my place, I don't mind staying. I'm sure you've done it often, Ned, for me."

"I am not in request, like you; but I have something I want to see to to-day."

"All right," said Harry. "Don't you go and overdo it, whatever it is."

"You are seedy with staying up, dancing and flirting," said young Merridew, with his imbecile laugh. "Nellie says she could not believe her eyes."

"I wish Ellen, and you too, would understand that dancing and flirting are entirely out of my way," said Edward, with a flush of anger, as he took his hat and went out.

Poor Algernon's innocent joke was doubly unsuccessful, for Harry stood perfectly glum, not moving a muscle. He had not been at all amused by the proceedings of the previous night.

"I wouldn't report it, if I were you, when Ellen says silly things," said her brother, as black as a thunder-cloud.

"By Jove!" said poor Merridew, falling from his eminence of satisfaction into the ludicrous dismay of undeserved depreciation. He told his wife after, "They both set upon me tooth and nail, when I meant nothing but to be pleasant."

"I wish you would learn, Algernon, that it's always wise to hold your tongue when I'm not there," Ellen said. "Of course I understand my own family. And not much wonder they were vexed! Edward that doesn't look at a girl because of Aunt Catherine, and Harry that she has snubbed so! You could not have chosen a worse subject to be pleasant upon," Mrs. Ellen said.

But it was not this subject that was in Edward's mind as he sallied forth with the step and the air of that correct and blameless man of business which already all Redborough believed him to be. He had taken that aspect upon him in the most marvellous way—the air of a man whose mind was balanced like his books, as regularly, and without the variation of a farthing. He was one of those who are born punctual, and already his morning appearance was as a clock to many people on the outskirts of Redborough. His hat, his gloves, his very umbrella, were enough to give people confidence. There was nobody who would have hesitated to intrust their money to his hands. But if Redborough could have known, as he passed

along the streets, causing a little wonder to various people—
for already it had become a surprising fact that Mr. Edward
should leave business at so much earlier an hour than usual—
what a wild excitement was passing through Edward's veins,
the town would have been scared out of its composure altogether. He scarcely felt the pavement under his feet. He
scarcely knew which way he was turning. The message for
Cordwainer went out of his head, though he went that way
on purpose. Several important questions had come before
him to be settled since he had taken his place at the head of
the bank. He had been called upon to decide whether here
and there an old customer who had not thriven in the world
should be allowed to borrow, or a new one permitted to over-
draw; and in such cases he had stood upon the security of
the bank with a firmness which was invulnerable, and listened
to no weak voices of pity. But this was far more important
than such questions as these. As his ideas disentangled
themselves, there seemed to be two possibilities before him.
If he threw himself into Ashton's scheme at all, to do it as a
partner in the business, not indeed with the sanction of his other
partners, but, if there was risk to the firm in his proceedings
at large, to make them profitable to it in case of success. In
case of success! Of course there would be success. It was
inevitable that they must succeed. On the other side, the
expedient was to use the money and the securities of the
bank, not for the aggrandisement of Vernon's, but for his
own. This would leave the responsibility of the action entirely
upon his own shoulders if anything went wrong. And he did
not refuse to give a rapid glance at that contingency. What
could it mean to the bank? Not ruin—he half-smiled as he
thought. It would mean coming down perhaps in the world,
descending from the *prestige* and importance of its present
rank. And to himself it would mean going to the dogs—
anyhow, there could be no doubt on that point. But on the
other side! that was better worth looking at, more worthy of
consideration. It would be like pouring in new blood to
stagnant veins; it would be new life coming in, new energy,
something that would stir the old fabric through and through,
and stimulate its steady going, old-fashioned existence. It
would be the something he had longed for—the liberating
influence, new possibilities, more extended work. He thought,
with an excitement that gradually overmastered him, of the
rush of gain coming in like a river, and the exhilaration and

new force it would bring. This idea caught him up as a
strong wind might have caught him, and carried him beyond
his own control. He walked faster and faster, skimming
along the road that led into the country, into the quiet,
where no one could note his altered aspect or the excitement
that devoured him, taking off his hat as he got out of sight of
the houses, to let the air blow upon his forehead and clear his
senses. And by and by things began to become more clear.
He read Ashton's letter over again, and with every word the
way seemed to grow plainer, the risks less. It was as near
a dead certainty as anything could be in business. "Of
course there is always a possibility that something unforeseen
may happen," Ashton wrote, "and it is for you to weigh this.
I think myself that the chance is so infinitesimal as not to be
worth taking into consideration; but I would not wish to
bias your judgment; the only thing is, that the decision must
be immediate." Now that the first shock of novelty was
over, he felt it in his power to "weigh this," as Ashton said.
Getting familiarised with the subject made him more impartial, he said to himself. The first mention of it had raised
a cowardly host of apprehensions and doubts, but now that
the throbbing of excitement began to die away, he saw the
matter as it was—a question of calculation, a delicate operation, a good *coup*, but all within the legitimate limits of
business. He had recovered, he felt, the use of his reason,
which the novelty, the necessity for immediate determination,
the certainty that he must take no counsel on the subject,
that Harry would be dumbly obstinate, and Catherine
anxiously, hortatively, immovably against it, had taken away.
Harry was an ass, he said to himself, recovering his calm, and
Aunt Catherine an old woman. What was the use of the
faculties he possessed, and the position he had gained, if in
such a crisis he could not act boldly and for himself !

   Thus it was with a very different aspect that Edward
walked back. He put on his hat, feeling himself cooled and
subdued ; his pulses returned to their usual rate of beating,
which was essentially a moderate one. And so rapidly had
he skimmed over the ground, and so quick had been the
progress both of his steps and his thoughts, that when he got
back, with his mind made up, to the skirts of the Common,
he saw the football party just beginning to assemble, and
recollected that he had never given Harry's message to
Cordwainer, and that accordingly no new umpire could have

been found in Harry's place. But what did that matter? He reflected benevolently, with a contemptuous good nature, that he could get back to the bank in time still to liberate his cousin, so that everybody would be satisfied. This he did, stopping at the telegraph-office on the way. His despatch was as follows:—" Proceed, but with caution. Needful will be forthcoming." He drew a long breath when he thus decided his fate; then he returned with all the ease and relief which naturally comes with a decision. The thing was done, whether for good or evil—and there could be very little doubt that it was for good. His countenance was cheerful and easy as he returned to the bank.

" I did not give your message, for my business did not keep me so long as I expected. Your football fellows are just collecting. You can get there, if you make haste, before they begin."

" Oh, thanks, awfully!" said Harry. " I hope you did not hurry, though I'm glad to go. I hope you understand I'm always ready to stay, Ned, when you want the time. Of course, you're worth two of me here, I know that; but I can't stand anything that's not fair, and if you want to get away—— "

" I don't, old fellow; I've done my business. It did not take so long as I thought. You had better be off if you want to get there in time."

" All right," said Harry. And he went off to his match in a softened state of mind, which, had he been able to divine it, would have astonished Edward greatly. Harry had seen Hester and her companion pass, and he felt a sad conviction that Edward's sudden business had something to do with that apparition. Well! he had said to himself, and what then? Hadn't he a right to try, the same as another? If she liked one better than the other, should the fellow she wouldn't have be such a cad as to stand in her way? This was what had made Harry " fly out," as Algey said, upon his brother-in-law; it had made him pass a very sombre hour alone in the bank. But in the revulsion of feeling at Edward's rapid return, and the likelihood either that he had not seen Hester, or that she would have nothing to say to him, Harry's heart was moved within him. Either his cousin was " in the same box" as himself and rejected, or else he was innocent altogether of evil intention—and in either case Harry's heart was soft to him : at once as one whom he had wronged, and as one who might be suffering with him under a common calamity.

CHAPTER XXVI.

STRAIGHTFORWARD.

"I HOPE, Cousin Catherine," said Emma, "that you will not think it is any want of civility on my part. I wished very much to come the first day. I went out with Hester Vernon, who is constantly at grandpapa's—and I was quite distressed, when I found we had to pass here, that she would not bring me in to call. But she seemed to think you would rather not. Of course I know that there are often tiffs in families, so I wouldn't say anything. There are times when Elinor wouldn't call on William's wife not if life and death depended on it; so I understand quite well, and of course a stranger mustn't interfere. Only I wish you to know that I had no wish to take sides, and didn't mean to be rude. That was the last thing in the world I intended. Elinor has always told us younger ones so much about you."

"It is very kind of Elinor, I am sure; and you have behaved most judiciously," said Catherine, with a twinkle in her eye." It is unnecessary to say to a person of your judgment that in the best regulated family——"

"Oh, you needn't tell me," said Emma, shaking her head. "Nobody can know better than I do. It is very awkward when you are the youngest, and when you are expected by everybody to take their part. Of course they have all been very kind to me. I live part of my time with one, and part with another, and that is why every one thinks I should be on their side. But now I am very independent," Emma said, "for Roland has taken me. I dare say he would tell you, Cousin Catherine, when he was here."

"That must be a very pleasant arrangement," said Catherine,

with a smile. "I suppose when you were with Elinor you had a good deal to do."

"I do Roland's housekeeping now. I don't wish to be idle," said Emma. "But to be sure when there are children to be seen after you are never done, and especially boys. Elinor has five boys!—it is something dreadful! The stockings and the mending you can't think! It is very nice being with Roland; he is most kind. He gives me a regular allowance for my clothes, which I never got before, and I am sure it is very good of him; but you can't have everything, you know, and it is a little dull. He is out all day, and often in the evenings, for of course I shouldn't wish him to give up his gentlemen-engagements for me. I don't think people should ever do that sort of thing. Tom Pinch is all very well in Dickens, but it would be inconvenient in actual life; for suppose you married?—and of course that is what every girl expects to do."

"To be sure," said Catherine. "Is there anything of that sort in prospect, if I may be permitted to ask?"

"Of course, I am quite pleased that you should ask," said Emma. "It would be such a comfort to have somebody like you to come and talk it over with, Cousin Catherine, if there was anything—for I should feel sure you could tell me about my trousseau and all that. But there is nothing, I am sorry to say. You see I have had so little chance. Elinor took me out sometimes, but not much, and she, was far more disposed to amuse herself than to introduce me. I don't think that is nice in a married sister, do you? And speaking of that, Cousin Catherine, I am sure you will be kind enough to help me here. Grandpapa will not take any trouble about it. I asked the gentleman whom we met coming out of here, Hester and I—Mr. Edward I think is his name."

"What of Edward?" said Catherine quickly, with a touch of alarm.

"But nothing seems to have come of it," said the persistent Emma. "He said he would try, and Hester made a sort of promise; but there has been one since and I have never been asked. It is your niece's dance—Mrs. Merridew, I think, is her name. She gives one every week, and both for a little amusement, and that I mayn't lose any chance that may be going, I should like very much to go. I don't doubt that you could get me an invitation in a moment if you would just say you would like it."

Catherine's consternation was ludicrous to behold. She was herself so much amused by the situation that she laughed till the tears stood in her eyes. But this matter-of-fact young woman who sat by and gazed upon her with such a stolid incapacity to see the joke, was of the side of the house to which Catherine could pardon anything—the old captain's grandchild, Roland's sister. What would have been vulgar assurance in another, was amusing *naïveté* in Emma. When she had got over her laugh she said, with amused remonstrance as if she had been speaking to a child—

"But you must know, Emma, that these family tiffs you are so well accustomed to, come in to prevent this too. Ellen would not care for my recommendation. She is a very self-willed little person, and indeed the chief rebel of the family."

"That is all very well, Cousin Catherine," said Emma with the downrightness of fact and certainty; "but you know you are the head of the family. You have got the money. If they were in trouble they would all have to come to you : and if you said 'I wish this,' of course nobody would venture to refuse you. The most stupid person must be sure of that."

There was a commanding commonsense in this view that silenced Catherine. She looked at the young philosopher almost with awe.

"Your arguments are unanswerable," she said; "there is nothing to be said against such admirable logic."

"Then you will ask for an invitation for me?" said Emma. "I am sure I am much obliged to you, Cousin Catherine. It is always best to come to the fountain-head. And it isn't as if I were going to cause any expense or trouble, for I have my ball-dress all ready. I have wore it only once, and it is quite fresh. It is my second ball-dress; the first I wore about a dozen times. Elinor gave it me, which was very kind of her. It was only muslin, but really it was very nice, and got up quite respectably. But this one I bought myself out of the allowance Roland gives me. Don't you think it is very thoughtful of him? for of course what a sister buys for you, however kind she is, is never just the same as what you would choose for yourself."

"I suppose not—I never had any experience," said Catherine, gravely. "I am afraid however, that you will not meet anybody who will much advance your views at Redborough. It is an old-fashioned, backward place. London would afford a much larger scope for any social operations.

Indeed it is very condescending in a young lady from town to give any attention to us and our little parties down here."

"Oh!" said Emma, eager to correct a mistake, "that just shows how little people in the country know. You think London means the London you read of in books, where you meet all the great people, and have half-a-dozen parties every night. But when London means Kilburn!" said Emma, shaking her head, "where all the gentlemen go to the city every morning, and there is perhaps one dance given in a whole season and only the people asked that you know! and we know scarcely one. You see the people there don't think of calling because they are your neighbours. There are so many: and unless you get introductions, or work in the parish, or something—. Working in the parish is a very good way," Emma added, with a sudden recollection; "you get invited to a great many evening parties where you just stand about and talk, or people sing: but not many dances. Unfortunately I never was much used to parish work. In Elinor's there was too much to do, and Bee was too worldly, and as for William's wife, though we should not like it to be known, Cousin Catherine, she is—a Dissenter."

Emma made this admission with the reluctance it merited.

"I have not told grandpapa," she said with bated breath.

"I think he could bear it," said Catherine. "I think you might venture on the communication. In some things he is very strong-minded."

"It was a very bitter pill to us," Emma said.

Here they were interrupted by the entrance of the captain himself, who had left his grandchild in a cowardly way to make Catherine's acquaintance by herself. But Emma had not minded. She had not even divined that his pretence of business was hypocritical. She had not been alarmed by Catherine, and now she was comfortably confident of having made a good impression, and secured a friend.

"I am quite ready, grandpapa," she said. "Cousin Catherine has been so kind. She says she will speak to Mrs. Merridew about my invitation, so you may make yourself quite easy on that subject. And grandmamma will be very pleased. Of course I could not expect such an old lady as she is to exert herself. But Cousin Catherine understands how important that sort of thing is to a girl," Emma said with an air of great gravity.

The captain gave Catherine a piteous glance. He did not
understand the new specimen of womankind of whom he had
the responsibility, and Catherine, whose powers of self-restraint
had been called forth to an unusual degree, responded with an
outburst of laughter.

" We have got on admirably," she said. " I like a straightforward mind, with such a power of applying reason to practical
uses. You must come to see me often, Emma. Never mind
grandpapa. He will tell you I am busy, but when I am
so, I shall tell you so. You are far too sensible to take
offence."

" Oh, offence, Cousin Catherine ? between you and me ! "
said Emma, " that would be too ridiculous. I hope I know
my place. When you are the youngest you soon learn that.
Your first lesson is that nobody wants you, and that you must
just do the best you can for yourself. There is only just one
thing I should like to mention, and that is, that the first time
it would be a great advantage to me if you would take me.
It is such a fine thing for a girl when she is known to belong
to the best people in a place. It is not even as if my name
were Vernon. But people will say ' Miss Ashton ! who is
Miss Ashton ? I never heard of her ! ' Whereas if I were
with you, the best partners in the place would ask to get
introduced to me, and that would give me a start. Afterwards I could get on by myself, as I hear Mrs. Merridew does
not care for chaperons," Emma said.

Once more Catherine was struck dumb. She pushed her
chair back a little and regarded this dauntless young woman
with a mixture of dismay, admiration, and amusement.

" But I assure you I never have gone to any of Ellen's
junketings," she said.

"That will not matter," said the persistent Emma. " Of
course she will be pleased to have you. It will be a great
honour. And then to me it would be such an advantage. I
should feel that I really was having my chance."

When she left the gate of the Grange, walking by the side of
the bewildered captain, Emma felt that she was tolerably sure
of getting all she wanted, and her triumph, though quite
moderate and serious, was great.

" I am very glad you left me to make acquaintance with
Cousin Catherine by myself," she said, "grandpapa ; I was a
little frightened, but she was so nice. She was very nice to
Roland too ; and it will be such an advantage to go into society

for the first time with such a well-known person. It makes all the difference. People see at once who you are, and there is no difficulty afterwards."

"And you think Catherine Vernon will depart from all her habits and take you to that butterfly's ball?" the captain said.

"Of course, grandpapa," said Emma, in the calm of simple conviction. It was not a matter which admitted of any doubt.

And the wonderful thing was, that she proved right. To her own great amazement, and to the consternation of everybody concerned, Catherine Vernon assumed her grey gown, the gayest of her evening garments, and most befitting a dance, and took Emma Ashton in her own carriage to Mrs. Merridew's house on the hill. Catherine was too genial a person in ordinary society to exercise any discouraging influence upon the young party in general; but upon the members of her own family there was no doubt that she did have a subduing effect. Ellen's face of consternation was the subject of remark in the family for years after; indeed, they spoke of "the night when Aunt Catherine came to the dance," dating things from it, as people speak of a great national event. Harry was the one who showed himself most equal to the occasion. He established himself by Catherine's side as a sort of guard of honour, relieving the frightened Algernon, who, what with pride and pleasure on his own part, and a wondering sympathy with Ellen's dismay, did not know how to conduct himself in such an emergency. Edward did not appear at all. He had said he was very busy, and did not think it was possible he could go, as soon as he heard of Emma's extraordinary request. And though Catherine was almost displeased by his defection, there was nothing to be said against so evident a necessity as that the most active partner in the bank should attend to his work. Her chief point of curiosity in the scene which she surveyed with amused disapproval and astonishment to find herself there, was Hester, to whom her eyes turned with the lively sense of opposition which existed always between the two.

Catherine's eyes, in spite of herself, turned from Emma's insignificance to the fine indignant figure of the girl whom (she said to herself) she could not endure, with the most curious mixture of curiosity, and interest, and rivalship. She, Catherine Vernon, the rival of a trifling creature of nineteen!

Such a sentiment sometimes embitters the feelings of a mother towards the girl of whom her son makes choice. But Catherine's mood had nothing to do with Edward. It was more like the "taking sides," which Emma was so anxious to demonstrate was impossible to her as a stranger. Hester had no separate standing ground, no might or authority, and yet it was no exaggeration to say that Catherine, with all of these advantages, instinctively looked upon her as a rival power.

Hester was in the blue dress, which was the alternative of her white one. In those days there were no yellows or sage greens; and even before Catherine remarked the girl's young freshness and beauty, or the high-thrown head, and indignant bearing, which denoted on Hester's side a sense of Catherine's inspection, her eyes had caught the glistening pearls on the young neck—her mother's pearls. Catherine looked at them with a mingled sense of pity and disdain. If that mother had been such a woman as Catherine, neither these pearls nor anything else of value would have remained in her hands. They were Catherine's, they were the creditors' by rights. Mrs. John was not wise enough to understand all that; but Hester, if she knew, would understand. Catherine could not keep her mind from dwelling upon these ornaments. If Hester knew, what would the girl do? Pocket the shame and continue to wear them as became Mrs. John's daughter, or tear them from her neck and trample them under foot? One or the other she would have to do— but then, Hester did not know.

As she walked about through the rooms, stopping to give a gracious word there, a nod here, a question about father or mother, Catherine's mind was not occupied either with the house or the company, but with this girl. Hester had been in the background till now. A glimpse of her in the corner of her own drawing-room, standing by her mother's side in her washed muslin, did not—though Hester's look was always one of indignation—impress her relation's mind. But here she stood like an equal, sending glances of defiance out of her brown eyes. Hester had come in the old fly with the white horse, while Emma was fetched from her grandfather's by Catherine's carriage. The contrast was striking enough; but Catherine, though she would not own it to herself, was more aware than any one else, that no one would look twice at Emma while Hester was by.

When the evening was about half over, Emma came to her patroness and kindly gave her her dismissal.

"Don't wait longer on my account, Cousin Catherine," she said. "I am quite nicely started; thank you so much. I have got my card filled; quite the nicest people in the room have asked me. I am sure I am very grateful to you, for it is all your doing; but don't think of waiting for me. Chaperons are not at all wanted, and I can go home in Hester's fly. I am so much obliged to you, but of course you want to get to bed. Don't stay a moment longer than you wish, for me."

Catherine smiled, but did not take any further notice. She walked about the rooms for some time after on the arm of Harry, who was always dutiful.

"And who do you think is the prettiest person in the room, Harry? I excuse you from telling me it is my young lady, whom for my own part I don't admire."

"I cannot see there is any doubt about it, Aunt Catherine," said Harry, in his sturdy way. "It is my cousin Hester. There is an air about her—I cannot explain it: I found it out long ago; but now everybody sees it."

"Thanks to her mother's pearls," said Catherine, with her laugh.

Harry looked at her with startled eyes.

"The pearls are very pretty on her; but they are nothing to me at least," he said.

"You should not let her wear them. She should not have them; knowing her father's story, as I suppose you do.—Don't you see," cried Catherine, with sudden energy, "that she ought not to appear in Redborough in those pearls?"

Emma had been standing near when this conversation began, and she drew closer to listen, not with any clandestine intention, but only with a natural curiosity. She caught up the words in a disjointed way. What reason could there be for not wearing your mother's pearls? She would have gone and asked the question direct of Catherine, but that just then her partner came for her; and for the rest of the evening she had no time to consider any such question; nor was it till she found herself in the fly in the middle of the night rumbling and jolting along the dark road that skirted the Common, by Hester's side, that this mysterious speech occurred to her mind. She had been talking of the advantage of being introduced by a well-known person and thus put at once "on a right footing."

" You don't want that. You know everybody; you have
been here all your life," she said. " And I am sure you got
plenty of partners, and looked very nice. And what a pretty
necklace that is," said Emma, artlessly entering upon her
subject. " Are they real? Oh, you must not be offended
with me, for I never had any nice ornaments. The youngest
never has any chance. If they are real, I suppose they are
worth a great deal of money; and you must be quite rich, or
you would not be able to afford them."

" We are not rich; indeed we are very poor," said Hester,
"but the pearls are my mother's. She got them when she
was young, from her mother. They have belonged to us for
numbers of years."

"I wonder what cousin Catherine could mean!" said Emma
innocently.

" About my pearls?" cried Hester, pricking up her ears,
and all her spirit awakening though she was so sleepy and
tired of the long night.

" She said you oughtn't to wear them. She said you
shouldn't have them. I wonder what she meant! And Mr.
Harry Vernon, that tall gentleman, he seemed to understand,
for he got quite red and angry."

" I oughtn't to wear them—I shouldn't have them!" Hester
repeated, in a blaze of wrath. She sat bolt upright, though
she had been lying back in her corner indisposed for talk.

" Oh, I dare say she didn't mean anything," said Emma,
" only spite, as you are on the other side."

Hester did not reply, but she was roused out of all her
sleepiness in a moment. She let Emma prattle on by her side
without response. As they drove past the Grange a window
was opened softly, and some one seemed to look out.

" Oh, I wonder if that was Mr. Edward," said Emma. " I
wonder why he stayed away. Is he after some girl, and
doesn't want Cousin Catherine to know? If it were not
that you would scarcely speak to each other when you met.
I should say it was you, Hester."

" I wish," said Hester severely, " that you would go to sleep;
at three in the morning I never want to talk."

" Well, of course, it may be that," said Emma somewhat
inconsequently, " but I never want to sleep when I have been
enjoying myself. I want to have some one in the same room
and to talk it all over—everything that has happened. Who
was that man, do you know who ——"

And here she went into details which Hester, roused and angry, paid no attention to. But Emma was not dependent on replies. She went on asking questions, of which her companion took no notice, till the fly suddenly stopped with a great jarring and rattling, and the opening of two doors, and glimmer of two small lights in the profound dark, gave note of watchers in the two houses, warned by the slow rumbling of the ancient vehicle, and glad to be released from their respective vigils. In Hester's case it was her mother, wrapped in a warm dressing-gown, with a shawl over her head, and two anxious eyes shining out with warm reflections over her little candle, who received the girl in her finery with eager questions if she were very cold, if she were tired, if all had gone off well.

"Run up stairs, my darling, while I fasten the door," Mrs. John said. "There is a nice fire and you can warm yourself, —and some tea."

In those days people, especially women, were not afraid of being kept awake because of a cup of tea.

"Mamma," said Hester when her mother followed her up stairs into the old-fashioned, low-roofed room, which the fire filled with rosy light, "it appears Catherine Vernon says I ought not to wear your pearls. Has she anything to do with your pearls? Has she any right to interfere?"

"My pearls!" cried Mrs. John almost with a scream. "What could Catherine Vernon have to do with them? I think, dear, you must have fallen asleep and been dreaming. Where have you seen Catherine Vernon, Hester? She gives us our house, dear; you know we are so far indebted to her: but that is the only right she can have to interfere."

"Had she anything to do with my father?" Hester asked.

She was relieved from she did not know what indefinable terrors by the genuine astonishment in her mother's face.

"Anything to do with him? Of course; she had a great deal to do with him. She was his first cousin. Her father had brought him up. It was intended——but then he met me," said the gentle little woman, not without a tone of satisfaction in the incoherent tale. "And she was a kind of partner, and had a great deal to do with the bank. I never understood the rights of it, Hester. I never had any head for business. Wait, darling, till I undo these buttons. And now, my love, if you have got warm, go to bed. My pearls! She must mean, I suppose, that they are too good for you to wear

because we are poor. They were my mother's, and her
mother's before that. I would like to know what Catherine
Vernon could have to say to them," Mrs. John said, taking
the pearls from her child's throat and holding them up, all
warm and shining, to the light, before she deposited them in
their carefully padded bed.

If there was anything in the world that was her individual
property, and in which no one else had any share, it was her
pearls : they had always been one of her household gods.

CHAPTER XXVII.

A CENTRE OF LIFE.

THERE are periods in life, and especially in the early part of it, when all existence gets, as it were, out of focus, and instead of some great and worthy centre, takes to circling round some point of outwardly frivolous meaning, some little axis of society entirely unfit to be the turning-point of even the smallest world of human concerns. This had come to be the case with the Vernons in those lingering weeks of winter just before Christmas. That the young, gay, foolish—nay, absurd —house on the hill inhabited by Algernon Merridew and his wife should become to all of this important family the chief place, not only in Redborough, but, for a time, in the world, was the most curious fact imaginable ; but yet it was so. To Edward it was the one place in the world where he was, as he hoped, free from observation and able to do as he pleased : which meant—where he was entirely free from Catherine, and need have no fear of any interruption from her to his amusement, or his pleasure, or, if you like it better, his love : to Hester it was the place where she had been recognised as part possessor in her own person, like the others, of the honours due to her family, and where the homage, to which a young woman sufficiently endowed has a right, was first given to her ; if it had a more close attraction still as the place where she met Edward, that was a dream as yet unacknowledged to her own heart. Harry, on the other hand, had a double interest—neither of them of a very cheerful kind—one of which was the necessity of standing by his sister, who his good sense told him was embarked in a very perilous way, and whose husband was quite incapable of controlling or guiding her erratic course ;

and the other was the painful fascination of watching Edward
and Hester through all the vicissitudes of their quarrellings
and makings up—the hours they would spend together,
followed by other hours in which they would mutually scowl
at each other and did not speak. Harry knew, poor fellow,
by a sort of instinct common to the rejected, that the quarrels
were as ominous, or more so, than the intimacy. Hester had
never quarrelled with himself, they had been on the best
terms, alas, as they were now! But Edward she would pass
with a flushed cheek and shining eye : she would address him
with haughty reluctance when it was necessary to speak to
him, and mark her reluctance with a decision which was never
employed towards those for whom she cared nothing. Harry's
eyes were opened, and he understood the duel between them.
The only mistake he made was in the belief that it had gone
further than the preliminary stage. He could not believe it
possible that no explanation had taken place between them.

And of all people to be interested in Ellen's silly parties, who
should be seized with an intense desire to know all about them
but Catherine Vernon herself ? She did know more about them
than any one else who was not present, and than a great many
who were present. Her suspicions had been roused by various
indications of something occult in Edward's mind. He was
no longer on his guard to the incredible extent which had been
common with him ; his mind was agitated with new hopes and
fears—the chance of being able to be altogether independent
of Catherine had made him relax in his caution, and there
had been moments when, in all the stir and elation of his
new life, he had been on the eve of disclosing everything.
Habitual prudence had saved him, but yet there had been
something in his aspect which had roused Catherine's suspicions. They had been, as she thought, in such entire
sympathy before, that she was deeply affected by this feeling,
which she could not explain to herself—this sense of being in
sympathy no longer. And it was all since Ellen's absurd
parties began, and he began to meet at them, *that* girl, born
for the confusion of all her plans, Catherine thought. There
were evenings when the strongest temptation to order her
carriage instead of going to bed, and to go suddenly—unexpected—to Ellen's party, and see with her own eyes what was
going on, would come over her mind. But there was in
Catherine's mind, along with her suspicions, that terror to
have them confirmed, which so often goes with love when it

begins to tremble in this way. Had she gone, Edward would
have declared contemptuously (within himself) that it was all
of a piece with her usual watchfulness, and the perfection of
her system—not being able to divine that Catherine would
have given the world to find herself in the wrong, and shrank
from proving herself to be in the right. In the meantime she
was kept informed of what was going on more or less by various
people, and above all by Emma Ashton, whose information,
though largely leavened by a great deal about herself which
did not much interest her hearer, also afforded revelations
about other people, especially Hester. Emma had become a
constant visitor at the Grange. She was allowed to prattle
for hours, and Catherine was always kind to her. Her insignificance, her little egotisms, her straightforward aim at her
own advancement, did not call forth the amused contempt of
that observer of the human comedy as they would have done
in any other specimen. Catherine's tradition in favour of her
mother's kindred covered this little person with a shield. But
those who were not aware of this fond superstition wondered
and scorned. And the feeling of the Redborough community
was not in Emma's favour.

"She is just a horrid little spy," Ellen cried. "I know she
goes and tells Aunt Catherine everything. I shouldn't have
her if I could help it; but everybody knows now that she is
Aunt Catherine's relation, and they are all civil to her."

"She cannot do us any harm, Nelly," said her husband,
"we are not afraid of any spy, I hope."

"Oh, don't talk so much nonsense, Algey," cried Ellen.
"Of course she can't do us any harm; but I hate spies for
all that."

They were wrong so far that Emma was not at all a spy.
Of all the interminable discourses she poured out upon
Catherine, the far greater part was about herself; only unfortunately the part that interested her auditor was not that
about herself, but the much smaller portion in which, quite
unconscious and without any evil motive, she dropped here
and there a chance hint as to the others.

"And whom did you say Edward was dancing with?"
Catherine would say.

"Oh, I was not talking of Mr. Edward, but of young Mr.
Merridew, who is always very attentive. That was our third
dance together, and I did feel it was a great pity there were
no chaperons, because I should have asked her, if I had been

with any one, whether it wasn't rather, you know—— for I wouldn't for the world do anything to get myself talked about."

"I thought you had been talking about Edward," Catherine said.

"Oh dear no. It was whether three dances together wasn't perhaps a little—— for I always feel the responsibility of belonging to the family, Cousin Catherine, and I wouldn't for the world do anything——it is quite different with gentlemen. Mr. Edward was just carrying on as usual."

"But, Emma, you must tell me what you mean by 'carrying on.' "

"Oh, I don't mean any harm," Emma would say. "I wonder what young Mr. Merridew is—if he is well off, and all that? Hester has cousins all round to tell her what's best, and of course she does not need to be on her p's and q's, like me."

Catherine had to follow a mazy, vague, and wandering clue thus, through acres of indifferent matter, and to piece together broken scraps of information which were never intended to affect her at all. But they did affect her sometimes so powerfully that she had her hand actually on the bell, not only that evening but on several other occasions, to intimate that she should want the carriage at ten o'clock—a proceeding which would have convulsed the household at home, and carried consternation to the recipients of the unlooked-for honour. But, on further consideration, Catherine always succeeded in subduing herself, often sadly enough saying to herself that it would be time enough when he told her—why should she go out to meet trouble? Her heart so took her strength from her, and changed her natural temperament, that Catherine restrained herself, with a shrinking, which nobody who knew her would have believed in, from any contact with irresistible fact, and decided that rather than find out the vanity of her confidence it was better to be deceived.

Thus the house on the hill, which flaunted forth every Thursday evening the great lamps of its lighted windows and the lines of Chinese lanterns in the conservatory, became the centre for the moment of a great deal of life and many anxious thoughts. It turned Ellen's head with pride and delight when she received indications of this, which indeed came to her on all sides. When a shade of alarm crossed Algernon's face at the amount of the bills, she took a lofty position which no man pretending to any spirit could have gone against. "Goodness, Algey, how can you look so glum about a pound or two, when you see we are doing a great work?" Ellen said. "Well! if it is not more important than mothers' meetings, I don't know what words mean: and Mr. Ransom says the mothers' meetings are a great work." Algernon laughed, but he, too, felt a thrill of pride. To have made the house, which though it was Ellen's was a Merridew house, and his own, into a centre for the great Vernon family, was, if not a great work, at least an extraordinary local success, such as old Merridew's son could never have hoped to attain to. And indeed Algernon's remonstrances about the bills were of the feeblest description. He was too much devoted to his wife to have interfered with her, even had not the balance of moral force been on her side; and he was proud of the extravagance and the commotion and the way in which the elders shook their heads. It is pleasant to make a sensation, and Algernon was comforted by the knowledge that he had already made a little money by his stockbroking transactions, and hoped to make a great deal more.

The young men had carried on their transactions with considerable vigour, though with little risk so far as Algernon and Harry were concerned. But Edward's was a different case. The venture upon which he had pondered with so much anxiety had turned out favourably, and he had gone on without telling his secret to any one, with a general amount of success which had made the operation of risking other people's money seem quite natural to him—a process without any practical consequences at all, except the accumulation of a good deal of money under his own name, which is one of the happiest of sensations. To his temperament indeed it is by no means certain that the vicissitudes of the career in which he had embarked, the tragic suspense in which he was occasionally held, and the transport of deliverance that followed, were not in themselves the highest pleasures of which he was capable. And even so early in his career as this, such crises would come. He had self-command enough not to betray himself when these moments arrived, and though there were eyes keen enough to see that something had produced a change in him, they were, as has been seen in Catherine's case, deceived as to the cause of his perturbation. Hester did not have so many opportunities of studying him, and she had no clue to the business complications in which he was involved; but she had many thoughts on her own mind

as to the reason of all the commotion which she saw
vaguely, without understanding it. Some of the members
of the general society, strangers who sometimes perceive a
departure from habit which does not strike the most intimate, had said of Edward on more than one occasion, that
he must be in love. Was he in love? Hester had felt that
a look was directed to herself when this was said, and
that a suppressed laugh had run round the little group.
She was herself agitated by tumults which she could not
understand, commotions in which Edward was certainly
involved, and his name thus mentioned brought the blood
to her cheek. Was he in love? She did not want to
turn the question upon herself, to bring the matter to any
conclusion, one way or another. He was very pale that
evening, yet would flush, as she herself did, growing red in
a moment and then pale again; and there was a watchful air
about him as of a man who expected to hear something or see
some one whom nobody else looked for. A man who was in
love did not behave so. He was absorbed in the being whom
he loved. He is not absorbed in me, the girl said to herself
involuntarily, then blushed, as if her thought had been found
out. Edward came up to her at this moment, which made her
confusion the greater.

"Why do you change colour so? What is the matter?"
he said to her.

"It is you who are changing colour," said Hester, not
knowing how else to defend herself.

Instead of contradicting her, or throwing off the accusation,
he suddenly took her hand and drew it through his arm.

"It is true," he said. "I have something on my mind.
You were going to dance this waltz with me. Come into the
hall, it is cool there, and let us talk instead?"

Every inch of available space in the house was given up to
the accommodation of the guests, and the hall was filled, like
the conservatory, with plants, among which little groups of
two could find corners. Edward established Hester in one
of these, and placed a chair for himself, so as to cut her off
from everybody.

"You are the only one that can understand," he said. "I
can speak to you. Don't mind me if I look like a fool. I am
too anxious to talk."

"What is it?" she said, with a tremor of sympathetic
anxiety.

"It is only business," he said, "but it is business so unexpected that even beside you I am obliged to think of it. Can a man say more than that?" he asked with something in his eyes which Hester had never seen there so distinctly before, and which silenced her. One great emotion clears the way for another. Edward in the commotion of his being was almost ready to rush into words that, being said, would have turned his life upside down, and shattered all his present foundations. He was saved by an incident which was of the most ordinary commonplace kind. There came a violent ring at the door which was within half a dozen steps of the spot where they sat. Half a dozen heads immediately protruded from among the little banks of foliage to see what this odd interruption could mean, for all the guests had arrived, and it was not late enough for any one to go away. Hester saw that all the colour ebbed immediately out of Edward's face. He did not even attempt to say a word to her, but sat perfectly still, slightly turned towards the door, but not looking out, awaiting whatever might come. It seemed to Hester that never in her life had she so understood the power of fate, the moment when Nature and life seem to stand still before some event. A minute after, the footman came up and handed a telegram to Edward. He tore it open with trembling hands. The next moment he jumped up from his seat with a suppressed cry of triumph. "Hurrah!" he said, and then with a laugh which was very unsteady held out the despatch to her. All that it contained were the words "All right." But somehow it was not to these words that Hester's eyes confined themselves. "From Ashton, London——" she said without knowing that she did so, before he thrust the pink paper into his pocket. "Come along," he said, "the waltz is not half over. We shall be in time yet." And for the rest of the evening Edward was in wild spirits, dancing every dance. He even asked the girls to take him with them in their fly as far as the Grange in his reckless exhilaration, and as he got out in the darkness, Hester felt a kiss upon her hand. This startled her still more than the telegram. "Till to-morrow," he said as they rumbled away.

"What does he mean by till to-morrow? He must be coming to make you an offer to-morrow—that is how they do. It often happens after a dance—when it is going to happen," Emma said in the darkness, with a little sigh.

CHAPTER XXVIII.

WAS IT LOVE?

WAS he in love? That this was a question very interesting to Hester there can be no reason to conceal. She did not even conceal it from herself, nor did she trifle with herself by pretending to suppose that if he were in love it could be with any one else. There was no one else who had ever appeared to attract him. To nobody had he so much as given his passing attention. When he had neglected her at the Grange it had been truly as he said, for no higher reason than that he might hand down the old ladies to supper or tea. No young one had ever been suggested as having any attraction for him. Hester did her best to enter calmly into this question. It is one which it is sometimes very difficult for a young woman to decide upon. What is conspicuous and apparent to others will often remain to her a question full of doubt and uncertainty; and it is to be feared that when this is the case it is all the more likely that her own sentiments will be capable of very little question. This, however, was not exactly the case with Hester. Her mind was very much interested, and indeed excited. She wanted to know what Edward meant. From the first morning when he had met her a child wandering on the Common, his manner had been different to her from the manner of other people, or from his own manner to others. His eyes had lingered upon her with pleasure even when his look had been stealthy; even when it had been but a glance in passing, they had said things to her which no other eyes said. His interest in her had never failed. It had not leaped like Harry's, after a good deal of indifference, into a sudden outburst. The very charm and attraction of it had

lain in the restraint which Hester had often considered to be
dishonest, and against which she had chafed. She had known
all through, even in those evenings when he had neglected
her, that he was always conscious what she was doing, and
knew without looking when any one went to talk to her,
when she left the room and when she came back. This had
kept her own interest in him unvarying. But Hester was
not any more sure of her own sentiments than of his. She
remembered with some shame that Roland Ashton's presence
had made a great difference in the state of her mind as
regarded Edward. She had felt but little curiosity about
him when that stranger was at the Vernonry. All the
foreground of her mind had been so pleasantly occupied by
that new figure which was in itself much more attractive
than Edward, that he had slid almost completely out of
her thoughts. And this fact, which was only quite apparent
to her after Roland was gone, had greatly discomfited Hester,
and given her a very small opinion of herself. Was it
possible that any new object that might appear would have
the same effect upon her? The effect had passed away, and
Edward had come slowly back to his original position as the
person who in all Redborough interested her most. But the
incident had been of a very disturbing character, and had
altogether confused her ideas. Therefore the question was
one of a very special interest. To know exactly how
he regarded her would much help her in deciding the other
question, not less important, which was, how she regarded
him? Everything thus depended, Hester felt, on Edward's
sentiments. If it should turn out that he loved her—
strange thought which made her heart beat! it could not
be but that in great and tender gratitude for such a
gift she should love him. She did not feel offended by his
efforts to disguise his feelings, or even to get the better of
them—never at least when she was cool and in command of her
judgment; but there could be no doubt that she was very
curious and anxious to know.

Was he in love? The appearances which had made the
lookers-on say so were not altogether to be attributed to this,
Hester knew. His paleness, his excitement, his absence of
mind, had all been from another cause. The discovery had
startled her much, and given her an uneasy sense that she might
at other times have referred to some cause connected with
herself manifestations of feeling which had nothing to do with

her, which belonged to an entirely different order of sentiments
—a thought which made her blush red with shame, since there
is nothing that hurts a girl's pride so much as the suggestion, that she has been vain, and imagined like the foolish
women, a man to love her who perhaps has never thought of
her at all. But the question altogether was one which was
too profound for Hester. She could not tell what to make of
it. Among the heads of the young party at the Merridews,
she was aware that no doubt was entertained on the matter.
Edward was allotted to her by a sort of unspoken right, and
in Ellen's jibes and Harry's gloom she read alike the same
distinct understanding. Ellen in her chatter, notwithstanding the warning to her cousin at the beginning, accepted it
entirely as a matter of course : and in a hundred things that
Edward had said as well as in his looks, which were still more
eloquent, there had been strong confirmation of the general
belief. But yet—Hester could not make up her mind that it
was beyond doubt. She watched him, not with anxiety so much
as with a great curiosity. If it was not so would she be deeply
disappointed ? she asked herself without being able even to
answer that question. And as to her own sentiments, they were
quite as perplexing. She was half ashamed to feel that they depended upon his. Was this a confession of feminine inferiority?
she sometimes wondered with a hot blush—the position here
being very perplexing indeed and profoundly difficult to
elucidate ; for it neither consisted with the girl's dignity to
give her love unsought, nor thus to wait as if ready to deliver
up her affections to the first bidder.

Such a matter of thought, involving the greatest interests
of life, is curiously mixed up with its most frivolous events.
They met in the midst of the dancing with a constant crash
and accompaniment of dance-music, amid chatterings and
laughter, and all the inane nothings of a ball-room, and yet
in the midst of this were to consider and decide the most important question of their lives. It was only thus, except by
concerted meetings which would have solved the question, that
they could meet at all, and the grotesque incongruity of such
surroundings with the matter in the foreground sometimes
affected Hester with a sort of moral sickness and disgust.
The scene seemed to throw a certain unworthiness, levity,
unelevated aspect upon the question altogether—as if this
thing which was to affect two lives was no more than an
engagement for a dance.

And though it is a strange thing to say, it is doubtful whether Edward was much more decided in his sentiments than Hester was. In such a case the man at least generally knows more or less what he wants; but partly because Edward's mind was in a high state of excitement on other subjects, he too was for a moment entirely uncertain as to what his wishes were. He knew with sufficient distinctness that he could not tolerate the idea of her appropriation by any one else, and it was his full intention that some time or other Hester should be his, and no one else's, which gave a foundation of certainty to his thoughts which was wanting to hers. But further than this, he too was in a chaos somewhat similar to that of Hester. Sometimes there was in his mind the strongest impulse to tell her that he loved her, and to settle the matter by an engagement, which must, however, he felt, be a secret one, giving satisfaction to themselves but no one else. And here it may be remarked that whereas Hester was apt to be seized by sudden fits of shame at the idea that perhaps, after all her thoughts on the subject, he was not thinking of her at all, Edward on the other hand felt no such alarm, and never thought it even presumptuous on his part to assume the certainty of her love for him, which, as the reader knows, was a certainty to which she had not herself attained. He believed with simplicity that when, if ever (nay, certainly it was to happen some time), he declared himself, Hester would respond at once. He acknowledged to himself that it was possible that in pique, or impatience, or weariness, if he did not keep a vigilant watch over the situation, it might happen that Hester would accept some one else. Her mother might drive her to it, or the impossibility of going on longer might drive her to it; but he had so much confidence in the simplicity of her nature that he did not believe that the complications which held him in on every side could affect her, and was sure that in her heart the question was solved in the most primitive way.

This was and generally is the great difference between the man and woman in such a controversy; until he had spoken, it was a shame to her that she should ask herself did he intend to speak; but Edward felt no shame if ever the idea crossed his mind that he might be mistaken in supposing she loved him; such a discovery would have made him furious. He would have aimed all sorts of ill names, such as coquette and jilt, at her; but he had no fear of any such mistake. He felt sure that he had her in his power, and when he did declare himself would be received with enthusiasm; and he always meant to declare himself some time, to reward her long suspense, and to make her the happiest of women. In words, this part is generally allotted to the lady, as it was in the days of chivalry. But the nineteenth century has modified many things, and if ever (out of America) it was really the woman who occupied the more commanding position, it is no longer so in the apprehension of the world. Only in this particular case, as has been seen, Edward was wrong. It is possible enough that in the curious position of affairs between them she would have followed his lead whatever it might be; but even this was by no means certain, and as a matter of fact, though her curiosity about him drew her mind after him, she had not even gone so far as he had, nor come to any ultimate certainty on the case at all.

Emma Ashton, who by means of propinquity—that quick knitter of bonds—had become Hester's frequent companion, had very different ideas on a similar subject. There was no sort of indefiniteness in her views. She was perfectly clear as to what she was likely to do in a given case, and the case in question occupied probably almost as great a share in her thoughts as the different yet similar question which agitated the mind of Hester. It was indeed to outward view, though with so many and subtle differences, a very similar question. Emma's wonder was whether Reginald Merridew would "speak" before she went away. She had no doubt that all the requisite sentiments were existing, and she had satisfied herself that when he did "speak" there was no reason why she should not reply favourably. The family was "quite respectable," it might almost be said also that it was "quite well off," but that there were rumours that Algernon was to be "made an eldest son of," which were somewhat disquieting. The suggestion was one which made Emma indignant, notwithstanding the gratitude she owed Algernon and his wife for giving her "her chance" in Redborough.

"When there is an estate I suppose it is all right," Emma said; "anyhow it can't be helped when that's the case: and there must be an eldest son. But when your property is in money it does seem such a mistake to make a difference between your children. Don't you think so? Oh, but I do; they are just one as good as another, and why should one be rich and another poor? If old Mr. Merridew does any-

thing of this sort I am sure I shall always think it is very
unfair."

"I suppose Mr. Merridew has a right to do what he
pleases?" said Hester; "and as it does not matter to
us——"

"You speak a great deal too fast," said Emma, offended.
"Say it doesn't matter to you: but it may to me a great
deal, and therefore I take a great interest in it. Do you
think parents have a right to do what they please? If they
make us come into the world, whether we wish it or not, of
course they are bound to do their best for us. I am the
youngest myself, and I hope I know my place; but then
there was no money at all among us. Papa spent it all
himself; so certainly we had share and share alike, for there
was nothing. When that's the case nobody can have a word
to say. But the Merridews have a good deal, and every one
ought to have his just share. Not but what I like Algernon
Merridew very much. He is always very agreeable, and I
think it very nice both of Ellen and him that they should
have been so kind to me and given me my chance, though
you say we're no relations. I am sure I always thought we
were relations, for my part."

"Did you think Reginald was your relation too?"

"Well, not perhaps quite so far as that—a connection I
should have said; but it does not matter very much now,"
Emma said, with a little simper of satisfaction. "What a
good thing Roland found out about grandpapa and grandmamma, Hester—and how fortunate that they should have
asked *me !* If everything goes right I shall feel that I owe
the happiness of my life to it. When a girl goes out upon a
visit, she never knows what may happen before she gets
home—or even she may never need to go home at all. I
don't know if I shall, I am sure. To talk about anything
taking place from Roland's house would be absurd. Why,
we don't even know the clergyman! and nobody cares a bit
about us. If there was any meaning in home it should be
from Elinor's, you know—for everybody knows us there."

"What do you mean about 'anything taking place?'—and
from—from what?" Hester asked, who never paid too much
attention to Emma's monologues, and had altogether lost the
thread of her discoursings now.

"Oh," cried Emma, clasping Hester's arm close, "how you
do make one blush! Of course you know very well what I

mean. If he speaks before I go away—and I am sure I hope he will, for it would be such a nuisance to have him following me up to Kilburn!—I don't suppose there would be any occasion for waiting long. Why should people wait when they are well off enough, and nothing to be gained by it? When the man has not got settled in a proper situation, or when there is not enough to live upon, then of course they must put it off; but in such a case as ours—I mean this, you know—it might as well be here as anywhere," Emma said, reflectively. "Cousin Catherine has always been very kind to me. Rather than let grandpapa and grandmamma be disturbed at their age, I shouldn't wonder if she would give the breakfast—especially considering the double connection, and that it is such a very good thing to get me settled. You needn't laugh, Hester. It is not a thing to laugh at. Unless I had settled, what should I have done? You are an only daughter, you don't know what it is to be the youngest and have no proper home."

These words mollified Hester, who had been in lofty opposition, half disgusted, half indignant. She was brought down by this appeal to her sympathy. "But you are happy with your brother?" she said.

"Oh, yes—happy enough; Roland is very kind. And though it's a small house, it is tolerably nice, and two maids with nothing particular to do. But it is very dull, you know, and I don't know many people. And you must always take into consideration that at any moment Roland might marry, and then where should I be? Why, he admires you very much. He might just as likely as not, next time he comes, make you an offer; and then where should I be?"

"You think, I suppose," said Hester, loftily, "that when a man makes an offer, as you say, that is all about it; there is no opposition to be looked for on the girl's side."

"Well, you know," said Emma, "I call you one of the high-flown ones. There are always some like that. But in an ordinary way what do girls want but their chance? And when they've got it, what folly to refuse—at least in my position, Hester. If I don't get settled, what have I to look forward to? Roland will marry sooner or later. He's an awful flirt, and though he admires you very much, I shouldn't advise you to have anything to do with him unless you just marry him out and out. I should think he'd make a good husband. But don't be engaged to him, Hester; mind my words. Be married in three weeks, or have nothing to say to him—that is my advice. Oh, you need not be huffy. I am sure I don't want you or any one to marry him, at least till I am settled. But if I don't settle now, he is sure, of course, to marry some time; and then where shall I be? This is what makes me wish that if—*he*, you know, is going to speak, he would do it, and not shilly-shally. It is astonishing how men shilly-shally. I think they take a pleasure in it. They would know better if they had to wait as we have, and wonder, and feel that we can't make any arrangements or settle anything till we know what's coming. If I have to go away and he never says anything, I don't know what I shall do."

"Is this because you — care so much for Reginald Merridew ? " Hester could not so form her lips as to say love.

Emma made a sort of reflective pause. "I like him well enough," she said. "I am not one to go on about love and so forth. Besides, that sort of thing is not becoming in a girl. You can't, till you are quite certain what *they* mean, don't you know? It is dreadful to go caring for them, and all that, and then to find out that they don't care for you. A girl has to wait till they speak."

Hester listened, not with her usual mixture of amusement and indignation, but with a curious feeling of shame and alarm growing in her. Was not this what she herself was doing? Emma's desire that her supposed lover should speak and settle the question, was it not much the same thing as her own curiosity and self-questioning in respect to Edward? Emma was always more practical. She was so in sentimental matters as well as in everything else. Things that other people leave indistinct, in a half light, she put clearly, without any pretences at obscurity. Her grieved sense of the shilly-shallying of men, her consciousness of all the inconveniences that arose from their way of putting off their explanations, her prudential conviction that a girl should not commit herself by " caring for " *them*, before they made it apparent that they cared for her—were these not so many vulgar, straightforward statements of the dilemma in which Hester too found herself? But this grotesque resemblance of sentiment and situation made Hester, as may be supposed, passionately angry and indignant, not with Emma, who was guiltless, and who pursued the subject endlessly, never tiring of it, nor of going over the matter again and again from the

beginning as they walked, but with herself and Edward, and
fate, which had placed her in such circumstances. It was
something like a caricature of herself that was thus presented
to her, and she could scarcely help laughing at it, even while
she resented it warmly as an insult offered to her by—
whom? not Emma—by circumstances, and evil fortune, and
the spite of a position which was intolerable, and Catherine
Vernon.   All these persons were conspiring against her, but
none of them were so hard upon Hester as this little purring,
deliberate Emma, holding up her little distorted mirror that
Hester in her pride might see how like was the image in it to
her own troubled face.

CHAPTER XXIX.

WHILE all these agitations were going on, it came to be Christmas, with the usual stir and commotion always produced in a large family and connections, by that often troublesome festival. The amount of reality in the rejoicings may be very doubtful, but yet there must be a family gathering, and the different branches of the race must seem to take kindly to it whatever may be their private sentiments. Dickens did wisely in finding his types of Christmas felicity among people to whom an accidental turkey is a benediction from heaven, and the mystery of the pudding has not lost its freshness. In such a family as the Vernons, the turkey and the pudding are unsatisfactory symbols—a return to the rude elements of plenty which were employed by a more primitive age ; and though it was certainly an excitement for the Miss Vernon-Ridgways, and Mr. Mildmay Vernon, and Mrs. John to be invited to dinner, it was by no means invariable that their feast improved the harmony of these much separated divisions of the family. It was a very big dinner, and there was no absolute breach of the peace. Catherine sat at the head of the table in a dress which, though very handsome, was by no means one of her best, and without the diamonds in which she appeared on very great occasions. This was kindly intended, in order that she might not make too evident the contrast between her own toilette and that of some of her visitors ; but the kindness of the intention was not appreciated.

"We are not considered worth dressing for," Miss Matilda said, in her sister's ear, after they had respectively kissed their relative, and, with effusion, wished her a merry Christmas.

"She thinks it better taste to be as shabby as we are," said the other, which indeed was very true, though no offence was meant.

As for Mrs. John, though she was quite willing to enjoy herself, her mind was kept in a state of nervous anxiety about Hester, who was in the defiant mood with which she always met her cousin. It had been her mother's desire to dress her plainly in one of the simple dresses made up on the foundation of the "silk slip," which by this time had been worn out as a ball-dress. These economies were very necessary, and indeed it ought to be said that the ball-dresses could not have been kept up as they were, but for the sacrifice of Mrs. John's Indian shawl, which, after Hester and the pearls, was the thing in the world which the poor lady held most dear.

Hester had not resisted the substitution of the simpler dress for those carefully preserved clouds of tarlatan which were sacred to the Dancing Teas. But she stood firm to the pearls, and insisted on wearing them. "Unless you will put them on yourself, mamma," she said.

"I wear them, Hester! Oh, no! They have been in their box all these years, and I have never put them on, you know. I kept them for you. But don't you think, dear, that just for a family dinner—no one is expected to be fine at a family dinner——"

"Don't you want Catherine Vernon to see them, mother? If it is so, tell me at once."

"Don't I want Catherine Vernon—to see them?" cried Mrs. John, stupefied with astonishment. "I wonder," she added, regretfully, "what there is between you that makes you lose your good sense, Hester—for you are very sensible in most things, and far cleverer than I ever was—the moment Catherine Vernon's name is mentioned? I cannot think what it can be."

"Oh, mother! You are too good—if that is what not being clever means. When I think how you have been allowed to stand in the corner of that room, and nobody taking any notice of you."

"My dear," said Mrs. John, mildly, "I did not require to go unless I liked."

"And now this dinner—a sort of Christmas dole for her relations—like the flannel petticoats to the poor women."

"We do not require to go unless we like," said Mrs. John ; "but if you will reflect a little, Hester, that is not how a lady should talk."

It was seldom that the mild little woman said so much. When Hester came up to Catherine, following her mother's little figure, clothed in a black silk gown which had seen a great deal of service, she read, with an excitement that made her glow, that Catherine's first glance was upon the pearls.

"You are quite fine," she said as she went through the Christmas formula, and dropped a formal kiss upon Hester's reluctant cheek ; "you have put on your lovely pearls to do us honour."

"She is fond of the pearls," said Mrs. John, who was very watchful to prevent any collision ; 'they were her grandmother's, and her great grandmother's, Catherine. It is not only for their value that one is fond of things like these."

"Their value is sometimes the worst thing about them," said Catherine, feeling that there was a sternness of virtue in what she said which justified her dislike. But Mrs. John stood her ground.

"I don't think so," she said simply. "I like them to be worth a great deal, for they are all she will have."

Hester, thus talked over, stood drawing back, in all her flush of youthful indignation, kept down by the necessities of the occasion. She gave a glance round at the little audience which was enjoying the encounter, the Miss Vernon-Ridgways in the foreground. She caught their keen inquisitive stare, and the mantling of delight upon their faces as they witnessed the little passage of arms ; and Mr. Vernon Mildmay craning over their shoulders with his sharp face projected to see what it was, and Mrs. Reginald's countenance half sympathetic, half-preoccupied (for to-day for the first time her eldest boy had accompanied her, and she was very anxious lest he should do or say anything that might injure him with Catherine). But the one thing Hester did not catch was Edward's eyes, which, surely if he had cared for her, ought now to have been raised in kindness. He was outside of the circle, his head turned away, taking no notice. When Mrs. John fell back to give way to Ellen Merridew, who came up rustling and jingling with all her bracelets, Edward still kept apart. He was talking to Harry, to Algernon, to everybody except the two who, Hester felt, wanted the succour of a chivalrous sympathy. But Mrs. John had no feeling of

this kind. She felt that she had held her own. She looked
with a mild pride upon the group of her neighbours all so
eagerly watching for mischief. It was natural, when you
think of it, that she should treat the ill-nature of the Miss
Vernon-Ridgways with gentle disdain. Poor things! they
had neither a daughter nor a necklace of pearls. And as she
had not been at the *Thés dansantes*, nor seen Edward in any
aspect but that he had always borne at the Grange, she felt
no anxiety as to his present behaviour. Harry's was the eye
which she sought. She beamed with smiles when he came and
stood beside her. Harry was always faithful, whoever might
be careless. She looked at him and at Hester with a little
sigh; but who could tell what might happen with patience
and time?

There was, however, one moment during the evening in
which Edward had the opportunity of setting himself right.
It was while the departures were going on, while the ladies
were being shawled and cloaked. Catherine had not come
down stairs, and in the darkness of the further corner of the
hall, under cover of the chatter of Ellen and Emma Ashton,
the young man ventured upon a hurried whisper—

"Do you despise me or detest me most?" he said in
Hester's ear. She started—what with the sudden proximity,
what with the unexpected character of the question.

"I wonder?" she answered coldly. He took the opportunity
of wrapping her cloak round her to grasp both her hands in
a sudden, almost fierce grasp.

"You could do nothing less: but I cannot be different
here. Suspicion produces treachery, don't you know?" he
said, with his face close to her ear. "I cannot be true here.
No, don't say anything. I ought, but I cannot. It is in the
air. All of us, every one except you, we are making believe
and finding each other out, yet going on all the same. But it
is only for a time," Edward cried, grasping her hands once
more till the pressure was painful, "only for a time!"

Next moment he was standing at the door, impassible, saying good-night to every one, paying no more heed to Hester
than if she had been, as indeed she was, the least important
of all the Christmas visitors. Ellen, as a married woman and
a social power, commanded his attention, and to Emma, as
the stranger among so many who knew each other, he was
very polite. But Hester got from him the coolest good-night.
The very servants who stood about, felt a passing wonder that

the prettiest person in the company should meet with such
scant observation, but explained it by saying to each other
that " Mr. Edward, he was the one as kep' hold of the main
chance."

And Hester went home, angry, yet somewhat soothed. It
did not make her less indignant, less wrathful; but it gave
an excuse which at least had to be taken into consideration.
Before she got home, indeed, she taught herself to lay that
offence too to the score of Catherine. She went home packed
into the fly with her mother and Emma and the Miss Vernon-
Ridgways, all together. Mr. Mildmay Vernon was mounted
on the box, and the old white horse had the six people,
besides his driver, to drag behind him. He took a great deal
of time over the short bit of road, thinking probably that it
was as well to take his time over one fare as to put it in the
power of his oppressors to send him out with another, or
perhaps compel him to kick his heels at the railway station
waiting for the last train. The ladies were packed very
close inside, but not too close to talk. The sisters immediately
plunged into that "criticism of life" which could scarcely be
called poetry in their hands.

" What a blessing it is," said one, "that we can't be called
upon to eat another Christmas dinner with Catherine for
another year."

" Dear Catherine! " said the other, " she always means so
well. It is our own fault if we don't carry out her
intentions."

"Indeed," said Mrs. John, " she gave us a very nice dinner,
and everything was very comfortable."

" Dear Mrs. John! you are always so charitable," said
Miss Matilda, " as we all ought to be, I am sure. Did you
ever see anything so insufferable as that little Ellen—like a
picture out of a fashion-book—giving herself as many airs
as if she were at the head of society? I never heard she had
any society, except the vulgar young people on the Thursdays.
I wonder she doesn't ask her shop people."

" Oh, hush, hush! " cried Mrs. John, alarmed.

"Perhaps she does ask the shop people," said Miss Matilda,
"it would be wise of her, for I should not think they'd ever
see the colour of their money. The old Merridews can never
keep up all that extravagance, and Algey is nothing more than
a clerk in his father's office. It is dreadful to see a young
man dragged on to destruction like that."

"Oh, I hope it is not so bad !" cried Mrs. John. "I am sure if I thought so, I should never let——"

"It is the talk of the town," said Miss Matilda. "A thing must be very bad before it comes to us, who never hear any gossip."

"Oh, everybody knows," said Miss Martha.

It was happy that Hester's mind was so fully occupied, and that the conversation passed harmlessly over her head. When they reached the Vernonry, Mr. Mildmay Vernon got down from the box where he had been seated wrapped up from head to foot, but which he protested against with a continuous volley of short coughs as he helped the ladies out one after another. He thought in his heart that if one of these strong young women had been put up on the box, who had no rheumatism, it would have been more appropriate.

"I hope you have enjoyed your evening, including your dinner," he said. "I have made up my mind to rheumatism to-morrow; but what does that matter in comparison with such a delightful entertainment ? "

"It was very nice," said Mrs. John, dubious as to his meaning, as she always was.

"Nice !" he said, with a grimace, "a sort of little heaven on earth ! "

"It is wicked to be so satirical," said one sister, with a laugh ; and " Dear Catherine ! I am sure she meant everything that was kind," said the other.

And then there was a little flutter of good-nights, the respective doors opening, and lights flashing out into the dark.

This entertainment was followed very shortly after by the larger gathering which Catherine had announced her intention of giving some time before, and to which all Redborough was convoked besides the immediate family. The period between these two parties was the climax of Hester's hostility to Catherine Vernon. She had never been so actively indignant, so angry, nor so impotent against her old and wealthy cousin as in these wintry days. Catherine was a kind of impersonation of injustice and unkindness to Hester. She felt not only that she herself was oppressed and injured, but that the persecution of which she was the object was of a kind which was most petty and miserable, degrading to the author of it as well as to its victim. The attempt at interference with her movements was not only a kind of meddling most irritating to a high-spirited girl, but it was also the kind of assault which her very pride prevented her from resisting openly. Hester felt that she would have lowered her own pride and wounded her own self-respect had she uttered a word of reply, or taken any notice of the small and petty attack upon her. The incident of the pearls, though so trifling, excited her almost as much as the other and more important grievance she had against Catherine. That Edward should be so cowed by this woman that he had to conceal his real sentiments, to offend the girl whom he loved, to compromise his own honour and dignity all because of Catherine's watch upon him, and the subjection in which it held him, was such a miserable thought to Hester, that it was all she could do to restrain herself at all. It is terrible to be compelled to endure one who has harmed those who are dear to you; but to enter her house and preserve a show of peace and good-feeling, though you are aware she is causing the self-debasement of those you love, that is the hardest of all. What should it matter to Edward that Catherine's eye was upon him? An honourable and fine spirit would not have been influenced by any such oppression. It made Hester's heart sick to think that he did this consciously, deceived his bene-factress, and pretended to obey her when in his heart he loathed his bondage ; and to think that she herself should be called upon to sustain this humiliation filled her with shame and rage. But though her heart was bitter against Edward, there was yet a softening in it, an involuntary indulgence, which made her glad to elude the question so far as he was concerned, and to fix upon Catherine, who was the cause of it, with all her force of indignation.

From Hester's point of view there was indeed little to be said for this woman who, to so many in the place, was the very impersonation of active benevolence and goodness — a tyrant who seized upon the very soul of the young man whom she favoured most, and whose prying and vigilant observation forced him to deception, and made him true to himself only when he was out of her sight—a woman, who while she gave with one hand closed a grasp of iron upon the people obliged to her with the other, and would prescribe their very dress if she could. Oh, how true it must be after all, the picture of the tyrannical, narrow despot, exacting, remorseless, descending to the lowest details, which a woman, when endued with irresponsible

power, was understood to make! Hester had rebelled as
a girl does against every such injurious picture of women;
but it occurred to her now that it must all be true. No
doubt it was unsafe to trust such a creature with any
kind of authority. She would not be content with less than
absolute sway. She would let no charity nor ruth, nor the
hearts of others, nor their wishes, stand in her way. She
would crush a young life with no more compunction than a
savage. Thus Hester took refuge from questions more trying—
from the aspect of Edward which within these last few days
had become more and more important to her. Her whole
being seemed to be flowing towards him with a current which
she felt herself unable to restrain. She did not any longer
ask herself questions about his love. She tried not to ask
any questions about him at all. In her secret consciousness
there was a distrust of him, and disapproval and fear, which
had never been breathed into any ear—scarcely even into
her own. Indeed, Hester was her own only confidant.
All the things which occupied her were uncommunicable.
She had grown a woman, everything that happened was
now more important to her than in earlier days. And
now there had come a crisis in her fate, and it was not she
who held the key of the problem, nor her lover, nor any
legitimate authority—but Catherine! Catherine controlled
her future and all its issues through him. Catherine could
have stopped all further development for both, she could have
checked their love ruthlessly, and made an end of their happiness. The girl began to feel that there was something in the
presence of this woman, in her influence, in her very name,
that was insupportable. That impulse of flight which always
presents itself to the impatient spirit came upon her strongly.
Why should not she and her mother shake themselves free
from the imbroglio—go away anywhere, it did not matter
where, and get peace, at least, and a life free of agitations
and complications? Away from the Vernons she would be
free to work as she pleased, and so make up for the aid that
Catherine gave—away from them there would be no more
question of love and hate, love afraid to declare itself, hate
veiled beneath the aspect of benevolence.

Hester had very little to do at home. She had not even
books to read. She had unbounded time to think; even
her visits to her old friends, the captain and his wife, had
grown less frequent since Emma came, for Emma's monologues

were not amusing to Hester's excited mind, and the captain
and Mrs. Morgan had both yielded to their granddaughter's
irrepressible talent of speech. Hester was more at home in consequence, more alone, less subject to wholesome distractions and
interruptions. She would think and think the whole evening
through. The *Thés dansantes* began to fill her with a sort of
sickening, of weariness, and disgust. She felt as if she too, like
Emma, had gone to get her "chance" there, and was, like
Emma, hung up in degrading suspense until he should
speak. The rage with her position, the scorn of herself
with which this filled her, is indescribable. She would burst
forth into wild laughter after one of Emma's calculations,
often repeated, about Reginald Merridew; then hide her
face in her hands to conceal the burning blush — the
bitter consciousness that her own circumstances were not
much different. The self-ridicule was more painful still
than the self-disgust. She shed no tears over the question,
but the laughter was a great deal more bitter than any
tears.

Mrs. John was as unconscious of this struggle as if it had
gone on in Kamschatka and not under her own eye, in her own
parlour, and the bedroom that opened into hers. She was not
one of the women who divine. She understood what was told
her, and not always that—never anything more than was told
her. She thought her child was not looking well, but then,
she had a cold; and there is nothing more oppressive than a
cold. The first thing that really startled her was Hester's
determination not to go to Mrs. Merridew's party on the first
Thursday that occurred after Christmas, which was to be a
particularly brilliant one. This struck her mother with
consternation.

"Do you think your cold is so bad as that? I would
not wish you to do anything imprudent, but I have often
heard girls say that a ball was the very best thing for a cold.
If you were to nurse up this evening, and have your breakfast
in bed, I can't help thinking you would feel quite yourself
to-morrow, my darling," Mrs. John said.

"It is not my cold," said Hester; and then she reflected
that it was a pity to throw aside so excellent a plea. "At
least it is not altogether my cold."

"Oh, I know how oppressed one feels, just good for nothing;
but, my love, you would feel sorry after. It is a pity to give
in. You shall have a foot-bath to-night with some mustard

in it, and a hot drink.   And you must not get up till mid-day.
You'll feel a great deal better after that."

"I don't want to go—I am tired of them," Hester said, her
impatience getting the better of her, "once a week is a great
deal too often.   I am sick of the very name of dancing."

"My love!" cried her mother in consternation.   Then she
came behind her and gave her a soft little kiss.   "I think I
shall give you quinine, for I am sure you're low," she said,
"and you must be bright and well, and looking your best for
Catherine's great party, which is next week."

"I don't——" cried Hester, then stopped short, for she had
not the heart to give her mother a double wound by declaring
she would not go to Catherine's party.   One such blow was
enough at a time.

The astonishment with which her non-appearance at Mrs.
Merridew's was regarded by all the connection was unbounded.
The discovery that Hester *was not going*, filled the Miss Ridg-
ways with excitement.   What could be the cause?

"I suppose there has been a quarrel," the sisters said.
"Ellen is a little minx: but still she is a true Vernon, and won't
stand any such airs as that girl gives herself.   Her mother and
she are insupportable, with their pearls and their pretences."

"Roman pearls," said Mr. Mildmay Vernon, "and Brumma-
gem pretences."

So they discussed the question.   When Hester went in
next day to Captain Morgan's, not without a little curiosity
to hear from Emma what had been said of her absence: "I
am glad you have recovered," Mrs. Morgan said, kissing
her, and looking into her face with an air of reproach and a
shake of the head.

"It is not like you to give in for a cold," the old captain
added; but fortunately for Hester all explanation on her
part, and all remonstrance on theirs, was cut short by the
persevering deliberate voice which now was the principal
circumstance in the old people's house.

"I assure you Ellen was very much astonished, Hester.
She looked at me as if she could not believe her eyes.   And
they all looked at me as if it was my fault.   How could it be
my fault?   I didn't give you your cold.   I think there were
more people than usual.   We had Sir Roger de Coverley, you
know, because it was Christmas.   I danced it with young Mr.
Norris, who has just come into his fortune, you know.   He is
very nice.   He asked me for four dances, but I only gave him

three. Don't you think I was right, grandmamma? That is
the worst of Ellen's parties, that there are no old chaperons
with experience, that could advise you on a point like that.
Two waltzes and then the Sir Roger, which is a sort of extra
you know, and doesn't count. I don't think there could be
anything wrong in that."

"You should not give in, Hester," said the old captain.
"That is not like you. What is a cold at your age? You
should always stand to your colours, and hold your— —"

"Oh, I said to everybody, Hester had such a bad cold,"
said Emma. "I said her nose was red and that it quite
affected her voice. So it does. You don't notice it so much
when she flames up like that. I wonder how you can blush
in that way, Hester. It is the difference of complexion, I
suppose. I always keep the same. It is nice in some ways,
for however hot it is you can be sure you are not a figure; but
in other respects I should like to change colour like that. It
makes you look interesting. People think you are so sensitive, and that sort of thing, when it's only just complexion.
Harry Vernon was more grumphy than ever because you
were not there, always standing about beside Ellen, and looking after her, which, considering she's married, is a great deal
more than any brother ought to take upon him. I am sure if
Roland did, I should not know what to think. But then
Ellen is an only sister, which makes a great difference, and I
am the youngest. Reginald Merridew was in such a way! I
was engaged for almost every dance before he came. I quite
enjoyed it. I filled up my card as soon as I could, just to give
him a lesson. Men should be kept in their proper places. I
never thought you showed half a spirit letting Edward Vernon
carry you off just as he pleased."

"My dear," said old Mrs. Morgan, making an endeavour to
strike in, "we have not seen half so much of you lately as we
like to do. My old man misses you on his walk. Do go and
take a walk with him, as your cold is better."

"Oh, don't send her away when I just want to talk over
everything," said Emma. "You never think what young
people like. I am sure you are very kind and nice, grandmamma, I always say so. Whatever any one may think, I
always maintain that you have been very nice and kind to me :
and kept me such a time—when I dare say you are tired
of me. But you don't remember what young people like. Of
course Hester wants to hear who was there, and how every

one was looking, and who danced with who, and all that.
There are always a hundred things that we have to say to each
other. Come up with me to my room, Hester, and then we
shan't bore grandmamma and grandpapa. I have such a lot
to tell you. Ellen had such a lovely new dress, old gold and
black. It sounds much too old for her, but it wasn't a bit. It
was quite a change among all the whites and pinks. I just went
in my grenadine. I don't pretend to cope with the rich girls,
you know. If the men want to dance with rich dresses they
must just leave me alone. I am always straightforward. I
say, 'Don't ask me unless you are sure you don't mind.' But
I suppose they like my dancing or something, for I always
have my card full. Sir Roger de Coverley was really fun.
We were all dancing, it seemed about a mile going down the
middle. It is such a pity you weren't there. Edward Vernon
danced it with—I really forget who he danced it with—one of
the Miss Bradleys or Mary Wargrave, or one of that set.
Are you really going out with grandpapa? That is awfully
self-denying of you, to please the old gentleman. And it
is so cold. Grandmamma, I do think you shouldn't let her
go."

"She can hear your report another time—indeed she has
heard a great deal of it already," said old Mrs. Morgan.
"You don't lose any time, Emma. But, Hester, if you are
afraid——"

" Oh, I shouldn't go on any account," cried Emma, "with a
bad cold. But then I have such dreadful colds when I do
have them. I am obliged to go to bed. I never get my nose
red like Hester's, nor lose my voice—but I get such a cough.
I am so thankful I have not had one here. It gives everybody so much trouble when you get ill on a visit, and you
lose all the good of the visit, and might just as well be at
home. There is grandpapa calling. I should just let him call,
if it was me. Well, Hester, if you will go I can't help it.
Come in again if you are not afraid of the evening air, and
you shall hear all the rest ; or if you'll have me at tea time,
perhaps that will be best. I'll go to you——"

The old captain sighed as he went out. Emma was, as it
were, left speaking, standing on the step of the door addressing
Hester as she followed her old friend out into the dusky afternoon of one of those black days that conclude the year. Very
black days they were on this occasion, not so cold as December often is, without snow or any of the harsher signs of

winter, but also without sun or any of the exhilarating sharpness of the frost. Everything was dry, but dark, the skies leaden, the very Common showing less green. The captain went on before with a woollen comforter wrapped in many folds about his throat, and woollen mittens on the hand which grasped his stick with so much energy. He struck it against the ground as if he had been striking some one as he hurried away.

"I think that girl will be the death of us," he said : then repented of his sharp utterance. "I told you I thought you were a spiritual grandchild, Hester. What the child of our child whom we lost, who never had a child, would have been. And you have spoiled us for the other thing—the grandchild of common life."

"It is a long time since we have been out together," said Hester, as the old man put his other hand in its large mitten within her slender arm.

"And you have been in the meantime getting into some of the muddles," he said. "It was kind of my old wife to hand you over to me, Hester. We all think our own experience the best. She would like to have had you to herself, to find out all about it, and give you the help of her old lights; but instead of that she was self-denying, and handed you over to me. And now let me hear what it is, and see if the old ship's lantern will do you any good."

"Am I in any muddles?" said Hester. "I don't know— Perhaps there is nothing to tell. It is so hard to divide one thing from another."

"So it is; but when it is divided it is easier to manage," said the old captain. He paused a little to give her time to speak : but as she did not do so he resumed on an indifferent subject, that the girl's confidence might not be forced. "I am always glad when the old year is over. You will say I am an old fool for that, as my days are so few. But the first of January is a great deal gayer than the last of December, though they may be exactly like each other. When you can say there will be spring this year——"

"Captain Morgan," said Hester, who had been taking advantage of the pause without paying any attention to what he said, "Catherine Vernon is angry because I wear my mother's pearls. How should that be?"

"You must be mistaken, my dear," said the old captain, promptly. "She has her faults, but Catherine is never paltry, Hester. That cannot be."

"Either you are very much mistaken about her, or I am much mistaken about her," Hester said.

The old man looked at her with a smile on his face.

"I don't say anything against that. And which of us is most likely to be right?" he asked. "I knew her before you were born."

"Oh, before I was born! Does that tell you anything about her conduct to *me*? Once I was not, but now I am; and somebody quite distinct from other people."

"Very distinct!" Captain Morgan said.

"Then what does she mean by it?" cried Hester. "She cannot endure the sight of me. Oh, I know she is not paltry in one way. She does not care about money, as some people do; but she is in another. Why should she care about what I wear? Did you ever hear anything about my father?" the girl said raising her eyes suddenly, and looking him full in the face. The old captain was so taken by surprise that he fell back a step and almost dropped her arm in his dismay.

"About your father!"

"About him and Catherine Vernon—and how it was he went away. He had as good a right to the bank as she had, had he not? I have not thought much about it; but I should like to know," said Hester with more composure, "how it was that she had it, and not papa?"

"That was all before my time," said Captain Morgan, who had recovered himself in the interval. "I did not come here, you know, till after. And then it is not as if I had been a Vernon to understand all the circumstances. I was not of the family, you know."

"That is true," said Hester thoughtfully, and she suffered herself to be led into safer subjects without any serious attempt to return to a question so unanswerable; while Captain Morgan on his side was too much alarmed by the possibility of having to explain to her the steps which had led to her father's expatriation to inquire any more into the "muddles" which he had read in her countenance. And thus they made their way home together without any mutual satisfaction. The captain was obliged to own to his wife afterwards that he had given Hester no aid or good advice.

"She asked me about her father: and was I going to be so brutal as to tell the poor child what has always been concealed from her?"

"Concealments are never good," Mrs. Morgan said, shaking her head. "It would be better for her to know." But the captain had an easy victory when he said "Should you like to be the one to tell her?" with defiance in his voice.

Thus the time went on for Catherine Vernon's great Christmas party, to which all Redborough was asked. It was not till the day before that Hester was bold enough to declare her intention not to go. "You must not be angry, mamma. What should I go for? It is no pleasure. The moment I am within Catherine Vernon's house I am all wrong. I feel like a beggar, a poor relation, a dependent upon her charity; and she has no charity for me. Don't make me go."

"Oh Hester, my darling," said Mrs. John. "It would never, never do to stay away, when everybody is there! And you her relation, that ought to wish to do her what honour you can."

"Why should I wish to do her honour? She has never been kind to us. She has never treated you as she ought to have done. She has never behaved to us as a relation should, or even as a gentlewoman should."

"Oh hush! Hester, hush!" said Mrs. John. "You don't know what you are speaking of. If you knew all, you would know that Catherine has behaved to us—better than we had any right to expect."

"Then let me know all, mother," said Hester, sitting upright, her eyes shining, her whole face full of inquiry. "I have felt lately that there must be something which was concealed from me. Let me know all."

Then Mrs. John faltered and explained. "There is nothing for you to know. Dear, dear, you are so literal. You take everything one says to you, Hester, as if one meant it. There are just things that one says——When I said if you knew all, I meant—if you were to consider properly, if you saw things in a just light—"

"I think you mean something more than that," Hester said.

"What should I mean more? We had no claims upon her. Your poor father had got his share. He had not perhaps been very prudent with it, but I never understand anything about business. He got his share, all that he had any right to expect. Catherine might have said that, when we came back so poor; but she did not. Hester, you have forgotten what she has done for us. Oh, my dear, if you knew all!

No, I don't mean that there is anything to know—but just
if you would think—Hester, you must not insult Catherine
in the sight of all Redborough by refusing to go to her party.
You must not, indeed you must not. If you do, you will
break my heart."

"What I do is of no importance to Catherine Vernon.
Oh, mother, do not make me go. It is more than I can bear."

"But you are of importance, and she would feel it deeply.
Oh, Hester, for my sake!" Mrs. John cried with tears in her
eyes. She would not be turned away from the subject or
postpone it. Her daughter had never seen her so deeply in
earnest, so intent upon having her way before. On previous
occasions it had been Hester that had won the day. But
this time the girl had to give way to the impassioned
earnestness of her mother, which in so mild a woman was
strange to see.

CHAPTER XXX.

THE PARTY AT THE GRANGE.

CATHERINE's Christmas party called forth all Redborough. It was an assembly to which the best people in the place considered themselves bound to go, notwithstanding that many of the small people were there also. Everybody indeed was supposed to come, and all classes were represented. The respectable old clerks, who had spent their lives in the bank, talked upon equal terms, according to the fiction of society, with the magnates of the town, and Edward and Harry Vernon, and others of the golden youth, asked their daughters to dance. The great ladies in their jewels sat about upon the sofas, and so did Mrs. Halifax, the cashier's wife, and Mrs. Brown, the head clerk's, in their ribbons. All was supposed to be equality and happiness; if it were not so, then the fault was upon the shoulders of the guests, and not of the hostess, who walked about from one to another, and was so civil to Mrs. Brown—so very civil—that Lady Freemantle could not help whispering to Mrs. Merridew that, after all, when a woman had once been engaged in business, it always left a mark upon her.

"She is more at home with those sort of persons than she is with the county," Lady Freemantle said.

Mrs. Merridew was deeply flattered with the confidence, and gave a most cordial assent. "It does give a sort of an unfeminine turn of mind, though dear Miss Vernon is so universally respected," she said.

This little dialogue would have given Catherine sincere enjoyment if she had heard it. She divined it from the conjunction of Lady Freemantle's diamonds with Mrs. Merridew's lace, as they leant towards each other, and from the expression and direction of their eyes.

On her side, Mrs. Brown drew conclusions quite as fallacious. " Miss Vernon is well aware how much the young gentlemen owe to Brown," that lady said afterwards, " and how devoted he is. She knows his value to the business, and I am sure she sees that a share in the bank is what he has a right to look to."

This delusion, however, Catherine did not divine.

It was with a reluctance and repugnance indescribable that Hester had come : but she was there, by the side of her mother, who, a little alarmed by the crowd, did not know what to do with herself, until Harry Vernon interposed and led her to the corner of a sofa, in the very midst of the fine people, which poor Mrs. John, divided between the pride which was too proud to take a chief place and the consciousness that this place was her right, hesitated greatly upon.

" I think I should like to be farther off," she said, faltering ; "down there somewhere," and she pointed in the direction of the Mrs. Browns — " or anywhere," she added, getting confused.

"This is your proper place," said Harry out of his moustache, with persistence.

The poor lady sat down in a nervous flutter in her black silk gown, which looked very nice, but had lasted a long time, and though it had been kept, so to speak, within sight of the fashion by frequent alterations, was very different from the elegant mixture of velvet and satin, fresh from the hands of a court milliner, which swept over the greater part of the space. Mrs. John had a little cap made of a piece of fine Mechlin upon her hair, which was still very pretty, and of the dark brown satin kind. Her ornaments were of the most modest description, whereas the other lady had a set of emeralds which were the admiration of the county. Hester stood behind her mother very erect and proud, in her white muslin, with her pearls, looking like a maid of honour to a mild, discrowned queen. A maid of honour in such circumstances would stand a great deal more upon her dignity than her mistress would be likely to do. This was the aspect they presented to the lookers-on who saw them in that unusual eminence. When Catherine perceived where her poor pensioners were placed, she gave way to a momentary impatience.

"Who put Mrs. John there?" she said to Edward, almost with anger. "Don't you see how thoroughly out of place she looks? You may think it shows a fine regard for the fallen, but she would have been much more comfortable at the other end among the people she knows."

"I had nothing to do with it. I have not spoken to them," said Edward with a certain sullenness. He was glad to be able to exculpate himself, and yet he despised himself all the more fiercely.

Catherine was vexed in a way which she herself felt to be unworthy, but which she said to herself was entirely justified by the awkwardness of the situation.

"I suppose it is Harry that has done it," she said, her voice softened by the discovery that Edward at least was not to blame. "It must be said for him, at least, that he is very faithful to his family."

Did she mean that *he* was not faithful? Edward asked himself. Did even she despise him? But he could not now change his course, or stoop to follow Harry's example, that oaf who was inaccessible to the fluctuations of sentiment around him, and could do nothing but cling to his one idea. It cannot be said, however, that either Mrs. John or Hester were at their ease in their present position. It was true, as Catherine had said, that with the curate's wife Mrs. John would have been much more comfortable, and this consciousness wounded the poor lady, who felt that she now was out of place among the people to whom she was allied by nature. She was accustomed to the slight of being put in a lower place, but to feel herself so completely out of her old position, went to her heart. She looked timidly, poor soul, at the great lady with the emeralds, remembering when she, too, used to be in the order of great ladies, and wondering if in those days she had ever despised the lowly. But when she thus raised her eyes she found that the lady of the emeralds was looking very fixedly at her.

"Surely," she said, after a little hesitation, "this must be Lucy Westwood."

"Yes," said Mrs. John wistfully, investigating the stranger with her timid eyes.

"Then have you forgotten 'Bridget—Fidget?'" said the other.

It was a school name, and it brought a glow upon Mrs. John's pale face. An old school-fellow! She forgot all the painful past and her present embarrassment, and even her

daughter. Hester stood for some time in her maid-of-honour
attitude and contemplated the conversation. She heard her
mother say, " This is my girl—the only one I have," and felt
herself crimsoning and curtseying vaguely to some one she
scarcely saw ; then the stranger added—

" I have three here ; but I think they are all dancing."

Yes, no doubt there was dancing going on, but Hester had
no part in it. She became tired, after a while, of her post of
maid of honour. Her wonderful indignant carriage, the poise
of her young head, the proud air of independence which was
evident in her, called forth the admiration of many of the
spectators. " Who is that girl ? " said the elder people, who
only came once a year, and were unacquainted with the gossip
of Redborough. " John Vernon's daughter ? Oh, that was
the man who ought to have married Catherine—he who nearly
ruined the bank ? And that is her mother ? How good of
Catherine to have them here." If Hester had heard these
remarks she would have had few questions to ask about her
father. But she was unaware of the notice she was attracting,
placed thus at the head of the great drawing-room. The
folding doors had been removed and the two rooms made
into one. The girl was in the most conspicuous position
without knowing ; her white figure stood out against the
wall, with her little mother in the foreground. She stood
for a long time looking out with large eyes, full of light,
upon the crowd, her varying emotions very legible in her
face. When a creature so young and full of life feels herself
neglected and disdained, and sees others about her whom
her keen eyes cannot help but see are inferior to herself,
promoted far above her, enjoying what is forbidden to her,
finding pleasure where she has none—yet is bound to the spot
and cannot escape, it is natural that indignation should light
fires in her eyes, and that her breast should swell and her
young countenance glow with a visionary scorn of all who seem
to scorn her. This sentiment is neither amiable nor desirable,
but it gave a sort of inspiration to Hester—her head so erect,
slightly thrown back, her nostrils a little dilated, her mouth
shut close, her eyes large and open, regarding in full face
the world of enemies against whom, whole or singly, she
felt herself ready to stand. All this gave a character
and individuality to her such as nothing in the room could
equal. But by and by she tired of standing, shut out from
everybody, holding up her banner. She stole away from her

mother's side, behind the chairs, to get to somebody she knew and could talk to. Flesh and blood cannot bear this sort of martyrdom of pride for ever.

An old man was standing in her way, who made a little movement to stop Hester as she passed. "You will excuse an old friend, Miss Hester," he said; "but I must tell you how glad I am to see you and your mother. I have been looking at you both ever since you came. She is very much changed since I used to see her, but her sweet expression is the same. That is a thing that will never change."

"I think I know you," said Hester, with the shy frankness which was so unlike her hostile attitude. "Did not I see you at Captain Morgan's? and you said something to me about my mother?"

"I had not much time to tell you then. I should just like to describe it to you," said the old clerk. "I have never forgotten that day. I was in a dreadful state of anxiety, fearing that everything was coming to an end; and the only place I could think of going to was the White House. That was where your parents were staying at the time. No, no, they were not your parents then; I think there was a little baby that died——"

"I was born abroad," said Hester, eager to catch every word.

"Yes, yes, to be sure; and she was quite young, not much older than you are now. It was in that long room at the White House, with a window at each end, which is the dining-room now. You will excuse me for being a little long-winded, Miss Hester. It was beautifully furnished, as we thought then; and there was a harp and a piano. Does your mamma ever play the harp now? No, no, I ought to remember, that has quite gone out of fashion. She had her hair high up on her head like this," said Mr. Rule, trying to give a pantomimic description on the top of his own grey head of the high bows which had once adorned Mrs. John's. "She had a white dress on, far shorter than you wear them now; and little slippers with crossed bands, sandals they used to call them. Oh, I remember everything like a picture! Ladies used to wear little short sleeves in those days, and low dresses. She had a little scarf round her over one shoulder. What a pretty creature she was, to be sure! I had been so wretched and anxious that the sight of her as I came rushing in, had the strangest effect upon me. All bank business and our troubles about money, and the terror of a run, which was what I was frightened for, seemed nothing but ugly dreams, without any reality in them. I dare say you don't know, Miss Hester, what I mean by a run?"

"No, indeed," said Hester, a little impatient; "but I should like to know what happened after."

"A run on the bank," said the old clerk, "is the most terrible thing in all creation. A battle is nothing to it—for in a battle you can at least fight for your life. It happens when the partners or the company, or whatever they may be, have had losses, or are reported to have had losses, and a rumour gets up against the bank. Sometimes it may be a long time threatening, sometimes it may get up in a single day—but as soon as the rumour gets the length of a panic, everybody that has money deposited comes to draw it out, and everybody that has a note of the bank comes for his money. In those days Vernon's issued notes, like all the other great country banks. I was in mortal terror for a run: I never was in such a state in my life. And it was then, as I told you, Miss Hester, that I went to your mother. Of course we had not money enough to meet it—the most solvent could scarcely hope to have that at a moment's notice. Next day was the market day, and I knew that, as sure as life——! I have passed through many a troublesome moment, but never one like that."

And, as if even the thinking of it was more than he could bear, the old clerk took out his handkerchief and wiped his forehead. Hester had listened with great interest, but still with a little impatience: for though the run upon the bank would have interested her at another time, it was more than her attention was equal to now.

"But was not my father here as well as my mother?" said Hester, in her clear voice, unconscious of any need to subdue it.

Mr. Rule looked at her with a startled air and a half-involuntary "hush!"

"Your father!" he said, with a tone of consternation. "Oh; the fact was that your father—did not happen to be there at the time."

Hester waved her hand slightly as a token for him to go on. She had a feeling that these words were of more import-ance than they seemed to be, but they confused her, and she did not as yet see what this importance was. She remembered that she had thought so when he told her this incident before.

"Where was I?" said Mr. Rule. "Oh, yes, I remember; just going into the White House with my mind full of trouble, not knowing what to do. Well, Miss Hester, when I found that your—I mean when I discovered that your—mother was alone, I told her the dreadful condition I was in—Nobody to say what to do, no chief authority to direct, and market-day to-morrow, and a run as sure as fate. Now, you know, we could have telegraphed all over the country, but there was no such thing as a telegraph then. I had to explain it to her just as I have to you, and I feel sure she didn't understand me in the very least. She only knew there was money wanted. She stepped across the room in her pretty sandals, with her scarf hanging from her shoulders, as if she had been going to play her harp, and opened a little bit of a desk, one of those gimcrack things, all rosewood and velvet, which were the fashion then, and took out all her money and brought it to me. It was in our own notes, poor dear," said old Rule, with a little laugh; "and it came to just twenty pounds. She would have made me take it—forced it upon me. She did not understand a bit. She was full of trouble and sympathy, and ready to give up everything. Ah, I have often told Miss Vernon since. It was not want of will; it was only that she did not understand."

"I am sure you mean to speak kindly of mamma," said Hester, with a quick blush of alarmed pride; "but I don't think it is so difficult to make her understand. And what did you do after that? Was there a run—and how did you provide—?"

She did not know what to say, the questions seemed to get into her throat and choke her. There was something else which she could not understand which must soon be made clear. She gave furtive glances at the old clerk, but did not look him in the face.

"Ah, I went to Miss Vernon. She was but a young lady then. Oh, I don't mean to say young like you. It is thirty years ago. She was older than your pretty young mamma, and though she had a great share in the business she never had taken any part in it. But she was come of a family that have all had fine heads for business. Look at Mr. Edward now: what a clear understanding he has, and sees exactly the right thing to do, whatever happens. She was a little

shocked and startled just at first, but she took it up in a
moment, no man could have done it better. She signed away
all her money in the twinkling of an eye, and saved the bank.
When all the crowd of the country folk came rushing to draw
out their money, she stepped in—well, like a kind of goddess
to us, Miss Hester—and paid in almost her whole fortune, all
her mother's money, every penny she had out of the business,
and pulled us through. I can remember her too, as if it had
been yesterday, the way she stepped in—with her head held
high, and a kind of a triumph about her; something like
what I have seen in yourself, my dear young lady."

"Seen in me! You have never seen me with any triumph
about me," cried Hester, bitterly. "And where have you
seen me? I scarcely know you. Ah, that was because of
the money she had. My mother, with her twenty pounds,
what could she do? But Catherine was rich. It was because
of her money."

"Her money was a great deal: but it was not the money
alone. It was the heart and the courage she had. We had
nobody to tell us what to do—but after she came, all went
well. She had such a head for business."

Hester could not stand and listen to Catherine's praises;
but she was entirely absorbed in the narrative. It seemed
terrible to her that she had not been there to be able
to step in as Catherine had done. But there was another
question pressing upon her which she had asked already, and
to which she had got no reply. She shrank from repeating it
yet felt a force upon her to do so. She fixed her large widely-
opened eyes upon the speaker, so as to lose none of the indications of his face.

"Will you tell me," she said, "how it was that you had,
as you say, nobody to tell you anything—no one at the head
—nobody to say what was to be done?"

Old Mr. Rule did not immediately reply. He made a little
pause, and shuffled with his feet, looking down at them, not
meeting her eyes.

"Hester," said Ellen Merridew, who was passing, and paused
on her partner's arm to interfere. "Why don't you dance?
What do you mean by not dancing? What are you doing
here behind backs? I have been looking for you everywhere."

"I prefer to be here," Hester answered, shortly; "never
mind me, please. Mr. Rule, will you answer me? I want
to know."

"You asked how it was that we—— What was it you asked, Miss Hester? I am very glad to see you so interested: but you ought to be dancing, not talking to an old man, as Mrs. Merridew says."

"I think you are all in a plot against me," said Hester, impatiently; "why was it you were left without a head? What had happened? Mr. Rule," cried the girl, "you know what I asked, and you know why I am so anxious. You are trying to put me off. What does it all mean?"

"It is an old story," he said; "I cannot tell what tempted me to begin about it. It was seeing you and your mother for the first time. You were not at Miss Vernon's party last year?"

"What has that to do with it?" cried Hester. "If you will not tell me, say so. I shall find out some other way."

"My dear young lady, ask me anything. Don't find out any other way. I will come and see you, if your mamma will permit me, and tell you everything about the old days. But I can't keep you longer now. And, besides, it would need a great deal of explanation. I was foolish to begin about it here, keeping you out of your natural amusement. But I'll come and tell you, Miss Hester, with pleasure," said the old man, putting on a show of easy cordiality, "any day you will name."

"Hester," said another voice over her head, "Ellen says I am not to let you stay here. Come and see the supper-room. And the hall is very pretty. I am not to go without you, Ellen says."

"Oh, what do I care for Ellen!" cried Hester, exasperated. "Go away, Harry; go and dance and amuse yourself. I don't want you or any one. Mr. Rule——"

But the old clerk had seized his opportunity. He had made a dart at some one else on the other side, while Hester turned to reply to Harry's demand. The girl found herself abandoned when she turned to him again. There had been a gradual shifting in the groups about while she stood absorbed listening to his story. She was standing now among people who were strange to her, and who looked at her curiously, knowing her to be "one of the family." As she met their curious eyes, Hester, though she had a high courage, felt her heart fail her. She was glad to fall back upon her cousin's support.

"I think you are all in a conspiracy against me," she said; but she took Harry's arm. He never abandoned her in any

circumstances. Edward had not spoken to her, nor noticed her
presence; but Harry never failed. In her excitement and
disappointment she turned to him with a sense that here she
could not go wrong. As for Harry, to whom she was seldom
so complacent, he drew her arm within his own with a flush
of pleasure.

"I know you don't think much of me," he said, "but surely
I am as good as that old fellow!" a speech at which Hester
could not but laugh. "I should like to know what he was
saying to you," Harry said.

"He was telling me about the run on the bank and how
Catherine saved it. Do you know—I wonder—— Had my
father never anything to do with it?" Hester said.

They were making their way through the crowd at the end
of the room. And Harry's countenance was not expressive.
Hester thought the stare in his eyes was directed to somebody
behind who had pushed against her. She was not suspicious that Harry could hide from her any knowledge he
possessed.

"That was ages before my time," he said very steadily.
"You might as well ask me about the flood;" and so led her
on through the many groups about the door, entirely unsuspicious that he, too, for whom she had an affectionate contempt, had baulked her. She allowed him to take her over all
the lighted rooms which opened into each other: the hall, the
library, the room blazing with lights and decorations, which
was prepared for supper. Hester had never been before at
one of these great assemblies. And she could not keep herself
entirely unmoved by the dazzling of the lights, the warmth and
largeness of the entertainment. A sort of pride came upon her,
surprising her in spite of herself: though she was so humble a
member of the family, and subject under this roof to slights
and scorns, yet she was a Vernon, and could not escape some reflection of the family glory which centred in Catherine. And as
she went into the hall a still more strange sensation suddenly
came over Hester. She caught sight, in a large mirror, of herself stepping forward, her head held high in its habitual poise of
half indignant energy, and a certain swiftness in her air and
movement, a sentiment of forward motion and progress, very
familiar to everybody who knew her, but which brought suddenly to her mind old Rule's description, "stepping in with
a kind of triumph about her, as I have seen yourself."
"Triumph!" Hester said secretly within herself, and coloured

high, with a sensation of mingled pain and pleasure, which no
words could have described. She did not know what it
meant; but it stirred her strangely. If she had been in
these circumstances she would have acted like Catherine. The
story of her mother in her gentle ignorance, which the old
clerk thought so much of, did not affect the high-spirited girl
as did the picture of the other putting herself in the breach,
taking upon her own shoulders the weight of the falling
house. Hester felt that she, too, could have done this. Her
breast swelled, her breath came short with an impulse of impatience and longing to have such an opportunity, to show the
mettle that was in her. But how could she do it? Catherine
was rich, but Hester was poor. In this way she was diverted
for the moment from her anxiety. The question as to how the
bank came into that peril, the suspicion that her father must
have been somehow connected with it, the heat of her research
after the key of the mystery, faded away for the moment in a
vague, general excitement and eager yet vain desire to have it
in her power to do something, she also —— a desire which
many a young mind has felt as well as Hester; to have that
golden opportunity—the occasion to do a heroic deed, to save
some one, to venture your own life, to escape the bonds of
every day, and once have a chance of showing what was in
you! This was not the "chance" which Emma Ashton desired,
but it appealed to every sentiment in Hester. The strong longing for it, seemed almost to promise a possibility, as she walked
along in a dream, without noticing Harry by her side. And
he did not disturb her by conversation. It was enough for
Harry to feel her hand on his arm. He had never very much
to say, and he did not insist upon saying it. He was content
to lead her about, to show her everything; and the sensation
of taking care of her was pleasant to his heart.

When they reached the hall, however, they became aware of
a late arrival, which had a certain effect upon both. Standing near the great door, which had been opened a minute
before to admit him, sending a thrill of cold night air through
the whole warm succession of rooms, stood Roland Ashton.
Hester was aware that he was expected, but not that he was
coming here. A servant was helping him off with his coat,
and Edward stood beside him in eager conversation. Edward's
countenance, generally toned down to the air of decorum and
self-command which he thought necessary, was excited and
glowing. And Harry, too, lighted up when he saw the new

comer. "Ah, there's Ashton!" he said; while from one of
the other doors Catherine Vernon herself, with a white shawl
over her shoulders, came out from amidst her other guests to
welcome her kinsman. It was a wonderful reception for a
young man who was not distinguished either by rank or
wealth. Hester had to hang back, keeping persistently in the
shade, to prevent her companion from hurrying forward into
the circle of welcoming faces.

"I felt the cold air from the door at the very end of the
drawing-room," Catherine said; "but though it made me
shiver it was not unwelcome, Roland. I knew that it meant
that you had come."

"I wish my coming had not cost you a shiver," Roland
cried.

"One moment; I must say how d'ye do to him," said Harry
in Hester's ear; and even he, the faithfulest one, left her for
a moment to hold out his hand to the new comer.

The girl stood apart, sheltering herself under the shade of
the plants with which the hall was filled, and looked on at
this scene. There was in the whole group a curious connection with herself. Even to Catherine she, perhaps, poor
girl as she was, was the guest among all the others who roused
the keenest feeling. Edward, who did not venture to look at
her here, had given her every reason to believe that his mind
was full of her. Harry had put his life at her disposal.
Roland—Roland had taken possesssion of her mind and
thoughts for a few weeks with a completeness of influence
which probably he never intended, which, perhaps, was
nothing at all to him, which it made Hester blush to remember.
They all stood together, their faces lighted up with interest
while she looked on. Hester stood under a great myrtle bush,
which shaded her face, and looked at them in the thrill of the
excitement which the previous events of the evening had called
forth. A sort of prophetic sense that the lives of all were linked
with her own, a presentiment that between them and among
them it would be hers to work either for weal or woe, came over
her like a sudden revelation. It was altogether fanciful and
absurd she felt; but the impression was so strong that she
turned and fled, with a sudden impulse to avoid the fate that
seemed almost to overshadow her as she stood and looked at
them. She, who a moment before had been longing for the
heroic opportunity, the power of interposing as Catherine had
interposed, felt all the panic of a child come over her as she

stood and gazed at the four people, not one of whom was indifferent to her. She hurried out of the comparative quiet of
the hall into the crowd, and made her way with a trembling
of nervous excitement to where her mother sat. Mrs. John
was still seated serenely on her sofa talking of old school-days
and comrades with the lady of the emeralds. She was serene,
yet there was a little gentle excitement about her too, a little
additional colour upon her soft cheek. Hester, with her heart
beating loudly and a strange tumult in her veins, took refuge
behind her mother with a sense of protection which she had
never felt before. The soft nature which was ready to be
touched by any gentle emotion, which understood none of
life's problems, yet, by patience and simplicity, sailed over them
all, is often a shield to those that see more and feel more.
Behind her unconscious mother Hester seemed to herself to
take refuge from her fate.

It was a great elevation to Mrs. John to sit there at the
upper part of the room, among the great ladies, out of the
crowd of less distinguished persons. Her feeling of embarrassed shyness and sense of being out of place had all
vanished when she discovered her old friend ; and from that
time she had begun to enjoy herself with a soothing consciousness that all proper respect was paid to her, and that at last,
without any doing of hers, all, as she said to herself, had come
right. She assented with gentle cordiality to all that was
said to her about the beauty of the house, and the perfection
of the arrangements.

" Catherine is wonderful," she said ; " she has such a head ;
she understands everything," and not a feeling in her heart
contradicted her words.

That evening was, in its way, a gentle triumph to the
gentle little woman. Hester had disappeared from her for a
time, and had been, she had no doubt, enjoying herself ; and
then she had come back and stood dutifully by her mother,
such a maid of honour as any queen might have been proud
of. She had a thousand things to say of the assembly ; of dear
Bridget Wilton, who recollected her so well, and who was now
quite a great person ; of the prettiness of the party, and the
girls' dresses, and all the light and brilliancy of the scene—
when at last it was all over and they had reached home.

" Now I am sure you are glad you went," she said, with
innocent confidence. " It is a long, long time since I have spent
so pleasant an evening. You see Catherine would not allow

me to be overlooked when it was really a great party. She knows very well what is due. She did not mind at those little evenings, which are of no importance ; but to-night you could see how different it was. Bridget insisted that Sir John himself should take me to supper. No, dear, it was nothing more than was right, but it shows, what I always thought, that no neglect was ever intended. And Catherine was very kind. I am sure now you are glad you went."

Was she glad she had gone? Hester could not tell. She closed the door between her and her mother as if she were afraid that Mrs. John in her unusual exhilaration might read her thoughts. These thoughts were almost too great to be confined within her own spirit. As she lay down in the dark she seemed to see the light shining all about her, the groups in the ball-room—the old man garrulous, deep in the revelations of the past, and the cluster of figures all standing together under the light of the lamps, exchanging questions which meant, though she could scarcely tell how, the future to Hester. Perhaps, on the whole, it was true, and she was glad she had gone.

CHAPTER XXXI.

BUSINESS AND LOVE.

ROLAND had but a few days to spend at Redborough, where he came on the footing of an intimate friend and relation, sought and courted on all hands. His time was already portioned out among the Vernons before he came to pay his respects to Mrs. John and her daughter, though that was on the morning after his arrival. At a still earlier hour Emma had rushed in very tearful and dejected to beg Hester to intercede for her that she might not go away.

"If I go now *he* may never speak at all," Emma said. "I am sure I did everything I could last night to bring it on. I told him Roland had come for me, that he couldn't do without me any longer ; and if you could only have seen him, Hester ! he grew quite white, poor fellow, and his eyes as big as saucers ! I don't believe it is his fault. It must be his people ; so often, when things are going just as you wish, their people will interfere. I am sure he is quite miserable. And if he doesn't speak now, I dare say he will never speak."

"How can you talk as if it were a matter of business ?" cried Hester ; "if he cares for you he is sure to ' speak,' as you call it. And as for bringing it on——"

"But, of course, it is a matter of business," said Emma, "and very important business too. What can be so important for a girl as settling ? It is all very well for you to talk, but I am the youngest, and I have no fixed home, and I must think of myself. If he comes forward it makes all the difference to me. Why, Roland and everybody will think twice as much of me if I have an offer. Hester, there's a dear, do persuade Roland to let me stay. He doesn't want

me a bit, that's all talk; he is just as happy without me.
Perhaps he will tell you they have had enough of me here;
but they don't say so, and you're not bound to go and inquire
into people's feelings if they don't say so. I do believe grandpapa is tired of having me, but he will never turn me out;
and when it is so essential to my best interests! Hester, I
think you might have a little fellow-feeling. There's Edward
Vernon, I'm sure you would be more comfortable if he were
to——"

Hester turned upon her indiscreet companion with a
blaze of indignation. The fact that there was truth in it
made it doubly odious. Her whole frame trembled with
angry shame. She threw up her hand with an impatient
gesture, which frightened and silenced Emma, but which
Hester herself afterwards felt to be a sort of appeal to her
forbearance—the establishment of a kind of confidence.

"What is that about Edward Vernon?" said Mrs. John,
whose tranquil ear had caught something, naturally of that
part of the conversation which it was most expedient she
should not hear.

Emma paused, and consulted Hester with her eyes, who,
however, averted her countenance and would not ask forbearance. A rapid debate ensued in Emma's mind. What is the
use, she asked herself, of having a mother if you cannot tell
her everything, and get her to help you? But on the other
hand, if Hester did not wish it spoken of she did not dare to
oppose an auxiliary who might be of so much service to her.
So she answered carelessly—

"Oh, nothing! but don't you think, Mrs. Vernon, you who
know the world, that for a girl to go away just when a gentleman is coming to the point, is a great pity? And just as likely
as not nothing may ever come of it if her people interfere
like this and drag her away."

"My dear," said Mrs. John, astonished, though mollified
by the compliment to her knowledge of the world, "I cannot call to mind that I have ever heard such a question discussed before."

"Oh, perhaps not—not in general society; but when we
are all women together, and a kind of relations, I am sure it
is only charity to wish that a girl like me might get settled.
And when you have had an offer you take such a different
position, even with your own people. I want Hester to ask
Roland to let me stay."

"Hester! but why Hester? If you wish it I will speak to Mr. Ashton—or your grandparents would be more suitable," Mrs. John said.

And it was at this moment that Roland himself came in to pay his respects. When he had said everything that was polite—nay, more than polite, ingratiating and devoted, as if in a subdued and reverential way he was paying his court to the mother rather than the daughter—he contrived to make his way to where Hester sat apart, working with great but spasmodic energy, and not yet recovered from the ferment into which Emma had plunged her. "I scarcely saw you last night," he said.

"There were so many people to see," Hester replied, with a cloudy smile, without lifting her eyes.

"Yes, there were a great many people. And to-morrow night, I hear, at the Merridews——"

"I am not going."

"No? I thought I should have been able to see a little of you there. A ball-room is good for that, that one—I mean, two—may be alone in it now and then—and there were many things I wanted to say. But I thought you did go."

"Yes, often; but I am tired of it!" cried Hester. "It is too much; one wants something more than folly in one's life."

"This is not folly," he said, looking round at the quiet little room, the tranquil lady by the fire, the work at which Hester's hands were so busy. She was seated near the side window which looked out upon the road.

"No; this is dulness—this is nothing," she said; "not living at all, but only going on because one cannot help it."

"I suppose, on the whole, the greater part of life is that; but you, with the power to make others happy, with so much before you——"

"I am sure the life that I know is all that," cried Hester; "we are here, we don't know why, we cannot get out of it, we must go on with it. It is a necessity to live, and prepare your dinner every day and mend your clothes, not because you wish to do so, but because you can't help yourself. And then the only relief to it is folly."

"Don't call an innocent little dance folly, with all its opportunities. If it gave me the chance of a long quiet talk —with you."

"If that is not folly, it is nonsense," Hester said, with a laugh, not unmoved by the tone, not unsubdued by the eyes.

"You may think so, but I don't. I have looked forward to it for so long. If life is nothing to you here, fancy what it is to me in the Stock Exchange."

"I have no doubt it is very interesting to you. It is something to do: it is change, and thought, and risk, and all that one wants."

"That is what Edward Vernon says," said Roland. "He, too, finds life monotonous—I suppose because he has everything he wishes for."

"Has he everything he wishes for?" said Hester, with a catch of her breath, and a sudden glance up with keen, questioning eyes. The next moment she bent her head again over her work. "What I want is not dancing," she said.

"It is work, according to the fashion of young ladies. You don't know when you are well off. You have always wanted work," said Roland, "and barbarous parents will not let you. You want to go and teach wretched little children, and earn a little miserable money. You to be wasted on that! Ah! you have something a great deal better to do."

"What?" said Hester, raising her eyes and fixing them upon him. "I should like, not that, but to do as Catherine Vernon did," she cried, lighting up in every line of her animated countenance. "I should like to step in when ruin was coming and prop it up on my shoulders as she did, and meet the danger, and overcome it——"

"I thought you hated Catherine Vernon," Roland cried.

"I never said so," cried Hester; and then, after a pause, "but if I did, what does that matter? I should like to do what she did. Something of one's own free will—something that no one can tell you or require you to do — which is not even your duty bound down upon you. Something voluntary, even dangerous——" She paused again, with a smile and a blush at her own vehemence, and shook her head. "That is exactly what I shall never have it in my power to do."

"I hope not, indeed, if it is dangerous," said Roland, with all that eyes could say to make the words eloquent. "Pardon me; but don't you think that is far less than what you have in your power? You can make others do: you can inspire (isn't that what Lord Lytton says?) and reward. That is a little highflown, perhaps. But there is nothing a man might not do, with you to encourage him. You make me wish to be a hero."

He laughed, but Hester did not laugh. She gave him a keen look, in which there was a touch of disdain. "Do you really think," she said, "that the charm of inspiring, as you call it, is what any reasonable creature would prefer to doing? To make somebody else a hero rather than be a hero yourself? Women would need to be disinterested indeed if they like that best. I don't see it. Besides, we are not in the days of chivalry. What could you be inspired to do—make better bargains on your Stock Exchange? and reward—— Oh, that is not the way it is looked at nowadays. You think it is you who——" Here Hester paused, with a rising colour, "I will not say what I was going to say," she said.

"What you were going to say was cruel. Besides, it was not true. I must know best, being on the side of the slandered. A man who is worth calling a man can have but one opinion on that subject."

Hester looked at him again with a serious criticism, which embarrassed Roland. She was not regarding the question lightly, as a mere subject of provocative talk, but was surveying him as if to read how far he was true and how far fictitious. Before he could say anything she shook her head with a little sigh.

"Besides," she said, "it was not a hero I was thinking of. If anybody, it was Catherine Vernon."

"Whom you don't like. These women, who step out of their sphere, they may do much to be respected, they may be of great use; but——"

"You mean that men don't like them," said Hester, with a smile; "but then women do; and, after all, we are the half of creation—or more."

"Women do! Oh, no; that is a mistake. Let us ask the company present—your mother and my sister."

Hester put out her hand to stop him. "That goes far deeper," she said, with a rising blush. What did she mean? Roland was sufficiently versed in all the questions of this kind, which are discussed in idleness to promote flirtation. But he did not know why she should blush so deeply, or why her forehead should contract when he claimed his sister and her mother together as representatives of women. They were so, better than Hester herself was. Mrs. John represented all the timid opinions and obstinate prejudices of weakness; all that is gently conventional and stereotyped in that creature, conventionally talked about as Woman from the beginning of

time ; while the other represented that other, vulgarer type
of feminine character which, without being either strong
enough or generous enough to strike out a new belief, makes
a practical and cynical commentary upon the old one, and
considers man as the natural provider of woman's comfort,
and, therefore, indispensable, to be secured as any other
source of income and ease ought to be secured. Hester was
wounded and ashamed that her mother should be classed
with Emma, but could say nothing against it ; and she was
moved with a high indignation to think that Roland was
right. But he had not the least idea what she could mean,
and she had no mind to enlighten him. Their conversation
came to an end accordingly ; and the sound of the others
came in.

"I don't see why I should go away," said Emma. "For,
whatever he may choose to say, Roland doesn't want me, not
a bit. Elizabeth is a very good cook, and that's all a man
thinks of. I couldn't do him any good at home, and he
doesn't like my acquaintances. A girl can't live without
friends, can she, Mrs. John ? If you are to have any amusement at all, you must be getting it when you're about twenty,
that is the time. But men never care : they go out, and they
have their own friends separate, and they never think of you.
But here, without bothering him a bit, I have lots of nice
people, and grandmamma has never said she was tired of me.
Then why should he take me away ? "

"There is no reason for talking of that just now at all,"
said Mrs. John politely, "for Mr. Roland is not going away
himself as yet."

"Oh, he cannot stay long," cried Emma, "he oughtn't to
stay ; he has got his business—not like me that have nothing
to call me. Edward Vernon wouldn't like it a bit if Roland
stayed away from his business."

"I am always hearing the name of Edward Vernon," said
Mrs. John ; "you mentioned it to Hester just now. What
has he to do with Hester or with Mr. Roland's business ?
Though Catherine Vernon thinks so much of him, he is not
one of my favourites. I like his cousin Harry better."

"And so do I," Roland said.

They all looked at him with surprise, and Hester with a
sudden increase of colour. She was angry, though she could
not have told why.

"He is very hot and eager in business," Roland said. "I

suppose I ought to like him the better for that. And he has
a keen eye too ; but it goes to his head, and that is what one
never should allow one's business to do."

"Ah!" cried Mrs. John, "if it can be prevented, Mr.
Roland. That was what happened to my dear husband.
He could not be cool as, I suppose, it is right to be. But
sometimes, don't you think one likes a person better for not
calculating too much, for letting himself be carried away?"

Roland looked more dark than he had ever been seen to
look before, and responded vaguely, "Perhaps," with a face
that had no doubtfulness in it.

"Why should he not be hot and eager?" cried Hester; "I
understand that very well. Everything is quiet here. A
man, when he gets out of this still atmosphere, wants a little
excitement, and to fling himself into it."

"Ah!" said Mrs. John, "that is what your poor father
always said."

But Roland had never looked so unsympathetic. "A man
may lose his head in love or in war, or in adventure, or in
pleasure, but he must not lose it on the Stock Exchange," he
said ; then, looking up, with an uneasy laugh, "I need not
warn you, ladies, need I? for you will never lose your heads
about shares and premiums. I am glad to think I am a
very steady fellow myself."

"Oh, steady!" cried Mrs. John, alarmed. "I hope, I am
sure, they are all *quite* steady. I never heard a word to the
contrary. It would be dreadful for poor Catherine ; after all,
though we are not very good friends—not such good friends as
I should wish to be—it would be dreadful ; for if Edward was
not steady—— Oh, I hope, Mr. Roland, you are mistaken.
I hope that is not so."

"He means a steady head, mother ; there is no question of
anything else," said Hester, very red and troubled. Her
secret consciousness in respect to Edward made life and
conversation very difficult for her : she could not bear any ani-
madversion upon him, though in her own heart she made
many ; and at the same time she could not defend him openly.
What was he more to her than Harry was? The same far-off
cousin—old friend : not so much, indeed, as Harry, for all the
world knew that Harry would fain have established another
relationship had it seemed good in Hester's eyes.

"I meant nothing against his morals," Roland said.

"That is a great relief to my mind," said Mrs. John, "for

Catherine Vernon is a good woman, though she and I have
never been great friends; and it is a terrible thing to
set your heart upon a child and have him turn out badly.
There is nothing so heartrending as that. One of my mother's
sister's, Aunt Eliza, of whom you have heard me talk, Hester,
had a son——"

"Oh, mamma, I don't think we want to hear about that."

"And you were coming out for a walk," said Emma, who
saw that her own affairs were slipping out of notice. "Didn't
she say she would come out for a walk? And if we are
going we had better not be long about it, for the days are so
short at this time of the year."

"Put on your hat, Hester; it will do you good. You
change colour so I do not know what to make of it," her
mother said.

"And so do I now," cried Emma; "they always tell me it is
indigestion, but that is not a nice reason to give when people
think you are blushing about something. It is very disagreeable. Mine comes on often after dinner when we dine early,
and all the afternoon I am just a fright! It is a blessing it
goes off towards evening when one is seeing people. Roland,
you must take Hester and me into Redborough. I want to buy
some gloves, and I dare say so does she, for the Merridews
to-night."

"She is not going to the Merridews," said Mrs. John, with
a plaintive sound in her voice.

"Oh, she told us something about that, but I didn't believe
it was true. Why shouldn't she go to the Merridews?—she
that is always made so much of, just like the sister of the
house. If I had that position I never should miss one
evening; and, indeed, I never have since I had my first
invitation. Grandpapa did not like it at first, but of course
he got reconciled. Oh, here you are, Hester; how quickly
you do dress! To be sure, you never put on anything but
that pea-coat of yours. But I don't like drawing on my
gloves as I go out, as you do; I like to put them on carefully,
and smooth them, and button them up."

"You are always so tidy," said Mrs. John, with a faint
sigh. She could not but feel it would be an advantage if
Hester, though so much superior, would get some of Emma's
ways. She was so neat: never a hair out of order, or a
shoe-tie loose. Whereas, now and then, in her own child,
there were imperfections. But she smiled as she looked after

them, going out to the door to see them go. Hester, with her varying complexion (which had nothing to do with her digestion), threw up her head to meet the wind with a movement so vigorous, so full of grace and life, that it was a pleasure to see. The mother thought that it was pretty to watch her drawing on her gloves, though, perhaps, it would have been tidier to button them carefully as Emma did, before she came down stairs; but then in those days gloves had few buttons and were easily managed. As soon as they had gone out of the gate of the Vernonry, Emma gave Hester a significant look, and even a nudge, if it must be told, and begged them to walk on while she ran in for an umbrella which she had forgotten. "For it always rains when one hasn't an umbrella," she said. It cost Hester an effort to remember what the look and the nudge meant. Then she laughed as she watched the schemer down to Captain Morgan's door.

"Why do you want to take Emma away?" she said. "She seems to be happy here."

"Do you think she makes the old people happier? They don't say anything, but she seems to me to worry my old grandfather. I don't want to take her away. She has her little schemes on hand, no doubt, and means to settle or something; but I cannot let her tire out the old people. They are part of my religion," Roland said. This, too, was meant as provocation to draw Hester on to discuss the question of religion, perhaps to an attempt to convert him to sounder views, which is a very fruitful method. He looked at her with a pleased defiance in his eyes. But Hester was not to be drawn out on this subject. She had no dogmatic teaching in her, and did not feel qualified to discuss a man's religion. Instead, she returned to the subject of their previous discussion, herself abandoning Emma's cause.

"What do you do on the Stock Exchange?" she said.

"That is a tremendous question. I don't know how to answer it. I should have to give you a lecture upon shares, and companies, and all the vicissitudes of the Funds."

"These, I suppose, are your material, just as written things are the material of a newspaper editor. I understand that," said Hester, "what I want to know is what you do?"

"We buy and we sell," he said, with a laugh. "We are no better than any shopkeeper. We buy a thing when it is cheap, and hold it till it becomes dear, and then we sell it again."

"But who," said Hester, with a little scorn, "is so silly as to buy things *when they are dear?* Is it to oblige you? I thought that was against political economy—and everything of that kind," she added vaguely. It was not the subject Roland would have chosen, but out of that, too, he could draw the thread of talk.

"Political economy is not infallible," he said. "We praise our wares so, and represent their excellence so warmly, that there comes a moment when everybody wishes to buy them. Sometimes they deserve the commendations we bestow, sometimes they—don't. But in either case people buy. And then political economy comes in, and the demand being great increases the value; so that sometimes we make a nice little bit of profit without spending a penny."

Hester looked at him with a blank face. She knew nothing about these mysteries. She shook her head.

"I don't understand business," she said; "but how can you buy without spending a penny? I wish I knew how to do that."

"I should like to do it for you," said Roland, with a look that said still more; for even stockbroking will do as a vehicle for flirtation. "I should like to buy you a quantity of Circassians, for instance, exactly at the right moment, neither too soon nor too late, and sell them next day, perhaps, when the market had turned, and hand you over a thousand pounds or two which you should have made without, as I said, spending a penny. That would make the profession romantic, poetic, if one could conduct such operations for *you.* Probably I shall put that money into the pocket of some bilious city person who does not want it, instead of into your fair hands——"

"Which do. I don't know if they are fair hands, but they want it certainly. A thousand or two! enough to make people comfortable for life. And what are Circassians?" Hester asked.

"They are stock. You must accept certain words as symbols, or we shall never make it clear. And my business is to watch the market for you, to catch the moment when the tide is turning. There is a great deal of excitement in it."

"And is that how Edward loses his head?"

She spoke in a low tone, and Roland stopped suddenly in what he was about to say, and turned upon her with real

surprise. After this he put on an air of mock mortification
—mock, yet not without a mixture of the true.

"Is it for this," he said, "that I have been devising delicate operations for you, and explaining all my mysteries? to
find you at the end not in the least interested in my work
or in your possible fortune, but considering everything in
the light of Edward Vernon? Acknowledge that this is hard
upon me."

"I was thinking only," said Hester, with again that sudden
flush of colour, "of what you said, that Edward lost his head.
It is not much wonder if what you say can be. He would
like to be rich; he would like to be free. He would prefer
to get a fortune of his own, especially if it can be done that
way, rather than to wait for years and years, till he has made
money, or till Catherine dies. That is generous, you know.
He does not want to wait till she dies, as if he grudged her
life. It would be terrible for her to think that he did not
wish her to live as long as she could. But at the same time
he wants, and so do we all, to be free."

"I am so much obliged to you for explaining Edward
Vernon's motives," said Roland, much piqued. It was an
experience he was not familiar with, to have himself forgotten
and his rival expounded to him. His rival! was he his rival?
In the sting of this sudden revelation of preference, Roland
all but vowed that he would enter the lists in earnest and
chase this Edward, this country fellow whom she thought so
much of, from the field.

Hester was confused, too, when her investigation into her
cousin's mind was thus received. It was true enough; it was
the problem which had interested her in the first place—not
directly Edward in person who was the subject of it. She
had tried to explain his position to herself. Now that her
interest was found out, and she discovered it to be an offence
to her companion, she threw herself back instinctively on a
less alarming question.

"I think a great deal about Catherine," she said.

"About Catherine—Cousin Catherine—whom I thought
you disliked with all your heart?"

"You may be astonished, but it is true. I think a great
deal about her. I think of her, after being kind to everybody
—for now that I am grown up I begin to understand, she has
been very kind to everybody; not loving them, which takes
the grace out of it—but yet kind, after being so kind, to be left

alone with nobody caring for her, and perhaps the one she loves best expecting when she will die. No," said Hester, "I am glad Edward loses his head—that is what he is thinking of. Not to wait or feel as if he would like by an hour to shorten her life, but only for himself, like a man, to get free. I am very glad of it," she added hotly, with another overwhelming blush, "for Catherine's sake."

Roland was bewildered and doubtful what to think, for truth was so strong in Hester that it was hard to believe she was sheltering herself behind a fiction. But he was very much mortified, too.

"I don't think," he said, plaintively, "that I want to talk either of Cousin Catherine or of Mr. Edward, whom she thinks a great deal more of than he deserves—as, perhaps, others do, too."

"And we have come on so fast and forgotten Emma!" cried Hester, with a sense of guilt. "We ought to go back and meet her. She has been a long time getting that umbrella. Don't you think you had better leave her with Mrs. Morgan a little longer, since she likes to be here."

"I shall not disturb her if—you wish her to stay," he meant to say if she wishes to stay, but changed his phrase and gave it emphasis, with a look of devotion. "If I thought you had any regard for my poor little sister how glad it would make me. It would do her so much good; it would alter her way of looking at things."

"Oh, you must not think," cried Hester, meaning, like him, to say one thing and saying another, "that Emma is likely to be influenced by me. She knows what she thinks much better than I do.—Mr. Ashton, would it not turn one's head and make one unfit for one's other business if one was trying to make money in *that* way?"

"Perhaps," Roland said.

"Has it not that effect upon you?"

"But it is my business. I don't act for myself. I am tempted sometimes to do things I ought not to do, and sometimes I fall. Even you, if you were tempted, would sometimes fall. You would dabble in Circassians, you would find a new company too much for your virtue; shares going to-day for next to nothing but sure to be at a premium next week—if the bubble doesn't burst in the meantime."

"And does it always happen that the bubbles burst?"

"Oh, not always; but after you have done with them you

don't care what becomes of them. I never thought I should have had you for half an hour all to myself, and talked of business the whole time. It is incredible; and there is that little Emma running this way as if she thought we were inconsolable for the loss of her. I wanted to tell you how much I have been thinking of all our talks since I have been in my little house alone. Did you never think of coming to London? The very feeling of being in a place so full of life and action, and thinking, makes your veins thrill. I think you would like to be there. There is so much going on. And then I might have the hope of seeing you sometimes. That is one for you and two for myself."

"We could not afford it," said Hester, colouring again. "I think I should like it. I am not sure. To look on and see everybody doing a great deal would be intolerable if one had nothing to do."

"What are you talking of?" cried Emma, coming up breathless. "I couldn't find that umbrella. I went up and down into every room in the house, and then I found I had left it in your drawing-room, Hester, and your mamma looked up when I went in, and said, 'Back already!' I think she must have been dozing, for we could not possibly have gone to Redborough and back in this time, could we, Roland? You two looked so comfortable by yourselves I had half a mind not to come at all: for you know two's company but three's none. And then I thought you didn't know my number, and Roland would never have had the thought to bring me my gloves. But don't be afraid, I dare say I shall pick up some one on the way."

They walked into the town after this, and bought Emma's gloves. Hester could not be tempted into a similar purchase, nor could she be persuaded to go to the Merridews. And she resisted all Roland's attempts to make himself agreeable, even after Emma encountered young Reginald Merridew, who was glad enough to help her to buy her gloves. Though it was not many months since she had seen him, Hester felt that she had outgrown Roland. His eyes were very fine, but they did not affect her any more. He brought no light with him into the problems of life, but only another difficulty, which it was more and more hard to solve. A sort of instinctive consciousness that something was going to happen seemed in the air about her. All was still, and everything

going on in its calm habitual way. There were not even
any heavings and groanings, like those that warn the surrounding country before a volcano bursts forth. Nevertheless,
this girl, who had been so long a spectator, pushed aside from
the action about her, but with the keen sight of injured pride
and wounded feeling, seeing the secret thread of meaning
that ran through everything, felt premonitions, she could not
tell how, in the heated air, and through the domestic calm.

CHAPTER XXXII.

A SPECULATOR.

Roland's Christmas visit to his friends was not the holiday it appeared. His engagements with them had been many during this interval, and attended both by loss and gain; but the gain had outbalanced the loss, and though there had been many vicissitudes and a great many small crises, the Christmas balance had shown tolerably well, and every one was pleased. Edward's private ventures, which he had not consulted any one about, but in which the money of the bank had been more or less involved, had followed the same course. He had a larger sum standing to his individual credit than ever before, and, so far as any one knew, had risked nothing but what he had a right to risk, though, in reality, his transactions had gone much further than any one was aware of, even Ashton; for he had felt the restraints of Roland's caution, and had already established, though to a limited extent, dealings with other agents of bolder disposition. And, indeed, his mind had gone further than his practice, and had reached a point of excitement at which the boundaries of right and wrong become so indistinct as to exert little, if any, control over either the conscience or the imagination. Through his other channels of information he had heard of a speculation greater than he had yet ventured upon, in which the possible gain would be immense, but the risk proportionate —almost proportionate—though the probabilities were so entirely in favour of success that a sanguine eye could fix itself upon them with more justification than is usual. It was so vast that even to Edward, who had been playing with fire for months back, the suggestion took away his breath,

and he took what was in reality the wise step of consulting
Ashton. It was wise had he intended seriously to be guided
by Ashton, but it was foolish as it happened, seeing that a
day or two's contemplation of the matter wrought in him a
determination to risk it, whether Ashton approved or not.
And Roland did not approve. He came down at the utmost
speed of the express to stop any further mischief if he could.
He had himself always kept carefully within the bounds of
legitimate business; sometimes, indeed, just skirting the edge,
but never committing himself or risking his credit deeply,
and he had never forgot the solemn adjuration addressed to
him by both the old people at the Vernonry. If Catherine
Vernon or her representatives came to harm it should not be,
he had determined, by his means. So he had answered Edward's
appeal in person; and, instead of communicating with him
only, had spoken of the matter to Harry, supposing him to
be in all Edward's secrets, a thing which disturbed Edward's
composure greatly. It was his own fault he felt for so dis-
trusting his own judgment; but he durst not betray his displeasure: and so the proposal which he had meant to keep to
himself had to be discussed openly between the partners.
Harry, as may be supposed, being passive and unambitious,
opposed it with all his might. Roland had been shut up with
them in Edward's room at the bank for hours in the morning, and the discussion had run high. He had been a kind of
moderator between them, finding Harry's resistance to some
extent unnecessary, but, on the whole, feeling more sympathy
with him than with the other. "It isn't ourselves only we
have to consider," Harry said; and he repeated this, perhaps
too often, often enough to give his opponent a sort of right to
say that this was a truism, and that they had heard it before.

"A thing does not become more true for being repeated,"
Edward said.

"But it does not become less true," said Roland; "and I
think so far that Harry is right. With all your responsi-
bilities you ought to go more softly than men who risk
nothing that is not their own. You are in something of the
same position as trustees, and you know how they are tied up."

"This is a statement which hardly comes well from you,"
said Edward, "who have been our adviser all along, and
sailed very near the wind on some occasions."

"I have never advised you to anything I did not think
safe," said Roland.

Edward was so eager and so confident of his superiority over his cousin, that it was difficult to keep the suspicion of a sneer out of his voice in this discussion, though for Roland Ashton, whatever his other sentiments might be, he at least had no feeling of contempt.

"And there's Aunt Catherine," said Harry. "Of course a great part of the money's hers. Her hair would stand on end if she knew we were even discussing such a question."

"Aunt Catherine is—all very well; but she's an old woman. She may have understood business in her day. I suppose she did, or things would not have come to us in the state they are. But we cannot permit ourselves to be kept in the old jogtrot because of Aunt Catherine. She departed from her father's rule, no doubt. One generation can't mould itself upon another. At least that is not what I understand by business."

"And there was John Vernon, don't you know," said Harry. "He was a caution! I shouldn't like to follow in his ways."

"John Vernon was a fool; he threw his chance away. I've gone into it, and I know that nothing could be more idiotic. And his extravagance was unbounded. He burned the candle at both ends. I hope you don't think I want to take John Vernon for my model."

"It seems to me," said Harry, "that it's awfully easy to be ruined by speculation. Something always happens to put you out. There were those mines. For my part I thought they were as safe as the bank, and we lost a lot by them. There was nobody to blame so far as I know. I don't mean to stand in the way, or be obstructive, as you call it, but we have got to consider other people besides ourselves."

Roland did not look upon the matter exactly in this way. He was not of Harry's stolid temperament. He heard of a proposition so important with something of the feelings of a war-horse when he sniffs the battle. But his opposition was all the more weighty that it was more or less against his own will.

"In your place I do not think I should venture," he said. "If I were an independent capitalist, entirely free——"

"You would go in for it without a moment's hesitation! Of course you would. And why should we be hampered by imaginary restrictions? Aunt Catherine—if it is her you are thinking of—need know nothing about it, and we risk nobody so much as we risk ourselves. Loss would be far more fatal to us than to any one else. Am I likely to insist upon anything which would make an end of myself first of all if it went wrong?"

But the others were not convinced by this argument. Harry shook his head, and repeated his formula.

"It wouldn't console anybody who was injured that you ruined yourself first of all," he said.

"Nor would it comfort me for the loss of a fortune that other people had rejected it," cried Edward, with an angry smile.

His mind worked a great deal faster than the conversation could go, and the discussion altogether was highly distasteful to him. Harry had a right to his say when the subject was broached, but it was beyond measure embarrassing and disagreeable that Harry should have heard anything about it. It was all Ashton's fault, whom he had consulted by way of satisfying his conscience merely, and whom he could not silence or find fault with for betraying him, since, of course, he wanted no one to suppose that he acted upon his own impulse and meant to leave Harry out. He could not express all this, but he could drop the discussion, and Ashton (he thought to himself) along with it. Let him prose as he would, and chime in with Harry's little matter-of-fact ways, he (Edward) had no intention to allow himself to be stopped.

"I would let it alone, if I were you," Roland said. "It is a great temptation, and of course if you were entirely independent—— But I would not risk a penny of other people's money."

"That's just what I say. We have others to consider besides ourselves," said the steadfast Harry.

Edward made no reply. He was outvoted for the moment by voices which, he said to himself, had no right to be heard on the question. The best thing was to end the discussion and judge for himself. And the contemplation of the step before him took away his breath; it took the words out of his mouth. There would be nothing to be said for it. In argument it would be an indefensible proceeding. It was a thing to do, not to think, much less talk about. No one would have a word to say if (as was all but absolutely certain) his operations were attended by success. In that event his coolness, his promptitude, his daring, would be the admiration of everybody; and Harry himself, the obstructive, would share the advantage, and nothing more would be heard of his stock phrase. Edward felt that in reality it was he who was considering others, who was working for everybody's benefit; but to form such a determination was enough to make the strongest head swim, and it was necessary that he should shake off all intrusion, and have time and solitude to think it over in private.

The way in which he thus dropped the discussion astonished both the other parties to it a little. Edward was seldom convinceable if he took an idea into his head, and he never acknowledged himself beaten. But Harry at first was simple enough to be able to believe that what he had himself said was unanswerable, and that as nothing could be done without his acquiescence, Ned showed his sense by dropping the question. Roland was not so easily reassured; but it was not his business, which makes a wonderful difference in the way we consider a subject, and it was not for him to continue a subject which the persons chiefly concerned had dropped. He strolled with Harry into his room presently on a hint from Edward that he had something particular to do. Harry was not very busy. He did what came under his special department with sufficient diligence, but that was not oppressive work: the clerks took it off his hands in great part. In all important matters it was Mr. Edward who was first consulted. Harry had rather a veto upon what was proposed, than an active hand in it; but he was very steady, always present, setting the best example to the clerks. Roland talked to him for a quarter of an hour pleasantly enough about football, which eased the minds which had been pondering speculation. The result of the morning's conference was shown in one way by his ready and unexpected adherence to Mrs. John's statement that she liked Harry best. Roland thought so too, but he did not give any reason for it; and indeed, so far as intellectual appreciation went, there was perhaps little reason to give.

After Emma's gloves were bought, the group sauntering through Redborough just at the hour when all the fine people of the place were about, were met in succession by the two cousins. Harry had time only to pause for a minute or two, and talk to the girls on his way to a meeting of the football club, at which the matches of the season were to be settled; but Edward, who was going their way, walked with them as far as the Grange. He was pale and preoccupied, with that fiery sparkle in his eyes which told of some pressing subject for his thoughts, and though those eyes shot forth a passing gleam when he saw that Roland kept by Hester's side, and that he was left to Emma, the arrangement perhaps on the whole was the most suitable one that could have been made, for Emma wanted little help in keeping up something which sounded sufficiently like conversation. Her voice flowed on, with just a pause now and then for the little assenting ejaculations which were indispensable. Edward said "Yes," sometimes with a mark of interrogation, sometimes without; and "Indeed," and "To be sure," and "Exactly," as we all do in similar circumstances; and the pair got on very well. Emma thought him much nicer than usual, and Hester going on in front, somewhat distracted from Roland's remarks by the consciousness of the other behind her, was perhaps more satisfied to hear his stray monosyllables than if he had maintained a more active part in the conversation. When they stopped in front of the Grange, where Catherine Vernon, always at the window, saw the group approaching, they were called up stairs to her by a servant—an invitation, however, which Hester did not accept. "My mother will be waiting for me," she said; and while the others obeyed the summons, she sped along the wintry road by herself, not without that proud sense of loneliness and shut-out-ness which the circumstances made natural. Edward lingered a moment to speak to her while the others went in, having first ascertained that they were shaded by the big holly at the gate and invisible from the window.

"I must not go with you, though I want to talk to you," he said. "When will this bondage be over? But at the Merridews to-night——"

"I am not going," she said, waving her hand as she went on.

She was half pleased, yet altogether angry, despising him (almost) for his precautions, yet glad that he wanted to talk to her, and glad also to disappoint him, if it is possible to describe so complicated a state of mind. She went along with a proud, swift step, her head held high, her girlish figure instinct in every line with opposition and self-will: or so at least Catherine Vernon thought, who looked after her with such attention that she was unaware of the entrance of the others, whom she liked so much better than Hester. She laughed as she suffered herself to be kissed by Emma, who was always effusive in that way, and fed upon the cheeks of her friends.

"So Princess Hester has not come with you," Catherine said. "I suppose I should have gone down to the door to meet her, as one crowned head receives another."

"Oh, she had to go home to her mother," said Emma, who never spoke ill of anybody, and always took the most matter-of-fact view of her neighbours' proceedings.

Catherine laughed, and was amused (she thought) by the girl's persistent holding aloof.

"All the same a cup of tea would not have poisoned her," she said.

When the Ashtons left the Grange it was nearly the hour of dinner, and Catherine did not remark the silence of her companion. Edward had been moody of late; he had not been of temper so equable, or of attentions so unfailing, as in the earlier years. But she was a tolerant woman, anxious not to exact too much, and ready to represent to herself that this was but "a phase," and that the happier intercourse would return after a time. She wondered sometimes was he in love? that question which occurs so unnaturally to the mind at moments when things are not going perfectly well with young persons, either male or female. Catherine thought that if his choice were but a good one, she would be very glad that he should marry. It would give to him that sense of settledness which nothing else gives, and it would give to her a share in all the new events and emotions of family life. If only he made a good choice! the whole secret of the situation of course was in that. At dinner he was more cheerful, indeed full of animation, doing everything that could be done to amuse and please her, but excused himself from following her to the drawing-room afterwards.

"You are going to Ellen's folly, I suppose," she said, which was the name that the Merridew entertainments held in the house.

"Very likely—but later," said he; "I have a great deal to do."

Catherine smiled upon his diligence, but held up a finger in admonition.

"I never approved of bringing work home," she said. "I would rather for my own part you stayed an hour longer at the bank. Home should be for rest, and you should keep the two places distinct; but I suppose you must learn that by

experience," she said, putting her hand caressingly upon his
shoulder as he held the door open for her ; and she looked
back upon him when she had passed out with a little wave of
her hand.   "Don't sit too long over your papers," she said.

He had *trop de zèle.* No fear of Edward shrinking from
his work.   But experience would teach him that it was better
to give himself a little leisure sometimes.   Would experience
teach him ? she asked herself, as she went up stairs.   He was
of a fervid nature, apt perhaps to go too far in anything that
interested him.   She reflected that she had herself been older
before she began to have anything to do with business, and a
woman looks forward to home, to the seat by the fire, the
novel, the newspaper (if there is nothing better), the domestic
chat when that is to be had, with more zest than a man does.
What she herself liked would have been to have him there
opposite to her as he used to be at first, talking, or reading
as pleased him, telling her his ideas.   Why was it that this
pleasant state of affairs never continued ? He preferred to sit
in the library now, to work, or perhaps only, she began to
fear, to be alone.   The idea struck Catherine sadly now she came
to think of it.   There was a great difference.   Why should men
prefer to sit alone, to abandon that domestic hearth which
sounds so well in print, and which from Cowper downward all
the writers have celebrated.   Even Dickens (then the master
of every heart) made it appear delightful and attractive to
everybody.   And yet the young man preferred to go and sit
alone.   A wife would alter all that, provided only that the
choice he made was a good one, Catherine Vernon said.   The
drawing-room was a model of comfort ; its furniture was not
in the taste of the present day, but the carpets were like
moss into which the foot sank, and the curtains were close
drawn in warm, ruddy, silken folds.   The fire burnt brightly,
reflected from the brass and steel, which it cost so much
work to keep in perfect order.   Catherine sat in the warmest
place just out of reach of the glare, with a little table by
her favourite easy chair.   Impossible to find a room more
entirely " the picture of comfort " as people say.   And few
companions could have been found more intelligent, more
ready to understand every allusion, and follow every suggestion, than this old lady who was not at all conscious of being
old.   Yet her boy, her son, her nephew, her chosen, whom she
had taken to her heart in place of all the other inmates who
once dwelt there, sat down stairs !   How strange it was ; yet

notwithstanding Catherine deposited herself in her seat by
the fire, with a sort of subdued happiness, consequent on the
fact that he was down stairs. This gave a secondary satisfaction if nothing better was to be had. It is all that many
people have to live upon. But if he had a wife that would
make all the difference. A wife he could not leave to sit
alone ; provided only that his choice was a right one ! If
Catherine had known that his choice, so far as he had made
a choice, had fallen upon Hester, what would her sentiments
have been ? but fortunately she did not know.

But if she could have looked into the library down stairs,
which had been given up to Edward as his room, what would
she have seen there ? The sight would have driven out of
her mind all question about a problematical wife : though
indeed Edward always prepared for domiciliary visitations,
and believing them to be the fruit of suspicion, not of love,
was ready in that case to have concealed his occupation at
the first sound of the door opening. He had an open drawer
close to him into which his materials could have been thrown
in a minute. He took these precautions because, as has been
said, Catherine would sometimes carry him with her own
hands a cup of tea in affectionate kindness, and he thought it
was inquisitiveness to see what he was doing ! She had not
done this now for a long time, but still he was prepared
against intrusion. The papers he was examining he had
brought himself in a black bag from the safe in the bank. He
had locked the black bag into an old oak escritoire till after
dinner. He was looking over them now with the greatest
care, and a face full of suppressed, but almost solemn excitement. They were securities of all kinds, and meant an amount
of money which went to Edward's head even more than the
chances of fortune. All that in his power ; no chance of being
called upon to produce them, or to render an account of the
stewardship which had been so freely committed to him ! It
was enough to make any man's head go round. To hesitate
upon a speculation which might bring in cent. per cent. when
he had all these to fall back upon, papers upon which he
could easily find, to meet a temporary need, any amount of
money ! and of course no such need could be anything but
temporary ! Edward was as little disposed to risk the future
of the bank as any one. He had wisdom enough to know
that it was his own sheet anchor, as well as that of the
family, and he had a pride in its stability and high

reputation, as they all had.   That Vernon's should be as safe
as the Bank of England was a family proverb which admitted
of no doubt.   But why should Vernon's be affected except to
its advantage by really bold speculation ?   It was the timid,
half-hearted sort of operations that frittered away both money
and credit, which ruined people, not anything which was
really on a grand scale.   Edward represented to himself that
ventures of this great kind were rarely unsuccessful.   There
was a security in their magnitude—small people could not
venture upon them ; and what even if it did not succeed ?   It
blanched his countenance and caught his breath to think of
this, but (he said to himself) every possibility, even the most
unlikely, must be taken into account.   If it did not, here was
what would keep the credit of the bank scatheless until
another luckier stroke should make up for failure.   For in
such pursuits the last word was never said.   Could you but
go on you were sure one time or another to satisfy your fullest
desires.   This was the worst in case of failure : but there was
in reality no chance of failure, every human probability was
in favour of a great, an almost overwhelming success.

   There was almost a sense of triumph, though the thrill
of excitement had alarm in it also—in the final calculations by which he made up his mind, to throw Ashton and
prudence to the winds.   He wrote with a heart leaping high
in his breast to the other broker, whom he had already employed, before he rose from his writing table.   Ashton was a
fool—he would lose a large commission, and make nothing by
his preachment ; and to think of that preachment made Edward
smile, though the smile was constrained and dry—not a cheerful performance.   Harry and Ashton—they were a sensible
couple to lecture him as to what was best !   It seemed to
Edward that he had himself far more insight and faculty than
a dozen such.   Ashton indeed might know a thing or two.
He had proved himself a fool in this case, but naturally he
was not a fool.   Advice might be received from him, but
dictation, never.   And as for Harry with his football, a
ninny who had never been trusted with any but the mechanical
working of the bank, it was too ridiculous that Harry should
take upon himself to advise.   Edward got his letter ready
for the post with something of the feeling with which a
conspirator may be supposed to light the match by which some
deadly mine is to be fired.   It may blow himself into atoms
if he lingers, and the strong sensation of the possibility is

upon him even though he knows it cannot happen except by some extraordinary accident. Edward put the letter where he knew the butler would find it, and send it away for the late post. It would thus be out of his power to recall, even though a panic should seize him. When he had done this, he felt an overwhelming need of the fresh air and movement to calm his nerves and distract his thoughts. Should he go to Ellen's folly as was his custom? He put on his coat and went out, forgetting that it was his usual custom to go up stairs and say good-night to Catherine before doing so. There was no intentional neglect in this, but only the intensity of his abstraction and self-absorbedness. When he got out the cold breeze in his face was pleasant to him, brain and all. Then he remembered that Hester had said she would not go to the Merridews, and obeying his impulse without questioning what he expected from it, he turned away from the lights of the town, and took his way along the moonlit road towards the Vernonry. He did not expect to see her—he expected nothing in particular; but his thoughts, his heart, drew him in that direction—or his fancy if nothing more.

Catherine, in the warmth and lonely luxury of her drawing-room, heard the door shut, and wondered, with a new little arrow of pain going into her heart—Was it possible that he could have gone out without saying good-night? She was like a mother who is beginning to discover that she is of no particular consequence in the economy of her child's life. When you seize upon the office of parent without being called to it by God, you must accept the pains as well as the pleasures. This new step in the severance between them hurt her more than she could have thought possible; the merest trifle! He might have forgotten; it might be fully accounted for—and, if not, what did it matter? It was nothing; but she stole behind the heavy curtains, and looked out at the corner of the blind with a wistful anxiety to see him, as if the sight of him would afford any comfort. Had Edward seen it he would have gnashed his teeth at her inquisition, at her watch and surveillance, without a thought of the trembling of profound tenderness, surprise, and pain which was in her. But Catherine was too late to see him. He had got into the shadow of the great holly, and there paused a moment before he turned his back upon Redborough and the dance. She saw a solitary figure on the road in the opposite direction, and wondered vaguely who it could be at that hour, but that was all. That it should be Edward did not enter into her thoughts.

But to Edward the silence and stillness were very grateful, emerging out of the very heat and din of conflict as he had just done. The cold too did him good; it refreshed his weary mind and excited brain, and composed and stilled the ferment in his whole being. The vast darkness of the world about him, the broad white light of the moon streaming along the road, but retiring baffled from the inequalities of the common; the spectral outline of every object, enlarged by the blackness behind of its own shadow—all had a vague effect upon him, though he made but little account of the features of the scene. He was in a state of mental exaltation, and therefore more open than usual to all influences, though it was not any lofty or noble cause which raised him into that spiritual suscepti- bility. He could see a long way before he reached it, the end window of Mrs. John's house shining along the road, its little light looking like a faint little ruddy earth-star, so near the ground. The mother and daughter were still sitting over their fire talking—or rather it was the mother who talked, while Hester sat with her hands in her lap, half-listening, half- thinking, her mind escaping from her into many a dream and speculation, even while she gave a certain attention to her mother's broken monologue, which was chiefly about the dances and parties of the past.

"I never refused a ball when I was your age," Mrs. John said. "It would have been thought quite unnatural; and though I am old now, I feel the same as ever. What can be nicer for a girl than to have a nice dance to go to, when she is sure of plenty of partners? If it was in a strange place, or you did not know the people, I could understand. It did hurt me a little, I confess, to hear that little Emma, with her white eyes, rolling away like a princess, to get all the atten- tion, while my girl, that had so much better a right, stayed at home."

"Never mind, mamma," said Hester, with a smile. "It was my own fault; there was no wicked stepmother in ques- tion. And even if there had been, you know, after all, it was Cinderella that got the prince."

"Stepmother!" cried Mrs. John. "My dear! my dear! how could you have had a stepmother, and me surviving your poor dear papa all these years? I dare say if it had been me that died you would have had a stepmother, for gentlemen

don't think of second marriages as women do. However, as
it could not have happened, we need not think of that. Don't
you hear steps on the road? I could be almost certain that I
heard some one pass the window about five minutes ago; and
there it is again. Can there be anything wrong with the
Captain or old Mrs. Morgan? Dear me! what a dreadful
thing if they should be taken ill, and nobody to send for the
doctor! Listen! it is coming back again. If it was some
one going for the doctor, they would not walk back and forward like that under our window. I declare I begin to get
quite frightened. What do you think it can be?"

"If you think they may be ill I will run round directly,"
said Hester, rising to her feet.

"But, my darling! it might be robbers, and not Captain
Morgan at all."

"I am not afraid of robbers," said Hester, which perhaps
was not exactly true. "Besides, robbers don't make a noise
to scare you. I must go and see if there is anything
wrong."

Mrs. John did all she could at once to arouse her daughter
to anxiety about the old people, and to persuade her that it
was dangerous to run round the corner at nearly eleven
o'clock. But eventually she consented to let Hester venture,
she herself accompanying her with a candle to the door.

"It will be far better, mamma," Hester said, "if you will
stand at the parlour window, and let me feel there is some
one there."

This Mrs. John, though with much trembling, at length
agreed to do. She even opened the window a little, though
very cautiously, that nobody might hear, reflecting that if it
was a robber he might jump in before she could get it closed
again. And her anxiety rose almost to the fever point in the
moments that followed. For Hester did not pass the window
on her way to the Morgans' door. On the contrary, Mrs.
John heard voices in the direction of the gate of the Heronry,
and venturing to peep out, saw two dark figures in the moonlight—a sight which alarmed her beyond expression. It was
nearly eleven o'clock, and all the inmates of the Heronry were
in bed or going to it. Was it really robbers?—and why was
Hester parleying with them?—or were these two of the robbers, and had they made away with her child? She was so
alarmed at last that she hurried to the door, carrying her candle,
and went out into the cold without a shawl, shading the light

with her hand, and looking wildly about her. The candle and
the moonlight confused each other, and though her heart beat
less loudly when she perceived it was Hester who was talking
across the gate, yet the sense of the unusual filled her with
horror. "Who is it?" she cried, though in a whisper.
"Hester! oh, what is the matter? Is it a doctor? Who
is it? Is there anything wrong?"

"It is Edward Vernon; may he come in?" Hester said.

"Then it is Catherine that is ill," cried Mrs. John. "Oh,
I knew something must be going to happen to her, for I
dreamt of her all last night, and I have not been able to
think of anything else all day. Surely he may come in.
What is it, Edward? Oh, I hope not paralysis, or anything
of that kind."

CHAPTER XXXIII.

A LATE VISITOR.

He was not a frequent visitor: indeed it is doubtful whether, save for a visit of ceremony, he had ever been there before. As it was so near bedtime the fire was low, and the two candles on the table gave very little light in the dark wainscoted room. Outside it had seemed a ruddy little star of domestic comfort, but within the prospect was less cheerful. They had been preparing to go to bed. Mrs. John's work was carefully folded and put away, even the little litter of thimbles and thread on the table had been "tidied," as her usage was. A book lying open, which was Hester's, was the only trace of occupation, and the dark walls seemed to quench and repel the little light, except in some polished projection here and there where there was a sort of reflection. Mrs. John hastily lit the two candles on the mantelpiece which were always ready "in case any one should come in," and which mirrored themselves with a sort of astonishment in the little glass against which they stood. She was eager to be hospitable, although she had a somewhat warm realisation of Edward as on the other side: perhaps, indeed, this of itself made her more anxious to show him "every attention," as a sort of magnanimous way of showing that she bore no malice.

"It is rather too late to offer you tea," she said, "but perhaps a glass of wine, Hester—for it is a cold night and your cousin has had a long walk. I am very much relieved to hear that Catherine is quite well. For the first moment I confess I was very much alarmed: for she has used her head a great deal, and people say that paralysis——"

"I don't think she is at all a subject for that: her nerves are in perfect order," Edward said.

"That is a great thing to say for the strongest of us," said Mrs. John, sitting down in her chair again and furtively drawing her shawl round her; for he could not surely mean to stay long at that hour, and it seemed a pity to put more coals on the fire; "nerves is the weak point with most ladies. I know to be sure that Catherine is a very remarkable person, and not at all like the ordinary run. She has a masculine mind I have always heard. You are like Hester, you are not at the ball to-night—but you go generally, I hope?"

"I go sometimes; there was no particular attraction to-night," said Edward.

He saw that Hester understood, and that the ready colour rose to her face. How he longed to take the little tedious mother by the shoulders and send her up stairs! A sort of longing for sympathy, for some one to share his second and hidden life with him had seized upon him. He could not have told her all, even if he could have got Hester to himself, but he would have told her something, enough to keep the too full cup from running over. But Mrs. John settled herself as comfortably as she could in her chair. She tried to keep awake and make conversation. She would not allow one of the opposite side to suppose that she was wanting in courtesy. Hester sat down in the background and said nothing. She did not share Edward's faith that her mother would soon be tired out and leave them to themselves, but it was impossible that she should not to some extent share his excitement of suspense and be anxious to know what he had to say.

"I like young men to go to balls," Mrs. John said; "where could they be so well as amusing themselves among their own kind of people? and though perhaps Ellen may be a little silly, you know, I am sure she means well. That is what I always say to Hester. Young people are apt to judge severely, but Ellen always meant well. She might promise too much now and then, but so do we all. It is so easy to make yourself agreeable by just saying what will please; but then sometimes it is very difficult to carry it out."

"Nothing could be more true," said Edward, with a little bow.

"Yes, it is very true," continued Mrs. John. "It seems all so easy at the moment: but afterwards you have to take into consideration whether it is suitable or not, and whether the person is just the right kind, and to make everything fit: and

all that is so difficult." Then there was a little pause, and
Mrs. John began to feel very sleepy. "Do you often—take a
walk—so late?" she said. "Oh, I know some gentlemen do.
Hester's poor papa; but then there was the club—I used
always to think it was the club——"

"Indeed I ought to apologise for venturing to ask admission
at such an hour," said Edward. "I should not have taken
it upon me had not Hester come out to the gate."

"Oh, that does not matter a bit," said Mrs. John, waving
her hand. She could scarcely keep her eyes open. After
eleven o'clock—for the hour had struck since he came in—
Catherine ought to have had "a stroke" at least to justify
such a late visit. "You are sure you are not keeping
anything from us about poor dear Catherine?" she said
anxiously. "Oh, I think it is always better if there is any
misfortune to say it out at once."

Thus the conversation, if conversation it could be called,
went on for some time. Hester did not say a word. She sat
a little behind them, looking at them, herself in a state of
growing impatience and suspense. What could he have to
say that made him come at such an hour—and was it possible
that he ever could get it said? There went on for some time
longer an interchange of hesitating remarks. Mrs. John got
more and more sleepy. Her eyes closed in spite of herself
when Edward spoke. She opened them again widely when
his voice stopped, and smiled and said something which was
generally wide of the mark. At last Hester rose and came
to the back of her chair and stooped over her.

"Mamma, you are very tired, don't you think you had
better go to bed?"

"I hope—" cried Edward, "I fear that my ill-timed
visit——"

"Not for the world, dear," said Mrs. John in an undertone: "no doubt he'll be going presently. Oh no, you must
not think anything of the sort—we often sit up much—later
than this—" and she sat very upright in her chair and
opened her eyes wide, determined to do her duty at all
hazards. Then Edward rose, and looked at Hester with an
entreaty which she could not resist. She was so anxious too to
know what he wanted.

"Don't come out, mother; I will open the door for
Edward," she said.

"But you don't know the right turn of the key. Well

then, perhaps—if your cousin will excuse me—but be sure you lock the door right. It is a difficult door. Put the key in as far as it will go—and then turn it to the right. Let me see, is it the right? I know it is the wrong way, not the way you generally turn a key. Well then, good-night. I hope you don't think it very uncivil of me to leave you to Hester," Mrs. John said, shaking hands, with that extremely wide-awake look which sleepy persons put on.

Edward went out into the dark passages, following Hester and her candle with a sense of something that must be said to her now. He had not thought of this when he set out. Then he had been merely excited, glad of the relief of the air and silence, scarcely aware that he wanted to pour out his soul into the bosom of some one who would understand him, of her who alone he thought could be trusted fully. But the obstacles, the hindrances, had developed this longing Why should he have made so inappropriate a visit except under the stimulus of having something to say? And she, too, was now expecting breathlessly, something which he must have to say. When she set down her candle and opened the door into the verandah, she turned round instinctively to hear what it was. The white moon shone down straight through the glass roof, throwing black shadows of all the wintry plants in the pots, and of the two who stood curiously foreshortened by the light above them. She did not ask anything, but her whole attitude was a question. He took both her hands in his hands.

"It is nothing," he said, "that is, I don't know what there is to tell you. I had come to a conclusion, after a great deal of thought. I had settled to begin in a new way, and I felt that I must talk it over, that I couldn't keep silent; and there is no one I could speak to with freedom but you."

She did not withdraw her hands, or show any surprise at his confidence; but only whispered, "What is it, Edward?" breathlessly, with all the excitement that had been gathering in her.

"I don't know how I can tell you," he said; "it is only business. If I were to go into details you wouldn't understand. It is only that I've made up my mind to a new course of action. I am burning my ships, Hester. I must get rid of this shut-up life somehow. I have gone in to win—a great fortune—or to lose——"

"Edward!" she said, with an unconscious pressure of his hands. "Tell me—I think I could understand."

"So long as you feel with me, that is all I want," he said. "I feel better now that I have told you. We shall make our fortune, dear, or—but there is no or—we must succeed. I know we shall ; and then, Hester, my only love——"

He drew close to her, and kissed her in his excitement. straining her hands. It was not a love-kiss, but the expression of that agitation which was in his veins. She drew back from him in astonishment, but not in anger, understanding it so.

"What is it? To win a great fortune, or—to lose—what? Edward, you are not risking—other people?" she said.

"Pshaw!" he said, almost turning away from her. Then, next moment, "Never mind other people, Hester. That will come all right. I hope you don't think I am a fool. I have made a new departure, that is all, and with everything in my favour. Wish me good luck, and keep my secret. It seemed too big for me to keep all by myself. Now that I have put half of it upon you I shall be able to sleep."

"But you have not told me anything," she said.

Upon which he laughed a little, in an agitated way, and said—

"Perhaps that is all the better. You know everything, and yet you know nothing. I have been kept in long enough, and done as other people would, not as I wished myself ; and now that is over. There is no one in the world to whom I would say so much, but you."

Hester was pleased and touched to the bottom of her heart.

"Oh, if I could only help you!" she cried ; "if I could do anything, or if you would tell me more ! I know I could understand. But anyhow, if it is a relief to you to tell me just as much as that ; I am glad ! only if I could but help you——"

"At present no one could help ; it is fortune that must decide."

"You mean Providence," said Hester, softly. She had never used the phraseology of religious sentiment as many girls do at her age, and was very shy in respect to it. But she added, under her breath, "And one can always pray."

At this Edward, which was a sign of grace in him, though she did not know it as such, drew back with a hasty move-

ment. It gave him a strange sensation to think of the success
which he was seeking by such means being prayed for, as if it
had been a holy enterprise. But just then Mrs. John stirred
audibly within, as if about to come and inquire into the causes
of the delay. He kissed her again tenderly, without any
resistance on her part, and said—

"Good-night—good-night! I must not say any more."

Hester opened the outer door for him, letting in the cold
night air. It was a glorious night, still as only winter is, the
moonlight filling up everything. She stood for a moment
looking after him, as he crossed the threshold. When he had
made a few steps into the night, he came back again hastily,
and caught her hands once more.

"Hester, we win or lose. Will you come away with me?
Will you give up all this for me? You don't love it any more
than I do. Will you come with me and be free?"

"Edward, you don't think what you are saying. You
forget my mother," she said.

He gave an impatient stamp with his foot; contradiction
was intolerable to him, or any objection at this moment.
Then he called "Good-night," again, more loudly into the air,
as though to reach Mrs. John in the parlour, and hurried
away.

"Edward was a long time saying good-night," said Mrs.
John. "I suppose you were talking about the ball; that is
always what happens when you give up a thing for a whim;
you always regret it after. Of course you would both have
preferred to be there. I suppose that is why he came in this
evening, a thing he never did in his life before. Well, I must
say we are all indebted, more or less, to Ellen Merridew,
Hester. She has drawn us together in a way there never
was any chance of in the old times. Fancy Edward Vernon
coming into our house in that sort of unceremonious way! It
was too late. I would never encourage a gentleman to come so
late : but still it showed a friendly spirit, and a confidence that
he would be welcome, which is always nice. I must tell him
next time I see him that I shall be delighted at any time to
have him here, only not quite so late at night."

"I dare say it will not happen again," Hester said.

"Why shouldn't it happen again? It is the most natural
thing in the world; only I shall tell him that usually we are
all shut up by ten o'clock. It did give me a great fright to
begin with, for I thought he must have come to tell us that

Catherine was ill. She has always been so strong and well that I shouldn't wonder at all if it was something sudden that carried her off in the end ; and whenever it does come it will be a great shock ; besides that, it will break up everything. This house will probably be sold, and——"

"Catherine Vernon does not look at all like dying," Hester said. "Please do not calculate upon what would happen."

"My dear, it does not make a thing happen a day the sooner that we take it into consideration; for we will have to, when the time comes. We shall all have to leave our houses, and it will make a great deal of difference. Of course we can't expect her heirs to do the same kind of thing as Catherine has done. No, I confess that was what I thought, and it was a great relief to me to hear—did you lock the door, Hester ? I hope you remembered to turn the key the wrong way. The fire is quite safe, I think, and I have shut the shutters. Carry the candle and let us go to bed."

Mrs. John continued to talk while they were undressing, though she had been so sleepy during Edward's visit. She would permit no hasty manipulation of Hester's hair, which had to be brushed for twenty minutes every night. She thought its beauty depended upon this manipulation, and never allowed it to be omitted, and as this peaceful exercise was gone through, and her mother's gentle commentary ran on, it is impossible to describe the force of repressed thought and desire for silence and quiet which was in Hester's veins. She answered at random when it was necessary to answer at all, but Mrs. John took no notice. She had been roused up by that curious visit. She took longer time than usual for all her own little preparations, and was more particular than usual about the hair-brushing. The fire was cheerful in the outer room, which was the mother's, and on account of this fire it was the invariable custom that Hester should do her hair-brushing there. Her mother even tried a new way of arranging Hester's hair, so full was she of that mental activity which so often adds to the pangs of those who are going through a secret crisis. It seemed hours before the girl was finally allowed to put out the candle, and steal back into the cold moonlight, into her own little room where the door always stood open between her and her mother. Hester would have liked to close that door ; her thoughts seemed too big, too tumultuous, not to betray themselves. Soon, however, Mrs,

John's calm, regular breathing, showed her to be asleep, and then Hester felt free to deliver herself up to that torrent of thought.

Was it possible that not very long since she had scorned herself for almost sharing Emma's ignoble anxiety that he should "speak." It had chafed and fretted her almost beyond endurance to feel herself thus on the same level as Emma, obliged to wait till he should declare his wishes, feeling herself so far subordinate and dependent, an attitude which her pride could not endure. Now he had spoken indeed—not in the conventional way, saying he loved her and asking her to marry him, as people did in books. Edward had taken it for granted that she was well aware of his love—how could it be otherwise? Had not she known from the beginning, when their eyes met, that there was an interchange in that glance different from and more intimate than all the intercourse she had ever had with others? Even when she had been so angry with him, when he had passed by her in Catherine Vernon's parties with but that look, indignant as she had been, was there not something said and replied to by their eyes such as had never passed between her and any other all her life long? —"My only love." She knew she was his only love. The remembrance of the words made her heart beat, but she felt now that she had known them all along. Since the first day when they met on the common, she a child, he in the placidity of unawakened life, there had been nobody to each but the other. She knew and felt it clearly now—she had known it and felt it all along, she said to herself—but it had wanted that word to make it flash into the light. And how unlike ordinary love-making it all was! He had come to her, not out of any stupid doubt about her response to him, not with any intention of pleading his own cause, but only because his burden was too much for him, his heart too full, and she was the only one in all the world upon whom to lean it. Hester said to herself, with fine scorn, that to suppose the question, "Do you love me?" to be foremost in a man's mind when he was fully immersed in the business and anxieties of life, was to make of love not a great but a petty thing. How could he fail to know that as he had looked upon her all those years so she had looked upon him? "My only love"—the words were delightful, like music to her ears; but still more musical was the thought that he had come to her not to say them— that he had come to lean upon her, upon her arm, and her

heart—to tell her that something had happened to him
which he could not tell to any one else in the world. To
think that he should have been drawn out of his home, along
the wintry road, out into the night, solely on the hope of
seeing her and reposing his over-full mind upon her, conveyed
to Hester's soul a proud happiness, a sense of noble befitting-
ness and right, which was above all the usual pleasure (she
thought) of a newly disclosed love. He had disclosed it in
the noblest way, by knowing that it needed no disclosure, by
coming to her as the other part of him when he was in
utmost need. Had Edward calculated deeply the way to
move her he could not have chosen better; but he did it
instinctively, which was better still—truly needing, as he
said, that outlet which only the most intimate unity of being,
the closest of human connections, could give. Hester could
think of nothing but this in the first rapture. There were
other things to be taken into consideration—what the momentous step was which he had taken, and what was the
meaning of that wild proposal at the end. To go away with
him, win or lose—— She would not spoil the first sweet impression with any thought of these, but dropped asleep at last,
saying to herself "My only love" with a thrill of happiness
beyond all words. She had believed she would not sleep at
all, so overflowing was her mind with subjects of thought,
but these words were a sort of lullaby which put the other
more important matters out of her head. "My only love"—
if it was he who had said them, or she who had said them,
she could scarcely tell. They expressed everything—the
meaning of so many silent years.

Edward was making his way as quietly as possible into the
house which had been his home for so many years, while Hester
turned over these things in her mind. He had loitered on
the way back, saying to himself that if Catherine should
chance not to be asleep, it was better that she should suppose
him to have gone to the Merridews. He felt himself something
like a thief in the night as he went in, taking his candle and
going softly up the carpeted stairs not to disturb her—a proceeding which was for his sake, not for hers, for he had no
desire to be questioned in the morning and forced to tell petty
lies, a thing he disliked, not so much for the sake of the lies as
for the pettiness of them. But Catherine, disturbed by a new
anxiety which she did not understand, was lying awake, and
did hear him, cautious as he was. She said to herself, "He

has not stayed long to-night," with a sense half of satisfaction, half of alarm. Never before during all the years he had been under her roof had this feeling of insecurity been in her mind before. She did not understand it, and tried to put it aside and take herself to task for a feeling which did Edward injustice, good as he was, and had always been, in his relations with her. If some youthful tumult was in his mind, unsettling him, there was nothing extraordinary in that—if he was "in love," that natural solution of youthful agitations. It is common to say and think that mothers, and those who stand in a mother's place, are jealous of a new-comer, and object to be no longer the first in their child's affections. Catherine smiled in the dark, as she lay watching and thinking. This should not stand in Edward's way—provided that he made a right choice! But whatever choice he made, it would be for him, not her, she reflected, with a magnanimity almost beyond nature, and it would be strange if she could not put up with it for his sake. She had not, indeed, the smallest idea in which direction his thoughts had turned. But there was something in the air which communicated alarm.

When Hester woke next morning, it was not with the same sense of beatitude which had rapt her from all other considerations on the previous night, notwithstanding her high certainty that the mere love declared was but secondary in her mind to the noble necessity of having to share the burdens and bear part in the anxieties of her lover. Everything else he said had in fact been little to her in comparison with the three words which had been going through her mind and her dreams the whole night, and which sprang to her lips in the morning like an exquisite refrain of happiness, but which gradually, as she began to think, went back out of the foreground, leaving her subject to questions and thoughts of a very different description. What had the crisis been through which he had passed? What was the new departure, the burning of the ships? There must be some serious meaning in words so serious as these. And then that wild suggestion that she should fly with him, whether they gained or lost, "away from all this; you don't love it any more than I do" —what did that mean? Alarm was in her mind along with the excitement of a secret half-revealed. An eager and breathless longing to see him again, to know what it meant, gained possession of her mind. Then there floated back into her ears

Roland's remark, which had half-offended her at the time, which
she had thought unnecessary, almost impertinent, that Edward
"lost his head." In what did he lose his head? She remembered the whole conversation as her mind went back to it.
Edward was too hot and eager; he had a keen eye, but he
lost his head; he was tired of the monotony of his present
life. And then there came his own statement about burning his
ships. What did it all mean? She began to piece everything
together, dimly, as she could with her imperfect knowledge.
She had no training in business, and did not know in what
way he could risk in order to gain—though of course this was
a commonplace, and she had often heard before of men who
had lost everything or gained everything in a day. But when
Hester thought of the bank, and of all the peaceable wealth
with which Vernon's was associated, and of the young men
going to their office tranquilly every day, and the quiet continual progress of their affairs, she could not understand how
everything could hang upon a chance, how fortune could be
gained or lost in a moment. It was scarcely more difficult to
imagine the whole economy of the world dropping out in a
moment, the heavens rolling up like a scroll, and the foundations of the earth giving way, than to imagine all that long-
established framework of money-making collapsing so that
one of the chief workers in it could talk of burning his ships
and suggest a moment when he should fly away from all this—
which could only mean from every established order of things.
That her heart should rise with the sense of danger, and that
she should be ready to give her anxious help and sympathy
and eager attention, to the mystery, whatever it was, did not
make any difference in Hester's sudden anxiety and alarm.
The earth seemed to tremble under her feet. Her whole life
and the action of the world itself seemed to hang in suspense.
She did what she had never in her life thought possible before.
She went out early, pretending some little business, and hung
about on the watch, with her veil down, and her mind in a
tumult impossible to describe, to meet Edward, if possible, on
his way to the bank. Could it be Hester, so proud, so reserved as she was, that did this? Her cheeks burned and
her heart beat with shame : but it seemed to her that she
could not endure the suspense, that she must see and question
him, and know what it was. But Edward had gone to the
bank earlier than usual, which was a relief as well as a
disappointment unspeakable to her. She stole home, feeling

herself the most shameless, the least modest of girls; yet
wondered whether she could restrain herself and keep still,
and not make another effort to see him, for how could she live
in this suspense? Punishment came upon her, condign and
terrible. She fell into the hands of Emma Ashton, who was
taking a little walk along the road in the morning, to wake
her up a little, she said, after the ball last night, and who,
utterly unconscious of Hester's trouble and agitated looks,
had so many things to tell her, and turned back with her,
delighted to have a companion. "For though a little exercise
is certainly the best thing for you, it is dull when you take it
all by yourself," Emma said.

CHAPTER XXXIV.

DOUBTS AND FEARS.

THE abruptness with which Edward Vernon retired from
the discussion with his partner and agent had a singular
effect upon both. Neither accepted it as done in good faith.
It surprised and indeed startled them. What they had looked
for was a prolonged discussion, ending in all probability in a
victory for Edward, who was by far the most tenacious of
the three, and least likely to yield to the others. So easy a
conclusion of the subject alarmed them more than the most
obstinate maintenance of his own views. They were so much
surprised indeed that they did not communicate their astonishment to each other on the spot by anything more than an
interchange of looks, and parted after a few bewildered
remarks about nothing in particular, neither of them venturing to begin upon a subject so delicate. But when they
next met reflection had worked upon both. Neither had been
able to dismiss the matter from his thoughts. They met
indeed in a most inappropriate atmosphere for any such grave
discussion, at Ellen Merridew's house, where they mutually
contemplated each other from opposite sides of the room,
with an abstraction not usual to either. It had a great effect
upon both of them, also, that neither Hester nor Edward
appeared. Roland had known beforehand and reconciled
himself as well as he could to the former want : but Harry
did not know it, and was full of curious and jealous alarm on
the subject, unable to refrain from a suspicion that the two
who were absent must have somehow met and be spending
at least part of the time together free from all inspection
—a thing which was really happening, though nothing could
be more unlikely, more unprecedented than that it should

happen. Roland did not think thus ; he knew very well that
Edward had not attempted to hold any intercourse with
Hester, and felt that as far as this was concerned there was
no extra danger in the circumstances : but Harry's alarm
seemed to confirm all his own ideas on the other matter. He
missed Hester greatly for his own part—not that he did not
do his best to make several of the Redborough young ladies
believe that to recall himself to her individual recollection
was the special object of his visit—but that was a mere
detail of ordinary existence. It was Hester he had looked
forward to as the charm of the evening, and everything was
insipid to him without her, in the feminine society around
him. It was not till after supper, when the fun had become
faster and more furious that he found himself standing close
to Harry whose countenance in the midst of all this festivity
was dull and lowering as a wintry sky. Harry did not dance
much ; he was a piece of still life more than anything else
in his sister's house : loyally present to stand by her, doing
everything she asked him, but otherwise enduring rather than
enjoying. This was not at all Roland's *rôle :* but on this
special evening when they got together after midnight the
one was not much more lively and exhilarating in aspect than
the other. They stood up together in a doorway, the privi-
leged retreat of such observers, and made some gloomy
remarks to each other. "Gets to look a little absurd don't
it, this sort of thing, when you have a deal on your mind ? "
Harry said out of his moustache. And "Yes. Gaiety does
get depressing after a while," Roland remarked. After which
they relapsed again into dead silence standing side by side.

" Mr. Ashton, what do you mean by it ? " cried Ellen. " I
have given up Harry : but *you* usually do your duty. Good
gracious ! I see *three* girls not dancing, though I always have
more men on purpose. I don't know what you boys mean."

"Let us alone, Ashton and I, Nell—we've got something
to talk about," said Harry.

His sister looked up half alarmed in his face.

" I declare since you've gone so much into business you're
insupportable, Harry," she cried. It seemed to bring the two
men a little closer to each other when she whisked off again
into the crowd.

" It's quite true," said Harry, " let's go into the hall,
where there's a little quiet. I do want awfully to talk to you.
What do you think about Ned giving up that business all at

once, when we both stood up to him about it? I was awfully
grateful to you for standing by me. I scarcely expected it;
but as for Ned giving in like that, I can scarcely believe it
even now."

"It was not much like him, it must be confessed," Roland
said.

"Like him! he never did such a thing in his life before;
generally he doesn't even pay much attention to what one
says. He has a way of just facing you down however you
may argue, with a sort of a smile which makes me fit to dance
with rage sometimes. But to-day he was as meek as Moses
—What do you think? I—don't half like it, for my part."

"You think after all he was in the right perhaps?"

"No, I don't. I never could do that. To risk other people
in that way is what I never would consent to. But a fellow
who is so full of fight and so obstinate, to give in—that's
what I don't understand."

"You think perhaps—he has not given in," Roland said.

Harry gave him a bewildered look, half grateful, half
angry. "Now I wonder what I've said that has made you
think that!"

"Nothing that you have said—perhaps only an uneasy
feeling in my own mind that it isn't natural, and that I don't
understand it any more than you."

"Well," said Harry, with a long breath of relief, "that
is just what I think. I don't believe for a moment, you
understand, that Ned, who is a real good fellow all through"—
here he made a slight pause, and glanced at Roland with a
sort of defiance, as if expecting a doubt, which however was
not expressed—"means anything underhand you know. Of
course I don't mean that. But when a man knows that he
is cleverer than another fellow, he'll just shut up sometimes
and take his own way, feeling it's no use to argue—I don't
mean he thinks himself cleverer than you, Ashton; that's
a different affair. But he hasn't much opinion of me. And
in most things no doubt he's right, and I've never set up to
have much of an opinion."

"There you are wrong, Vernon," said Roland, "you have
the better judgment of the two. Edward may be cleverer
as you say, but I'd rather throw in my lot with you."

"Do you really say so?" cried Harry, lighting up; "well
that is very kind of you anyhow. My only principle is we've
got others to consider besides ourselves."

"Precisely so," said Roland, who had heard this statement
already, "and you were quite right to stick to it : but I confess I am like you, not quite comfortable about the other
matter. Has he means enough of his own to go in for it?
If so, I should think that was what he intended."

Harry shook his head. "We had none of us any means,"
he said. "Aunt Catherine took us, as you might say, off the
streets. We were not even very near relations. She's done
everything for us : that's why I say doubly, don't let us risk a
penny of her money or of what she prizes above money.
You may think we were not very grateful to her," Harry
continued, "but that's only Ellen's way of talking. If there
was anything to be done for Aunt Catherine that little thing
has got as true a heart as any one. But we were not wanted,
as you may say. Ned was always the favourite, and so Nell
set up a little in opposition, but never meaning any harm."

"I feel sure of that," said Roland, with a warmer impulse
than perhaps Mrs. Ellen in her own person would have moved
him to. And then he added, after a pause, "I think I'll open
the subject again. If Edward Vernon means to do anything
rash, it's better he should be in my hands than in some,
perhaps, that might be less scrupulous. I'll see him to-morrow
about it. There's no time lost, at least——"

"That's capital!" cried Harry, warmly ; "that's exactly
what I wanted. I didn't like to ask you ; but that's acting
like a true friend : and if, as a private person, there's anything
I could do to back him up—only not to touch Vernon's, you
know——"

Their privacy was broken in upon by the swarm of dancers
pouring into the coolness of the hall as the dance ended ;
but up to the moment when the assembly broke up Harry
continued, by an occasional meaning look now and then across
the heads of the others, to convey his cheerful confidence in
Roland, and assurance that now all would go well. Ashton,
too, had in himself a certain conviction that it must be so.
He was not quite so cheerful as Harry, for the kind of operations into which Edward's proposal might bring him were not
to his fancy. But the very solemn charge laid upon him by the
old people had never faded from his memory, and Catherine
Vernon in herself had made a warm impression upon him.
He had been received here as into a new home—he who knew
no home at all ; everybody had been kind to him. He had
met here the one girl whom, if he could ever make up his

mind to marry (which was doubtful), he would marry. Everything combined to endear Redborough to him. He had an inclination even (which is saying a great deal) to sacrifice himself in some small degree in order to save a heartbreak, a possible scandal in this cheerful and peaceful place. Edward Vernon, indeed, in himself was neither cheerful nor peaceable; but he was important to the preservation of happiness and comfort here. Therefore Roland's resolution was taken. He had come on purpose to dissuade and prevent; he made up his mind now to further, and secure the management of this over-bold venture, since no better might be. He knew nothing, nor did any but the writer of it know anything, of the letter which Catherine Vernon's butler had carefully deposited in the postbag, and sent into Redborough an hour or two before this conversation, to be despatched by the night mail. The night express from the north called at Redborough station about midnight, and many people liked to travel by it, arriving in town in the morning for their day's business, not much the worse if they had good nerves—for there was only one good train in the day.

Next morning, accordingly, just after Hester had returned with Emma from that guilty and agitated walk, which she had taken with the hope of meeting Edward, and hearing something from him about his mysterious communication of the previous night—Roland too set out with much the same purpose, with a grave sense of embarking on an enterprise he did not see the end of. He met the two girls returning, and stopped to speak to them.

"Hester has been at Redborough this morning already," Emma said. "I tell her she should have been at Mrs. Merridew's last night, Roland. It was a very nice dance— the very nicest of all, I think; but perhaps that is because I am so soon going away. A regular thing is so nice—always something to look forward to; and you get to know everybody, and who suits your steps best, and all that. I have enjoyed it so very much. It is not like town, to be sure, but it is so friendly and homely. I shall miss it above everything when I go away."

"It was unkind not to come last night, my only chance," said Roland. He had no conception that Hester could have the smallest share in the grave business of which his mind was full, and, grave as it was, his mind was never too deeply engaged in anything for this lighter play of eye and voice

She seemed to wake up from a sort of abstraction, which
Emma's prattle had not disturbed, when he spoke, and
blushed with evident excitement under his glance. There
was in her, too, a sort of consciousness, almost of guilt, which
he could not understand. " I hope you were sorry," he added,
"and were not more agreeably occupied : which would be an
additional unkindness."

" I am afraid I can't say I am sorry."

Her colour varied ; her eyes fell. She was not the same
Hester she had been even last night ; something had happened to the girl. It flashed across his mind for the moment
that Edward had been absent too, which gave a sting of pique
and jealousy to his thoughts : but reassured himself, remembering that these two never met except at the Merridews. Where
could they meet ? Edward, who conformed to all Catherine
Vernon's ways, though with resentment and repugnance, and
Hester, who would conform to none of them. He was glad to
remind himself of this as he walked on, disturbed by her look,
in which there seemed so much that had not been there before.
She seemed even to have some insight into his own meaning
—some sort of knowledge of his errand, which it was simply
impossible she could have. He told himself that his imagination was too lively, that this little society, so brimful of
individual interests, with its hidden motives and projects,
was getting too much for him. He had not been in the
habit of pausing to ask what So-and-So was thinking of,
what that look or this meant. In ordinary society it is
enough to know what people say and do ; when you begin
to investigate their motives it is a sign that something is
going wrong. The next thing to do would be to settle down
among them, and become one of the Redborough coterie,
to which suggestion Roland, with a slight shiver, said
Heaven forbid ! No, he had not come to that point. Town
and freedom were more dear to him than anything he could
find here. Hester, indeed (if he was sure he could afford it),
might be a temptation ; but Hester by no means meant
Redborough. She would not cling to the place which had
not been very gracious to her. But he could not afford it, he
said to himself, peremptorily, as he went on. It was not a
thing to be thought of. A young man making his way in
the world, living as yet a bachelor life, may have a little
house at Kilburn with his sister ; but that would not at all
please him with a wife. And Hester meant her mother as

well. It was out of the question ; it was not to be thought of.
But why did she look so strangely conscious? why was she so
pale, so red, so full of abstraction and agitation to-day? If
anything connected with himself could have caused that
agitation, Roland could not answer for it what he might be
led to do,

This thought disturbed him considerably from the other
and graver thoughts with which he had started ; but he
walked on steadily all the same to the bank, and knocked at
the door of Edward's room. Edward was seated at his table
reading the morning's letters with all the calm of a reasonable
and moderate man of business—a model banker, with the
credit and comfort of other men in his hands. He looked up
with a smile of sober friendliness, and held out his hand to
his visitor. He did not pretend to be delighted to see him.
The slightest, the very most minute shadow of a consciousness
that this was not an hour for a visitor, was on his tranquil
countenance.

"You man of pleasure," he said, "after your late hours
and your dances, how do you manage to find your way into
the haunts of business at this time in the morning!" and he
glanced almost imperceptibly at his letters as he spoke.

"I am in no hurry," said Roland. "Read your letters.
You know I have nothing particular to do here. I can wait
your leisure ; but I have something to say to you, Vernon, if
you will let me."

"My letters are not important. Of course I will let you.
I am quite at your disposal," Edward said ; but there was
still a shade of annoyance—weariness—as at a person im-
portunate who would not take a hint and convey himself
away.

"I wanted to speak to you about the subject of our conversation yesterday."

"Yes, which was that?"

"It was important enough to have remained in my memory,"
said Roland, with a little offence, feeling himself put in the
wrong from the beginning. "I mean the proposals we were
discussing—your ideas on the subject of the——"

"Oh that! but you put a stop to all my ideas, Harry and
you in your wisdom. I thought you must have meant that
little matter about Aunt Catherine's books. Yes, it seemed
to me, so far as my lights went, that the proposals were very
promising : and I might have stood out against Harry, who

will never set the Thames on fire; till you came down upon me with your heavy guns—you whom I expected to be on my side."

"Then you have really given it up?" cried Roland, with a sigh of relief.

"Didn't you mean me to do so? That is what I thought, at all events. You were so determined about it, that I really don't see what else I could have done, unless," he said, with a smile, "I had been a capitalist, and completely independent, as you said."

"I am most thankful to hear it, Vernon. I had not been able to divest myself of the idea that you were still hankering after it," said Roland; "and I came, intending to say to you, that if your heart was really set upon it—rather than that you should put yourself into hands, perhaps not so scrupulous——"

"Ah! I see: rather than that a rival should get the business—let us speak plainly," said Edward, with a pale smile.

"That is not speaking plainly. It is altogether different from my meaning; but take it so, if you please. I am glad to know that there is no necessity for my intrusion anyhow," Roland said; and then there was a little pause.

At last Edward got up, and came forward, holding out his hand.

"Pardon the little spite that made me put so false an interpretation on your motive, Ashton. I know that was not what you meant. I was annoyed, I confess, that you did thwart me yesterday in a matter I had so much at heart."

"I felt that you were annoyed; but what could I do? I can only advise according to my judgment. Anyhow, Vernon, I came here intending to say, 'Let me do the best I can for you if you persist; don't throw yourself among those who promote that kind of speculation, for they are not to be trusted to.' But I am above measure glad to find that you have no hankering after it. That is far the best solution. You take a weight off my mind," Roland said.

Edward did not answer for the moment. He went back and reseated himself at his table. When he showed his face again, Roland saw he was laughing.

"After all you said to me yesterday, and Harry! think of Harry's grand argument coming down upon me like a sledge-hammer, as potent, and alas, quite as heavy—how

could you think it possible that I should persist? I am not
such a determined character. Besides, don't you know I have
never been trained to act for myself?"

His laugh, his look, were not very convincing, but at all
events they were conclusive. After another pause, Roland
rose.

"I am interfering with your work," he said. "I thought
it my duty to come at once; but now that it's all over, I must
not waste your time. Pardon my officiousness."

"Nothing of the sort," said Edward, smiling cheerfully;
"the kindest feeling. I know it is. Are you going to see
Harry? He is in his room, I know."

"Yes, I think I'll just speak to him. There is some football match that Emma wants to see."

"More pleasuring," said Edward, and laughed again.
There was in him such an air of having found his visitor
out, that Roland could not divest himself of a certain embarrassment. Edward, he felt, knew as well as he did, that
he was going to report his failure to Harry. It fretted him
beyond description to be thus seen through, he, who had
thought himself so much more than a match for any provincial fellow of them all. "But you are quite right to consult Harry about football; he is the greatest possible authority
upon that subject," Edward said.

"Oh, it is not of the slightest importance; it is merely
that Emma, who does not really care a straw for football,
and only wants something to do, or see——"

"That is surely reason enough," said Edward, and his com-
plaisance went so far that he left his papers again, and led the
way to Harry's room, where he looked in, saying, "Here's
Ashton come to inquire about that match."

"Eh? Match?" cried Harry, in much surprise. Then his
faculties kindled at the sight of Roland's face. "Will you
play for us, Ashton? I didn't know you went in for football.
I just wanted a man to be——"

"It was for Emma; your sister told her she must go and
see it."

"I'll leave you to your explanations," said Edward, with a
laugh of triumph. And indeed the two conspirators looked
at each other somewhat crestfallen, when he had gone away.

"He takes it quite lightly," said Roland, with the sense of
talking under his breath, "as if he had never thought of the
matter again—does not conceal that he was vexed, but says

of course there was an end when I came down upon him with
my heavy guns."

Then they looked at each other guiltily—ashamed, though
there was nothing to be ashamed of, like plotters found out.

"Well, that's something tided over," Harry said.

"I hope so : but I must not stay, to confirm his suspicions.
Tell me when the match is for Emma, for she does want to go
and see it, that's quite true."

"I don't care for girls about," said Harry; "they never
understand the game, and it makes fellows nervous. It's on
Saturday if she wants to come."

"I'll tell her it makes fellows nervous," said Roland, as
he went away. He said it in a louder tone than usual,
that he might be heard in Edward's room, and then despised
himself for doing so. Altogether he had seldom felt more
small or more completely baffled and seen through than
when he retired from those doors which he had entered
with so kind a purpose. It is embarrassing to have the
tables turned upon you, even in the smallest matters. He
felt that he had been made to appear officious, intrusive,
deceitful, even to himself, making up plots with one man
against another, prying into that other's purposes, attributing
falsehood to him. This was how his generous intention was
cast back upon his hands. He tried to smile cynically, and to
point out to himself the foolishness of straining to do a good
action; but he was not a cynic by nature, and the effort was
not successful. In any way, however, in which it could be
contemplated, it was evident that all had been done that it
was possible to do. If Edward had made up his mind to the
risk, he could not stand between him and ruin. The matter
was taken entirely out of his hands.

Edward, for his part, returned to his room, and shut himself in with feelings much less victorious than those he made
apparent. The excitement of the great decision had a little
failed and gone off. He was in the chill reactionary stage,
wondering what might befall, feeling the tugs of old prejudice,
of all the traditions of honour in which he had been brought
up, dragging at his heart. No man brought up as Edward
had been could be without prejudices on the side of right. It
alarmed and wounded him to-day to think that he had last
night considered the property of the bank and its customers
as a foundation upon which to start his own venture. The
sophisms with which he had blinded himself in his excitement

failed him now—the daylight was too clear for them. He
perceived that it was other people's goods, other people's
money, which he was risking; that even to take them out,
to look at them, to think of them as in his power, was a
transgression of the laws of honour. Those chill drawings
back of customary virtue, of the prejudices of honour, from the
quick march of passion which had hurried him past every
landmark in that haste to be rich, which would see no obstacle
in its way, plunged Edward into painful discouragement. He
seemed to himself to have fallen down from a height, at which
he had been master of his fate, to some deep-lying under-
ground where he was its slave, and could only wait till the
iron car of necessity rolled on and crushed him. He had set,
he felt, machinery in motion which he could not stop, which
might destroy him. He sat and looked out affrighted upon all
the uncomprehended forces which seemed to have got into movement against him. He, a poor adventurer, with nothing that
was his own, to thrust himself into the midst of the commercial movements in London, which nobody out of them
could understand fully; he to risk thousands who had nothing; he to "go in to win" who had nothing to stand
upon! He saw all round him, not only destruction, not
only ruin, but contempt and outrage. He had once seen a
miserable "welsher" hunted from a racecourse, and the
spectacle, so cruel, so barbarous, yet not unjust, came back
to his mind with a horrible fascination. He remembered the
poor wretch's hat battered down upon his head, blinding him—
the clothes torn from his back, the cruelty with which he was
pursued, and still more, the mud and dirt, that meant not
only punishment but unutterable contempt. Under that recollection Edward sat shivering. What was he better than the
welsher? Though he sat there, to all appearance, spruce and
cool, reading his morning's letters, he was already in this
state of miserable depression and terror when Roland came in.
The post that morning had brought him no fresh alarm, no
new excitement. He was safe for that day; nothing could
yet have been done in his affairs that was not remediable.
It was possible even that by telegraphing now he could stop
all those horrible wheels of destiny, and undo the decision of
last night. As a matter of fact, no intention of doing so was
in his mind; but the idea came uppermost now and then in
the boiling up and ferment within him: to stop everything
still, to relapse into the Edward of three months ago—

submissive, respectable, keeping every punctilio of the domestic
laws, as well as those of recognised honesty and prudence.
But he never meant it ; he was alarmed at himself, shaken out
of all that ease which excitement gives, that possibility of
believing what we wish ; but though everything that last
night pointed to success seemed now to point to despair, he
felt himself clinging on to the chance with desperation com-
mensurate with the gloomy prospect. Whatever it was to
lead to, he must yet go on. After all, prudence itself sometimes fared as badly as hardihood. An investment that had
been calculated upon as the surest and safest would sometimes turn out disastrous. Who could tell ? The chances of
money were beyond all calculation. And, after all, no one
could say that the ruin of the bank would be for his good.
It would be ruin to himself. It was not a thing that anybody
could suppose he would risk without deliberation.

He was in this condition, surging and seething, when Roland
visited him, and brought him suddenly to himself with the force
which an encounter with the world outside so often gives to a
struggling spirit. He felt, with a wonderful sense of self-satis-
faction, that he was equal to the emergency, and confronted
it with a sudden gain of calm and strength which seemed to
him almost miraculous, like what men engaged in holy work
are justified in considering help from above. It could not be
help from above which supplied Edward with self-possession
and strength for his first steps in the career of evil, but still
the relief was great. He got the better of Roland, he extinguished the little virtuous plot which he divined between him
and Harry, and he returned to his room with a smile on his
face. But once back again there he did not feel triumphant.
He felt that he was not trusted—that already they suspected
him of having broken loose from their society and acting for
himself. He said to himself angrily that but for this he would
probably have telegraphed to contradict that momentous letter
of last night. But how could he do it now ? it would be pander-
ing to their prejudices, owning that he had taken an unjustifiable step. And how was it unjustifiable ? Was it not he
who was the virtual head, upon whose judgment and insight
everything depended ? Supposing Catherine to be consulted,
as had ceased to be the case for some time, partly with,
partly against, her own will—but supposing her to be consulted now, would not she certainly give her adherence to
Edward's judgment rather than Harry's ? It was not a

question there could be a moment's doubt about. She would shake her head, and say, "You are far more venturesome than ever I was, but if Edward really thinks——" Was not that always what she had said? And ten years of experience had given him a right to be trusted. He was acting for the best; he looked for nothing but success. It was nerves, mere nerves that had affected him—a reaction from the excitement of last night.

And thus everything settled down. When he had got over it, Edward was the most serene of all the doubtful group which surrounded him, not knowing what to make of him. Harry, who took a matter-of-fact view, came next. He now thought it highly probable, on the whole, that his cousin had thought better of it. How could he do anything else?—he had not means of his own to risk to such an extent, which was a thought very satisfactory to Harry. Roland Ashton was as much dissatisfied as men usually are who endeavour in vain to see into the minds of their neighbours, and offer good offices which are not wanted. But the most uneasy of all was Hester, who that day, for the first time, took upon her the most painful burden of women—the half knowledge which is torture, which the imagination endeavours to supplement in a thousand unreal ways, knowing them to be unreal, and dismissing them as quickly as they are formed—and the bitter suspense, the sensation that at any moment things may be happening, news coming which will bring triumph or misery, but which you cannot foresee or accelerate, or do anything but wait for. She did her best to pray, poor girl! breathing broken petitions for she knew not what, as she went about her little occupations all that lingering day. Surely he would try to see her again, to satisfy her, and tell what it was he had done, and how it could be possible, winning or losing, to fly, as he had suggested, from everything here. To fly—how could it be? Why should it be? All the other mysteries came in that to wonder unspeakable and dismay.

CHAPTER XXXV.

A DISCOVERY.

THERE was a dinner-party that evening at the Grange. It was given on account of Ashton, now well known in Red-borough ; and Catherine Vernon had taken the trouble to go herself to beg Captain Morgan to be of the party : but the old man had refused steadily.

"I will have none of your fine company," he said. "No, no ; you do enough for me here. When you come to see us it always is a pleasure, both to my old woman and me : but a dinner, no. I have not had on my evening coat this dozen of years. It's not likely it would be in the fashion now."

"What does it matter about fashion ? You shall come as you are if you would like that better," Catherine said ; but she did not mean it, and of that they were all perfectly aware. "It is to do honour to Roland. You are no longer so anxious to separate yourself from Roland as when he came here first," she said.

The old man did not say anything, but his wife answered for him.

"We will not commit ourselves, Catherine, you know our way ; but we think the boy does us credit. I think it might be that if we were left to ourselves we might even do a little match-making for him if we could."

"Are you come to that ?" said Catherine : but there was an echo of a sigh in her voice. "That seems to me to mean a confession—that we are not enough for them any longer, but still that we will not give in ; we will be enough for them in another way."

"Why should we be enough for them ? We could not

think that was possible, living far off as we do, and in a different way. No, but out of pure love, which is just as foolish as anything else. I am the wisest in this respect, for I know it will not do."

"And who is the lady?" Catherine asked, with a smile.

The next moment she saw very well who it was, for they did not make her any reply. Old Mrs. Morgan folding her hands said quietly, "It will never answer," and the Captain, leaving the mantel-piece against which he had been leaning with his face fully presented to her questioning, went and sat down in his usual place near the window, which afforded no such facilities to a penetrating eye. They did not mean to tell her, and she knew. She laughed to carry off the little annoyance with which this preference and prejudice, as she called it, always moved her, and said, "You should exert yourself in his sister's favour; by all she tells me she would not be ungrateful," in a way which communicated the annoyance she felt back again to her friends.

"We will not meddle with Emma," said old Mrs. Morgan. "I am tempted to think sometimes that the blood gets thin in a race when it runs too long, like the last cup of my tea—which he says is just hot water."

"Not so, not so," said old Captain Morgan. "You are growing a materialist in your old age; that is sometimes just the very essence and cream of all. In story-books, when there are an old couple left like you and me, the last child left with them to make them happy is a creature that is perfect."

"Oh, this is heresy indeed," cried Catherine. "I will not have you compare Emma to your last cup of tea. There is nobody I meet with so original; and is she to stay longer and have her chance? or has she come to the height of her desires and persuaded the gentleman to speak—there is nothing I want so much to know."

But here Catherine became vaguely sensible of a sentiment which, according to their own account, had died out long ago in these old people. They had declared themselves above prejudice in respect to their own flesh and blood. The captain indeed had thrown off all responsibility, and announced at Roland's first coming that he was not prepared to answer for him; and Emma had not been so congenial to them as Roland. Notwithstanding, when their grandchild

was thus freely criticised it galled them both.   The old lady
betrayed a little rising colour of vexation and shame, and
Captain Morgan got up again restlessly and went and stood
against the window, shutting out half the light, and turning
his back—which was a very strong step, though but for a
moment—upon his guest.

"She has not been brought up like other girls," said Mrs.
Morgan.   "Perhaps it was none of our duty ; it is hard to
say.   We knew nothing of her : poor little motherless thing,
we might have brought her away with us ; but these are
all questions it is little use going into now.   Such as she
is, she is a good girl in her way.   When she is married,
for she will be sure to marry, she will make a good, careful
wife."

"One would think I had been saying harm of Emma,"
cried Catherine, with some quickness ; "when the fact is I
am one of those that like her most.   She is the most piquant
variety of her species.   There is nobody that amuses me so
much.   She knows what she wants, which so few do, and she
means to have it.   She is quite honest and straightforward.
You do me injustice in this."

There was nothing said in reply, and Catherine did not like
the position.   Perhaps the universal submission to which she
was accustomed had spoilt her, though she was so sure of
seeing through it.   She got up to go away.

"I must do without you then, uncle, if I am not to have
you ; though I think it is a little hard upon me—and upon
Roland too."

"We are always here when you want us, Catherine ; as
much as is in us is always at your service.   It is not much,"
said the old man, hobbling after her to the door ; "but your
fine house and your fine people are not in *her* way nor in
mine.   And what should I do going back to the world,
and *her* in the arm-chair ?   You see yourself that would
never do."

"It would delight her !" said Catherine, pausing at the
door ; "you know that.   Fancy her keeping you by her
because she is not able to go out too !   It almost looks as if—
but that is impossible—you did not understand a woman
yet."

The old captain laughed and shook his white head.

"Persuade yourself that !" he said ; "make yourself think
that : that will chime in with the general opinion, Catherine.

If I were an old man on the stage I would say, there's no
understanding women.   If I don't understand her and all
her ways, I am a sillier old blockhead than you think."

"Then you know that what I say is true—that she would
like you to come—that it would please her——"

"Then it is she that is the silly old woman that does not
understand her old man," Captain Morgan said.

Catherine left them with the impression that they were in
a mood beyond her comprehension.   It was a fine, clear,
almost warm day, and the roads dry and walking pleasant.
She had come on foot, as was not very usual with her, and
meant to walk home.   She set out on her return waving her
hand to Mrs. Morgan, but in no very cheerful frame of mind.
She had not been cheerful when she left home.   Her mind mis-
gave her as it had not done before for more years than she could
count.   What was the reason she could scarcely tell.   Edward
was not really less kind, less observant of her comfort.   The
change she saw in him was one indescribable, which no one
else would have suspected, which in all probability existed in
her imagination alone.   Why should she suppose evils that
had no existence ?   There was no one like him, no son so
dutiful to his mother, no one so ready to make any sacrifice
for the pleasure of his home.   If his looks had been a little
abstracted lately, if he had spent his time away from
her, if his work in his own room, which she had made so
comfortable for him, which she had been so anxious to assure
him the exclusive proprietorship of, had increased of late,
perhaps this was merely the natural course of events.   Or if
he had fallen in love—what then ?   Did the boy perhaps
think that she would be jealous and stand in the way of his
happiness ?   How little he knew !   Provided only his choice
was a right one ; she would open her arms and her heart.
She would be ready to do anything for their comfort.   There
was no sacrifice she would not gladly make.   Notwithstanding that somewhat nonsensical mystical flourish of the old
Captain's about his understanding of his wife, Catherine
believed, and with much show of truth, that men rarely
understood women, and never knew how ready they were to
arrange everything, to give up everything for the comfort
and pleasure of those they loved.   What a welcome she
would herself give to Edward's wife, though he was trembling
and putting off and afraid to tell her !   What a reception that
young woman should have !   Provided always—but with

Edward's good taste and good sense how could he go wrong in such a choice?

It was at this moment that a shuffling light step became audible, hurrying along the road, and a voice calling "Catherine—is it really Catherine?" followed by another step and another voice, with a fainter sound in the repetition, but also calling upon "Catherine!" Catherine Vernon paused and looked round, her face losing its gravity and brightening into its usual humorous look of half-contemptuous toleration.

"It is Catherine!" cried Miss Vernon-Ridgway; "I told you so. Dear Catherine, isn't this long walk too much for you, and on such a cold day? Take my arm—please take my arm: or won't you come back to our little house and rest, and we'll send for the carriage? It is a long walk for us who are not used to luxury, and what must it be to you?"

It was true that the Miss Vernon-Ridgways were under fifty, and Catherine was sixty-five; but she was far more vigorous than they were, and more capable of exercise. She turned round upon them smiling, but kept her arms close by her side, and refused any support.

"I assure you," she said, "I am quite capable of walking. You know I have always been accustomed to exercise."

"Ah yes," said the sisters, "you were brought up sensibly, dear Catherine, not spoiled darlings as we were. We have never quite got over it, though we should have known better long ago, if experience was all: no one can tell how we miss our carriage; and when we see you on foot, who can command every ease, it quite wounds our feelings," said Miss Martha, coming in at the end in a little provocation by herself.

"It is very kind of you: but it does not at all hurt my feelings. This is a fine day for a walk, and I hope you are enjoying yours, as I do," said Catherine, with her laughing look.

They both shook their heads.

"We do what we have to do, and I hope we don't complain. But I declare I feel hurt that you should have been at the Heronry and not paid us a visit. I wish not to be jealous. You were no doubt talking things over with Mrs. John?"

"I know nothing that there is to talk over with Mrs. John," said Catherine, tartly. "I was visiting my old uncle, which is a duty I never like to neglect."

"Oh!" said one sister, and "Ah!" said the other. Then
they cried eagerly each to each, "I knew it was a vile story.
Of course we have been misinformed."

"What was there to be misinformed about?" said
Catherine; then as she looked from one to another, a sensation of coming trouble shot across her. "And what," she
added with a smile not so easy as the former one, "am I
supposed to have to say to Mrs. John?"

"Oh, it was all an accident of course," said Miss Matilda.
"But you might tell Catherine all the same. It is best that
people should know; and then they know what steps to take,"
said Miss Martha. "To be sure Catherine would know
what steps to take," Matilda added again.

"This may all be very amusing," said Catherine, "but
as I don't know the word of the puzzle, I don't see the joke,
you know. One would think something had happened in
which I was concerned."

"I am not sure if you would think anything had happened. Oh yes, I am sure we thought so last night," cried
the sisters one after another. "You see the least little
thing looks important when you are going to bed—after eleven
o'clock at night."

"What was this great event?" said Catherine with a certain
sternness in her tone.

There was a great flutter of nods and looks between the
sisters. They came close to her, one on either side, and Miss
Matilda, always the boldest, put a hand to Catherine's elbow
by way of supporting her if support were needed.

"Dear Catherine, do turn back with us to our little place!
it is close by, and we can give you an easy chair and a cup of
tea. You will bear it better there than here."

"Did you say *bear* it better?"

"Oh! did I say it—*bear* it—Martha? I am sure I don't
know. I think I said hear it, Catherine. Oh! for Heaven's
sake don't look so stern. Perhaps you will think nothing of
it——"

Catherine gave her foot a stamp upon the ground. She
said—

"Tell me at once what you have got to tell," in a voice
which was almost threatening. They looked at each other
again, and then Miss Matilda began—

"I don't want to get any one into trouble, I am sure," she
said in a faltering but eager voice. 'It frightened us so—

that was the thing. It frightened us about you. I said to
Martha, ' Dear Catherine must be ill; nothing less than that
would bring him here at such an hour.' You see the voices
roused us just as we were going to bed. Mrs. John's door was
locked, for I had heard her do it; she always does it herself,
and, judging by her usual hours, she must have been in bed—
when we heard voices at the gate : oh, I was not surprised
at that. Sometimes it is old Captain Morgan himself, who I
am sure, with every respect for him, ought not to be out of
doors at such hours; sometimes the young gentleman, the
grandson—I don't remember his name ; or it used to be Harry
Vernon in his time. We all know that girl ; we needn't say
anything more on that subject. I merely remarked, ' There
she is at the gate again.' And Martha said——"

"Oh, I said, ' Fiddlesticks, she is at the ball ; it must be
one of the maids.' I am so unsuspicious," said Miss Martha.

"And then we listened as you may suppose. There was
just a little corner of the window open. Of course if it had
been one of the maids I should have thought it my duty——
Catherine, you are getting quite tired."

"I freely confess, yes—of your story. What do I care for
your maids and their lovers? You can settle these surely
without me."

"Oh, if you will only wait a little ! Very soon we could
hear that it was, if you please, Miss Hester's voice, and she
was inviting some one in. Oh, pressing him—almost forcing
him. Shouldn't you say so, Martha ? like the woman in the
Pilgrim's Progress."

"Yes, just like that kind of woman. Won't you come in,
just for a moment—just to rest a bit," said Martha, changing
her voice into a sort of squeak of the most unseductive kind.
"And he resisted as long as he could ; but she would take no
denial. You can't expect a young man to say ' No ' if a girl
puts herself at his feet like that. So he yielded at last,
poor young fellow. We didn't blame him a bit, did we,
Martha ?"

"Oh, not a bit ! poor young man, with such a creature as
that laying herself out—"

"And who was this whom you are so sorry for ? " Catherine
said.

As if she did not know ! She had been rather glad of all
the delays and *longueurs* of the tale, and marched along
through it, glad to make them out of breath, almost hoping

to be at her own door before the crisis; but in this she did
not succeed. She did not look at them even, but kept her
eyes upon the path with steady indifference.

"Dear Catherine!—but you won't blame him, poor young
fellow! It was your own Edward, that dear boy—"

Prepared as she was, the name gave her a shock, as perhaps
Miss Matilda, still holding her elbow, felt; but if so, it was
only for a moment. "Edward!" she said with a laugh.
"You mean Harry, I suppose? Edward was at home and
busy, occupying himself in a very different sort of way."

At this the sisters interchanged glances again, and shook
their heads in unison. "Ah, Catherine, that is just how
you are deceived. We know Harry Vernon's voice very well.
It was Edward."

Catherine turned upon them with a countenance perfectly
cloudless, a laugh upon her lips. "When I tell you," she
said, "that he was in my own house! he could not, I think,
be in two places at once—my house, his house—it is all the
same. He was at home—" she added after a moment, in a
deeper tone, "and with me."

"Oh! with you!" The sisters broke off with sudden
fright, not venturing to persevere. So sudden a check
quenched Miss Matilda's lively genius altogether. It was her
sister, the practical member, who added with a spasmodic
gasp, "Oh, of course, Catherine, if he was with you——"

"Yes, of course he was with me; he is only too attentive.
I could wish he took a little more amusement. So your fine
story is at an end, you see. If it had been any one else I
might have thought it my duty to inquire into it; but as I
can prove it not to be Edward—not that I see much harm in
it if it had been Edward," she added, turning upon the
accusers again. "I am not fond of Hester Vernon, but she
is his cousin all the same."

"Oh, no harm! oh, I never thought so," cried the gossips,
alarmed and faltering. "It was only just—it was merely—
it frightened us, thinking that dear Catherine must be ill, or
something happened—"

"Did you think then that your dear Catherine, if she were
ill, would send for Hester Vernon?—as her prime favourite,
I suppose, and the one that loved her best among all those
who——"

Catherine paused; the native magnanimity in her, beneath
all the pettiness which her laughing cynicism had taught her,

would not insult even these heartless women by a reminder in so many words of their dependence. It cost her all her strength to stand up erect before them and put off their assault. They had got at her heart, but they should never know it. She stood ample and serene between the two slim shabby figures and smiled defiance. Never were talebearers more completely discomfited. They turned upon each other with mutual reproaches in the confusion of the moment. "You need not have made such a fuss, Matilda." "I told you, Martha, you oughtn't to be so confident about a voice."

"Come," said Catherine, "we had better say nothing more about it; evidently there has been a mistake. Hester, who ought to be more careful if she is to live at the Vernonry, must have another admirer with whose voice you are not acquainted. But it is unwise to form conclusions on no better ground than the sound of a voice, and perhaps not very charitable or kind of you, so much older than she is, to tell anything that is uncomfortable about that girl, who is no favourite of mine already, to me. Don't you think you would do better if you warned her, or her mother?" Catherine's countenance was so calm, her eyes so commanding, that the Miss Vernon-Ridgways, altogether defeated in their malicious intention, which was chiefly to wound herself, felt their knees tremble under them, and were genuinely awestricken for perhaps the first time in their lives.

"Oh, as for that—it was not Hester we were thinking of —it was you," they faltered between them, "that you might not allow—or be exposed—" Their words got incoherent and ran away to nothing, into breaks and frightened lapses. And when Catherine, opening her eyes still wider, said, "For me! to warn me!" and laughed them to scorn, Matilda, who being the most forward was at the same time the most sensitive, was so overcome by anger and alarm and mortification that she began to cry for sheer despite, and felt in her inmost heart that she hated the woman who could humiliate her so.

"You were kindly afraid that I should be tired a few minutes ago: and standing does tire me, though I like a walk," Catherine said. "I will say good-bye now. Perhaps you meant it kindly; and if so, I'll thank you too—all the more as it's a mistake—for that is the best of it," she said with a laugh, waving her hand: and leaving them, walked on homewards with an alert and energetic step. But it would have been balm to their feelings if they had been able to see how

very little like laughter was her face when she had once
turned her back upon them.   There was nobody to observe
her along that quiet road. The nursemaids with their children
had all turned townwards some time ago.   There was not a
soul between her and the gate of the Grange.   Catherine's
face lengthened and darkened as if by a sudden effect of
years ; the sanguine life and confidence and force went out
of it.   She looked an old woman in that moment, as indeed
she had a right to do, but did not, nature interposing for
her aid.   She said to herself that she would not think, would
not ask herself what it meant, until she should get home, and
could feel the shelter of her own walls about her.   She wanted
shelter and privacy before she faced the fact which had been
dimly shadowing before her, but never in this form.   She was
a very resolute woman, and had not come so far in life without
having to confront and overcome many things that looked
terrible enough at the first glance.   But never since those
early days which were so far off that they were half forgotten,
had she been called upon to face those troubles which sap
the strength out of heart and will, the disappointments and
bitterness brought upon us by those we love.   She had few
of these sufferings for what seems the saddest reason, that
she had nobody to love.   But it was not so sad as it appears.
She had a number of people whom she loved well enough
to be delighted by their prosperities, and overcast by their
troubles.   She had all the advantages of affection without
being so closely knit to any as to have its drawbacks too.
But this easy position changed when she became, so to speak,
the mother of Edward Vernon.   It was not the doing of
providence, it was her own doing.   She had taken it upon
herself, and for years past she had said to herself that the
boy had made her know, as she had never known before,
what happiness was.   But now here was, swinging round
slowly, revealing itself to her in glimpses, the reverse of the
medal, the other side of the picture.   Was he deceiving her ?
She had taken up his defence boldly, not caring what she said :
but she had believed what she heard all the same, and had known
it to be true.   Was this why he had not cared to see her, to bid
her good-night, before he came out to have that meeting with
Hester—like a shopgirl and shopboy, she said to herself, her
lip quivering with passion, vexation, derision, all bound
together by the pain that produced them—at the gate ?   The
commonplace character of the meeting, the look of petty

intrigue in it, humbled her pride in her boy. If they had met at Ellen's dance, or in any legitimate way, she thought it would not have mortified her so much—but like a lady's maid and a footman, like Jane the scullery-girl and her young man ! She laughed to herself at the thought, but the laugh was more painful than tears.

By and by, however, Catherine came to take a little comfort out of the fact that Edward had not come to bid her goodnight. Not considering for a moment that any incident of all this might be accidental, though everything was so, she concluded that his heart had failed him, that he had felt himself incapable of the treachery of kissing her cheek in the usual tender way when about to do a thing which he knew would be so displeasing to her. When this occurred to Catherine the whole aspect of the matter changed : her features relaxed, her colour came back. This, no doubt, was how it had been. The girl had met him at Ellen's folly—how truly a folly had never been proved till now : and she was pretty and clever. Catherine was too proud to deny her her natural advantages ; and men were fools, as was well known—the best of them, the wisest of them !—where women were concerned. She had led him into some engagement, some light wager perhaps, some defiance of what he would venture to do. And Edward had been silly enough to be led away. She did not want him to be too wise. If he was silly, it was no more than everybody else had been before him. But he, dear boy, true boy, having involved himself in a piece of folly, had shown that high respect to her, that he would rather let her suppose he had forgotten and neglected her, than come to her with the usual greeting when he knew he was doing something which would seem treachery to Catherine. Thus she, who for the first moment had known no wish but that of pushing homeward and hiding her sudden downfall within her own house where nobody could intrude upon her, had so triumphantly explained all that trouble away before she got home, that she entered the Grange radiant, with no sense of having a downfall to hide. The casuistry of love is more skilful than any device of philosophy. She explained everything to herself. She wondered that she had not read it in his face all the evening. She felt that it had been there, if she had only had eyes to see. A foolish talk carried a trifle too far—a bold girl, not bad, no, not bad—that was not necessary, and Catherine would be just—pleased to get a little triumph when she could over the other side : and a foolish promise, not intended, had drawn him, perhaps against his will. By this subtle demonstration— which no faculty less keen than that of love could have made— Catherine proved to her full satisfaction, the fundamental truth in him which no little trumpery deceit (of a kind so innocent as this !) could undermine. All this fine fabric was raised on the most insignificant foundation of fact. But what did that matter ? it was enough. And if Catherine had been told that Edward's forgetfulness of the good-night had been accidental, and that his meeting with Hester was accidental, and that no incident of the night had been planned beforehand, she would have simply and flatly denied the possibility. She knew better ; and she preferred the matter as it stood.

The dinner-party was an insignificant affair to her after this. She did full justice to it, and to Roland Ashton, the chief guest, the man whom she delighted to honour, and for whose pleasure and profit the best people in Redborough were called together. He was already known to many of them, and it was Catherine's pleasure to make her relationship and interest in the young visitor clear. But her mind was eager to get through the commonplace courtesies of the evening—to come to the moment when Edward and she should meet alone. She could not pass her discovery over without note. She would tell him what she had heard, and what she had divined. She would give him the tender warning which such an affection as hers had a right to offer. If it was more than a passing flir- tation (which she did not believe), to beg him to reconsider it ; if his heart should be touched (which Heaven forbid ! but the thought made her smile, it was so profoundly unlikely), to intreat him to reflect, 'and see how little satisfaction could come to him from such intercourse. She went over and over again the interview that was to come—so often, indeed, that she exhausted it, and when the moment did come, did not remember half of what she intended to say. It came, indeed, in a way entirely contrary to that she had imagined. After the party had dispersed, Edward took Roland into his room to smoke with him—which she ought to have recollected he was in the habit of doing—and then, what was more dis- appointing still, went out with him to accompany him part of the way. She was going down stairs to Edward's room, that she might get these explanations off her mind without a moment's delay, and was taken entirely by surprise when she heard the door close, and two voices continuing outside.

"Has Mr. Edward gone out?" she asked, with a trembling she could scarcely control, of the butler, when he came up to put out the lights.

"I was to say, ma'am, as he'd be back in half an hour," said the man.

Catherine sent her maid to bed, and kept her particular lamp burning on her little table, waiting there in the dimness of the large deserted room, hearing every crackle and rustle of the night. It seemed to her far more than half an hour before she heard Edward's key in the door; but she was resolved not to be balked now. She had no idea, poor lady, that he thought her suspicious, inquisitive, and watchful, making domiciliary visits in order to find him out in something, which was very far from Catherine's disposition. She went down accordingly to lose no time, and met him in the hall. He was astonished to see her, as was natural enough; and she had an uneasy tremor upon her, which was natural too, but which looked like cold. He was full of apologies for having kept her up.

"If I had known you would have waited for me, Aunt Catherine——"

"You did not say good-night to me last night, Edward. I did not like that to happen two nights running. I will go into your room, not to hurry you up stairs."

"I can't think how that happened," he said, following her into the cosy room, with its red curtains and cheerful fire, and all the conveniences and prettiness she had accumulated for him there. "I had been thinking hard, and my mind was full of balance-sheets and figures. I entirely forgot I had not seen you."

She turned round upon him, taking his arm between her hands, and looking with a tender smile into his face.

"No, my dear boy, I know better than that. You had a reason—which shows me how well I have divined you, and how true you are, Edward. I have been told where—you went to last night."

This startled him greatly for the moment. He looked at her with an alarmed expression: but seeing no anger in her face, said quickly—

"That was all quite accidental, Aunt Catherine. You don't think I went there on purpose, do you?" without shrinking at all from her eyes.

"Yes, Edward, I thought you did. Perhaps I was wrong.

I thought there might have been some silly bargain—some promise made without thought : and that you felt a little treacherous—that is a harsh word—deceitful—that is worse—to me, and would not come back and kiss me when you might be supposed to be going against me. I forgave you entirely, Edward, for that good thought."

He was a little touched in spite of himself.

"You are very good, Aunt Catherine—far better to me than I deserve ; but, as a matter of fact, it was all purely accidental. I had been very busy, and felt feverish and sleepless. I went out to have a turn in the moonlight : chance took me that way. There was light in Mrs. John's window. They heard my steps, and looked out in great surprise, and asked me to come in. I could scarcely satisfy her," he said, with an embarrassed little laugh, "that you were not ill, and had not sent for her to nurse you. It was as good as a play," he went on, still laughing, followed in every word by her anxious eyes, "to see poor Mrs. John's struggle between politeness and sleep. She was very sleepy, poor little woman! but dreadfully polite. You may suppose I was surprised enough to find myself there."

"Yes," she said, still holding him, still reading his face with her anxious eyes, but feeling the ground cut from under her feet. She was a little breathless with anxiety and excitement. "I wonder—that you did not tell me of it—this morning."

"Dear Aunt Catherine," he said, "pardon me, but you have a little prejudice, you know, against these people. And it was so entirely accidental. You might have thought, had I told you, that it had been done on purpose."

"Did I ever doubt what you said to me, Edward ?"

"No," he said, taking her hands in his tenderly, as she thought ; and indeed the action was not without real tenderness, for his heart was touched. "No," he said, smiling. "but yet you would have had a little doubt—a little wonder whether it was really so."

"And it *was* really so?" she said, looking into his face, "really—really—no little shadow of a wish for—a little provocation, a little talk, a little fun if you like, Edward? Oh, no, I have no prejudice. I should know it was quite natural. And you mean that there was nothing at all, nothing of this—a mere accident, nothing more ?"

He kissed her cheek, and he laughed at her in a filial way.

"Didn't I tell you, Aunt Catherine? You believe me—oh, yes; but then you ask me if really—really I am saying what is true? Really—really as often as you like; it was accident, and nothing more."

This was how all the eloquent things which Catherine had prepared to say were never said. She went up to bed pleased and happy, yet not so pleased as if he had confessed her version of the story to be the true one. She did not doubt his word—oh no, no—but yet—the other version looked more true to nature. She could have understood it better that way.

CHAPTER XXXVI.

IN THE LABYRINTH.

AFTER these events there seemed a lull, in which nothing more seemed to happen. Though time is so short, and our modern pace of living, we flatter ourselves, so much more rapid than of old, how few after all are the periods in which things happen, and with what long stretches of vacant days between! Hester could hardly explain to herself how it was that Edward Vernon's sudden evening visit, so unexpected, so unprecedented, had made an entire revolution in her life. There had been no mutual confessions of love, no proposal, no acceptance such as are supposed to be necessary. There was nothing to confide to her mother, had it been possible to take any one into that strait union of two suddenly become one. The effect bewildered her entirely, and she could not tell how it had been produced; but yet it was so. They had been on the eve of this, she felt, for years, and the first time that they met, in a moment of complete freedom, their souls flowed together, flowed into one. Perhaps he had not meant it when he came. The dim parlour and the sleepy mother, trying hard to be polite, quite unconscious how unnecessary her presence was; the young man, with his eager eyes, scarcely keeping himself in—came before her like a curious picture a hundred times in a day: and then the sudden sweep of the torrent after it, the almost involuntary, impetuous, unalterable junction of these two hearts and lives. But the shock even of happiness when it comes so suddenly is great; and Hester was not sure even that she was happy. He seemed to have led her to the edge of some labyrinth, without freedom to leave it, or to advance into its mysteries. There

was a clue, indeed, but it was lying in loose coils at her feet,
and who could tell if it ever could be sufficiently straightened,
sufficiently tightened, to give any real guidance? There was
no habit of meeting in their lives, no way of seeing each other
even, without attracting suspicion. He sent her a letter next
morning, full of love, and of ecstatic realisation that she
was his, and that in all his difficulties he was sure of her
sympathy, but it was understood that he was not to make
such a breach of all his habits as to come to see her; and
Hester was too proud to break through hers, as she had done
that one morning in order to see him. So that everything
remained a secret between them, and save for the sudden
understanding into which they had leaped, the sort of be-
trothal which both took for granted, there was no difference in
their outward lives; which was a state of things infinitely
painful to the girl who lived her usual daily life with her
mother and her friends in a state of guilty abstraction, thinking of *him* all the time, and feeling herself a domestic traitor.
She felt that it was but the shell of her that remained,
following mechanically the usual occupations, talking from
the lips outward, absorbed in a long perpetual reverie of
new consciousness, new hopes and fears. That secret world
had need to have been bright to make up to her for the
sense of guilt and treachery with which she entered into it :
and it was not bright. The air was dark and tremulous
as in that sad valley, sad yet sweet, which, in Dante, lies
outside of hell. She never could tell at what moment some
dark unknown shape of calamity might appear through its
twilight coming towards them; for Edward had been driven
to her by anxiety and trouble, and the sense of a burden
which he could not bear alone. What was it? He did not
tell her in his letter. The other little notes he wrote were but
appeals to her sympathy—petitions to her to love him, to think
of him. Ah! Hester thought to herself, no fear of that—but
how? What was she to think? in what way was her imagination to follow him, groping dimly amid scenes she did not
understand? His secret was as a germ of fire in her heart—
which by times blazed up into hot flames, devouring her with
all the anguish of that thirst to know which is one of the tor-
tures of uneasy love. What was it that troubled him so, that
alarmed him so, that might ruin and overwhelm him—that
might make him fly, which was the most mysterious hint of
all? But to all these questions she got no satisfaction. For

the first few days she had a little furtive outlet to her anxiety
in questioning Roland, which she did with a vague sense of
treachery to Edward, as if she were endeavouring to surprise
his secrets by a back way, but very little perception of the
false impression which her interest in his communications
was making upon Roland, who himself became day by day
more ready to believe that marriage might become a possible
venture, and that the decision of it rested chiefly with himself.
He knew no other reason why she should question him than
interest in himself, and it was with a grateful zeal that he attempted to satisfy a curiosity which was so legitimate, yet so
unusual. He explained his trade with that pleasure which
the wisest of men feel in talking about themselves, and never
divined that her rapid mind passed everything through one
narrow test, *i.e.* whether it was possible that it could concern
Edward. She did not even remark the *attendrissement* with
which he received her questions, with eyes that said volumes.
These eyes overflowed with pleasure and sentiment as he made
his little disquisitions.

" After this," he said, with a laugh, " you will be armed
cap-à-pied against any doubtful agency, and able when you
like to speculate for yourself."

" And why should not I speculate," said Hester, " if I had
any money? It is like fighting, I suppose. It feels like
living, they say. But after all it is no true life—only figures,
as you tell me."

" Figures," said Roland, " mean so much ; in this elemental
way they mean money. And money means——"

" Figures over again," Hester said, with a certain weary
disdain. It was not possible that this alone could be the
tragic danger, the burden of the soul that Edward meant.
But Roland was thinking his own thoughts, and interpreted
her comments in a way of his own.

" It means most things in this world," he said ; " unfortunately, however high-minded we are, we can do nothing
without it. It means of course show and luxury, and gaiety,
and all the things you despise ; but at the same time——
It means," he said, after a little pause, " the house which two
people could make into paradise. It means ease of mind, so
that a man can rise every day without anxiety, knowing that
he has enough for every claim upon him. Ah! how can I
say all that it means—you would laugh, or be frightened.
It means the right to love, and the right to say it." Roland

was making use of all his well-worn artillery, but of something more besides which he had not quite understood the
existence of—something which lent a very eloquent tremor to
his voice and doubled the seduction of his eyes.

"Oh! I was not thinking of anything half so sentimental,"
said Hester. She never looked at him, to be affected by his
glances, or paid any attention to his voice. And yet there
had been a moment when Roland's departure made the world
itself shrink and look narrow : but she remembered nothing
about that now. "To tell the truth, all I was thinking of
was buying and selling," she said ; "for business means that,
doesn't it ? Of course I suppose, as we must have money to
live, you may say that money is the first thing in life, more
necessary than bread ; but I did not mean that."

Conversations which ended in this way were, however, very
little serviceable to Hester, for how could she tell which of
these mysteries of the craft had entangled Edward, or if any
of them could justify the seriousness of his excitement, the
tragic sense of a possible catastrophe, the wild expedient of
flight, which had been in his words! All this talk about the
vicissitudes of money was too petty to satisfy her mind as a
reason. And still less was that talk calculated to promote
Roland's purpose, who did not care very much what he was
saying so long as he could recommend himself to her favourable opinion. What he wanted was to show her that the
future had large possibilities of advancement. He wanted,
without committing himself or doing anything that could be
afterwards commented upon as "behaving badly," to leave
upon Hester's mind a delicate intimation that he meant to
come back, to speak more plainly, to say things more worthy
of her attention ; and that she might be able to make up her
mind in the meantime and not be taken by surprise. Roland
was not so romantic as to be unaware that the advantages
lay on his own side ; he had solid gifts to give, and a position
to offer, which could not be carelessly considered by any person
of sense. And he was well aware that there was no crowd
of candidates contending for Hester's hand. She had to him
the air of a girl neglected, altogether out of the way of
forming any satisfactory engagements, almost painfully
divested of that "chance" which Emma looked at with such
sensible if matter-of-fact eyes. Roland, to do him justice,
was all the more willing to show her a romantic devotion on
this account, but it kept him free from anxiety about his own

hopes. There had been Harry indeed—but she would not
have Harry. And Edward he was aware had paid her furtive
"attentions" at Ellen Merridew's parties; but what could
Edward do? He could not pay serious addresses to any one,
in his circumstances, far less to Hester : and he was not the
fellow to marry a girl without money and under the cold
shade of Catherine's disfavour. This last was one of the
things that made Roland himself hesitate—but he thought
it might be got over. And there could be no doubt that his
mind had made great strides towards making itself up during
this Christmas visit. But it was a short visit on the whole,
for he had not much time to spare for pleasure and his business had been summarily ended. Emma thought it was
owing to Hester's interference that she was left behind,
Reginald Merridew having not yet "spoken;" but there was
in reality a certain sympathy in Roland's mind with his
sister's honest desire to be settled, and there would be much
convenience in it could it be accomplished, he felt. He went
away accordingly, slightly depressed by Hester's indifferent
farewell, and remembering the look of over-clearness in
her eyes when he had gone away the first time with a sort
of fond regret. He was sure that day that she had shed a
few tears over his departure, of which there was no appearance now. But soon he recovered his spirits, asking himself
to look the situation in the face. Who else was there?
What rival could he have? There was nobody. She was
stranded in that old house as if it had been a desolate island.
And she could not be content to vegetate there for ever, a
girl of her spirit. There was a practical element in Roland's
character, notwithstanding his romantic eyes.

And Hester was so ungrateful that his departure was almost
a relief to her. She forgot altogether that she had cried the first
time when he went away, and she was glad to be set free from
the hope, which at the same time was a fear, of finding out something about Edward's troubles from his chance revelations.
Her mind turned now with unbroken eagerness to the sole
means of intercourse which she had with her lover, which
could be calculated upon with any freedom, which were
Ellen's parties—the *Thés Dansantes!* It seemed incredible
that her entire existence should be concentrated in a weekly
assembly so frivolous, so thoughtless, and nonsensical, and
that all those grave and troublous thoughts should seek interpretation in a dance. But so it was. The first of them

brought her only disappointment, and that of a kind that she felt almost maddening—for Edward did not appear. He gave her no warning, which was cruel, and when she found; after hours of waiting, that he was not expected, the shock of resentment and shame and dismay almost stunned her : but pride carried the day. She threw herself into the current with a sort of desperation, and held her place with the gayest : then entered, sombre and silent, upon another week of suspense. The second occasion was not so bad. He was there, and appropriated her as usual, and breathed hints into her ear which kept her in a whirl of excitement.

"How can I explain to you," he said, "here ? And even if I could explain to you, I don't want to do it, for it is all miserable trade, which you would not understand—which I don't wish you to understand."

"But I want to understand it, Edward. You don't think how cruel it is to me to tell me just so much, then leave me outside."

"Should I *not* have told you so much ? " he said, looking at her. "You are right. I believe you are right, Hester ; but my heart was running over, and to no one else could I say a word. I could not put a little bit of my burden upon any one but you. I know it was selfish, dear."

"Oh, Edward ; it is not that. I will bear your burden ; I am glad to help you ; I would bear it all for you if I could," she cried with her bright eyes widening, her cheeks glowing with enthusiasm. "Don't you *know* that I would bear it all if I could ? It is not that. But tell me, only tell me a little more."

He shook his head.

"Hester," he said, "that is not what a man wants in a woman ; not to go and explain it all to her with pen and ink, and tables and figures, to make her understand as he would have to do with a man. What he wants, dear, is very different—just to lean upon you—to know that you sympathise, and think of me, and feel for me, and believe in me, and that you will share whatever comes."

Hester said nothing, but her countenance grew very grave.

"Don't you think that a woman could do all that—and yet that it would be easier for her if she understood what it was, and why it was ? " she said, after a pause.

"Dear," said Edward, gazing at her with glowing eyes. He was in a hopeful mood, and he allowed himself to

indulge the love and pleasure he felt in her, having bound
her to him with a chain more fast than iron, "Darling!
was it ever known that a woman, a girl like you (if there ever
was a girl like my Hester), thought of what would be easiest?
And you who would bear it all, you said."

"So I should—gladly; but then I should understand."

"My only love! understanding is nothing, it matters
nothing; another fellow, any man, a clerk in the office, would
understand. I want your sympathy. I want—you."

"Oh, Edward!" she cried, "you have me and my sympathy— even if you were wrong you should have my sympathy. But is it just, is it good do you think, that you should
ask all that and tell me nothing? I am a woman, but I am
not a fool. I can understand most things. Try me—tell
me—I will set my mind to it. Sympathy that is ignorant
cannot be so good as sympathy that knows."

He made a little pause, and then he said, looking at her,
she felt, severely, with a scoff in his voice—

"And where is this explanation to take place? Will you
appoint to meet me somewhere with my balance-sheet and
my vouchers? Perhaps you will come to my room at the
bank? or appoint an accountant whom you can trust?"

"Edward!" she drew her hand out of his arm and then
put it back again after a moment's hesitation, "do you want
me to look a wretch even to myself? Why should you say
all this? and why—why be so unjust to me? You forget
that when one knows nothing one thinks all sorts of things,
and invents a hundred terrors. Tell me how it is in the
general, not details. You do not want silly sympathy."

"I want all your sympathy, silly or not. I want you.
Hester, if we are to escape notice we must dance like the rest;
we cannot stand and talk all night. And I am just in the
mood for it!" he cried.

Many people no doubt have waltzed with very little inclination for it, people who were both sad and sorry, disappointed, heartbroken; but few more reluctant than Hester,
who felt her position intolerable, and by whom the complacent
injustice of it, the calm assertion that such blind adherence
was all that was to be looked for from a woman, was more
irritating and offensive than can be described. Was it
possible that he thought so? that this was what she would
have to encounter in the life she should spend with him? Her
advice, her intelligent help, her understanding, all ignored

and nothing wanted but a kind of doggish fidelity, an un-reasoning belief? Hester felt it cruel to be made to dance even, to be spun through the crowd as if in the merest caprice of gaiety while at such a crisis of her fate.

But neither this nor their subsequent conversations made any difference; the evening passed for her as in a dream. Edward, who was not much of a dancer, and seldom cared to perform these rites with any partner but herself, danced repeatedly with others that night, while Hester stood by looking on with gathering bewilderment. She had a headache, she said. It was her mother's way of getting free of every embarrassment, and Hester was acquainted with the expedient, though she had not hitherto been tempted to use it. She sat by Mrs. Merridew, the mother of the house, who was a kind woman, and disposed to be good to her. "Just say the word, my dear, and as soon as our carriage comes I will take you home," this lady said; "for to sit with a racking headache and watch other young folks dancing is more than flesh and blood can bear." But alas! Mrs. Merridew's carriage was not ordered till two o'clock, and Hester had to bear her burden. And of course it was not thus that the evening ended. He came to seek her at Mrs. Merridew's side, and heard the account of her headache with a sympathetic countenance.

"This was our dance," he said; "but come into the hall instead, where it is cool, and let me get you some tea." He placed her there in the shelter of the evergreens, when all the hubbub of the next dance was in full progress. They were quiet, almost alone, and Edward was in a fever of high spirits and excitement. He had said little about love in that strange moment when he had taken possession of her. Now he made up for all deficiences. She endeavoured at first to bring him back to what she called the more important subject. "Can any subject be more important?" he said with tender reproach. And she was silenced, for what could she say? And the moments flew too fast and were too brief to be lost in any struggle. They parted with a few mysterious words whispered into her ear, which did much however to bring back the painful tension which had relaxed a little in his presence. "If I send to you, you will see me, Hester?" he whispered. "You won't think of proprieties? I might have to put your love to the test—to ask you——"

"What?" she cried with almost a spasm of alarm. He

gave her hand a warning clasp as he put her into the fly,
and then stooping to arrange the shawls around her, kissed it
secretly. And that was all. She drove home in the silence
and dark, feeling every word thrill her through, going over it
again and again. What was this test of love that might be
required of her? What did he expect her to do for him, in
ignorance, in blind trust? Hester had too high a spirit to
accept this *rôle* with ease. She was bewildered—dazzled by
the lavish outpouring of his love; but all that did not blind
her to the strange injustice of this treatment, the cruelty of
her helpless position. For what could she do? She could
not desert him in his hour of need; if he made this call upon
her which he spoke of so mysteriously, it would no doubt be
in his utmost need, when to desert him would be like a
traitor. And Hester knew that she could confront any
danger with him or for him—but what was it? A dilemma
so terrible had never presented itself to her imagination.
There was a cruelty in it, a depreciation of all the nobler
parts of her, as if only in ignorance could she be trusted.
Her mother's questions about the ball, and whether she had
danced much, and who her partners had been, were insupportable, as insupportable as the maunderings of Emma. In
short, if there was anything that could have made this
mystery and darkness in which her way seemed lost, more
hard to bear, it was the background of amusement and supposed light-heartedness against which it was set. "My head
ached," she said. "I scarcely danced at all," by way of freeing
herself ; but this opened only another kind of torture, for
poor Mrs. John, well used to the feminine indulgence of head-
aches, had a whole surgery of little remedies, and bathed her
child's forehead, and drew back her hair, and would have
administered sal-volatile, tea, eau-de-cologne—there was no
telling how many other cures—if she had been allowed.

"Let me fan you then, my love : sometimes that does me
a great deal of good. Just let me pour a little eau-de-cologne
first ; you don't know how cooling it is."

"Oh, mamma ! let me be still; let me be in the dark ; go
to bed, and don't mind me," cried Hester.

"My love ! how could I do that and leave my child to
suffer," said Mrs. John heroically—and it was heroic, for
the night was cold, the fire burning low, the hour three o'clock.
Hester, with her brain throbbing, all inaccessible to eau-de-
cologne, did not know how to free her mother from this

too generous unnecessary martyrdom. She began to talk
to break the spell.

"Emma is very happy," she said, "she danced with
Edward Vernon. She thinks perhaps it may make the other
speak, or that even Edward himself—" Hester broke off
with a quiver in her lip. "I am becoming malicious like the
rest," she said.

"That is not malicious, dear," said Mrs. John. "Emma
is very amusing, being so frank, but she is right enough when
you come to think of it ; for what can she do if she does not
marry? And I am sure, Edward Vernon, though Catherine
makes such a fuss about him, is nothing so very great. I
wonder what he meant coming here that one night, and so late."

"It was by accident," Hester said.

"It was a very odd accident," cried her mother, "no one
else ever did so."

"He had been sitting late over his work, and his head was
very full of—business."

Mrs. John looked in all the confidence of superior wisdom
into her daughter's face. A smile dawned upon her lips.

"Perhaps you think he was coming to confide his troubles
about his business, Hester, to you and me."

"And why not?" said Hester, raising herself from her
bed.

Mrs. John dropped her fan in her surprise, and sat down
abruptly upon the little chair by Hester's bedside, to her
daughter's great relief.

"Why not?" she said. "I think, though you are my
own, that you are the strangest girl I ever knew. Do you
think a man *ever* talks to women about these things? Oh,
perhaps to a woman like Catherine that is the same as a
man. But to anybody he cares for—never, oh, never, dear!
I suppose he has a respect for you and me ; think of any man
venturing to bring business into my drawing-room, though it
is only a poor little parlour now, not a drawing-room at all.
Oh, no, that could never—never be! In all my life I never
descended so low as that," Mrs. John said, with dignity. "I
used to be brought into contact with a great many business
people when your poor dear papa was living ; but they never
talked 'shop,' as they call it, before me."

"But my father himself?" said Hester, her eyes blazing
with the keenest interest ; "you knew all his affairs?"

Mrs. John held her delicate little hands clasped for a

moment, then flung them apart, as if throwing the suspicion
away.

"Never!" she cried; "he respected me too much. Your
poor papa was incautious about money, Hester, and that has
done a great deal of harm to both of us, for we are poor, and
we ought to have been rich; but he always had too much
respect for me to mix me up with business. You are very
inexperienced, my dear, or you would know that such a thing
could not be."

Hester followed her mother with her large eyes, with a
wondering wide gaze, which answered well enough for that of
believing surprise, almost awe, which Mrs. John was very
willing to recognise as a suitable expression. And there was
indeed a sort of awe in the girl's perception of her mother's
perfectly innocent, perfectly assured theory of what was right
in women. What wonder that a man should think so, when
women themselves thought so? This strange discovery composed and stilled her when at last she was left in the dark
and in peace.

Hester kept gazing through that wintry blackness, with
eyes still wide open, and her clear brows puckered with wonder
and alarm. Was it natural, then, a thing she could accept as
just, that it was enough for her to sympathise, to share the
consequences, to stand by the chief actor whatever happened,
but never to share in the initiative or have any moral concern
in the motive or the means of what was done? A sense of
helplessness began to take the place of indignation in her mind.
Was that what they called the natural lot of women? to suffer
perhaps, to share the blame, but have no share in the plan, to
sympathise, but not to know; to move on blindly according
to some rule of loyalty and obedience, which to any other
creature in the world would be folly and guilt? But her
mother knew nothing of such hard words. To her this was
not only the right state of affairs, but to suggest any better
rule was to fail in respect to the lady whose right it was to be
left ignorant. Hester tried to smile when she recalled this,
but could not, her heart being too sore, her whole being
shaken. *He* thought so too perhaps, everybody thought so,
and she alone, an involuntary rebel, would be compelled to
accept the yoke which, to other women, was a simple matter,
and their natural law. Why, then, was she made unlike
others, or why was it so?

Edward had been in great spirits that night. The next

time they met was in the afternoon late, when Hester was
returning from a visit to Mrs. Morgan. It was nearly dark,
and it startled her to see him standing waiting for her under
one of the trees past the gate of the Heronry. She went
slowly, somewhat reluctantly, to join him on the sign just
discernible in the dark which he made her. He caught her
hand quickly, as she came up, and drew it within his
arm.

"You have been so long with that old woman, and I have
wanted you so," he cried, leading her away along the deserted
country road, which struck off at right angles with the Common. "Couldn't you divine that I wanted you? Didn't you
know by instinct I was longing for consolation?"

"Oh, Edward! what is wrong? What has made so great
a change in you?" she cried.

He drew her arm closer and closer through his, and leaned
upon her as if his appeal for support was physical too.

"I told you it was too long to explain," he said; "it is all
the worry of business. Sometimes things seem going well, and
then I am top-gallant high, and vex you with my levity, as
the other night—you know you were vexed the other night:
and then things turn badly, and I am low, low down in the
depths, and want my love to comfort me. Oh, if you only
belonged to me, Hester, and we had a home somewhere where
I could go in to you and say ' Console me ! ' "

"But Edward, your business never used to be a fever and
an excitement like this."

"How do you know? I did not dare to come to you; and
you were a child then. Ah, but you are quite right, Hester;
it was different. But a man cannot vegetate for ever. I
endured it as long as I could. Now it is all on a turn of
the cards, and I may be able to face the world to-morrow,
and have my own way."

"On a turn of the cards! Edward, you cannot mean it is
play? You are not a—gambler?" Hester gave a little
convulsive cry, clutching him by the arm with both her
hands.

He laughed. "Not with cards, certainly," he said. "I
am a respectable banker, my darling, and very knowing in
my investments, with perhaps a taste for speculation—but
that nobody has brought home to me yet. It is a very
legitimate way of making a fortune, Hester. It is only when
you lose that it becomes a thing to blame."

"Do you mean speculation, Edward?"

"Something of that sort; a capital horse when it carries you over the ford—and everything that is bad when you lose."

"But do you mean—tell me—that it is simple speculation—that this is all that makes you anxious?" Hester had never heard that speculation was immoral, and her mind was relieved in spite of herself.

"Only—simple speculation! Good Lord! what would she have?" he cried, in a sort of unconscious aside, with a strange laugh; then added, with mock gravity, "that's all, my darling; not much, is it? You don't think it is worth making such a fuss about?"

"I did not say that," said Hester, gravely, "for I don't understand it, nor what may be involved; but it cannot touch the heart. I was afraid——"

"Of something much worse," he said, with the same strange laugh. "What were you afraid of?—tell me. You did not think I was robbing the bank, or killing Catherine?"

"Edward!"—she did not like these pleasantries—"why do you talk so wildly? Come in with me, and my mother will give you some tea."

"I want you, and not any tea. I should like to take you up in my arms, and carry you away—away—where nobody could know anything about us more. I should like to disappear with you, Hester, and let people suppose we were dead or lost, or whatever they pleased."

"I wonder," said Hester, "why you should have lived so long close to me, and never found out that you wanted me so much till now. Oh, don't laugh so! You have always been very cool, and quite master of yourself, till now."

"It was time enough, it appears, when you make so little response," he said; "but all that is very simple if you but knew. I had to keep well with so many. Now that it is all on a turn of the dice, and a moment may decide everything, I may venture to think of myself."

"Dice! What you say is all about gambling, Edward."

"So it is, my sweetest. It is a trick I have got. Chance is everything in business—luck, whatever that may be: so that gambling words are the only words that come natural. But don't leave the talking to me; you can talk better than

I can ; you are not a silent angel. Tell me something, Hester. Tell me what you thought that night. Tell me what this little heart is saying now."

Hester was not touched by that reference to her little heart, which was not a little heart, but a great one, bounding wildly in her breast with perplexity and pain, as well as love, but ready for any heroic effort.

"If I were to tell you perhaps you would not like it, Edward. It makes me happy that you should want me, and lean on me, and give me your burden to bear ; but I want so much more. Perhaps I am not so gentle as women ought to be. My mother would be content, but I am not. I want to know everything, to help you to think, to understand it all. And besides, Edward—— No, one thing is enough ; I will not say that."

"Yes, say everything ; it is all sweet from you."

"Then, Edward, come home and let my mother know. She will betray nobody. We ought not to meet in the dark like two—— to send little hidden notes. We are responsible to the people who love us. We ought to be honest—to mamma, to Catherine Vernon."

"We ought to go and hand in the banns, perhaps," he said, with sudden bitterness, "like two—honest shopkeepers, as you say. Catherine Vernon would give me away. And is this all you know of love, Hester ?—it is the woman's way, I suppose—congratulations, wedding presents, general triumph over everybody. How should you understand me when I speak of disappearing with my love, getting lost, dying even, if it were together—— ? "

There was a pause, for Hester was wounded, yet touched, both to the heart. She said, after a moment, almost under her breath, "I can understand that too." The faltering of her voice, the droop of her head, and his own need for her, more urgent than either, changed Edward's sarcastic mood. He drew her closer to him, and put down his face close to her ear.

"We must not fight," he said, "my only love. I am going away, and I can't quarrel with you, my only love ! And I am your only love. There has never been anybody between us. I will come back in two or three days ; but Hester, another time, if it should be for good, would you come ? —you would come ?—with me ? "

"Elope!" she said, breathless, her eyes large in the darkness, straining upon the face which was too near her own to be very clear.

He laughed. "If you like the word; it is an innocent word. Yes, elope then," he said.

"But why?—but why? It would wound them all—it would break their hearts; and for what reason?" Hester cried.

CHAPTER XXXVII.

ALARMS.

EDWARD was about a week away from home. He had often been away before, and his absence had caused no particular commotion : but now it affected a good many people. To Catherine, if it were possible, it might be said to have been a certain relief. He and she had got over that explanation when she had intended to say so many things to him, and had found the words taken out of her mouth. All things had gone on again in their usual way. But the suspicion which he had supposed to exist so long without any reason now had actually arisen in her mind. She showed it less than he had supposed her to show it when she had no such feeling. She was on her guard. She did not worry him any longer by her old affectionate way of going to the window to watch him when he went out ;. that had been simple love, admiration of his orderly, regular ways, pleasure in the sight of him : but somehow instinctively since she had begun to doubt she came to perceive the interpretation he had put upon it, and she did it no longer. But at night when all was still in the house and Edward down stairs at work in his room, or supposed to be at work, if any sound of the door closing echoed upwards, Catherine would steal behind the curtains and watch if it was he who was going out, and which way he took. She believed him, of course ; but yet there was always in her soul a wish to ask—was he really, really sure that he was true ? Doubts like these are beyond the power of any but the sternest self-command to crush, and Catherine was capable of that in his presence. She would not betray her anxiety to him : but when he was not there no such effort was necessary, and she betrayed it freely, to the silence, to the night, when there was nobody to see.

And her thoughts had travelled fast and far since that

evening. She had no longer any doubt that he loved somebody, and she had made up her mind that it was Hester who
was the object of his love. This had caused her perhaps the
greatest mental conflict she had ever known in her life—for
her life had this good thing in it, that it had been wonderfully
free from struggle. She had been the arbiter of all things in
her little world, and nobody had made any actual stand
against her will. Many pretences had surrounded her, feigned
assents and furtive oppositions, but nobody had stood out
against her. It was a great wonder to her that he or any
one should do so now (though he did not : he had opposed her in
nothing, nor ever said a word from which it could be inferred
that he rejected or questioned Catherine's sway), but with all
her natural strength of mind she set herself to reconsider
the question. If she disliked Hester before, if for all these
years the bright-eyed, all-observant girl, mutely defiant of
her, had been a sort of Mordecai to Catherine, it is not to be
supposed that she could easily receive her into favour now.
Her parentage, her looks, her mind, her daring setting up of
her own personality as a child, as if she were something important, had all exasperated Catherine. Even the consciousness of her own prejudice, of the folly of remembering against
a girl the follies of her childhood, helped to aggravate this
sentiment ; nor was it likely that the fact that this girl was
Edward's chosen love should make her heart softer. She said
to herself that she could not endure Hester ; but yet she prepared herself for the inevitable from the first day. Perhaps
she thought it well to propitiate fate by going to the very
furthest length at once, and forecasting all that the most
evil fortune could bring her.

It cost her a sharp and painful struggle. No one knew
what was going on in her mind in those wintry days of
the early year : her preoccupation was attributed to other
things : afterwards, when events seemed to account for it,
her wonderful prevision was admired and wondered at.
But in reality the previsions in Catherine's mind were all
of one kind. She saw a series of events happen in succession, as to which she was as confident as if they were past
already ; and in her imagination she did the only thing
that nobody expected of her, the thing which fate did not
demand of her—she made up her mind that she would make
no stand against this hateful thing. What was the use of it ?
If the young but held out, even the most unwise and the most

cruel, they must win in the end. It would not be for her dignity, she said to herself, to stand out. She would make no opposition to Edward's choice. The separation that must ensue she would bear as she could—with dignity at least if nothing else. The elevation of her enemy and her enemy's house she must submit to. She would withdraw, she would have no hand in it; but at least she would not oppose. This, by dint of a hard fight, Catherine obtained of herself. She would say nothing, forestall nothing, but at the same time oppose nothing. All the long hours which a lonely woman must spend by herself she appropriated to this. She must lose Edward; had she not lost him now? He had been her sole weakness, her one delusion; and it was not, she said to herself, a delusion—the boy had loved her and been true to her. He had made her happy like a mother with a true son. But when that vagrant sentiment comes in which is called love (the fools! as if the appropriation of the name to one kind of affection, and that the most selfish of all, was not a scorn to love, the real, the all-enduring!) what was previous virtue, what was truth, and gratitude, and everything else in life, in comparison? Of course they must all give place to the fascination of a pair of shining eyes. Father and mother, and home and duty, what were they in comparison? Everybody was aware of that, and the old people struggled often enough, as was well known. Sometimes they appealed to heaven and earth, sometimes were hysterical and made vows and uttered curses. But in the long run the battle was to the young ones. They had time and passion, and universal human sympathy, on their side, whereas the old people had none of all these, neither time to wait, nor passion to inspire, nor sympathy anywhere in heaven or earth. Catherine said to herself proudly that she would not expose herself to the pity which attends the vanquished. She would retire from the fray. She would clothe herself in double armour of stoicism, and teach herself to see the humour in this as in so many things. Was not seeing the humour of it the last thing that remained to the noble soul amid the wonder of life?

Her sense, however, of this great downfall which was approaching, and in which she meant to enact so proud and magnanimous a part, was so strong and bitter that Edward's absence was a relief to her. She expected every day that he would present himself before her, and burst forth into some agitated statement—a statement which she would not help

out with a word, but which she would receive, not as he would
expect her to receive it, with opposition and wrath, but with
the calm of one who knew all about it, and had made up her
mind to it long ago. But when he was absent she felt that
here was a respite. She was freed from the eager desire she
had, against her will, to know what he was doing, where he
went, who he was with, which tormented her, but which she
could not subdue. All this ferment of feeling was stilled
when he was away. She did not ask why he should go away
so often, what the business was that called him to London.
For the first time in her life she was overmastered by a conflict of individual feeling ; and she was glad when there came
a lull in it, and when the evil day was postponed. She went
on seeing her friends, visiting and being visited, keeping a
fair face to the world all the time. But it began to be
whispered in Redborough that Catherine Vernon was beginning
to fail, that there were signs in her of breaking up, that she
began to show her age. People began to ask each other about
her. "Have you seen Catherine Vernon lately? How did
you think she was looking?" and to shake their heads. Some
said she had been so strong a woman always, and had taken
so much out of herself, that probably the break-up would be
speedy if it was true that she was beginning to break up ;
while others held more hopefully that with her wonderful
constitution she might yet rally, and see twenty years of
comfort yet. The fact was that she was not ill at all. It
seemed to herself that she was more keenly alive, more highly
strung to every use of existence than ever. She saw better,
heard more quickly, having every sense on the alert. Nothing
had so quickened her and stimulated her powers for years.
She was eager for every new day which might carry some
new crisis in it. She did not even feel the deadly chill of
Edward's desertion for the intense occupation which the whole
matter brought her. And then, though she said to herself
it was certain, yet it was not so certain after all. It might
turn out that she was mistaken yet. There was still an
outlet for a secret hope. Sometimes indeed a flattering
unction was laid to her heart, a feeling that if it is only the
unforeseen that happens, the so carefully thought out, so elabo-
rately calculated upon might not happen. But this Catherine
only permitted herself by rare moments. For the most part
she felt very sure of the facts, and almost solemnly cognisant
of what was to come.

In this way the spring went on. It had appeared to
Edward himself as certain that some great *coup* must have
settled his fate long before. It was his inexperience, perhaps,
and the excitement of his determination to act for himself,
which had made everything appear so imminent; but after
all it did not turn out so. The course of events went on in
that leisurely current which is far more deadly in its sweep
than any sudden cataract. He did not lose or gain anything
in a moment, his ventures either did not turn out so vast as
he imagined, or they were partial failures, partial successes.
Step by step he went on, sacrificing, jeopardising, gradually,
slowly, without being himself aware of what he was doing,
the funds he had under his control. He had been ready in
the first passion of his desire for wealth to risk everything and
finish the whole matter at one swoop; but that passed over,
and he was not really aware how one by one his counters
were being swept out of his hands. It went on through all
the awakening time of the year, as it might have gone on for
half a life time, and he was impatient of the delay. Besides,
this new accompaniment, this love which he would not have
suffered himself to indulge had he not believed everything on
the eve of a crisis, became a great addition to his difficulties
when the crisis did not come. The habit of resorting to
Hester was one which grew upon him. But the opportunities
of indulging in it were few, for he was as anxious not to
betray himself nor to let Catherine suspect what was going
on, as at the beginning, when he believed that all would be
over in a week or two. And Hester herself was not a girl
with whom it was easy to carry on a clandestine intercourse.
The situation chafed her beyond endurance. She had almost
ceased now to think of the mystery in which he hid his
proceedings, or to rebel against the interest and sympathy
which he demanded from her blindly, out of the keen humiliation and distress which it cost her to feel that she was deceiving
her friends and the world, conspiring with him to deceive
Catherine. This consciousness made Hester disagreeable to
live with, an angry, resentful, impatient woman, absorbed
in her own affairs, little accessible to the world. Her
mother could not understand what had come to her,
and still less could the old Morgans, who loved and had
understood her so completely, understand. She avoided them
now, she cared for nobody. Week by week with a joy-
less regularity she went to Ellen Merridew's dances, where

half the evening at least was spent with Edward in a curious
duel of mingled love and dislike — yes, sometimes hatred
almost. It seemed to her that her distaste for everything that
was going on was more than her love could balance, that she
so hated the expedients he drove her to, that he himself took
another aspect in her eyes. Sometimes she felt that she
must make the crisis which he had so often anticipated, and
instead of consenting to fly with him must fly by herself,
and cut the tie between them with a sharp stroke. It was
all pain, trouble, misery — and what was worse, falsehood,
wherever she turned. As the year slid round into sunshine,
and the days grew longer, everything became intolerable to
Hester. His absence was no relief to her. She had his secret
to keep whether he was there or away, or rather her secret : for
nothing she felt could be so dreadful to her as the secresy
in which her own life was wrapped, and which he was
terrified she should betray.

And though it was now nearly six months after Christmas
Emma Ashton still lived with the old Morgans, and pursued
her adventures with her bow and spear in the dances and
entertainments of the neighbourhood. Reginald Merridew
so far from "speaking" had been sent off by his father to
America, professedly on business, but, as was well known in
the family, to put a stop to the nonsense which at his age was
so utterly out of the question ; and though other expectations
had stirred her from time to time, nothing had given certainty
to her hopes of being settled. She was going home at last,
to Roland, in the beginning of June, and the old people were
looking forward to their deliverance with no small impatience.
Emma never failed at the *Thés Dansantes*. The old fly with
the white horse rumbled along in the dusk of the early
summer nights and mornings, carrying these two young
women to and fro almost as regularly as the Thursday came—
Hester reluctant, angry, and pale, obeying a necessity which
she resented to the very depths of her being ; Emma placid,
always with a certain sense of pleasure animating her
business-like arrangements. Catherine, who did not sleep
very well on these nights, got to recognise the sound, and
would sometimes look out from her window and wonder
bitterly whether *that girl* too was glancing out, perhaps with
triumph in her eyes as she passed the shut-up house,
thinking of the day when it would be her own. It gave her
a little pleasure on the first of June when she heard the slow

vehiclé creeping by to think that Edward had been called away
that afternoon, and that if Hester had expected to meet him
she would be disappointed. That was a little consolation to
her. She heard it creeping back again about one in the
morning earlier than usual, with a satisfied smile. There had
been no billing and cooing that evening, no advance made
towards the final triumph. She thought there was a sound of
disappointment even in the rumble of the fly; and so indeed
there might have been, for Emma was sobbing, and discoursing
among her tears upon the sadness of her prospects. It was the
last *Thé Dansante* to which Emma could hope to go. "And
here I'm going just as I came," Emma said, "though I had
such a good opening, and everybody has been so kind to me.
I can't say here that it has been for want of having my
chance. I have been introduced to the best people, and grandmamma has given me two new dresses, and you have never
grudged me the best partners, I will say that for you,
Hester; and yet it has come to nothing! I am sure I sha'n't
be able to answer Roland a word if he says after this that
balls are an unnecessary expense—for it is not much I have
made by them. To think that not one single gentleman
in all Redborough——! Oh, Hester, either Elinor and Bee
tell awful stories of what happened to them, or things have
changed dreadfully, quite dreadfully, since their day!"
    Hester could find no words in which to console this victim
of the times. She listened indeed somewhat sternly, refusing
compassion. "To be sure, there was poor Reginald, it was
not his fault," Emma sobbed. "If I should live to be a hundred I never should believe it was his fault. But, after all,
he was very young, and he could have had no money to speak
of, and what should I have done with him? So perhaps that
was for the best. But then there was Dr. Morris, whom I
could have got on with; that was his mother's doing :—ladies
are always jealous, don't you think?—and I should not have
minded that Captain Sedgely, that volunteer captain. But it
is of no use talking, for this is my last Thursday. Oh, you
don't mind; you have a good home, and a mother, and everything you can desire. There is no hurry about you."
    Hester made no reply. It seemed to her that she would
be willing to change lives even with Emma, to fall to her
petty level, and estimate the chances of being settled, and
count the men whom she could have managed to get on with,
rather than carry on such an existence as hers. It was no

glance of triumph, but one of humiliation, that she hád cast,
as they past, upon the shuttered windows and close-drawn
white draperies at the Grange. In her imagination she stole
into the very bedchamber where Catherine had smiled to
think of her disappointment, and delivered her soul of her
secret. "I am not ashamed that we love each other : but I
am ashamed that we have concealed it," she imagined herself
saying. She was very unhappy ; there seemed no consolation
for her anywhere. Edward had warned her in a hurried note
that he was called to town. "I think it is coming at last,"
he said. "I think we have made the grand *coup* at last."
He had said it so often that she had no faith in him ; and
how long was it to go on like this—how long?

Meanwhile the house of the young Merridews was still
ringing with mirth and music. There was no restraint, or
reserve, or prudence or care-taking, from garret to basement.
Algernon, the young husband who was now a father as well,
had perhaps taken a little more champagne than usual in
honour of his wife's first re-appearance after that arrival.
She was so brave, so "plucky," they all said, so unconven-
tional, that she had insisted on the *Thés Dansantes* going on
all the same, though she was unable to preside over them,
and was still up, a little pale but radiant with smiles, at the
last supper-table when every one was gone. Harry had been
looking very grave all the evening. He had even attempted
a little lecture over that final family supper. "If I werè you,
Algy and Nell," he said, "I'd draw in a little now. You've
got your baby to think of—save up something for that little
beggar, don't spend it all on a pack of fools that eat you up."

"Oh, you old Truepenny," Ellen said, without knowing
what she meant, "you are always preaching. Hold your
tongue, Algy, you have had too much wine ; you ought to
go to bed. If I can't stand up for myself it's strange to me.
Who are you calling a pack of fools, Harry? It's the only
thing I call society in Redborough. All the other houses are
as stiff as Spaniards. There is nobody but me to put a little
life into them. They were all dead-alive before. If there's
a little going on now I think it's all owing to me."

"She is a wonderful little person is Nell," cried her husband, putting a half-tipsy arm round her. "She has pluck
for anything. To think she should carry on just the same,
to let the rest have their pleasure when she was up stairs.
I am proud of her, that is what I am. I am proud——"

"Oh, go to bed, Algy! If you ever do this again I will divorce you. I won't put up with you. Harry, shut up," said the young mistress of the house, who was fond of slang. "I can look after my own affairs."

"And as for the money," said Algy, with a jovial laugh, "I don't care a —— for the money. Ned's put me up to a good thing or two. Ned's not very much on the outside, but he's a famous good fellow. He's put me up," he said, with a nod and broad smile of good humour, "to two—three capital things."

"Ned!" cried Harry, almost with a roar of terror and annoyance, like the cry of a lion. "Do you mean to say you've put yourself in Ned's hands?"

Upon which Ellen jumped up, red with anger, and pushed her husband away. "Oh, go to bed, you stupid!" she cried.

Harry had lost all his colour; his fair hair and large light moustache looked like shadows upon his whiteness. "For God's sake, Ellen!" he said; "did you know of this?"

"Know of what?—it's nothing," she cried. "Yes, of course I know about it. I pushed him into it—he knows I did. What have you got to do with where we place our money? You may be sure we sha'n't want you to pay anything for us," she said.

Harry had never resented her little impertinences; he had always been submissive to her. He shook his head now more in sorrow than in anger. "Let's hope you won't want anybody to pay for you," he said, and kissed his sister and went away.

Harry had never been in so solemn a mood before. The foolish young couple were a little awed by it, but at last Ellen found an explanation. "It's ever since he was godfather to baby. He thinks he will have to leave all his money to him," she said; and the incident ended in one of Algy's usual bursts of laughter over his wife's *bons mots*.

Harry, however, took the matter a great deal more seriously; he got little or no sleep that night. In the morning he examined the letters with an alarmed interest. Edward was to be back that evening, it was expected, and there was a mass of his letters on his desk with which his cousin did not venture to interfere. Edward had a confidential clerk, who guarded them closely. "Mr. Edward did not think there would be anything urgent, anything to trouble you about," he said, following Harry into the room with unneces-

sary anxiety. "I can find that out for myself," Harry said,
sharply, turning upon this furtive personage. But he did
not meddle with any of the heap, though it was his right to
do so. They frightened him, as though there had been
infernal machines inside, as indeed he felt sure enough there
were—not of the kind which tear the flesh and fibre, but the
mind and soul. When he went back to his room he received
a visit very unexpectedly from the old clerk, Mr. Rule, with
whom Hester had held so long a conversation on the night of
the Christmas party. It was his habit to come now and then,
to patronise everybody, from the youngest clerks to the young
principals, shaking his white head and describing how things
used to be "in John Vernon's time." Usually nobody could
be more genial and approving than old Rule. He liked to
tell his story of the great crisis, and to assure them that,
thanks to Miss Catherine, such dangers were no longer possible. "A woman in the business just once in a way, in five
or six generations," he thought an admirable institution.
"She looks after all the little things that you young gentlemen don't think worth your while," he said. But to-day
Mr. Rule was not in this easy way of thinking. He wanted to
know how long Edward had been gone, and where he was,
and when he was expected back? He told Harry that things
were being said that he could not bear to hear. "What is
he doing away so often? Is it pleasure? is it horse-racing,
or that sort of thing? Forgive me, Mr. Harry, but I'm so
anxious I don't know what I'm saying. You have always
taken it easy, I know, and left the chief management to
Mr. Edward. But you must act, sir, you must act," the old
clerk said.

Harry's face had a sort of tragic helplessness in it. "He's
coming back to-night—one day can't matter so much. Oh,
no, it's not horse-racing, it's business. Edward isn't the sort
of fellow——"

"One day may make all the difference," cried the old man,
but the more fussy and restless he was, the more profound
became Harry's passive solemnity. When he had got rid of
the old clerk he sat for a time doing nothing, leaning his head
in his hands : and at last he jumped up and got his hat, and
declared that he was going out for an hour. "Several gentlemen have been here asking for Mr. Edward," he was told as
he passed through the outer office. "Mr. Merridew, sir, the
old gentleman : Mr. Pounceby : and Mr. Fish has just been to

know for certain when he will be back." Harry answered impatiently what they all knew, that his cousin would be at the bank to-morrow morning, and that he himself would return within the hour. There were some anxious looks cast after him as he went away, the elder clerks making their comments. "If Mr. Edward's headpiece, sir, could be put on Mr. Harry's shoulders," one of them said. They had no fear that *he* would be absent when there was any need for him, but then, when he was present, what could he do?

Harry went on with long strides past the Grange to the Heronry; it was a curious place to go for counsel. He passed Catherine sitting at her window, she who once had been appealed to in a crisis and had saved the bank. He did not suppose that things were so urgent now, but had they been so he would not have gone to Catherine. He thought it would break her heart. She had never been very kind to him, beyond the mere fact of having selected him from among his kindred for advancement; but Harry had a tender regard for Catherine, a sort of stolid immovable force of gratitude. His heart melted as he saw her seated in the tranquillity of the summer morning in the window, looking out upon everything with, he thought, a peaceful interest, the contemplative pleasure of age. It was not so, but he thought so—and it seemed to him that if he could but preserve her from annoyance and disturbance, from all invasion of rumour or possibility of doubt as to the stability of Vernon's, that there was nothing he would not endure. He made himself as small as he could, and got under the shadow of the trees that she might not observe him as he passed, and wonder what brought him that way, and possibly divine the anxiety that was in him. He might have spared himself the trouble. Catherine saw him very well, and the feeling that sprang up in her mind was bitter derision, mixed with a kind of unkindly pleasure. "If you think that *you* will get a look from her, when she has *him* at her feet?" Catherine said to herself, and though the idea that Hester had *him* at her feet was bitter to her, there was a pleasure in the contempt with which she felt Harry's chances to be hopeless indeed. She was very ungrateful for his kindness, thinking of other things, quite unsuspicious of his real object. She smiled contemptuously to see him pass in full midday when he ought to have been at his work, but laughed, with a little aside, thinking, poor Harry, he would never set the Thames on fire, it did not matter very much after all whether he was there or not. The master head was absent, too often absent, but Edward had everything so well in hand that it mattered the less. " When he is settled he will not go away so often," she said to herself. What a change it would have made in all her thoughts had she known the gloomy doubts and terrors in Harry's mind, his alarmed sense that he must step into a breach which he knew not how to fill, his bewildered questionings with himself. If Edward did not turn up that night there would be nothing else for it, and what was he to do ? He understood the common course of business, and how to judge in certain easy cases, but what to do in an emergency he did not know. He went on to the Heronry at a great rate, making more noise than any one else would with the gate, and catching full in his face the gaze of those watchful observers who belonged to the place, Mr. Mildmay Vernon in the summer-house with his newspaper, and the Miss Vernon-Ridgways at their open window. He thought they all rose at him like so many serpent heads erecting themselves with a dart and hiss. Harry was so little fanciful that only an excited imagination could have brought him to this.

Mrs. John was in the verandah, gardening—arranging the pots in which her pelargoniums were beginning to bloom. She would have had him stay and help her, asking many questions about Ellen and her baby which Harry was unable to answer.

" Might I speak to Hester?" he said. " I have no time to stay ; I would like to see her for a moment."

" What is it?" cried Mrs. John. Harry's embarrassment, she thought, could only mean one thing—a sudden impulse to renew the suit which Hester had been so foolish as to reject. She looked at him kindly and shook her head. " She is in the parlour; but I wouldn't if I were you," she said, her eyes moist with sympathy. It was hard upon poor Harry to be compelled thus to take upon himself the credit of a second humiliation.

" I should like to see her, please," he answered, looking steadfastly into Mrs. John's kind, humid eyes, as she shook her head in warning.

" Well, my dear boy; she is in the parlour. I wish—I wish—— But, alas! there is no change in her, and I wouldn't if I were you."

"Never mind, a man can but have his chance," said magnanimous Harry. He knew that few men would have done as much, and the sense of the sacrifice he was making made his heart swell. His pride was to go too; he was to be supposed to be bringing upon himself a second rejection; but "Never mind, it is all in the day's work," he said to himself, as he went through the dim passages and knocked at the parlour door.

Hester was sitting alone over a little writing-desk on the table. She was writing hurriedly, and he could see her nervous movement to gather together some sheets of paper, and shut them up in her little desk, when she found herself interrupted. She gave a great start when she perceived who it was, and sprang up, saying, "Harry!" breathlessly, as if she expected something to follow. But at first Harry was scarcely master of himself to speak. The girl he loved, the one woman who had moved his dull, good, tenacious heart—she whom, he thought, he should be faithful to all his life, and never care for another; but he knew that her start, her breathless look, the colour that flooded her face, coming and going, were not for him, but for some one else, and that his question would plunge her into trouble too; that he would be to her henceforth as an emissary of evil, perhaps an enemy. All this ran through his mind as he stood looking at her, and kept him silent. And when he had gathered himself together his mission suddenly appeared to him so extraordinary, so presumptuous, that he did not know how to explain it.

"You must be surprised to see me," he said, hesitating. "I don't know what you will think. You will understand I don't mean any impertinence, Hester—or prying, or that sort of thing."

"I am sure you will mean to be kind, Harry; but tell me quick—what is it?" she cried.

He sat down opposite, looking at her across the table. "It is only from myself—nobody's idea but mine; so you need not mind. It is just this, Hester, in confidence. Do you know where Edward is? It sounds impertinent, I know, but I don't mean it. He's wanted so badly at the bank. If you could give me an address where I could telegraph to him? Don't be vexed; it is only that I am so stupid about business. I can do nothing out of my own head."

"Is anything going wrong?" she cried, her lips quivering, her whole frame vibrating, she thought, with the beating, which was almost visible, of her heart.

"Well, things are not very right, Hester. I don't know how wrong they are. I've been kept out of it. Oh, I suppose that was quite natural, for I am not much good. But if I could but telegraph to him at once, and make sure of getting him back——"

"I think, Harry—I have heard—oh, I can't tell you how! he is coming back to-night."

"Are you quite sure? I know he's expected, but then—— So many things might happen. But if he knew how serious it was all looking——"

Her look as she sat gazing at him was so terrible that he never forgot it. He did not understand it then, nor did he ever after fully understand it. The colour had gone entirely out of her face; her eyes stared at him as out of two deep, wide caves. It was a look of wonder, of dismay, of guilt. "Is he wanted—so much?" she said. Her voice was no more than a whisper, and she gave a furtive glance at the door behind her as if she were afraid some one might hear.

"Oh, wanted—yes! but not enough to make you look like that. Hester, if I had thought you'd have felt it so! Good Lord, what can I do? I thought you might have told me his address. Don't mind, dear," cried the tender-hearted young man. "I've no right to call you dear, but I can't help it. If it's come to this, I'd do anything for him, Hester, for your sake."

"Oh, never mind me, Harry—it is—nothing. I have got no address: but I know—he's coming to-night."

"Then that's all right," Harry said. "I wanted to make sure of that. I don't suppose there is anything to be frightened about so long as he is on the spot, you know—he that is the head-piece of the establishment. He is such a clear-headed fellow, he sees everything in a moment, and he has got everything on his shoulders. It's not fair, I know. I must try and shake myself up a little and take my share, and not feel so helpless the moment Ned's away—that's all," he said, getting up again restlessly. "I have only given you a fright and made you unhappy; but there's no reason for it, I assure you, Hester, so long as Ned is to be here."

What he said did not comfort her at all, he could see. Her face did not relax nor her eyes lose their look of horror.

He went away quite humbly, not saying a word to Mrs. John, who on her part gave him a silent, too significant, pathetic grasp of her hand. Harry was half tempted to laugh, but a great deal more to weep, as he went back again to Redborough. He reflected that it was hard upon a fellow to have to allow it to be supposed that he had offered himself to a girl a second time when he was doing nothing of the kind. But then he thought of Hester's horrified look with a wonder and pain unspeakable, not having the remotest idea what such a look might mean. Anyhow, he concluded, Edward was coming home. That was the one essential circumstance after all.

CHAPTER XXXVIII.

THE CRISIS.

HESTER sat still after Harry had left her as if she had been frozen to stone. But stone was no fit emblem of a frame which was tingling in every nerve, or of a heart which was on fire with horror and anguish and black bewilderment. The look which Harry could not understand, which stopped him in what he was saying, and which even now he could not forget—was still upon her face. She was contemplating something terrible enough to bring a soul to pause, a strange and awful solution of her mystery; and the first glance at it had stunned her. When she had assured him that Edward was coming back that night, a hurried note which she had received that morning seemed to unfold itself in the air before her, where she could read it in letters as of fire. It was written on a scrap of paper blurred as if folded while the ink was still wet :—

"The moment has come that I have so long foreseen. I am coming home to-morrow for a few hours. Meet me at dusk under the holly at the Grange gate. The most dangerous place is the safest; it must be for ever or no more at all. Be ready, be calm, we shall be together, my only love.—E.V."

This was how she knew that he was coming back. God help her! She looked in Harry's face, with an instantaneous realisation of the horror of it, of the falsehood that was implied, of her own sudden complicity in some monstrous wrong. "I know he is coming home to-night." What was it that turned Medusa into that mask of horror and gave her head its fatal force? Was it the appalling vision of some unsuspected abyss of falsehood and treachery suddenly opening at her feet, over

which she stood arrested, turned into an image of death, blinding and slaying every spectator who could look and see? Hester
did not know anything about classic story, but she remembered
vaguely about a face with snaky locks that turned men to
stone. She told Harry the truth, yet it was a cruel lie. She
herself, though she knew nothing and was tortured with terror
and questionings, seemed to become at once an active agent
in the dark mystery, a liar, a traitor, a false friend. Harry
looked at her with concern and wonder, seeing no doubt that
she was pale, that she looked ill, perhaps that she was unhappy, but never divining that she was helping in a fatal
deceit against her will, contrary to her every desire. He
did not doubt for a moment what she said or put any meaning
to it that was not simply in the words. He never dreamt
that Edward's return was not real, or that it did not at once
satisfy every question and set things if not right, yet in the
way of being right. He drew a long breath of relief. That
was all he wanted to know. Edward once back again at the
head of affairs, everything would resume its usual course.
To hear him say "Then that's all right!" and never to say
a word, to feel herself gazing in his eyes—was it with the
intention of blinding those eyes and preventing them from
divining the truth? or was it in mere horror of herself as the
instrument of a lie, of him, him whom she would fain have
thought perfect, as falsehood incarnate? There was a moment
when Hester knew nothing more, when though she was on
fire and her thoughts like flame, lighting up a wild world of
dismay about her, she yet felt as if turned into stone.

The note itself when she received it, in the quiet freshness
of the morning, all ordinary and calm, her mother scarcely
awake as yet, the little household affairs just beginning, those
daily processes of cleaning and providing without which no
existence can be—had been agitation enough. It had come
to her like a sudden sharp stroke, cutting her loose from
everything, like the cutting of a rope which holds a boat, or
the stroke that severs a branch. In a moment she was
separated from all that soft established order, from the life
that had clasped her all round as if it would hold her fast for
ever. Her eyes had scarcely run over those hurried lines
before she felt a wild sensation of freedom, the wind in her
face, the gurgle of the water, the sense of flight. She put out
her hands to screen herself, not to be carried off by the mere
breeze, the strong-blowing gale of revolution. A thrill of

strange delight,. yet of fright and alarm, ran through her veins—the flood of her sensations overwhelmed her. Its suddenness, its nearness, its certainty, brought an intoxication of feeling. All this monotony to be over ; a new world of adventure, of novelty, of love, and daring and movement, and all to begin to-night. These thoughts mounted to her head in waves. And as the minutes hurried along and the world grew more and more awake, and Mrs. John came down stairs to breakfast, the fire in Hester's veins grew hotter and hotter. To-night, in the darkness—for ever or no more at all. It seemed incredible that she could contain it all, and keep her secret and make no sign. All this time no question of it as of a matter on which she must make up her mind, and in which there was choice, had come into her thoughts. She was not usually passive, but for the moment she received these words as simple directions which there could be no doubt of her carrying out. His passion and certainty took possession of her : everything seemed distinct and necessary—the meeting in the dusk, the hurried journey, the flight through the darkness For great excitement stops as much as it accelerates the action of the mind. Her thoughts flew out upon the wind, into the unknown, but they did not pause to discuss the first steps. Had he directed her to do all this at once, in the morning instead of in the dusk, she would have obeyed his instructions instinctively like a child, without stopping to inquire why.

But this mood was changed by the simplest of domestic arguments. Mrs. John, fresh and smiling in her black gown and her white cap, came down to breakfast. Not a suspicion of anything out of the ordinary routine was in Mrs. John's mind. It was a lovely morning ; the sunshine pleased her as it did the flowers who hold up their heads to it and open out and feel themselves alive. Her chair was on the sunny side of the table, as it always was. She liked to sit in it and be warmed by it. She began to talk of all the little household things as she took her tea ; of how the strawberries would soon be cheap enough for jam. That was the one thing that remained in Hester's mind years after. In a moment, while her thoughts were full of a final and sudden flight, that little speech about the jam and the strawberries brought her to herself. She felt herself to come back with a sudden harsh jarring and stumbling to solid ground. "The strawberries!" she said, looking at her

mother with wild eyes of dismay as if there had been something tragic in them. "In about a fortnight, my dear, they
will be quite cheap enough," Mrs. John said, with a contented
nod of her head. In a fortnight! a fortnight!—a century
would not mean so much. A fortnight hence what would
the mother be thinking, where would the daughter be? Then
there came to Hester another revelation as sudden, as all-
potent as the first—that it was Impossible—that she must be
mad or dreaming. What! fly, go away, disappear, whatever
might be the word? She suddenly laughed out, her mother
could not tell why, dropping a china cup, over which Mrs. John
made many lamentations. It broke a set, it was old Worcester
worth a great deal of money. It had been her grandmother's.
"Oh, my dear, I wish you would not be so careless!" But
of anything else that was broken, or of the mystery of that
sudden laugh which corresponded with no expression of mirth
on Hester's face, Mrs. John knew nothing. Impossible!
Why there was not a word to be said, not a moment's hesitation. It could not be—how could it be? Edward, a young
man full of engagements, caught by a hundred bonds of duty,
of work, of affection—why, if nothing else, of business—to
whom it was difficult to be absent for a week, who had sometimes to run up and down to town in twenty-four hours—that
he should be able to go away! He must mean something else
by it, she said to herself; the words must bear a second
signification. And she herself, who had no business, or duty, or
tie of any sort except one, but that one enough to move
heaven and earth, her mother—who in a fortnight would be
making the jam if the strawberries were cheap enough. The
thought moved her to laughter again, a laugh out of a strangely
solemn, excited countenance. But this sudden revulsion of
feeling had given the whole matter a certain grotesque
mixture of the ludicrous: it demonstrated the impossibility
of any such overturn with such a sarcastic touch. Hester
said to herself that she must have been nearly making some
tragical mistake, and compromising her character for good
sense for ever. Of course it was impossible. Whatever he
meant by the words he did not mean that.

After breakfast, when she was alone and had read the note
over again, and could find no interpretation of it but the first
one, and had begun to enter into the agonies of a mental
struggle, Hester relieved the conflict by putting it down on
paper—writing to Edward, to herself, in the first instance,

through him.   She asked him what he meant, what other
sense there was in his words which she had not grasped?   He
go away ! how could he, with Catherine trusting in him, with
Vernon's depending upon him, with his work and his reputation, and so much at stake ; and she with her mother?   Did
not he see that it was impossible ?   Impossible ! He might say
that she should have pointed this out before, but she had
never realised it ; it had been words to her, no more ; and
it was words now, was it not ? words that meant something beyond her understanding—a test of her understanding ; but she had no understanding it appeared.   Hester
thought that she would send this letter to await him when
he reached the Grange, and then she would keep his appointment and find him—ready to laugh at her, as she had
laughed at herself.   She put it hurriedly into her desk
when Harry appeared, with a guilty sense that Harry, if
he saw it, would not only divine whom it was addressed to,
but even what it said.   But Harry was no warlock, and though
he saw the hurried movement and the withdrawal of the
papers never asked himself what it was.

But after Harry was gone, she wrote no more.   She gave
one glance at the pages full of anxious pleading, of tender
remonstrances, of love and perplexity ; then closed the lid
upon them, as if it had been the lid of a coffin, and locked
it securely.   They were obsolete, and out of date, as if her
grandmother had written them.   They had nothing to do
with the real question ; they were as fictitious as if they
had been taken out of a novel.   All that she had said was
foolishness, like the drivelling of an idiot.   Duty ! she had
asked triumphantly, how could he disengage himself from
that ? how could she leave her mother behind ?—when,
great heaven ! all that he wanted was to shake duty off,
and get rid of every tie.   Harry's revelation brought such
a contrast before her, that Hester could but stare at the
two pictures with dumb consternation.   On one side the bank
in gloomy disarray, its ordinary course of action stopped, the
business " all wrong," poor people besieging its doors for
their money, the clerks bewildered, and not knowing what to
do ; and poor Harry faithful, but incapable, knowing no better
than they.   On the other, Edward, in all a bridegroom's excitement, with the woman he loved beside him, travelling far
away into the night, flushed with pleasure, with novelty, with
the success of his actions whatever they were, and with the

world before him.   It seemed to Hester that she saw the two
scenes, although she herself would have to be an actor
in one of them if it ever came to pass.   She saw them to the
most insignificant details.   The bank (Vernon's—that sheet-
anchor of the race, for which she herself felt a hot partisan-
ship, a desire to build it up with the prop of her own life if
that would do it), full of angry and miserable people cursing
its very name—while the fugitives, with every comfort about
them, were fast getting out of sight and hearing of everything
that could recall what they had left.   Deserter ! traitor ! were
these the words that would be used ? and was he going to fly
from the ruin he had made ?   That last most terrible question
of all began to force itself to her lips, and all the air seemed to
grow alive and be filled with darting tongues and voices and
hissings of reply.   And then it was that Hester felt as if her
very hair began to writhe and twist in living horror about her
shoulders, and that her eyes, wide with fright and terror, were
becoming like Medusa's, things that might turn all that was
living to stone.

But to think through a long summer day is a terrible
ordeal, and many changes and turns of the mind are inevitable.   It was a pitiless long day, imagine it ! in June, when
not a moment is spared you.   It was very bright, all nature
enjoying the light.   The sun seemed to stand still in the sky,
as on that day when he stopped to watch the slaughter in
Ajalon ; and even when he disappeared at last, the twilight
lasted and lingered as if it would never be done.

Hester had put away her long letter of appeal, but she
wrote a brief, almost stern note, which she sent to the Grange
in the early evening.   It ran thus :—

"Harry has told us that all is going wrong at the bank,
that you are wanted urgently there, that only you can set
things right.   You cannot have known this when you wrote
to me.   I take it for granted this changes everything, but I
will come to-night to the place you name."

She sent her note in the afternoon, and then waited, like a
condemned criminal, faintly hoping still for a reprieve ; for
perhaps to know this would stop him still ; perhaps he had
not known it.   She went out just after sunset, escaping not
without difficulty from her mother's care.

"It is too late for you to go out by yourself," Mrs. John

said. " I do not like it. You girls are so independent. I never went beyond the garden by myself at your age."

" I am only going to the Common," Hester said, with a quiver in her voice. She kissed her mother very tenderly. She was not in the habit of bestowing caresses, so that this a little startled Mrs. John ; but she returned it warmly, and bade her child take a shawl.

Did Hester think she might yet be carried away by the flood of the other's will, against her own, that she took her leave so solemnly ? It was rather a sort of imaginative reflection of what she might have been doing if—— She had gone but a little way when she met Captain Morgan.

"Why did not you tell me you were going out ? " he said. " I have tired myself now ; I can't go with you. I have been inquiring about the midnight train for Emma, who did not get off this morning after all."

"Is she going by the midnight train ? " Hester asked, with a sense of inconvenience in it that she could hardly explain.

"Yes, if it is possible to get her off," said the captain ; " but, my dear, it is too late for you to walk alone."

" No, oh no. It is only for this once," Hester cried, with involuntary passion unawares.

" My dear child ! " said the old man. He was disturbed by her looks. " I will go in and get an overcoat, and join you directly, Hester ; for though I am tired I would rather be over-tired than that you should walk alone."

The only way that Hester could defend herself was to hurry away out of sight before he came out again. She had a dark dress, a veil over her face. Her springy step indeed was not easy to be mistaken, nor the outline of her alert and vigorous figure, which was so much unlike loitering. She got away into the fields by a lonely path, where she could be safe she thought till the time of her appointment came. What was to happen at that appointment she could not tell. Excitement was so high in her veins that she had no time to ask herself what she would answer him if he kept to his intention, or what she should do. Was it on the cards still that she might follow him to the end of the world ?

Edward had arrived late, only in time for dinner. He got Hester's note and read it with an impatient exclamation.

" The little fool," he said to himself, " as if that was not the very——" and tore it in a thousand pieces. He dressed for dinner very carefully, as was his wont, and was very pleasant at table, telling Catherine various incidents of his journey. "You must make the most of me while you have me," he said, "for I have a pile of letters in my room that would make any one ill to look at. I must get through them to-night—there may be something important. It is a pity Harry doesn't take more of a share."

"I think for my part it is one of the best things about him," said Catherine, "that he always acknowledges your superiority. He knows he will never set the Thames on fire."

"And why should he?" said Edward; "a man may be a very good man of business without that. I wish he would go into things more; then he would always be ready in case of an emergency."

"What emergency?" said Catherine, almost sharply. "You are too far-seeing, I think."

"Oh, I might die, you know," said Edward with an abrupt laugh.

"Anything might happen," she said; "but there are many more likely contingencies to be provided for. What is that?" she added quickly.

The butler had brought in and presented to Edward upon a large silver salver which called attention to it, a small, white, square object.

"Return tickets, ma'am," said the butler solemnly, "as dropped out of Mr. Edward's overcoat."

"Return tickets! you are not going back again, Edward?"

"I am always running up and down, Aunt Catherine. I constantly take return tickets," he said quietly, pocketing the tickets and giving the butler a look which he did not soon forget. For there were two of them, which Marshall could not understand. As for Catherine, this gave her a little pang, she could not tell why. But Edward had never found so much to tell her before. He kept her amused during the whole time of dinner. Afterwards he took her up stairs into the drawing-room and put her into her favourite chair, and did everything that a tender son could have done for her comfort. It was growing dusk by this time, and he had not been able to keep himself from giving a glance now and then at the sky.

"Do you think we are going to have a storm, Edward?" Catherine asked.

" I think it looks a little like it. You had better have your window shut," he said.

He had never been more kind. He kissed her hand and her cheek when he went away, saying it was possible if his letters were very tough that he might not come up stairs again before she went to bed.

" Your hand is hot," she said, " my dear boy. I am afraid you are a little feverish."

" It has been very warm in town, and I am always best, you know, in country air," was what he said.

She sat very quietly for some time after he had left her, then seeing no appearance of any storm rose and opened her window again. He was almost too careful of her. As she did so she heard a faint sound below as of some one softly closing the door. Was it Edward going out notwithstanding his letters? She put herself very close to the window to watch. He had a small bag in his hand, and stood for a moment at the gate looking up and down; then he made a quick step beyond it as if to meet some one. Catherine watched, straining her eyes through the gloom. She was not angry. It brought all her fears, her watchfulness, back in a moment. But if it was true that he loved Hester of course he must wish to see her—if she was so unmaidenly, so un-womanly as to consent to come out like this to meet him. And was it at her own very door that the tryst was? This roused Catherine. She heard a murmur of voices on the other side of the great holly. The summer night was so soft, every sound was carried by the air. Here was her opportunity to discover who it was. She did not pause to think, but taking up her shawl in her hand threw it over her head as she stole down stairs. It was black and made her almost invisible, her dress being black too. She came out at a side door, narrowly escaping the curi-osity of Marshall. The bright day had fallen into a very dim evening. There was neither moon nor stars. She stole out by the side door, avoiding the path. Her footsteps made no sound on the grass. She crossed the gravel on tiptoe, and wound her way among the shrubberies till she stood exactly under the holly-tree. The wall there was about up to a man's shoulders; and it was surmounted by a railing. She stood securely under the shadow of it, with her heart beating very loudly, and listened to their voices. Ah, there could be no

doubt about it.   She said to herself that she never had any
doubt.   It was the voice of *that girl* which answered Edward's
low passionate appeals.   There are some cases in which
honour demands a sacrifice scarcely possible.   She had it in
her power to satisfy herself at once as to the terms upon
which they were, and what they expected and wished for.
She had no intention of eavesdropping.   It was one of the
sins to which Catherine was least disposed; but to turn back
without satisfying herself seemed impossible now.

CHAPTER XXXIX.

It seemed to Hester that she had been for hours out of doors, and that the lingering June evening would never end. Now and then she met in the fields a party of Redborough people taking a walk—a mother with a little group of children, a father with a taller girl or boy, a pair of lovers. They all looked after her, wondering a little that a young lady, and one who belonged to the Vernons (for everybody knew her), should be out so late alone. "But why should she not have a young man too?" the lovers thought, and felt a great interest in the question whether they should meet her again, and who *he* might be. But still it could not be said to be dark—the wild roses were still quite pink upon the hedges. The moments lingered along, the clocks kept chiming by intervals. Hester, by dint of long thinking, felt that she had become incapable of all thought. She no longer remembered what she had intended to say to him, nor could divine what he would say. If it were but over, if the moment would but come! She felt capable of nothing but that wish; her mind seemed to be running by her like a stream, with a strange velocity which came to nothing. Then she woke up suddenly to feel that the time had come. The summer fields all golden with buttercups had stolen away into the grey, the hedgerows only betrayed themselves by a vague darkness. She could not see the faces, or anything but ghostlike outlines of those she met. The time had come when one looks like another, and identity is taken away.

There was nobody upon the Grange road. She went along as swift as a shadow, like a ghost, her veil over her face. The holly-tree stood black like a pillar of cloud at the gate, and some one stood close by waiting—not a creature to see them far or near. They clasped hands and stood together enveloped by the greyness, the confused atmosphere of evening, which seemed to hide them even from each other.

"Thank Heaven I have you at last. I thought you were never coming," Edward said.

"It was not dark enough till now. Oh, Edward! that we should meet like thieves, like——"

"Lovers, darling. The most innocent of lovers come together so—especially when the fates are against them; they are against us no more, Hester. Take my arm, and let us go. We have nothing to wait for. I think I have thought of everything. Good-bye to the old life—the dreary, the vain. My only love! Come, there is nothing to detain us——"

It was at this moment that the secret listener—who came without any intention of listening, who wanted only to see who it was and what it meant—losing her shoe in the heavy ground of the shrubbery, stole into that corner behind the wall.

"Oh, Edward, wait—there is everything to detain us. Did you not get my note? They say things are going wrong with Vernons'—that the bank—— I can't tell what it is, but you will understand. Harry said nothing could be done till you came."

"Harry is a fool!" he said, bitterly. "Why didn't he take his share of the work and understand matters? Is it my fault if it was all thrown into my hands? Hester, you are my own love, but you are a fool too! Don't you see? Can't you understand that this is the very reason? But why should I try to explain at such a moment—or you ask me? Come, my darling! Safety and happiness and everything we can wish lie beyond yon railway. Let us get away."

"I am not going, Edward. Oh, how could you think it! I never meant to go."

"Not going!" he laughed, and took her hands into his, with an impatience, however, which made him restless, which might have made him violent, "that is a pretty thing to tell me just when you have met me for the purpose. I know you want to be persuaded. But come, come; I will persuade you as much as you can desire when I get you safe into the train."

"It is not persuasion I want. If it was right I would go if all the world were against it. Edward, do you know what it looks like ? It looks like treachery—like deserting your post—like leading them into danger, then leaving them in their ignorance to stumble out as they can."

"Well?" he said. "Is that all? If we get off with that we shall do very well, Hester. I shouldn't wonder if they said harder things still."

"If the bank should—come to harm. I am a Vernon too. I can't bear it should come to harm. If anything was to happen——"

"If it will abridge this discussion—which surely is ill-timed, Hester, to say the least—I may admit at once that it is likely to come to harm. I don't know how things are to be tided over this time. The bank's on its last legs. We needn't make any mystery on the subject. What's that?"

It was a sound—of intolerable woe, indignation, and wrath from behind the wall. Catherine was listening, with her hands clasped hard to keep herself up. It was not a cry which would have betrayed her, but an involuntary rustle or movement, a gasp, indistinguishable from so many other utterances of the night.

"I suppose it was nothing," he added. "Hester, come ; we can't stand here like two—thieves, as you say, to be found out by anybody. There's that villain Marshall, Catherine's spy, always on the outlook. He tells his mistress everything. However, that does not matter much now. By to-morrow, dear, neither you nor I need mind what they say. There will be plenty said—we must make up our minds to that. I suppose you gave your mother a hint——"

"My mother, a hint? Edward ! how could I dare to say to her— What would she think ? but oh, that comes so long a way after ! The first thing is, you cannot go ; Edward, you must not go, a man cannot be a traitor. It is just the one thing-- If all was plain sailing, well ; but when things are going badly— Oh no, no, I will not hear you say so. You cannot desert your post."

He took hold of her arm in the intensity of his vexation and rage.

"You are a fool," he said, hoarsely. "Hester ! I love you all the same, but you are a fool? Didn't I tell you at first I was risking everything. Heavens, can't you understand ! Desert my post ! I have no post. It will be better for them that I should be out of the way. I—must go—confound it ! Hester, for God's sake haven't you made up your mind ! Do

you know that every moment I stand here I am in danger?
Come! come! I will tell you everything on the way."

She gave a cry as if his pressure, the almost force he used to
draw her with him, had hurt her. She drew her hand out of his.

"I never thought it possible," she said, " I never thought
it possible! Oh, Edward! danger, what is danger? there's
no danger but going wrong. Stop: my love—yes, you are my
love—there has never been any one between us. If you have
been foolish in your speculations, or whatever they are, or
even wrong—stay, Edward, stay, and put it right. Oh, stay,
and put it right! There can be no danger if you will stand
up and say 'I did it, I will put it right;' and I—if you care
for me—I will stand by you through everything. I will be
your clerk; I will work for you night and day. There is no
trouble I will not save you, Edward. Oh, Edward, for God's
sake, think of Catherine, how good she has been to you; and
it will break her heart. Think of Vernon's, which we have
all been so proud of, which gives us our place in the country.
Edward, think of— Won't you listen to me? You will be a
man dishonoured, they will call you—they will think you——
Edward!"

"All this comes finely from you," he cried; "beautifully
from you! You have a right to set up on the heights of
honour, and as the champion of Vernon's. You, John Vernon's
daughter, the man that ruined the bank."

"The man that— Oh, my God! Edward, what are you
saying—my father! the man——"

He laughed out—laughed aloud, forgetting precautions.
"Do you mean to say you did not know—the man that
was such a fool, that left it a ruin on Catherine's hands?
You did not know why she hated you? You are the only one
in the place that does not. I have taken the disease from
him, through you; it must run in the blood. Come, come,
you drive me into heroics, too. There is enough of this; but
you've no honour to stand upon, Hester; we are in the same
box. Come along with me now."

Hester felt that she had been stricken to the heart. She
drew away from him till she got to the rough support of the
wall, and leant upon it, hiding her face, pressing her soft
cheek against the roughness of the brick. He drew her
other arm into his, trying to lead her away; but she resisted,
putting her hand on him, and pushing him from her with all
her force.

"There is not another word to be said," she cried. "Go
away, if you will go; go away. I will never go with you!
all that is over now."

"This is folly," he said. "Why did you come here if you
had not made up your mind? And if I tell you a piece of
old news, a thing that everybody knows, is that to make a
breach between us? Hester! where are you going? the other
way—the other way!"

She was feeling her way along the wall to the gate. It
was very dark, and they were like shadows, small, vague,
under the black canopy of the tree. She kept him away with
her outstretched arm which he felt rather than saw.

"I never knew it—I never knew it," she said, with sobs.
"I am going to Catherine to ask her pardon on my knees."

"Hester, for God's sake don't be a fool— To Catherine!
You mean to send out after me, to stop me, to betray me!
but by——"

The oath never got uttered, whatever it was. Another
figure, tall and shadowy, appeared behind them in the opening
of the gate. Edward gave one startled look, then flung from
him the hand of Hester which he had grasped unawares, and
hurried away towards the town, with the speed of a ghost.
He flung it with such force that the girl's relaxed and drooping figure followed, and she fell before the third person, the
new comer, and lay across the gateway of the Grange, half
stunned, not knowing at whose feet she lay.

Edward hastened onward like a ghost speeding along the
dark road. He was miserable, but the greatest misery of all
was to think that even now at the last moment he might be
brought back—he might be stopped upon the edge of this
freedom for which he longed. He wanted Hester, he wanted
happiness, and he had lost them—but there was still freedom.
Had there been only the risks of the crisis, the meeting of
alarmed and anxious creditors, the chance even of criminal
prosecution, he might have faced it; but to return again to
that old routine, to take up his former life, was impossible.
He flew along like the wind. There was still an hour or more
before the train would start. Would the women gather themselves together, he wondered, soon enough to send after him,
to prevent his journey? As much to avoid that risk as to
occupy the time, which he did not know what else to do
with, he resolved to walk to the junction, which was at a

distance of two or three miles. So strange is the human
constitution, that even at this tragic and sombre moment he
almost enjoyed the dark night walk, though it was that of a
fugitive ; the present is always so near us, so palpable, so
much more apparent than either the future or the past. He
arrived at the junction just in time, and jumped into the first
carriage he could find in his hurry. He had no luggage,
having left everything in town—nothing but the small bag in
his hand, in which there were various things which he had
meant to show to Hester, to amuse her, distract her thoughts
on the night journey, and keep her from too many questions.
Among these things was a special licence, which he had
procured that morning in town. He jumped into the carriage
without perceiving that there was any one in it ; and it annoyed
him to see, when he settled in the furthest corner, that there
was a woman in the other. But the light was low, and it could
not be helped. Thus shut up in close and silent company, two
strangers, each wrapped in a world of their own, they went
swinging through the night, the lights of the stations on the
road gleaming past, while with a roar and rush they ran
through covering sheds and by empty platforms. After a
while Edward's attention was caught, in spite of himself, by a
little measured sob and sigh, which came at intervals from the
other corner. The lady was very quiet, but very methodical.
She put back her veil ; she took out her handkerchief ; she
proceeded to dry her eyes in a serious matter-of-fact way.
Edward could not help watching these little proceedings. A
few minutes after, with a start, he perceived who his companion was. Emma, going home at last, just as she came, no
one having spoken, nor any event occurred to change the
current of her life. Her little sniff, her carefully-wiped off
tears were for her failure, and for the dulness of Kilburn,
which she was about to return to. A sudden idea struck
Edward's mind. He changed his seat, came nearer to her,
and at last spoke.

"I am afraid, Miss Ashton, you don't like travelling by
night," he said.

She gave a little start and cry. "Oh, is it you, Mr. Edward?
I thought, when you came in, it must be somebody I knew.
Oh, I am afraid you must have seen me crying. I am very
sorry to go away ; everybody in Redborough has been so kind to
me, and there is always so much going on."

"But in London——" Edward began.

"Oh, that is what everybody says. There is always so much going on in London. That just shows how little they know. Perhaps among the fashionable sets. I don't know anything about that ; but not in Kilburn. It's partly like a little village, and partly like a great huge town. You're not supposed to know the people next door ; and then they are all just nobody. The men come home to their dinner or their tea, and then there is an end of them. When you are in the best set in a place it makes such a difference. Roland is very kind, and I have nothing to complain of, but I can't bear going back. That's what I was crying for : not so much for having to leave, but for having to go back."

"You are tired of your life too, I suppose ? "

"Oh, so I am ! but it can't be helped. I must just go back to it, whether I like it or not."

"Would you be glad of an alternative ? " asked Edward. He spoke with a sort of wanton recklessness, not caring what became of him.

"Oh ! " said Emma, waiting upon providence, "that is a different thing ; perhaps it would be better not : I can't tell. Yes, I think I should, if you ask me. Anything new would be a blessing ; but where am I to look for anything new ? You see, Roland has his own engagements ; you never can interfere with a brother."

It took away her breath when Edward rose from the opposite side where he was and came and sat beside her. "I am going away too," he said ; " I want change too. I can't bear the quiet any longer. I want to travel. Will you come with me ? We could be married to-morrow morning and start immediately after——"

"Mr. Edward ! good gracious ! " cried Emma. It took away her breath. This was coming to the point indeed. " Was this what you were thinking of when you asked me to dance the Thursday before last ? I never thought of such a thing. I thought it was Hester. Goodness me, what would they all say ? Did you know I was coming to-night ? Were you only pretending about Hester ? Were you struck with me from the beginning, or only just at the last ? I am sure I don't know what to say."

"Come with me, that is the best thing to do," Edward said.

CHAPTER XL.

THE HOUR OF NEED.

CATHERINE stood upon the threshold of her own gate : her house still and vacant behind, the lamps just carried into the vacant place up stairs, the windows beginning to show lights. She stood, herself a shadow, for the moment regardless of the shadow at her feet, looking out into the dim world after the other shadow which went along swift and silent into the darkness. "Edward!" she cried; but he did not hear. He had disappeared before she turned her eyes to the other, who, by this time, had raised herself to her knees, and remained there looking up, her face a paleness in the dim air, nothing more. Catherine Vernon looked at her in silence. She had heard all that had been said. She had heard the girl plead for herself, and it had not touched her heart. She had heard Hester beaten down to the ground by the reproach of her father's shame, and a certain pity had moved her. But a heart, like any other vessel, can contain only what it can contain. What time had she to think of Hester, what room? Edward had been her son, her creed; whoso proved that he was not worthy of faith even in Catherine's interest was her enemy; everything else came in a second place. He had stabbed and stabbed her, till the blood of those wounds seemed to fill up every crevice in her being. How could she think of a second? She looked after him with a cry of sorrow and anger and love that would not die. "Edward!" No doubt he could explain everything—he could tell her how it was, what had happened, what was the meaning of it all. Only when he was gone, and it was certain that he meant to explain nothing, did she turn to the other. They looked at

each other, though neither could see anything but that
paleness of a face. Then Catherine said—

   " If you are not hurt, get up and come in. I have to ask
you—there are things to explain——"

   " I am not hurt : he did not throw me down," said Hester,
" it was an accident."

   Catherine made an impatient gesture. She did not even
help the girl to get up ; the dislike of so many years, raised
to the tragic point by this association with the most terrible
moment of her life, was not likely to yield in a moment, to
give way to any sense of justice or pity. She motioned to her
to follow, and led the way quickly into the house. The great
door was ajar, the stairs and passages still dark. They went
up, one shadow following another, without a word. In the
drawing-room Marshall had just placed the two shaded lamps,
and was closing the windows. His mistress called to him to
leave them as they were, and sat without speaking until, after
various flittings about the room, he went away. Then she
hastily raised the shade from the lamp upon her own table,
throwing the light upon her own face and the other. They
were both very pale, with eyes that shone with excitement
and passion. The likeness between them came out in the
strangest way as they stood thus, intent upon each other.
They were like mother and daughter standing opposed in civil
war.   Then Catherine sat down and pointed Hester to
another chair.

   " We are not friends," she said, " and I don't think I can
ever forgive you ; but you are young, and perhaps you are
strained beyond your strength. I would not be cruel. Will
you let me give you something to restore you, or will you not,
before you speak ? for speak you must, and tell me what this
means."

   " I want nothing," said Hester. " If I should be killed,
what would it matter ? I recognise now that I have no right
to your kindness—if that was true——"

   " It was true."

   " Then I ask your pardon," said the girl, folding her hands.
" I would do it on my knees, but you would think that was—
for effect. I should think so myself in your place. You do
right to despise us : only this—oh, God help us, God help us
—I never knew——"

   " Girl," cried Catherine roughly, " the man you love (I
suppose) has just fled away, so far as I can see, dishonoured

and disgraced, and leaving you for ever! And yet you can stop to think about effect. I do not think you can have any heart."

Hester made no reply. She had reached that point which is beyond the heights of sensation. She had felt everything that heart could feel. There were no more tears in her, nor anger nor passion of any kind. She stood speechless, let any one say what they would to her. It might all be true.

"I do not think you can have any heart," cried her passionate opponent. "If it had been me at your age, and I had loved him, when he threw me from him so, I should have died."

There came a ghost of an awakening on Hester's face, a sort of pitiful smile of acquiescence. Perhaps it might be so. Another, more finely tempered, more impassioned, more high and noble than she. might have done that : but for her, poor soul, she had not died. She could not help it.

Catherine sat in her seat as in a throne, with a white face and gleaming eyes, and poured forth her accusations.

"I am glad of it," she said, "for my part! for now you will be queen's evidence, which it is fit and right your father's daughter should be. Do not stand there as if I had put you on your trial. What is it to me if you have any heart or not? I want information from you. Sit down there and husband your strength. How long has this been going on? It was not the first time he had talked to you of flying, oh no. Tell me honestly : that will be making some amends. How long has this been going on?"

Hester looked at her with great liquid eyes, dewy in their youthfulness and life, though worn with fatigue and pain. She asked in a low, wondering voice, "Did you hear all we said?"

"I heard—all, or almost all. Oh, you look at me so to accuse me, a listener that has heard no good of herself! I am not sorry I did it. It was without intention, but it was well. I can answer for myself. Do you answer for yourself. How long has it been going on?"

Hester stood still, clasping and unclasping her hands. She had nobody to appeal to, to stand by her : this was a kind of effort to get strength from herself. And her spirit began to come back. The shock had been terrible, but she had not been killed. "What can I say to you beyond what I have said," she cried, "if you heard what we said? There was no more. His life has been intolerable to him for a long time ; the monotony, the bondage of it, has been more than he could bear. He has wanted change and freedom—''

Hester thought she was making excuses for Edward. She said all this quickly, meaning to show that these were innocent causes for his flight, motives which brought no guilt with them. She was brought to a sudden pause. Catherine, who had been gazing at her when she began with harsh, intent earnestness, suddenly threw up her hands with a low cry of anguish. She sank back into her chair and covered her face. The girl stood silenced, overawed, her lips apart, her eyes wide staring. The elder woman had shown no pity for her anguish. Hester, on her side, had no understanding of this. She did not know that this was the one delusion of Catherine's soul. Miss Vernon had believed in no one else. She had laughed and seen through every pretence—except Edward. Edward had been the sole faith of her later life. He had loved her, she believed ; and she had been able to give him a life worthy of him. Heaven and earth ! She had heard him raving, as she said to herself, outside. The boy had gone wrong, as, alas, so many have gone : out of a wicked, foolish love, out of a desire to be rich perhaps. But this was different. A momentary temptation, even a quick recurring error, that can be understood. But that his life should have been in-tolerable, a monotony, a bondage, that change had been what he longed for—change from her house, her presence, her confidence ! She gave vent to a cry like the cry of a wild animal, full of horror and misery and pain. The girl did not mean to hurt her. There was sincerity in every tone of her voice. She thought she was making his sins venial and defending him. Oh, it was true, true ! Through Catherine's mind at that moment there ran the whole story of her later days, how she had used herself to the pretences of all about her, how every one around had taken from her, and snarled at her, eaten of her bread, and drunk of her cup, and hated her —except Edward. He alone had been her prop, her religion of the affections. The others had sneered at her weakness for him, and she had held her head high. She had prided herself on expecting no gratitude, on being prepared, with a laugh, to receive evil for good—except from him. Even now that she should be forced to acknowledge him ungrateful, that even would have been nothing, that would have done her no hurt. But to hear that his past life had been a burden, a

bondage, a monotony, that freedom was what he longed for—
freedom from her! The whole fabric of her life crushed
together and rocked to its foundations. She cried out to
Heaven and earth that she could not bear it, she could not
bear it! Other miseries might be possible, but this she
could not endure.

Hester stood motionless, arrested in what she had to say.
She did not understand the sudden effect of her words;
they seemed to her very common words, nothing particular
in them : certainly no harm. She herself had experienced the monotony of life, the narrowness and bondage.
But as she stood silenced, gazing, there came over her by
degrees a faint comprehension; and along with this a
sudden consciousness how strange it was that they should be
both heartbroken on one subject and yet stand aloof from each
other like enemies. It was not possible to mistake that cry—
that sudden gesture, the hiding of Catherine's face. Whatever
was the cause of it, it was anguish. And was there not
cause enough? For a moment or two, Hester's pride kept
her back—she had been already repulsed. But her heart was
rent by trouble of her own. She made a step or two
forward, and then dropped upon her knees, and touched
Catherine's arm softly with a deprecating, half-caressing touch.

"Oh, Catherine Vernon!" she cried, "we are both in great
trouble. We have not been fond of each other ; but I am
sorry, sorry for you—sorry to the bottom of my heart."

Catherine made no reply. The shock was too great, too
terrible and overwhelming. She could not answer nor show
that she heard even, although she did hear in the extraordinary tension of her faculties. But Hester continued to kneel
beside her. Youth is more simple than age even when it is
most self-willed. The girl could not look on and refuse to be
touched, and she herself wanted fellowship, human help or
even human opposition, something different from the loneliness in which she was left. She touched Catherine's arm
with her hand softly two or three times, then after a while in
utter downfall and weakness drooped her forehead upon it,
clasping it with both her hands, and sobbed there as upon
her mother's breast. The room was perfectly still, stretching
round them, large and dim : in this one corner the little sted-
fast light upon the group, the mother (you would have said)
hiding her face from the light, hiding her anguish from both
earth and Heaven, the daughter with that clinging which is

the best support, giving to their mutual misery the pathetic broken utterance of tears.

Catherine was the first to rouse herself. The spasm was like death, but it came to an end. She tried to rise with a little wondering impatience at the obstacle. It was with the strangest sensation that she turned her eyes upon the hidden head lying so near her own, and felt, with an extraordinary thrill, the arms clasped round her arm as if they never would detach themselves. What new thing was this? Hester had lost all her spirit and power. She had got within the sphere of a stronger than she. She was desolate and she clung to the only arm that could sustain her. Catherine's first impulse was to snatch her arm away. What was this creature to her—this girl who one way or other had to do with everything that had happened to her, and was the cause of the last blow? She could have flung her away from her as Edward had done. But the second glance moved her more and more strangely. The helplessness had an appeal in it, which would not be resisted. It even did her the good office of withdrawing her thoughts for a moment from the emergency which claimed them all. She half rose, then fell back again and was silent, not knowing what to do. What appeal could be more strong than that of those arms so tightly holding by her own? She tried to speak harshly, but could not. Then an impulse she could not resist, led her to lay her other hand upon the drooping head.

"Hester," she said gravely, "I understand that you are very unhappy. So am I. I thank you for being sorry for me. I will try, in the future, to be sorry for you. But just now, understand, there is a great deal to do. We must stand between—him," her voice faltered for a moment, then went on clear as before, "between him and punishment. If he can be saved he must be saved; if not, we must save what we can. You have overcome me, I cannot put you from me. Free me now, for I have a great deal to do."

She had felt, by the closer straining of the clasping arms, that Hester heard every word. Now the girl raised her face, pale, with a look of terror.

"What can you do? Are you able to do it?" she said.

"Able!" said Catherine, raising herself upright with a sort of smile. "I am able for everything that has to be done. Child, get up and help me! Don't cry there and break my heart.'

Hester stumbled to her feet in a moment. She could scarcely stand, but her heart sprang up like a giant—

"I will do—whatever you tell me," she said.

Catherine rose too. She put away her emotion from her as a workman clears away all encumbering surroundings. She made the girl sit down, and went out of the room and brought her some wine.

"Perhaps," she said, "we may help each other; at all events we have a common interest, and we have no time to give to lamentations to-night. The first thing is—but your mother will be unhappy about you. What shall I do? Shall I send her word that you are here and staying with me all night? Your mother is a happier woman than you or I. She will accept the reason that is given her without questioning. Probably she will be pleased. Be calm and rest yourself. I will do all that is needful."

She went to her writing-table and began to write, while Hester, shattered and broken, looked on. Catherine showed no signs of disablement. The butler came in in his stealthy way while she was writing, and asked if he must "shut up." She said—"No," going on with her writing. "You will go, or send some one, at once to the Heronry with this note. And afterwards you can go to bed. I wish no one to sit up. I expect news, for which I must wait myself. Let all go to bed as usual. No, stop. Go to the White House also and tell Mr. Harry— What do you think, Hester? is it worth while to call Harry?"

She turned round with the clear eyes and self-controlled aspect of use and wont. Even Marshall, who had the skill of a well-trained domestic in spying out internal commotion, was puzzled. She seemed to be asking a question on a matter of business in which the feelings were no ways involved. Hester was not equal to the call upon her, but she made a great effort to respond.

"He is very—anxious."

Catherine made a movement with her footstool which partly drowned the last word.

"You can wait a little, Marshall. I will write a note to Mr. Harry too."

The two letters were written at full speed, and given with a hand as steady as usual into the man's keeping. "Let them be taken at once," Catherine said. Then she began to walk up and down the room talking in her usual tones.

"Don't mind me pacing about—it is a habit I have. I can talk best so. It is my way of taking exercise now." She went on until Marshall was out of hearing, then turned upon Hester, with a changed tone. "He meant to take you away by the midnight train," she said. "That was so? He cannot leave Redborough till then. I am going to meet him there, and endeavour to persuade him to return. Quiet, child! This is not the moment for feeling. I—feel nothing," she said, putting her hand as nature bids with a hard pressure upon her heart. "We have got to do now. Are you strong enough to come with me, or must I go alone?"

Hester rose up too, quickly, with a start of new energy. "I can do anything that you will let me do," she said.

"Come, then." But after a moment Catherine put her hands on the girl's shoulders, and drew her into the light. "You are very young," she said, "not twenty yet, are you? Poor little thing! I was full grown before I was brought to this. But show what mettle is in you now. Come with me and bathe your face and put yourself in order. We must have no look of excitement or trouble to bring suspicion. Everything is safe as yet. What? Do you know anything more?"

"I know only—what I said," said Hester. "Harry is very anxious. He came to ask if I knew where—*he* was. I did not. He said all was wrong, that no one could put things right but he, that——"

"Yes, yes," Catherine said, with a little impatience; she could not bear any repetitions. "I have told Harry to come here at half-past twelve. If we find *him*, if *he* comes back with us—here is your work, Hester, to see Harry and dismiss him. If Edward is with us all will be well. If he comes, if he only comes! Oh God! I will deny nothing, I will oppose nothing, let but honour be saved and his good name! And in that case you will see Harry and send him away. But if he does not come——"

"He will, he will!—for you."

Catherine shook her head; but a faint smile came over her face, a kindling of hope. Surely, surely the old love—the old long-enduring bond would tell for something. It could not be possible that he would throw everything—love and duty, and honour, and even well-being, all away—when there was still a place of repentance held out to him. She took Hester to her room, where she dressed herself carefully, tying on her

bonnet, and drawing out the bows with an elaboration at
which the girl looked on wondering. Then they went down
stairs where all was now in half light, one lamp burning
dimly in the hall. As Catherine drew the heavy door behind
her it sent a muffled echo into the air. It was after eleven
o'clock. The world was wrapped in a soft darkness more
confusing than blacker night : there was not a creature
visible on the road. She had not walked, save for her
pleasure, in the sunshine, just so far as was agreeable, for
years, and it was far to go. To Hester this strange walk
through the dark was at once novel and terrible. She did
not know what interruptions they might meet. She kept
close by her companion, who went along with a free and
rapid step, as if she had shaken off half her weight of years.
Deep down in the recollection of many a woman of whom the
world knows no such history will lurk the recollection of such a
walk taken in terror and sorrow, to call back some wanderer,
to stop some shame. The actors in such scenes never speak
of them, though they may be the noblest in their lives.
Catherine said something not uncheerful from time to time,
keeping up her own courage as well as her companion's. Nobody
noticed them as they came within the lighted streets, which
were deserted at this late hour, except round the railway
station, where Catherine sped along without a pause. The
train had not arrived ; there were a number of people about
upon the platform waiting for it, among them a little group
composed of Emma and her trunks, with old Captain Morgan
standing like a pillar in the midst of the confused heap.
"Wait here and watch," Catherine said, putting Hester into
a quiet corner, where the girl stood trembling, gazing at the
shifting groups, hardly able to sustain her fatigued and
tottering limbs, but following with a kind of fascination the
movements of her companion, who seemed to penetrate every
knot, to scan every countenance, not a creature there escaping
her inspection.

If he had been there, would all this page of history
have been changed, and wrong become right again ? These
strange turns for good or evil, that seem to hang upon
the quiver of a balance, are too bewildering for mortal
senses. Catherine by that time had no doubt. Had she
but found him, quivering with love and strength and
passion as she was, she would have saved him still. But he
was not there. She made no affectation of secrecy. She

called the guard to her, and gave him a succinct reason for
wishing to find her nephew. "Some news have come for him
since he left the house. Find him for me," she said, with a
smile, and a half-crown ready. But by and by she came back
to the girl in the corner, reproving her with an impatient
touch on her shoulder. "Don't look so scared," she said.
"What is there to be frightened for?" She took hold of
Hester by the arm. She was trembling from head to foot:
for by this time she knew that he was not there.

There was still the chance left that he might dart in at the
last moment, and it was for this reason that she placed herself
by the doorway, her face full in the lamplight, with a smile
upon it, her look of expectation frank and cheerful. Then
came the deafening clang of the arrival, the confusion and
bustle and leave-takings, the little pause full of voices and
noises, and then the clang of the train getting under weigh, the
sweep and wind of its going, the emptiness and blackness left
behind : all so vulgar and ordinary, yet all tragic sometimes
as the most terrible of accessories. She drew Hester aside
almost violently, and let the other spectators stream away.
Among the first old Captain Morgan stalked forth, tired but
contented, noticing nobody. Of all people in the world he
would least have recognised these two standing in agitation
inconceivable, subduing as they could the heart-throbs that
took away their breath. When he had got well on his way
the two women came out into the light. They were holding by
each other, Hester clasping her companion's arm, and guiding
her as she had once guided her mother. A sombre cloud had
come over Catherine's face. She had allowed herself to hope,
and the second disappointment was almost worse than the
first revelation. It was all her self-command could do to
prevent her from flinging off from her the girl whose share in
all this—what was it? perhaps the whole was her doing,
perhaps the suggestion of everything, perhaps, God knows,
craft enough to make this final effort to recover the boy a
failure. Who could say if Hester had not known from the
beginning that the attempt would be fruitless? And the other,
too, Harry, whom she had called to her by an impulse which
seemed now to have been put into her head by some one, and
not to be her own. Harry, too. He would be brought into
the secret! Her humiliation would be complete. The boy
she had scoffed at, the girl she had disliked, turned into
her confidants, and Edward, her own, her heir, her son, the

successor she had chosen !—Catherine's heart cried out within
her with a mother's passion. In the quiet of the country
road she could hold her peace no longer. She drew her arm
out of Hester's abruptly.

"No doubt," she said, "no doubt! he was to carry you
away, a fine lady like you, with posthorses in a romantic way
—not by the vulgar method of a train; and you have deceived
me, and lost me my last chance. Edward! Edward! Oh where
are you, my boy, my boy?"

Here, had she but known it, poor Catherine's comedy of
human nature was complete. Edward, upon whom she called
with tragic passion as great as that of a Constance, was just
then approaching Emma, in a fierce farce of self-compensa-
tion, determined to make the adventure complete, to cut every
tie and tear every remnant of the past to pieces. Her laugh
of contempt at the poor farce-tragedy would have been
supreme had it been any case but her own.

CHAPTER XLI.

A NIGHT'S VIGIL.

THEY had been sitting through all the night, examining
everything. Catherine was not a woman to be the slave of
passion, even when that was the one delusion of her life.
She got over it with a stern and fierce struggle before they
reached the gate of the Grange, whither Hester followed her,
trembling and half stupefied, unable either to resist or to think
of any course of action for herself. Catherine paused at the
gate, and looked round her with a curious quivering smile.
" Here is where I saw him going away," she said ; " here is
where I heard the last words from him." She laughed ; her
heart was throbbing with the wildest suffering. She dashed
her hands together with a violence of which she was unaware.
"Such words!" she cried. It was scarcely one o'clock, but in
summer there is little night, and already the air had begun to
whiten with some premonition of day. She held up her face
to the sky—an old face, with so many lines in it, suddenly
smitten as with a death blow. Her eyes, under the curve of
pain, which makes the eyelids quiver, looked up to the pale
skies with what is the last appeal of humanity. For why?—
for why?—an honest life, an honourable career, a soul that
had shrunk from no labour or pain, a hand that never had
been closed to human distress—and repaid with misery at the
end! Is there no reason in it when God's creature lifts a
face of anguish to His throne, and asks why? She paused
on the threshold of her house, which was desolate, and made
that mute appeal. It was beyond all words or crying, as it
was beyond all reply. The other, who was the companion of
her misfortune, stood beside her, looking, not at heaven, but

at her. Hester had got far beyond thinking of her own share
in it. Fatigue and excitement had brought sensation almost
to an end. She was not angry with Catherine, who had
thrown her off. Everything was blurred to her in a sense
of calamity common and universal, of which Catherine seemed
the sign and emblem. She made no interruption in the
silence. And it was only when Catherine turned to go in
that she was recalled to a recollection of Hester by her side.

"I think—I had better go home—to my mother," the girl
said, looking along the road with a dreamy terror. She was
afraid of the dark, the solitude, the distance—and yet what
was there left to her but to go home, which she seemed to
have quitted, to have fled from, with the idea of never returning, years ago. Catherine put out her hand and grasped
her. She was far the more vigorous of the two. She could
have carried the girl into the house, where she now half led,
half dragged her. They found Harry already waiting for them in
great bewilderment and distress. He could not account for
the entrance of these two together, or for their apparent
union—but Catherine gave him no explanation. She made
him sit down and tell her at once everything he knew of the
state of affairs: and when this was made plain to her, she
flew out upon him with a wrath that made Harry shrink.

"Why did you leave everything in one person's hands? Is
it not a partner's business to look after his own interests?
You have piled all upon one man's shoulders. He has had
everything to do. It has been too much for his mind—it has
turned his head. If it had been yours, what would have
happened to you?"

"I have been saying all that to myself, Aunt Catherine,"
Harry said, humbly; "but you know I am not clever, and
poor Ned——"

She stamped her foot on the floor. "Let me have none of
your commiserations," she cried. "There is nothing poor
about it at least."

She put Hester down at the table with pen and ink to
write for her. She had not said a word of compassion to
her; this had been the way she had chosen to express her
feeling, whatever it was. When Harry had interposed, begging
to be allowed to do it, she had stopped him summarily; and
had gone on thus, collecting information, dictating to Hester,
examining papers with Harry, asking a hundred questions,
till morning was blue in the skies. When she saw by that

strange light stealing in how wan and wretched her two
companions looked, Catherine rose from her chair. She was
not tired—her colour was as fresh and her eyes as bright
as ever, her mind full of impatient energy; but the powers of
the others had flagged.

"Go home and rest," she said to Harry. "Have old Rule
there to-morrow morning to meet me. I will come to the
bank to-morrow—I mean to-day—at eight, before you open.
Go home and go to bed."

"Not if I can be of any use to you, Aunt Catherine—or to
poor Ned."

Her foot made the same impatient movement upon the
carpet. "You can be of no use," she said, "dropping asleep
as you are: go and rest; at your age few can do without sleep.
And Hester, go too, you can do no more." It was not without
a half contempt that she saw the overpowering of their young
faculties by that which to her was nothing. There are so
many things in which youth has the best of it, that age has
a right to its dolorous triumph when that comes. She went
down with Harry to the door to let him out, glad of the
movement, and stood in the early light for a moment breathing
in the fresh air. The birds were all twittering, making their
morning thanksgiving, expressing their joy in the new day.
Catherine looked out sternly upon the light and gladness in
which she had no share. She thought again—should she ever
think of anything else?—of the last words she had heard, and
of his figure hurrying away in the darkness, deaf to her cry.
It was a relief to go in again, even to see the poor little lamp
flickering, and the light bursting in at every crevice of the
ineffectual shutters. When she reached the room in which
they had been at work, Hester, who had answered as far as
her faculties could to every call upon her, had dropped back
into the great chair in which she had been sitting, and had
fallen asleep in utter exhaustion. It was a curious scene.
The windows were all closed, and candles upon the table still
burning: but the light swept in from above, over the top of the
shutters, which were not so high as the glass, and lighted up
the room in a strange abstract way like a studio or a prison.
In the midst of this pale and colourless illumination Hester's
white face, with the blue veins showing in it, in an attitude of
utter abandonment and exhaustion, pillowed upon the dark
cushions of the chair, was the central point; her hand with the
pen in it was still on the table, the candles flickering with a

yellow uncertain blaze. Catherine went and stood by her for
a moment and looked at her. Tears were upon the girl's long
eyelashes, her mouth seemed still quivering, the faint sound
of a sob came out of her sleep. She looked younger even
than she was, like a child that had cried itself asleep. Catherine looked at her with many a thought. John Vernon's
daughter, who had all but ruined her father's house, and had
wounded her own pride, if not her heart, in the way women feel
most—and bitterer still, Edward's love, she, for whom he had
planned to betray her own better claims, for whom he would have
deserted her, for whom he had ruined her, this time perhaps
without remedy. With a strange bitterness she looked at
the young creature thus fatally connected with all the miseries
of her life. It was not Hester's fault. The table was covered
with proofs of her submission and obedience. If it was true
that but for her perhaps Catherine's power would never have
been disturbed, it was also true that but for her Catherine
might have been ruined irretrievably, she and all she prized
most. But this argument did not tell in the mind of the
woman who stood gazing at her, so much as the look of utter
infantile weariness, the broken sound of the sleeping sob, the
glitter upon her eyelashes. She stood for a long time, and
Hester never moved. Then she took a shawl and covered the
sleeper as tenderly as her mother could have done it, and
began to pace softly up and down in that weird clearness.
She did not even extinguish the candles, but left them there
amid all the disarray of the table, the scattered papers,
covered with notes and figures. The young can sleep, but not
the old. The romantic interest would be with Hester worn
out with wretchedness and weariness; but the heavier burden
was her own.

Perhaps had the truth been pursued to its depths it
gave a certain satisfaction to Catherine to find herself at
last left to contemplate alone that uttermost and profoundest
loss which was hers. The girl slept though her heart might
be broken ; the woman whose last hope he was, whose faith in
human nature was wound up in him, who believed in Edward,
but on earth in no one else, slept not, rested not, could not
forget. She walked from end to end of the room, her hands
clasped, her face in all its comely age paled in a moment to
the pallor of an old woman. People had said that her colour
was like a girl's still : her eye was not dim nor her natural
force abated. But over her there had come this chill in a

moment. And where was he, the cause of it all? Flying fast
across the country somewhere, directing his way, no doubt, to
some port where he could get out of England. For what, oh
Heaven, for what? Was there any sacrifice she would not
have made for him? He might have had his Hester, his own
house like the others, if that was what he wanted. There
was nothing, nothing she would have grudged him! She
would have asked no gratitude, made no conditions. He
should have had his freedom, and his love—whatever he wanted.
All this swept through her mind as she went to and fro in
that blue clearness of the morning which swept down upon
her from the skies over all the weariness and disarray of the
night. Catherine did not ask herself what she would have
said, all things being well, if she had been asked to consent
to the effacing of herself, which now it seemed would have
been so easy a solution of the problem. It seemed to her
now that in love she would have granted all he could ask for,
and in pride she certainly would have done it, scorning to ask
how he could resign her so easily. Love and pride combined
wrung her heart between them now. Up and down, up and
down with a soft monotonous motion she walked unsubdued
while the others sank. Her old frame felt no weariness, her
old heart was yet high. She could no more sink down and
acknowledge herself beaten, than she could drop her head
and sleep like Hester. With impatience and an energy
unbroken she waited for the day.

Catherine's carriage stood outside the bank at eight o'clock
in the morning, to the wonder yet admiration of the town.
"Old as she is, she's an example to the young ones," the people
said: though there were darker rumours, too, that one of the
young men had gone wrong, and that it was a sharp and
speedy inquiry into this that had brought Catherine into the
town without delay. The still closed door was opened to her
by Harry, who was pale with his sleepless night and with the
anxiety from which he could now find no escape. Behind
Harry was old Rule, who came forward with a face like a
mute at a funeral, his hands held up, his countenance distorted with grief and sympathy. "Oh, my dear lady!" he
cried; "oh, Miss Catherine, has it come to this? Who could
suppose that you and I should meet together a second time
in this way?"

Catherine made a sudden gesture of impatience. "How
do you know what the way is until you hear?" she said.

She sat down at the table where she had sat so often. Her
old look of command, the energy and life of old, seemed in
her face ; if it was paled and jaded, the others, who were
more shaken still than she, had no eyes to see it. The three
were deep in their work before the clerks appeared, one by
one, all those who were of any weight in the place, or cared
for Vernon's, asking anxiously if anything was known of Mr.
Edward. When they were met by the astonishing statement
"Miss Vernon is here," the announcement was received in different ways, but with great excitement. "Then all is right," said
one ; but another shook his head. "All must be very wrong,"
he said, "or Catherine Vernon would not be here." It was
the cashier who uttered these words. He was an old servant
of the bank, and had been a junior at the time when old Rule
was head clerk and Catherine the soul of everything. After
a while he was sent for into the mysterious room towards
which the attention of every one was now directed. There
old Mr. Merridew was shown in with solemnity on his brows,
and various others of the fathers of the town. Even outside
there seemed a little excitement about to the anxious spectators within. If it had been market-day there might have
been a run on the bank. As it was, there were one or two
little groups about, anxiously noting the grave faces of the
visitors. All day long they came and went ; the great books
were all spread about upon the table within, and when the
door opened sometimes one anxious face would be seen, sometimes another. One of the younger men passing the door saw
Catherine herself explaining and urging something upon the
chief of the Bank of England in Redborough, who had joined
the conclave. It was clearly then, they all felt, a matter of life
and death. Some wine and biscuits were taken in in the middle
of the day, but no one went away for luncheon, no one had
time or leisure for any such thought. Mr. Pounceby, who was
Catherine's solicitor, stayed by her all day long, while the
others went and came. The clerks, when their day's work
was done, left this secret conclave still sitting. The cashier
and the head clerk were detained after the others. The
younger men went away with an alarmed sense that Vernon's
might never open again.

And this impression was so far justified that the councillors,
almost without exception, thought so too. There had been found
in Edward's room at the Grange a bundle of papers, securities
taken by him from the safe at the bank. The greater part

had been abstracted, but the few that were left showed too
clearly what methods he had adopted. The bank itself was
worth aiding. Its prestige as yet was scarcely touched;
but how were these deficiencies to be made up, how was
it to be worked without money, and how was its credit
to be restored? Catherine had not now the independent
fortune which on the former occasion she had thrown into
the common stock with proud confidence in Vernon's. It had
all been repaid her, but it had remained in the business, and
if Vernon's now were to be made an end of, was gone. That
did not affect the mind of the proud old woman. She thought
nothing of herself or her fortune. She sat unwearied, meeting
one man after another, who a week or two ago had been
obsequious to her, without wincing, ready to hear all their
doubts, to bear the shakings of their heads, their blame of
the culpable negligence that had left everything in one man's
hand—their denunciations of Edward, the eager advantage
they took of that right to find fault and reproach which
is put into the hands of every man who is asked to help.
Catherine faltered at first, when she found that to save
Edward's character, to smooth away his guilt, and make
excuses for him was impossible. These angry men would not
hear a word of apology. He was a swindler to them and
nothing more. "Pardon me, my dear Miss Vernon, but I
always thought the confidence you showed in that young fellow
excessive." "He should not have been permitted a tithe of
the power he had. It was not just to others who were far
more deserving." "If you mean me, I was no more to be
matched with Edward than a tortoise is with a hare," said
Harry. Catherine put out her hand to him under the table
and gave his hand such a pressure, delicate as hers was, as
almost made the strong young fellow cry out; but at the
same time she silenced him with a look, and bore it all. She
bore everything—the long hours of contention, of explanation,
of censure, of excuse, of anxious pointing out again and again
of the strong points in her case. She argued it all out with
every individual, and again with every combination of them,
when two or three together would return to the old objections,
the difficulties they had originally started, and which again
and again had been argued away, with no doubt the natural
special pleading of all who speak in their own defence. During
this continually repeated process Harry would stand behind
her with his face of trouble, watching the countenances of the

speakers, now and then blurting out something (the reverse
of judicious in most cases), shuffling with uneasy feet upon
the floor ; sometimes, poor fellow, there being nothing else in
his power, holding her elbow with the idea of supporting her,
kneeling down to put her footstool straight ; while old Mr.
Rule, sitting at a little distance, equally anxious, equally
eager, not of importance enough to speak, would come in
with a quavering " Miss Vernon explained all that, sir—"
" As Miss Vernon has already said, sir——"

She alone showed little anxiety and no distress. She was
as dignified as if she had been entertaining them at her
table, as she had done so often. She bore those repetitions
of the old objections with composure. She did not get
impatient, twisting and turning in her chair like Mr. Rule,
or crushing her impatience under foot like Harry. She was
like an Indian at the stake : or rather like a prime minister
in his place in Parliament. The hundred times repeated
argument, the old doubt brought up again, all afresh with
shakings of the head, the stolid little compliments to her as
a woman so much superior to her sex, her masculine understanding (good lack! wonderful, though not equal to those
whom she had convinced over and over again, yet who began
again next moment where they had left off), all this she put
up with without shrinking. Oh, the dulness of them, the
unconvinceableness, the opaque vision, the impotent hearts!
But she made no sign that she perceived. She sat still and
held her own. She had the best of the argument in logic,
but not, alas, in power. Ten mortal hours had struck by the
time the last of her visitors hastened away to his dinner,
promising to think of it, yet shaking his head. Catherine
leant her head upon the back of her high chair and closed her
eyes ; the tears came to them in the relief of having no more
to say. She was so pallid and so worn now that they both
rushed to her in silent terror. She opened her eyes with an
astonished look. " I hope you do not think I am going to
faint ; I never faint," she said.

Ten hours ! She walked to her carriage with a foot lighter
and firmer than that of Harry, upon whose fine physique and
troubled soul this day had wrought more havoc than the
severest football. She would not allow her old friend and
servant to come to the door with her.

"Don't tire yourself," she said. " You have so much to
do for us yet. I think we shall pull through."

"God bless you, Miss Catherine," said the old man; "if we pull through it will be your doing."

"What merit is that?" she said quickly. "Why should God bless me for that? It is for myself."

"Oh, my dear lady," cried the old clerk. "I know you better than you do yourself. It is for Vernon's and not for you. And Vernon's means the honest living of many a family. It means——"

"Don't tell me what it means," she cried, putting up her hands. "It means downfall and shame now. It means a broken heart, Mr. Rule."

"No, no," he cried. "No, no, we'll get through. I'll come back if you'll let me, and Mr. Harry will work like a hero."

She gave Harry a strange glance. There was in it a gleam of repugnance, an air of asking pardon. She could not endure the contrast which it was not possible to refrain from making. He, standing by her, so dutiful, so kind, while the other who had ruined her, fled away. She could have struck him with her nervous hand, which now was trembling; she could have made a humble confession to him of the injuries she had done him in her heart. She could bear the old town dignitaries, the men of money, better than this.

"May I go with you?" he said, supporting her with his arm, bending over her with his fair countenance full of trouble and sympathy.

She could have struck him for being so good and true. Why was he true, and the other—— Better, better if they had both been alike, both traitors, and left her to bear it by herself.

"No, Harry," she said; "no, Harry, let me be alone."

He kissed her hand, poor boy, with a piteous look, and she felt it wet with a tear. Nor did she misunderstand him. She knew it was for her he was sorry. She knew even that he was the one alone who would stand up for the absent, and excuse him and pity him. All this she knew, and it was intolerable to her, and yet the best and sweetest thing that was in her lot.

CHAPTER XLII.

HESTER woke next morning in an unfamiliar room with a consciousness of something strange and terrible that had happened, she could not tell what, that first sensation before memory awakens which is one of the most bitter indications of having entered upon the world of evil. So the guilty pair in Paradise, in the morning of the world, must have woke out of their sleep, and felt, before remembrance came, the sense of ill. She scarcely remembered how she had been transported to that bed. She had slept for sorrow, calamity crushing all her unused faculties, and her first waking sensation was one of trouble and wonder what it was. She had not long to wait before the whole came rushing back upon her mind. She gave a low cry, and all her wounds began to bleed anew—nay, she felt them as for the first time, for last night's terror and commotion and misery were like a dream to her. When she uttered that cry, there was a soft stir in the room, and a little, noiseless figure, and anxious face appeared at her bedside.

"Mother!" Hester cried, with a voice of dismay.

"Yes, my darling, I am here. Catherine was so good as to send for me. She said you had received a great shock. She went out herself very early, so that you need not be afraid of being disturbed, Hester. And what is it, my dear? She would not give me any satisfaction. She said you had behaved very well, and had been the means of giving her valuable information. I am very glad of that anyhow, Hester. I always told you she was kind in the main. If you and she should be better friends after this it would be a great pleasure to me."

There was anxiety in Mrs. John's plaintive face, but it was confined to the fear lest her daughter's health should be affected, and to a little uncertainty whether the relations with Catherine might be improved or injured by this mysterious event, whatever it was.

"She has been very kind, mamma."

"I was sure of it, my dear. Catherine has a way with her that is not very—*nice*—sometimes. But then we all have some fault. I was to ring for tea as soon as you were awake. That maid, after all, though I have always had a prejudice against her, is kind too, in her way. She has made me most comfortable. I have always observed in my life, Hester, that when you get to know people you so often think better of them than when—— That has been my experience. Do you feel able to take some breakfast, dear? or will you get up first? You are to do exactly as you please."

Hester lay still with a little moan, and made no reply. She would have liked to turn her face to the wall, to beg that the light of day might be shut out, that she might be left to make acquaintance with her trouble. But none of these things were possible. Her mother's gentle face shining upon her with so much easy anxiety, and so little conception of anything under the surface, brought her to herself as nothing else could have done. Why should she be troubled with these anguishes that were beyond her? The girl raised herself with that heroism of necessity which is more effectual than mere will. Mrs. John would weep with her, and make up to her with a thousand caresses for the loss of her lover, when she came to understand it ; but she would never understand the burden that was on Hester's soul. The girl said to herself that it must be borne silently, that there must be no further betrayal. She begged her mother to leave her a little, while she got up.

"I have had a long sleep. I am quite myself again," she said.

"You look pale," said Mrs. John, kissing her. "You have had a shock, and you have never told me yet what it was. But perhaps, on the whole, the best thing you can do is to get up ; breakfast in bed is not very comfortable. I will go and have a good look at Catherine's pretty things in the drawing-room—she has some nice china—and come back in half an hour or so. Don't hurry, my darling, but it is such a lovely morning ; it will do you good to have some fresh air."

When Hester was left alone she tried to think, but could

not. ' Scenes came back to her as in a theatre—the meeting
at the gate, and all that passed there ; Catherine's appearance, and the force with which Edward flung her away from
him, and set out into the dark, into the unknown. Why—
why had he done it ? Was it in a sudden fit of passion,
which he had repented of ? Was it in the terror of being discovered—and out of that suspicion and opposition, and gloomy
distrust which had always been in his mind towards Catherine?
And then the railway would rise before her mind—the crowd
and noise, and wild unnaturalness of everything, the disappointment which to her at heart was a relief. Had he not gone
after all ? What if a better thought had struck him ? What
if, when they all went to the bank, thinking him a traitor,
they should find him there, throwing light on everything,
putting the wrong right ? Hester raised her head again when
this thought came into her mind. Was it not after all the most
likely, the most natural thought ? A man does wrong by temptation, by evil companions, by the leading on of one wrong
thing after another ; but when he is brought to a pause, when
there is a distinct call upon him, when he is made to see
beyond dispute what his duty is, is it not natural, certain that
he must do it ? So she said to herself. For a moment all
the clouds flew away, a warm exhilaration took possession of
her. Then there floated up before her eyes another scene—
the table round which they had sat in the dead of night ;
Harry with his troubled face opposite to her ; Catherine
paramount in her energy and rapidity ; she herself putting
down upon paper, so quickly that her fingers alone moved and
her mind had no share but the most broken and imperfect one,
what she was told to write. If he had come back, if he was
working now at the re-establishment of everything, could
Edward ever forgive them ? What matter, what matter,
she cried, so long as he set himself right, so long as Vernon's stood by his help and did not fall ? From all this it will
be seen that nothing of the despair which in reality and
in reflection had overwhelmed all the other chief actors in
the drama, had touched Hester. To her everything was still
possible, and Edward's vindication, Edward's repentance, the
chief, the most natural event of all.

"Well, my dear, are you ready ? " said Mrs. John. "There is
quite a nice breakfast waiting for you down stairs. Catherine's
maid (whom I really was unjust to, Hester, for she is a very
nice woman when you come to know her) insisted upon

making you some chocolate instead of tea : for it would be more sustaining, she said, in case you should not be disposed to eat. I don't know why she should think you would not be disposed to eat. I told her you always liked your breakfast. But come, my dear, come, I am sure you must want something. Did you find the clean things I brought you? Oh! I thought you would be better in a nice clean print, instead of that dark thing ; but you have put on the old one all the same."

"It is best for me to-day," Hester said.

She thought to herself if it all turned out as she hoped, with what joy she would return to her summer garments in the evening, even if it might be that Edward had broken with her for ever. She thought this almost certain, for had she not turned against him? but this was not the question paramount in her mind. There was but one thing all important, that he should have returned to his post. Mrs. John was greatly surprised at the wisdom of that prevision on the part of Catherine's maid. How could she have foreseen that Hester, a healthy girl, with generally a healthy appetite, would turn away almost with loathing from the dainty food, the pretty tray, the careful provision made for her? She swallowed the chocolate hastily at her mother's entreaty : the very air of the house, those stairs and passages, all flooded with light, which had painted themselves on her recollection in the darkness, filled Hester with a sense of the intolerable. She made haste to get out, to get away, to take her mother home.

"Don't you think it will only be polite to wait till Catherine comes back?" Mrs. John said. " You must remember, dear, that she has been very kind to you ; and nothing could be kinder than her note, and sending the carriage for me this morning, and all. I think we ought to wait and thank her for her kindness. She will think it strange that we should go away without a word. Well, if you think it will really be better to come back in the afternoon, Hester—Has Catherine gone out to spend the day? That is quite unusual, surely for her—but however, of course it is not our business. Lean on my arm, my dear. I am sure, as you say, the air will do you good."

The air did not do Hester good : the shade of the holly-tree lying motionless upon the road, the half-open gate at which Catherine had appeared in the darkness, the strange intelligence that seemed to be in every bush, as if these inanimate things knew and remembered what had been done

and said in secret, seemed to bring conviction, and force back
upon her all the scenes she had gone through of which her
innocent mother knew nothing. And every inch of the way
recalled her own proud, eager thoughts of the night before,
the desperation with which she had gone to that meeting,
determined upon her protest and refusal, yet never sure that
she would ever retrace these steps again. To retrace them
now as she was doing, with her mother's gentle talk in her
ears, the occasional mild question which it was so easy to
elude, the praises of Catherine which her supposed kindness
called forth so easily, seemed an incredible thing. Mrs. John
enjoyed the walk. It was seldom she went out in the morning, and the excitement of her daughter's absence all night,
of Catherine's explanations, of the drawing together of some
new and closer bond between Hester and the head of the
Vernon society—the most important person of all the kindred
—gave her a secret exhilaration. There had not been such a
sensation in the Vernonry for months as that which had been
caused that morning by the sight of Catherine's well-known
brougham, sent for Mrs. John ! It might be that in future this
would be no such rare sight : it might be—but the poor lady
scarcely knew how to contain the satisfaction with which she
saw the vista opening up before her of Hester's promotion
and favour with Catherine. Valuable information ! She was
proud of what seemed to her like the highest praise. She
always knew that her Hester, so much superior as she was to
other girls——if Catherine but knew her as she deserved to be
known. And then she asked with pleasant expectation—

"What was the information, Hester, that you gave Catherine ? I am so glad that you were able to tell her something
she didn't know. I was quite in a flutter when I got her note
last night; but of course it was perfectly right for you to
stay when she wished it. I shall tell her I am so much
obliged to her for having taken such good care of you. It
gave me quite a fright for the moment, but I soon got over it.
And Emma, you know, went away at last by the night train."

Thus Mrs. John diverted her own attention and never
pressed a question. But it is impossible to tell how deserted,
how silent, how far out of the world and life the little rooms
at the Vernonry looked after the agitation of the night.
Hester could not rest in them : the summer forenoon seemed a
twelvemonth long. She could not take up any of her usual
occupations. She was afraid to meet any one, to be questioned

perhaps more closely than her mother had questioned her. Her heart was away, it was not in this place. In the pauses of Mrs. John's gentle talk she felt her own thoughts thronging upon her almost audibly. It seemed impossible that other people, that even her mother, unsuspicious as she was, should not find her out. And how slow, how slow were those sunshiny minutes, sixty of them in an hour! The time of the early dinner came, and again Hester turned from the food. Mrs. John began to be alarmed. "If it goes on like this I shall have to send for the doctor," she said.

Hester hastened out as soon as the meal was over to escape from her mother's comments. It seemed to her that she recognised some new knowledge in the keen glances of the sisters, and in Mr. Mildmay Vernon's grin as he sat over his newspaper in the summer-house. And she was afraid of the old Morgans, who had more insight. The surroundings of the house altogether were odious to her—unnecessary things that had nothing to do with those real affairs and mysteries of living which were being solved elsewhere. She asked herself wistfully, whether it was not time for her to go back: though if Catherine had not returned, what could she do but cause suspicion if she went to the empty house? To be even in the empty house would be something—it would be so much nearer the scene in which everything was going on. While she stood with her hand curved over her forehead looking out upon the road, with her eyes " busy in the distance shaping things that made her heart beat quick," the old captain came up to her. She thought he was paler than usual, and his eyes were troubled. He had laid his hand on her shoulder before she heard his approach, so absorbed was she in her own thoughts. He took her by the arm in his fatherly way—

" Come with me, Hester, and talk to my old woman?" he said.

It was with a great start that she turned to him, trembling with a nervousness all unknown to the Hester of yesterday.

"Is she ill?" she cried, scarcely knowing what she said; and then with a vague smile, "I forgot. Emma is gone, and she is missing—"

"It is not Emma we are thinking of. Hester, tell me," said the old man, leading her away with her arm in his, " what is this about Catherine? What has happened? Your mother told us you were there all night, and now to-day——"

" What do they say has happened ? " cried Hester with a gasp of suspense.

" I cannot make head nor tail of it.   I hear that one of the young men has gone wrong ; that Catherine is at the bank ; that there are great defalcations ; that he went off last night ——I can testify," cried Captain Morgan querulously, " that he did not go away last night, for I was there."

Hester looked up at him with a face from which all colour had fled.

" Is it known who it is ? are you sure he has not come back? Oh, I have a feeling," she cried, " a feeling in my heart that he has come back ! "

" My child," said the old captain, " you may trust her and me.   Whatever it is, it is safe with her and me."

Mrs. Morgan was sitting at the window in her summer place ; her placid brow had a cloud upon it, but was not agitated like her husband's.

" Have you come back to us, Hester ? " she said.   " We thought we had lost you.   If you can satisfy his mind with anything you can say, do it, my dear."

" What can I say ? " Hester cried.   " We are all in great trouble.   I don't know which is the greatest, but I cannot tell you secrets that are not mine.   Dear Mrs. Morgan, tell the captain so.   Whatever I know it is by accident.   I think I shall die with anxiety and suspense, but there is nothing I can say."

" My dear, you will not die, you will live to be anxious many another day.   Rowley, my old man, you hear the child. We must not ask her another question.   Wait, as you have waited many a time before.   It is all in the Lord's hands."

The old man was wiping the moisture from his forehead : he had seated himself as soon as he came in, his old limbs were shaking under him.   His large, colourless hands shook, holding his handkerchief.

" Mary," he said, " if it is my flesh and blood that has brought this disturbance into the place, that has seduced her boy, and brought down ruin on her house, how am I ever to lift my head again ? "

The old lady looked at him with pathetic eyes, in which there was a suffering as acute as his own, softened and made almost bright by the patience and calm that were habitual to her.

"Rowley, we are not thinking of Catherine, we are thinking of ourselves," she said.

And then there was a pause. It seemed to Hester that her own brokenheartedness was a sort of child's passion in comparison. She said humbly—

"Will you tell me what you are afraid of? There is nobody blamed but one. There is not a name spoken of but one. I don't know if that is any comfort to you, Captain Morgan."

"And the one is her boy, the apple of her eye, the only one that she has trusted, her choice out of all the world," the old lady said. "Oh be silent, be silent, my old man! What is your pride to that? I would rather I had a share of the burden—I would like to be suffering with her." The tears stood in the deep wells of those old eyes, which had wept so much. She was past weeping now. "The Lord forgive him and bring him back," she said.

"You mean punish him, you mean give him over to the powers of darkness that he belongs to! What does he deserve, a man that has used a woman like that?"

"I am not asking what he deserves. I will tell you what he would get if he would come back. Pardon!" said the old woman with a sob, instinctively putting out her old soft hands.

"I am not for pardon," said the captain vehemently, his head moving in his agitation, his hands shaking. "I am for every soul bearing its own burden. Here is a woman that has spread prosperity around her. She has been kind, even when she has not been merciful. The grateful and the ungrateful, she has been good to them all. She has been like the sun shining and the rain raining upon both just and unjust. And here is the end of her, stung to her heart by the child of her bosom. For it will be the end of her. She is a grand woman. She won't bear being deceived."

"Do not say that," said Hester; "she is so strong, stronger than any of us—if you had seen her last night!"

"Where could I have seen her last night?" he said quickly; then with a smile, "that is all you know, you children. Yes, stronger than any one of you, able to do everything. Do you remember the French boy in Browning's ballad, Hester, that could not bear it when his Emperor asked if he were wounded? 'I'm killed, sire!' That is like Catherine. She stands like a tower. I can see her in my mind's eye. She needs no sleep, no rest : but she is killed for all that."

Hester rose to her feet as he spoke in an excitement she could not control.

"I must go," she said. "I must go—I might be wanted."

The old man rose and hobbled out after her. He followed her to the gate.

"I will wait while you get your hat. I am coming with you," he said. "We cannot rest, Hester, neither you nor I."

Mrs. John was dozing in her chair as she generally did in the afternoon. She opened her eyes and said, "Are you going for a walk, dear?" then closed them tranquilly again. The very atmosphere in the brown wainscotted parlour breathed of peace and quiet uncongenial with any such throbbings as those in Hester's heart. She joined the old man, who was waiting for her at the door, and they went on together, saying little. The great window in the Grange where Catherine usually sat commanding the road was vacant. There was a certain deserted air about the place. They knew without a word that Catherine was still out of it.

"It is too far for you to go," Hester said.

Though they had not spoken for a long time they understood each other à demi-mot.

"It is too far for me," said he, "but what does that matter? everything will soon be too far for me. Let me go on while I can."

They walked as far as the bank, where their anxious eyes made out the people lingering about, the air of curiosity and excitement. Old Captain Morgan hobbled up to Mr. Merridew, who was making his way out with a serious face. "You will excuse me for my anxiety, sir," he said, "but will you tell me if Miss Vernon is there, and what is going on?"

"That is an easy question you are asking me," said Mr. Merridew, eying him closely; "certainly Miss Vernon is there."

"I am her near relation," said the old man, "and you are connected with her by marriage."

"I know very well who you are, Captain Morgan: a distinguished officer, though people have not found it out here. If you can lend Miss Vernon substantial help I advise you to do it at once."

Captain Morgan drew back a little: he gave Hester a pathetic glance. They retired slowly with lingering steps from the vicinity of Vernon's. They understood all without knowing anything.

"There is the bitterness of having nothing," said the old captain, "and that man knew it, Hester. I would coin myself if I could for her, and yet I cannot help her." Neither of them knew about business, nor how men like Mr. Merridew, who had been listening all day long to Catherine's explanations and arguments without being moved, could save the bank still if they would. But they felt in their hearts the dull opposition of his face, the shake of his head, the nature of his advice to one whom he knew to be a poor man, to help her now. "Money is a wonderful thing," said Captain Morgan; "it can do so much and yet so little. If you or I were rich as we are poor we could make Catherine think for half an hour that she had surmounted everything."

"Why for half an hour, Captain Morgan?" said Hester.

"Because, my dear, at the end of that time Vernon's being safe, there would come back upon her that from which neither heaven nor earth can deliver her."

"Oh, Captain Morgan, do not say so. Cannot Heaven, cannot God, deliver from everything?" cried Hester with a sense of horror.

"Ay, in a way that He uses always at the end—by death. At least we think death will do that for us; but it is only a guess even then. How otherwise?" said the old man, raising his dim old eyes beneath their heavy lids. "What is done cannot be undone. If the boy were to be touched with compunction too late and come back, even that would not restore the past."

"Why not?" she said, "why not? We could forgive him." It was the first acknowledgment she had made of any share in the catastrophe.

"Forgive him! You speak as if that could change anything! What is your forgiveness? You seem to think it is a thing, not so many words." Then after they had gone a little while in silence the old man burst forth again. "You could forgive him! A man wants not forgiveness, but to make up for his sins. You think it is like giving him a fortune to give him your pardon, as if he could set up again, and make a new beginning upon that. Forgiveness may save a man's soul, but it does not save his honour or his life. You could have him back and let him live upon you, and eat out your hearts with his baseness, trying to make it show like virtue. But Catherine is too noble a creature for that," cried the old captain. "Thank God she has never been broken down to that."

This torrent of words overwhelmed Hester; they had turned into the quiet road again, and the girl fell into a low sobbing and weeping as she went. She was too much over-strained to be able to control herself. Yet her heart struggled against this sentence.

"If you love any one is it only while he is good?" she said. "Is it noble to cast him from you because he has gone wrong? Then what is love or faithfulness? Are they nothing —nothing?"

She knew now that he had not come back. Honour had not moved him, nor love, nor any nobler impulse. She could have flung herself upon the earth in her misery. She felt that a touch now would be too much—that she could bear nothing further. And her companion saw that she was beyond the reach of any argument. He was silent, and they moved slowly along together, he tottering on his aged limbs, scarcely able to get along.

"Soon everything will be too far for me," he said with a half-pleased, almost satisfied nodding of his head. It took them a long time to get home, and the old captain was so worn out that he could not rise from his chair again that evening. He and his old wife sat sadly, saying something to each other once in half an hour. They could think of nothing but Catherine. They kept up their broken musing discussion upon her and her fate as the slow summer evening again crept silently by.

But Hester could not rest. She satisfied her mother easily that it was right she should go back to the Grange and find out if she could be of use.

"It is what I was going to suggest, my dear," said Mrs. John. "If Edward Vernon is away, as you say, and nobody with her, she must be lonely. And if there is any trouble besides—though you have never rightly explained to me what it was. No, no, dear, I don't mean to say it is your fault. No doubt you have told me, and I have not taken it up. To be sure, Hester, you must go; and though I cannot bear to be without you, yet if Catherine wants you, and she is in trouble, stay. I am sure she would do as much for me," said the simple soul, without any cold breathings of doubt. She went to the gate with Hester, and when she came back

could not help giving her neighbours a little sketch of the
state of affairs. " My Hester has gone back to the Grange,"
she said, " she will probably stay there all night. Catherine
Vernon wrote me the nicest note to tell me my child had been
of so much use to her ; that is always gratifying to a
mother."

" Of use ! " cried the ladies both together. " Gracious goodness, what can be going to happen ? Hester of use ! " cried
one sister. " And to Catherine ! " said the other. " Dear
Catherine, she tells you so to please you—when probably she
is thinking you the greatest bore—"

"She likes something new to experiment upon," said Mr.
Mildmay Vernon with a snarl. Mrs. John was much dis-
couraged by this reception of her news. She said—

" You little know my child if you think she will be ex-
perimented upon," holding her head high ; but when she got
indoors she cried a little over their ill-nature. If it had
been one of them who had been chosen how different would
have been their tone. Had the brougham been sent express
for Miss Matilda or Miss Martha, what airs they would have
given themselves ! and Mrs. John knew that she had given
herself no airs : she had not said a word. But she could not
be silent about the promotion of her child.

CHAPTER XLIII.

AN INTERRUPTION.

CATHERINE was in her usual chair in the familiar room where she had lived for so many years. These walls had witnessed most of the pleasantnesses and disappointments of her life ; within them she had grown into that amused spectatorship of all the pranks of human creatures which it had pleased her to think was her characteristic attitude, indulgent to everybody, seeing through everybody. They had never seen her in the aspect which she bore now, beaten down under the stroke of fate. She was too far gone even to be conscious of the extraordinary irony of life which had made of the one only creature to whom she had been consciously unjust, whom she had considered from her childhood as an enemy, her sole ministrant and sympathiser now. But she was not conscious even of Hester's presence, who, overpowered by a great awe of the suffering which she shared, kept herself in the background, recognising, as so few watchers do, that she was there for the sake of the sorrowful woman whom she watched, and not at all for her own. Catherine lay back in her chair, her head thrown back, her eyelids half closed. She did not move, except now and then to put up her hand and dry the moisture which collected slowly under her eyelids. It could not be called tears. It was that extorted dew of pain which comes when the heart seems pressed and crushed in some giant grasp. She was not thinking, any more than it is inevitable to think as long as life remains. She was only suffering, nothing more. She could not make any head against it. Her last stronghold had fallen. This it is which makes calamity so terrible to the old. She could not get beyond it. There was nothing, nothing in her path but this, blocking it across with a darkness that would never be dispersed. If he had died she would have known she could not remain long behind him, and the gloom would have been but a mist between; but he had not died. The thought of searching for him through the world, of holding out succour to him when he came to need, of forgiving, that last prerogative of love, was scarcely in her nature. It was hers rather to feel that deep impossibility of re-beginning, the misery and pain of any struggle to make tho base seem noble, which is as true a sentiment as the other. She could not have done it. To many women it is the highest form of self-abnegation as it is the bitterest lot that can be borne on earth; but to Catherine it would not have been possible. The blow to her was final. There was but one thing—to fight for Vernon's to the last gasp, to ward off disgrace and failure from the name, to keep the ground it had occupied so long, against possibility, against hope; but after that no more—no more. She had borne herself bravely as long as any eye was upon her, betraying nothing; and had sat down to table and tried to eat, with that utter self-mastery which will sustain the life it loathes with sedulous care so long as it is necessary—talking to Hester at intervals, giving Marshall directions as if nothing had happened. She had been first impatient, then satisfied to find the girl there. Her presence was a help in that needful struggle.

Catherine went up stairs after dinner as usual. Nothing was changed; but when she had attained to that shelter, she could do no more. She put back her head and closed her eyes, and gave herself up to the endurance of her deathblow. At the other end of the room Hester sat motionless. A keensighted spectator would have seen the outline of her figure in her dark dress, but nothing more. She was watching, forgetting her own share, intent upon the other. Her mind was full of what the old captain had said, "I'm killed, sire." Hester watched with a great awe, wondering if even thus, in the silence, without any more demonstration, a woman might die. She thought in her heart it would be well; but being so young she was afraid. And the silence was so deep, more deep than life could tolerate. She watched eagerly for that sole movement, the lifting of Catherine's hand to dry away the moisture from her eyes.

This stillness was broken suddenly by a loud knocking at the door—a continued volley of knocks, accompanied by the sound of voices outside. Then this sound surged inwards, and hasty steps were heard rushing up stairs. Hester's heart leaped to her mouth. It could not be that *he* would come back with such a noise and outcry; but yet a sort of frantic hope took possession of her as she rose to her feet. Catherine had raised herself too, and sat with her eyes widely open fixed upon the door. They had not long to wait. The door was flung open, dashing against a cabinet which stood near, with a superfluity of noise and emphasis, and, sweeping away the silence before her, and every possibility of calm, Ellen Merridew burst into the room, her eyes inflamed with crying, her fair countenance streaked with red, her light locks standing up round her face. She was followed by her husband, trying to hold her back, and by Marshall in the rear, eager—under a respectful semblance of attending the hasty visitors —to give accuracy to the floating suspicions of the servants' hall, and find out what it was all about. Ellen rushed in, and gazed about her wildly.

"Where is he?" she cried. "Oh, Aunt Catherine, where is he? You are hiding him. I said you would hide him, whatever he did. Oh, is it nothing to you if he goes and ruins people that never did him any harm?—young people like us that have all our life before us, and a dear baby to be turned out upon the world. Oh, Aunt Catherine, if you have any heart at all, where is he, where is he? I'll have him to justice!" cried Ellen. "I'll not sit under it. I won't—not if he should kill me! I want Edward. Where is Edward? I sha'n't go out of this till you give him up to me. He has ruined us, he has ruined us!" cried the excited creature, bursting into a transport of passionate tears.

There had been a moment of bewildered struggle in Catherine's face; then she rose up with what seemed to the excited new comers her usual composure.

"What does all this mean?" she said, in her quiet voice.

Hester had shut the door upon the servant's curiosity; Ellen crying violently, and poor Algernon, endeavouring vainly to console her, stood between the two, in the centre of the room. It was all that poor young Merridew could do not to weep too.

"I am sure you will forgive her, Miss Vernon," he said, in faltering tones. "We are nearly out of our senses. Oh, don't cry, my dearest; whatever they do they can't part us, and I'll work for you and baby. I'll work till I drop. Miss

Vernon, if Edward's here—she doesn't mean any harm. She is just off her head, poor girl! and baby not a month old yet. If you will only let us see him, I'll pledge my word——"

"Algy, hold your tongue!" cried Ellen amidst her sobs, stamping her foot. "Hold your tongue, I tell you. She'll never, never give him up—never till she's forced, I know that. She has always liked that fellow better than the whole of us put together. And we've every one kotoued to him for her sake. He's been the head of everything, though he was nothing but a poor—— And as frightened of her as a dog, and hated her all the time. Oh yes, Aunt Catherine, you may believe me or not, but whenever there was a word about you, Edward was always the worst. Of course we all had our remarks to make, I don't say anything different; but he was always the worst. And now he's gone, and led Algy to his ruin," she cried, with another wild outburst. "We have lost every penny. Do you hear me, Aunt Catherine, do you hear me? We're ruined, with a dear baby not a month old, and I that have never got up my strength. Oh yes, Algy, yes, dear. I know you'll work till you drop. But what good will that do to me, to have you work yourself to death, and to be left a widow at my age, with a baby to support? And, Aunt Catherine, it will all be your fault," cried Ellen. "Yes, it will be your fault. If you hadn't made such a fuss about him, who would have ever trusted him? It was because of you I gave my consent. I said Aunt Catherine will never let him come to harm. And now here it has all come to smash, and me and Algy are ruined. Oh, how can you have the heart? and a dear innocent baby without a word to say for himself! And me at my age—and poor Algy that thought he was making so good a marriage when he got one of the Vernons——"

"Nelly, Nelly, darling!" cried the poor young fellow, "I married you because I loved you, not because you were one of the Vernons."

"And he had a good right to think so," said Ellen, pushing away his caressing arm. "And they all thought so—every one; and now they've turned against me, and say I'm extravagant, and that I've ruined him. Oh! me to have ruined him that thought I was making a man of him. Aunt Catherine! Will you let us all be sacrificed, every one, only to keep Edward from harm?"

Catherine Vernon had sunk into her chair, but there was something of the old look of the spectator at a comedy again upon her face. The evening was beginning to fall, and they did not see the almost ghastly colour which had replaced the wonderful complexion of which everybody once spoke.

"Make her sit down, Algernon, and stop this raving," she said. "What has happened? I know nothing of it. If you have any claims upon Vernon's you will be paid with the rest—if we stand, till the last penny, if we fall, to the utmost that can be paid. I cannot say any more."

They both sat down and gazed at her with consternation on their faces; even Ellen's tears dried up as by magic. After she had stopped, they sat staring as if stupefied. Then Ellen got up, and threw herself at Catherine's feet with a cry of wild dismay.

"Aunt Catherine! you don't mean to say that you cannot help us, that you cannot save us? Oh, Aunt Catherine! don't be angry with me. I did not mean to make you angry. I was always silly, you know. You will help us, you will save Algy, you will pay the money, won't you?" She crept close to Catherine, and took her hand and kissed it, looking up piteously, with tears streaming down her face. "You'll do it for me, Aunt Catherine? Oh, though I am silly I am fond of my husband. And he's so good; he's never said it was my fault. And I always knew you would put it right. Aunt Catherine! you will put it right?"

Her voice rose into a shrill, despairing cry; then she dropped down helpless, sobbing and moaning, but still holding by Catherine's hand and her dress, whatever she could grasp at, in a passion of incredulity and despair.

Then Catherine, who had been so stately, sank back into her chair.

"I can't bear any more," she said, "I can't bear any more. For the love of God take her away!"

But it was only the sudden appearance of Harry which put an end to this painful scene. He gathered his sister up in his arms, while her husband was ineffectually intreating and reasoning with her, and carried her out of the room, with a severity and sternness which silenced the young pair.

"Look here," he said, taking them into the deserted library which had been Edward's room, "we are all in the same box. He has ruined her and us all. You, out of your own confounded folly, the rest of us—I can't tell you how. He has

ruined *her*. God—forgive him!" cried Harry, with a long
pause, bringing out the last words with a violent effort.
"But, look here! The only hope we have of pulling through
is in her. They can't let Catherine Vernon be ruined in Redborough. I don't think it's in the heart of man to do it;
but if we drive her into her grave, as you've been trying
to do——"

"Oh, Harry, how dare you say so! I only went to her—
where should I go?—and I thought it would be all right. I
thought it was dreadful, but I never believed it, for I know
Aunt Catherine——"

"Ellen, hold your tongue, for God's sake! If we kill her,
it's all up with us. Hasn't she got enough to bear? I
brought a cab when I knew you were here. Take her home,
Algy, and keep her quiet, and let's meet and talk over it
like men," Harry said, severely.

He had never so asserted himself in all his life before.
They hurried her out between them to the cab, much against
Ellen's will, who wanted explanations, and to know if it was
true that Aunt Catherine couldn't, couldn't if she would; and
then told them, sobbing, that if it was so, none of them could
afford to pay for a cab, and why, why should ruined people
spend a shilling when they had not got it? The cabman
heard part of these protestations, and Marshall another part.
But on the whole both Algernon and Harry were more
occupied with her in her transport, more anxious for its
consequences, more tender of her than if she had been the
most self-commanded and heroic woman in the world.

When this tempest of interruption swept away, Catherine
was still for a few minutes more. Then she called Hester to
her in a voice of exhaustion.

"I think," she said, "it has done me no harm. Anything
is better than that which—is always behind. And I must
do nothing to hurt myself before to-morrow. Was not
Harry there? He may have something to tell me. Let him
come and say it to you. You are quick witted, and you will
understand; and if it is worth writing, write it down. I will
not take any part. I will keep still here. If it rouses me so
much the better. If not, you will listen for me with your
young ears, and forget nothing. I must save myself, you see,
for to-morrow."

"I will forget nothing," Hester said.

Catherine smiled faintly, with her eyes closed.

"I had thought of making you bring me some wine. There is some Tokay in the cellar; but one always pays for a strong stimulant, and this is the better way. You are young, and you are a Vernon too. Bend your mind to it. Think of nothing but the business in hand."

"I will," said Hester, with solemnity, as if she were pronouncing the words before a judge.

Catherine took hold of her dress when she was going away. "One thing," she said. "I think you and I have hated each other because we were meant to love each other, child."

"I think I have always done both," said Hester.

The faint sound that broke through the stillness was not like Catherine's laugh. She patted the girl's arm softly with her hand. Their amity was too new to bear caresses.

"Now go and do your work, for your honour and mine," she said.

It appeared that Harry had much to say. It was strange to have to say it all to the young and eager listener, her eyes glowing with interest and anxiety, who was not content with any one statement, but questioned and investigated till she had brought out every point of meaning, while the real authority sat by silent, her eyes closed, her hands clasped, like an image of repose. Both the young people kept their eyes upon her. There was not a movement which Hester did not watch, while she exerted her faculties to comprehend everything that Harry told her, and put down everything that seemed at all important. The impulse carried her over her own share of the individual misery. Everything else disappeared before the paramount importance of this. When all that Harry had to say was said, there arose a silence between them which had the effect which nothing before had of rousing Catherine. She opened her eyes and looked at them kindly.

"Everything has been done as I wished," she said. "I have gleaned something, and the rest you will tell me, Hester, to-morrow. It has been a rest to me to hear your voices. You can expect me, Harry, at the same hour."

"Is it not too much for you, Aunt Catherine? It is everything for us that you should come."

"I will come," she said. "It is easier than staying at home. Fatigue is salvation. Now I am going to bed, to sleep. Oh, I mean it. I cannot do my work without it. You will come too in the morning, Hester, when I send for you? Then, good-night."

They watched her go away with her step still stately. Her faithful maid, whom Mrs. John had found so kind, but who had not always been kind, was waiting for her. The two young people stood and looked after her with eyes of tender respect and awe.

"I thought once," said Hester, in a hush of subdued feeling, "that she might have died sitting in her chair."

"Ah," said Harry, who had a little more experience, "it is seldom that people get out of it so easily as that. I want to tell you something more if it will not—upset you more."

Hester smiled.

"Is there anything that can upset me more?" she said.

He looked at her wistfully. He did not know what her individual part in this trouble had been; whether Edward was more to her than another, or what the position was in which they stood to each other.

"I don't know how to take it," he said, "or how to understand it. There are news of—Edward."

The last gleam of hope shot across Hester's mind.

"He is coming back?" she said, clasping her hands.

Harry shook his head.

"Will you come with me to the door? It is such a lovely night."

She had not the courage or the presence of mind to say no. She went down stairs with him where the lamps were lighted again, and out to the gate—the same hour, the same atmosphere as last night. Was it only last night that all had happened? She could have turned and fled in the tremor, the horror of the recollection. Just there she lay at Catherine's feet. Just there Catherine had stood and listened.

Hester stood her ground like a martyr. She knew she must learn to do so, and that it would not be possible to avoid the place made so bitter by recollection. Harry did not know how to speak. He shifted uneasily from one foot to another. "He has been traced to town; he got in at the junction, not here. He reached London this morning, very early—with a lady."

"With a lady!"

Hester had expected a great shock, but the astonishment of this took its sting away.

"They left this afternoon, it is supposed, to go abroad," Harry said.

"Still with the lady? That is very strange," said Hester, with a little quiver in her lips.

"There is reason now to suppose that he—married her in the meantime."

Hester had grasped by accident the post of the gate. She was glad she had done so. It was a support to her, at least. Married her! It gave her no immediate pain in her astonishment, which was unspeakable. In the dusk Harry did not see her face. He had no conception of the real state of the case. The fact that Edward had been discovered with another woman had confused Harry and diverted the natural suspicions which had risen in his mind when he had found Hester so linked with Catherine after the discovery of Edward's flight. He watched her with a little alarm, wondering and anxious. But the only sign of any emotion was the tightening of her hand upon the iron gate.

"You will know," he said, "whether it will be best to say anything of this. If it will hurt her more, let it alone till the crisis is past."

"If it will hurt her—more? I do not think anything—can hurt her more."

"And you are nearly over-worn," he said, with a tender and pitying cadence in his voice. "I can't say spare yourself, Hester. You are the only one she deserves nothing from. She ought to feel that : if he is gone who owes her everything, yet you are standing by her, who never owed her anything."

Hester could not bear it any longer. She waved her hand to him and went in—into the house that was not hers, where there was no one who had a thought to bestow upon her. Where was there any one? Her mother loved her with all her heart, but had nothing to say to her in this rending asunder of her being. She thought she was glad that it was all happening in a house which was not her home, which after, as Harry said, the crisis was past, she might never need to enter again. She went up stairs, to the unfamiliar room in which she had spent the previous night. There she sat down in the dark on the bed, and looked at it all, passing before her eyes, like a panorama. For this was the only description that could be given. The conversation just recorded occurred over again, as if it had been in a book. "With a lady!" "They left this after-noon." "Reason to suppose that in the meantime—" And

then this talk, suspended in the air as it seemed, came to
a pause. And Hester, through the interval, saw all her
own long stormy wooing, its sudden climax with so much
that was taken for granted—" My only love !—and I am your
only love." That was all true. Those agitated scenes, the
dances that were nothing but a love duel from beginning
to end, the snatches of talk in the midst of the music
and tumult, the one strange blessed moment in the verandah
at home, the meeting so tragical and terrible of last night.
That was a sort of interlude that faded again, giving place
to Harry's steady subdued voice—

" Married her in the meantime !   Married her ! "

Hester said these words aloud, with a laugh of incredulous
dismay and mockery. The sound terrified herself when she
heard it. It was Catherine's laugh made terrible with a sort
of tragic wonder. Married her ! Had there been no place
for Hester at all, nothing but delusion from beginning to
end ?

CHAPTER XLIV.

THE SETTLEMENT.

THE records of the next few days were agitated and full of excitement. Day after day Catherine spent at the bank, immersed in calculations and consultations with every one who could throw the slightest light upon the matter. Everything oozed out by degrees, and it was said now that Edward was being hunted down by detectives, now that he had escaped altogether, now that his defalcations were so tremendous that nothing but absolute ruin was possible for Vernon's, now that there was enough left to make a fight upon if only the creditors would be merciful, and give time, and have patience. The usual panic with which such news is received was somehow tempered in this case. It was thought in the district that Catherine Vernon was enormously rich, and independent of the bank, and when it was known that she had not abandoned it, but in her old age had come back, and was in the office every day, struggling to retrieve affairs, there was nobody short of the financial authorities of the place who did not believe that all was safe. Catherine Vernon would not see any harm come to the bank; Catherine Vernon would see everybody paid. This popular faith held up with a certainty of obstinate prepossession which was worth so much solid capital to the tottering house. Catherine herself placed everything she had in the world in the common stock. She it was who took the lead in all the discussions. She rejected the provisions for her own comfort which everybody concerned was anxious to make. The prevailing feeling among all who had any power was at first that the re-establishment of the old concern was hopeless, but that enough might be saved out of the wreck to enable Catherine to end her days in peace. To this she opposed a determined negative. She would have no arrangement made on her behalf. "Do you think I want," she cried, "to end my days in peace? I am ready to die fighting, on the contrary, rather than sacrifice the place my father lived and died in and his father before him. Don't speak of peace to me." It was when they perceived that she was immovable in this point and was determined to denude herself of everything, that the old contemporaries who had stood by her before in her gallant struggle, and had been her competitors, and had lived to see themselves distanced by Catherine, had felt it impossible to persevere in their refusal to help. She would have no charity, she declared with a flushed cheek. Help for Vernon's, yes, to set them on their feet again, with the certainty that nobody should lose a penny in the long run—for that she would thank them with a full heart; but help for herself, to keep her in a show of comfort when the reality was gone, no! "not a farthing," she said. "I am not afraid of the workhouse," said Catherine, with proud calm, "and I have a right to a Vernon almshouse, the first that is vacant. Nobody will deny that I am Redborough born, and of good reputation. I will not take a penny. Do you think I could not live in a single room and eat my rations like another? It is because you don't know Catherine Vernon yet."

The old men who had known Catherine Vernon all her life could not withstand this. "We must manage it for her, we must do it somehow," they said. "Vernon's is an old name among us. There is no name in all the district that the people have such confidence in. We must try, sir, we must try," they began to say to each other "to help her through." The young men, many of them, were impatient, and would have refused to consider the question at all. What had an old woman to do with business? She ought to be thankful if she was allowed a maintenance, and to terminate her days in comfort. But on this point there was not another word to be said. The Grange and everything in it was to be sold, the White House and the old furniture, part of which Mrs. John still remembered so fondly. There was no question as to that. "We are prepared to sacrifice everything," Catherine said. "What we desire is not to keep up any false pretence, but to carry on our business and recover ourselves by your help. Dismiss me from your mind. I will take my chance; but think of Vernon's, which is not hopeless, which has life in it

yet." Old Mr. Rule on his side had pages upon pages of
statements to put before the gentlemen. The week was one
of terrible suspense and misery, but at the end, though with
conditions that were very hard upon the pride of the family,
it was decided at last in favour of the bank. Certain great
capitalists came forward to prop it up, "new blood" was put
into it in the shape of an enterprising manager, who was to
guide Harry's steps. There were bitternesses, as there is in
every cup that is administered by strangers. But Catherine
had gained her object, and she made no complaint. Vernon's
would continue, and Harry might have it in his power still to
retrieve the family fortunes. As for all the rest, what did it
matter? She was a woman who was, or thought herself, very
independent of material conditions. Whether she lived in
the Grange or one of the Vernon almshouses, what did it
matter to her? She did not care for fine eating or fine
clothing. "Besides, my clothes will last out my time," she
said with a smile. The week's struggle had been good for her.
She had not forgotten the great and enduring grief which lay
behind all this. But she had not had time to think of it.
She had put it away out of her mind as a strong nature can,
till her work was done. It was waiting for her to overwhelm
her : but in the meantime she was strong.

Roland Ashton hurried down as soon as the terrible
news reached him. He was eager to tell her his own connection with it, to prove to her that it was not he who had
led Edward into speculation, that he had done his utmost to
restrain him, and had even in his anxiety been willing to
embark in what he felt to be a hazardous course in order to
save Edward from the rashness he feared. He came down
with all his details ready and a burning anxiety to set himself
right. But when he reached the scene of all their troubles,
Roland never said a word to Catherine on the subject. Such
details were beyond the case. She had never willingly spoken
of Edward ; when it was possible she ignored him altogether ;
the investigations which had been set on foot, and which
had revealed the greater part of his secrets, she had been
compelled to know of, but had spoken to no one about them.
Since the first day his name had scarcely passed her lips.
Harry only had been allowed to tell her that he had baffled
all the attempts made to find him, and had escaped—The search
after him had been indeed made rather to satisfy anxiety than
with any design of punishment, for the other partners in the

bank were responsible for everything, and it was on their
shoulders that the burden had to fall. He disappeared as
if he had fallen into the sea or been lost in a railway accident.
The most wonderful complication of all, the companionship
in which he had left England, was not told to her then. It
threw to all the others a horrible mockery upon the whole
story. There was a bitter sort of smile upon Roland's face
when he sat with the old people, and told them all the
investigations he had made, the incredulous indignation
with which he had received the first idea that Emma's dis-
appearance could be connected with that of Edward, the
growing certainty that it was so, and finally the receipt of her
letter which he brought them to read. The old people were
very sad for their beloved Catherine and little inclined to
laugh, but the old captain indulged in a tremulous roar which
was half a groan, and the old lady, who allowed that her
sense of humour was small, gave a grieved smile when it
was read to her. This is what Emma said :—

"DEAR ROLAND,—I think it my duty to let you know, as it
was, so to speak, in your house I was living at the time, how
it is that I had to make up my mind at a very short notice,
and couldn't even go through the form of referring Edward to
you. I met him in the train, as you will probably have
heard. I was rather sorry about leaving Redborough, and so
was he too till he saw me beside him. And then it turned out
that he had been very much struck with me at Ellen
Merridew's parties, and would have spoken then but for some
entanglements that were of old standing, and that he could
not shake off. I need not mention any names, but if I say it
was some one that was quite out of the question, some one
that was detested at the Grange, you will know. He told me
he was leaving England for ever, and would I come with him?
You know I have always thought it my first duty to get
settled, being the youngest and without any fixed home. So
after thinking it over for an hour or two, and him being so
anxious to come to the point, which is generally just where
gentlemen are so slow, I thought it best to consent. We were
married before a registrar, but he says that is just as legal as
in church. It was at the registrar's in Holywood Street,
Trentham Square. We are going to travel, and may be
moving about for a good while ; but when we settle I shall
let you know. I am glad to tell you that we shall be quite

well off, and have everything very handsome ; and Edward
never grudges me anything I fancy. Give my love to them
all, and let them know I am as happy as possible, and that I
am Mrs. Edward Vernon now, which is one of the prettiest
names I know.

" Your affectionate sister,
" EMMA."

This was the last that was heard of this strange pair for a
number of years. They discovered that Edward, after many
losses, had made a sudden successful venture which had
brought him a sum so large as to turn his head. He had
been utterly demoralised by all the excitements he had passed
through, and the sense of a reckoning which he could never
meet, and he had not given himself time to think. He
disappeared into the unknown with his ill-gotten gains and
the wife he had picked up in the midnight train, and was
seen no more. As for poor Algernon Merridew, who was his
victim, although only as his own eagerness and that of his
wife to get money anyhow, made him so, he had to descend,
like all the rest, from his temporory grandeur and gaiety. Old
Merridew was as stern now as he had been indulgent before, and
Ellen, who had been almost worshipped as one of the Vernons
when she glorified the family by entering it, was now the
object of everybody's scoffs and accusations. But Ellen was
a girl of spirit, and equal to the circumstances. Algernon got
a humble place in the bank, and the little family lived with
Harry, putting their small means together until better days
came ; but adversity and a determination at least not to let
herself be insignificant had so inspiring an effect upon Ellen,
that she kept the impoverished household as gay as the
extravagant one had been, by cheaper and better means. The
Merridew girls, once so subservient, learned what she called
"their place" when she was poor more effectually than they
had done when she was rich. And her brother, always by her,
who, though he had losses, was still the chief partner in the
bank, Catherine Vernon's nephew, and the bearer of a name
which commanded respect in all the district, kept the balance
even. When Vernon's flourished again Algernon became a
partner, and all the past grandeurs of the beginning were
more than realised.

In the meantime, however, when it had just been decided
that Vernon's, bolstered up by a great deal of supplementary

aid, was to go on again, there was much commotion among all
the dependents of the house.   For one thing it was decided
that as the Grange was to be sold, the most natural refuge
for Catherine was at the Vernonry, her own house, from which
some of her dependents must go to make room for her.   This
was the one point upon which she had made no personal
decision, for it hurt her pride to be obliged to dismiss one of
those for whom she had provided shelter so long.   There had
been a great effort made to make her retain the Grange, and
continue her life in its usual course, a little retrenched and
pared away, yet without any great disturbance of the habitual
use and wont.   This she would not consent to, making the
protest we have seen, that external circumstances were nothing to her, that one of the Vernon almshouses would be as
good a shelter as any other for an old woman.   But she shrank
from bidding any one of her pensioners to make room for her
in the Vernonry.   It raised a wonderful commotion, as may
be supposed, in the house itself.   All the dwellers on the
garden side were disposed to think that Mrs. Reginald, whose
boys were now growing up, and two of them in what their
mother called "positions," was the right person to go.   But
Mrs. Reginald herself was of opinion that her house, a good
deal battered and knocked about by the boys in the course of
their bringing up, was not in a fit state to receive Catherine
Vernon, and that the other side, which was the best, was the
natural place for her.   The Miss Vernon-Ridgways could
think or speak of nothing else.

"Our little place," they said, "is far too small for Catherine.   She could not turn round in it.   Of course we would
turn out in a moment; it would be our duty.   But dear
Catherine, used to such large rooms, what could she do in
ours, which is the size of a pocket-handkerchief?   And if
Mrs. Reginald will not budge, why there is Mrs. John.   She
is so intimate with Catherine nowadays.   Hester, that used to
be such a rebel, and whom Catherine, we all know, could not
endure, is always there.   Dear me, of course there cannot be
a doubt about it.   Mrs. John's house is the right thing; she
must have that," which was a great relief to their minds.

Mr. Mildmay Vernon made a great many faces over his
newspaper as he sat in the summer-house.   He reflected that
the hot water pipes would be sure to get out of order in
winter, and who would now repair them?   He did not commit himself by any remark, but he thought the more.   When

Mrs. John told him of the opinion of the sisters, and consulted him with a troubled countenance, he only shook his head.

"I am sure I would do anything for Catherine," Mrs. John said, "especially now when she is in trouble ; but we cannot go far from here, for Hester is so much with her ; and where are we to get a house ? There is nothing within reach but that little cottage on the road. I am sure, if I were Mrs. Reginald, with no particular tie, and her boys in town, such a long way to come, I don't think I should have any doubt as to what my duty was."

It was a question which Hester at last solved in her hasty way, declaring that wherever they lived Catherine must have the best place in her own house—a principle to which her mother was obliged to make a faltering adhesion. But while every one was thus resisting, Mr. Mildmay Vernon was carrying on his reflections about the hot water-pipes.

"She put me next the trees on account of my rheumatism," he said to himself. "I know she did, and I shall never live through a winter if the apparatus gets out of gear. And I can't afford to pay for the fire, that's clear." The result of which reflection was that Mr. Mildmay Vernon made it known that he had received a legacy which would make a little addition to his income, and he could not think any longer of taking up room which he believed was wanted. "Besides, one may accept a favour from one's cousin," he said, "especially when it is not much of a favour, being the damp part of the house which few people would have taken had they been paid for doing so—but to be indebted to a firm of bankrupts is impossible," Mr. Mildmay Vernon said.

He took his departure in the beginning of the winter, just when the want of the hot water-pipes would be beginning to make itself felt. And it was almost without consulting her mother that Hester made arrangements for removing their few household goods into his house, to leave their own free for the mistress of all. Mrs. John consented to the arrangement, but not without a few tears.

"It is not that I mind the difference," she said, "in the size of the rooms, or anything of that sort. But it feels like coming down in the world."

"We have all come down in the world," said Hester ; "and Catherine most of all."

And then Mrs. John cried for Catherine, as she had first done for herself, and resisted no more.

CHAPTER XLV.

THE END.

It was early in November when the time came for Catherine to leave the Grange. She had made a selection of a very few things to go with her, and all the others had been valued for the sale. She spoke quite cheerfully about the sale. She had gathered a great many valuable things about her, and it was thought they would sell very well. She had some pictures which had been in the house for generations, and some things which her great-uncle had picked up when he made the *grand tour*. And there was a great deal of valuable china and quantities of old silver, the accumulations of a family that had not been disturbed for generations. She showed no feeling about it, people said; and indeed Catherine felt that neither about this nor any other external thing was she capable of showing much feeling. She cared nothing about leaving the Grange. Had she been actually brought down as far as the almshouse, in all likelihood she would have taken it with the proudest placidity. What was there in that to move a soul? One room was very much like another if you went to general principles, though it might be larger or smaller. Were these matters to make one's self unhappy about? So she said, fully meaning it, and with a smile. She was at the office every day. It seemed a matter almost of economy to keep for the present the brougham with its one horse which took her there; but of everything else she divested herself with the frankest good will. To the outer world she kept her good looks, though she was thinner, and her complexion paled; but those who watched her more

closely found that there were many changes in Catherine.
"I'm killed, sire," old Captain Morgan still said. He himself had given them a great alarm; he had had "a stroke"
in the beginning of the winter, but it had passed away,
though he still said everything was too far for him, and
found his evening hobble to the Grange too much. He went
as often as he could, sometimes to bring Hester home, who
was always there to receive Catherine at her return, sometimes only to sit and talk for an hour in the evening. With
other people, when they came, Catherine employed the same
plan which she had first set on foot with Harry. She made
Hester her representative in the conversation. She said it
did her good, while she rested, to hear the voices and to take
into her mind now and then a scrap of the conversation.
But it seemed to Hester that she paid less and less attention
to what people said. She was very cheerful in her time of
business, but when she lay back in her chair in the evenings,
she was so still sometimes that but for her hand now and
then stealing to her eyes, her anxious companion would
scarcely have known that she lived. She thought nothing
of her health for her own part, and constantly said that she
was quite well and that her work agreed with her. There
had been a little excitement in her appearance when she came
home in the evening of the last day she was to spend at the
Grange. Hester thought it was the coming change that
occasioned this, though Catherine declared her indifference to
it. She talked with a little haste and excitement during
dinner, and when they were alone afterwards did not flag
as was her wont, but continued the talk. "It is a great
pity," she said, "a girl like you, that instead of teaching
or doing needlework, you should not go to Vernon's, as you
have a right to do, and work there."

"I wish I could," Hester said, with eager eyes.

"They tell me you wanted to do something like what I had
done. Ah! you did not know it was all to be done over again.
This life is full of repetitions. People think the same thing
does not happen to you twice over, but it does in my
experience. You would soon learn. A few years' work,
and you would be an excellent man of business; but it
can't be."

"Why cannot it be? You did it. I should not be
afraid——"

"I was old. I was past my youth. All that sort of thing

was over for me. It could be in one way—if you could make
up your mind to marry Harry——."

"I could not—I could not! I will never marry."

"It is a great pity you cannot—I think it is a mistake.
I have done him a great deal of injustice in my time; but
one finds out sooner or later that brains are not everything.
There is another man, and he has brains, who would marry
you if you would have him, Hester—Roland Ashton. Take
him—it is better in the end."

"Oh, do not ask me! I will never marry," Hester cried.

Then Catherine suddenly sat upright in her chair, and
clasped her hands together with almost wild emphasis. "I
would marry," she cried, "if I were you! I would wipe out
every recollection. Did they tell you the pitiful story of a
meeting in the train, a marriage suddenly made up—and who
it was that went away into the darkness in what was to have
been your place?"

"Yes, they have told me," said Hester, in a low voice.

"Lord in Heaven!" cried Catherine, "what a world, what
a world this is!—all mockery and delusion, all farce except
when it is tragic. And after that you will not marry—for
the sake of——"

"How can I help it?" cried the girl, with wistful eyes.
"You do the same yourself.'

"Myself? that is different. Your heart will not be empty
for ever, Hester. It cannot close itself up for ever. With
me that was the last;—this is one thing that makes a mother
like no one else. Hold the last fast, they say. It was everything one had to look to. I am very cheerful, and I shall
live for years—many people do. But I have got my death
blow," Catherine said. Then the silence dropped again
between them. It was before a cheerful fire, with a lamp
burning—altogether a more cheerful scene than in those sad
summer days.

"There are some people who would not take much interest
in it," Catherine continued, "but you do. I think you are
like me, Hester. We were kept apart by circumstances;
perhaps it is possible we might have been kept apart on purpose. "He"—Catherine made a pause before and after, and
said the word with a sob—"never understood me. They say he
was—afraid of me, never could trust me with what he really
wished. Alas, alas! It must have been my fault——"

"Oh no, no!"

"Ah, yes, yes. I had rather think that; and there is a great deal that is base in me. I could not but laugh even at that story of Emma—even now. Human nature is so strange —it is a farce. I am not angry though, not at all : all things seem floating off from me. I could think we were floating away altogether, you and I——"

"You are not well. You are doing too much. I should like to send for the doctor."

"I believe in no doctors. No, no ; I am quite well, only tired with the day's work and ready for rest."

And the silence resumed its sway. She laid herself back as before—her pale head against the dark curtains stood out like ivory. Some time afterwards she sighed two or three times heavily, then there was no sound at all. The fire burned cheerfully, the lamp shed its steady glow upon Hester's book, to which after this talk she did not, as may be supposed, pay very much attention. But Catherine did not like a vacant watcher, and the book was a kind of safeguard, protecting her from the sense of an eye upon her. Perhaps an hour passed so. A chill crept into the room like nothing Hester had ever felt before, though all was still, serenely warm and bright to outward appearance. She rose softly at last and touched Catherine's hands, that were folded in her lap, to wake her. It was from them the cold had come that had crept to her heart.

There was, then, no need that Catherine Vernon should ever live in cramped rooms, in another house from that in which she had been born. When they carried her out from it a week after, the whole population came out to meet the procession, and followed her weeping, lining the path, filling the streets. Her misfortunes, and the noble courage with which she had stood up against them at the end, brought back all the fulness of the love and honour with which she had been regarded when she first became supreme in the place, and all bounty flowed from her. There was not any one connected with her, high or low, not only the poor Vernons who had snarled and scoffed while they accepted her favours, but the very men of money who had of late taken upon themselves the air of patronising Catherine, but was proud to be able to repeat now, on the day of her burying, what she had said to them, and how they had come in contact with her. The doctors were not clear as to how she died. She had never been suspected of heart disease, or any other disease.

But it was her heart somehow, with or without a medical reason for it, that had failed her. The last touch, those who loved her thought, had been too much. Derision such as she had delighted in in other circumstances, had over- taken the last tragic occurrence of her life. Catherine had not been able to bear the grim mockery, the light of a farce upon that tragedy of her own.

And as for Hester, all that can be said for her is that there are two men whom she may choose between, and marry either if she pleases—good men both, who will never wring her heart. Old Mrs. Morgan desires one match, Mrs. John another. What can a young woman desire more than to have such a possibility of choice?

FINIS.